Praise for

"Powerful and suspenseful, *Son of Avonar* will keep you up long past your bedtime."

—*The Davis Enterprise*

"Imagination harnessed to talent produces a fantasy masterpiece, a work so original and believable that it will be very hard to wait for the next book in this series to be published." —*The Midwest Book Review*

"*Son of* ...
series. . .

"A gooc...
thor's w...
intensity...
publishe...
tion, an...
stronger...
sors; it's...

"The plo...
taining characters."

—*Locus*

"Dragons' voices and one man's sheer, indomitable will blend to produce a powerful story of courage and faith. *Song of the Beast* is this summer's sleeper hit."

—*The Davis Enterprise*

continued . . .

Praise for *Transformation, Revelation,* and *Restoration,* the acclaimed Rai-Kirah saga by Carol Berg

"Vivid characters and intricate magic combined with a fascinating world and the sure touch of a Real Writer—luscious work!" —Melanie Rawn

"This well-written fantasy grabs the reader by the throat on page one and doesn't let go. . . . Wonderful."
—*Starburst*

"Berg greatly expands her world with surprising insights." —*The Denver Post*

"Both a traditional fantasy and an intriguing character piece. . . . Superbly entertaining."
—*Interzone Magazine*

"The prince's redemption, his transformation, and the flowering of mutual esteem between master and slave are at the story's heart. This is handled superbly."
—*Time Out* (London)

"Vivid characters, a tangible atmosphere of doom, and some gallows humor." —*SFX Magazine*

"An exotic, dangerous, and beautifully crafted world."
—Lynn Flewelling, author of *Traitor's Moon*

"Powerfully entertaining." —*Locus*

"Berg's characters are completely believable, her world interesting and complex, and her story riveting."
—*Kliatt*

"Epic fantasy on a gigantic scale. . . . Carol Berg lights up the sky with a wondrous world."
—*Midwest Book Review*

"Ms. Berg's finely drawn characters combine with a remarkable imagination to create a profound and fascinating novel." —*Talebones*

"Carol Berg is a brilliant writer who has built her characters carefully and completely. The magic is subtle and vivid, and the writing is compelling."
—BookBrowser

"A much-needed boost of new blood into the fantasy pool." —*Dreamwatch Magazine*

Also by Carol Berg

The Rai-Kirah Series
TRANSFORMATION
REVELATION
RESTORATION

SONG OF THE BEAST

The Bridge of D'Arnath Series
SON OF AVONAR
GUARDIANS OF THE KEEP

GUARDIANS OF THE KEEP

Book Two of The Bridge of D'Arnath

CAROL BERG

A ROC BOOK

ROC
Published by New American Library, a division of
Penguin Group (USA) Inc., 375 Hudson Street,
New York, New York 10014, U.S.A.
Penguin Books Ltd, 80 Strand,
London WC2R 0RL, England
Penguin Books Australia Ltd, 250 Camberwell Road,
Camberwell, Victoria 3124, Australia
Penguin Books Canada Ltd, 10 Alcorn Avenue,
Toronto, Ontario, Canada M4V 3B2
Penguin Books (NZ), cnr Airborne and Rosedale Roads,
Albany, Auckland 1310, New Zealand

Penguin Books Ltd, Registered Offices:
80 Strand, London WC2R 0RL, England

First published by Roc, an imprint of New American Library,
a division of Penguin Group (USA) Inc.

First Printing, September 2004
10 9 8 7 6 5 4 3 2 1

Cover art by Matt Stawicki

ROC REGISTERED TRADEMARK—MARCA REGISTRADA

Printed in the United States of America

For the boys. And you thought the garage was tough. . . .

The builders did bow before the castle lord and say to him that his fortess was complete. But the lord declared the castle not yet strong enough, for his enemies were powerful and many. And so the lord commanded the builders to set an iron ring into the stone on the battlements at each compass point of the keep, and he chose his four strongest warriors to sanctify his fortress with their lives. One of the four was chained to each of the rings and charged to watch for marauders who might appear from any point along the sweeping horizon. At every hour the watch bells were rung to ensure the warriors did not sleep, and none were allowed to speak to them lest they be distracted from their duty. Through burning autumn and into bitter winter the four stood watch, allowed no shelter, no comfort, and no respite, believing that their faithfulness and honor would protect their lord's stronghold long after their eyes and ears had failed. And when they died, they were left in place until their dust had filtered into the stones and mortar. They were called the Guardians of the Keep and are said to protect it still, and the symbol of the Four Guardian Rings is the shield of Comigor. Indeed, the four must have been potent warriors, for never in six hundred years has Comigor fallen to its enemies.

The History and Legends of Comigor Castle

CHAPTER 1

Seri

My driver rang the bell for the third time. No doubt the castle was in mourning. Black banners flew from the squat towers alongside the duke's pennon. And the severe façade of the keep's entry tower, broken only by the tall, narrow glass windows near its crown, was draped with myrtle branches, wound and tied with black crepe. But for all the activity I could see, one might think the entire household dead instead of just the lord.

At last, almost a quarter of an hour after we'd driven through the unguarded outer gates, one of the massive doors was dragged open. A red-faced under-housemaid carrying a water pitcher on her shoulder gestured frantically and disappeared into the house, leaving the door ajar.

Renald hurried back across the courtyard to the carriage, scratching his head. "The girl says you're to go right up to her mistress' rooms. She didn't even wait to hear my introduction."

"How could they know I was coming today?" Not waiting for Renald's hand, I jumped from the carriage and directed him to the kitchen wing where he might get refreshment and perhaps a bit of gossip. I ran up the broad steps. Thirteen years since I'd been banished from this house—

A blood-chilling wail from the upper floor precluded reminiscing, as well as any puzzling over the lack of proper guards at the gates of a wealthy house with a newly dead lord. Hurrying across the tiled floor of the entry tower and up the grand staircase, I followed the commotion through a set of double doors at the end of the passage and into a grand bedchamber.

The chamber, larger and airier than most of the dark rooms in the old keep, had once been my mother's. But only the location was recognizable. The graceful, Valloreanstyle furnishings had been replaced by bulky, thick-topped tables of dark wood, ornate gilt chairs, and carved benches of a lumpish design with thin velvet cushions added for "comfort." The bedstead sat on a raised platform, bedposts reaching all the way to the plastered ceiling. Heavy red draperies hung at the windows, blocking the bright sun and soft air of the autumn morning, and a fire roared in the hearth, making the room dim, stuffy, and nauseatingly hot.

The place was in chaos. A gray-haired woman in black satin hovered near the bed, waving ineffectually at a host of chambermaids in black dresses and winged white caps. The girls ran hither and yon with basins and towels, pillows and smelling salts, while from behind the gold-tasseled bedcurtains, the screams faded into whining complaints punctuated by great snuffles.

The gray-haired woman regarded me with dismay. "Well, where is the physician, then?"

"I know nothing of any physician. I've come to wait upon the duchess and the young duke. What's the difficulty here?"

Another wail rose from the bed.

"You're not with the physician?" The woman spoke as if she were sure I was mistaken or as if somehow it were my fault that I was not the person expected.

"No. But perhaps I could be of some help."

"Has Ren Wesley come, Auntie?" came the voice from the bed. "Truly, I cannot get a breath."

If breathing were the problem, I thought a clever application of the damper at the hearth and a brief wrestling match with the iron casements might improve the patient's health considerably.

"It's a stranger, my pet. Walked in bold as a thief. Says she's here to see you and the young duke, but she's not with the physician." The black-clad woman wagged a bony finger at me. "You've no business here, young woman. Leave or I shall call the guards."

"I'll die before he comes, Auntie. I shall expire with only you and the servants and this thief to attend me. I shall die here in this wretched house and what will become of Gerick, then?"

The old woman poked her head between the bed-curtains. "Now, now, child. It is quite possible you will die, but you will have me beside you every moment."

"Where is the damnable physician? And where is that cursed Delsy who was to bring me brandy?"

I made my way through the fluttering maids to the side of the bed and peered over the old woman's shoulder. She was dabbing a towel on the brow of a round-faced young woman, whose fluffy white bed gown made her look like a great hen, roosting in a nest of pillows so large an entire flock of geese must have sacrificed their feathers for them. Long fair hair was piled atop her head; teasing curls and wisps floated about her pink, tear-streaked cheeks. I saw nothing to explain the mortal predictions I'd heard, though the thin red coverlet couldn't hide the fact that my sister-in-law was most assuredly with child. I doubted Tomas had even known.

I nudged the bed-curtain open a little wider. "Excuse my intruding unannounced, Philomena. When I heard your call, I came up straightaway. May I offer assistance?"

"Moon of Jerrat!" The young woman removed the handkerchief and stared at me with her great green eyes, all present agonies seemingly forgotten in shock and recognition. My brother and I had resembled each other closely. And she'd seen me often enough.

My long estrangement from my brother Tomas had never allowed me to become acquainted with his wife. Only in my ten years of exile after my husband's execution, when I was forced to appear once each year before the king and his courtiers to renew the parole that spared my life, had I met her face to face. Each year during that ritual humiliation, my giggling sister-in-law had used the public questioning to pose the most vulgar and intimate queries.

I reminded myself that I had not come to Comigor for Philomena, only for the boy. "I sent word," I said. "I promised Tomas I'd come. Are you ill?"

"Who is this woman, child?" asked the woman in black, scowling at me. "What kind of impudent person disturbs a poor widow so near death from her travail?"

"Well, I'm no thief and assuredly no stranger to this house," I said. And the invalid looked nowhere near death, though I didn't insult either of the ladies by saying so.

Philomena poked out her rosy lower lip. Her tears flowed freely, though exactly what sentiments induced them remained a question. "Tomas said he'd never lose a match, that I'd never be left alone in this vile place. Bad enough he was forever away, but at least he would take me to Montevial in the winter. And now I'm so ill, and it's just as well I should die, for by the time this is over, it will be almost spring. I shall be fat and ugly and everyone at court will have forgotten me. Curse him forever!"

With every shuddering sob Philomena set the twittering chambermaids aflutter like a flock of birds disturbed by a prowling cat.

"Oh, my sweet girl," said the old woman, patting Philomena's coverlet. "You must calm yourself or the child will be disfigured, even if you should manage to bring it alive this time."

Philomena howled. Half the maids wailed in unison with their mistress.

Neither affection nor sympathy persuaded me to take charge of the sickroom, but only purest pragmatism. If I couldn't speak with Philomena in a rational manner, then I couldn't discharge my obligation and get on with my life.

It was my duty—and my wish—to tell Tomas's wife and son how he had died with the honor befitting the Duke of Comigor, the Champion of Leire, the finest swordsman in the Four Realms. No matter now that he had never been intended to survive the battle that took his life, that he had been a pawn in a much larger game than the challenge of some petty chieftain to his king. No matter that his hand was fouled with the blood of those I most loved. In the end, set free of his madness, he had asked my forgiveness, and his last thoughts had been of his son. I had promised him I would tell the boy of his regard. In some way I did not yet fully understand, the enchantments that had corrupted my brother's life had been my responsibility, and I liked to think that fulfilling his last wish might in some measure repay him for what had been done to him.

"Look here, madam," I said to the old woman, drawing her away from the bed, "this excitement is doing your niece no good. And you yourself look exhausted. I'm a relation of the late duke—family, just as you are—and I'd be happy to look after Her Grace while you take a rest. For her sake, you must take care of yourself, must you not? Take you to your room for an hour. I promise to call you at the slightest difficulty."

"Why I could never— Who do you—?"

I caught the arm of a passing maid and ordered her to escort Philomena's aunt to her chamber, seat herself outside it, and wait upon the lady's every whim. I then commanded the hovering attendants out of the room, sending one to make broth to be brought only at my call, another to polish all the glassware in the house in case the physician was to need it, and one to count the clean linen for when it might be wanted. Only one quiet girl called Nancy did I keep with me. I asked Nancy to hang up my cloak, open a window, and keep everyone out of the room so her mistress could rest. Then I pulled up a chair to the side of the huge bed and waited.

It was not surprising that my sister-in-law was difficult. Her father was the Chancellor of Leire. A political marriage that obliged her to live in a place as removed from court as Comigor would seem like slow death for a pampered young woman reared amid the royal intrigues and scandals of Montevial.

After a brief interval of steadily decreasing moaning, Philomena took a shaking breath and looked about. "Where is everyone?" She sniffed and blinked.

"I told them that their highest duty was to serve you, and that they'd serve you best by giving you room to breathe. Now tell me what's the matter. You're not giving birth, nor look even close to it."

Philomena wailed again. The serving girl jumped up from her seat by the door, but I waved her away. I folded my hands in my lap.

The wail ended with a hiccup. The duchess dabbed her eyes. "It's dreadful. If I'd not lost the others, you see . . . The physician tells me I must stay abed or I'll lose this one, too. To suffer such wicked travail and have them all dead, save for Gerick, of course, my darling . . . though he's not quite as affectionate as one might want, nor at all interested in the things he should be, and such a vile temper . . . The physician Ren Wesley tells me to stay abed, so Aunt Verally says he must think that I will die, too. Then today I wake with such awful pain in my back that I know the end must be near."

"Ah. I understand now. How many have you lost, then?"

"Two. Both stillborn." I handed her an embroidered handkerchief from a stack of them beside the bed. She blew her nose.

"It's a terrible thing to lose a child at birth."

Philomena glanced up quickly, as if it had just occurred to her who was sitting at her bedside. She pulled the red satin coverlet tightly to her chin.

"I mean you no harm, Philomena. What Tomas did wasn't entirely his fault. Certainly, I hold neither you nor your son responsible."

Months ago, even before Tomas was free from his corrupting blindness, he had begged me to return to Comigor, hoping that I could protect his child from some unnamable evil. I had refused him then. I had seen no reason to heed my brother's fears when my brother had watched my husband tortured and burned alive for being born a sorcerer. I had seen no reason why I should care for my brother's child when my brother's knife had slit my own newborn son's throat, lest he inherit his gentle father's magical gifts. How had Tomas reconciled what he had done? Madness, enchantment—I had to believe that. It was the only way I could forgive him.

She averted her gaze. "Tomas's men brought your message when they brought the news that he was dead. I thought you were trying to make me afraid."

"Let's not speak of those things now. If the physician has sent you to bed, then I'm sure it's for the child's health, and not because of any danger to your own. If your back hurts, perhaps it's because you have so many pillows so awkwardly arranged." I reached around her and pulled about half of them away, straightening the others so she could change position without being smothered. I had Nancy bring a warmed towel, which I rolled into a firm cylinder and inserted behind Philomena's back.

"Oh! That's marvelously better."

"Good. Nancy can replace the towel whenever you wish. Now you should rest. When you're awake again, I'll tell you and your son what I've come to tell you of Tomas."

"It won't bring him back," said Philomena, settling into her nest and yawning.

"No," I said, feeling guilty at the joyous anticipation that prickled the boundaries of my skin. Ten years after his horrific death, *my* husband had indeed been brought back to life, a mystery and a marvel I could not yet fully comprehend. Only a few months had passed since Midsummer's Day, when a sorcerer prince with a damaged memory had intruded on my life. Only a few weeks had passed since the day I realized that somehow Karon lived again within that prince, and a sorcerer named Dassine had confirmed my guess. At the end of that day, when the two of them had walked through the fiery Gate of D'Arnath's Bridge and vanished, Karon could not yet remember either his own life or that of D'Natheil, the Prince of Avonar, in whose body he now existed. But Dassine had assured me that Karon's recovery was only a matter of time and work and sorcery. He would come back. He would know me again.

Sighing deeply, Philomena dropped off to sleep. To look on her drew me back to the lingering grief that even such a miracle as Karon's life could not allay. Philomena had a living son.

Appointing Nancy to guard the bedchamber, I wandered out into the passage and gazed from the top of the stairs into the great echoing well of the entry tower. Hazy beams of sunlight poured through the tall, narrow windows. This tower was young by the standards of Comigor history, but Tomas and I had found it marvelous as children. The giant black and gray slate squares of the floor tiles had been a magnificent venue for a hundred games. Our favorite was chess, and we were forever coaxing servants, visitors, dogs, and cats into our games as living chess pieces. When the light was just right, the thick, leaded panes of the high windows would transform the sunbeams into a rainbow. I would sit at the top of the stair and let my imagination sail up the shafts of red and blue and violet to places far beyond the lonely countryside of my home.

At no time in all my girlhood dreaming had I ever imagined anything resembling the strange courses of my life, or the mysteries of a universe that was so much larger than I had been taught. Wonder enough that I had married a sorcerer, reviled as evil incarnate by the priests and people of the Four Realms. But in these past months I had learned that another world existed beyond the one we knew—a world called Gondai, embroiled in a long and terrible war, a world of sorcerers, the world of my husband's people, though he and his ancestors, exiled in this most unmagical of realms, had forgotten it.

Lost in reminiscence, I made my way down the stairs. Just off the entry tower, near the bottom of the stair, was my father's library, one of my favorite rooms in the house. I laid my hand on the brass handle of the library door. . . .

"Now just hold there a moment, young woman," spoke a crusty, quavering voice from behind me. A familiar voice. "Might I ask who you are and what business you have in the duke's library, much less ordering the servants about like you was mistress here?"

I smiled as I spun about to face her. "Was I not always the one to get my way, Nellia?"

The elderly woman was propped up on a walking stick, but she came near toppling over backward in surprise. "Seriana! May the gods strike me blind and dumb if it not be my darling girl . . . after so long and so dark a road . . . oh my . . ." She fumbled at her pockets.

I caught hold of her and guided her to a leather-covered bench. "I was beginning to doubt there was any familiar face to be found here, but if I were to choose one to see, it would be yours. It makes me think the place must be properly run after all."

"Oh, child, what a blessing it is to see you. There's none but me left that you'd know, to be sure. The mistress"—the word was dressed with scorn enough to tell me the old woman's opinion of Tomas's wife—"brought mostly her own people from the city. She was of a mind to dismiss us all. But His Grace, your brother, wouldn't allow her to send me away, nor John Hay nor Bets Sweeney, the sewing woman. But you can see as things are sadly out of sorts. The new girls care only for the mistress and her things. John Hay died two years ago, and Bets is pensioned off to live with her daughter in Graysteve, so I'm all as is left. Little worth in me neither. But these eyes is good enough to see my little sprite come home when I never thought she would."

She patted my knee and dabbed at her eyes with a handkerchief. "Shall I have one of the girls open up your room? I've kept it set to rights in hopes you and your brother might make it up between you. We never believed what was said about you. Great wickedness we were told, but I knew my little Seri could no more do a great wickedness than she could eat a frog. The master wouldn't speak of it. And mistress—well, she has little good to say of anybody—and so's Bets and John Hay and myself would never credit ought she said of you." Quite breathless, Nellia stopped. Waiting, perhaps. . . .

The tales she'd heard of me were likely *quite* wicked—treason, heresy, consorting with sorcerers and all the evils attendant on such sordid association—crimes that would have cost my life had my brother not been the boyhood friend and sword champion of the King of Leire.

I wrapped my arm about her bony shoulders. "You mustn't worry about anything you've heard. It was all a terrible misunderstanding. And I appreciate so much that you've cared for my things, but I'm not to stay. I've only come to speak to Philomena and her son. I was with Tomas when he died, and all was well between us at the last."

Nellia's pink-rimmed eyes filled with tears. "I'm glad to

hear it. He was always a prideful boy, and the same as a man. Never learned to bend. Came by most everything as was his desire, but he'd no peace from it. Broke my heart it did, who knew him from a babe, to see him so high, but troubled so sore."

"But his son—he spoke of him with great affection. Surely the boy brought him happiness."

The old woman frowned and shook her head. "You've not met the young master, then?"

"No. I've been here only half an hour."

"It's right to say the duke—may holy Annadis write his name—took pride in the boy and had great hopes for him, but he's not an easy child."

"Tomas and I weren't easy either."

The old lady chuckled. "No. Easy was ne'er a word used in the servants' hall about either of you, but this one . . . Well, you must meet him." She glanced up and wrinkled her brow. "Shall I find out where he is?"

"I think it would be prudent if we were introduced in Lady Philomena's presence." I desired no personal relationship with the boy.

"That mightn't be easy. He's not one to sit at his mother's knee or—" She broke off and waved a hand. "Ach, I'm too free. You must be perishing thirsty, and hungry, too, I'd guess. Shall I have a tray brought to the library?"

"That would be marvelous. And it would be kind if you would send someone to your mistress's room to tell Nancy where I can be found. I'd like to know when the duchess wakes."

"Done, my dearie." Nellia wiped her eyes once more, patted my hands, and hobbled away.

My father's library was almost the same as I remembered it—leather chairs, dark woods, and ceiling-high shelves stuffed with leather-bound books and rolled manuscripts. On the end wall farthest from the hearth was his giant map of the Four Realms: our own Leire colored in red, subject kingdoms Valleor in blue, Kerotea in brown, and the ever-rebellious Iskeran in yellow. And yet a great deal of dust lay about, along with a general air of neglect. The tables and desks had seen no oil or polish; the brass lamps were tarnished; and my father would have threatened to behead the hapless servant who had allowed the bindings of his books to crack or his priceless maps to curl in their display.

My father had been, first and foremost, a warrior. For twenty years he had fought his sovereign's battles with skill and pride, always with more notches on his sword than his most grizzled veterans. But even more than fighting and glory, he had relished strategy and tactics, the marvelous interplay of soldier and general. Though not a scholarly man, he had accumulated a library of military history and philosophy unrivaled even at the University in Yurevan. He had collected maps, too, of all known lands and seas, ranging from ancient, primitive brushstrokes on silk or parchment that would crumble at a whisper to the most detailed, modern charts made by King Gevron's military cartographers.

But long before the books and maps held any fascination for Tomas and me, we were drawn to the library by the contents of two glass-fronted display cases. The treasure inside was a wonder unknown in any other house of our acquaintance—hundreds of miniature soldiers, cast in such perfect detail that you could read the expressions on their tiny lead faces and distinguish the individual links in their chain mail. Foot soldiers and cavalry, knights and flag bearers, trumpeters and generals, heralds and kings were crafted in every possible position. There were horses, too: battle chargers rearing, racing, wheeling, and beasts of burden laden with water casks the size of a thumb or pulling tiny baggage wagons. Along with a miniature flotilla, awaiting a young admiral's command, were armaments enough for a nation of finger-sized warriors.

Sometimes we would find the diminutive hosts deployed upon the maps of some ancient battlefield, poised to relive a day of blood and glory. Sometimes they were arrayed on the long, polished library tables as our father considered a new plan for smiting the enemies of Leire. But we couldn't touch the armies if they were in use, so our delight was to find them captive in their velvet-lined cases. Then had we released the leaden hordes and devised our own games.

The soldiers were the first thing I looked for in the library. To my delight, the cabinets were just as I had last seen them, flanking my grandfather's suit of plate armor. One cabinet held an army painted silver and blue, and the other a host of red and gold. I pulled open the door and reached for a silver swordsman and a horse caparisoned in blue, but passed them by when I saw the silver king, his sword still raised in royal majesty and his crown still bent from the days when Tomas and I would forever fight over him. Beside him was his herald, blowing an invisible trumpet, his instrument lost when Tomas sat on him in the dining room to hide from our father his terrible crime of removing a piece from the library.

"You're not to touch them!"

I turned in surprise, still holding the silent herald, and glimpsed the shadow of someone sitting in the window seat, all but his boots obscured by green velvet draperies.

"But they do no good, sitting so quietly in their case. They are meant to be out and about, defending their king from his enemies, are they not? No soldier hides in his encampment forever."

"You needn't speak to me as if I were five."

"I had no such intent. I just believe that it's a shame when any things so fine as these soldiers are left idle. Someone ought to use them, whether to give military insights or just for the pure pleasure of playing with them."

"No one plays with them."

"More's the pity," I said.

"Who are you?"

"When your mother is awake, we can be properly introduced."

"One of her friends. I might have known. Are you here to steal something from us?"

"It's not my habit. Have there been a rash of thefts in the neighborhood, that everyone here seems to suspect a stranger of thieving?" I drifted to my left, trying to get a glimpse of the boy in the niche, but the glare from the window behind him left him in shadow.

"Why else would anyone come here?"

"To visit your mother?"

"No one enjoys visiting her. And now she's a widow. Not worth knowing."

"To visit you, then?"

"I can grant no favors yet." How old was this child?

"Then perhaps to visit this marvelous house and the beauteous lands of the north?"

"No one—"

"No one would consider them marvelous or beautiful? I'll not dispute your assessment of your mother or even of yourself, but I will argue with any attempt to discount the attractions of Comigor Keep. Once you've held one of the Guardian Rings and imagined what it was like to be chained there for months on end with everyone you valued depending on your faithful watch, or hidden in the secret room in the north tower and watched the colors of the hills and sky change or the lightning dance across the roof as a summer thunderstorm rolls through . . . Well, I'll hold it up to you for marvels any day of any week. But for now, I'll leave you to your business. Excuse me for intruding."

Without waiting for a response, I left the library, narrowly avoiding a collision with a young footman who bore a tray loaded with jam pots, butter, and steaming oatcakes. "I've changed my mind," I said. "I'll sit in the music room. Leave the door ajar, if you please, so I can see if anyone looks for me in the library."

The footman set the tray on a low table, and I sat where I could see the library door. After only a few moments I saw a thin face peep out of the carved double doors that led to the library.

Tomas had said his son had our looks. There was no disputing that. The boy could have been his father as a child or a masculine version of myself at ten or eleven. Deep brown eyes, too large for the immature face, a body gangly and bony, already starting to get his height. Shining hair that waved about his face, hair of the same dark brown color with the tinge of red as my own. Bitter resentment at fate's cruel jests took a moment's grip on my heart. My son might have looked just the same as this boy.

The boy surveyed the hall and seemed annoyed at finding

no one about. He threw something to the floor and ran toward the stairs, out of my range of vision. Such an odd child. So angry.

I restored my equilibrium by devouring Nellia's oatcakes until some half an hour later when a chambermaid scurried across the tiles to the library doors. I jumped up. "Are you looking for me?"

"Aye, miss. The mistress is waked. Nancy's sent me to find the lady in the library."

"Well done. Tell her I'm coming."

The girl hurried away, and I followed more slowly. Halfway across the black and gray tiles, I saw a lump on the floor and stooped to retrieve it. It was the silver king, his bent crown now totally askew, and his mighty blade twisted so that it could never harm his enemies, only himself.

CHAPTER 2

When I arrived at her room, Philomena was yelling again, but not for pain or fear of dying. A stooped, middle-aged man, soberly dressed and unremarkable, was the recipient of a diatribe being laid on like a flogger's cane. "How can there not be enough silver to pay the wine merchant? You've likely put it all in your own pocket. I'll have you hanged!"

"But my lady—"

"Comigor is the richest hold in the Four Realms, and you are paid exorbitantly to manage it. Perhaps if we were to take your wage out of your flesh, you would find what's needed."

"But, if you please, my lady, we have spent . . . prodigiously . . . in the past year: the new furnishings, the gem dealer, the dressmakers. And now the roof is leaking in the west wing and the forge is unusable since the fire, and we cannot even hire laborers—"

"How dare you accuse me! My husband denied me nothing, but my steward dares tell me 'no more'? I suppose you would have me wear rags. I suppose I am to suffer completely."

"But my lady, the rents are eight months overdue." The steward blotted his forehead with a wide kerchief.

"Then get them, fool. Must I hold your hand?"

"Duke Tomas—may blessed Annadis write his name—left instructions at the first of this year that my lady must see to collecting the rents, as he was to be away on the appointed day. The Lords of Comigor have honored their covenant with the tenants for more than five hundred years.

Only the lord or a member of his family may receive the rents. The tenants are not permitted to deliver their coins to anyone else."

The bruised patience in the steward's voice gave me the sense that this was not the first time for such an argument.

"You insufferable prig. It was certainly not my choice to rot here while my husband went charging all over the Four Realms, but of course he never consulted me in this or any other matter. 'For Gerick's inheritance,' he said. 'To keep the vultures in Montevial from getting any ideas.' As if I knew nothing about inheritance and ambition. At least he can't pester me about it any longer. A new lord rules here—though he listens to me no better than his father." The painted fan that Philomena had been flapping like a pennant in a gale fell still, and her rosy face beamed with sudden inspiration. "Of course! My son can do it! He is the castle lord now. I'll command him to collect the cursed rents."

The long-suffering steward replied patiently. "Until he comes of age, the young duke cannot collect the rents, Your Grace. He is too young to be held to account, and therefore he cannot fulfill the terms of the covenant."

Philomena uncorked a silver vial she had snatched from her bedside table, inhaled deeply, and closed her eyes for a moment, then motioned to one of her maids. "Even if I could escape from my bed, I would not spend an entire tedious day nodding and smiling to filthy peasants. I care nothing for their nasty children or their cows or their wheat. Find some other way to get the money. Send the soldiers. Take hostages. I don't care."

"My lady, please . . . the dishonor of it . . ."

The steward seemed on the brink of tears, but Philomena turned her attention to a silver-backed mirror a maid had brought her, instantly rapt as the girl began to brush her golden hair. The steward stood his ground for a few moments, but when the lady began directing the maid in how to braid her tresses, he bowed and slunk out of the room.

I knew well of the Comigor Covenant. How many times had I been forced to dress in my stiffest clothes and sit in endless boredom beside my mother and Tomas as my father collected his rents? The ceremony played out like an elaborate dance figure. On the first day of every year, Covenant Day, the line of tenants would stretch through the great hall, across the outer ward and far into the outer bailey. One by one they would step forward, and my father would graciously invite the man to sit with him at a small table, offering him the glass of wine that sat on the table. Inevitably, the man would refuse the wine. The tenant would inquire politely after the health of the lord's family. We were always "quite robust," even when my mother was so weak from her last illness that she had to be carried up the stairs at the end of the day. Then my father would inquire after the health of the tenant's wife and his parents and the progress of his children, each of them by name, and ask whether the man needed new tools or a new goat. After a suitable time, the tenant would stand and bow, and, almost as an afterthought, offer his coins to his lord. My father would salute the man and wish him a good season, then turn his full attention to the next man and begin the dance again.

When Tomas and I got restless and speculated between ourselves on the dire consequences to the state of the universe should one of the tenants actually *drink* the glass of wine, our mother whispered that we were being disrespectful. For many years, I believed that she meant we were disrespectful to my father—a terrifying prospect that instantly corrected my behavior. Only later did I understand that our behavior was disrespectful to the tenants, who fed us, clothed us, and kept us in comfort in return for the use of the Comigor land and the protection of its lord.

When my father was away on campaign, my mother sat at the little table with Tomas and me beside her. Tomas had been awkward the first few years after his coming of age, when our mother was dead and our grieving father too drunk to do his duty, but he had grown into it. Until my banishment from Comigor, I had sat with him as always. To change the practice had been unthinkable.

I entered my sister-in-law's bedchamber in great disturbance of mind. "Did you rest well, Philomena?" I said.

Philomena's aunt lurked glowering on the far side of the

bed, half hidden behind the bed-curtains. The duchess's attention remained focused on her mirror. "I don't know what was in my head this morning, Seriana," said Philomena, smoothing a strand of her hair. "I should have told you to go immediately. My husband didn't want you here and neither do I. I've only your word that he sent you."

"You may accept what I say as truth or lies. But your son has a right to know how his father died, and there's no one else to tell him of it."

"For all I know, you may have killed Tomas yourself," said Philomena, more from annoyance than conviction. "You were married to a sorcerer and conspired with traitors. My husband caught you at it and called down the law. You're probably here for revenge."

"I told you, I hold neither you nor your child responsible. Tomas is beyond knowing, so vengeance has no purpose. Nothing will bring back my son." I pulled a small gray silk bag from my pocket and laid it on the bedclothes in front of Philomena. "I brought this for you. It's not dangerous." I smiled at the old woman, who had backed away from the bedside as if the little pouch might conceal a snake.

From the bag Philomena pulled out a lock of Tomas's red-brown hair tied with a green silk thread. She twined it about her fingers thoughtfully.

"Let it make peace between us," I said. "If for nothing else than this—your son is the Duke of Comigor. I've brought him the Comigor signet ring. I have no child to rival him, and I'm not likely to. This is the house of my father and his fathers before him for thirty generations. I'd not see it destroyed for pointless revenge."

"I think that's what Tomas was most angry about," said Philomena. "That you would do what you did and risk bringing ruin to this decrepit pile of rock. I never understood it."

My conviction that Tomas had been controlled by the Zhid, the ancient enemies of Karon's people from the magical world across D'Arnath's Bridge, was unsupported by physical evidence. But I would have wagered my life on it. "If Tomas had been allowed to think on his own, he would have known that I'd never take such a risk lightly. He might have tried to understand what I told him about my husband and his people. Whatever else, I think he believed me at the end. Will you summon the boy?"

Philomena tossed the lock of hair onto her coverlet and picked up her mirror, first polishing it with a lace handkerchief and then observing her pretty face twisted into a flirtatious pout. "He might not come. He was so much nicer when he was small and the nurse would bring him to us for an hour in the evening. We would dandle him about and then send him off to bed. Now he says such awful things when he's angry, and he's angry so often and for no reason." She pursed her lips, pinched her cheeks, and smoothed the skin over her brows, but she also dispatched one of the maids to find the young duke and tell him his mama most urgently requested him to wait on her.

Philomena continued her self-absorbed activities while we waited. I wandered to the window, unsure of how to broach the subject of the rents. Managing Philomena would be a full-time study. I was delighted that I didn't have to cope with her for more than a day.

The expansive view from the window behind the heavy draperies was serenely beautiful. The southern face of Comigor fronted wheat fields, a golden ocean that lapped at the stone walls and stretched into the midday haze as far as I could see to east and south.

A glance over my shoulder confirmed that the hissing sound was Philomena's aunt whispering vehemently in the duchess's ear. Philomena was not so circumspect with her replies. "She was not the sorcerer. She was only married to one—" When she found my eye on her, the old woman paled and stepped away from the bed. Astonishing how many people believed that marrying a sorcerer must surely imbue a woman with magical powers of her own. I had often wished that to be the case. "—and he's long dead."

More time passed. Philomena tapped her teeth with the corner of the silver mirror. "I think you should give the ring to me," she said abruptly.

I perched on the narrow window seat, where I could both enjoy the prospect and keep an eye on the bedchamber. "I'll give it only to its proper owner."

"Why would you care who has it? He's too young to wear it, and I can take it from him as soon as you leave."

"If I give it to him, and you take it away, then he will know who has it and who does not. There'll be no misunderstanding." I trusted Philomena no further than I could see her.

Philomena sulked until the boy strode into the room. "Gerick, my darling boy. Have you come to brighten your poor mama's day?"

Philomena didn't wait for an answer, and the boy didn't seem inclined to provide one. I didn't think his answer would be to his mother's liking anyway. His thin face was contemptuous and aloof, and I would have thought he cared about nothing in the world, except that he so studiously avoided looking at me. Though I stood in a direct line with the door, he proceeded directly to his mother's bedside and allowed her to peck him on the cheek.

"Gerick, this woman has brought you something that belongs to you. She insists on giving it directly to you, as is her right, but Mama must keep it for you until you come of age."

The boy turned to me and bowed politely, his eyes devoid of emotion, even curiosity. I waited for Philomena to make a proper introduction, but she said nothing more. So I motioned for the boy to join me on a settle padded with thin red velvet cushions. He positioned himself, stiff as a starched collar, in the farthest corner of the bench.

"I was with your father when he died," I said. The boy's eyes grew large, their chilly disdain melted in an instant. "I want to tell you something of that day. . . ."

I had prepared carefully what I would tell him of the strange, fog-bound cavern hidden in the snowy peaks of the Dorian Wall, and of the cruel, empty-eyed warriors who had sought to ensure their dominion over the Four Realms as well as their own far-distant lands by luring the finest swordsman in Leire, the King's Champion, to fight the Prince of Avonar. I told the story sparingly, so that all I spoke was truth, yet withholding the parts a child could not understand or that it would be dangerous for him to hear. The boy's attention did not waver through all my telling.

". . . . And so, you see, they never intended for your

father to win the match. They made him confused and angry and didn't tell him what they planned, for the Prince was pledged not to slay anyone from our lands. It was a most sacred vow that his ancestors had made, and the wicked men wanted to corrupt the Prince. But despite their tricks, your father discovered how he'd been deceived, and he refused to fight the Prince any longer. He told the evil men that there was no honor for King Evard in the match."

Now came the most difficult part to explain. I dared not touch on the subjects of sorcery and enchantment and D'Arnath's magical Bridge that linked our world to the world called Gondai and its royal city of Avonar. How could I explain that a soulless warrior Zhid had raised his fist and with terrible enchantments had driven Tomas to madness so that he impaled himself on D'Natheil's sword? How could anyone, adult or child, comprehend that Prince D'Natheil was truly my husband, Karon, who had once let himself be burned to death rather than betray his Healer's principles?

"These men were so wicked," I said, "and their leader so lacking in honor and truth, that they drove your father to fight once more. It was difficult—impossible—for him to see in the fog and the dim light, and when he charged, thinking to slay the evil warriors, he ran right onto the Prince's sword. The Prince was furious at what the wicked men had done, and he fought the villains until they could do no further harm. The Prince and I tried our best to save your father, but his wounds were terrible, and we could not. I held your father in my arms, and he told me he didn't suffer. And then he spoke of you."

The boy's great eyes were shining, flecks of blue and amber in their rich brown depths, displaying a child's pain that tugged at my heart no matter my disinterest or resentment. I was pleased that Tomas's son mourned him. It should be so.

"He said that you were fair and had his looks, and so you do. And he said you were intelligent and opinionated, and that he wanted very much to tell you what a fine son you were. He was very proud of you."

The boy took a shallow breath with the slightest trace of a quiver in it.

"He died in my arms soon after that. I buried him by that lonely lake with a sword in his hands as was proper for the King's Champion. When you're older, if you wish it, I'll take you there."

From a green silk bag much like the gray one I had given Philomena, I drew the heavy gold ring with the crest of the four Guardian Rings on it, and I placed it in the boy's hand. "This is yours now. When the time comes, wear it with the dignity of your father and grandfather. They were not perfect men, but they always did what they thought was right. Great responsibilities come with such a fine thing as this, and you must learn of them as your father would wish." But, of course, as I watched the boy wrap his slender fingers about the ring so tightly that his knuckles turned white, I wondered who would teach him. Not his mother or her aunt or her fluttering maids.

The child looked up at me as if seeing me for the first time. His voice was no more than a whisper. "Who are you?"

"My name is Seri. I'm your father's sister. That would make me your aunt, I suppose."

I thought I was prepared for whatever his reaction might be to the story I had told him, whether childish tears or controlled sorrow, confusion, or the more common disinterest of an aristocratic child whose parent was preoccupied with great events, but Gerick caught me entirely by surprise.

"The witch!" he screamed, as he jumped up and ran to his mother's bed. "How dare you come here! How dare you speak of my father! He banished you from Comigor for your crimes. You're supposed to be dead. Mama, make her go away!" Never had I heard such abject terror. Beasts of earth and sky, what had they told him?

"Hush, Gerick," said Philomena, nudging him aside and smoothing the bedclothes he had rumpled. "Calm yourself. She's leaving right away. Now, give me the ring before you drop it."

The boy clung to the red coverlet, shaking and completely drained of color. His voice had faded to a whisper. "Go away. You shouldn't be here. Go away. Go away."

Philomena's aunt looked triumphant.

I didn't know quite what to do. Controlled retreat seemed best. "I am certainly not a witch, and the last thing in the world I would want is to harm an intelligent boy such as yourself. Your father and I were strangers for many years, believing terrible things of each other, but by the time he died, we had learned the truth—that the evils in our lives were done by the wicked men who killed him. All was made right between us then, and that's why he sent me to you. But I know it's complicated. I hope that as you learn more about me, you'll not be afraid. And if there comes a time when you would like me to tell you more about your father, what he was like when he was your age, what things he liked to play and do, I'll come back here and do so. For now, I'll leave as you've asked."

They must have filled the child with all the worst teaching about sorcery. Even so, I would never have expected Tomas's child to be so dreadfully afraid. I nodded to Philomena, who was paying more attention to the signet ring than to her trembling child, and left the room. A wide-eyed Nancy stood outside the doorway. Unhappy, unsatisfied, I asked her to bring my cloak and summon my driver. It was certainly not my place to comfort the boy.

As I descended the stairs, I met a small party coming up. Nellia was leading a gentleman so formidable in appearance that you could never mistake him once you'd met. His dark curly hair and tangled eyebrows were streaked with gray, but his cheerful, intelligent black eyes, giant nose, and drooping earlobes, heavy with dark hair, had changed not a whit since the last time I'd seen him.

"Lady Seriana, have you met the physician Ren Wesley?" asked the housekeeper.

"Indeed so," I said. "Though it was many years ago."

"My lady!" said the gentleman, his bow only half obscuring his surprise. "I never would have thought to find you here. I was not even sure— Well, it is a considerable pleasure to see you in good health."

Ren Wesley had once been my dinner partner at the

home of a mutual acquaintance. The animated conversation with the well-read physician had turned a dreary prospect into a stimulating evening. On the day of Karon's trial the sight of the renowned physician among the spectators had prompted me to argue that a healer's skills were not usually considered evil, but rather marvelous and praiseworthy.

"I'm surprised to find you here also, sir, a full day's journey from Montevial. My sister-in-law is fortunate to have such skill at her call."

"Her Grace is difficult to refuse," said the physician. "And, indeed, she *is* in need of care." He pursed his lips thoughtfully. "May I ask—I never expected to have the opportunity—but I would very much appreciate a few words with you once I've seen to the duchess."

"I was just leaving."

"Oh dear. I'm sorry to hear that. I assumed—hoped—that you might be here to care for the young duke while his mother is unable to do so." The physician's broad face creased into a disappointed frown, and he lowered his voice. "The boy is in desperate need of some looking after, especially since his father's death. You've seen it, have you not—how troubled he is?"

"I've only met the boy today."

Philomena's aunt appeared at the top of the stair. "Sir physician, your dallying is insupportable. The duchess awaits."

Ren Wesley called up to her. "Madam, I have journeyed for most of a day to wait upon the good lady. Inform Her Grace that a portly old man, stiff from a long carriage ride, does not move so quickly up the stairs as sylphlike creatures such as yourself. Only a moment more and I shall be at her side." His scowl gave way to a raised eyebrow and a twinkle in the eye as soon as he turned back to me. "I would speak to you on the boy's behalf, my lady. Now, if no other time is available."

Unlike my nephew, I had never been the master of my own curiosity. "You should go up," I said. "I can postpone my departure for a little while. I'll be in the music room."

"Thank you, my lady. I will rejoin you as speedily as may be."

I sent word to Renald that our departure was delayed and returned to the music room. Sadly, this room was more neglected than the library, cobwebs draped over a standing harp as if the spiders were trying to add new strings to it. I straightened the portrait of my mother that hung over the hearth. My fragile, lovely mother had brought music and grace to this musty warriors' haven. She had been afraid of war and hated talk of it. When she had died so young—I was but nine years old—people had said that life as a Leiran warrior's wife had been too harsh for her. I had vowed to be stronger. Strange how things work out.

I ought to go. No need to concern myself with the child. By spring Philomena would be mobile again and would take her children to Montevial. Though I would be sorry to see Comigor left vacant, perhaps it would be better for the boy. Surely in the capital city some friend of Tomas's would take him under his wing.

As I picked idly at the strings of a lute that hung on the wall, that consideration led me to think of Darzid, Tomas's cynical, unscrupulous military aide. Darzid was an enigma, a charmingly amoral man who had attached himself to my family eighteen years before. With only flimsy proof, I was convinced that Darzid's mysteries were connected with my brother's terrible deeds, and, ultimately, with the soulless Zhid warriors who had killed Tomas and tried to destroy D'Arnath's Bridge. Darzid was unlikely to concern himself with Tomas's child. But the possibility that Philomena might turn to him for the boy's tutelage kept me in the music room waiting for Ren Wesley. If I could discourage any such association through the good offices of the physician, I had to do so.

Almost an hour later the leonine head poked itself through the music-room door. "May I?"

"Please, come in. I hope everything is well with my sister-in-law."

Heaving a massive sigh, the physician lowered himself to a high-backed chair that creaked woefully at the burden. "As I expected, the duchess needed only a good measure of reassurance. I've recommended that she keep close to her bed this time in hopes we may bring this child into the world for more than a single day. The last two arrived well beforetime, and, as such infants will, they lacked the stamina to survive more than a few hours. Every day we can prolong Her Grace's confinement gives the little one a better chance. But I ramble. You desire to be off."

"I do, but it's not for lack of interest in renewing our acquaintance. I've nothing but good memories of our evening's encounter."

The physician clucked his tongue. "What dreadful dinner parties the countess concocted! That particular evening was the only one in my memory when I did not return home swearing to renounce society completely. I looked forward to meeting you again. But the next time I saw you, you were in a witness box before the king, vowing it was possible for a healer to bring his patient back from the dead." Elbows resting on his thick knees, chin propped on his clasped hands, Ren Wesley examined my face as if I were some rare symptom to be added to his store of knowledge. "Ah, madam, do you understand what questions your story raised in me? The appalling truth of my own ignorance . . ."

"Surely you know that to discuss such matters would put us both in violation of the law." His frankness was disarming, but I had lived too long to ignore the consequences of unbridled speech. Any door or window could conceal an informer. Only sorcerers were burned alive, but those who countenanced sorcery, even by speech, likewise paid a mortal price: beheading or hanging, according to their rank. So Leiran law had stipulated for four hundred and fifty years.

"Yes . . . well . . . there are those among us who listen and think somewhat more independently than we have the courage to display. But in the interests of timeliness as well as safety, I will concede. Truly your nephew is of more immediate concern. You say you've met him?"

"He's the reason I'm here. . . ." I told Ren Wesley of my promise to Tomas and the message he had sent to his son.

"They did not get on, you know," mused the physician. He leaned back in his chair and took out a pipe, proceeding through the rituals of filling and tamping. "Gerick clearly admired his father a great deal, yet from the time the child left the nursery, he would scarcely open his mouth in his father's presence. The duke was quite concerned. Knowing I had sired six sons of my own, he consulted me several times, even asking me to examine the boy for any sign of disorder."

"And what did you find?"

"Never had the opportunity to discover anything. Twice I attempted an examination, and twice the child went into a fit, almost making himself ill."

Just as he had in Philomena's room.

The physician tapped the unlit pipe in his large hand. "Many children throw tantrums, especially children who are wealthy and indulged and permitted to be willful. But what's so worrisome is that the boy is not at all prone to such behavior. Your brother was a good father, and unless I attempt to examine him, Gerick is invariably polite and respectful to me, just as he was to Duke Tomas. He is very much in control of himself. Too much so for a child of ten."

"I noted the same. That's why I was so surprised at his outburst." I told the physician about the boy's terror when I revealed my identity. "I assumed that the tales he's been told of sorcery and my connections with it were just too frightening for one so young."

"For any other child you might be correct, but Gerick is not subject to foolish frights. No. The boy has built a wall about himself and will let no one beyond it. When anyone attempts to breach his defenses, he throws himself into this morbid frenzy. It's not healthy. He needs someone to take him in hand, someone who cares for him."

I sat on a cushioned stool beside the standing harp and began brushing cobwebs off the tarnished strings. "Why are you telling me this? I've just met the child. Though I grieve to hear of his trouble, surely there are better ears to hear of them." Someone who did not begrudge the boy's life. "His mother—"

Ren Wesley harrumphed like a volcano belching fire before its eruption. "I wouldn't trust his mother with the training of my dogs. But the woman isn't stupid, either. Where it comes to her abiding interests, she's been known to listen to reason. When I spoke with her just now, I took a great liberty. The duchess was complaining of a problem with the tenants and the rents. . . ."

"I heard it. I hope she can be made to understand the importance of the Comigor Covenant."

"What she understands, madam, is how painful is her lack of silver and how her own position depends on the security and prosperity of her son's inheritance. I told her that it was important to her health to ease these worries . . . certainly true. And I told her that I could see only one solution to her problems."

"What was that?" A blindly innocent question.

"I told her that *you* must collect the rents." His great eyebrows leaped skyward.

"You're mad! Philomena would never consent to such a thing."

"On the contrary, my lady; once her eyes were opened, she began to think it her own idea."

"Then *she's* mad."

"Not at all. Consider. The boy is not of age. The traditions of this house require that an adult, a member of the family or a guardian appointed by the king, carry out this covenant. His mother sees dealing with the rents as tedious and common and would as soon hang the tenants as shake their hands. But by persuading you to stay, she can have money in her pocket at the turn of the year without putting herself out in the least. I told her that your familiarity with the castle could perhaps relieve her of a number of burdens and allow her to concentrate on her health."

I was not sure whether to laugh hysterically or throw the harp at the monstrous eyebrows that waggled in delight at my discomfiture.

"I apologize for failing to take into account whatever it is that currently occupies your days, but the opportunity presented itself. I cannot but think the boy would flourish in your care."

The only thing that kept me from laughing at his foolish presumption was the way my heart warmed, even as I accused him of madness. I fingered the rose-colored, thumb-sized stone that hung around my neck. At some time in the coming months, so I'd been told, the stone would glow of its own light, and its unnatural chill grow warm. The next morning Dassine would bring Karon to visit me in hopes I might provide some small help as the sorcerer restored Karon's memory.

I had no good plan for what to do with myself while I waited. I could not bear to return to the primitive life I had lived for ten years in Dunfarrie, nor, even if I had the means, could I resume the life of aristocratic dabbling that had been interrupted by Karon's arrest. For the past few months I had been caught up in events that shaped the universe, and now neither sphere felt like home. I hadn't believed that I belonged at Comigor either. But if I could do some good with the time, shore up Comigor's neglected future, then staying here might be a decent way to spend my time. As for the boy . . .

"If I allow myself be talked into this foolishness, whatever would I do about my nephew?" I said. "He was trembling at the sight of me." And to think that I, of all people, could break down the boy's unnatural reticence . . . I could scarcely endure looking at him.

The furrows in the physician's broad forehead deepened. "A gamble, to be sure. If he cannot come to tolerate you, we'll have to reconsider. I told the duchess that I would speak to him." His last words were phrased as a question. He cocked his massive head, waiting for my answer.

I couldn't seem to think of another argument. "You're a wicked man, Ren Wesley. You remind me of another I met just recently, a healer, too, who with his conceits sets himself up to order the fate of men and women and worlds. I don't think either Philomena or her son will thank you for this. Nor will I."

The physician burst into thunderous laughter. "It should be a match of historic proportions. I might have to set myself a regular schedule of visits just to make sure you've not murdered each other."

So it was that the Duchess of Comigor sent me an urgent message, requesting me to delay my departure so she could set me a proposition. While I stood in the window of a second floor sitting room, waiting for my interview and wondering at the change a few hours could make, I watched Ren Wesley stroll about the inner ward. Hands clasped at his back, he examined the crumbling sundial that marked the exact center of the castle. He was just moving toward the curved border of the well when he spun on his heel. My nephew hurried across the courtyard, bowed politely to the physician, and joined him on his walk. Gerick stopped after a moment and seemed to be making a point, shaking his head vigorously. But he displayed no hysteria, no screaming or other irrational behavior, and soon the two resumed their stroll, disappearing through the arched gate into the fencing yard. A short time later, a maid brought the physician to me.

"Your nephew is greatly disturbed by your presence, my lady," said a bemused Ren Wesley, "and he repeated his accusations that you are—pardon my frankness—condemned and wicked. He says that his father banished you, and that you have no right to be at Comigor."

"That's that, then. He's absolutely correct. I'll go at—"

"But when I told him that your stay was in the best interests of Comigor and his mother's health, he accepted the decision quite reasonably. Unquestionably something about you disturbs him, but I don't believe he is half so terrified as he acts."

A bit later, when I was invited to Philomena's room, my sister-in-law sweetly begged my pardon, claiming that her lack of welcome earlier was due to her anxieties over her health. Her husband had obviously trusted and forgiven me, for she had received word of the royal pardon granted at Tomas's behest. Truthfully, said the duchess, in blushing humility, she had been quite taken by my words to Gerick about the honor and responsibilities of the family. When the physician had given her the dire news that she must abandon all serious thoughts and occupations such as the running of the household, the only thing that prevented abject despair was the realization that the Holy Twins had sent me to be the salvation of the family's honor and my nephew's heritage. After an hour of Philomena's wheedling and an hour of serious negotiations touching on my rights, duties, and privileges while in her house—the woman indeed knew her business where it came to matters of inheritance and ambition—we agreed that I would stay.

By nightfall Ren Wesley had departed, and my driver had been dispatched with letters to my friends in Dunfarrie, informing them of my change in plans. I had no need to send for my things. The few articles of clothing that I had acquired on my return to city life had traveled with me. By midnight, I lay again in the little room in the north wing where I had slept from the day I left the nursery until the day my brother had forbidden me ever to come home again.

CHAPTER 3

The autumn days quickly fell into a routine. I breakfasted with Nellia in the housekeeper's room, and then spent the morning either with the steward, going over the accounts or inspecting those parts of the castle in need of repair, or with Nellia, poking into the storerooms, guest rooms, linen rooms, or pantries. I had agreed with Philomena that in exchange for my help in collecting the rents, I would be allowed to put right what was needed with the house and estate, setting it in good order for my nephew.

Though the servants were universally shy of me—the infamous, corrupted conspirator of sorcerers, allowed to live only by the king's grace—my respectful manner to Giorge and his clerks quickly soothed the anxious steward. After a few awkward sessions in which I demonstrated both my understanding of the estate's complex finances and my regard for the unique arrangements between the lord's family and the tenants, the steward became my most ardent defender save for Nellia. With delight he dispatched his assistants to every tenant, notifying them that the world was in order once again. Covenant Day was set for the first day of the new year.

Afternoons I reserved for myself, walking out every day to enjoy the northern autumn, a luxury I had sorely missed in my impoverished exile, when autumn labors might be the only thing to stave off starvation in a hard winter. I returned from my walks to write letters on estate business or work on some household project: taking inventory of the linen, or showing the maids how my father's maps and books should be cared for.

I had agreed to spend an hour with my sister-in-law every evening after dinner. At first, Philomena required me to expound upon the most minute details of my activities and investigations, from how many napkins I had found in the dining-room cupboards to the state of the hay supplies in the stables. After a few days of verifying every item with Giorge or Lady Verally, her sour aunt, she must have satisfied herself that I was dealing with her honestly. I never again got beyond, "Here is what transpired today. . . ." without her saying, "Good enough, good enough. Let's talk of more interesting matters."

As I knew no court gossip and had no insight into current fashion, her "more interesting matters" seemed to be the private details of my life with a sorcerer. She wheedled and teased, calling me boorish, stupid, and cruel for refusing to amuse a poor bedridden woman, but I was not at all inclined to provide anecdotes to titillate Philomena's friends when the duchess returned to society. One night, in exasperation at our abortive attempts at conversation, I asked Philomena if she would like me to read to her.

"Anything that will pass this interminable time," she said. I suppose she thought that to dismiss me early would grant me some mysterious advantage in our contract.

After rejecting the first ten titles I brought as too serious or complicated, she allowed me to begin one of the books of romantic adventure that had been my mother's. Soon she was wheedling me to read beyond our hour's time. I always shut the book firmly; one hour of my life a day was all I was going to give her. But reading made these interludes more than tolerable and set our relationship on a reasonable, if not intimate, course.

Which left me to the matter of my nephew. An uncomfortable and unclear responsibility. My love for my brother was built in large part on our common history. We had been two very different people connected by the people, things, and experiences we had shared as children in this house. Yet our attachment had been much stronger than I had ever imagined, surfacing at the last after so many horrors seemed to have destroyed it. But I could see no way to stretch my affection for Tomas to encompass this strange boy. Someone needed to discover what was troubling the child, but I didn't even know how to begin and was little inclined to try.

Any presumption that casual interaction might break down Gerick's barriers was quickly dismissed. My nephew seemed to have abandoned all the public rooms of the house. Except for an occasional glimpse in the library, I saw him only at dinner. Formal and genuinely polite to the servants, he spoke not a word to either Lady Verally or me.

"Has Gerick a tutor?" I asked Nellia over breakfast one morning. I had never lived around children. A tutor might serve as a source of advice or insights.

"He's had a number of them," she said, "but none for long. He tells them how stupid they are, how he can't abide them as they're no better than beggars. If they're stubborn and put up with that, he'll start with the mischief, putting tar in their ink pots or lamp oil in their tea. Or he'll put on screaming fits with the duchess to make her send them away. Out of all the poor gentleman, only one ever stuck at his post for more than a week. But didn't the boy carry a tale to his mother that the man was getting overly friendly . . . in a nasty sort of way, if you take my meaning? So, of course, the man was dismissed right off. That was almost a year ago, and none has taken up the position since then."

And this was the boy that Ren Wesley claimed was polite and well behaved! "He doesn't seem to treat the servants so wickedly."

"Oh, no! He's as sweet a body as one could wish. Always polite and so grateful when you do him a service. James—the young master's manservant—he's never had a cross word from the boy, and spends more than half his time sitting idle because the child takes care of himself and his own things. He's ever so proper. Just not friendly as you and your brother always were."

Strange. "Does he have any friends that visit?"

"A few times children have come to stay with their parents—even the king's own daughter has been brought here—but the young master might as well not live here for all he shows his face. From what I hear, when the family goes to Montevial it's much the same. It don't seem right."

"So there's no one close to him, no one who could tell me anything that might help me understand him better?"

Nellia shook her head and poured more tea in our cups. "The only one ever got on with him was Lucy, his old nurse, but she's been off her head for nigh on five years now. Of course, she couldn't tell you ought anyhow as she don't speak. Then there's the fencing master. The young master does dearly love his sword fighting. I always thought it a sorry thing that he never let Duke Tomas teach him. The lad would only work at it—and right fiercely too—when his lordship was away. He—the duke that is—heard about the boy's practicing. He hired the finest fencing master he could find to come and teach the lad."

"And has Gerick allowed the fencing master to stay?"

"Indeed so. Swordmaster Fenotte. But he'll be of no help to you. He's Kerotean. Speaks not a word of decent Leiran. I just never understood why the boy wouldn't learn sword fighting of his father who was the finest in the kingdom."

"Actually, I think that's the most understandable thing you've told me."

Nellia looked puzzled.

"Tomas would have had no patience with a beginner. If the boy admired his father, wanted to be like him . . ."

The old woman nodded her head. "I'd not thought of it in that light. It's true the duke, grace his memory, was not humble about his skills."

I laughed, with no little sadness. "Perhaps he had the wisdom to see it and spare the boy his impatience." My brother had loved his son very much.

One of my first duties in the house was to make some ceremony of Tomas's death. King Evard would likely mount an elaborate rite for his sword champion, but with Philomena confined to her bed and Gerick so uncomfortable with me, I could not see us traveling to Montevial for such an event. Yet I felt the need of some ritual of closure for the family.

Most Leirans had long lost interest in the only gods sanctioned by our priests and king—the Holy Twins, Annadis the Swordsman, god of fire and earth and sunlight, and Jerrat the Navigator, god of sea and storm, stars and moon. History, most particularly fear of sorcery, had wiped out any public acknowledgement of other deities. And the cruelties of life had convinced most everyone that the Twins must be more concerned with controlling the legendary beasts of earth and sky and monsters of the deep than with the trials of mortals. But warriors like my brother and my father had found some solace in thinking that Annadis and his brother would write the history of their deeds in the Book of Heroes and tell their stories around their mythical campfires.

I had grown past blind acceptance of myth when I learned to think and explore for myself, and I had lost all faith in supernatural benevolence when I saw the slit throat of my newborn son. Yet experience had taught me the comfort of ritual, and it was not my place to refuse Tomas or his son the rite my brother would have chosen for himself.

So I brought in a priest of Annadis, and Gerick and Philomena and I, along with representatives of the servants and the household guard, sat in Philomena's room and listened to the stories of the Beginnings and the First God Arot's battle with chaos and how, after his victory, Arot had given dominion over the world to his twin sons. Rather than have the priest recite the entirety of my brother's military history—some of which I could not stomach hearing—I had the aging cleric list the matches Tomas had fought to defend the honor of his king in his fourteen years as Evard's sword champion. That evening, Gerick and I stood on the hill of Desfiere outside the castle walls and watched as a stone was raised to Tomas beside my father's stone and my grandfather's and the hundreds of others that stood on the treeless hillside like a forest of granite. My nephew remained sober and proper throughout the day, so I didn't know if the rite meant anything to him or not. But I felt better after.

* * *

It was nearing four weeks of my stay when I began to sense I was being watched. At first I told myself I was just unused to living with other people. Seventy-three house servants worked at Comigor: clerks and maids, cooks and footmen, boot boys and sewing women and Philomena's gaggle of personal attendants. There were about half that number of outside servants, grooms and pot boys, a smith and an armorer, carters and gardeners. Tomas's personal guard numbered some ninety men; they lived in the barracks across the inner bailey from the keep. And hundreds of other people lived on the estate and in the villages close by. So plenty of eyes were on me every day. But a day came when I became convinced that the creeping sensation was not just my imagination.

The day was hot and bright as only an autumn day can be, the sky a regal blue, the light golden, the angle of the sun and the sharp edge of the wind hinting at the season's change. I trudged through a deep rift that split the grass-carpeted hills to the west of the castle, risking a stumble on the rocks that littered the rift bottom and pricks and scratches from the draggle bushes in compensation for the shade.

As I walked, the hairs on my neck began to rise, the creeping sensation that had become so familiar over the past days. Calling myself fifty names for foolish, I hurried my pace and then made a sudden stop beyond the next bend of the rift. Peering back around the corner, I strained to catch some telltale movement or hear a soft footstep. But I didn't glimpse so much as a hare.

Feeling ridiculous, I tramped back toward the castle. But on the return journey, my eyes were momentarily blinded by an arrow of light from the west battlements. I blinked and caught the glint again. The third time, I smiled in satisfaction. So I wasn't mad. The only thing out this way for anyone to be observing with a spyglass was me.

The thought of a spyglass turned my thoughts to the Comigor spyholes. When I was ten and sorely lamenting the disdain heaped upon me whenever my eleven-year-old brother ventured into manly pursuits not permitted little sisters, my father had supplied me with a powerful weapon in sibling combat. One of the former lords of Comigor, desiring to know everything that went on in his domain, had installed squints into the Comigor walls and ceilings. The small holes were hidden in the decorative stonework or the capitals of columns or in the intricate carving of a wooden mantelpiece or door frame. If one knew just the right place to stand, in a niche or behind a column, or in the crawls left by stairs or corners or angles, one could press eye or ear to the hole and gain possession of castle secrets. I almost laughed in relief. To spy on the suspicious intruder was such a natural thing for a child. Perhaps I could turn the situation to good purpose.

No spyholes opened into my bedchamber, thank goodness, nor into the little study I'd made from the adjoining room in the north wing, but one of them overlooked the passage outside my door. The passage joined the north wing to the northwest tower stair, and the spyhole was concealed in a stepped molding that matched the rectangular wing to the circular tower. To look through the hole, one had only to lie flat on the first landing of the tower stair and peer through a slot in the dusty wooden floor.

On a day when I had the clear impression that my shadow was with me, I dug about in a cluttered storeroom until I found an old metal box that had a hasp, a working lock, and a key. I set the box in the passage outside my bedchamber door in clear sight of the spyhole. Over the next few days I found occasion to place several wrapped bundles in the box, making sure to lock it carefully after each entry. Having installed no telltales, I had no idea if the box had been moved or examined, but I didn't believe my spy could get into it.

On a crisp autumn morning, I inserted a last bundle into the box and carried it up the tower stair. Only because I knew to expect them did I notice the disturbed dust on the floor beside the lumpy shape of a moth-eaten rug, crumpled in the corner of the landing. I climbed slowly past the hidden spy.

The narrow triangles of the tower steps spiraled about the walls, expanding into a landing as they penetrated each of four levels. Tall arrowslits laid a barred pattern of light on the worn steps. A keen observer might note that the walls narrowed near the top, the spiral of the stair closing just a bit tighter than it should have. No more stairs existed beyond the fourth landing. Were an invading enemy to harry him so far, a besieged warrior could make his last stand there with no escape but his blade. The enemy could not know that the lady or the heir of the house had preceded this last defender into a secret place.

Pausing at the eighth stair past the third landing, and making a great show of sneaking, I twisted the head of a stone gargoyle and pressed hard on the blank stone beneath the ugly carving. Though I worried briefly that my scheme might be foiled by time and neglect, the stone slab soon swung away from me, revealing a steep narrow stair between the inner and outer wall of the tower. Narrow shafts in the outer stonework, invisible from below, supplied light and air.

Carefully I slipped through the opening and pushed the door closed, but not quite enough to let the gargoyle slip back into position. I ran up the steps to the tiny room at the top of the tower, the secret room where the lady and the heir could huddle terrified until their champions repelled the invaders, or where they would die by their own hands if all hope was lost.

The wind gusted through a small door to the outside. Past the door, five more steps led up to an open stone platform, centered by a firepit. This platform, hidden behind the crown of the tower, was the highest point in all of Comigor Castle, commanding a view that stretched to the horizon in every direction. The vast forest of Tennebar made a dark line in the west, while the snowcapped peaks of the Dorian Wall were just visible far to the southwest.

I smiled as the door from the inner stair creaked slightly, and I counted the steps it would take him to see where I had gone. . . . *Six, seven paces across the room and peer out the door. . . . Four, five steps. Now peek around the low wall that faces the platform and open your mouth in astonishment.*

"In this place only a bird can look down on you," I said. I was perched on the parapet between two merlons, eating an apple, my feet dangling over the wide world. "To my mind it's quite the most spectacular view in all of Leire."

As I had thought it might, the wonder of the place stole away the boy's determination to remain apart. He was soon leaning over the wall on which I sat.

He moved slowly around the parapet, his eyes wide, his red-brown hair blowing wildly. I said nothing more until he completed his survey and stood beside the metal box that sat in the crenel beside me. He glanced up at me quickly.

"Do you want to see what's in it?" I was careful not to smile.

He shrugged and said nothing, backing away a few steps.

"You've been interested in my doings these past days."

He flushed, but didn't run away.

I opened the box and pulled out a cloth bag. "When I was a girl and wanted to be alone, I often came up here. I didn't want anyone to spy me going in and out of the secret door, so I made sure to keep a box of supplies up here—a metal box to keep out the mice. I pretended I was the lady of the keep, and I needed enough food to sustain me until I could be rescued. That's what all this was built for, you know. At one time a supply of wood was kept in the secret room, so a balefire could be lit in this firepit to let the lord's troops know survivors were waiting for help."

From the bag I pulled out two more apples, a chunk of dry bread, and a lump of cheese, and set them beside me. From another bundle came a flask of wine and two mugs, then a tightly rolled shawl, a cloak, three candles, flint and steel, and a book.

I held up the shawl and the cloak. "It's nice to have something soft to sit or lean on, and, of course, the wind never stops, so at sundown, even in summer, it can get chilly. But the stars make it worth the wait. That's everything in my box. As with most things that look mysterious or frightening, it is really quite ordinary."

The boy narrowed his eyes, waiting.

I poured a mug of wine, stuck the rolled cloak between my back and the merlon, and picked up the book. "Help yourself to something to eat if you like," I said and began to read.

After only a few moments, the boy turned on his heel and disappeared down the steps. Too much to expect he'd say anything.

Gerick continued to watch me for the next few days, though he was quieter and more careful in his stalking. I was pleased in a way, for it meant he was still interested, and there was some hope that my scheme would succeed. Late one afternoon, as I started up the tower stair once again and passed the lumpy rug on the first landing, I said, "If you come, I'll show you how to open the door. Then you can go up whenever you like."

He didn't answer, but when I reached the eighth step past the third landing, the boy stood at my elbow. Without saying a word, I demonstrated how to turn the gargoyle's head and push on the proper place. Once I had it open, I shut it again and let Gerick try. He struggled a bit with the stiff and balky mechanism, but I didn't offer to help. When he managed to get it open, I acknowledged his success with a nod and started up the inner stair. "You can come too if you wish," I said. "I won't bother you."

He stayed well behind me, and he sat himself in his own crenel while I settled down once more to read. I poured myself a mug of wine, but didn't offer him any or attempt any conversation. After an hour or so of pretending not to watch me, he left.

After that, I went up to the northwest tower every few days, and on occasion found Gerick there. I always asked him if he minded my staying, and he always shook his head, but inevitably he left within half an hour. Had I not heard his voice on my first day at Comigor, I might have believed him mute.

Every morning he worked with the Kerotean swordmaster in the fencing yard. Although Gerick tried hard, he wasn't very good. His form was poor and his attacks more earnest than effective. But he was still young. The language difficulty was surely part of the problem. Once the Kerotean master had demonstrated a move, all his coaching and teaching was in the way of waving his hands and stamping his feet.

Three more weeks passed, and it seemed I was getting nowhere, but at least matters were no worse. And then on one evening I found ink spilled over the papers on the writing desk in my study. There had been little of importance on the desk: a letter to my friend Tennice's father asking for advice about roofs and forges, a shopping list for Nancy's next trip to Graysteve, half a sheet of musical notation for a melody I was trying to remember. But of course, the value of what was destroyed was not the measure of the loss. Nor was it the invasion of my privacy, for I had clearly left myself open to such a violation. I almost laughed when I realized what bothered me so sorely. It was the lack of imagination. I had been consigned by a ten-year-old to the company of weak-willed tutors and spineless schoolmasters. All my cleverness had advanced me not a whit. I was insulted.

Soon I found myself devising one scheme after another to crack Gerick's shell. One day when I visited the tower, I brought a small wooden box that held chess pieces and unfolded into a small game board. I asked Gerick if he played. He nodded, but refused to have a game with me. Another day, I brought my knife. Surely knives were irresistible for young boys still practicing swordplay with wooden weapons. I made a flute from a hollow reed, proud that I got it to play passably. When I offered to show Gerick how to make one, he flared his nostrils in distaste. "You are a wicked, evil woman. Everyone knows it. Why do you stay here? Go away!" At least I had evidence he was not struck dumb by my presence. On another day I brought a bundle of tall meadow grass and spent an entire afternoon weaving figures of animals as my old friend Jonah had taught me to do when I lived in Dunfarrie. Gerick stayed, pretending to shoot arrows at birds, only leaving the tower once I had used up my supplies. I considered that a victory.

Only one certain conclusion resulted from my activity. The boy was not afraid of me. Though he still maintained his reserve, he would sit on the windy parapet all afternoon, separated from me only by the empty firepit or a stone merlon. He watched me for hours at a time while I was at my business, though he knew I was aware of him. So, if fear that I might somehow ensorcel him was not keeping him silent, he must have some other reason, well calculated and determined. It made me look at him with new eyes. What could prompt a child to maintain such control?

Not for the first time I wished I had the ability to steal the boy's thoughts as Karon's people could. Scruples prevented the Dar'Nethi from using their power without permission, but for my part, the puzzle of my nephew would have quickly overcome any such ideals.

Philomena paid no attention to Gerick's attempts to be rid of me. She was pleased with our arrangement, she told me. No one bothered her with tedious business, yet the house was calm, the servants well ordered, the food excellent, and, most importantly, it would soon be Covenant Day, and silver would flow into the Comigor coffers once more. "You've been a great blessing, Seri," she told me one evening after our reading time. She had just finished detailing Gerick's latest complaints. "I told him he's acting the selfish little pig."

"Tell me, Philomena, have you considered getting some friend of Tomas's to foster Gerick?"

"Well, of course. Not that anyone I know would put up with him. One would think someone might offer out of sympathy, but only the captain has said he'd do it. He's such a nosy."

"The captain?"

"You know him. Tomas's trained dog. Captain Darzid."

Hatred bubbled up from my depths for the immaculately groomed courtier who had stood in every dark place of my life. Karon's arrest and trial. My son's murder. Darzid had hunted the sorcerer prince who had come to me at midsummer, and I believed he had lured Tomas to his death, making him a pawn in the long war between Karon's people and the three sorcerers who called themselves the Lords of Zhev'Na. "Darzid has offered to train Gerick?"

"Of course, I would never consider him." Philomena

fanned herself with a flat of stiff, painted paper cut in the outline of a rose. "He's no more than a common soldier really, not even knighted. Not at all suitable for a duke's companion."

"Very true. How perceptive of you to see that a relationship with your son would be only to Darzid's advantage and not Gerick's at all."

"Gerick loathes him. He'd probably kill the man if forced to be with him. I told the captain not even to think of it."

I almost patted Philomena's head that evening. I read to her for an extra hour, which put her quite to sleep. "Your snobbery has served you well for once," I whispered as I blew out her lamp.

Common sense told me to waste no more time trying to befriend a child who so clearly wanted nothing to do with me, but somehow that answer was no longer acceptable. I could not shake the image of his red-brown hair blowing wildly in the wind on the roof of the northwest tower. Whatever was troubling Gerick had cut him off from the most basic human contact. No child should be so alone.

One morning in late fall, Allard, the head stableman, came to me with an odd story. Two days previous, a boy had come to the stables asking for work. Being unknown to anyone, he was sent away. "An ordinary kind of boy," said Allard. "But yestermorn, that same boy was at the kitchen door, asking cook for work. Cook sent him away, too, though she gave him a morsel of food as he looked so forlorn. I hope that's all right, ma'am, as I wouldn't want to get cook in trouble."

"Of course, that's all right," I said.

"Then last night late," said the stableman, "I woke with the feeling that all was not right with the horses. When I went to the stable, I found that boy again! I thought to take a whip to him, but he started talking about how Quicksilver was getting a twist in his gut that was hurting him terrible, and how Slewfoot had a crack in his hoof and would soon go lame if it weren't fixed, and about how Marigold was going to foal a fine colt, but we needed to keep her quiet as she was delicate. . . ."

I almost burst out laughing. Paulo! No other boy in the Four Realms had a feel for horses like Paulo. It was hard to let Allard talk his worries out.

". . . and he sounded so true, that I took a look and Quicksilver was tender in the belly just as the boy said. All the rest was right, too. The boy is lame, which some would hold against him, but I could see as he was a natural with the horses, far past any lad in the stable. But I didn't want to take him on without your say. I thought there might be something odd, as he was asking if this was where 'the lady called Seri was set up to run things.' "

"Allard, would it make you feel better if I were to speak to this boy before you took him on?"

Relief poured out of the man like summer ale from a barrel. "Aye, my lady. That would be just what I was thinking."

"Send him to me in the housekeeper's room."

The old man touched his forehead in respect and looked relieved to have shed the burden of the extraordinary. I hurried to Nellia's sitting room and shooed her away, saying I was to interview a new lad for Allard. When Allard brought Paulo to the door, the boy grinned shyly.

"You can go, Allard," I said. "No need to interrupt your work. Come in, young man."

Paulo limped in, his twisting gait the result of one leg misshapen since birth. The old man bowed and closed the door. The boy grinned shyly at me and touched his brow.

Only the certainty that Paulo would be mortified with embarrassment kept me from embracing him. I offered my hand instead. "What in the name of the stars are you doing here, Paulo?"

"Sheriff sent me."

Graeme Rowan, Sheriff of Dunfarrie, had sheltered the homeless thirteen-year-old since our adventures of the summer. Rowan, Paulo, and Kellea, an untrained young sorceress from Valleor, had become valuable, if unexpected, allies, as I helped the mysterious Prince of Avonar evade pursuit and accomplish his mission in our world.

"Is anything wrong?"

"Nope. Just checking on things. Not heard from you in

a while. Sheriff thought you might want one of us about to take letters or help out or whatever. Easiest if it was me."

"I've just been a bit busy. I'll write a letter to send back, but before you go, I want to hear all the news from Dunfarrie."

Paulo's brown hand twisted the tail of his tunic, and his eyes roamed everywhere in the room except my face. "Course, I don't *need* to go back. You got horses here need a good hand."

"I'd be delighted to have you here, but don't you think the sheriff would worry?"

"Time I was getting me a job. Don't want to be a burden. He and Kellea are . . . well, you know. Don't need me about all the time."

I knew that the courageous sheriff, bound by his office to hunt down sorcerers and burn them, had lost his heart to a talented, short-tempered young woman who was probably the last living Dar'Nethi sorcerer born in the Four Realms. But I also knew that neither of them begrudged Paulo a home. "It's not that Graeme's making you work at your lessons?"

It wasn't easy to make Paulo blush, but a spring radish would have paled in comparison. "Horses don't care if a man can read."

"I'll give you a job in the stables. Allard needs the help. But later this winter, we might have to work on your schooling a bit."

I returned Paulo to Allard, who was waiting in the kitchen, and I said I could find no fault with the boy except that he needed a bath even more than he needed a meal. Paulo scowled and followed the old man back to the stables.

Paulo and I seldom had occasion to speak. But as I made my rounds of the estate with Giorge or rode out for pleasure, I saw him limping about the place. He always grinned before he ducked his head and touched his brow. Allard swore that Paulo had been born in a stable, perhaps of equine parentage. Soon I couldn't go into the yard without seeing the two of them, heads together.

I never told anyone that I had known Paulo in my former

life, though I could not have explained why. I was certainly not ashamed of him. He was a good and talented boy who had been my companion in adventure, brave and steady in circumstances that would daunt many grown men. It just felt good to have a private friend.

Seille came, the midwinter season when we observed the longest night of the year and the ten days until the new year. Seille and Long Night were celebrations bound up with the legend of a wounded god brought from despair by the generous offering of food, entertainment, and gifts from the poorest of his subjects. I found the truths of sorcery, two worlds, and the magical Bridge that somehow linked them and kept them in balance more fascinating than any Long Night myth. But I had always loved the trappings of Seille: gifts bound with silk ribbons, storytelling, pageants, pastries, evergreen boughs, hot cider fragrant with cinnamon and cloves, and splurging with hundreds of scented candles to brighten the cold, dark nights.

With the holidays came the first evidence of real progress with my nephew. I was surprised and pleased to find Gerick in Philomena's room when I went to her for our nightly hour on the Feast of Long Night. It had seemed a bleak holiday having no family gathering to parallel the festivity in the servants' hall, so I had asked the maids to garland Philomena's mantel with evergreen, ordered a special supper for the duchess, and invited Gerick to join us. Though matters between the boy and me had been more detached than hostile of late, I had never expected him to come. But he was dressed in a fine suit and had already lit the candles that Nellia had sent on the tray, adding their perfume to the scent of balsam that filled the air.

"A joyous Long Night, Philomena," I said, "and to you, Gerick."

Philomena sighed. Gerick bowed politely, but didn't say anything. One couldn't expect too much.

Gerick sat on the edge of his mother's bed while I pulled up a chair. I poured the wine and shared around the roasted duck, sugared oranges, and cinnamon cakes. There was no conversation, but no hostility either. When we were finished eating, Gerick and I moved the table out of the way. Philomena frowned and said, "Aren't you planning to read tonight?"

"On the contrary . . ." From my pockets I pulled two wrapped parcels and gave one to each of them. I had ordered the two books from a shop in Montevial. Philomena's was an exotic Isker romance, and she insisted I begin it immediately. Gerick's was a manuscript about Kerotean sword-making, so beautifully illustrated that I had hesitated to give it to him. I hated the thought that he might destroy it because it came from me. But while I read to Philomena, he sat cross-legged on her bed turning every page. His cheeks glowed in the candlelight.

When he closed the book at last, he jumped off the bed. I paused in my reading while he pecked his mother on the cheek. "Excuse me, Mama. I'm off to bed." Then, his eyes not quite settling on me, he made a small gesture with the book. "It's fine. Thank you." Tucking the book securely under his arm, he ran off, leaving me feeling inordinately happy. Even Philomena's gleeful report on his most recent demand that I be sent away did not spoil it.

A mere two days before the turning of the year and Covenant Day, I took my afternoon walk on the south battlement, forced to confine myself to the castle because of a snowstorm that had raged throughout the day. The wild whirling snow made me dizzy, and a sudden gust sent me stumbling toward the crumbling southernmost cornice. As I grabbed the cold iron ring embedded in the stone, thanking the ancient guardian warriors for protecting the daughter of Comigor yet again, I began to feel a burning sensation in the region of my heart. I thought I had frosted my lungs or developed a sudden fever in them, or perhaps something I'd eaten was bothering my digestion.

Before going back inside, I pulled on the silver chain about my neck as was my custom when I was alone, drawing Dassine's talisman from my bodice, expecting to find it cold and dull as always. But, as the storm wind whipped my hair into my face, the snow swirled about me in a rose-colored frenzy, picking up a soft glow from the translucent stone, banishing all thoughts of storms or loneliness or difficult children. I wrapped my cold fingers about the stone until my hand gleamed with its pink radiance, and I relished every moment of that burning, for I had been assured that when the stone grew warm and glowed with its own light, Karon would arrive with the next dawn to visit me.

CHAPTER 4

I could not remember feeling so anxious in all my life, not when I was first presented at court, not on the day I was married. I knew so much of this man who was coming, all those things that had drawn me to him even when I believed him a stranger. Yet I was not foolish enough to think a man could die in agony, be held captive for ten years as a disembodied soul, and be brought back to life in another person's body without being profoundly changed. So much less difficult had been my own lot, and I was not the same person I had been. He was my beloved, and he was alive beyond all hope, but I was very much afraid.

What would he be like? Though his soul was unquestionably my husband's, Dassine had said that D'Natheil would always be a part of him as well. I had seen the conflict between Karon's nature and the instincts and proclivities of the violent, amoral Prince of Avonar that remained in that body. How would the balance between the two have settled out after four months of Dassine's care? Perhaps he would seem more like Aeren again, the half-mad stranger I'd found in the forest six months before who was somehow both of them.

First I had to decide where we would meet. Large as it was, Comigor Castle provided few places where I could receive visitors unobserved. Privacy was a rare commodity in a great house. I had only just persuaded Nellia not to come walking through my bedchamber door at any hour as she had when I was a little girl. But my bedchamber was hardly suitable. I wasn't sure whether Karon would even remember me as yet. Dassine had said he would have to "take him back to the beginning" to restore his memories. It was all so strange!

I considered the battlements. No one went there but me, fair weather or foul, but despite the emerging stars' promise of fair skies, the bitter wind still howled from the wild northlands as fiercely as the wolf packs of famine years. And the snow lay deep on the surrounding countryside, so I couldn't ride out.

One other place came to mind. Located on the eastern flank of the keep, where morning sun could warm the stone, was a walled garden, wild, neglected, locked by my father on the day my mother succumbed to her long illness. Once the garden had been thick with flowers and herbs native to the far southeastern corner of Leire whence my mother had come at seventeen to wed the Duke of Comigor. The customs of Comigor, a strictly traditional warrior house, allowed a bride to bring only one of her father's retainers to her new home, and my mother had chosen, not her personal maid or some other girlish companion, but a gardener. The poor man had spent eleven years fighting Comigor's bitter winters and hot summers to reproduce the blooms and fragrances of his lady's balmy homeland, only to be sent away when she died because my father could not bear the reminder of her.

For many years after her death, I had climbed over the wall to read and dream in the peaceful enclosure, watching the carefully nurtured plants grow wild and die away like a fading echo of my young girl's grief. Now I held the keys to the house, and with them the key to my mother's garden, a place deserted, secluded, and most importantly, invisible from any vantage point within the castle.

Unable to sleep for my anticipation, I wrapped myself in a cloak, let myself through the garden gate, and strolled among the bare trees and shrubs and the sagging latticework of the arbors. The Great Arch of the stars still lit the darkness like a reflection of D'Arnath's enchanted Bridge.

I didn't question that they would come. "At the sun's next rising," Dassine had said, "at whatever place you are." If I'd told anyone in the world what it was that I anticipated so anxiously as I awaited dawn in my mother's garden, that person would have thrown me in an asylum. I wrapped my hand tightly about the pink stone, allowing its heat to warm my freezing fingers.

The sun shot over the garden wall, causing me to blink just as a streak of white fire pierced the rosy brilliance. Squinting into the glare, I spied a short, muscular man, who leaned on a stick as he hobbled toward me along the gravel path. His white robe flapped in the breeze, revealing a rumpled shirt, knee breeches, and sagging hose. Dassine. Alone. Bitter disappointment welled up in my throat. But when the sorcerer raised his hand in greeting, I glimpsed another figure. That one remained at the far end of the path, almost lost in the fiery brightness. Tall, broad in back and shoulder, he too wore a white robe. A white hood hid his face.

"Good morning, my lady," said Dassine, his breath curling from his mottled beard like smoke rings. Though tired lines surrounded them, his blue eyes sparkled. Gray-streaked brown hair and beard framed his ageless face like a striped corona. "Am I never to find you in a warm place? This weather makes my bones brittle. One snapped limb and you will never be rid of me!"

"There aren't many private places here."

He craned his neck to survey the pile of ancient rock that was my home. "Indeed. I am astounded to discover where you have settled yourself. Is that not your brother's pennant?"

"It's a long story."

"And you're not particularly interested in dwelling on such trivialities while my companion stands at the far end of the path alone. Am I correct?"

I was near bursting. "How is he? Does he remember—?"

"Patience! I told you it would take time. Do you remember my condition for bringing him?"

"That I must follow your instructions exactly."

"And you still agree to it?"

"Whatever is best for him."

"Precisely that. Sit down with me for a moment." He plopped himself heavily on a stone bench. I sat beside him, but my eyes did not stray from the distant, still figure in white.

"You are not a prisoner here?" said Dassine.

"I'm here of my own will and have full freedom of the house."

"Your brother's house seems an odd place to welcome the very one who caused the black flag to fly over these battlements. Is it safe?"

"Safe enough. I'd never endanger either one of you. Only one old woman here causes me any discomfort, and I can deal with her. I'm only here because I came upon an opportunity to repay my brother for all that happened."

"Just so. Well, then . . . we have made progress. Over the past four months I have given the Prince the memories of his youth—both of them. He remembers his life as D'Natheil up to his twelfth birthday, when he was sent to the Bridge the first time. I don't think I can take him farther than that, for as I told you, the disaster on the Bridge left little soul in D'Natheil. It's as well. Karon doesn't need to know more of what D'Natheil became in those next ten years. Sufficient that he knows of D'Natheil's family—his family—and Avonar, and most importantly, he knows of the Lords and the Zhid, the Bridge, and his duty as the Heir of D'Arnath. I think he will be able to pass examination if it comes."

"Examination?" Gondai, the world that lay across the Bridge, was such a mystery. I knew only bits and pieces about the Catastrophe—a magical disaster that had destroyed nine-tenths of their world—and the ensuing centuries of war between the Dar'Nethi and the Lords of Zhev'Na.

"D'Natheil's body has clearly aged more than these few months that have passed since he came to you last summer. If the Preceptors have doubts about the Prince's identity, they will examine him to determine whether he is truly the son of D'Marte, and thus the rightful Heir of D'Arnath. His physical makeup will be examined, and his patterns of thought will be read and matched to those of his ancestors. The tests will question knowledge and conviction, flesh and spirit."

"So he must *believe* he is D'Marte's son."

"Exactly. For him merely to accept that he was Prince D'Natheil *at one time* is not enough. He must live as D'Natheil, as well as Karon, now and forever."

"And what of his other life?" His true life, as I thought of it: his childhood in Valleor, his education at the University, his years in hiding, his scholarly posts, our meeting, our marriage. And then the horror that had ended it all: arrest, torture, burning, death . . . until this man beside me had snatched his soul before it could cross the Verges into the afterlife and held it—him—captive for ten terrible years, believing Karon was the last hope of the Dar'Nethi and their world.

"We still have some years, some of the best and all of the worst, yet to travel. He remembers his youth as Karon, twenty-odd years of it, through the time of his return to the University after his years in hiding. But he remembers nothing of the twenty years since that time or why he has two lives when others have only one."

"So he does not yet know he was dead?"

"No."

"And he does not remember me or our son?"

"He has not 'met' you in his past as yet. Nor has he yet confronted the decision that caused his execution—the decision that abandoned your child and your friends to death and you to humiliation and exile. My aim is to restore the man that made that decision, not to change him into someone else whose choice might have suited you better. Can you leave aside your feelings about those events as you speak to him?"

His gaze was penetrating, and as unrelenting as his harsh words. When he had been arrested, Karon had chosen not to use his power to save himself or the rest of us, believing that use of sorcery to injure others—even his captors—was a fundamental violation of the healing gift he had been given, sacrilege. Anger and bitterness at his choice had blighted my life for ten years. "My feelings about his decision are unchanged, Dassine, but neither would I change the heart that made it. I'll wait until he is whole again to resolve our disagreement."

Though his eyes lingered on my face, the sorcerer jerked his head in satisfaction. "Understand that he also remembers nothing of the events of last summer or your journey together. They will need to be relived in their turn. He is, to put it mildly, in a state of confusion, a most delicate state which you must do nothing to upset. This is really not a good time to bring him. Not at all." Clearly, this argument with himself was not a new dispute.

"Then why did you?"

Dassine sighed and leaned his chin on his white cane. "I know you think me cruel to have imprisoned Karon's soul for so long, and wicked to have arranged D'Natheil's mortal injury. And so I may be. What I do with him now is painful and exhausting as well. Every memory I give him must live again. Every sensation, every emotion, every sound, every smell . . . the experiences of days or months compressed into a few hours until his senses are raw. I press him hard, for though we have this interval that he won for us by his actions at the Gate, I don't know how long it will last. "

"Your war is not ended, then?"

"The assaults on Avonar have ceased—a blessing, of course. But our peace is uneasy and unaccustomed. No one knows quite what to do. The people of Avonar rejoice that the Heir of D'Arnath lives, and they know that he was somehow changed by his journey here in the summer and his victory at the Bridge, but they've not yet seen him. He has managed to put off the Preceptors with a brief audience, but their patience is wearing thin. And the Lords of Zhev'Na . . . our enemies, too, wait . . . and we do not know for what. I must use this time to bring back our Heir to lead us." Dassine rapped his stick on the frozen ground as if some Zhid warrior were hiding under the snow. A rabbit scuttered out from under the bench and paused under a fallen trellis, twitching indignantly. "But I've no wish to kill him. He needs an hour's respite . . . and someone other than his taskmaster to share it with."

"What must I do?" I said.

"Follow my instructions precisely. Say nothing of your acquaintance and marriage. Nothing of your friends.

Nothing—absolutely nothing—of his death. They are not his memories yet, and to mention them could do irreparable harm. If he speaks of himself—either self—then let him. As far as he knows, you are a friend of mine and know his history, but have met him only this year."

"Then what can I say to him?"

"Be a friend to him. Ease him. You were his friend before you were his wife. Now go. He thinks I'm here to consult an old ally, but, in truth, I'm tired and plan to take a nap."

Before I could ask even one of my hundred questions, Dassine leaned back, closed his eyes, and vanished. There was nothing to do but walk toward the end of the path.

He stood motionless, solitary, bathed in winter sunlight, facing a gnarled, bare-limbed tree that creaked in the cold. The white hood masked his profile, and his arms were folded into his white cloak, so that he might have been some strange snowdrift left in the garden by the passing storm, something only an enchanter could transform into human shape. I didn't even know what name to call him. "Good morning, Your Grace," I said, dipping my knee.

He bowed to me in answer to my greeting, but said nothing and did not raise his hood to reveal his face. He remained facing the tree.

"The tree is a lambina," I said, "native to lands well east and south of here, lands less extreme in their climate. In spring it flowers, brilliant yellow blossoms as large as your hand, their scent very delicate, like lemon and ginger. When the flowers fade in early summer, they don't fall, but float away on the first breeze like bits of yellow silk. Then the tree blooms again, almost immediately, small, white, feathery flowers with bright yellow centers, each in a cluster of waxy green leaves. It's very beautiful."

"I've seen it," he said, so softly that I almost didn't hear him. "The leaves turn dark red in autumn."

"This one hasn't bloomed in many years. I'm hoping it's only dormant."

With movements spare and graceful, he stepped across the snowy lawn to the tree and laid a hand on its gnarled trunk. "There is life in it."

Beneath my warm cloak, the hairs on my arms prickled. "I'm glad to know that."

"You're Lady Seriana, Dassine's friend." So strange to hear the disembodied voice coming from the shapeless robe and drooping hood. I strained to hear some trace of the person I knew in the quiet words.

"He said you might like someone to talk to while he was about his business."

"Please don't feel obliged. It's cold out here, and you'd be more comfortable inside. I'll await my keeper as he commanded. He knows he needn't set a guard on me."

"I don't consider it a burden to speak with you."

"A curiosity, perhaps."

"I'll ask no questions."

"And answer none? Dassine's not very good at it—answering questions, that is. I can't imagine he would permit someone else to answer things that he would not."

I smiled at this wry disgruntlement, even as I blinked away an unwanted pricking in my eyes. "I'll confess that he's asked me to be circumspect."

"Then you *do* know more than I." His curiosity tugged at the conversation like a pup.

"About some things."

"It sets quite a burden on an acquaintance when one knows more than the other." The note I detected in his voice was not anger. Nor did it seem to be resentment that kept his countenance hidden under his hood. I felt the blood rush to his skin as if it were my own. Earth and sky, he was embarrassed.

I shook the crusted snow off a sprangling shrub, and the branches bounced up, showering me with ice crystals and almost hitting me in the face. "I think this could be considered an interesting *variation* of acquaintance," I said, brushing the chilly dusting off my cloak. "And, as many things have happened since I met you last, we should start again anyway, don't you think?"

"*I* certainly have no choice in the matter." His tone demonstrated a most familiar irony and good humor. My heart soared.

"All right, then. We shall ignore all past acquaintance

and begin right now. You may call me Seri. I am thirty-six years old, and I live in this hoary edifice you see before you. A temporary situation, though there was a time— Ah, I forget myself. No past. I am a poor relation to the lord who rules here, though circumstances have placed me in charge of the household—not an inconsiderable responsibility. I am well educated, though not as up-to-date in many areas as I'd like, and I have a secret ambition to teach history in our kingdom's center of learning. Now tell me of yourself."

"I believe you already know who I am."

"No, sir. If I must begin again, then you must do the same."

"It is required?" His voice was low.

I let go of my teasing for a moment. "Only if you wish it. I am not Dassine."

With another bow, he turned to me and lifted the hood from his face. His eyes were cast down, and his cheeks were flushed as I had known they would be. "It seems I have several names. You must choose the one that suits."

"Aeren," I said without thinking. Tall. Fair hair grown long enough to tie back with a white ribbon. Wide, muscular shoulders. Square jaw and strong, narrow cheeks that might have been sculpted to match the fairest carvings of our warrior gods. Wide-set eyes of astonishing blue.

At the time of his death, Karon had been thirty-two, slight of build, dark-haired and boyishly handsome, with high cheekbones and a narrow jaw. The rough-hewn stranger who had dropped into my life on Midsummer's Day looked nothing like Karon. I had called him Aeren, for he had no memory of himself except that he shared a name with the bird—a gray falcon—that screeched over Poacher's Ridge. I had learned that his own language named him D'Natheil, but this man was not D'Natheil either. I felt no scarcely restrained menace from him. The threadwork of lines about his eyes, the strands of silver in his fair hair, the air of quiet dignity stated that the one who stood in my mother's garden was older, wiser, more thoughtful than the violent twenty-two-year-old Prince of Avonar. But he was not my husband . . . or so I told myself.

"As you wish." Even as he accepted my judgment, he glanced up at me.

My breath caught. In that brief moment, as had happened four months ago in an enchanted cavern, I glimpsed the truth that lived behind his blue eyes. This was no one but Karon.

I started to speak his true name, to see if those syllables on my lips might spark some deeper memory. But no light of recognition had crossed his face when his eyes met mine. *Patience*, Dassine had said. *You were his friend before you were his wife.* He looked very tired.

"Would you like to walk?" I said. "There's not much to see in this garden, but walking would be warmer as we wait."

"I'd like that very much. I can't seem to get enough of walking outdoors."

Inside, I danced and leaped and crowed with delight; Karon had *never* gotten enough of walking out of doors. Outwardly, I smiled and gestured toward the path.

My boots crunched quietly as we strolled through the frosty morning. Karon broke our companionable silence first. "Tell me more of yourself."

"What kind of things?"

"Anything. It's refreshing to hear of someone who isn't me."

I laughed and began to speak of things I enjoyed, of books and conversation, of puzzles and music, of meadows and gardens. He chuckled when I told him of my first awkward attempts at growing something other than flowers. "Jonah couldn't understand why his plants produced no beans, until the day he found me diligently picking off the blooms. I told him that my gardener had once said that plants would grow larger if we didn't let them flower. Poor Jonah laughed until tears came, telling me that until we could eat the leaves I had best leave the flowers be. I had ruined the entire planting, a good part of their winter sustenance. It was devastating for one so proud of her intellect as I, but it was only the first of many gaps in my experience I was to discover."

"This Jonah sounds like a kind gentleman. He was not

your family, though, for if his crop was a good part of his winter sustenance, he was not the lord of this manor."

Careful, Seri. Careful. "Jonah and Anne were like parents to me. I was estranged from my own family at the time."

"But now you are reconciled?"

"They're all dead now, my mother and my father and my only brother. The lord of this house is my ten-year-old nephew, and the lady is his mother, a somewhat . . . self-absorbed . . . young widow."

"We have something in common, then. I've gained and lost two families in these past months, one I loved and one I hardly knew. And now I'm left with only Dassine."

"And does Dassine teach you to grow beans, or does he pout, whine, and tell you nasty gossip?"

His laugh was deep and rich, an expression of his soul's joy that had nothing to do with memory. "He has taught me a great deal, and done his share of pouting and cajoling, but no interesting gossip and certainly nothing of beans. Beans must be beyond my own experience also." They were. I knew they were. I laughed with him.

The path led us toward a sagging arbor, a musty passage so hopelessly entangled with dead, matted vines that the sun could not penetrate it. Without thinking I followed my longtime habit and looked for an alternate way. But to avoid traversing the arbor we would need to trample through a muddy snarl of shrubbery or retrace our steps.

"Is there a problem with the path?" Karon asked, as I hesitated.

"No," I said, feeling foolish. "I just need to let my eyes adjust so I won't trip over whatever may be inside. I must get a gardener out here to clear all this away." I led him quickly into the leafy shadows. The air was close and smelled of rotting leaves, and our feet crunched on the matted vines.

"Why are you afraid?" His voice penetrated the darkness like the beam of a lantern.

"I'm not . . . not really. A silly thing from childhood."

"There's nothing to fear." His presence enfolded me.

Less than fifty paces and we rounded the curve and emerged into the sunlight. "No," I said, my voice trembling ever so slightly. "Nothing to fear. This was my mother's garden." I walked briskly, stopping only when I reached the lambina tree again. From the corner of my eye I could see Dassine hobbling slowly toward us. *Not yet!* Not even an hour had passed.

Suddenly a quivering trace of enchantment pierced the morning, and the lambina burst into full bloom, each great yellow blossom unfolding like a miniature sunrise, its pungent fragrance wafting through the sharp air. In a few moments of wonder, the huge blossoms floated away like enormous, silken butterflies, only to be replaced by the soft white blooms of summer, heavy with sweet and languid scent, each cradled in its nest of bright green. And then the glorious dying, the white blossoms fading into burnished gold and the waxy green leaves into deep russet, falling at last to leave a royal carpet on the frozen ground.

"Thank you," I said, my breath taken away by the marvel. "That was lovely."

"It's too cold to wake it completely, and I know I must be wary in this world, but I thought perhaps it might ease your sadness."

"And so it has." I hadn't meant for him to see my tears. Perhaps he would think they were for my mother. "You'll come again to visit me?" Dassine was almost with us.

"If my keeper allows it. I'd like it very—" Both voice and smile died away as he stared at my face. Knitting his brow, he touched my tears with his finger, and his expression changed as if I had grown wings or was a dead woman that walked before him. "Seri . . . you're . . ." Pain glanced across his face, and the color drained out of him. Rigid, trembling, he whispered, "I know you." He raised his hands to the sides of his head. "A beacon in darkness . . . Oh gods, so dark . . ." Eyes closed, head bent, he groaned and stepped backward. I reached out.

"Do not!" commanded Dassine angrily, shoving me aside and grabbing Karon's arm to steady him. "What have you done? What did you say?"

"Nothing. Nothing that was forbidden. We walked and talked of the garden. Nothing of the past. He made the tree bloom for me."

Dassine laid his hands on Karon's temples, murmuring words I couldn't hear. Instantly, Karon's face went slack. When his eyes flicked open again, they were fixed on the ground, and the light had gone out of them.

"What is it? What's happened?" I whispered.

"As I said. It was not a good time to bring him. You are too strong an influence." The old man took Karon's arm. "Come, my son. Our time here is done. We've a hard journey home." They started down the path toward the eastern wall.

"Dassine!" I called after them. "Will he be all right?"

"Yes, yes. He'll be fine. It was my fault. It was too early, and I left him too long. A setback only."

Before I could bid him farewell or ask when they might come again, the two white figures disappeared into a flickering fog.

CHAPTER 5

Karon

Surely I am the sorriest of madmen. These hands . . . they are not *the hands that lifted the wine goblet to my father on the day he became the Lord of Avonar, my Avonar of the mundane world, the Avonar that is no more. The shape is wrong. They're too large; the palms too wide. The hair on the backs of them too fair. This face . . . I peer into this placid pond that mimes so truly the tree and the stone beside me and the clouds that travel these azure skies, and the face I see is not the face that looks back at me from the ponds that exist in my memory. And my left arm . . . only four scars. Into what reality did the hundreds of them vanish, each one a painful ecstasy so clearly remembered, each one a reminder of the gift I know is still a part of me? It is a loss beside which the loss of the limb itself would be no matter at all. Where has the first of them gone, the long, ragged one made when I embraced my dying brother and a future that terrified me—the day I first knew I was a Healer? With this gift I have brought people back from the dead.*

So. These are a stranger's hands. Yet, I know their *history, too. Know and feel and remember . . . They have been anointed with oil of silestia, that which consecrates the Heir of our ancient king, D'Arnath, to the service of his people. With them I raised the Preceptors of Gondai from their genuflections on the day I was made Prince of Avonar, this other Avonar that still lives. These hands wield a sword with the precision of a gem cutter and the speed of lightning. And they have taken life, a deed that fills my soul with revulsion.*

How is it possible that I've killed and thought it right? And I'm good at it and proud of my prowess. . . .

As I sat in Dassine's garden, I pressed my hands—the stranger's hands—to my face, digging the heels into my eye sockets so perhaps the world wouldn't come apart on this bright, windy winter morning—or if it did, at least I wouldn't see it. As always after a session with Dassine, my search for understanding had left me stranded on a mental precipice, facing . . . nothing. Absolutely nothing. If I stayed at the precipice too long, tried too hard to shape some coherent image in this gaping hole in my head, the universe would fall apart in front of me, not just in the mind's realm, but the physical world, too. Jagged cracks of darkness would split whatever scene I looked on and break it into little fragments—a tree, a stone, a chair, my hand—and then, one by one, the fragments would fade and vanish into the abyss.

The effort of holding the world together always felt as if it were tearing my eyes right out of my skull. Even worse than the physical discomfort was the paralyzing, suffocating horror that always accompanied it. And I knew in my very bones that if ever I let the whole world disappear, I would never find my way back. If I was capable of speech, I would beg Dassine to make it stop, to wipe clean all he had returned, to excise that mote of cold reason that told me I would never be whole until I knew everything.

And what did my teacher, my companion, my keeper, answer when I begged his mercy? He would pat my throbbing head and remove my shaking hands from their desperate hold on his wrinkled robe, and say, "We've pushed a little too hard today. Take an extra hour's rest before we begin again." For, of course, my questioning, my feeble attempt to unravel the meaning of the person I was and the lives I had lived, was but the inevitable result of Dassine's schooling.

In my life as a Healer in the mundane world, I had once come upon a remote village where the inhabitants had discovered a tree whose fruit, dried and powdered and mixed with wine, gave them terrifying visions that they believed came from their gods. Drinking this potion also caused them to forget to eat and to care for themselves. When I found these people, the corpses of their starved, neglected children lay all about their village. The few adults who yet breathed were wasted with starvation and disease. Though they knew well that their insatiable foolishness had led them to this piteous state, they could not refuse the call of their gods. I understood them now. Even when so weary I could neither eat nor lift a cup, even when I wept from exhaustion and madness, neither could I refuse another taste of Dassine's gift. Dassine—my master, my subject, my jailer, my healer, my tormentor.

A cold gust caught the hood of my white robe, yanking it off my head and dumping the snow from a bare tree limb onto my neck. With leaden arms, I reached around and brushed off the snow, feeling a few icy droplets trickling down my back. Shivering, I drew my stranger's hands into the folds of the wool robe. *Who am I? What's happened to me?*

"Come on. Time to sleep." I hadn't heard Dassine open the door.

He had already disappeared back into the house, leaving the door open. He wouldn't expect me to answer. Words were always an effort by this time. I rose and padded through the garden after him, shedding my flimsy sandals at the door. I needed the fresh air, even on such a cold day, to remind myself that a world existed beyond my broken mind. Our latest session had ended better than most. No panic. No raving. No begging.

Once I'd stepped inside the house and closed off the world again, Dassine pointed to a cup of tea sitting on the table. "You shouldn't go out on days like this. I don't like you getting so cold."

I shook my head, refusing the tea and his worries in one efficient motion. In two heartbeats, I would be asleep and wouldn't care.

My bedchamber was a small, unadorned room that adjoined Dassine's workroom. Its walls and floor were bare, constructed of thick stone that eliminated all vagary of noise or climate that might disturb its utter monotony. Despite its construction, the chamber was neither cave nor prison cell, for it was clean and dry, and had a large, unbarred window of thick but exceptionally clear glass, a bed and a washing table, and no door at all, only an empty opening to the cluttered workroom. The bed was comfortable, though I was never allowed a full night to enjoy it.

Dassine would rouse me after only a few hours' rest, day or night, and lead me stumbling into this chilly, untidy jumble of books and tables, pots and jars he called his lectorium. He would remove my robe and seat me, shivering and naked, within a circle of tall candlesticks. Always he would ask for my consent to go on, and like the skeletal villagers of Pernat, I would tell him I was ready to seek my visions once again. Then he would begin a low chanting—quiet, rhythmic, peaceful, seemingly benign—until the candle flames grew taller than my head and roared with the thunder of a hundred waterfalls. By that time I could encompass no sensation but the light. It forced its way into my eyes, my head, and my lungs. It seeped through the very pores of my skin until I thought my body must glow with it.

Very quickly, then, would come to birth another day that had been hidden from me. In Dassine's light I saw again the face of my mother as she sang me to sleep, her intricate compositions of word and melody taking physical shape and weaving themselves into my childish dreams. In that light I heard once more the voice of my father whom I loved, watched him sit in his hall of justice, ruling with benevolence and honor those who would burn him alive if they knew what he was—a sorcerer of uncommon power. In that candlelight I learned again the art of healing from my mentor, Celine, and felt again the fiery kiss of my knife as I shared my life's gift with the sick and the dying. There I heard the reports of the slaughter of my family and my people and the devastation of my home. There I reread the books that I loved and those that bored me. I suffered the indignities of childhood and the revelations of youth, and I rediscovered my love of archeology, reacquiring my knowledge of the culture and history and art of peoples that were not my people, but whom my ancestors had embraced as their own.

Hours and days and weeks I lived in the light of Dassine's candles. And when the light died away at last and my mind limped back to his dim study, Dassine would tell me how long I had been away—four hours, perhaps, or five of present time.

After he had put the candles away and given me my robe, he would share food and drink that had been set on a tray in the middle of his scuffed pine table. The meal was wholesome and plentiful, but always plain. I'd eat what I could, and then I'd walk in Dassine's garden to bask in the sun or the starlight and inhale the sweetness of the open air. Inevitably I would begin to ponder what I had learned . . . until my questions drove me to the edge of the precipice. Then Dassine would send me to sleep and, a few hours later, wake me to begin it all again.

I had no idea how long I had been with Dassine. Time had lost its pristine simplicity, and every sunrise signaled a further distortion. Somewhere in the months and weeks just past was a beginning . . . an eternity of stupefied confusion while Dassine laid a foundation in my head so that he could speak with me of D'Arnath's Bridge between the worlds and what my actions to prevent its destruction had done to me. He spoke now only in the vaguest generalities, saying that the truth of my experiences must come from inside myself as I relived them.

On this very early morning—the bright, windy cold morning when the world had held itself together for once—the Healer watched from the doorway to the lectorium as I shed my robe and burrowed into the mound of rumpled pillows and blankets. My eyes were already closed when I felt a blanket drawn up over my bare shoulder and a hand laid on my hair. "Sleep well, my lord."

"D'Natheil! Wake! You must be up. The hounds are baying, and we must ride with them a while." Dassine shook me awake with unaccustomed vigor.

It was unusual for him to call me by that name—mine, yes, but not the one I had come to believe was closest to me. If I'd not been so groggy, I might have wondered more at his use of it, but it had been just after dawn when I had last collapsed on the bed. The light told me it was still early morning, and cramps and stiffness told me that I'd not even had time to change position.

"Have mercy, old man," I groaned and buried my head in the bedclothes. "Can't you give me an hour's peace?"

"Not this morning. We have visitors, and you must see them."

"Tell them to come back." I could muster no enthusiasm, even for such a glorious variation in our regimen as a visitor.

As far as my own sight or hearing witnessed, no other beings existed in the universe, though I suspected that someone else shared the house with us. On the table in the lectorium I often found two glasses smelling of brandy that I'd not been allowed to taste. And I could not imagine the testy Healer making soup or filling my washing pitcher with tepid water.

"The Preceptors of Gondai have come to wait upon their Prince. I've put them off for more than three months, and if I don't produce you, they'll cause trouble. I can't spare the energy to fight them, so you must get up and present yourself."

"The Preceptors . . . Exeget, Ustele, the others?" The urgency of his words prodded me to function at some minimal level. I sat up, trying to stir some blood into my limbs.

"Yes, you blithering boy. They sit in my library at this very moment in all their varieties of self-importance and deception. I told them you were sleeping, but they said they would await Your Grace's pleasure. So if you would like another hour's sleep before we begin work again, rouse yourself, get to the library, and get rid of the bastards. We've no time to dally with them."

"What will I say? I know nothing more than a twelve-year-old." My faith in Dassine's assurances that all I now remembered was truth took an ill turn. What if the memories he had instilled were only wild fictions and not the unmasked remnants of my own experiences? But a glance at the sagging flesh around his eyes reminded me that he slept no more than I. I couldn't swear that his mysterious game was the only hope of the world as he insisted, but I believed that he did nothing from cruelty or indifference. I had to trust him.

"You will say as little as possible. They're here to verify that I'm not grooming some impostor to supplant the line of D'Arnath."

I couldn't help but be skeptical. "And how am I to prove that? I doubt I can reassure them by telling the story of my life—lives."

Dassine jabbed at my chest with his powerful fingers. "You are D'Natheil, the true Heir of D'Arnath. You can pass the Gate-wards, walk the Bridge, and control the chaos of the Breach between the worlds. The blood in your veins is that of our Princes for the last thousand years, and no one—no one—can deny or disprove it. It's true that you've had experiences others cannot understand, and we cannot tell these fossils about them quite yet, but I swear to you by all that lives that you are the rightful Prince of Avonar."

It was impossible to doubt Dassine.

"Then they'll want to know what I'm doing here with you all these months, which, lest you've forgotten, you've never explained."

"They have no right to question you. You are their sovereign."

Ah, yes. It didn't matter that in my life in the mundane world, my younger brother, Christophe, had inherited the gift of Command from my beloved father, the Baron Mandille. In my life here in the world of Gondai—in this Avonar of sorcery and magic—I, D'Natheil, the third son of Prince D'Marte, had been named Heir of D'Arnath when my father and two older brothers had been slain in quick succession. When my name had been called by the Preceptorate—the council of seven sorcerers who advised the Heir and controlled the succession—I could scarcely write the letters that comprised it, because no one had ever thought that a third son, so wild, and so much younger than the others, would ever be needed to rule my devastated land.

My memories of D'Natheil's life ended abruptly on the day I turned twelve, the day my hands were anointed and

I came into my inheritance. On that day these same Preceptors waiting for me now had decided that I must essay D'Arnath's enchanted Bridge and attempt to repair the weakness caused by years of war and neglect and the corrupting chaos of the Breach between the worlds.

Gondai and the mundane world—the human world—had existed side by side since Vasrin gave shape to nothingness at the beginning of time. Dar'Nethi sorcery and human passion created a delicate balance in the universe that no one quite understood. At the time of the Catastrophe, when the Breach came into being and separated the two worlds, upsetting this balance, we Dar'Nethi found ourselves diminished, left without power enough to reclaim our devastated land. And so our king, D'Arnath, built his Bridge of enchantment to span the Breach, hoping to restore the balance. The long war with the Lords and the corruption of the Breach threatened to ruin the Bridge, and only by the power and labor of D'Arnath and his Heirs had it endured a thousand years.

But at twelve I had not known what to do to preserve the Bridge. Dassine told me that my attempt had damaged me so dreadfully that further memories of D'Natheil's life were impossible. When these Preceptors had last spoken to me, I had been a crass, amoral youth, one whose life was consumed in a passion for war. They would not know me as I really was, Dassine said. It was my *other* life—Karon's life—that had transformed me.

My head started to ache with the contradictions and convolutions, and I pressed my fist against my forehead to keep it from splitting.

"Stop!" said Dassine sharply. "This is not the time to think. The Preceptors are not your kindly grandparents. You must be clear-headed."

"Empty-headed?"

"If that's the only way. Prepare yourself. I'll return for you shortly. I'll bring saffria."

I dragged myself back from the precipice without looking over it. "Make it strong, Dassine."

He tugged at my hair. "You'll do well."

There was not much preparation to make. I wished I could fit my entire head into the small basin of water on the stand in my room, but splashing the grit from my eyes would have to do. And I had nothing to wear but my white robe. From my first days with him, Dassine had forbidden me to use sorcery to obtain anything beyond his meager provision. Neither of us could afford to squander power, he said, and in truth, I rarely had enough to conjure a candle flame. By the time I knew that I was the ruler of Avonar with the authority to command comforts to be brought to me, I was beyond caring.

Dassine reappeared almost immediately with saffria. I downed it in one long, hot gulp, hoping its pungent sweetness would find its way to those of my extremities that had still not come to the conclusion that they must function. With no more conversation—we had spent more words that morning than during an entire week of our usual business—he led me down a long hallway. Tantalizing telltales of early morning sneaked into the cool, shadowed passage through a series of open doorways: birdsong, dust motes dancing in beams of gold light, the scents of mint and damp earth. It would be so much more pleasant to follow them than to go where Dassine led.

I stood behind him as he pulled open a wide door. "You are greatly favored this morning," he announced. "The Prince has agreed to a brief audience. My friends and colleagues, His Grace D'Natheil, Heir of the Royal House of D'Arnath, Prince of Avonar, sovereign and liege of Dar'-Nethi and Dulcé. May Vasrin Shaper and Creator grant him wisdom as he walks the Way."

Now for the test. I walked through the doorway, fighting that part of me which insisted I did not belong here, that words of royal homage did not apply to me. I tried to focus on this world and its customs and to convince myself I had a place in it. Conviction is everything in a ruler, the father I had loved once told me.

Seven people stood up as I entered the wide, airy room: four men, two women, and one—not a child, but a slight, dark-haired, olive-skinned man, who hovered in the background. A Dulcé. One of the strange race that cohabited this world, a people with an astonishing capacity for knowledge and astonishing limitations in its use.

The six that were not Dulcé arranged themselves in an expectant and diverse half-circle in the center of a scuffed wood floor. One of the six was shorter than average, another enormously fat, one cadaverous, two in the fine tunics and breeches of men of rank, the others in robes of the type worn by scholars, variously brightly colored, dull, shabby, or fine. They, with Dassine as their seventh, were the Dar'Nethi Preceptorate. Though I knew these six only with the unshaded colorations of a child's mind, I knew what was required to greet them properly. The rituals of kingly politeness had been battered into me by the well-dressed man on the far left, a puffy, balding man with full lips and deep-set eyes. He looked soft but was not. My back ached with the memory of his beatings, and my spirit shriveled with the echo of his self-righteousness.

I had been an angry nine-year-old when courtiers dragged me away from the grimy comfort of a palace guard firepit and took me to the Precept House, the large, austere building that housed the meeting chamber of the Preceptorate and served as the residence of its head. On that night Master Exeget had announced that, as my father and brothers were all dead, I was to be raised up to be Heir, ignorant, filthy beast that I was, no better than a dog, fed on the scraps from the soldiers on the walls.

No one had told me that D'Seto, my last living brother, a dozen years older than me, and the most dashing, talented, and skillful of princes, had been slain by the Zhid. He was the only one of the family who had ever had a kind word for me, and all my awkward, childish striving, played out in alleyway throne rooms and stableyard sword fights, had been to be like him. Exeget did not grant me even the simple courtesy of believing that I might grieve for my brother. Instead he spent an hour telling me how unlike D'Seto I was. I hated Exeget from that moment, for he made me believe it. There was no justice in a universe that infused the blood of kings in such as me, he said, while condemning nobler spirits to lesser roles. Only strict discipline and rigorous training might improve me, and so I was not to return to the palace, but live with him in the Precept House. He had crammed his red face into mine and sworn that if his efforts failed and I was not made worthy of my inheritance, I would not live to disgrace it.

And so, on this morning as the Preceptors gathered to inspect me, I could not look at Exeget without loathing. I began my greetings at the other end of the line, hoping to find the right words to say by the time I got to him. Moving from one of the Preceptors to the next, I turned my palms upward as a symbol of humility and service. Each in turn laid his or her hands on mine, palms down, accepting what I offered, kneeling before me in honor of my office. As I raised them up, one by one, each greeted me in his or her own way.

The giant Gar'Dena, a powerful, prosperous worker of gems, wheezed and grinned, for I gave him more than a princely touch to help raise his bulk from his genuflection. I hoped no more sorcery would be needed, for the simple assistance had used up my small reserve of power. Once standing at his full height, dwarfing everyone in the room, Gar'Dena straightened his red silk tunic, blotted his massive forehead with a kerchief the size of a sail, and hooked his thumbs into an elaborately jeweled belt. "*Ce'na davonet, Giré D'Arnath*!" All honor to you, Heir of D'Arnath. This traditional greeting, which he pronounced in an ear-shattering bellow, was deeply respectful. Cheered by his generous spirit, I moved down the row.

Ce'Aret, an ancient, wizened woman with the face and humor of a brick, poked at my cheek with a sharp finger and snorted, whether in disbelief or general disapproval I didn't know. I gripped her finger and returned it to her firmly, which didn't seem to please her at all. Ce'Aret had taken on herself the duty of ferreting out those who secretly aided our enemies. Everyone feared her.

Ustele was almost as old as Ce'Aret, but his quick and incisive probe of my thoughts belied any impression I might have had of diminished faculties. Touching my mind without consent was an unthinkable offense, an invasion of my privacy that would permit me to summarily dismiss him from the Preceptorate, if not banish him from Avonar . . . assuming I was accepted as the true Prince. No one in the room, save perhaps the Dulcé, would have failed to register it. If I wished to retain any semblance of respect from the others, I could not ignore such an attempt.

"This day's grace I will give you, Ustele, because you were my grandfather's mentor. But no more. Age grants you no privilege to violate your Prince, because age has clearly not dimmed your gifts. The Wastes await those who take such liberties. Be warned." To my relief, my voice neither croaked nor wavered.

The old man curled his lip, but withdrew. Dassine's satisfaction wafted through the air from behind me like scented smoke. In truth, my thoughts were in such confusion, no one could have learned anything from them.

Y'Dan, a thin, dry stick of a man, would not rise when I touched his shoulder. He shook his hairless brown skull vigorously, chewed on a bony knuckle, and refused to look me in the eye. "My lord"—he dropped his voice to a whisper so that I had to bend close to his mouth to hear—"listen, my lord. I beg you listen." He wanted me to read his thoughts.

I nodded, uneasy, for this was an act I had not been capable of performing as D'Natheil, and that custom had been strictly forbidden in my other life. But the Preceptorate had been told that whatever I had done to restore the Bridge had changed me, so I left off worrying and opened my mind to him.

. . . murder . . . conspiracy . . . treachery . . . your forgiveness, my lord. . . . we did not know you . . . our faith lost . . . the Zhid among us . . . we thought it was the only way. . . . Searing, consuming guilt. Impossible to sort out the flood of incoherent confession that accompanied it. Who had been murdered? My father perhaps or my brothers? What was the conspiracy of which he spoke?

Confused and wary, I put my finger to his silent lips, telling him to stop. "Another time," I said. "I'll hear you in private." Sometime when I knew what he was talking about.

Madyalar looked more like a fishwife than a Preceptor

of Gondai. Rawboned and red-cheeked, her gray hair tangled, she stood almost as tall as I. The soft-hued stripes of her billowing robe kept subtly shifting their colors, confusing the eye. Madyalar had been an Examiner when I was a boy, one who supervised Dar'Nethi mentoring relationships such as mine with Exeget. Though I had counted no one as a friend in those days, she had fought a running battle with Exeget over my care. That lent her a bit of grace in my sight, though, in truth, the course she had espoused was no more dignified than Exeget's, only less violent. She had declared that the only humane path was to teach me enough of duty, manners, and cleanliness that I could father a new Heir as soon as possible.

When she stood up after her genuflection, she probed me, not illicitly with her mind as Ustele had done, but with warm, rough hands that quickly and firmly traced every contour of my face.

"I hope I have exceeded your expectations, Mistress Madyalar," I said to her. I started to add, "even though I've produced no son." But in a moment's unsettling clarity, I realized that I didn't know whether I had fathered any children. I—Karon—was forty-two years old, so Dassine had told me. Twenty of those years were still missing. The thought was disconcerting, one I could ill afford in my present situation. I closed my eyes for a moment, afraid the world might disintegrate.

Madyalar drew me back. "You are no longer the boy I examined for so many years, my lord."

My eyes flew open. She had a curious smile on her face. "My bruises tell me that I am."

She cast her eyes slightly to her right where Exeget was studiously gazing out of the window. "I don't doubt that. Childhood bruises sting long after their discolor has faded. Though I would like to avoid contributing to Dassine's inflated opinion of himself, you seem changed for the better. Whether it is the old devil's skill in teaching or merely the fact that he saved your life until you matured on your own, the air is quiet about you now, whereas before it was a constant tumult. You bear many burdens that you did not when we saw you last, and you carry them with a strength that is different from that you displayed as a youth. And you have gray in your hair, Your Grace."

"Years will do that." No sooner had I said the words than I knew I'd made a mistake. The tension in the room drew tighter, and the dozen calculating eyes fixed on me widened.

"True," said a puzzled Madyalar. "But you must tell us how a few *months* can work such an alteration."

Although I remembered nothing of D'Natheil's life since I was twelve, Dassine had told me that it had only been a few months since I—D'Natheil, a prince of some twenty-odd years of age—had been sent onto the Bridge a second time, crossing into the mundane world on a mission I could not remember. These people had witnessed my departure. But the details of that journey were embedded in the lost years of one life and buried under twenty missing years of another. Spirits of night . . . what had happened to me?

My tongue stumbled onward. "I've worked hard at improving myself and continue to do so." Without further word, I moved on to Exeget.

Permit no questioning. Keep silent. Satisfy them. Get rid of them. These commands burst into my head as if I had thought them myself. *Concentrate, fool.* That command was my own.

"Our hopes and good wishes are with you, my lord Prince"—Madyalar spoke quietly to my back—"and, of course, the wisdom of Vasrin."

I nodded, hoping I hadn't offended her.

By an immense act of will I did not flinch when Exeget laid his perfectly manicured hands on mine. I knew he watched for it, hoped for a hint of cowering to demonstrate that he had power over me. For the greater part of the three years I'd spent in his custody, I had devoted my entire being to making sure he never received such a demonstration. I had never feared him, only despised him, but his hands had been heavy. Neither cold nor warm, neither soft nor hard, no roughness or other mark of age marring their smooth perfection. He took great pride in his hands, and had always required a servant to bathe and care for them after he beat me. In those vile years he had claimed that he could allow no one else to take on the onerous task of my discipline, as only a parent or mentor was permitted to chastise a child of my rank. But his apologetic disclaimers had not deceived me. He had enjoyed it immensely.

I confess I left him kneeling longer than the others, not so much to prove I could, but for the simple fact that I didn't want to touch him again. Perhaps he felt the same. I had scarcely brushed his shoulder when he popped to his feet.

"We rejoice, my lord, in the happy outcome of your journey." A nice sentiment, belied by his demeanor that expressed little of rejoicing and much of suspicion and arrogance.

I kept my mouth closed and my expression blank.

He spoke as much to the others as to me. "Master Dassine says that your ordeal in the mundane world has been a great strain, requiring a period of withdrawal from your duties, duties you've scarcely begun. Will you require ten more years in Dassine's care before your people have the benefit of your service?"

"I'll do whatever I think best, Master Exeget," I said. To speak in calm generalities with a straight face is much easier when one is absolutely ignorant. An advantage in a confrontation such as this. It's difficult for barbs and subtle insinuations to find their mark when the expected mark is missing.

"Whatever *you* think best? Please tell us, my lord Prince, what is it you think best? For more than three months we have sought your counsel and have been rudely put off by our brother, Dassine. For ten years before your journey, you failed to seek any counsel but that of this same man, and we were not allowed to speak with you unsupervised. You had no experience before you left us and have had no experience since your return. What assurance can you give us that your ideas of what is *best* have any foundation in reality? Why does Dassine keep you hidden?"

Ce'Aret and Ustele had not moved a step, yet I felt them close ranks, flanking Exeget like guardian spirits. "The Heir of D'Arnath is the servant of his people, yet he does not even know his people, nor do his people know him," croaked Ce'Aret. "As Madyalar says, you are much changed. I wish to understand it."

"Perhaps Dassine has hidden him all these years so we would *not* know him," said Ustele. "Can any of us say that this is, in fact, D'Natheil?"

The room fell deadly silent. Expectant. I knew I should say something. What sovereign would permit such an accusation? But my head felt like porridge, leaving me unable to summon a single word of sense.

"Master Ustele, what slander do you speak?" To my astonishment it was Exeget who took up my cause, donning the very mantle of reason. "Who else would this be but our own Prince? True, his body has aged, and his manner is not so . . . limited . . . as it was. But he has fought a battle on the Bridge—done this healing that has preserved and strengthened the Bridge and given us hope. Such enchantments could surely change a man."

"As a boy he was touched by the Lords. We all knew it," snapped Ce'Aret. "Never did this prince demonstrate any gift of his family. He killed without mercy and did not care if the victim was Zhid or Dar'Nethi or Dulcé."

"And where was it the beastly child finally found some affinity?" asked Ustele. "With our brother Dassine who had just returned from three years—three years!—in Zhev'Na. Dassine, the only Dar'Nethi ever to return from captivity. Dassine, who then proclaimed wild theories that contradicted all our beliefs, saying that our determination to fight the Lords and their minions was somehow misguided, that training our Prince in warfare was an 'aberration.' And when he could not convince us to follow his way of weakness, of surrender, he took the Heir and hid him away. What more perfect plot could there be than for the Lords of Zhev'Na to corrupt our Prince?"

The others talked and shouted all at once: denials, affirmations, and accusations of treason.

"Impossible!" shouted Exeget, silencing them all. "D'Natheil has done that for which we have prayed for eight hundred years! The Gates are open. He has walked the Bridge, healed the damage done by the Lords and the chaos of the Breach. We have felt life flow between the worlds.

He has foiled the plots of the Lords that would have destroyed the Bridge. All we ask is to understand it. His duty is to lead us to the final defeat of the Lords of Zhev'Na and their demon Zhid. We only want to hear how and when that will come about."

I couldn't understand why Exeget was defending me. Their arguments had *me* half convinced.

"We've all heard the rumors of what passed in the other world," said Ce'Aret. "That D'Natheil allowed three Zhid warriors to live, claiming to have returned their souls to them. That the only ones slain in that battle were the loyal Dulcé Baglos and a noble swordsman from the other world. Has anyone seen these Zhid who were healed? Was D'Natheil successful? Perhaps the victory at the Gate resulted from the sacrifice of another of the Exiles and not D'Natheil at all. Perhaps the Prince failed at his *real* task—his traitorous task—of destroying the Bridge."

The accusation hung in the air like smoke on a windless day. Gar'Dena's broad face was colorless, his eyes shocked. "Tell them these things are not true, my lord," he said softly. Exeget spread his arms wide, waiting for my answer. Madyalar's face was like stone. Even Y'Dan's head popped up. They were all waiting. . . .

Permit no questioning. Keep silent. Dassine stood just behind me. Though his fury beat upon my back like the summer sun, he held his tongue. No one spoke aloud. Yet from every one of the Preceptors came a similar pressure, the throbbing power that was so much more than spoken anger or demanding trust, the battering insistence that I speak, that I explain, that I condemn myself with truth or expose myself with lies or justify the faith some held in the blood that filled my veins. These seven were the most powerful of all Dar'Nethi sorcerers. I felt myself crumbling like the wall of a besieged citadel. I had to end it.

"Master Exeget, I'll not explain myself to you . . ." I began, wrapping my arms about my chest as if they might keep me from flying apart.

"You see!" said Ce'Aret, shaking her finger at me. "Dassine has made us a tyrant!"

". . . until I have completed my time of recovery with

Master Dassine. Then I will appear before the Preceptorate to be examined. If you find that I am indeed who I claim to be, and you judge me worthy of my heritage, then I will serve you as I have sworn to do, following the Way of the Dar'Nethi as holy Vasrin has freed us to do. If you find me wanting in truth or honor or ability, then you may do with me as you will."

Dassine exploded. "My lord, they have no right! You are the anointed Heir of D'Arnath!"

I turned on him, summoning my convictions as a flimsy shield against his wrath. "They have every right, Dassine. They—and you are one of them—are my people, and I will have only trust between us."

I believed what I said, and though it might have been wise to press the point with Gar'Dena and Madyalar and even Y'Dan, I had no strength to argue. I had to get out of that room. "I cannot say how long until I am recovered fully. I ask you all to be patient with me and to tell . . . my people . . . to be of good heart. Now, I bid you good morning." I turned my back on them and fled.

The Dulcé opened the door for me. I believed I saw a glint of humor in his almond-shaped eyes. Unable to shuffle my bare feet fast enough to suit me, I made my way along the route we had come. The stark simplicity of my little cell welcomed me—the barren stone that offered no variation to the eye, that kept the air quiet and stable and blocked out the clamoring questions that had followed me down the passage. My only evidence that I fell onto the bed before going to sleep was that I was in the bed that afternoon when Dassine roused me to begin our work again.

CHAPTER 6

Many days passed before Dassine and I had the time to sort out what had happened at the meeting with the Preceptors. He allowed no slacking off in our work, and my journeys of memory were increasingly troubling, leaving me no strength to spare for politics.

I was reliving the time when the Leiran conquerors had learned that sorcerers lived in Avonar—the Avonar of the mundane world, the Vallorean city where I was born. By virtue of my position at the University in Yurevan, I had escaped the subsequent massacre. But I had immediately abandoned my studies and gone into hiding, telling my few unsuspecting mundane friends that I had tired of academe and was off to seek my fortune in the wider world.

Rather than traveling in the spheres my colleagues might have expected, I had melted into the poorest of the masses haunting the great cities of the Four Realms, taking almost any kind of job that would feed me, intending to bury my former life for as long as it took for people to forget me. I dared not use the most minuscule act of sorcery. Such self-denial was physically painful as well as mentally distressing. Yet I was a Healer, and inevitably I would come across those who needed my gift. I could not refuse them. So I stayed nowhere long, wandering in the farthest reaches of Leire and Valleor, Kerotea and Iskeran, and into the strange wild lands beyond. It had been a fearful time, and I could not shake an ever-present foreboding when I returned to Dassine's candlelit lectorium.

During all these days, Dassine fumed. He snorted at any hint of weakness on my part, and his lectorium looked as if it had been ransacked by looters. We had never conversed much, but our silence had always been deep and comfortable. After the Preceptors' visit, the very air was angry.

To define my relationship with Dassine was impossible. He never asked what I had experienced in my journeys, though he always seemed to know whether they had been pleasant or especially difficult. I wondered whether he could "listen" as I relived my lives. Or perhaps he knew everything already. For my part, I could predict his actions with phenomenal accuracy, from the way he closed a book or the moment he picked to rub his game leg when the weather was damp, to the very words he would use to wake me. His moods colored my days. The vague impressions I had of him from my memories of D'Natheil's childhood did not explain our familiarity.

Exeget's assertion that I had lived with Dassine for ten years before my second foray onto the Bridge intrigued me. Dassine had told me that my first failed attempt to walk the Bridge when I was twelve had left me incapable of analytical thought or human sympathy. If that were true, and it was only *after* that incident that I lived with Dassine, then why did I feel such close kinship with him? Had I known him in my other life as well?

I had long sworn not to damn myself to incipient madness by asking such questions, and now I had to add the Preceptors' accusations to my list of nagging mysteries. But the days passed, and Dassine continued to slam our plates of soup and bread on his table, kick the well-fed cats that wandered in and out of the study, and throw his candlesticks into a heap instead of packing them away carefully when we were done.

"Get up. The world won't wait on you forever."

I slid my toes out from under the blanket, trying to keep my eyes closed and my head on the pillow for as long as possible. But just as one foot touched the stone floor, a hand whisked the blankets off, exposing my bare flesh to the cool air, and yanked the pillow out from under my head, letting my head flop most uncomfortably. The stars outside my window told me it was sometime in the midnight hours. I had to find out what was bothering Dassine.

I fumbled for my robe and slogged into the lectorium. After my journeys I was often incapable of speech, and he would brook no delays when he was ready to begin, so I had to act quickly. "Dassine—"

"So, are you ready?" He mumbled and swore under his breath as he placed the candlesticks in the circle.

"Dassine, I'm sorry if I disappointed you with the Preceptors. Was it my offer to let them examine me? I could see no other way to put them off."

"You had no need to put them off." Had he been a bear from the frozen northlands of Leire, he could not have growled so expertly. From a lacquered box, he selected a new candle as thick as my wrist and ground it into one of the tall candlesticks.

"But you know quite well that I had no idea of what they were talking about. How else could I answer their charges?"

"I told you they had no right to question you. You should have listened to me . . . trusted me." The last two words burst out of him as if unbidden, laden with bitterness.

"Is that what all this is about? Gods, Dassine, I've trusted you with my life, my sanity, with the future of two worlds, if what you tell me is true. I do everything you wish, though it makes no sense, and I accept it when you tell me that it will all fit together someday. I've met no one in either of my lives that I would trust in such a fashion. No one. Not my parents or my brothers or any friend. I can't even explain why, except that I seem to be incapable of doubting you. But despite my irrational behavior toward you, I cannot demand blind obedience from others. I will not, cannot, rule that way. You must know that as you know everything else about me. How can you ask it?"

He scowled and stopped his fussing, sagging into a chair by his junk-laden worktable. He drummed his wide fingers on the table for a bit, then said vehemently, "Then you should have kept silent."

"Perhaps you should have told me more."

"I'll not distort your past by interpreting it for you. You must become yourself again, not a version of yourself crafted by Dassine. Believe me when I say it is not easy to withhold the answers you seek. I have quite healthy opinions about many things, and it would gratify me if you were to come to share them. I believe you will . . . but I will not plant them in you now." He hammered one finger on the table repeatedly to emphasize his point.

"Then you can't be angry when I do what I think is right, even if you don't agree."

"Pssshh." He averted his eyes.

I pressed the slight advantage. "If I accept that I am truly D'Natheil, as you've sworn to me, then what harm is there in an examination? Even Exeget, as much as I detest him, would not go so far as to distort the findings of an examination by the Preceptorate. They'll learn that I am who you say I am, and they'll decide whether or not my mind is whole enough to lead them. It might do me good to have that reassurance."

Dassine pushed a pile of books from his table onto the floor and reached into a battered cabinet behind him, pulling out a green flask. He thumped it on the table and rummaged in a pile of water-stained manuscripts, dirty plates, ink pots, sonquey tiles, and candle stubs to come up with a pewter mug. When he uncorked the flask, the woody scent of old brandy made my mouth water. He poured a dollop into his mug, but didn't offer me a drop.

I must have looked disappointed, for he said, "You need all your faculties," and slammed the cork back into the flask. "If you think you've deferred our work by this yammering, you're wrong. When we've made a little more progress . . . closer to the end of all this"—he waved the mug at the circle of candles that had started to burn of their own accord—"I'll explain the realities of life to you, a little more about your friends on the Preceptorate, and why it would behoove you to stay as far away from them as possible."

"One of them . . . Y'Dan tried to tell me about conspiracies . . . murder. I didn't understand it."

"You have no concept of the twistings and turnings of

deception. Just today I've discovered that I am not the master at such that I believed. But for now"—he slammed the empty mug on the table and shoved the flask back into the cabinet—"we have work to do."

I berated myself for wasting my limited strength in the belief that I might change Dassine's mind about anything. But as he hobbled around behind me to finish his preparations, he used my shoulder for a handhold. Something in his firm grip told me it hadn't been such a waste after all.

In a few moments he was ready, and he took my robe and motioned me into the circle. I took up my position seated on the cool stone. As he began his chanting, I would have sworn he was grinning at me, though it was impossible to see through the ring of fire.

That night I journeyed back to the university city of Yurevan to study archaeology, the passion I had discovered in my three years of wandering. I lived just outside the university town with Ferrante, a professor and friend who was the only living person who knew the secret of my power. Just at the end of my night's vision, he introduced me to a friend of his, a fascinating man of far-reaching intellect, deep perceptions, and irresistible charm. His name was Martin, Earl of Gault, a Leiran noble, but far different from the common run of his warlike people.

When I returned from that fragment of time I had lived again, I sat in Dassine's garden, watching the dawn light paint the faded dyanthia blooms with a brief reminder of summer, and I found myself enveloped in overwhelming and inexplicable sorrow. Such things as Preceptorate politics seemed as remote as the fading stars. Dassine did not have to fetch me to send me to bed as was the usual case, for on that morning I wanted nothing more than to lose myself in unthinking oblivion.

Not long after this—in terms of my remembered life, six or seven months, so perhaps a fortnight of current time—Dassine said he needed to do an errand in the mundane world, and that he would allow me to visit his friend, Lady Seriana, while he was occupied. I was delighted at the prospect of any change, but made the mistake of asking Dassine if the lady was someone I knew. He tried to avoid the question and then to lie about it, but my mind was not so dulled as to mistake the answer.

"Yes, yes. All right," he grumbled. "She knows of you. Has met you. Yes." In his infuriating way, he would say no more.

The lady was not what I expected any woman friend of Dassine's to be. Not just intelligent, but witty and overflowing with life. Beautiful—not solely in the way of those on whom my young man's eyes had lingered, though she was indeed fair. Every word she spoke was reflected in some variance of her expression—a teasing tilt of her lips, a spark of mischief in her eye, the soft crease of grieving on her brow. I began to think of ways to draw more words from her, just to observe the animation of her face, the richness of a spirit that opened itself to the world in so genuine and generous a fashion.

From the first moment of our conversation, I knew she had been no casual choice, no acquaintance who just happened to be available to converse with me while Dassine went about his business. I knew things about her with a surety I could not apply to myself, and felt as if I were just on the verge of knowing more. But when I reached for memory I found myself once again at the precipice. The universe split apart as had become its disconcerting habit—on one fragment stood the lady, on another the lambina tree, Dassine on another, and between each fragment the terrifying darkness. To my shame, pain and dread overwhelmed me, and I could not even bid the lady farewell.

When next Dassine hauled me from my bed to begin my ordeal once more, I did not beg him to erase what he had returned to me, but instead I asked if he could return something of the woman, Seriana—Seri she called herself. She was so substantial, so real. If I knew something of her place in my history, then I might be able to veer away from the precipice when the terror came on me the next time. My jailer did not scoff or ridicule me as he often did when I pleaded for some variance in his discipline. He only shook his head and said, "Soon, my son. Soon you will know it all."

CHAPTER 7

Seri

I sat for a long time in my mother's garden. To interpret what had passed was like trying to analyze a streak of lightning. Already the event itself was fading, leaving only the bright afterimage. I tried to hold onto the moment of his laughter, the sound of his voice, and the look in his eyes as he made the tree bloom for me, and to ignore the disturbing ending of his visit.

Many wild dreams had grown unbidden in the past months. Though I had succeeded in dismissing most of them, one had lingered. Somewhere beyond my disbelief I'd held a secret hope that I might see Karon's face again. Clearly, that was not to be. His face was Prince D'Natheil's. Though aged by more than fifteen years in our few months together the previous summer, sculpted by his struggle to fuse body and soul, his appearance had changed no further since he had vanished through the Gate-fire with Dassine four months before.

Yet how could I be disappointed? Dassine had said I was not yet a part of his memory, and such was clearly not the case. He understood my fear of the dark and knew what would ease my sadness. As we walked through the arbor, his manner had been so like Karon's that I could never have guessed he was not the man I married. He *would* remember me.

On the previous night I had told Nellia that I was not feeling well, and under no circumstances was I to be disturbed until noon at the earliest, but my subterfuge now seemed a bit foolish. As I locked the garden and walked through the herb and vegetable beds toward the kitchen door, it was not even mid-morning.

I pushed open the door to the kitchen and stepped into bedlam. Nellia was directing two white-faced serving girls to carry jugs of hot water upstairs as soon as they were ready, and another girl to take a stack of clean towels to the mistress' room. When the housekeeper caught sight of me, she hurried toward me. "Oh, my lady, I've just sent Nancy to wake you. Though you said not to disturb, I knew you'd want to be told. It's the duchess. Lady Verally has sent word."

Philomena's child. Weeks too early. "Has Ren Wesley been sent for?" I climbed the servants' staircase alongside Nellia.

"I dispatched Francis right away, but—"

". . . but it will be an entire day before he can be here. Has anyone on the staff had experience as a midwife?"

"Only Mad Lucy, the young duke's old nurse."

"She still lives here at the castle? Somehow I'd thought . . ."

"Aye, Duke Tomas let her stay as she'd nowhere else to go. But her mind's long gone. She's done naught but sit and rock in her chair for nigh on five years now."

"Perhaps if we talked to her, even if she's feeble in the mind, she might be able to help. Even when they can't remember whether they've eaten dinner, old people can often remember what's important to them—how to make bread or play a game or deliver a child."

"No use. She's a mute, you know. Even if she'd a thought to share, she couldn't do it."

"Then we must send to Graysteve for a midwife."

Nellia puffed with effort as we passed through a door to the first floor passage. "But the duchess will have naught to do with anyone from the village. She says they're common and ignorant. That's why she hired Ren Wesley to come and stay for her last weeks, though, alas, it don't appear the time was set right for him to come."

"If the child is really on its way, I don't think she'll care. Send for the midwife."

"As you wish, my lady."

Nellia turned back, while I continued on to Philomena's bedchamber, only to find the door barred by an iron-faced Lady Verally. "You'll not come in. The duchess is in her last travail. We must have a physician or a priest, not a witch. You may have weaseled your way into this house through my niece's kindness, but I've a clear eye yet, and I can see what you're up to. I won't have you anywhere near her."

"Ren Wesley has been sent for and also a midwife from the village, but it will take time."

"I've already done all that can be done. Her fate is in the hands of the Holy Twins."

Poor Philomena. I never imagined I could feel sorry for her. To face the loss of another child born early with only the grim Lady Verally to comfort her would be a dismal ordeal indeed. And neither the High God Arot, retired to his celestial palace in mythical Cadore, nor the Twins—male warriors as they were—were going to be much help with a woman's labor.

"Will you tell me her condition then, so I can inform the young duke? He'll likely be quite distressed by rumors. Tomorrow is Covenant Day, and we must be prepared for all eventualities."

"I'll tell you nothing, witch. I've advised the young duke to stay away from you until we have you removed from this house. Your deceptions will be uncovered, and you will burn as you should have long ago." She slammed the door in my face.

Beastly woman. I hurried downstairs and sent a message to Gerick, telling him that it was possible that his mother would deliver her child early and reminding him that, no matter what happened, he would be expected in the great hall at first light on the next day to receive his tenants. Difficult though it might be, nothing must interfere with it.

For the rest of the day everyone in the house walked softly, as if an untoward disturbance of the air might precipitate disaster. The mourning banners that still drooped heavily on the castle doors took on an ominous new significance.

I occupied myself with preparations for receiving the tenants, trying to concentrate on the lists of names and families that Giorge had prepared, but I chafed sorely at being barred from Philomena's room. Though I had no idea what I might be able to do to help, I believed I should be there. Nellia brought me periodic reports, gleaned from the chambermaids. Philomena's labor had stopped after only a short while, but could resume at any time.

The midwife from Graysteve arrived, but Lady Verally insisted we dismiss her straightaway. I spoke to the woman, a neat, trim person of about my own age, and asked if she would be willing to stay through the afternoon and evening, in case the duchess were to overrule her aunt's decision. The midwife said she would wait as long as necessary. Infants should not be held responsible for the concerns of their relations, she said, putting a polite face on our foolishness. I asked Nellia to see to the woman's comfort.

I received no response from Gerick. Giorge had told me that the boy had sat with Tomas every Covenant Day since he could walk and had behaved himself admirably. I had to trust that he would do so again.

It was dark and cold when I rose on the next morning, and I dressed quickly. The custom was for the family members to dress in their best, but I had nothing fine. As I pulled on the better of my two dresses, I told myself that my dignity would have to be my adornment for the day. Even as I said it, I had to laugh. I sounded just like my mother.

I hurried down to the kitchen and pounced on Nellia as she came out of the larder. "Any word of the duchess?"

"The girls say the night was quiet," she said, as she set a wedge of cheese on a plate in the middle of a tray filled with plates, bowls, and pots. "Lissa! Take this on up." When the girl in the white cap hoisted the heavy tray, I was sure one moment more would see us all splattered with fruit porridge, boiled fish, sausage, scalding cider, and seedcakes. But the maid steadied her load and scurried away. "Lady Verally slept in the mistress' room," Nellia continued. "She's pushed a chair up to block the door and will only let her own girls in. I had the midwife stay the night with me. I thought to ask you should we just send her home. Don't seem needful to keep her from her own children when she's not wanted here."

"No, the duchess needs her. I've had an idea. . . ."

Though I bore no love for Philomena, I would not see her life stolen if I could prevent it, so I gathered Nellia, Giorge, the midwife, the captain of the household guard, and two of the footmen whom Nellia recommended as highly loyal to Tomas, and I directed them to stand ready. As soon as we had a report that the duchess was in true labor, the midwife was to be taken to her. If Lady Verally refused to admit the woman, then the footmen were to remove Lady Verally from the room and confine her to her apartments until such time as Her Grace's child was born or the aunt was sent for. I invoked my authority in the absence of the duchess for the purpose of preserving Her Grace's life and that of her child. All agreed. I left them waiting for Nellia's word to implement the plan. My own duties were in the great hall.

Comigor's great hall was a long, narrow room, its floor area modest only in proportion to its immense height. Its arched ceiling was so tall that as a child I had marveled at the clouds that drifted there, and believed that if I were ever allowed to be in the chamber when it was dark, I might see a whole new universe of stars. Of course the clouds had been only the lingering smoke from the ancient hearths that gaped taller than a man, and the hundreds of lamps and candles required to light the place.

On this morning the banqueting tables and chairs had been pushed to the sides of the room. My footsteps echoed as I hurried across the wood floor to the far end of the hall. Giorge and his assistants had everything arranged: the small table with the flask of wine and two glasses, the two cushioned chairs for Gerick and me, and the plainer ones for the tenant and for Giorge and his assistant who would sit behind me and record the payments in their ledgers. Everything was the way the tenants would expect it to be. There is great comfort in five-hundred-year expectations fulfilled.

"Is the young master on his way?" Giorge joined me, his hands smoothing his gray velvet doublet. Rustling and murmuring could be heard through the front doors that had been flung open, and beyond the narrow windows of the hall, gray shapes moved about the courtyard, stamping their feet in the cold.

"I'm sure he'll be here." Of course, I was not sure at all, and I breathed at least as great a sigh of relief as Giorge when Gerick hurried into the hall. My nephew was outfitted in close-fitting breeches of black satin, white hose, a wide-collared shirt of patterned green silk, and a tight-fitting doublet of yellow satin, heavily embroidered in gold. His red-brown hair was shining, and his eyes could have frozen a volcano.

"You look quite handsome this morning, Your Grace," I said.

Without deigning an answer, he sat down next to me, his back straight and stiff. He seemed a great deal older than ten.

"Have you spoken with your mother or Lady Verally this morning?" I asked. He shook his head. "Then perhaps you'll want to know. . . . I understand that all is well with your mother as of yet." I didn't expect him to dance with joy, but was astounded when he shot me a look of such unmitigated hatred that my skin burned with it.

I had no time to consider the cause of his current displeasure, for the first rays of the sun angled through the windows. The clatter and scrape of a hundred nailed boots echoed at the far end of the hall as a long line of sturdy, plainly dressed men surged toward us through the door. I rose from my chair and motioned to Gerick to do the same.

Giorge leaned forward from behind me and whispered, "This man is—"

"Goodman Castor," I said, nodding to the squat, toothless man who stood proudly at the front of the line.

I had asked Giorge to prompt me discreetly if I hesitated on a name, as there was no way to learn all the new faces in a short few months or to be sure that I could remember the old. But this man had worked the Comigor land since my father was a boy.

I gestured toward the chair. "In the name of His Grace,

the young duke, I welcome you to Comigor. Please rest yourself."

"An honor, ma'am," the roughly dressed man said loudly, his eyes narrowed as he touched his forehead and settled himself carefully into the wooden chair.

"Would you have a glass?" I asked.

"Thank'ee, ma'am, but not this morning. I've work as must be done."

"Tell me, Goodman, how is it with your Kate? And Bon and Ceille must be quite grown up since I was here last. Do they still switch dresses to fool everyone into thinking one is the other?"

The man's face lost its wary sobriety. "It *is* you, then!" He swallowed hard, and blinked. "No . . . no, ma'am. Ceille has done gone and got herself with child four times, but Bon's not chosen a man, so they turn out quite different now. And my Kate fares well. Still has all her teeth."

"I'm glad to hear it."

"How is it with the young duke and his family?" The man dipped his head to Gerick, who nodded silently. A gracious and proper response.

"We are quite robust," I said, "and give thanks to all who honor us with their service."

We talked briefly of crops and the weather, and I had Giorge write a note that Goodman Castor could use an extra half-bag of seed, for he was farming the portion of his son-in-law who was gone to the war in Iskeran. The young soldier had no one else to work his plot, for his own father was dead and his eldest son only six years old. When all was duly noted, I stood up to conclude the interview. "We wish you a healthy winter and a good season, Goodman Castor."

The man rose and touched his forehead again. "And for the lord and his family, my lady." Then he reached into his pocket, pulled out a grimy handkerchief, and carefully unwrapped it to reveal eight small silver coins. Reverently, he placed them in my hand.

"Thank you, Goodman Castor," said Gerick, with a polite bow of respect for the senior tenant, surprising me almost as much as he surprised the farmer. Then the man was gone, and another stood in his place, eyeing me anxiously.

Many of the tenants I knew, heads of the families that had worked the Comigor land for generations, whose children had grown up alongside me, though our paths had never been allowed to cross. Others were new to the estate. A few refused to open their mouths even in response to my questions. Their reluctance might just have been unfamiliarity, but more than one made the flick of the fingers that was supposed to call the Holy Twins' attention to a bit of the evil from which they were supposed to be guarding us. One after the other the tenants came. All morning, only a few moments apiece, and it was necessary to greet each one as if he were the first.

"Goodman Phinaldo, I welcome you . . ."

". . . an honor, my lady . . ."

". . . no wine this morning . . ."

". . . a healthy winter, and a prosperous year . . ."

Two hours into the long day, a footman brought me a note written in Nellia's threadlike scrawl.

The duchess is full into her labors and does not fare well. The lady aunt has been removed and the midwife brought in as you directed.

"Goodman Helyard, I welcome you . . ."

". . . a new scythe, as the old one has been sharpened until naught but a nubbin . . ."

". . . quite robust, thank you . . ."

There was nothing to do. We couldn't stop. In between tenants, I passed the note to the boy, for he had the right to know. His grave expression remained unchanged after he read it, and he nodded graciously to the next man. I felt inordinately proud of him.

". . . and for the lord and his family . . ."

"With seven children, you surely have a goat. No? Giorge, please make a note. Goodman Arthur must have a goat."

". . . quite robust . . ."

At midday, the footman returned.

The duchess has been delivered of a daughter. The child is frail. The duchess sleeps and seems well.

I passed the message to Gerick, and he reacted exactly as before.

". . . many thanks for your good service . . ."

". . . my son is ready to take a wife . . ."

". . . a note, Giorge. Goodman Ferdan's son, Gerald, should be next on the list for a plot. If we reopen the western fields as we plan . . ."

We did not stop for a midday meal. I had nagged at my mother unmercifully about how unfair it was that the tenants got to go home after their duty was done, but we had to sit all day with neither a drink nor a bite. She never dignified my complaining with anything but a single comment. "Someday you will understand, Seri, that asking a man to hold his year's work so that you may fill your stomach is unworthy of one in the position you have been given in life." Gerick did much better than I had done at ten, looking each man in the eye as he thanked him for his payment. Tomas had taught him well. I smiled as I welcomed the next man.

". . . loathly ashamed, my lady. 'Tis the drink what done it . . . makes me a madman it does . . . and the thieves took advantage. . . ."

". . . but this is the third year with no rent, and we have five young men waiting for land. It is time you yielded your place to those who will work honestly."

"But where will I go? My wife . . . my kindern . . ."

"You should have thought of your family when you drank away your responsibilities. They will not reap the bitter harvest you have sown, but you will work your own portion no longer. You will serve Goodman Castor who works two plots while his son-in-law is away. He is to give you only a common laborer's sustenance. Pay him heed, and he'll teach you honor and duty."

So passed Covenant Day until the last brushed and scrubbed man departed the great hall hours after the last shreds of daylight had faded. The glowing Giorge directed his assistant to pack up his ledgers and the plain steel box that now held the wherewithal to repair the forge and the west wing roof, to pay royal tax levees, the servants, the soldiers, and the wine merchant, and to ensure the security of the young duke and his family for another year. When he had sent the pale clerks on their way, the steward bowed deeply.

"A good day, my lady, young master. Properly done." High praise indeed from the taciturn steward.

The carafe of wine sparkled deep red in the light of the candles that had been set out to illuminate the steward's business. On a whim, I poured a little into each of the two glasses that had sat so neglected all through the day, and offered one to Gerick who slumped tiredly in his chair. He sat up straight, took the glass, and put it to his lips.

"Your father would have been proud of you today," I said, smiling.

But my words seemed to remind him of whatever it was that had worsened the state of affairs between us. With a snarl, he threw the wineglass at my feet, shattering the glass on the floor and splattering my skirts with the ruby liquid. Then, he ran out of the hall. I was beyond astonishment.

The two notes from Nellia lay crumpled in Gerick's chair, reminding me that I had not yet finished the business of the day. I thanked the wide-eyed servants, who came to clean up the mess and put the hall to rights, and started up the stairs to see Philomena.

Before I reached the first landing, a harried servant accosted me with a message from the chamberlain. A visitor was waiting in the small reception room, asking to see the duchess on urgent business. Perhaps Lady Seriana could see the man. I decided to get rid of the visitor first, leaving me uninterrupted time for Philomena and Gerick. I couldn't imagine what might bring someone to Comigor so late of an evening, so with curiosity as well as impatience, I hurried into the plain anteroom that was used to receive messengers and low-ranking visitors.

"Good evening, sir," I said to the cloaked figure that stood by the fire with his back to me. "Please tell me what is your urgent business with the duchess."

"Only if you happen to *be* the duchess," said the man in a supercilious tone that one did not usually hear from those consigned to the small reception room. He turned toward me as he spoke, and my retort died on my tongue. A handsome man of middle years, narrow face, dark, close-trimmed hair, conservatively dressed in garb suitable for a soldier of middle rank with connections at court. He had let his beard grow longer since I had seen him last, but I could not fail to recognize him. "Darzid!"

"You!" He gathered his self-control quickly, but I had seen astonishment, displeasure, and yes, an undeniable streak of dismay before he donned his usual mask of detached amusement. It gave me an unseemly jolt of pleasure to see him discomfited—even if only for a moment. "Lady Seriana. Never in all the vagaries of time would I have expected to find you settled in your brother's house. Has her ladyship gone mad?"

Wariness kept my loathing on a tight rein. Only hours since Karon and Dassine had walked in a Comigor garden, and now here was the man I believed the most dangerous in the Four Realms. "Her Grace is not receiving visitors this evening, Captain. State your business, and I'll do what I can for you."

I had once considered Tomas's darkly charming guard captain no more than a clever and somewhat amoral courtier, one who found cynical amusement in hanging about the edges of power and observing the foolish antics of those with high ambition. We had been friends as much as Darzid's nature was capable of friendship. But I had lost interest in Darzid as I became involved with the greater mysteries of falling in love with a sorcerer. And then the captain's amusements had taken a murderous turn. He had been instrumental in Karon's arrest, trial, and execution, and those of our dearest friends. Darzid himself had brought my dead infant to show me, observing my grief as if I were some alien creature with whom he had no kinship. And on the day Karon had first returned to this world in the body of D'Natheil, Darzid had come hunting him in the company of three Zhid—sorcerer-warriors from the world of Gondai. Whether he was a pawn, a dupe, or a conspirator, I wasn't sure, but he was certainly not innocent.

He stepped close, uncomfortably close, for I could smell anise on his breath from the sweets he favored. But I did not retreat. "Oh, this is very amusing," he said, studying my face, "a twist in the paths of fortune that could never have been anticipated. But my business is *quite* urgent. A critical opportunity, I might say. The lady duchess will have someone's head if it passes her by—yours, I suppose."

"Either *I* deal with the matter or it will have to wait. The duchess has given birth to a daughter today."

He smiled broadly, his cheeks flushed. "A daughter, you say. Poor Tomas. His last try at immortality comes only to another girl. And is this one as weak as the others?"

"I don't see that as any of your business, Captain."

"A fine thing he got a son the first time, is it not, else who would carry on the holy Comigor traditions?" He burst into entirely incongruous laughter. If he had not been standing so close, I might have missed the unamused cold center of his eye.

"Your urgent business, Captain? The hour is late."

He flopped on the high-backed wooden bench beside the fire, his thin, sprawling, black-clad legs reminding me of a spider. "I've brought the duchess the answer to her prayers, but clearly circumstances have changed. Perhaps my news is out of date, undesired, or unnecessary. . . . Tell me, my lady, how fares your nephew?" His voice was casual, drawling, but his gaze did not waver.

"Why would the young duke be of concern to you? When my brother died, so did your relationship with Comigor. Tomas forged no contract with you."

Darzid smiled broadly. "Have no fear, my lady. I'm not here to insinuate myself onto the Comigor paylist, but only to do a last favor for my late, esteemed master. Deeming me unworthy to tutor a lord's son, the duchess asked me to make some private inquiries as to proper fostering. Indeed, I have found someone who is both of sufficient rank to satisfy the duchess's pecuniary ambitions and of sufficient tolerance to take on the task of making a man out of your brother's, let us say, uniquely difficult progeny."

"And who might this person be?" As if any selection of Darzid's might be appropriate!

"Oh, you will delight in this. It is a matter of such delicacy that I shouldn't tell anyone before I inform the duchess, but the chance to see your reaction is just too amusing. Can you not guess who might agree to such a responsibility?"

I didn't answer. My skin burned where his eyes rested. I folded my arms tightly, so perhaps he would not notice my involuntary shudder.

"You will not give me the pleasure of a joust? Ah, lady, I do regret— Well, too bad." He leaned forward. "It is our king himself who offers." And then he sagged back against the spindled arm of the bench, smiling hugely.

"Evard wants to foster Gerick?" Only the fatigue of the long day prevented my disgust from exploding.

"Who else? His feelings for your brother were quite fraternal, and he wants to do for him as any brother would. I'd say that there's a good chance young Gerick will get a royal bride out of the arrangement, if he can be made civil. Ironic, is it not? Comigor linked to the Leiran throne—the connection Tomas most wanted, only a generation late. And he is far too dead to appreciate it."

It was not out of the range of belief; that was what was so appalling about the idea. Evard, King of Leire, had indeed loved Tomas, as much as a shallow, ambitious, unscrupulous man could love anyone. He might well be persuaded that if he were to give a home to his friend's son and groom the boy as a suitable mate for his only child, the Princess Roxanne, then he would be ridding himself of two irksome responsibilities at once. And there would be no stopping it. The offer was, as Darzid said, the answer to Philomena's prayers.

Darzid sat awaiting my response like the crowd before a gallows awaits the springing of the trap. No use for artifice.

"You'll be delighted to hear that I have no say whatsoever in this matter, Captain. But I wouldn't condemn the most deprived peasant child to life with Evard, so I'll do everything in my power to convince the duchess that her son needs a mentor with some rudimentary concept of honor . . ."

"And woe to him who underestimates the Lady Seriana. I've come near it myself. Very near."

". . . but the decision, of course, rests with my sister-in-law. She may be able to see you tomorrow, but I won't promise anything. Are you staying nearby?" I was not going to offer him a billet in the castle.

"I'm at the Vanguard in Graysteve and will return in the morning. The matter cannot wait. His Majesty expects the boy to be in residence by tomorrow night. But then . . . perhaps the game is changed now you're here . . . yes, I think so. . . . Even the soundest strategy must respond to an unexpected play."

"I'll have the servants bring your horse."

Without shifting his languid posture, he gave me a smirking nod. "As you wish, my lady. As you wish."

Still puzzling over Darzid's position in the scheme of things, I made my way upstairs to Philomena's bedchamber. The room was dim, only a few candles sitting on the mantelpiece, casting a pale light on Philomena who slept soundly in the great bed, her cheeks and lips rosy and her golden hair tangled on the fluffy pillows. Lady Verally sat at attention in a straight chair beside the bed, but her chin had sagged upon her black satin bosom, and she snored in a prim and ladylike manner. One could find many faults in the dismal woman, but she was indeed a devoted companion.

I found Eleni, the midwife, in the nursery, crooning softly to a white bundle in her arms.

"How are they?" I asked quietly.

Eleni shook her head and pulled back the wrappings so I could see the child. Never had I seen features so small. My smallest fingertip would cover her nose, my thumb her eyes. Surely even the gentle forces that hold us to earth must crush such frailty. A golden down covered her head. She was beautiful.

"We had a wet nurse in, but the little one has no strength to suckle. We gave her a few drops of milk from a spoon, but it will not sustain her. You can already hear the trouble in her breathing."

"And what of the duchess?"

"She'll be quite well, ma'am. The babe gave her no trouble, though the older lady made her believe it so. It's clear neither one of them ever carried a full-term child to birthing."

"I don't believe Lady Verally has any children, but the duchess has a son who is quite healthy."

The woman looked puzzled. "If I didn't hear it from your lips and profoundly respect your saying, I'd say you are mistaken, ma'am. The duchess's womb is weak and will always give way beforetime. I've never seen such a womb bear a child strong enough to live."

"Thankfully her son is a sturdy child," I said. "I suppose he was from the beginning. It's good you were here, Eleni. I thank you for your patience and skill."

The woman opened her mouth as if to argue the point, but instead dipped her head politely. "We've sent to Graysteve for a more experienced wet nurse. Another hour should see her here. I've been told to wait for her here, though it's past time I got back to my own brood."

"Certainly, you should go home. Pick up your payment from Nellia and get some supper before you leave. Tell her to send up the nurse when she arrives. I'll watch the child until then."

The infant didn't weigh anything. Her hand was no bigger than a kitten's paw and her tiny fingers wrapped themselves about one of mine. I walked her around the room, whispering to her of Tomas, and I shed a few tears for lost lives and lost years and lost promise. Then the wet nurse arrived and took the child, settling into the plain chair that had been left for her in a dark corner of the room.

Despite the late hour I went in search of Gerick, willing to intrude upon his anger so that he might see his sister while she lived and perhaps give his mother some comfort when she woke. James, his underemployed manservant, said the young duke had stopped by his apartments earlier and picked up his cloak. No one had seen the boy since then. Unusual for him to retire so late.

I retrieved my cloak and a lamp from my bedchamber and set out for the northwest tower. As a girl, I had often sought refuge there when I was upset. All the way up the stairs and into the secret room, I was unable to rid myself of a vague and growing anxiety.

He was not there. A bitter wind gusted through the doorway leading to the outer steps, the roof, and the parapet. My lamp cast eerie, dancing shadows on the curved walls. Gathering my cloak about me, I climbed to the tower roof. Gerick wasn't there, either, but someone had been there quite recently. An acrid odor wafted from the firepit. I held my lamp close to see what caused such a vile smell. The smooth stone pit was perfectly clean save for a large, shapeless gray mass still radiating heat. I saw no clue as to the nature of the stuff until I searched beyond the stone ring and found a tiny arm of blue-painted metal. The soldiers. Somehow Gerick had dragged wood up here and battled the wind to set a fire, all so he could melt every one of my father's lead soldiers. I didn't know whether to scream or to weep.

CHAPTER 8

I would leave the next morning. Neither screaming nor weeping would be of any use, but removing myself from Gerick's life might. Even if I had to walk to Graysteve and hire a farm hack to carry me, I would not stay and watch a child destroy himself and his home on account of me. Nothing I had done in the past four months seemed at all important. Philomena's baby would die. Gerick desperately needed a firm, kind hand to lead him away from his hatred and isolation. I could help none of them.

Rummaging about my room, I furiously stuffed my things into my traveling bag. What had happened to make the child so angry? For the last few weeks we had lived without warmth, but with tolerance at least. Our Long Night celebration had left me with great hopes. What had changed? I was filled with foreboding that no rational consideration could dispel. Nothing made sense.

I woke in the middle of the night, huddled on top of the coverlet, still in my Covenant Day garb. My lamp had long since burned out. I pulled the blankets around me, letting the darkness drag me back into wild and fearful dreams.

The furnishings of my room lay shrouded in gray when my frantic beating on the door of some dreamworld prison faded into an insistent hammering on the quite real door of my bedchamber. "My lady, please. Nellia says you must come right away." The terrified whisper drew me instantly awake. "Please, my lady, answer me. It's terrible. I'm sorry to wake you, but Nellia says to. Won't you please open the door?"

"Nancy? I'm here. One moment." The knocking continued as I fumbled at the latch.

The serving girl was white and trembling. "Nellia says please to come right away."

"Is it the young duke? The duchess?"

Nancy shook her head until her white cap threatened to take off on its own. "No, my lady. Her ladyship is still asleep. A message has come that the physician will arrive this morning, but this other business . . . it's too awful, and we don't know what to do." She crammed a reddened knuckle in her mouth and closed her eyes, forcing herself to patience while she waited for me.

No further enlightenment was going to come from Nancy. I slipped on my shoes and let her lead me through a maze of passages into the servants' quarters, a hive of small, plain rooms on the upper floor of the south wing. We turned into a short passageway, lit by a single grimy window, and found a distraught Nellia wringing her hands in front of a door that stood slightly ajar.

"Oh, my Lady Seri. I didn't know what to do. With the duchess so delicate and all . . . to take such terrible news . . . and the scandal of it as soon as word gets around . . . But it can't be dismissed, and I don't know what to do." Ten years' worth of new wrinkles crowded Nellia's already weathered cheeks.

I wrapped my arms about her shaking shoulders and hushed her like a babe. "Nellia, take a breath and tell me. What is it? Why are we here?"

"It's Mad Lucy. Nancy was bringing her breakfast as she does every day. . . ." Nellia's words drowned in a sob.

"The feebleminded nurse? Is this her room?" I felt vaguely guilty at not having realized the woman yet lived at Comigor.

Nellia nodded, burying her face in her hands.

I pushed the door open a little further. The room was unlike any servant's room I'd ever seen. Straw was scattered about the floor, and tucked into every corner were crates and baskets. A small table was piled high with scraps of fabric and wood, papers, nails, and balls of colored yarn. On one wall were stacked rough plank shelves loaded with all manner of oddments. In one corner lay a pallet where a yellowed sheet covered a shape of ominous dimensions.

"Has the old woman died, then?" I asked. Without reason, my voice came out a whisper, though no one was nearby to overhear.

Nellia pressed a hand to her breast. "Not peacefully, though, my lady. Not as she should. She's done for herself."

I picked my way through the debris and knelt beside the pallet. Nellia remained by the door, her spine firmly aligned with the doorpost. With great misgivings, I pulled back the sheet.

She was a woman of some fifty years, not ancient as I had expected, tall and sturdily made, her skin unwrinkled and her gray hair combed and twisted into a knot on the top of her head. She was laid out neatly on her back, legs straight, skirt and apron smoothed, arms straight at her sides, but she could have had no blood in her. The wool blankets of the pallet were soaked with it, and the color and texture of her garments were indistinguishable beneath the stiff and rusty coating. Ugly slash marks marred her wrists.

But shocking and terrible as these things were, they were but a whisper beside the shouts of warning that filled my head when I saw her face. I knew her. For almost half a year she had brought me food I did not want, and she had urged me without words to eat it. She had brought me water, and when I was too listless to use it, she had silently washed my face and hands. She had brought me a brush in the pocket of her shift and shyly offered it as if it were a priceless treasure, and when, in my anger, I had thrown it against the door of my prison, she had picked it up and gently brushed my hair every day until it was cut off in the name of penitence. They had told me her name was Maddy, and I had ignored and despised her because I believed any servant chosen by my jailers must be a partner in their evil. But she had bathed my face and moistened my lips and held my hands while I labored to deliver my child who could not be allowed to live. She had wept for my son when I could not, and she had taken him from the room as soon as she had cut the cord that was my only contact with him. All these years I had believed they had killed her, too, the unspeaking witness to their unspeakable crimes. What was Maddy doing in my brother's house? How could he have kept her—a constant reminder of the murder he had done?

"What are we to do?" Nellia's quavering whisper intruded on my horrified astonishment. "Such a thing to happen on the day when the little one is born so frail. It's too wicked a burden."

"We must think of it just as if her heart had failed, Nellia." I was surprised at my own calm voice. "The appearance is awful, but if she was mad, then there's really not so much difference. Just a different part of her that has given out."

"She was daft. Done nothing but rock in her chair and sit in all this clutter for all these years, but I never thought as she'd do this to herself. Such a gentle soul she was with the young master."

"She was Gerick's nurse? You told me that, but I didn't realize . . ." I didn't realize she was someone I knew.

"Aye. She cared for him from the day he was born."

Nellia was crying again, and to calm her I set her to work. I sent Nancy for a clean blanket, and asked Nellia to find some rags and water so we could clean things up a bit.

"We'll set her to rights, and then call the other servants to help us take her downstairs," I said.

Nellia nodded, and we set to work replacing the bloodied blankets with fresh and putting a clean tunic and apron on the dead woman. While Nancy and Nellia scrubbed the floor, I wandered about the room, looking at the things on Maddy's shelves. They were a child's things: a ball, a writing slate with childish characters printed on it, a rag doll pieced together from scraps and stuffed with straw, a pile of blocks, a puzzle, and a small game board with dried beans set on it like game pieces. She must truly have been in a second childhood.

"How long ago did Madd . . . Lucy become feebleminded?" I asked Nellia, who seemed much more herself now she had something to do.

"It was when the young master was close on six years old, and mistress thought he was not so much in need of a nurse. I guess it took Lucy's spirit right away when she wasn't needed no more. She took herself to rocking and moaning on the day she had to leave the nursery, and no one was able to get her to do nothing else ever again. But when the physician said that her mind had left her, His Grace, your brother, wouldn't let her be sent away, as she'd no place to go but an asylum, and the child loved her so."

"Gerick loved her?"

"Aye, indeed he did. They was always happy together when he was a wee one, even though she couldn't say no word to him. She talked with her eyes and her hands, I guess. They'd look at books together, and he'd tell her what was in them. She'd teach him games and take him for walks and was a blessing to the little mite."

I was happy to hear that Gerick had known such care and affection and had been able to return it. I ran my fingers over the slate and the ball. "He came to see her here, didn't he?"

"Well, I suspect as how he did—though the duchess forbade him to. She said Mad Lucy might harm him, but she'd never, no matter she had lost her mind or what."

Did he still visit her, I wondered, and found the answer at hand quickly. On the shelf beside some broken knitting needles and a tin box of colored stones sat a small menagerie made of straw: a lion, a cow, a deer, a bear. I looked a little further and found a flute. Crude, but a reasonable replica of the reed flute I had shown him how to make.

So many things bothered me about all this, but I couldn't name them, as if sunbeams were dancing through storm clouds, illuminating a roof here or a tree there, but just as you would turn to look at it, the gap would close, and gloom shroud everything once more.

Why would Maddy have taken her own life? The malady Nellia had described seemed no violent mania. Could those with failed reason feel the pangs of despair that precipitated self-murder? Had they enough calculation left to accomplish such a horrific deed?

When Nellia and Nancy were done, Maddy looked far less fearsome. Nellia wanted to know if we should send for some of the men to carry the body downstairs. Though I hated the thought of it, I knew Gerick should be told before we buried his friend.

"Nellia, when was it that the young duke took on his present . . . moodiness?"

"About the same time as Lucy took ill. I've oft said to myself as maybe he took her being dismissed from the nursery as hard as she did. Though, since she didn't have to go away, and he came here to see her, you might not think it would come to that."

"Then this will be difficult for him, her dying like this."

"Aye. Poor child. Losing the two who ever loved him so close together—his papa and his Lucy."

"Then someone will have to break the news to him before the word gets out. Keep it to yourself for now. I'll let you know when you may tell everyone and have her taken care of. And when the time is right, the staff may have a wake for Lucy if they wish. I don't think it would be seemly to do so until all is settled with the duchess and her daughter."

"I understand, my lady," said Nellia, and she wagged her finger at Nancy, who nodded, wide-eyed.

After a brief visit to my room to wash the sleep from my eyes, I hurried to Philomena's bedchamber. Voices from the adjoining room were arguing, quietly but vehemently.

". . . dragged me away from her like I was a piece of rubbish. I've never been so humiliated. I'll have the witch arrested." Lady Verally.

"But what she has done, madam, for which you would have her arrested, is save your niece's life." The rumbling bass voice was Ren Wesley's. "Her Grace's labor was of such poor effectiveness that it could have lasted for many more hours. Having experienced hands to deliver the child was the difference between a tragedy and a double tragedy. If your authority had been allowed to prevail, your niece would be dead from it, and you would find yourself responsible for the death of a special friend of King Evard. In short, you should thank the Lady Seriana for saving you from a murder charge of your own."

I walked in and greeted my defender. If Lady Verally had been possessed of a weapon, I might have ended up in the same condition as Mad Lucy.

The physician returned my greeting with robust gravity. "Good morning, my lady. It seems my timing was abysmal, and the very thing we hoped to prevent has occurred, but as I was just informing the good lady here, you've saved her ladyship's life by your good judgment in summoning the midwife."

"How are they?" I asked.

"You know it well, witch," snarled Lady Verally. "You didn't want my precious girl to die. It would have spoiled your evil fun, wouldn't it? You want to watch her suffer."

Ren Wesley turned his back on the seething lady. "Thanks to you and the most excellent midwife, the mother is resting comfortably and will soon be on her feet, none the worse save in her sorrow. It grieves me to say that the child has not survived the dawn. There was nothing to be done."

"I feared as much," I said, ignoring Lady Verally's haughty departure.

"I've given the duchess a sleeping draught, and now I am on my way to find some breakfast."

"I was hoping to speak with you for a moment," I said. "I've a great boon to ask."

"At your service." The physician poked his head into Philomena's room to let the maids know where he could be found. Then he took my arm, and we walked through the upper corridors to the galleries that overlooked the great hall.

I told him of Mad Lucy and how she had been found, and that Gerick had not yet been told. "He shouldn't have to hear such news from me," I said. "I'm too much a coward to face his wrath. I'm worried . . ."

". . . that he'll blame you."

"With Lady Verally's constant harping on revenge, it seems certain." And how could I face the child, withholding the fact that I knew his Lucy and had ample reason to despise her?

"Perhaps it would be well if I saw the dead woman first, then spoke to the boy. I'll remind him of the dangers of age and senility, and also that his mother bore two dead children long before you were in residence."

"I'd be most grateful. It grieves me to be unable to comfort him. He is such a sad child."

"You've become quite attached to him."

"I suppose I have." Somehow, what had begun as a challenge had become a work of affection I hadn't thought possible. Yet, even after so many months, I scarcely knew the child.

Ren Wesley shook his massive head. "I wish we'd been able to speak with this nurse before she chose to withdraw from life. Perhaps she could have explained the boy to us in some fashion."

The physician took his leave, following Nancy to Maddy's room. Meanwhile I sent a message to Gerick, requesting him to meet Ren Wesley in the small reception room in half an hour.

A short time later Gerick's young manservant sought me out with a worried look on his face. "The duke is not in his rooms, my lady," he said. Then, with concern overshadowing discretion, he added, "And what's more, his bed has not been slept in this past night. I asked the guards as were on duty through the night, and none's seen the young master since yestereve."

Thinking of my own troubled sleep, and the evidence I had found of Gerick's disturbance of mind, I wasn't surprised. "Yesterday was a very trying day for him, James. My guess is that you'll find him curled up on a couch or chair somewhere. Take two others and search him out. We must speak with him."

No sooner had James left than Nancy skittered into the gallery, saying that Ren Wesley respectfully requested my presence in Lucy's room. I hurried along the way, leaving Nancy to intercept James should he return with word of Gerick.

Ren Wesley stood contemplating the still figure that lay

on the pallet in the cluttered room. His arms were folded across his wide chest and he was twisting the end of his exuberant mustache with two thick fingers. When I came in, he whirled about, scowling.

"What is it, sir?" I asked.

"My lady, there is something you must know about this woman's death. There is foul play here."

"I don't understand."

"You must pardon the vulgar description, madam. There is no pleasant way to phrase it. Look at the depth of these gashes; they pass not only through skin and sinew, but right into the bone."

He expected me to understand, but I shook my head.

"What it means is, she could not have done it to herself."

"But she was a strong woman."

"Look here." He picked up Maddy's hands and showed me her swollen joints and crooked fingers. I had seen such in several old servants, the painful inflammation that robbed strong and diligent men and women of their livelihood. One who had shod wild horses could no longer grip the reins of a child's pony. One who had carried the heaviest loads or sewn the finest seams could no longer lift a mug of beer or grasp a sewing needle. "She may have had the strength to do such injury, but never could she have applied it with these hands."

"Then you're saying—"

"This woman was murdered."

I was speechless . . . and appalled . . . and my skin flushed with unreasonable pangs of guilt. If anyone learned of my connection with Lucy—Maddy—the finger of accusation would point directly at me.

"Who would do such a thing? And for what possible cause?" Ren Wesley demanded in indignation.

"She was mute," I stammered, shamed that my first thought had been of myself and not this poor woman. "And, from what I was told, a gentle soul. It doesn't make sense."

People were murdered because of passion: hatred, jealousy, fear. Lucy had neither physical beauty nor the kind of attractions or influence that could generate such emotions. People were also murdered for business: politics, intrigue, secrets. She had been involved in such things, but what could she know that could provoke murder? And why now? For ten years she had been out of sight; for five of those she had rocked in her chair and puttered about with children's toys.

Ren Wesley was looking at me intently. Waiting. "What am I to tell the boy?" His words were precise, his voice cold.

"It would be difficult enough to tell him that she did it herself, but this . . ." The temptation to hide the truth strained my conscience. What if the woman had somehow let Gerick know of her connection with me?

"He has to be told," I said at last. "However painful it is, hiding the truth will only compound the hurt." Someday he would know, even if he figured it out for himself. "And when the duchess is well enough, we'll have to inform her also."

The physician nodded. I thought I saw a flash of relief cross his face. "I was hoping you would say that." My reputation was wicked. If even so liberal-minded a soul as Ren Wesley had felt it reason to doubt me, I couldn't blame him.

By late afternoon, Gerick had not been found. With my permission, James had started inquiries among the other servants, but no one had seen the boy since he had taken his cloak from his room the previous evening. I directed the servants to start at one end of the castle and search every nook and cranny, inside and out, high and low, no matter how improbable.

Meanwhile, the day dragged on, and we had to take care of Lucy. I dispatched a gardener to prepare a resting place in the frozen hillside beyond the family burial ground at Desfiere. As Nellia, Nancy, and I rolled the dead woman in her blankets so the men could carry her out, Nancy picked up something from the corner and laid it on top of the grim bundle. "She must've kept it since summer," whispered the girl. "Nice for her to have a flower, even if it's old."

I looked at what the girl had found and touched it, not quite believing the evidence of my senses. It was wrong, jarringly wrong, like so much I had seen and heard in the past two days. But like a catalyst in an alchemist's glass, the wilted blossom drew the pieces of the puzzle together: Philomena, whose womb could carry no children to full term . . . a firepit with no trace of ash or soot, yet bearing a lump of molten lead . . . a child who would allow no one to know him, not a tutor, not a kind physician, not even the father he loved . . . a child who lived in terror of sorcery . . . a woman who was living where she had no reason to be . . . And now, a lily . . . in the middle of winter, a lily, wilted, but not dead, its soft petals still clinging to the stem . . . a lily that had been fresh not twelve hours earlier. I knew only one person who loved Maddy enough to give her a flower, as he had given her straw animals and a reed flute and a hundred other childish creations. But where in the middle of winter would any child find a lily to give the woman who had tended him . . . from the day of his birth . . . ?

"Nellia," I said in a whisper, scarcely able to bring words to my tongue. "What is Gerick's birthday?"

The old housekeeper looked at me as if I were afflicted with Mad Lucy's malady. "Pardon, my lady?"

"The young duke . . . on what day and in what year was he born?"

I knew what she was going to say as clearly as I knew my own name.

"Why, it's the twenty-ninth day of the Month of Winds, ten years ago, going on eleven in the coming spring."

It was as if the world I knew dissolved away, leaving some new creation in its place, a creation of beauty and wonder that crumbled into horror and disaster even as I marveled at its birth. How could I find my place in such a world? What could I call truth any longer, when that which had been the darkest, most bitter truth of my life was now made a lie? To none of those questions could I give an answer, but I did know who had murdered Lucy and why, and it was, indeed, because of me.

Darzid had never expected to find me here, had not believed I could ever find out. When he discovered his miscalculation and my laughable ignorance of the truth sitting in my hand, he took swift action to remedy his mistake. Lucy had never been feebleminded, but brave and clever and devoted, feigning a ruined mind in order to keep the child she loved safe. She had taught him to hide what he could do. When she was told that she was no longer needed in the nursery, she knew better, and she did what was necessary to make sure she was close by to watch him, to be his friend when he dared not let anyone close enough to discover his terrible secret.

Ten years ago on the twenty-ninth day of the Month of Winds . . . two months to the day after Karon's burning . . . the day the silent, gentle Maddy had helped me give birth to my son.

From my breast burst a cry of lamentation that would have unmanned the Guardians of the Keep, making them snap the chains that bound them to their sacred duty. I ran like a madwoman through the corridors of Comigor, knowing as well as I knew the sun would set that Gerick would not be found in any corner of the world I knew.

CHAPTER 9

Karon

The forest was dense, shady, and incredibly green. The bearded mosses hung down and tickled my face as I fought my way through the thick underbrush. No trail lay before me, only a distant speck of light piercing the emerald gloom. My destination . . . if I could but shove the masses of greenery out of my way, I had no doubt that I could reach the light. Well rested, bursting with strength, I swept aside the verdant obstacles. But as I traversed the forest, the light got no closer and the green faded to gray. . . .

The cool brush of pine boughs hardened into cold, rough stone, the wispy mosses into a white linen sheet and gray wool blankets. Only the light was constant, unwavering. Through the thick glass of my window the sun glared from the eastern sky, demanding that my eyes come open to greet the morning.

Such a strange sensation. How long had it been since my eyes had opened of their own volition, no hand on my shoulder rattling my teeth, no sarcastic taunting? "Must I get my scraping knife? Your limbs have attached themselves to this couch like barnacles to a coastal schooner." Or, "What dream is this that holds you? You lie here like an empty-headed cat in a sunbeam, dreaming only of your full stomach while two worlds hold their breath, awaiting your pleasure."

I stretched and sat up. My dream had not lied. I felt rested as I had not in waking memory, and I was ravenously hungry. Had Dassine succumbed to pity at my lamentable state? We had been through five or six sessions in the circle of candles since my collapse in Lady Seriana's garden on the far side of the Bridge, and from each I had emerged a ragged refugee, taking longer each time to orient myself in the present.

When I was a child in Avonar, the lost Avonar of the mundane world, my brothers and I had a favorite place. A small river tumbled down from the snowfields of Mount Karylis in the summer, clear and icy. At certain places on the forested slopes, the water would be captured by great boulders forming deep clear pools, perfect for swimming. High above one of these pools was a chute of smooth rocks, worn away by a spring that raced down the rocks to join the river. We would slide naked down the chute and fly through the air before plunging into the pool far below. The experience teetered on the glorious edge of terror.

In these latest sessions of reliving my lost memories, I had felt as if I were on that long downward slide again, racing along a path that would soon leave me hanging helplessly in the air, ready to plunge into icy darkness. Whatever awaited me beyond the smooth surface—the enchantments that hid my own life from me—was terrifying, yet I could no more stop myself than I could have checked my careening path down that rocky chute.

Dassine had shown no inclination to let my difficulties slow my progress, and so, on the morning that my eyes opened of themselves, I was immensely curious as to what had caused this change of heart. Our last session had ended in late morning, and I had not dallied before falling into bed. Unless the sun's course of life had taken as strange a turn as had my own, I had slept the clock around.

I shivered in the unusually cold air and put on my robe, expecting Dassine to burst in on me at any moment, raising his exuberant eyebrows in disdain. The water in my pitcher was frozen solid. Another oddity. My washing water had never been anything but tepid, even on the coldest mornings. Having no implement to crack the ice, I touched it with a bit of magic, only enough to melt the crust, not to make the water warm. Liquidity was sufficient.

Even the use of power was not enough to bring Dassine. The first time I had attempted any magical working in his house—putting out a small fire from a toppled lamp—he had pounced like a fox on a dallying rabbit, berating me for wasting my strength on "frivolities."

As I stepped through the doorway into Dassine's lectorium, the air began to vibrate with a high-pitched keening. The old villain had put a ward on my door. Dassine and I would have to talk again about honesty and trust. Annoyed far beyond the irritation of the noise, I searched for some way to quiet the screech, but to my amazement I couldn't even find the door opening. Filling the space where the doorway should have been was a span of dingy plaster and shelves laden with books and herb canisters and uncounted years' accumulation of dust and miscellany—all quite substantial. Instinct told me I should experience a "hair-on-end" sensation when encountering such an illusion, but the enchantment was so subtle, I couldn't sense it at all.

The noise soon died away with nothing to show for it. My wonderment at his skill and annoyance at his cheek were snuffed out by the weight of the silence. "Dassine," I called quietly. No answer.

Along with his restrictions on use of power, dress, speech, and questioning, Dassine had forbidden me to leave his lectorium unaccompanied. He enjoined me repeatedly not to trespass his limits, saying that if I trusted him in all else, I had to trust that they were necessary. Truly, I hated to cross him, and so I decided to wait before searching further, despite the strangeness of the morning.

The remnants of our last meal sat on the worktable: a basket of bread, now cold and dry, a plate with a few scraps of hardened cheese, not two, but three dirty soup bowls, and two mugs smelling of brandy—"Bareil's best" Dassine had always called the contents of his green bottle. The candlesticks were still put away, the newest crate of tall beeswax candles unopened on the floor beside them. The chamber seemed no more and no less cluttered than usual. I sat at the table for a while, pushing around a few of the red and green sonquey tiles scattered on the table. Half of the tiles were arranged in a pattern bounded by finger-length silver bars, as if a game had been interrupted.

A small wooden cabinet lay toppled on the floor, its painted doors fallen open and several oddments spilled out: a gold ring, a small enameled box holding a set of lignial cards, used for tracing the lines of magical talent through a family, and one other item that fit in no easy classification—a plain circle of dull wood about the size of my palm. Embedded in the wood was a small iron ring, and within the ring was set a highly polished, pyramid-shaped crystal of pure black, its height half the span of my hand. I righted the cabinet and picked up the things, setting them back on the shelves. While mulling what to do next, I idly rubbed a finger on one smooth facet of the shining crystal . . . and my body vanished, along with the world and everything in it. . . .

I hung in void of pure black midnight, shot with threads of fine silver, as if someone had taken the stars and smeared them across their dark canvas on the day of their creation. So quiet . . . so still . . . though beyond the silence rang a faint chime of silver, as if the threads of light were speaking . . . singing. In the farthest reaches of my vision shimmered a line of light, shifting slowly from serene rose to glittering emerald to deep, rich blue.

"I need to be there, I belong beyond that light. Oh gods, what is this hunger?" My nonexistent eyes burned with tears. My incorporeal hands reached through the darkness toward the light.

How do you measure desire? Those things left behind? To leave this physical being was not an obstacle; I'd grown to no comfort with it. To abandon my work, the memories of two lives so dearly bought in these past months, gave me no pause. The friends and family who populated my past were but ghosts who would be exorcised with the passage of that distant marker—the light that now shot violet, mauve, and purple trailers to either side, up, down, right, left in this directionless universe of darkness . . . so far away, teasing, tantalizing, luring me from all other concern. My kingdom? "I'm a cripple, half a madman, no matter what Dassine says. Better they find someone whole to lead them." Like long, thin fingers, the silent bursts of color beckoned.

How do you measure desire? Those things to be endured? The void itself was colder than the winter morning on which I had waked unbidden, but the perimeters of my being burned—not the cold fire of the smeared stars, not the colored fire of the distant aurora, but a conflagration that seared through the barriers of memory . . . from the boundaries of reason. Roaring, agonizing fire . . . hot iron about my wrists and ankles eating its way through flesh and bone . . . I was enveloped in darkness, abandoned in unbounded pain and horror. The tongue I had so carelessly wished away cried out, yet I would endure even this if I could but pass beyond the barrier of light. . . .

Karon, my son, do not . . . not yet. Come back. From outside the holocaust called a voice so faint . . . almost unheard against the roar of the fire and my own cries.

Dassine. My mentor, my healer, my jailer. I had to tell him where I was going. If he understood about this hunger, about the beckoning fingers of amber and blue, he wouldn't hold me. I didn't belong with Dassine. But he didn't answer my call, and I could not ignore his summoning. I dropped the crystal, and the world rushed back. . . .

My robe was drenched with sweat. Shaking, chilled, I stepped back from the fallen artifact that lay so innocently on the floor. Once I'd found Dassine, I would come back for it. "Dassine! Are you here?" I called. No answer.

Two doors opened out of the lectorium. One led into the garden, the other to a short flight of steps and the passage that took one into the main part of the rambling house. Taking the second, I wandered down the passageways, peering into the rooms to either side. Dassine was nowhere in the house. I wandered back to the lectorium, stopping in the kitchen long enough to grab a chunk of bread, a slab of ham, and two pears from the larder. As I sat at the worktable and ate the bread and ham, I stared at the odd device that lay on the floor and hovered so disturbingly on the peripheries of my thoughts. What could be the purpose of such a thing?

Karon . . .

I almost missed it. The call was half audible and half in

my mind, and its origin was behind the second door, the door to the garden. Fool! I hadn't looked there. I yanked the door open. Tangled in his cloak, Dassine lay huddled against the wall, a trail of blood-streaked snow stretching behind him to the garden gate. His lips were blue, and only the barest breath moved his chest and the bloody wound that gaped there.

"Oh, gods, Dassine!" I carried him into the study and laid him on the couch by the cold hearth. With a word and the flick of my fingers, the pile of twigs and ash in the fireplace burst into flames, and I bundled him in everything I could find that might warm him. He shuddered, and his eyes flew open. Blood seeped from his chest. Too much of it.

A knife . . . I needed a knife and a strip of linen.

"No!" The old man gripped my wrist. "I forbid it! I need to tell you—"

"But I can heal you," I said. "The power is in me." Even as I spoke I gathered power . . . from my fear . . . from the bitter winter . . . from the pain and awe and terror of my vision. I just needed to make the link. . . .

"No use. No time." His voice was harsh and low, broken with strident breaths. "Listen to me. They have the child."

"What child? Why—?"

"No time . . . everything is changed. Your only task . . . find the child. Save him. Only one . . . only one can help. . . ." His words came ragged . . . desperate . . . "Bareil . . . your guide . . ."

"Who's done this to you?" I would not listen to words that rang so of finality. "Tell me who." And when I knew, that one would die.

"No, no, fool! Leave it be. If they take . . . boy to Zhev'Na, then . . . oh, curse it all . . . no time . . . the only way . . ." He faltered, choking as blood bubbled out of the corner of his mouth. I thought he was gone, but he snarled and forced the words past his clenched jaw. "If they take the boy to Zhev'Na, give yourself . . . to the Preceptorate."

"But—"

"Go defenseless. Tell them . . . ready to be examined. Let it play out. The only way. The only way . . ." His cold hand touched my face tenderly, his voice sunk to a ferocious whisper, his eyes boring holes in my own. "Dearest son, do *not* use the crystal. Not until you are whole, and you have the boy. Promise me."

"Dassine—"

"Promise me!" he bellowed, grabbing my robe and raising himself off the cushions.

"Yes, yes, I promise."

He jerked his head and sagged onto the cushions, his eyelids heavy, the grip on my robe relaxing. I did not beg or argue or rage about how little I understood. He had no strength to remedy my ignorance. But his finger fluttered against my arm, and I bent close to hear him. With a sighing breath, he whispered, "Trust me." And then he breathed no more.

My friend, my mentor, my keeper. Without thought of Bridge or worlds or any of the larger consequences of his passing, I held the old man in my arms until the sun was high. Though keeping vigil with the dead for half a day was the Dar'Nethi custom, love, not custom, compelled me to stay with him. Dassine had willingly forfeited every last drop of his life's essence to give me his instruction. No Healer could bring him back before he crossed the Verges.

Eventually, I laid Dassine in his garden, hacking at the frozen ground until my arms could scarcely raise pick or shovel. When I was done, I sat beside the grave, sweat and anger hardening into ice. I tried to recall everything he'd said, while trying to ignore how empty the world had become.

It is said that those who live long in close companionship come to anticipate each other's words and actions, and even that one of the pair comes to resemble the other in physical appearance. If such were true, then surely when I next looked in a glass, I would see wild, gray-streaked eyebrows sprouting from my face. Only now did I realize how closely bound our minds had been. Lacking his abundant presence, my thoughts felt thin and watery. Whatever else I retrieved of the years still missing, I vowed to learn someday how we had become so close.

So what to do? Nothing made sense. I could believe Dassine's last words were the product of delirium had it been anyone but Dassine who voiced them. A mysterious child to be saved from someone I didn't know. Someone named Bareil to guide me. No doubt that I needed help, but who was Bareil and where was he to be found? I had heard his name before . . . yes, the brandy. "Bareil's best." Dassine had spoken as if I should know him, but I'd met no one in Avonar save the Preceptors, the six . . .

No . . . a seventh person had been in that room when I met the Preceptors—a Dulcé. So perhaps he didn't mean an ordinary guide, but a *madrissé.* With their strange intellectual limitations, Dulcé on their own did not figure in the equations of power in Gondai. But a Dulcé could give a Dar'Nethi a significant advantage in life's games by placing his immense capacity for knowledge at that person's service. When a Dulcé bound himself in this rare and privileged relationship, he was called a madrissé, one whose knowledge and insights could guide the Dar'Nethi in decision-making. Bareil was likely Dassine's madrissé. He would have been the other presence I had felt in Dassine's house, the note-taker, the user of the third bowl, the one who would drink brandy with Dassine while I was enraptured with candlelight and the past. He could hold a number of answers, if only I could find him. To imagine it was a comfort.

In the matter of the crystal, I had to follow Dassine's judgment. From the corner of my mind where I had pushed the unsettling experience, the fingers of light beckoned dangerously, causing my blood to churn. When I was whole, Dassine had said, implying that such was still possible. The crystal, whatever it was, would have to wait. I had promised him.

As for his command to give myself to the Preceptorate, I was confounded. For how many days had Dassine fumed about my offer to be examined, warning me to stay away from the Preceptors' multitudinous deceptions? Now he told me that circumstance might demand I surrender to the Preceptorate while yet incomplete. Defenseless . . . helpless. The world would surely crack at their first probe, and they would judge me mad . . . or Zhid. Was that what he wanted? If not for his last words, I would have dismissed it entirely. Trust, in this matter, was very difficult.

"I thank you for my life, old man," I said, as I took my leave of the snowy garden. "But I mislike being a pawn in a dead man's game. However will I hold you to account for it?"

I returned to the silent house warily. The house would surely have formidable wards, the masterful illusion that hid my room but one example. But Dassine's enemies would themselves be formidable, and they would know that Dassine was severely weakened if not dead. As I was so unsure of my own strength, it seemed sensible to take whatever might be useful and leave Dassine's house as quickly as possible. Then I could watch and confront the murderers on my own terms. Not friendly terms.

Rummaging about the kitchen, I located a capacious rucksack. Careful not to touch the black crystal itself, I wrapped the unsettling artifact in a small towel and stuffed it into the bottom of the bag. I didn't question the motive that made me make sure of it before anything else. Next I searched the room for something I knew would never be far from Dassine's hand. Indeed, the small leather case sat on the shelf by the door. Inside it lay an exquisitely sharp, palm-length knife with a curved blade—a Healer's knife—and in a separate compartment, a narrow strip of linen, scarcely less fine than a spider's web. For a moment I felt almost whole. I put the case in the pack.

Next went in the flask of "Bareil's best" and the two pears I had not eaten earlier. From the larder I grabbed enough food for at least a day—a considerable amount since I was still ravenous. Clothes were more difficult. Dassine had given me nothing but the white wool robe. Citizens of Avonar who specialized in the study of sorcery wore traditional scholars' garb—loose robes and sandals or slippers. Warriors, tradesmen, those who tended gardens and fields, the Dulcé, and most others wore garments more like those to which I was accustomed: shirts or tunics, breeches, leggings, and boots. I didn't wish to proclaim myself a scholar—far from it. But I was more than two heads taller than Dassine. His more ordinary garments would do nothing to make me inconspicuous. Clothing would have to wait.

Money would be useful, but I had no idea where any might be. Masses of notes and manuscripts cluttered the house, some relevant to my situation, I had no doubt, but I'd no time to sort through them. Perhaps this Bareil would know what was valuable, if I could find him.

The instincts and habits I had so recently redeveloped from my memories of hiding from the law prodded me to move, to get away from the place my enemies expected me to be. My teeth were on edge, and despite the paltry supplies in the pack, I was ready to bolt.

But just as I hefted the pack, quiet footsteps sounded in the passageway from the house. I flattened myself to the wall beside the doorway, realizing at the same time that I had forgotten to acquire a most important piece of equipment—a weapon. I—Karon—had never carried a weapon, yet my hand demanded a blade. The Healer's knife was too small, and it was unthinkable to use an instrument designed for healing to harm another person.

But I was out of time. The sneaking villain tiptoed down the lectorium steps. I glimpsed a dagger in a bloody hand. Stupid brute. I grabbed his wrist and dragged him off balance. Remembering Dassine and the jagged wound in his chest, I was not gentle. I wrapped one arm about his neck and twisted his arm behind his back until his weapon clattered to the floor.

"Did you think to finish your work or simply add another to your tally?" I growled in his ear. Tightening my grip on his throat, I snatched the dagger from the floor, vowing to rip him open the same way he had murdered Dassine.

"Help Master Dassine . . . please." The man, small and light, went limp in my arms. An amateur's ploy. He deserved to die. But even as I poised the dagger at his belly, I noted the color of his skin . . . a creamy brown like strong tea with milk in it. Slender oval face. Dark eyes the shape of almonds. A Dulcé . . . I lowered the knife and shifted him in my arms. Black, straight hair cut short around his ears. A trim beard. An ageless face, his lips mortally pale.

Holy gods, he was the one, the seventh person in the room with the Preceptors! And his slight body was bleeding from no less than ten stab wounds. Whoever had taken a blade to him had wanted to make sure. I laid him on the couch still wet with Dassine's blood, grabbed the leather case from the pack, and pulled out the knife and the strip of linen.

No sorcery can blunt the pain of a Healer's knife. To cut your own flesh and mingle your blood with that of your patient is the only truly effective way to unleash your Healer's power. And pain is part of the working every bit as much as the words that open your mind to the light of the universe, as much as the gathering of power that lies hidden in the recesses of your being, as much as the smell of blood. Pain opens the door to the heightened senses needed for putting right what is wrong, a connection that binds Healer to patient more intimately than any strip of white linen.

The first time I had drawn a knife across my arm, on the day when I was desperate to save my dying brother and did not know I was a Healer, I had tried to ignore the hurt, to link myself with Christophe's broken body unscathed by my own senses. Surely a true Healer would be inured to pain, I thought, fearing that the tears that threatened and the cry that escaped me on that day were signs that I was nothing of what I needed to be. I struggled for so long that my brother's soul almost fled beyond the Verges before I could see the truth—that his senses were blocked to me as long as were my own. When the insight came and I released my control . . . only then did I share the realm of the other, allowed to see the shattered bones, feel the torn tissue, and hear the ragged heartbeat that had to be put right. There was no getting used to it, even after so many years. The magnificence of the whole more than compensates—a thousandfold is not too large a reckoning—but it is a truth that experienced Healers do not cry out, yet neither do they smile as they begin their work.

CHAPTER 10

There is no sense of time passing when one is engaged in the art of healing. You could count heartbeats, but there are usually more important matters to deal with, such as reconnecting damaged blood vessels or destroying the toxins that flock to the site of a wound like ravening vultures. So when I triggered the enchantment that would close the incision on my arm and slipped the knot that bound my arm to that of the injured Dulcé, I didn't know how long he had been staring at me.

"Ce'na davonet, Giré D'Arnath," he said, quietly. All honor to you, Heir of D'Arnath. "And my gratitude for that which can never be repaid."

"Your name is Bareil?" I asked.

He nodded tiredly. "Clearly Vasrin Shaper has a place in her heart for the foolish and disobedient, else I'd not be here to answer to it."

"You're fortunate that I'd not picked up a weapon. I was sure you were one of the murderers, come to confirm their work . . . or add me to their tally."

Though his voice and demeanor were steady, the Dulcé's eyes filled with tears. "Then he was able to get back here. You know what happened."

"I know nothing that makes any sense. Only that he's dead. Tell me who did this . . . if you're able, of course."

Dulcé have an immense capacity for knowledge and an extraordinary ability to search, analyze, and connect what they know into useful patterns of information. But only a small amount of their knowledge is usable at any particular time, so that a Dulcé might know the names of every star in the heavens on one day, but no more than two or three on the next, or have only the vaguest recollection of a name in one hour, but recall the entire history of the person in the next. A Dar'Nethi who is fortunate enough to be linked to a Dulcé in the rite of the madris can command any bit of that information to the front of the Dulcé's mind where it can be used. Because I had not been linked to Bareil, I had only royal authority, no power to control his mind.

"You'll find I have a somewhat larger threshold of knowledge than most Dulcé, my lord, and I will most certainly provide you with all that I am able"—the Dulcé's frown was not at all reassuring—"but if, as you so wisely assume, those who killed my madrisson will want you next, then we must be away from here as soon as possible. And I've had to breach the house defenses to get back inside. I hope my folly will not cost us the way."

"I was on my way out when you came," I said, and told him of my attempts at preparation.

He nodded thoughtfully. "There are a few things here that you must have. I'll get them." He struggled to get up, but I kept a firm hand on his chest.

"You've lost a great deal of blood, Dulcé—a condition my skills cannot reverse. Tell me what we need, and I'll get it."

He settled into the cushion. "As you say, my lord. First, in the wooden drawer case, the lower drawer, under the glass pipes and sharpening stones, you'll find a small pink stone, cold to the touch . . . yes, that's it. You must guard it carefully. I cannot emphasize it enough."

I shoved the stone into the pack. "What else?"

"Money—I'll get that on our way out. Clothes—you underestimate us, my lord. If you would open the door of the chemist's cabinet . . ."

Well, it looked like a chemist's cabinet—a tall wooden structure with glass doors. Through the glass you could see shelves of jars and flasks, small vials of blue and purple, boxes, pipes, and brass burners. Nothing of interest. Only, when I opened the door and looked inside, all the paraphernalia had vanished, and I found a tidy wardrobe filled with an array of clothing that could never have fit Dassine.

"Mine?" I said.

"I believe they may happen to fit you properly." When I looked askance at the reclining Dulcé, a spark in his eyes and a set of his mouth echoed the good humor I had noted in our earlier encounter. I shed my white robe, the front of it stiff with blood, and quickly donned a nondescript brown shirt, soft leather breeches and vest, and woolen leggings, all exactly the right size. As I pulled on a pair of doeskin boots, exactly my measure and so well made that my feet did not protest even after four shoeless months, I said, "You have Dassine's knack for avoiding answers."

"I have been Master Dassine's madrissé for thirty years. He entrusted me with his knowledge and his purposes. If you so desire, I will submit to the madris and allow you to command me, but I must and will refuse you in anything that contradicts Master Dassine's wishes as I understand them. Is my position clear, my lord?" He eased the blunt edge of his words with a delightful smile.

"Bareil, the assurance that someone knows what, in the name of all that lives, is going on with me is such a delight that I'll cheerfully respect whatever boundaries you set." I pulled a heavy wool cloak from the wardrobe. "And now, perhaps we should leave this place before those who are destroying the doors upstairs can find us."

A loud thumping reminiscent of an earthquake resounded from the upper levels of the house.

"Quickly, before we go. In the very back of the wardrobe," said the Dulcé, grunting as he shoved his legs off the couch.

Behind the shirts, breeches, and ceremonial robes hung a plain sword belt. A great-sword, its simple hilt finely engraved, its guard a graceful sweep of vines and leaves, and a silver knife were sheathed in its finely tooled scabbards—D'Arnath's weapons, heirlooms so precious that the safety of worlds had depended on them for a thousand years. I buckled the sword belt beneath my cloak and helped Bareil to his feet.

The Dulcé took a moment to open the painted cabinet and rummage about on the worktable and shelves, then clucked in frustration, rubbing his head tiredly. "There's one more thing you should have, but I can't find it. An odd little thing—"

A monstrous crash sounded from upstairs—the front door giving way.

"I believe I have what you're looking for. And I really think we should go." I grabbed a short cloak from a hook by the garden door to replace his ripped and bloody one. I would have him tell me about the crystal later.

"Indeed. This way, my lord," he said, and while still frowning at the jumbled mess of the study, he turned and vanished through the study wall. I could see no evidence of where he'd gone. When I traced my fingers along the wall, it was as solid as the floor on which I stood. I felt like an idiot trying to figure out how to escape through immutable stone.

"My apologies," said a grinning Bareil as he re-entered the room through the very place I had deemed impenetrable. "Step to the corner of the table, just so, and then turn left"—he angled his hand and jerked his head to his left—"and left again immediately. No enchantment is required." He swiveled and disappeared once again.

It was as he said. I stepped to the corner of our worktable, made an immediate left turn, but instead of banging my hip bone on the table, found myself in a gray stone passage. From the corner of my eye I could still see Dassine's lectorium. The trampling of boots on the stair induced me to forego wonder and make the second left turn.

I stepped into a small study, crowded with a writing desk, a hanging lamp, a bookcase, and a large leather-bound chest that Bareil was already unlocking. From the depths of the chest, the Dulcé pulled out two small cloth bags. He tossed one to me, and the heavy, fist-sized bag clinked pleasantly. After relocking the chest and using the desk to haul himself back to his feet, he stared at the jumble of papers and manuscripts littering the desk. He sighed deeply. "If you please, my lord . . . burn them all."

"Are you sure?"

"Master Dassine could protect his work, but we cannot. Quickly, if you would."

With so much paper to work with, fire was easy, and

in a moment nothing was left but a whirling cloud of ash and smoke.

"All of the information is inside me," said the Dulcé wryly, as he pulled open a door and nudged me into the cold sunlight of a deserted alleyway. "If you ever hope to know what was written here, I suppose you'll have to keep me safe."

"One of my highest priorities," I said, keeping my voice low as he did. "Now, can you tell me where we are? I'd like to see who's coming after us."

"Unfortunately we've no vantage that will allow us to observe our pursuers; we've left them well behind. I'd think you might recognize this place, my lord," he whispered cheerfully, as he led me between two buildings of pink brick and peeked about the corner into an expanse of empty courtyard, paved with white flagstones. "We're just outside the westernmost walls of *S'Regiré Monpassai d'Gondai*—the Palace of the Kings of Gondai. The structure you see across the way has been the home of your family for at least twelve hundred years. This is the very courtyard where Master Exeget's servants found you huddled by a burning barrel on the night you were named Heir."

My eyes were drawn upward by the graceful, rose-colored towers beyond the white flagstones. A banner of white and gold flew atop the tallest tower: two lions rampant supporting an arch, topped by two stars. The banner of D'Arnath. Indeed, I remembered the night of which the Dulcé spoke. . . .

Bitter cold. No one had enchantments to spare to keep the fires burning, so anything that could burn was dragged out, broken up, and tossed into the flames to keep the soldiers warm: crates, tables, chairs. Three soldiers were drinking wine and telling of a bloody encounter on the walls the previous night and how the Seeking of the Zhid had crept over the walls like a pestilence, seeping into those who stared into the darkness too long alone. Sleet pelted our faces and dribbled down our necks. . . .

"My lord!" Bareil was shivering in the frigid breeze. "If you please, we must move on. I know a hiding place close by. We can sleep and eat safely, and you can decide our next step."

"Lead on." I shuddered and pushed the memories aside. Like a stargazer who witnesses his first eclipse, or a student of history who stands atop a ridge watching his first battle, I was beginning to believe there might actually be some truth to all I'd learned in the past months.

We hurried across the courtyard and down a short flight of broken steps that descended between two short walls, ending at a narrow, shaded lane clogged with dead leaves and dirty clumps of snow. But instead of following the lane to right or left, Bareil glanced back at me, angled his hand left and then left again, raised his eyebrows, and disappeared. I tried to remember exactly where he'd stood. Then I made the turns and stepped into a stuffy passage that smelled like cooking bacon. Two oil lamps on the wall left the passage no better than dim, especially after the brilliance of mid-afternoon.

Bareil was moving carefully down the passage, past six or eight plain wood doors. No side passages. No people. No ornamentation that might be expected in a palace. Perhaps these were servants' quarters. With a key pulled from his pocket, the Dulcé unlocked a door at the far end of the passage. He stood aside for me to enter and bowed me in.

The chamber was small and plain, holding little more than a low bed, a square table, two straight-backed chairs, and a small tiled hearth with a clean brazier. On the table sat four pewter mugs and small brass urn, the steam rising from it the source of the fruity, pungent aroma of saffria that pervaded the room. Above the entry door was a small bronze mask of a single head with two faces, one male, one female—the common image of Vasrin. Daylight, extraordinarily bright, clean, and sharp-edged, spilled through a clean casement onto a smooth wood floor. Drawn to the window, I gazed out on a scene of such beauty and wonder that I could explore its marvels for a year and never note half of them. A cityscape of white-and rose-colored spires sprawled across the steep foothills of a range of snow-capped peaks that stood starkly white against a deep blue sky. Arched bridges spanned at least five sparkling waterways, and smooth paved streets wound between the houses and gardens, up and down the steep hillsides, coming together in a broad commard spread out before me.

The grand open space was paved with the same luminous white flagstones as the small courtyard we had crossed to get here. Crowds of men, women, and children of all stations and appearances hurried across the commard amid winter-bare trees that glittered with frost, and fountains poised in frozen exuberance. In the center of the space, a monumental sculpture depicted five leaping horses, the middle one ridden by a woman, her hair and garments and the horses' manes and tails flying in the imagined wind.

Around the edges of the commard, vendors dressed in costumes of red, green, and yellow satin hawked sausages on sticks and drinks dipped from steaming pots, sets of colored balls, silk birds, and fluttering banners that twirled and spun in the air above their heads. Two women in silver masks sold small glittering clouds the size of one's palm. Standing almost directly under my window, a young girl opened her hand and released one of the clouds, scattering its sparkling elements about her head. The music of a lute and viol drifted upward, fading only as the girl walked away. Sword-makers and armorers spread samples of their wares on broad tables to lure wandering warriors to their shops down the side lanes. It was as if I gazed on some fantastical painting, brought to life by a Singer like my mother.

But my perception took another jolt as I gaped, for beyond the commard, perched on the hillside above the steeply sloping sprawl of gardens and open commard, was the same palace I believed we had just entered by a hidden door—rose-colored towers, white and gold banners flying. What's more, though we had gone down from the courtyard and ascended no steps, we were now situated well above ground, perhaps on a third floor, overlooking what appeared to be the front gate of a modest inn.

I spun about to inquire what was going on, but Bareil had sagged onto a wooden chair, leaned his small hands on his knees, and dropped his head forward. "Your pardon, my lord, but I find myself a bit soggy at the knees."

Pulling the flask of brandy from my pack and yanking

the cork, I knelt in front of him. "I understand the vintage is exceptional," I said. He reached for it, but his hand was shaking, so I held the flask as he drank. "Can you tell me this, Dulcé, did you not say we were at the west wall of the royal palace?"

"Yes, my lord." He took another sip from the green flask, then leaned back in the chair, sighed, and closed his eyes. "Thank you, my lord. Most thoughtful."

I left the flask beside his feet and returned to the window. "So, do my eyes play tricks or is that the same palace there beyond at least twenty acres of open ground and halfway up a steep hillside, its west wall tucked securely up beside it?"

"It is."

"Then these hidden 'doorways' do not connect one space to an adjoining one as a person might expect?"

"It would depend upon whose expectations were being satisfied, my lord. If one recalled one's childhood lessons—that were evidently not well attended by certain royal children—one might recall the ways of portal-making. To connect one place to another is not a simple practice, but not uncommon either. Master Dassine was better at it than most. He was able to make undetectable portals that would change direction at his will. I suppose they'll all remain fixed now he's gone, and thus less secure. As soon as I can remember the steps needed, you must destroy the one we just used lest it lead your enemies here." The Dulcé smiled as he looked about the room. "Master Dassine enjoyed this house—The Guesthouse of the Three Harpers—and would often come here to play a game of sonquey or drink saffria with friends in the salon downstairs."

I wanted to know more. Much more. The touch of the world, the breath of fresh air, and the sight of the strange and marvelous city awakened excitement I'd not known in long months. But my hands were grimy from the garden soil where I had buried Dassine, and Bareil's tunic was stained with blood that should have been running through his veins and putting some color in his pale lips. I moved away from the window and sat on the floor by the Dulcé's feet. "Tell me what happened, Bareil."

He sighed and closed his eyes, the pleasure draining from his face. "Master Dassine received a message yesterday morning, just after he had put you to sleep. I can recite the message for you, if you wish. . . ."

"Please."

"It said, 'I have learned news of the most dreadful import. Our time has run out, and we are forced to deal with each other. The Third lives, and has obtained the prize he always wanted. Come to the observatory sculpture garden at sunset.' "

"And that was all? Who sent it? What does it mean?"

"That was all. Though the message carried no signature, I believe Master Dassine knew who sent it. He did not tell me. Something in the substance of the message caused him to cast aside any misgivings, as if it had confirmed his worst expectations."

"What expectations?"

In some way the Dulcé's words were made more worrisome by the calm sobriety with which he delivered them. "My master feared this unnatural quiet. Night after night he would worry at it. He has watched the Zhid closely since you were a boy, listened to rumors and speculations and the changes in the world, charted Zhid movements and their preparations, trying to understand the Lords who manipulate them. Over the past few years he has seen disturbing signs that he did not understand. I am unable to tell you of these particular concerns now, although, when you are ready, you may ask me again and learn of them. You understand?" He opened his eyes to make sure of my answer.

"I understand." How strange it must be to have more knowledge than can be touched with one's own mind, to know that another person must command your intellect to make it truly useful. Did it bother him? Perhaps when I knew him better, I could ask.

Bareil continued. " 'We have become complacent,' Master Dassine has said ever since your victory at the Bridge. 'We go about our lives as if the past thousand years have not happened. Why were the Zhid pulled back from battle? The Bridge is strong and the Gates are open, but the Zhid are not diminished. . . .' " Bareil left off and sat staring at the blank walls of the room as if continuing Dassine's monologues within himself.

"And so he went to this meeting?"

"Yes. Though he expected to be gone a slightly longer span than he usually left you, you were unlikely to wake before his return. As was usual when leaving the house, he commanded me to stay with you. There was always a risk that something would happen to him. That's why he stored the knowledge of his purposes and methods in me, so I could help you if the worst befell. Last night he commanded me doubly"—the Dulcé closed his eyes again—"but I disobeyed, and the worst befell."

"You followed him."

The Dulcé nodded. "The open nature of the sculpture gardens forced me to remain at a distance, so I could not hear what was said or get a close look at the one who awaited my master at the appointed time. They talked for perhaps half an hour until the murderers attacked. When Master Dassine fell, I, like a fool, drew my sword and ran to his defense. Nowhere is there a Dulcé less likely to win swordfame than I, and I knew my duty lay here . . . but I could not abandon him."

"I'll not argue with your choice. Did he put up no defense?"

"The assassins bore swords and knives, not enchantments. Master Dassine distracted their swords and snagged their feet with confusion, but there were too many of them. I noticed only one thing as I fell. The one who had called him there remained standing."

"Who was it?"

"I could not see a face, only that the person wore a blue Preceptor's robe with a gold stripe down the side of it."

"What happened next?"

"I was afraid the murderers would discover that I yet lived, so I crawled under a bench, hoping to regain some strength, but I fell out of sense. Later in the night I became aware of people with torches, hunting Master Dassine. One searcher said, 'I'll not believe Dassine is dead until I see his body. You must find him. I will destroy whoever is responsible for this.' "

"And who was it?"

"The Preceptor Madyalar. I tried to call out to her for help, but no one could hear me. Some time later, others came to search the gardens—in stealth, my lord. Quiet voices, hooded lamps. Master Exeget led this second party—I recognized his voice—and he was furious that Master Dassine was nowhere to be found. I remained hidden until they were gone. I trusted no one to help, so it took me a long time to get back to the house. Too long, it seems."

"And did you see what Master Exeget wore?"

For a long moment Bareil did not answer. "His robe was blue, my lord, with a gold stripe down the side of it."

Bareil's testimony only confirmed my suspicions. From the moment Bareil had implicated a Preceptor, I had believed Exeget guilty. Madyalar must have got wind of the attack and come to aid Dassine, giving Exeget no time to make sure of his old adversary. I would give Exeget a hearing before I passed judgment, but if he was responsible, I would kill him. Dassine could not have intended me to give myself to his murderer.

So then, what of Dassine's mystery? "Dassine told me that a boy has been taken," I said. "Abducted by the Zhid, I presume. He said that if they took the boy to Zhev'Na, then I was to surrender myself to the Preceptorate for examination. Do you know what he was talking about?"

"Not at present, my lord. If I possess this knowledge and you wish to command me to speak it, we must perform the madris."

"If you're willing, it would be a great service," I said.

The Dulcé grinned. "I'm honored that you would consider my sentiments in the matter, Your Grace, but as you have surely concluded and I know for certain, Master Dassine intended us to be joined. My guess is that if we do not, he will fly back from beyond the Verges to hound us until we do so."

"So I'm not the only one he bullied into obedience?"

"Oh no, my lord, far from it . . . though I think perhaps with you he enjoyed it more . . . you being his prince and all."

At that we both burst into delicious laughter laced with grief, and raising the green flask, we drank to the memory of our demanding master.

CHAPTER 11

The first time I participated in the madris, it had been a hurried business. The Dulcé Baltar and I and the seven Preceptors stood in the Chamber of the Gate next to the curtain of roaring white fire. All of twelve years old, I had feared nothing in my life until I understood that I was to step through that wall of flame into the Breach between the worlds, balanced on a thread of enchantment. My mouth had gone dry and my stomach had churned, my terror so overwhelming that I could not attend to the rite that was taking place.

The memory still confused me, for sometimes I envisioned Baltar, a solemn young Dulcé, who, though he was not a mote taller than me, had been lean and hard with powerful shoulders that emphasized my boyish stringiness. But sometimes Baltar wore another face, a rounder, older one, that burst into laughter, tears, worry, or delight with the ease and frequency of a child. I towered over him. It made me wonder if I had actually linked with a different madrissé—perhaps before my latest attempt to repair the Bridge—the one I could not yet remember. I could retrieve no name to go with the second face.

Exeget had performed my madris rite with Baltar, for I had not possessed the power required. With Bareil, of course, I was on my own. But he told me what to do, practicing the words with me until I had them right. "Give me a moment to prepare myself, my lord, and then you may begin."

Bareil knelt on the plank floor of the tidy chamber, held his hands palms up and open in front of his breast, and fixed his gaze on something in the vicinity of the door latch. Gradually his eyes lost their focus, and the light of awareness faded from his face. When his withdrawal from conscious activity seemed complete, I placed my hands on either side of his head, as he had instructed me, and touched his mind. He had made himself completely quiescent and completely open.

"Kantalo tassaye, Bareil. . . ." I began. Softly I touch thee.

To leave his mind so exposed was an incredible act of trust, for at that moment I could have filled him with anything: fantasies, delusions that bore the stamp of truth, sensations of pain or pleasure, desires that could induce him to murder or madness. I could revise his whole identity, his whole emotional bearing. But instead, I reached into the space he had left clear and uncluttered for me, and I carefully touched the centers of knowledge and memory, the places of instinct and reasoning, imprinting on each of them a trace of myself—a connection that would allow me to command their functioning.

Only one step of the madris did I skip, that part which would place my mark on his will, giving me the power to compel his obedience. He had not asked me to forego it, trusting that I would not command him when he wished otherwise. Perhaps he knew me better than I knew myself, for I could not say that I would never press him against his wishes. Better to leave the connection unmade, even if it left our bond incomplete.

For my part of the bonding rite, I simply gave the Dulcé a silent command to draw whatever he pleased from my own head. A sorry lot of miscellany that would be. The sensation was odd and unsettling, something like a thousand spiders scurrying across the skin with pricking bristles on their feet—only it was all inside my head. When it was done, I touched Bareil's face to rouse him, helped him to his feet, and we clasped hands.

"Well done, my lord . . . my madrisson," he said, smiling. "You are more than your memories. No memory can teach you to be so generous with your gifting or so careful in your mind's touch. I am honored and humbled to be your madrissé."

I tried to think of something equally kind to say, but he seemed to have used up all the eloquence in the room. "Thank you, Bareil. The honor is mine."

Though I was anxious to question Bareil, I encouraged him to sleep for a while. He took no time at all to accept the offer. The madris is a draining ritual for a Dulcé, and he had stood at the brink of death a few short hours earlier.

"One more thing," he said, as he moved to the bed, his eyelids already half closed. "You must destroy the portal that connects this place with Master Dassine's house and the palace courtyard, lest someone follow us here. Command me, and I can tell you how to accomplish it."

And so I did. By the time I had stepped down the passage to the spot where we had entered, fumbled my way through the destructive enchantment Bareil had given me, and returned to the sunny little room, the Dulcé was deeply asleep.

I spent the ensuing hours in the most elemental fashion—eating and wishing I could *not* think. Dassine, the child, the murderer . . . Several times that afternoon I came close to the precipice and had to tiptoe backward.

What was I to do about Exeget? If my old mentor had killed Dassine, then he would die for it. Yet such conviction in a matter of life-taking disgusted me. As I had relived the past in these months with Dassine, coming of age in the mundane world, traveling its poorest places and learning of suffering and the art of healing, I had come to the conclusion that for a Healer to take a life was unforgivable. And to do it for so crass a purpose as vengeance doubly condemned the act. But neither could I support mercy in this case.

The Lords had begun this war. A thousand years ago Notole, Parven, and Ziddari, three close friends, all of them powerful Dar'Nethi sorcerers, had discovered a new method of gathering power for sorcery, more efficient, they said, than the slow accumulation of experience, the acceptance and savoring of life that we called the Dar'Nethi

Way. They had devised a way to borrow the life essence from plants or trees or animals, and once they had used it to build their power, to return the essence to its source, leaving the source richer, more beautiful, more complete than it had been before. In joy, excitement, and deserved pride in their talents, they claimed that with such an increase in our abilities, we Dar'Nethi would be able to heal the sorrows of the universe.

But our king and his Preceptors, as well as many other wise men and women, judged that such practice was a dangerous and risky perversion, a temptation too easily distorted. All of nature was balance: light and dark, summer and winter, land and sea, intellect and passion, even as our god Vasrin was both male and female, Creator and Shaper. If the return of essence enriched the source, then something else must be diminished—and thus the balance of the world disrupted. Every enchantment had its price, and King D'Arnath forbade them to continue until we understood the cost of what they did.

Disappointed, but not ready to forego their greatest accomplishment, the three proceeded in secret, planning a monumental working designed to convince everyone of the innocence and rightness of their ideas—using themselves as the objects of their enchantment. But, as the wise had predicted, it all went wrong. Catastrophe. Oh, the three had indeed become immensely powerful, even immortal, so the stories said—Lords, they called themselves. But they had not returned anything of beauty to the world. They had left themselves, our beauteous land, and the universe itself corrupt and broken. Untold thousands of our people who had been in the path of their destruction had been transformed into soulless Zhid. All the realms of Gondai had been destroyed in the Catastrophe or the war that followed, only the High King D'Arnath's royal city and the nearby Vales of Eidolon enduring, surrounded by a desert wasteland.

How could it be wrong to destroy the Lords or the tools they used to draw the rest of us into their corruption? If Exeget had killed Dassine, then he would kill others, and

I was sworn to protect the people of both worlds. The argument left my skull ready to crack.

At dusk, I woke Bareil. Odd to be on the shaking end of it, rather than the shaken. "The sun is taking itself off, Dulcé," I said, "and I think we must do the same."

"You've let me sleep too long."

"I've just recently been reminded of how blessed it is to get a full measure."

"So what to do, my lord?"

"I must find out about this child."

"Command me."

I shared out bread and cold chicken from the pack, and filled two cups with hot, pungent saffria from the small urn sitting on the table. As we ate, I commanded Bareil, "*Detan detu, madrissé*. Tell me of the child that is lost." Such were the proper words to unlock the knowledge of a Dulcé.

He considered for a moment. "I'm sorry, my lord, but I know nothing of a child that is lost."

"Abducted, then. Any abducted child?" One had to be very specific when trying to access information that was not at the front of the Dulcé's mind. "Or any connection of an abducted child with me or with my family?"

"There have been many cases of children abducted by the Zhid, but nothing to distinguish one from another." Deep in thought, he pulled a bite of meat from the chicken leg. "Throughout history the Zhid have tried to abduct royal children as they do other Dar'Nethi children. None of those attempts have been successful. In the years before Master Exeget took you under his protection, there were three attempts to abduct you. I know of no specific connection of any abducted child with you or your family."

I came at the problem from a different tack. "Tell me of the place called Zhev'Na."

Bareil laid down his bread and set his cup aside. "Since the Catastrophe, we have called the ruined lands Ce Uroth—the Wastes—or, as those who serve the Lords say, the Barrens. Zhev'Na is the stronghold of the Lords in the heart of Ce Uroth. Dassine believed it was one of the great houses ruined by the Catastrophe, but even if that is true, no one knows which one or where to find it."

So Dassine knew, or feared, that the Lords had taken this mysterious child. But Bareil had already told me that he knew nothing of any child taken by the Zhid.

"Do we know why the Zhid capture children?"

"To steal an enemy's children has a profoundly demoralizing effect. It destroys his hope for the future and often will make him act rashly. In addition, Master Dassine surmised that children are especially susceptible to the corruption of the Lords. Some Zhid commanders are Dar'Nethi who were captured as children and raised in Zhev'Na under the tutelage of the Three. Only when they came of age, their minds twisted by the life they had led, were they made Zhid—the most wicked of all their commanders. And, of course, the Zhid can no longer produce children of their own, a condition that manifested itself in the early centuries of the war. The enchantments of the Lords are in opposition to creation—to life—so Master Dassine explained it."

As the daylight faded, lingering in the pearly glow given off by the paving stones of the city, I tried a hundred more questions, sideways, backward, arranging and rearranging them to elicit any scrap of information about one particular unlucky boy. To no avail. Dassine had made no references to any living child save the child I had been.

The luminous commard outside the window emptied and fell quiet. Bareil told me that even with the more peaceful times of the past few months, people were not accustomed to going about freely at night. The Seeking of the Zhid—the creeping invasion of the soul that led to despair—had always been strongest in the dark hours. Watchers yet manned the walls at night, but had neither seen any sign of the Zhid nor felt their Seeking since I had returned from the mundane world after doing . . . whatever I had done there.

"Stars of night, what does he expect of me?" I flopped onto the rumpled bedcovers, burying my face and my confusion. Dassine had said Bareil was the one who could help me. He must have thought it would be easy, or he would have slipped in some further word of instruction, even in his last distress. I rolled to my back. "*Detan detu, madrissé.* Tell me the ways Master Dassine gave you to help me. Anything more than the expected things like answering questions and leading me around the city."

Bareil nodded. "Master Dassine has allowed me to know the reasons for your present condition, and the means he has used to cause it and to remedy it. He has permitted me to know what things it might do you harm to know before you remember them properly, and what things would be of more benefit than harm. He has given me the purposes and instructions for the use of the device which we collected—the pink stone—and the second device which you must allow me to hold safe until the time is right for me to explain its history. He has entrusted me with the knowledge of shifting the exit point of the Bridge and several other such matters which may be spoken only in your presence, else my tongue will become mute for the duration of my life. He has entrusted me with the complete story of his sojourn in the Wastes, which he has told to no other living person, and how you must use his knowledge to chart your course for the future. He has entrusted me with the knowledge of those men and women that he mistrusts and those whom he trusts. Shall I go on?"

"Stars of night, Bareil . . ."

"My madrisson honored me with such confidence as no one has ever given a Dulcé."

"Do either of these devices—the pink stone or the other one—have anything to do with a child or any of the matters we have discussed?"

"Not that I can see, my lord. It seems I can be no help to you in the matter of the child."

Staring at the smoke-stained plaster of the ceiling, I thought back to Dassine's words yet again, reciting each one exactly as he had burned it into my head. *Holy stars!* I sat up. How could one man be so unendingly thickheaded? I had been misstating them all along. *Only one can help,* he had said. *Bareil . . . your guide.* But he *hadn't* said that Bareil and the person who could help were one and the same. "Dulcé, who in Avonar did Dassine trust?"

"Trust? No one, my lord, save myself. He often said it."

"None of the Preceptors?"

"Most especially none of the Preceptors. He has long suspected that one or more of his colleagues is a tool of the Lords."

That would explain a great deal. "Outside Avonar, then. Did he trust anyone outside of Avonar that might have knowledge of this matter?"

"I know of only one person that he trusted unreservedly, my lord, or whom he told anything of his work with you."

"Who was that?"

"Lady Seriana." The Dulcé looked away and closed his mouth tight. Dangerous ground that, and Bareil knew it. She had undone me once.

"She is across the Bridge."

"Yes, my lord."

"Is it possible that she might have knowledge of this mystery?"

"It is possible, though I have no direct information that says it to be true."

"And you know of no one else who might?"

"The Preceptors might. It is my presumption that Master Exeget might."

"You mean that Dassine may have learned of the abduction from Exeget before the attack?"

"I was told nothing of this matter, my lord. Though I'm sure there are matters which Master Dassine did not discuss with me, I believe he would have made sure I knew anything of vital importance to you . . . if he had the opportunity."

"But why would Exeget give him such important information and then have him killed?"

"I agree that such actions make no sense at all. Perhaps Master Exeget was taunting Master Dassine. I don't know."

There was a great deal more I wanted to learn from Bareil, but more than anything, I wanted to act. I had thought and questioned, lived in memory and dreams and confusion for so long that I was about to burst from the desire to ride, to run, to fight, to stretch my muscles for anything more than easing the cramps of too-short sleeping.

So. Two choices. We could find Exeget and force answers

from him, or we could seek out the Lady Seriana and discover if she knew anything of the mystery. My earlier conflict about the merits and justice of revenge induced me to choose the latter. Confronting the lady might damage my mind a bit, but I could not rid myself of the disturbing suspicion that confronting Exeget, with the image of the dying Dassine still so clear in my head, might do considerable damage to my soul.

"The Bridge, then," I said. "I will speak to the lady first."

Bareil bowed. "Command me, Lord."

"*Detan detu, madrissé.* Tell me what I must do to cross the Bridge and find the Lady Seriana."

"First, you will need the pink stone. . . ." In a quiet monologue, Bareil told me the words to raise the light of the stone, telling the lady we were on the way, and then how to reverse the enchantment so that I could set the exit point of the Bridge to the place where she was to be found. When he had schooled me enough, he motioned me to the door. I took our pack from him and followed.

We left the guesthouse in a more conventional manner than we had entered it, down the stairs and through a large room—a salon, Bareil had called it—that was quite different from the common rooms of inns in the Four Realms. This was a soft-lit, quiet place with many small groups of men and women engaged in lively discussions or storytelling, or testing their skills at sonquey—a game of strategy played with square tiles of red and green, finger-length bars of silver, and a dollop of sorcery. At another table, two men and a woman bent their heads over a pattern of exquisitely painted lignial cards, representing Speakers, Singers, Tree Delvers, and others of the hundred Dar'Nethi talents. The woman was pregnant, likely calculating the prospects of her coming child's magical gifts. A burly man served out mugs of saffria and ale, and laughter rolled through the room from here to there like summer showers. No fights. No filth. No grizzled veterans building the edifice of their valor larger with each tankard. No contests of manhood proving only that the stink of ale, sweat, piss, and vomit was the price of good humor. Steady-burning lamps hung about the room, and their light had nothing to do with fire. In fact, there was no smoke at all, save the marvelous emanations of a roasting pig, generously dripping its fat into the firepit in one corner of the room. If I could have borne the thought of sitting still another moment, I would have insisted on a plate of it.

Bareil pulled up the hood of his cloak and looked neither right nor left as we walked through the room. Having been the madrissé of a Preceptor for thirty years, perhaps he would be recognized. I, on the other hand, had less occasion to worry; few people had ever laid eyes on the present Heir of D'Arnath, or so I understood. But I pulled up my hood, too, as if in preparation for stepping into the cold night.

"We must take the long way around and come up behind the palace," Bareil said, as soon as we were in the street. "It is not time for you to walk in the front gate."

We passed like shadows through the soft glow of the city, hurrying past wonder after wonder: tiny yellow frost flowers with petals like crystal, blooming in a window box; a faint bluish eddy in the air over a well, where you could hold your freezing fingers and have them pleasantly warmed; an unfrozen pond whose dark waters reflected the complete bowl of the heavens, but nothing else, no structure, no tree, not even my own face as I peered into it.

"My lord, please," said Bareil, tugging at my arm. "We must get out of the streets. Those who wish you harm will be watching."

On we sped, crossing a district that had been reduced to skeletal towers and blackened rubble, where only vermin and wild cats could find refuge. We climbed narrow lanes that wound steeply up the hill past the palace, past sights that spoke of the long years of war: deserted houses, ruined shops and bathhouses, neglected gardens, crumbling bridges and dry pools. Even the intact bathhouses were closed and locked. What had once been a favorite recreation for Dar'-Nethi had fallen out of favor. Many people felt it unseemly to enjoy the pleasures of recreational bathing when thousands of our brothers and sisters were enslaved so cruelly in the desert Wastes.

We padded through a university, its cloistered walkways

broken up by weeds, its lawns and gardens long overgrown, entangling fallen statuary and broken stone benches in an impenetrable blanket of briars. At one end of a weed-choked quadrangle stood a ruined observatory. The domed roof that had once housed seeing devices used to study the heavens had caved in long ago, and many of the intricate carvings of heavenly objects that banded its walls were damaged beyond repair. The overgrown sculpture garden, the site of Dassine's murder, lay quiet.

Bareil said the palace was defended against hidden portals, so we would have to enter by one of its five gates. Almost an hour after leaving the inn, we stood across a courtyard from two slender towers that sheltered a single thick wooden gate into the palace precincts. This courtyard, tucked away behind the palace, almost hacked out of the rock of the mountainside, was not one of the commonly used entries, Bareil told me, but one used for prisoners being brought to the palace for trial or the royal family's personal visitors who wished to be discreet. No guard was in sight.

"This gate is sealed except when it is needed," said Bareil. "Guards are unnecessary except under a direct assault."

"Then how are we to get in?"

He smiled up at me, and whispered, "This is your house, my lord. The locks and seals will know you."

I hadn't considered that I could just walk in. I was not stealing into a place where I had no legitimate business. If I wanted, I could stroll through the front doors of this place and proclaim myself home—though I didn't think that would be clever.

We slipped around the shadowed edges of the courtyard and came to the great wooden door banded with steel. When I laid my hand on the thick latch, barbs of enchantment pricked my arm all the way to the shoulder.

"Press down as you would on any door handle," said Bareil. "It should open to your hand."

I did so. Nothing happened.

The Dulcé frowned. "I don't understand. No one could change the locks without your permission, and you used this gate many times when you were a boy."

True . . . In my first nine years, no one had ever really cared where I was or what I did, but fussy courtiers and tutors would forever attempt to ingratiate themselves with my father by reporting on my ignorance and undisciplined behavior. So I had sneaked away from them, down the narrow stair through kitchens and barracks and through the open doorway into the cluttered courtyard that lay on the other side of this very gate, knowing that everything I wanted awaited me just beyond it: freedom and adventure, weapons, combat, fear, blood, and death . . . war. Out on the walls of Avonar my friends the soldiers stared over the walls at the misty gray wall that was the Zhid encampment, gulped from flasks of ale, and laughed. I had wanted to laugh at fear and blood and death. No one in the palace would teach me how, but my friends, the soldiers, had. Yes, this was my door, in my house.

I pressed down again. This time the brass handle moved smoothly and quietly, and the massive gate swung open without the slightest pressure from my hand.

Now I led Bareil. Across the courtyard, through the labyrinthine way to the stair behind the kitchens. Only a few voices echoed through the passages—guards and servants who cared for the palace itself and functionaries who performed the hard daily work of governing. No royalty had lived in the palace since I'd been taken to Exeget when I was nine.

Our destination was not the living quarters I had so rarely graced, but the Chamber of the Gate, buried deep in the roots of the mountain underneath the palace. Downward and inwards, through minor galleries and guest quarters, past armories and long-silent ballrooms, into the ancient heart of the palace, burrowed deep into the rock. The stone of these corridors had not been cut and laid by any mason, even one who could cut with his singing or polish with a brush of his hand. Rather the walls were native stone that had been shaped and smoothed until the sworls of jasper and lapis shone of their own colored light. My steps accelerated.

I thought we'd made a wrong turn when the passage we traversed ended in a blank wall. But before I could turn to

Bareil, the stone shifted—a mightily unsettling sight—and revealed a door of age-darkened wood that swung open at my touch. I had forgotten the door wards. Beyond the door lay the circular chamber of white and rose, its ceiling lost in white frost plumes. Only when I stepped through the door could I see the Gate—a towering curtain of white flame, rippling, shifting, shimmering, reaching exuberantly for the heights in the uncertain light. Cold fire that left the room frigid and sparkling like the clearest of winter mornings. Rumbling fire, exploding geysers of flaming brilliance that created constantly shifting patterns. Though the fire didn't terrify me as it had when I was twelve, it still took my breath away. This was the legacy of my ancestors, one endpoint of a link that spanned the universe itself. My soul swelled and thrilled and wept all at once with the glory of it.

Bareil gave me the rose-colored stone. As he had instructed, I roused it to glowing life, creating a pool of warmth in the hollow of my hand. Then, with will and power, I shaped the path of the Bridge that lay beyond the Gate, so that it would lead me to the stone that matched the one I held.

"Shall I await your return, my lord? No one will alter the Gate path while I live."

I had to leave the pink stone behind to keep the return path open. If anyone removed it from the chamber or reworked my enchantment, then I would have to travel to the Exiles' Gate—the mundane world's counterpart of this, the Heir's Gate—in order to return to Avonar. That might be a journey of many days, depending on where the Lady Seriana was to be found. But I dared not get separated from Bareil and the information he carried.

I shook my head, unable to speak while I held the enchantment in my mind. Motioning him to leave the stone and stay close, I stepped through the curtain of fire and onto the Bridge that was my singular inheritance.

CHAPTER 12

Seri

Gerick was my son. Karon's son. My heart stumbled on the words, yet of their truth I had no doubt. There was no other answer to the puzzle he was.

Had Tomas known it? Surely not. Law and custom had convinced him that my child had to die for the safety of our king and his realm, and Darzid had convinced him that his own knife must do the deed. Not even the knowledge of his own child's frailty would have persuaded him to spare a sorcerer's child. Yet, I wondered . . . Had there been somewhere within my brother a mote of suspicion, a seed of doubt that never made its way to the light of his waking mind, but blossomed into the incessant nightmares and overpowering dread that made him beg me to return to Comigor? Never could he have permitted that seed to grow into the light, for it would have told him that the babe he had murdered was his own. If my fear and grief had left me any tears, I would have wept for Tomas.

On the evening of my discovery, I paced the library, waiting for news. The cabinets that had housed the lead soldiers gaped at me in reproach.

Every servant and soldier of Comigor had been called to the hunt. Troops of guardsmen scoured the Montevial road, inquiring for Darzid or the boy at every private or public house all the way to the capital. Other soldiers and servants followed every road, trail, and footpath that came anywhere near the castle. Giorge and his assistants were querying the tenants. I had done everything it was possible to do. Now I had to wait—until the last man came back and told me he'd found nothing. I knew it would be so. I had no idea of Darzid's capabilities, but every instinct screamed that they would be enough to hide Gerick from one who had no talent but that of her own prideful imaginings. Where would he take a sorcerer's child? Dassine had said that Zhid could not cross the Bridge without the complicity of powerful sorcerers in Avonar . . . but Zhid had crossed the Bridge last summer, and Darzid had been hunting with them. What if Zhid could take Gerick across the Bridge?

I slammed the door of the soldiers' cabinet so hard one glass pane shattered.

I had dreaded telling Philomena. When I had gone to her room that afternoon, I'd found her sitting up in bed, a maid brushing her hair. Her fingers toyed idly with the gray silk bag in which I'd brought her the lock of Tomas's hair. All evidence of her dead infant had been stripped from the room. Not the least trace remained of that short, sweet life, and I wondered if anyone had given the little girl a word of farewell as she was laid in the frozen earth. "I'm so sorry about your daughter, Philomena," I said.

"Gerick has run away, hasn't he?" she said calmly, not taking her eyes from the gray silk that was wound about her fingers.

I could not understand her composure. "How did you know?"

"The servants say men are searching the house. I've not slept as much as everyone thinks."

"No one has seen him since last evening. I've sent—"

"Is he dead?"

"We've no reason to believe it. I won't believe it." *Worse . . .* The stone that settled in my stomach whenever I thought of him grew colder, heavier. Some things were worse than death.

Philomena wrinkled her brow as if trying to decide on white wine or red with dinner. "It's not as if he was ever very affectionate. He didn't like playing cards or dice with me, and I never knew what else to do with him. Boys are so beastly. They like fighting and dirt and nasty things."

"He's not dead, Philomena. I believe Captain Darzid has taken him. Many people know the captain; he's easy to identify. Do you know of any place he might take Gerick? Did he ever mention any town or city or person to which he might go?"

"I never listened to Captain Darzid. He was boring." She looked up, her fair brow in an unaccustomed wrinkle. "Some say *you* are responsible for these terrible things. Auntie says it. But others whisper that the gods make me pay for my husband's sin—because he killed your child and helped King Evard burn your husband—and that's why all of them are taken from me. Do you think that's true?"

"Don't ask me to explain the workings of fate. Life is incomprehensible enough without believing we have to pay for someone else's faults in addition to our own."

"Ren Wesley says you saved my life."

"I only fetched the midwife."

"Did you want me to live so that I would know that all my children are gone—so I would suffer? I don't understand you at all." She sighed and tossed the gray silk bag onto the floor. "You'll come read to me tonight?"

I was ready to scream, *Are you mad, stupid woman? My son—mine—has been stolen away by a smooth-tongued villain, and I don't know where in this god-cursed universe they've gone.* Yet, what else had I to do but wait? Losing myself in fantasy for an hour might be the very thing to save my reason. I bit my tongue. "I'll be here at the usual time."

"Do whatever you need to find him," she said as I left the room.

"You can be sure I will." But how and where?

And so I had dispatched more searchers and a message to Evard, and when evening came, I read to Philomena until she fell into the image of peaceful sleep. Since then I had waited, gripping the rose-colored stone that hung around my neck as if sheer force of will might bring it to life and send my plea to Avonar along the paths of its enchantment. Our child had been abandoned at his birth—by his dead father's idealism and his living mother's bitterness and self-pity. He had grown up in fear, not understanding what he was. If I had to walk the Bridge myself to fetch help for him, I would do it. Somehow.

* * *

Just after dawn a footman came to me in the library, saying that a stable lad was causing trouble. "It's the cripple. I caught him sneaking through the kitchens and threw him out. Then I caught him again, coming through the windows of the wash house. I told him Giorge would have him flogged, but he insists he has to see the Lady Seri—pardon the liberty, ma'am, but that's how he put it—as he had information you would want to know. I didn't want to bother you with it, but Allard said that with the hunt and all—"

"Bring him to the housekeeper's room." Any distraction was welcome.

"Yes, my lady. As you say."

The footman dragged Paulo into the little office next to the kitchen, holding him at arm's length by the neck of his shirt. "Here he is, my lady. I'll stay close by."

"No need." I closed the door firmly, then laid on the table a packet of ham and bread I'd fetched from the larder. Paulo's eyes brightened, and he reached for it. But I laid a hand on the packet and said, "First a question, my friend. What's so urgent that you risked punishment to get in here?"

Paulo crammed his dirty hands in his pockets. "Just wanted to tell you she's on the way."

"She?" Paulo never liked to use four words when two would do.

"You know. Sheriff's friend what saved him and me last summer."

"Kellea? Kellea is on her way here?"

He nodded and eyed the packet of food under my hand. Paulo had every intention of making up for thirteen lean years living with a drunken grandmother. I pushed the bundle toward him, still not understanding.

"But why? I mean, what brings her this way?"

Stuffing the bread in his mouth, he mumbled. "Told her you needed her."

"You told her. . . ." Needed Kellea? Of course . . . she was absolutely the one person in this world that I needed, and I hadn't even thought of it. Kellea, the last survivor of

Karon's Avonar, newborn the week before the massacre, was a Finder. Herbs, lost objects, people . . . given the proper materials to create a link with the thing or person she sought, she could locate almost anything.

The first spark of hope glimmered in my head. "She's coming to search for Gerick?"

Paulo nodded. "Be here tonight."

"That's the best news I've heard in two days. But how, in the name of heaven, did she know?"

He gave me the same long-suffering sigh he used whenever I asked how he knew that a horse wanted to run faster or graze in the next clearing rather than the one we were in. "I *told* her."

"I think you'll have to explain that."

He took the bread from his mouth, but not too far. "When I come here, she said that every once in a while she'd talk to me, tell me about the horses and Sheriff and all. You know, like she can, that way we can't say nothing about?" Dar'Nethi—J'Ettanne, as Karon's people had called themselves in this world—had rarely used their ability to read thoughts and speak in the mind, aware of the potential to abuse such power, especially when living in a world where no one else could do it.

"Mind-speaking? I didn't think she knew how." Or cared to know.

"Well, she learned it of that woman"—he leaned close and dropped his voice even lower—"the swordwoman."

The "swordwoman" was one of the three Zhid who had pursued us to the Bridge in the summer. After his battle with Tomas, Karon had healed the three of them, returned or reawakened the souls they had lost in their transformation. I believed that their healing had been the very act that had strengthened the Bridge and kept the Gates open. Karon had been too weak to take them back across the Bridge to Avonar, and, indeed, they had had little reason to hurry. Their own families and friends had died centuries before, and they were unlikely to find welcome among the other Dar'Nethi whose family and friends they had slaughtered or enslaved. So the three had taken up residence in Dunfarrie under Kellea's and Graeme Rowan's protection.

"Kellea taught me how to talk back to her when she was with me in my head," said Paulo. "Just think real hard about her and what I want to say and nothin' else at all for as long as it takes. Thought my head might burst while we were working at it, but I learned how. The swordwoman says not many non-magical folk can do it so well as me." The rest of the bread and a good measure of ham cut off any further discussion.

"Paulo, I knew it was a good day when you came here."

The boy wiped his mouth on his sleeve and jerked his head at the door. "Best go now. Got work to do."

"Yes. Not a single word to anyone about these things. You know that?"

He gave me a bready grin, pulled open the door, and disappeared through the hot kitchen.

My revived hopes were quickly swallowed by grim reality. Throughout the day—the second since Gerick's disappearance—searchers returned empty-handed. I sent them out again, telling them to go farther, ask again, be more thorough, more careful, more ruthless. Even for a Dar'-Nethi Finder, the trail was growing cold.

I wandered down to the library and curled up in the window seat where I had first laid eyes on my son. For half the day I stared at a book of which I could repeat no word. The bright winter sun glared through the window glass. . . .

A rapid tapping startled me awake. Someone had built up the fire and thrown a shawl over me to ward off the evening chill. My book had slipped to the floor. The insistent tapping came again from the direction of the library door. "My lady? Someone's asking to see you." It was Nellia. "A young woman. Says she's expected."

"Bring her right away"—I jumped to my feet, fully awake in an instant—"and hot wine . . . and supper. Whatever there is. She's come a long way."

The small, wiry young woman who strode into the room a few moments later could almost pass for a youth with her breeches, russet shirt, leather vest, and the sword at her belt. Her black, straight hair hung only to her shoulders. "Here almost before you thought of me, right?" she said, displaying the quirky smile people saw so rarely.

All my grief and guilt and terror, so closely held for two long days, was unleashed by Kellea's arrival. I embraced her thin shoulders fiercely and engulfed her in a storm of tears. The poor girl . . . shy, uncomfortable with people, especially awkward with anyone who knew of her talents . . . Knowing how such behavior would unnerve her, I swore like a sailor even as I wept.

"What is it? Has the boy been found dead or something?" Kellea said, shifting awkwardly as I gained command of myself and pulled away. "I know he's your brother's child, but—"

"He's not Tomas's son, Kellea. . . ." I drew her close to the fire, speaking low as I told her everything, built up the case again, one point at a time, hoping she could tell me that my fears were overblown.

But when the story was told, she shook her head. "Oh, Seri . . . and you've no way to contact anyone across the damnable Bridge."

"It could be a year until I hear from Dassine again."

"You don't think this Darzid means to arrest the boy, take him to Montevial . . . to execute him?"

That had been my first terror—that my child might suffer the same horror as Karon had. But I had persuaded myself that a trial was the least likely result.

"Without substantial proof Evard would never harm a child he believed to be Tomas's son. And how would Darzid explain switching the two infants without condemning himself for condoning sorcery? Darzid must have done the switch; he brought the dead infant to me himself. He has preserved Gerick's life all these years, knowing what he is. Why would he harm him now?"

Why? Why? Darzid's motives had always been a mystery. His deeds had taken him well beyond the common reasoning of greed and ambition. In the days of our friendship he had confided in me his dreams of a "horrific and fantastical" nature and professed a growing conviction that somehow he did not belong in his own life. In my months of imprisonment between Karon's death and Gerick's birth, Darzid had badgered me to tell him of sorcerers, to explain Karon and his people, claiming that "something had changed in the world" in the hour Karon died . . . which of course it had. But I hadn't understood the world back then, and had no concept that Karon's death had opened the Gates to D'Arnath's Bridge, renewing an enchanted link designed to restore the balance of the universe. How had Darzid perceived such a thing? The gleeful hunter and persecutor of sorcerers had demonstrated no sympathy, no kinship, and most importantly, no knowledge that might imply that he himself could be one of the Dar'Nethi Exiles. I refused to countenance any such possibility. So what was he?

"Sounds like we've no time to waste," said Kellea. "Bring me something that belongs to the boy, and I'll try to pick up his trail. Meanwhile, if you don't mind, I'm going to dig into this little feast. Didn't stop much on the way."

I hurried upstairs, leaving the young woman slapping butter and cheese on the toast Nellia had brought in. Gerick's room was perfectly arranged: bed, wardrobe, washing cupboard, a set of elaborate chess pieces meticulously aligned on an otherwise bare shelf. I searched the wardrobe and a small writing case, looking for some article that might hold enough of Gerick's ownership to trigger a Finder's magic. Clothing did not usually work well, Kellea had told me. For most people, too little of the self was invested in them. The dust on the chess pieces hinted they'd rarely been used. I settled for a pair of fencing gloves, thinking of Gerick's intense desire to master the sword. Clearly his life had been lived elsewhere—in Lucy's room, I guessed, where he felt safe. Inspired by the thought, I hurried to Lucy's room and snatched up the reed flute he had made for his nurse.

Kellea tried the gloves first as they were Gerick's own possession, but eventually she threw them aside and reached for the flute. Closing her eyes, she ran her fingers over the hollow reed, around the ends and over the holes. Then, she laid the flute on the table, and, motioning me to be patient, she sat on a stool beside the fire, propping her elbows on her knees and her chin on her clasped hands as she stared at nothing. Just as I concluded that time had come to a halt, she jumped to her feet. "They're heading west."

CHAPTER 13

West. I scribbled a message for Philomena, saying I'd received word of Gerick and was taking two companions to investigate. While Nellia helped Kellea pack food from the larder, and Paulo readied the horses, I changed into riding clothes, found us blankets and supplies, and rummaged through Gerick's wardrobe for a heavy cloak and thick gloves for Paulo. I dared not bring soldiers along: Kellea was risking her life by using sorcery in the Four Realms.

Within two hours of Kellea's declaration, Paulo, Kellea, and I rode into the night.

The moon was full and newly risen, its blue-white light so bright on the snow that we cast long shadows ahead of ourselves. Only the ring of hoofbeats on the frozen road and the occasional howl of a wolf broke the silence. We rode hard. By the time the moon shadows had shifted to lie long on the road behind us, the barren heath had yielded to more substantial hills, dotted with pine and oak scrub. Ahead of us lay a dark line that looked like the edge of the world—the Forest of Tennebar, an immensity of trees that stretched to north and south, and well beyond the rugged borderlands to the west, deep into Valleor.

Why Valleor? I could not shake the nagging suspicion that Darzid was taking Gerick to the Zhid. Yet, as far as I knew, the only way to take Gerick to Gondai was across D'Arnath's Bridge. And the Exiles' Gate—the fiery chamber where my brother had died and Karon had restored the Bridge—lay not in Valleor, but in the high mountains of southwestern Leire, many days' journey from here. Were more of the empty-eyed warriors hiding in the wretched places of this world, feeding off of our misery?

Our heads were nodding, and we were about to lose the light of the setting moon, so we halted at the edge of Tennebar. The trees gave us some protection from the bitter wind that gusted from the north.

Kellea had taken the last watch. She woke Paulo and me shortly after dawn. Within moments we headed into the forest, eating bread and cheese as we rode. Tennebar stretched for leagues in every direction, its vast expanse scored by wide logging trails, as its tall, straight pines were much prized for building. The sun glittered on the frosty branches. Rabbits and foxes, startled by our passing, scampered across the sparkling snow, almost invisible in their winter white fur.

By midday we were climbing the first slopes of the Cerran Brae, the low range of forested peaks that formed the natural boundary between Leire and Valleor. As the way grew steeper, the road split. A wide wagon road angled south to cross the Cerran Brae by way of Cer Feil—the South Pass. From there one could descend into the valley of the Uker River and travel south to Yurevan or Xerema or angle northwest across the Vallorean Spine to Vanesta. The northern fork was a more direct route to Vanesta, but less traveled, for Cer Dis—the North Pass—was narrow and steep, reputed to be a haven for bandits. Traders generally stayed with the safer, if longer, southern route.

Kellea dismounted and walked a few steps along each branch of the road. For each way, she found a spot bare of snow, crouched down, and picked up a handful of damp dirt from the road, letting it fall through her fingers. When she returned and remounted, she led us north toward Cer Dis.

Night fell. We forged onward, able to follow the narrowing track for a while in the dappled moonlight. But as the way became steeper, Paulo worried about the horses' footing in the inky shadows, so, despite my chafing, we made camp. Clouds rolled in, smothering the moon and stars. Late that night, at the end of my watch, it began to snow.

The next day was a blur of misery. The light never advanced beyond dawn gray, and the air grew colder as we climbed higher. We led the horses up the steep switchbacks, each turn looking exactly the same as the one before, each made more treacherous by the lightly falling snow. Every time we saw a break in the trees on the forested ridge above us and thought that at last we were nearing the end of the ascent, we would find yet another step in the contour of the land, another slope to be traversed.

By mid-afternoon we were above the tree line, climbing a rocky defile that did little to shelter us from the bitter wind and stinging snow. The light, such as it was, was going. We were exhausted, but we dared not stop. I wasn't sure we could survive a night in such an exposed place, and I cursed my stupidity at setting out, two women and a boy on an unfamiliar road in the middle of winter.

Paulo was in the lead. He had sharp eyes for the trail and for anything that might be difficult for the horses. I kept my eyes on the too-large, slouch-brimmed hat he'd inherited from Graeme Rowan. It bobbed up and down with the boy's twisting gait.

About the time the light failed, I realized that Paulo was disappearing downhill. The burning muscles in my legs rejoiced, and I mustered a few words of encouragement for my horse who had plodded along gamely throughout the grueling day. If we could just get down into the trees, find grazing for the horses, build a shelter, make a fire . . .

Any assumptions that the downhill path would be easier were quickly swept aside. The track was steep, narrow, and icy. We descended another series of switchbacks, scarcely able to see for the snow and the settling gloom. Darzid, Gerick, the search, everything receded in importance. The whole world was reduced to the next step. . . . *One foot in front of the other . . . don't slip, don't stumble, don't imagine what lies down the impossible, dark slope at the end of each steep traverse. Shift the reins to the other hand so your fingers don't get numb and drop them altogether. . . .*

A yelp from in front of me broke my concentration. The

slouch-brimmed hat vanished into the murk. Paulo's horse stopped dead in the track.

"Paulo!" I yelled over the blustering wind. No answer. I picked my way carefully around Paulo's horse and the packhorse. It was fortunate I took care, for we had come to a set of snow-covered steps that signaled the end of one descent and the reversal of direction that would begin another. It appeared that at least one of the steps had been a false one, carved of snow instead of rock. Slide marks led right off the edge into the dark unknown below the trail.

"Paulo!" I screamed again. In a moment's lull in the gale, I believed I heard a soft moaning just below me and to the left.

"Holy gods . . ." Kellea had crept up behind me. "He's down there."

Without taking my eyes from the spot where I thought I'd heard him, I told her to get a rope . . . and to watch her step. She was back in moments.

"One of us has to go down," I said. "Is there anything to tie the rope to?"

"Only his horse."

"Can you steady the beast and hold the rope if I go down? You're likely the stronger."

"I think so."

We tied the rope to the horse and to my waist. I forced my frozen fingers to remember the sailors' knots my friend Jacopo had tried so hard to teach me. When all was as secure as I could make it, I told Kellea to start paying out the rope a little at a time. She murmured to the horse about what a good boy Paulo was and how important it was to hold fast.

I told myself the same and stepped backward over the edge. My boot found no purchase on the steep slope, leaving me sprawling face first in the snowy embankment. Shaking, I held on tight until I was sure the rope was taut and the knots around my waist snug. When my heart was out of my throat and my voice would come out in more than a croak, I started calling for Paulo. "Hold on," I said. "I'm coming. Make a noise so I can find you."

The next step down. Better. I found rock. If only I had a little light. I could scarcely see the darker patches where rock and dirt protruded from the snow. Estimating the angle of Paulo's slide, I tried to stay to one side of his path. I called again, but heard only the wind and the rush of fear in my ears. Down another step. The upper part of the embankment was incredibly steep. I slipped again and got a mouthful of dirt and snow. Was this what it was like to be blind, every step fraught with terror, stomach lurching, not knowing if your destination was within a finger's breadth or ten leagues away? How could Paulo have survived such a fall? This could be the very edge of the world for all I could see.

Kellea yelled something that was snatched away by the wind.

I stretched for a foothold. Stepped down again, trying to be sure of it. Where was he? "Paulo, help me find you."

To your right! screamed Kellea, directly into my head.

I moved to the right. Gods, where did the earth go? I flailed about in panic when my hand and foot found only a pitch-black void instead of a solid hillside. No, it was just that a piece of the slope had slumped away, leaving a scooped-out bowl of snow. A darker patch lay on the far side of it, and I heard the faint moan once again.

A little farther . . .

The snowy shelf angled outward. I eased onto it, digging in the uphill edge of my boot to make decent footing, scarcely daring to let down my weight in fear it would give way. I crept toward the sprawled figure, unable to determine his position, until I realized that one of his feet was pointed at a totally impossible angle. *Oh, curse it all. . . .* Even insensible he was holding on, his fingers dug into the snow and the dirt. Probably better if he could stay asleep. He wouldn't want to feel what it was going to be like to get him up the embankment.

Carefully I scrabbled into the snow at the back of the shelf, trying to make a spot that was fairly level, not at all happy to discover that the outsloping snow lay over outsloping rock. The snow would have to hold me in. I settled myself into the spot; then, hating every moment of it, I untied the rope.

"We're going to haul you up, Paulo. Hold on. It's going to be all right. . . ." Carefully . . . carefully I knotted the rope about Paulo as snugly as possible. No way to immobilize his leg until we got him up. Then, I gave three hard tugs on the rope. At the first creeping movement, Paulo screamed in agony. *Slowly, Kellea,* I begged silently.

I've known nothing that's taken so long as it did to drag Paulo up that embankment. After the first scream he never cried out, but I could hear his muffled sobs for a long while. When he at last fell quiet, I prayed that he wasn't dead. In fate's cruelest perversity, the broken leg was *not* the one that was already crooked, the one that gave the clumsy twist to his walk and made the children of Dunfarrie call him donkey.

He's up. Watch for the rope. Soon the rope dangled in front of the ledge. Unfortunately it was just out of reach. Gingerly I shifted forward, outward, until I could grab it and tie it about me. Three tugs and I started to climb, scrabbling upward and eating a good deal of dirt and snow as I went. I didn't really care, as long as the rope held.

When I crawled over the edge of the path, I lay in the snow panting beside a motionless Paulo. Kellea sat beside me, her head bowed. "We've got to get him downhill and get a fire going," she said, nudging my aching shoulder.

I nodded, and we stumbled to our feet. Together we bundled the limp Paulo in blankets, using our rope to bind one of them tightly about his leg to hold it as still as possible. Then we laid the boy across the saddle and tied him to his horse. Kellea took the lead as we crept down the trail.

The next hour passed in a misery of snow and cold, wind and exhaustion. When Kellea made an abrupt halt and scrabbled about in the snowy hillside on our right, I could do nothing but stand huddled in my cloak, numb, dull, too tired even to ask what she could possibly be doing. To my astonishment, she, her horse, the packhorse, and the spare mount we'd brought for Gerick disappeared abruptly in a direction that couldn't possibly be right. But I forced my frozen feet to follow . . . into a cave, deeper and wider than I could reach with my arms, and wonderfully out of the wind. I vowed never again to travel without a Dar'-Nethi Finder.

We lifted Paulo down first. Then, while I felt my way carefully with hands and feet, leading the horses a little deeper into the cave where they couldn't step on us, Kellea worked at starting a fire. She had never learned how to manage it with sorcery. From the mumbled oaths as she worked her balky flint, I guessed that fire-making would be the next thing she learned from the Dar, Nethi swordwoman.

Carrying blankets and what extra clothes I could grab from our packs in the blackness, I crept my way back to Paulo. I bundled him up and wrapped my arms around him, trying to share what little warmth I had, willing Kellea's flashing sparks to catch whatever she had found to burn. When the first sickly flame split the darkness, long before it provided any warmth, I sobbed silently in gratitude.

The cave looked like a way station for bandits. All manner of odd things lay about: broken crates, a few barrels, a spilled bag of blue-dyed yarn, chewed by generations of vermin. The blackened fire pit lay near the mouth of the cave, filthy with half-charred animal bones and unrecognizable muck. But a good supply of dry firewood was stacked beside it.

Paulo was awake and shivering uncontrollably, eyes glazed with misery, lips bloody from holding back his cries. His skin was pale and clammy. "We'll soon have you warm," I said, as Kellea ripped twigs from the larger pieces to feed her hungry flames. Fumbling with a waterskin and my handkerchief, I wiped the dirt and blood from the boy's mouth.

As soon as the fire was blazing, I turned to Paulo's injuries. Kellea knelt beside me, stroking his forehead while I cut away his muddy breeches and leggings. I tried not to let my voice reflect the grim sight I was uncovering. "About time we got you some new clothes, Paulo." *Oh, gods have mercy. . . .*

"I've brought a few things," Kellea said quietly over my shoulder. "I'd best get them."

Kellea's herbs weren't going to do much for Paulo. His lower left leg was broken in at least two places that I could see, possibly one more from the way he moaned when I touched his swollen knee. A shard of bone protruded through mangled flesh and sinew above his ankle, and he was bleeding profusely. At the least we had to straighten the breaks and stop the bleeding. Yet, even if we could keep the injury from killing him with sepsis or blood loss, I doubted the limb would ever be usable.

Kellea unrolled a small leather bundle containing a number of paper packets and small tin boxes. Tearing open a packet, she crushed several dark green leaves in her palm, transferred them to Paulo's tongue, then gave him a sip of wine to wash them down. "This'll make you sleepy, so it won't hurt so very much. We'll give it a little time to work before we see to your leg. Same as we did for Graeme when he was hurt. You remember."

He nodded ever so slightly.

I tried to blot away some of the blood from his ankle, but when I so much as touched the grotesque wound, he sucked in his breath and his face went even whiter. Little whimpering moans caught at the back of his throat. "Ah, Paulo, I know it's awful. But we have to press on it a bit to stop the bleeding. Can't have you leaking all over the blankets."

While Kellea stoked the fire to roaring and put a pot of water on to boil, I held the ragged remnant of Paulo's breeches on his wound. First we cleaned the wound with wine and boiled oak bark from Kellea's packet and forced the bone back inside, and then I held his upper body while Kellea pulled and twisted his poor limb into some semblance of alignment. Gripping my arms, he buried his face in my breast and did his best not to scream. But he couldn't manage it. His racking sobs tore me to the heart. After a while he fell insensible again and we finished the horrid task as best we could. From a small tin, Kellea extracted an oily yellow paste and spread it onto his torn flesh, then bandaged and splinted his leg with pieces of a broken crate, binding it with lengths of our rope. So pitifully little we could do.

Kellea was almost as pale as the boy when she was done. "It's far from straight, but I just can't get it to move any more," she said. "We'd have to use rope and pulleys to make it right, but even then I'm afraid we'd just do more damage. I'm no surgeon."

I threw Kellea's cloak over her shoulders as she dribbled willowbark tea into Paulo's mouth. Then I moved the horses farther into the deep cave and unsaddled them, giving them a cursory wipe-down with a piece of sacking Paulo kept for that purpose. We couldn't afford to have them die on us. I dared give them only half a ration of grain from Paulo's emergency supplies. Who knew how long we'd be here? By the time I had done what I could for the beasts and hauled the rest of our supplies close, Kellea had fallen asleep.

All through the night we took turns watching Paulo and feeding the fire. I forgave the bandits their crimes in thanks for the wood. Paulo shivered and moaned quietly, and I gave him more of the willowbark tea. What on earth were we to do?

At some time, I fell asleep without waking Kellea. When my shoulder was touched lightly, guilt set me apologizing even before I could unglue my eyelids. "Is he all right? I didn't mean to fall asleep." I fought my bone-weariness to sit up, but my dream refused to be banished with the opening of my eyes. Paulo lay beside me, his cold hand gripping mine. His face was pinched and pale, but bore a trace of his old grin as he gazed up at the one who knelt on the other side of him.

"This will hurt for a moment," said the newcomer, his voice quiet, weaving a cocoon of peace and reassurance, "but nothing as to what you've done already. Then I'll be with you, and we'll take care of it. All right?"

Paulo nodded, a silver knife flashed in the firelight, and Karon's words of healing scattered embers of enchantment like fireflies through the cave.

CHAPTER 14

A Dulcé had shaken me awake. "My lady," he whispered. "Would you be kind enough to step outside where we could speak? I would most appreciate it. The Prince has said it will take him a goodly time to care for the boy."

"Yes . . . yes. Of course." This could not be a dream if I was stammering so foolishly. "Of course I'll speak with you."

Kellea's blankets lay empty, no sign of her in the cave. I wrapped my cloak tight, dragged my eyes reluctantly from Karon, who was binding his bleeding arm to Paulo's, and stepped into the dawn light. Kellea wasn't outside either. The only tracks in the snow were the sun-melted muddle of our foot-and hoof-prints from the previous night.

The Dulcé followed me out of the cave.

"I didn't even feel it change," I said in wonder, pulling the pink stone from my tunic and clasping it in my hand to savor its lingering warmth. "We had a difficult evening."

"So it would appear." The bearded man's eyes glinted with good humor. "And, in our great hurry, we most rudely gave you little warning."

Recovering some measure of politeness, I said, "You seem to know me, but I've not had the pleasure. . . ."

"My name is Bareil," he said, bowing in the way of the Dulcé, with one arm extended and one behind his back. "Dulcé, as you see. Guide to Master Dassine for thirty years and now privileged to perform that service for Prince D'Natheil."

"Where is Dassine? I've news of such urgency . . ."

His smile dimmed. "Master Dassine is dead, my lady. Two days ago at the hand of unknown assassins."

"No! But what of the Prince . . . his recovery . . . his future . . . ?"

"I'll tell you all that I may, but if you please, a question first. What's happened here? The boy inside . . . who is he?"

"His name is Paulo. He was leading us down the mountain last night. Lost his footing and fell. We didn't know—"

"The peasant boy who accompanied you and the Prince to the Bridge last summer." The certain eagerness that had sparked Bareil's question sagged into disappointment. It put my hackles up.

"A brave and honorable boy, who was as responsible for saving the Bridge as anyone. If you know his name, then you know—"

"Please, madam"—Bareil flushed and held out his hands in an eloquent apology—"I am quite familiar with the merits of the boy Paulo and honor him as I do all who aided us in that great victory. But I will confess that I was hoping— Ah, the Prince must explain."

Biting my tongue, I stepped away from the cave mouth to the edge of the path. Pink and orange harbingers of the sun spilled over the peaks we had crossed, tinting the snow-blanketed landscape all the colors of flame. Below us, much closer than the forever distance of my night's imaginings, were the trees—pine and fir of deep green, flocked on this morning in snow, colored rose and coral. But my heart was behind me in the cave, and I could not keep silent, no matter the moment's irritation. "How does he manage with Dassine dead?"

Bareil stepped up beside me, his arms folded under his cloak. His low voice bore everything of kindness. "You must understand, my lady, that a madrissé may not discuss his madrisson or his madrisson's business with anyone, no matter how close. It is a violation of the absolute trust that must exist between them."

"I understand that." Of course, understanding did nothing to heal resentment.

"Master Dassine had a unique confidence in you, Lady Seriana. Because I must enlist your aid in carrying out his last wishes, I will stretch my oath so far as to say this: if you question the state of the Prince's heart, then he grieves sorely; if you question his will and courage, they are undiminished. But if you question the state of his recovery, it is not complete, and so I must ask you— The Preceptor Dassine entrusted me with the knowledge of his purposes and his plan for D'Natheil, so I must beg you to abide by all that he required of you."

"If it is necessary."

"Quite necessary. To look closely into the unresolved contradictions of his past or to strain too hard to understand those things still hidden is very difficult for the Prince."

"Yes. I saw it."

"Master Dassine believed that, even if he failed to pursue his course with the Prince, eventually the memories of the Prince's life as the man born in this world would return. They might be in differing order, however, or, due to the influence of present-day events or D'Natheil's life that is also his, they might spur different emotions and interpretations. Such was not my master's desire. He tried to submerge the Prince in his past by isolating him from everything, anything, that could distract him or burden his senses. And he gave my lord little time to analyze or react to his recovered memories. Master Dassine believed it imperative that nothing prevent the Prince from becoming the person that he was . . . as you knew him. This is still possible. I bear the knowledge, and there are those in Avonar who have the skill, to complete Master Dassine's plan. But the terrible events of the past few days and the mission that Master Dassine laid out for the Prince before he died . . . those must take precedence."

The sun warmed my face even as a sharp wind gusted off the snow, chilling my back. "I can't judge the importance of your mission, but I bring news of such significance that I would believe it was my willing it so that brought you here. Yet from what you say I shouldn't tell Karon . . . D'Natheil.

My news involves him so deeply and is connected with the most painful part of his past . . . and perhaps with the future as well."

Why? Why? Why would the Zhid and their masters, the Lords of Zhev'Na, want Gerick? A possible answer had come to me in the long night's journey, forgotten for a time in the horror of Paulo's injury, now recaptured in the clarity of the morning.

Bareil's small face crinkled into a frown. "Would you please consider trusting me with your information? Though we have just met, I feel as if I know you very well. I've been privy to all of Master Dassine's work in these past ten years. My only desire is to complete it and serve the Prince as I may."

I saw no choice. I could not risk harming Karon with what I knew. And beyond that, Bareil had already impressed me as imminently trustworthy.

"All right, then," I said, "tell me what would be the result if the Zhid gained possession of a child . . . a child who is the son of your prince?" I had seen it often, my own king taking hostage the children of his enemies.

"The legitimate son of the Heir of D'Arnath? The eldest living son?"

"Well, yes." Eldest, youngest . . . a hostage was a hostage.

The Dulcé did not turn pale, or cry out, or do any of those things we associate with uttermost dismay. He just became absolutely still, the pleasant animation of his exotic features wiped out in an instant. "Madam, if the boy had not yet come of age, it would be a day of such woe for my world and yours that there has been no day to compare with it since the day of the Catastrophe itself. Have you reason to believe such an event has occurred?"

"It's why you find us in such desperate circumstances," I said. Then I told him everything.

"The Third lives and has obtained the prize he has always wanted. . . ." he murmured to himself. "Would I had died with my late master before I heard such ill news. A child alive beyond all understanding, the reprieve of a life we mourned, a tale that should bring only rejoicing. And yet— The circumstances are so extraordinary, the father's soul now living in the Prince's flesh. But if the Prince and the boy were to pass the test of parentage . . ."

"No 'test of parentage' is needed. I'm certain Gerick is Karon's child. He can work sorcer—"

"No, no, my lady. I do not doubt you. Don't you see? Matters are far worse than you believe. If the boy is proven before the Preceptors of Gondai as the legitimate eldest son of the Heir, child of his flesh and spirit—no matter what circumstances have caused it to be true—then that boy will become the Heir's legitimate successor—the next Heir of D'Arnath."

Gerick the next Heir . . .

Bareil shook his head. "You have seen truly. We dare not tell the Prince. Master Dassine's strictures were clear. Your husband must not know this child is his own until he has relived the path to his own death."

"Then tell me how I am to convince the Prince that this rescue is of paramount importance, if I can't tell him the victim is his own son?"

"That will perhaps be easier than you think. Ah"—he glanced up, shaking his head and raising one hand as if to refuse temptation—"I speak too freely. I'm truly sorry that I'm unable to discuss the matter with you further. You must speak with the Prince and decide for yourself what to tell him of the child. Master Dassine had great faith in your judgment."

"I feel as if I don't know anything any more."

When Bareil smiled, it was with all of himself. Master Dassine had a knack of leaving people in impossible situations. "But only because the universe itself is in an impossible situation. He enjoyed doing battle with the universe—the only opponent he ever found challenging. And in you, madam, he was convinced he had found his worthiest ally."

The Dulcé excused himself, saying he would go in to check on D'Natheil's progress with the "most excellent boy." Restless, shaken, I climbed up on a rock that promised a good vantage. Still no sign of Kellea. The crumpled ridges of the Cerran Brae ran southward, their faces still shadowed, a contrast to the bright plains that stretched to the western horizon. The northern prospect was dominated by a single peak, its massive, forested shoulders topped by a snowy crest. Nestled at its feet was a frost-shrouded valley, plumes of pink-tinged mist rising from it as if the fires of the netherworld burned below its veil.

Out of my chaotic thoughts emerged one dreadful comfort. The Lords would want Gerick alive.

After perhaps three quarters of an hour the Dulcé popped out of the cave. "The healing is done. Perhaps we should eat while you speak with the Prince. He will need sustenance, and my guess is that you and your companions would not be averse to a hot meal." He offered me a hand down from my perch.

"Are you a cook, too, then?" I asked, remembering the first Dulcé I'd met—a charming, pitiful betrayer who thought murder and an ancient sword could have his city.

A shadow crossed his face, quickly smiled away. "Alas, no. Poor foolish Baglos was a chef without peer, even in Avonar where there are many fine cooks. This company will have no such pleasure from me, though I am not immodest to say that the brandy I lay down is considered to be a unique pleasure. We have a bit with us, if you should have need of a drop. . . ."

"Not now. Last night I might have traded my horse for it." I followed him into the cave.

Paulo slept peacefully next to the snapping fire. His chest rose and fell, slow and deep, and the color in his thin face was a healthy brown. Most incredibly, he had rolled over on one side, his fist tucked under his chin, and his legs—both legs—curled up under his blankets. The bloody rags and splints lay in a pile near his feet.

Karon sat on the ground beside the boy, his arms about his knees and his chin dropped to his chest as if he were sleeping. But he looked up as Bareil and I walked in, and the marvelous smile that had always been the sign of Karon's true nature illuminated his tired face. "You invited me back to visit you, my lady, but you didn't say you would find an even colder spot to meet and provide a challenge such as I've not seen in a very long time."

"How's that, my lord?" said the Dulcé. "I thought the saving of my own life had been your fairest challenge!"

"Ah, Dulcé, a few pinpricks such as you had cannot begin to compare."

"I thought you timed your return visit extremely well, sir," I said, trying not to stare. "But I cannot quite shake the conviction that you are only a convenient fantasy."

"I'm sure that if I were your fantasy, I would be able to leap up from this frigid floor and greet a lady properly, and then work some marvelous feat of sorcery to transport us all to southern Iskeran where it's warm." He rubbed his head vigorously with his fingertips, tousling the hair that had come loose from its tie at the back of his neck. "I make a most inadequate fantasy, my lady. You should conjure another."

"How is Paulo?" I asked, offering him a waterskin.

"Once we fill his stomach, he should be able to resume your journey with no difficulty," said Karon, accepting the water gratefully. He drank deeply and wiped his mouth on the back of his hand.

"You've saved his life or at least his limb, which is much the same. I—all his friends—are grateful beyond words."

"I believe I've only begun to repay him." After a quick glance at me and an almost imperceptible shake of his head, all pleasantry vanished from his face. "My debts are innumerable. Bareil told you of Dassine?"

"A grievous loss," I said.

He nodded. "Did he also tell you of the task Dassine set us?"

"He said only that you have business with me beyond bringing this dreadful news." I held patience and let him speak first.

"We're searching for news of an abducted child. . . ." He told me his story, then, of Dassine's murder, of the note, and the Healer's dying words of a child that must be rescued from the Zhid. ". . . so you see, even though it makes no sense, I must discover what I can. Bareil tells me that Dassine trusted you beyond any other, and so I begin with you."

This could be no coincidence. My mind raced. What should I tell him? Instinct insisted I claim that Gerick was a descendant of D'Arnath's line who had been placed in my world for his own protection. Or perhaps that he was simply a Dar'Nethi child who had shown immense power. Anything to convince him that Gerick was the boy he sought. Karon had so many holes in his reality anyway, so what if one was filled with untruth or exaggeration.

But my heart forbade me to lie to him. Once, in the years of our marriage, I had kept a terrible secret from Karon, glossing over it with misdirection. I could still feel his hurt on the day he'd learned the truth, wounded not so much by the secret itself, but by the barrier the lie had built between us.

Gerick had grown up as the son of my brother, and I didn't know why he had been taken. That was truth. I had no evidence that Darzid or the Zhid knew that Karon and D'Natheil were one and the same, and despite my convictions, I had no direct proof that Gerick was our son. Best stay with what I knew and say nothing beyond it. Keep silent where truth would not serve.

And so I told Karon the story of my brother's child who had disappeared from his home four nights previous. Treading carefully, I told him, too, of my brother's mysterious aide who had disappeared on the very same night as Gerick. Though I could not mention Darzid's role in his own arrest, I explained about Darzid's strange fancies and how he was a known hunter of sorcerers, yet had been seen consorting with the Zhid in the year just past. ". . . and so with no hard evidence, I've come to believe that Darzid is more than he seems and is surely in league with the Zhid."

"Why would the Zhid want a child of your world?" Karon asked. "You say your brother was a noble, and a worthy swordsman, and a close ally of your king, but he was not Dar'Nethi. I can't see why Dassine would consider this particular abduction to be so much more worrisome than any other."

And this, of course, was where the difficulty lay. Bareil came to my rescue. "My lord, I wonder. . . . You remember when I told you of the Zhid's delight in taking children, raising them in Zhev'Na, and thereby creating their most formidable captains?"

Karon dipped his head, his brows knit in puzzlement.

"What if they have decided that with this child, the noble son of this world's most potent warrior, they could do something the same? Create a Zhid warrior of the mundane world to command the Zhid hosts if they were to find some way to transport Zhid across the Bridge? Such would be a terrible blow to those of this world who would try to resist."

And how much worse it would be if that commander held the power of the Heir. . . .

Karon nodded slightly. "Could that be what was written in the note, 'the Third lives and has the prize he has always wanted'?"

Bareil was slow in responding to Karon's question, and Karon glanced up at him sharply. "*Detan detu, madrissé.* Do you know the meaning of this phrase?"

But the Dulcé did not retreat at Karon's show of impatience. "I cannot answer you, my lord. Forgive me."

Before Karon could reply, someone burst through the curtain of blinding sunlight at the mouth of the cave.

"We've got to get out of here. They're com— Fires of Annadis! D'Natheil!"

Karon was on his feet, already poised to strike, sword in one hand, silver dagger in the other.

"Hold, my lord!" I cried. "She's our friend. Your friend. Kellea, what is it?"

The Dar'Nethi girl kept her eyes on the unwavering blades and her hands well away from her own weapons. "Bandits. Five or six, at least, halfway down from the summit. They'll be here in half an hour, and from what I saw, they're not anyone we would like to meet. They fell on a pair of travelers up the pass. Stole the poor sods' clothes and boots and chased them naked through the snow. Played them for sport, wounding them a little worse each time, then letting them loose again until they butchered them. Earth's bones, I never saw such savagery. If I'd not been alone . . ."

"I'll get the horses," I said.

"But perhaps I've got help now," said Kellea, grinning at Karon and lowering her hands as he lowered his weapon. "The Prince and I could rid the world of the beasts. And we wouldn't have to move Paulo."

"The Prince has healed Paulo," I said. "If we can make it down to the trees, the bandits won't find us." We had no time for this. No resources to spare.

"Wake the boy and get you gone—all of you." Karon's quiet self-assurance—or was it D'Natheil's?—implied the discussion was ended. "I'll take care of the vermin and join you down the road."

"Indeed you will not," I said. "Dassine gave you a task to do." No purposeless gesture was going to endanger the life of my child.

"Such brutes must not be allowed to enjoy the fruits of their crimes."

He stepped toward Kellea and the cave mouth, but I dodged into his path, blocking the exit. "This is not your business," I said. "If you set out to right every wrong in this land, you'll be as old as D'Arnath before you've even begun."

"But I can take care of this one," he said, trying to step past me.

I didn't budge. "Your responsibilities are far more important than petty vengeance."

Anger flared in his blue eyes. "My responsibilities are with me every moment. I must do what I think is right."

Like lightning in a dry forest, his words sparked such a blaze of anger in me that I lost all caution. "You must do what is most *important*! The child you were sent to save is two days' journey ahead of us, perhaps more than that by now. His safety is your responsibility. Nothing else. You will not abandon him to his fate, not this time."

"Madam, please . . . have a care. . . ." Bareil stepped in between Karon and me.

But caution had deserted me. "As for the rest of us, Kellea must lead you to the child, and Bareil holds the keys to your reason. They cannot be put at risk. Paulo and I are the only ones who can be spared to aid you, and I'll carry Paulo down this mountain on my back before I'll allow you to sacrifice another life to your moral certainties. We will go down now. All of us."

Karon stared at me, as white and still as if I'd stabbed him. His sword slipped from his hand into the dirt. I crouched down to the scatter of pots and blankets beside Paulo. Hands shaking, I wadded up the blood-soaked rags, rolled up blankets, emptied and stacked pots and cups, cramming everything into the scuffed leather bags and panniers.

After an interminable silence, the others moved as well. Kellea shook Paulo's shoulder with hushed urgency and helped the groggy boy pull on her spare wool leggings, the two of them whispering, marveling at the pale white scars on his straight leg. As I poked at the refuse in some ridiculous attempt to cover the evidence of our stay, the two of them saddled the horses in the back of the cave.

I glanced over at Karon again. He stood rigid, scarcely breathing, his bloodless hands clenched and pressed to his forehead, eyes squeezed shut. What had I done?

Bareil murmured to Karon, one hand on Karon's shoulder and the other gesturing to the fire and the cave. Moments passed. With guilty satisfaction, I watched Karon start moving again. He retrieved his weapon and sheathed it, and then began to work with the fire, dousing its flames with a motion of his hand, leaving it cold and dead, unable to bear witness to our presence. A cold wind swirled through the cave, dispersing the smoke and the scent of the horses, masking our footsteps with cold ash and sand and a dusting of snow. The blessed Dulcé stayed close to him, murmuring in his ear, having no eye or word for anyone else.

After only a quarter of an hour, we were riding on the steep, downward trail, Bareil in the saddle behind Paulo, Kellea leading the packhorse, Karon at the back, riding the extra mount we'd brought for Gerick. Every little while I sensed a brush of enchantment; behind us the snow on the trail appeared undisturbed. As the tense silence continued, a frowning Paulo looked from one of us to the other.

I couldn't think of anything to say. No words could soften the sting of the ones already spoken. But I'd done only what was necessary. If it was too much for his fragile mind, best to know it now.

Once on the gentler trails in the sheltering trees, we picked up speed, riding at a brisk walk for several hours through the frosty woodland, making good time on a decent hard-packed road that headed northwest along the side of a gently sloping ridge. The sun was well past the zenith when we came to a sunny, snow-patched meadow, and Kellea called a halt. "We should rest the horses," she said. "We've had no sign of pursuit, so I think we're out of danger. And there's a crossroads up ahead; I need to take my bearings."

Though I could not bear the thought of slowing, I knew the wisdom of preserving both horses and riders.

"I'll see to the horses," Paulo said, dropping from the saddle easily and reaching for my reins.

"You should rest for a while," I said, taking his reins instead. "We'll care for your horses this time." With a little persuasion, Paulo sat on a log and allowed me to provide him with enough cheese and oatcakes for three men. While Bareil collected the animals and led them to the water, Karon strode down through the muddy snowfield and leafless tangle of vines and willow thicket toward the stream, stretched out on a sunny rock, and closed his eyes without a word to anyone.

"How are you feeling?" I asked, when Paulo had slowed his intake to a reasonable pace.

The boy's eyes shone as he stretched both legs out in front of him and stared at them as if they were forged of gold. "He put it all back straight. Don't hurt a bit. And he fixed the other one, too, as has never been right since I was born. I thought I was done for, and now I'm whole. I don't even have the right things to say about how it is with me."

His brow clouded as he looked down by the stream where Karon lay on the rock. "But he didn't remember Sunlight. I told him as I had been taking good care of him since he left. Never thought he'd forget that horse. Horse didn't forget him, not by a long ways." The boy glanced up at me. "Didn't think he'd forget you neither."

I sat on the log beside Paulo, pulled an apple from my pocket and stared at it, discovering that my own appetite had entirely disappeared. Stuffing the apple away again, I tried to explain that, although the Prince had finally remembered a great number of things that he couldn't when he was with us before, it unfortunately meant he no longer recalled anything about our journey together. "If he asks you questions about it, you can answer him. But it would be best not to volunteer too much. It makes his head hurt."

"Guess it would," said the boy thoughtfully, "having things goin' in and out all the time. It's easier with people like me." He tapped his head. "Not much doin' in here. But then I don't have to bother with nothing but my belly and my horses. If Sheriff'd just quit fussing at me about learning to read, I could do without my noggin altogether."

I couldn't help but laugh. Paulo always had a wonderfully pragmatic perspective.

CHAPTER 15

Karon

I knew our destination. From the moment I followed the lady and the Dulcé out of the cave and saw Karylis baring its hoary white chest to the blue of the northern sky, I knew it. Karylis, where I had learned to hunt, to climb, and to heal, the mountain that spread its mighty arms and embraced the fertile valley where I was born.

Hundreds of years in the past, my people—Dar'Nethi sorcerers exiled from a world they had forgotten and condemned as outlaws in this world—sought out places where they could begin a new life. Three families, including that from which I am descended, came to Karylis with its sweet air, rich soil, and clear rivers, and from their settlement grew a city of grace and beauty that they called Avonar. No man or woman of them could remember why they revered that name, only that it was a part of each one of them, so precious that it came to every tongue unbidden. They had long lost their memories of the other Avonar, the royal city of the world called Gondai, whence their ancestors had been sent here to maintain D'Arnath's Bridge.

We were never very many. Of the thousands who lived in Avonar when I was a youth, probably fewer than three hundred were sorcerers, but you could not walk through the streets without seeing the wonders our people had created there: the gardens that bloomed long after frost, graceful roads and bridges that did not age or crumble, a society of generous people who lived in mutual respect and civilized discourse.

I had been away at the University on the day my city died. Reports said the valley had been completely surrounded by Leiran troops just after dawn, and that by nightfall every sorcerer—man, woman, and child—had been identified by informers, tortured, and burned. Every other resident had been put to the sword. My father, the lord of the city, had been the last to die. The Leirans would have made sure that he witnessed the completeness of their victory. At midnight they had torched the city, so that as far away as Vanesta, people could see Avonar's doom written in the heavens.

I had not gone back after the massacre. Even for a Dar'-Nethi there are limits on the sorrow that can be inhaled with the breath of life. I wanted to carry with me the image of a living city, not the funeral pyre of everyone I loved.

I had embraced the grief of that terrible loss as was the way of our people, and yet, I think I always knew that someday I would have to look on Avonar again. From what I could remember of my life in this world, I had never yet done so.

Only one thing would draw a Zhid sympathizer like this Darzid to the ruins of my home. Was it possible he had learned the secret revealed to me just before I left for the University? My father had said we were going hunting that day, but I'd found it odd that he invited me alone, without any of my brothers who enjoyed it more. . . .

The soft folds of Karylis's foothills were draped in mist. The trail was new to me, and I found myself increasingly reluctant to penetrate the sweet-scented vale. "There's nothing here, Father," I said. "We've seen no sign of any game, large or small. There are a hundred more likely trails."

"Not for what we hunt today," he said, riding onward, his strong back and broad shoulders commanding me to follow, even as my hands itched to tighten the reins and turn back.

The white-trunked birches were scattered over the grassy slopes, the glades open and smoothly green, and as the morning waxed, the sun banished the mist into the rocky grottos that stood as reminders that it was Karylis's domain we traveled. The mountain itself was hidden by trees and swelling ground. A sheen of dewdrops lay on the grass and quivering leaves.

"We'll leave the horses here," said my father, when we came to a stream of deep blue-green that emerged from a towering granite wall.

"We shouldn't be here," I said as we dismounted, whispering as if my voice might divert some unwanted attention our way. "What is this place?"

My father laid his hands on my head, saying, "Be easy, my son. We've come to a place most precious and most secret. Only the one who bears the sign of the sovereign can know of it . . . no, do not protest. I am not rebelling against the Way laid down for us. Though of all my sons, I would entrust our future to you, I know that the thread of your life draws you along another path. Christophe is young yet, but he'll be a fine lord, and I'll bring him here when it's time. But you, Karon . . . you cherish our history and our Way as no one else, and I cannot but think that this is a place you should know."

At his touch my reluctance vanished, and we climbed alongside the stream until we came to two massive slabs of granite embedded in the hillside. They leaned together, leaving a triangular shadow of indeterminate depth between them. Power pulsed from the shadow, throbbing in my blood like the noonday sun in high summer.

"What is it?" I asked.

"It is our birthplace, one could say. From this place, some four hundred and fifty years ago, stepped three families seeking a new life."

"The portal from the stronghold! But I thought all the portals were destroyed."

Somewhere, in a place far from this hillside, lay the fortress where our people had held out in times of trouble. In the time of the Rebellion, when the extermination laws were passed, even the fortress had not been safe enough. Imminent discovery had forced our people to scatter, leaving behind a mystery, so our legends told us, something precious and holy that had existed since before our oldest memory. Though drawn to the secrets of the stronghold since I was a boy, I had assumed the portal destroyed.

My father traced the cracks and seams of the great stone with his strong fingers. "Those who remained in the stronghold said this portal was a link to the holy mystery and hoped that someday we would be able to practice our arts openly again and discover its true purpose. And so, to my distant great-grandsire they entrusted the words with which it could be opened, words in a language we didn't know, a secret to be guarded until times would change. We've waited all these years, scribed the words in stone so that time and faulty memory would not alter them—I'll show you where they're hidden. But, of course, times have not changed."

I stuck my hand into the opening and felt nothing out of the ordinary. "Have you never been tempted to venture the passage, Father? To discover whether anything remains of the stronghold? Perhaps we could unravel the mystery, learn more of the past, make things better. . . ."

"Yes, I ventured it once, as did my father and his." He shook his head. "We found only this cleft in the rock. Perhaps our power was not enough. Or perhaps there is nothing to find any more. But you . . . who knows? You should try, I think." He whispered the words in my ear, and his hand on my back urged me forward.

And so I stepped into the small alcove of granite. To an observer who could not sense the power of enchantment, the place would have been unremarkable, save perhaps for the feel of the air. While springtime lay a soft breath on the vale outside, within the alcove it was winter. Or perhaps the cold frost was only my first reaction to an enchantment that was not meant for me. As I walked the narrow passage that led me deep into the rock and ran my hands over the rough surfaces of the walls, speaking the words my father had whispered, the scars on my left arm began to sting as if newly incised. The longer I stayed, the more a bitter frost spread from my arm to the rest of me. Enchantment was everywhere, thrumming, pounding, swelling, filling my veins as if I had twice the blood of a normal man. So close . . . I summoned my power, drawn from life and healing and the beauties of the mountains and the morning . . . releasing it into the enchantment. So close . . . I could feel the walls thinning. So close . . .

But something wasn't right. The enchantment would not yield, and soon I was shivering so violently that I couldn't think. I ran back up the passage and into the daylight. "We're missing something," I said, my teeth clattering like a woodpecker's beak on dead wood. "We need to learn what the words mean."

Quickly my father bundled me in his cloak and built a fire.

"I'm all right," I said, "except that I feel like I've spent the night naked on Karylis in midwinter." I had no feeling in my left arm—or so I thought. When my father ran his fingers over my scars, I cried out, for his touch felt like hot iron. My left arm stayed numb and lifeless for almost a week . . . numb and lifeless and so cold . . .

I sat up abruptly. I must have fallen asleep as I lay in the winter sunlight. Idly, I rubbed my left arm where it had gone numb and looked about for my companions.

The boy Paulo was communing with the horses that grazed on a few patches of brown grass exposed on the stream bank. When he noticed my eye on him, he grinned at me and performed a hopping dance step, a spin, and an awkward bow. I could not remember ever receiving so winning a thanks. I grinned back at him.

The boy had been in tremendous pain when I joined with him, and in such a case, the relationship of Healer and patient can be very intimate. His fears were exposed for me to share: the terror that he would be more a cripple than he was already, more of a burden on the friends he so admired, beside which dying was of no matter at all. Yet he demonstrated an absolute trust in me. And as I worked and his pain eased, his thoughts kept returning to a horse called Sunlight . . . as if I might know the beast. This boy knew me.

The girl, Kellea, a Dar'Nethi girl, born in Avonar just before it fell—what a wonder that was—she had recognized me, too, and the Lady Seriana . . . The lady had called me Aeren when she looked on me that first time in her garden.

Dassine had told me that Aeren was another of my names, but that it was only an alias, not a third life to be remembered. I was grateful for that. The name was connected with my recent history—my mysterious second journey to the Bridge. Perhaps all three of them knew me from that time.

Lady Seriana . . . earth and sky, who was she? On this morning, when she was so angry with me, jagged rents had again appeared in the span of my vision. Through the terrifying gaps of darkness had poured such an oppression of guilt and sorrow that I would have done almost anything to escape it. But for Bareil nudging me to action, I might never have moved again. No, best not think of the lady.

I lay on my sunny rock as mindless as a cat, half asleep when Bareil came, bringing oatcakes and wine. "Is there some other service I may offer you, my lord?" The lines of worry carved so deep on his brow grieved me sorely.

"I can ask no more than you've already done today."

"I do only as Master Dassine instructed me. Are you fully recovered?"

"For now. You were quick."

"Then perhaps . . . The Lady Seriana would very much like to speak with you."

Speak with the lady? The sunlit meadow suddenly wavered before my eyes, as though I gazed through the heat shimmer of a fire. "No. Not now. Tell her . . ."

How could I tell her that I was afraid of her? Clearly she knew more than she was telling me, yet I had to trust her, because Dassine did so. But whatever she knew and whatever she was drove me to the brink of madness. Any further along that course, and I would have to abandon the search, just to get away from her. Then I would be left with only the disturbing task of avenging Dassine. Better she think me a boor.

"Just tell her I won't speak with her now. Perhaps later."

"Nothing more?"

"Nothing more."

CHAPTER 16

Seri

Though I tried to brush off Karon's refusal to speak with me as a passing pique, he didn't make it easy. As we left the snowy meadow, he vaulted into the saddle and rode out with Kellea before I'd even closed up my pack. When nightfall mandated the next halt, I tried to sidestep our disagreement. "Though the weather's no warmer, at least the sky's stayed clear," I said, sitting down on the log next to him as Kellea doled out our supper, "but a night in Iskeran would still feel better."

"Indeed." His porridge might have been the most delicate roast quail for the close attention he paid it.

I jumped up. A mistake to sit too close. Even so near the fire, I felt the chill. "Would you prefer ale or wine? We've a bit of both left."

"Wine, if you please." He raised his head at that, but his gaze flitted from woods to sky to muddy earth as if I had no physical substance.

Surely this was D'Natheil's reaction to my scolding and not Karon's. Dassine had warned me that the lingering echoes of the temperamental Prince would remain with Karon forever. But I would not apologize. I had been right to keep him focused. We had to keep moving.

On the next morning, Paulo discovered the remnants of a camp just off the road. Kellea confirmed that Gerick had been there. Karon said the fire was more than two days dead. Though we rode harder after that, no one pretended optimism. The greater the gap between us and Gerick, the more difficult for Kellea to follow.

Late in the afternoon of the second day from the bandit cave, Kellea called a halt in order to take her bearings. We had ridden all day on a narrow road that was half overgrown with birch saplings and tangled raspberry bushes. Carved stone distance markers, broken and toppled over well back in the dense undergrowth, testified that the road had once been well traveled and much wider. Indeed, when we emerged from the thinning trees onto a broad slope, carpeted with winter-brown grass, the faded ruts and indentations showed the roadway to have been more than forty paces wide, sweeping up and over the top of a gentle ridge. A snowcapped peak was just visible beyond the hilltop, but my uncertain geography gave no clues as to our destination, and I'd found no inscription remaining on the shattered distance markers.

Kellea dismounted and knelt to examine two paths that split off of the main track. Karon did not wait for her direction, however, but pushed on up the hill, halting only when he reached the top.

"He's chosen the right way," said Kellea at last, motioning us after him.

We joined Karon on the hilltop and found a view that was indeed worth a pause—the broad valley I'd seen from the bandit cave, no fire-shot frost plumes hanging over it any longer, only heavy gray clouds that promised snow before morning. The valley was much larger than I had imagined, a sweeping vista of grasslands and woodlands, small lakes and streams. The wide-thrown arms of the mountains were softened by leagues of rolling hillsides clad in winter colors, on that day a hundred shades of gray and blue. The valley's beauty seemed virginal—unscarred by human activity. But for the contrary evidence of the road, I might have believed we were the first to look on it.

Yet the longer we gazed, the more disturbing the quiet. No bird chirped; no insect buzzed. Nothing at all dripped or trickled, hopped, or scurried. And somewhere just beyond the center of the valley was a line of demarcation, straighter than anything nature could devise. Whatever lay beyond that line was dark and indecipherable in the gray light. Uneasy, I turned to ask the others if they knew the place. Paulo, Kellea, and Bareil were staring at Karon, who gazed unblinking on the valley, tears flowing freely down his cheeks. And then I knew.

By more than twenty years he had outlived his family and his birthplace. Before I could speak, he urged his mount forward, moving slowly down the hill.

As we followed Karon into the valley, we saw remnants of human habitation: stone houses overgrown with brambles and dark windows like hollow black eyes, a lone chimney standing in a bramble thicket, rotting fences, fields gone wild, roadside wells and springs so wickedly fouled that only black-and-green sludge lay within twenty paces on any side. But these sights were benign compared to the view as we passed beyond the barrier we had seen from the ridgetop.

A desolation of frozen mud, no remnant of twig or leaf or stubble saying that anything had ever grown in these fields. A few stunted thistles poking through the crumbled highroad seemed to be the only living things within a half a league of the city. Charred and broken towers stood starkly outlined against the heavy clouds. Bare white walls rose from the center of the wasteland like the bleached bones of some ancient beast. Everything dead. Everything destroyed. And lest one retain some hope that some remnant of life had escaped their wrath, the destroyers had set tall poles to flank the gate towers, and upon each one had strung a hundred heads or more—now reduced to bare skulls.

"Demonfire!" Paulo muttered under his breath.

Karon halted just outside the walls at the point where a faint track branched off from the main road. His gaze remained fixed on the eyeless guardians. "Our destination is a small valley in the foothills beyond the city," he said softly. "I'm sure of it. But to make use of what we find there, I must go into the city. Take this path outside the walls and wait for me where it meets the main road once again. I'll join you as soon as I can."

"Let us ride with you," I said. "You don't have to do this alone."

Bareil spoke at the same time. "I think I should be at your side, my lord."

A rueful smile glanced across Karon's face. "This is my home. I'll see nothing I've not imagined a thousand times over. Power awaits me in its contemplation, just as in those things I might prefer to look on. Ours is a perverse gift." He clucked to his mount, but immediately pulled up again, turning to Kellea. "Come, if you wish. This was your home, too."

Kellea wrenched her eyes from the grisly welcomers atop the poles. "My home was in Yurevan with my grandmother. Horror holds no power for me." But her cheeks were flushed, and she would not meet Karon's gaze.

"Don't blame yourself that you're not ready," he said, "or even that you may never be. I believe it's taken me a very long time to come back here." He spurred his horse toward the black gash in the wall that would once have been the wooden gates.

The cold wind gusted across the barren fields as the rest of us rode around the mournful ruin. I rued my angry words that had increased the distance between Karon and me. Long ago I had promised him that I'd go with him to Avonar when he was ready, a promise lost in the past he did not yet own.

The leaden evening settled into night as we rounded the city's eastern flank and picked up the road again close to the boundary of the desolation. Once Kellea had made sure of the way, we dismounted to stretch our legs. After only a brief wait, an agitated Bareil said he was going back. "He should not be alone in such a place," said the Dulcé. "Not in his fragile state."

I touched his hand before he could mount up. "Let him be, Bareil. He said he could manage it. In this . . .I think it's important that we trust him."

When the time had stretched far longer, I was on the verge of contradicting my own judgment.

But just as the first glimmer of the rising moon broke

through scudding clouds beyond Karylis, the weak light outlined a dark figure riding toward us at a gallop from the east gate of the dead city, such urgency in his posture, I bade the others mount and be ready. In moments Karon shot through the clearing where we waited, crying out, "Ride! We're racing the moon!"

Half a league up the road, he turned north into a narrow vale. The moon danced in and out of the clouds as we rode, revealing smooth slopes, broken by groves of slender trees and great boulders of granite, tumbled and stacked atop each other. As we followed the faint track, the faithless moon was swallowed by thickening clouds. Soon snowflakes stung my cheeks. We slowed to a walk in the uncertain light. But a burst of enchantment swept over us, and the horses surged forward, sure-footed again as if the way had been lit for them. After half an hour, perhaps a little more, Karon pulled up suddenly, all the beasts halting at the same time. I had never even tightened the reins.

"Quickly," Karon whispered as he dropped from his saddle, drawing us close as we did the same. From his hand gleamed a faint light, revealing his face ruddy with the wind and the cold, his eyes shining. "They're just ahead of us. The enchantment requires the proper angle of the moon, so we've a chance to take him. But you must be prepared to follow. Leave everything behind. Paulo, unsaddle the horses and bid them wait in this valley. They'll find grazing enough here, even in winter." Paulo nodded and hurried to do as he was asked, Bareil assisting him. Karon looked at Kellea, jerking his head to our right. "Does your sense agree with me?"

"Yes. Up the hill."

"Then follow me, quickly and quietly."

As Paulo shoved the last saddle under a bush, tied our blankets tight over them, and patted the last horse's rump, we started up a gentle slope alongside the stream, rippling and bubbling in its half-frozen shell. Karon let his light fade. Soon, from ahead of us, yellow light flickered from a triangular opening formed by two massive slabs of granite set into the hillside. To the right of the doorway stood a riderless horse, and to the other side was a pile of boulders.

Something about the place teased at my memory. Karon had once mentioned an incident with his father. . . .

Karon gathered us together again, whispering, "We must draw them out here at least as far as the opening. It's too cramped to attack him inside—a risk to the boy. Count to ten, my lady, then call the man out. Be convincing. I'll take him from the left. You," he said to Kellea, "be ready to grab the child. Bareil and Paulo, help us where it's needed most." Without waiting to hear an acknowledgment, he disappeared into the darkness.

When the interminable interval had passed, I stepped from the sheltering trees and stood before the torchlit entry. "Darzid!" I called. "Bring him out. I know who he is. You can't hide him." My plea sounded futile and stupid, even to me. "Please, just come and talk to me."

"Our time for conversation passed many years ago, Lady." His laughter rippled from inside the doorway just as the moon broke through the clouds, its beams shooting straight through the opening in the rock. The dim yellow light inside the cleft flared to eye-searing white, and every other sound was lost in a low rumble like a buried waterfall. Earth and sky—a Gate to the Bridge!

"Karon!" I screamed.

The Breach between the worlds was a boundless chasm of nightmare and confusion, of the corrupted bits and pieces left from the beginning of time, of horrific visions and mind-gnawing despair. Even if this Gate was open, how could Darzid and Gerick survive the passage or pass the wards D'Arnath had created to bar easy crossing? Only the Heir of D'Arnath could pass, so I had been told. Only the most powerful of sorcerers could control the terrors of the Breach.

"Hurry! Stay close!" Karon shouted as he leaped from the boulder pile. Sprinting across the patch of light, he disappeared through the doorway.

With Paulo, Bareil, and Kellea, I followed him through the cleft in the rock and down a brilliantly lit passage toward a wall of white flame. Karon was barely visible beyond the blazing veil, moving rapidly away from us. I hesitated. A few moments on the Bridge at Vittoir Eirit had almost destroyed my reason.

"He'll shield us," shouted Bareil over the roar of the fire. "Don't be afraid." The Dulcé took Paulo's hand in one of his; Paulo reached for Kellea; and together the three stepped through the curtain of fire. With a fervent plea to any benevolent god that might take an interest, I followed.

Pits of fire and bottomless darkness yawned beside my feet. Murmurs, growls, wailing laments, and monstrous roaring tore at my hearing. Shadowy figures took shape at my shoulders, one of them a woman with rotting flesh. She flicked her tongue toward me—a tongue the length of my arm with razor-sharp spikes.

My steps faltered; my hand flew to my mouth. A glance in any direction revealed horror in a thousand variations. From the left an ocean of blood rose up in a towering wave, threatening to engulf my three companions.

Kellea hesitated, shielding her eyes with one arm; Paulo flung his arms around her, ducking his head into her shoulder.

"Look straight ahead!" shouted Bareil, urging them onward with his small hands. "Nothing will harm you."

A cobra with the girth of a tree towered over me, spreading its hood, its hiss like a finger of ice caressing my spine. Shuddering, fighting my urge to retreat, I dragged my eyes from the vileness to either side and fixed them in front of me.

A smooth band of white light stretched before us into the gloom, and as if his arms had reached out and enfolded me, I felt the embrace of Karon's protection. The wave of blood fell short. The spiked tongue did not reach so far as my face. When a blood-chilling scream pierced the tumult, and a shrike with a wingspan wider than my arms sailed toward us through the tempest, its hooked beak ready to tear the flesh from our bones, the scream was quickly muted, and no horror touched us.

The journey seemed to take an eternity. But eventually, ragged and breathless, Bareil, Kellea, Paulo, and I stepped through another fiery veil into a circular chamber of white and rose tiles. The ceiling was lost in a soft white brilliance high over our heads. So familiar . . . yet I was enormously confused. I would swear that we were standing in the Chamber of the Gate in the ancient mountain stronghold where Karon had fought the Zhid and my brother had died. Why did we remain in the human world after traversing the Bridge?

I whirled about in panic, only Bareil's silencing gesture preventing my cry. Karon was nowhere in sight.

In the far wall, a thick wooden door clicked shut softly. The Dulcé tiptoed across the empty chamber and pulled open the door. Distant running footsteps echoed in the passage.

"He's gone after them," whispered Bareil, motioning us to hurry. "We must stay together and keep close if we can do so without being seen."

The passage emptied, not onto the gallery overlooking the cavern city of the lost stronghold, but into a network of increasingly wider passageways—smooth stone walls, veined with vibrant yellows and blues, softly lit by no source that we could see. Our direction was always up, though we traversed no steps, and I felt no ache in my legs to tell me that the slope was anything but illusion.

Before very long, I heard no footsteps but our own. Bareil sighed and drew us into a sheltered alcove. "Vasrin Creator," he said, panting, "never has my heart pounded so. But we've lost them in spite of it. Can you lead us?" he asked Kellea.

The girl shook her head in disgust. "You'd do better to ask Paulo. I've lost all sense of the boy since we stepped past the fire. There's . . . too much here. It's as if someone dropped a bag over my head and stuffed it with noise."

"Well, we can either return to the Chamber of the Gate or proceed to a hiding place where D'Natheil and I have agreed to meet if ever we are separated."

No. No. No. "No retreat," I said, forcing my voice low, but firm. "Not until Gerick is safe." Dread weighed in my belly like an anvil.

"I agree," said Kellea. "And I prefer a place that has more than one usable exit."

The Dulcé nodded. "Very well. Then you must do exactly as I say. All right?" Though he wrinkled his face seriously at Paulo, a smile danced in his almond-shaped eyes. "This place may seem strange."

The boy shrugged and pulled down his hat. "I've been about. Seen lots of things lately nobody'd believe."

"We'll not be remarked if we seem sure of ourselves and don't gawk." The Dulcé led our ragged group through passageways and deserted kitchens and dusty storerooms to an iron gate. Past the gate was a dimly lit, cloistered courtyard, the sheltered walkways lined by a double row of slender columns. A few trees grew in garden beds, thick-branched evergreens with long needles, but of no variety I recognized. Their light dusting of snow sparkled in the glow of white lanterns mounted on the cloister walls.

I grabbed the Dulcé's arm. "Before we go further, Bareil. Tell us. Where are we?" I needed to hear him say it before I could believe.

"Have you not guessed, my lady?" He smiled. "We've come to Gondai. You walk in Avonar."

CHAPTER 17

Gerick

I guess I have been scared my whole life. When I was little, I was scared of the dark, and Lucy always left me a candle or stayed with me until I went to sleep. And I was scared that when I grew up to be a soldier, I'd end up with only one arm or one leg or with my eye cut out like the men that came back from the war. But Papa told me that if I worked hard at sword training then I'd never have to be crippled like that. So I decided to train harder than anyone, though I knew I would never be as good as he was. Everyone said he was the best in the world.

Of course, I didn't really know what being scared was until the night Lucy caught me making the lead soldiers march around Papa's library. It was terrific fun, and I wondered why Papa hadn't shown me how to do it earlier that evening when he'd finally said I was old enough to play with them. The idea of it came to me when I was in bed. I couldn't sleep for wanting to try it, so I crept downstairs after Lucy had turned down the lamp and gone to bed. Mama and Papa had guests, so nobody would bother me in the library. Well, Lucy must've come back to the nursery to check on me that night. She ran down to the library—she was always good at guessing what I was thinking—and she saw what I was up to.

I never saw anyone so afraid. I thought she would be pleased like she was when I learned how to turn a somersault, or how to ride my horse without falling off, or how to write my name without getting ink all over. But on that night, if someone had given her a voice, she would have screamed every bit of it away again. She backed up against the door, looking like she wanted to run away, but instead she waved her arms and shook her head and pointed to the soldiers.

"But Lucy, it's all right. Honest. Just tonight Papa told me I could use them," I said, showing her how I could make the silver king climb over my leg.

But she wouldn't hear anything or even move until I let them all drop down still. Then she ran over and held me tight until I thought I was going to be squashed. She was crying and rocking me like I was a baby even though I was five years old.

I didn't like her to cry. Mostly Lucy and I had the best time. She knew lots of fun things to do, and of course because she was mute, she couldn't yell or whine like Mama. Even if she thought I'd done something bad, she'd just show me again how to do it right and give me her "disappointed" look. I had never made her cry before. I told her over and over that I was sorry that I was out of my bed, but I just wasn't sleepy and thought it wouldn't hurt to play with the soldiers a while, since Papa did say I was old enough.

She acted like she didn't even hear what I said, like she was thinking of something else altogether, something that she didn't like at all, and she made me put the soldiers away and go back to the nursery with her. We sat by the nursery fire, and with her mixed-up way of signs and making faces and drawing pictures, Lucy told me that if anyone ever, ever saw me do anything like what I did with the soldiers, they would kill me. Even Papa.

"I don't believe you!" I yelled at her. "You are an ignorant servant!" That's what Mama always said when one of the servants told her something she didn't like. "Papa loves me more than anybody. He'd never hurt me." I turned away from her so I couldn't see her tell me anything else, but she took me by the shoulders and marched me all the way through the castle to a room near the northwest tower. It was a girl's bedchamber. Everything was tidy and clean, but it smelled closed up, like no one had lived there for a long time. Dolls and little carved horses sat on a shelf, and books and writing things lay on a desk. On the wall was a painting of four people: a man, a woman, a boy, and a girl. I couldn't understand why Lucy was showing me that room, until I caught sight of myself in the looking glass that hung next to the picture. The boy in the picture could have been me, and the woman in the picture looked a lot like the portrait of Grandmama that hung in the music room.

"Is that boy Papa?"

Lucy nodded, and then pointed to the little girl in the picture and to the room we were in.

"That must be Papa's sister, Seriana, and this is her room."

Lucy nodded again. No one ever talked about Papa's sister. Whenever she was mentioned, people looked upset and clamped their lips tight. I'd thought she must be dead and that it made people sad to think of her. That gave me a terrible idea. "Lucy, did someone kill Seriana for making the soldiers march?" Lucy started to cry again and bobbed her head. I didn't ask her to explain any more, and I didn't ask her who had done the killing. I just let her hold me for a long time and told her I really didn't mean it when I called her ignorant. She showed me that she understood.

Only after Lady Verally came to live with us when I was seven did I learn that it wasn't Papa's *sister* that had been killed, but her *baby,* and that Papa had done it. I learned that the things I could do were called sorcery and that sorcery was the most evil thing in the world. Seriana's husband had been burned alive for doing it. I didn't *feel* wicked when I made the soldiers march around, or when I made the cats stay out of my room when they made me sneeze, or when I made the sharp thorns fall off the draggle bushes when I went exploring in the hills, but I knew that what Lady Verally said had to be true, because Papa would never kill anyone who wasn't wicked.

So Lucy hadn't been exactly right in what she told me. Some things were just too hard for her to explain in her signs and pictures. Probably she thought I was too little to understand, but she got me scared, which is what she was trying to do. From that first day she watched everything I did even closer than before. She taught me to stay away from anyone who might guess that I could do such wicked things, and how I always would have to think about everything I did and everything I said so they would never know the truth about me. I certainly couldn't stay around Papa any more. I figured that if he could see the wickedness in a little baby, then he would be able to see it in me, too. Lucy didn't think I was wicked, but she was not near so wise as Papa.

After that night in the library, I only felt safe when I was with Lucy. When Mama said it was time for Lucy to be sent away, because I needed a tutor rather than a nurse, I planned to run away to wherever they would send Lucy. I should have known she would find a way to stay with me. Lucy was my best friend in the whole world.

I couldn't believe it when Seriana—Seri, she said to call her—came to live with us. Lady Verally said she'd heard that Seri had killed Papa, and that she was a witch and had stolen Mama's senses, though everyone knew Mama didn't have much sense to steal. I didn't see how I was going to keep my secret if Seri was around. She would be used to sorcery and would see it in me even easier than Papa. The first time I met her, she went right to the soldiers in the library. That scared me, even though I didn't know who she was. I wondered if she could tell what I'd done with them. So I decided that I had to get rid of her right away. Lady Verally said that Seri had come to Comigor for revenge, and I was certain that when she found out about me, she would make sure I was burned like her husband was.

But all that thinking was at first, before I started watching her. She wasn't at all like I expected. When she told me about Papa dying . . . well, it didn't sound like she hated him, even though she must have thought I was a stupid five-year-old, who couldn't guess she was leaving out a lot of the truth. She worked hard and treated everyone with respect, even the servants and Mama. She didn't seem vengeful, and she knew all sorts of interesting things about the weather and history and making things, and especially about Comigor. Even though I didn't dare trust Seri, I started to wonder if maybe Lady Verally had the story wrong.

When Lucy heard that Seri had come to stay at Comigor, she was almost as scared as the night I made the soldiers march. I asked her if she thought Seri was come to kill me for revenge or if she would tell King Evard and have me burned if she found out about me. Lucy just let me know over and over that I must stay away from Seri. When I talked about Seri, she would start to cry, so I couldn't ask all the things I wanted. And so, as the weeks passed, I didn't tell Lucy that I had come to think that Seri might actually be a good person to have as a friend. Seri might not think I was so evil as everyone else would. Maybe she had loved her wicked husband and her wicked baby like Lucy loved me, even though they were evil and deserved to be killed. Then came the day before Covenant Day, when I found out how I'd been fooled.

I had given up watching Seri all the time. She knew about the spyholes and always guessed when I was around, though she didn't seem to mind very much. One day when we were both up on the secret tower, she had told me that there were only a few places in the castle where there were no spyholes: Papa's study, some of the bedchambers, the guard towers, the small reception room, the banquet kitchen, and the locked garden that had been Grandmama's. I thought it might be fun to see if I could make spyholes for those places. Then there would be something I knew about the castle that Seri didn't. Some of the places were too hard, and I decided I oughtn't spy on the bedchambers, but I got up every night when everyone was asleep and worked on the others.

On the morning before Covenant Day I got up while it was still dark to work on the spyhole in the reception room. But I got sleepy and decided to go back to bed. Before I reached my room, Seri came down the stairs, bundled up in her cloak like she was going outside. I thought that was strange, as it was still at least an hour before dawn and she always took her walks in the afternoons. I followed her down to Grandmama's garden, and used my new spyhole to watch her. For a long time it wasn't interesting at all. She just walked up and down the paths, but she looked excited, and at every sound she would jump and look behind her.

Just at dawn, I started feeling hot and prickly all over, like the sun was coming up inside of me instead of in the sky. Then, even stranger than that, two people walked right out of the sunrise. There wasn't a gate or a door, or any place they could have been hiding. They wore white robes, and it was clear Seri had been expecting them. She sat down with one of them, an older man that looked wild and strange. A lot of what they said I didn't understand, but some things—the important things—I did.

Seri said, "I'd never endanger either one of you. I'm only here because I came upon an opportunity to repay my brother for all that happened."

Repay my brother for all that happened . . . . Revenge. Lady Verally was right.

The old man said that the younger, taller man that walked with Seri in the garden was the prince who had killed Papa. I couldn't hear everything she said to the younger man, but there came a time when they stopped in front of a dead tree, and he lifted his hand to it. Suddenly the tree leafed out and bloomed and died again, a whole year's worth of living all while I watched. I knew what evil could make such things happen, so I knew what evil Seri had brought to my house. Lady Verally had been right all along. A sorcerer had killed Papa. That sorcerer was Seri's friend, and she had brought him to Comigor to finish her revenge.

I didn't wait to see where they all went. Instead, I hurried inside so I could tell somebody what was happening. I ran to Mama's room, but Lady Verally told me that Mama couldn't see anyone and that it wasn't proper to tell me why. That meant the baby was being born. Maybe Seri had persuaded the sorcerers to make this baby come early so it would die like the others.

"You won't let Seri into Mama's room, will you—or any strangers?" I said. "I know she's a witch, just as you've told me."

Lady Verally used my chin to pull my face up into her old, wrinkled one. "Have you seen signs of evil? We'll send for the royal inquisitors and have them question her." Her eyes burned.

I didn't know what to answer. The thought of royal inquisitors made my stomach hurt. If they started looking for sorcery, then they would be sure to find me. I tried really hard not to do anything evil, but I didn't always know what was evil and what was not. Some things just happened. That's why Lucy always watched me so close. No, I couldn't tell Lady Verally what I had seen, so I just said I didn't want Seri to hurt Mama or the new baby.

"She'll never get close, my little lambkin, and you stay away from her, too. I'm going to have her sent away from here. Captain Darzid is on his way here from Montevial. The captain helped your papa destroy that woman's evil husband and demon child. When the captain arrives, I'll tell him about her sneaking in here with your papa not even cold in the ground. He'll see she's taken away."

I had never liked Captain Darzid. He was always putting his arm around my shoulders, asking what I was doing or what I was studying or who were my friends, and all the time watching me. If I was practicing in the fencing yard, he would lean on the wall and watch, or if I was reading in the library, he would read over my shoulder. Lots of times he would give me a particular sneaking smile as if we were special friends. I was glad when he moved away from Comigor after Papa died.

If Darzid was coming, and Lady Verally was going to set him looking for sorcery, I had to be ready to bolt. It was no use wishing I was older or bigger or better at sword fighting, so that I could protect Mama or the baby from Seri and the sorcerers. I would be doing good to protect myself. I planned to run so far away that no one would ever find me. I spent the rest of that day getting some things together in a pack: a knife that someone had lost in the fencing yard, some cold buns that I saved from breakfast, some cheese that was set out on the sideboard for dinner, a warm shirt and gloves, and five silver coins that Papa had given me the last time we went to Montevial. I argued with myself about it, but finally went to the locked case in the library and took out the green silk bag with the Comigor signet ring in it. It belonged to me now, and I might have need of it someday. I hid my pack in the cellar.

I would have gone that very afternoon, but the next day was Covenant Day, and no matter what, I had to be there. Papa would expect it of me. Some things you just have to do, even if you hate them in the worst way. I would have to sit with Seri all day, and she would pretend that she didn't have friends that were sorcerers, and that she hadn't brought them to Comigor to kill us all. I stayed awake all that night so they couldn't sneak up on me.

I didn't see how anyone could do things as right as Seri could, and yet be so wicked underneath. She tried hard to take care of the tenants in the right way, just like Papa always said we had to do, showing them how they were important and respected. By the end of the day, I was tired and confused again. But then Seri made a mistake. I was ready to drink a glass of wine with her, but she started talking about Papa and how he would be proud of me. That made me think of him and how he wouldn't ever be there for Covenant Day again because of her and her sorcerer prince. It made me angry to know she'd brought Papa's murderer to our house. I wondered if maybe the wine was poisoned, so I threw it at her and ran away. I felt like a coward.

When I left the great hall, I made a quick trip to my room to grab my cloak and down to the cellar to get my pack. I was ready to go except for one thing. I couldn't leave without saying goodbye to Lucy. I hoped to slip in and out of her room without anyone seeing me, but the servants' quarters were as busy as an anthill, what with Covenant Day and the baby being born and all. I had to hide in an empty room until everything quieted down. Hours passed. I could have bitten a brick in half by the time Tocano went around turning down all the lamps. Even then I gave it a bit more time just to be sure. I wished I could make myself invisible.

When I finally got to Lucy's room, light shone out from underneath the door. Lucy never seemed to sleep very much. Whenever I came to her, she would be rocking in her chair, facing the doorway and smiling, as if she were just waiting for me to walk in. That night though, when I scratched on the door, I didn't hear her chair creaking, or her tapping that would tell me to come in, or any other sound. I almost didn't go in for fear of waking her. But I had to leave and I had to tell her, so I pushed open the door.

I'd never seen a dead person before, but even if there hadn't been all the blood, I would have known Lucy wasn't there any more. Her room had always been friendly, full of the things we played with and things we made, but on that night it just seemed dirty and cluttered. I sat beside her chair for a long time, too stupid to do anything but cry. Then I finally told myself that she wasn't coming back, and that the ones who killed her were probably looking for me. That made me angry again, and I guess I went crazy for a while.

Seri and her friends had killed Lucy. Seri had told the old man how there was only one old woman who gave her cause to worry, and how she could "take care of her." I wanted to hurt Seri for what she'd done. I could think of only one way to do it, because Seri only cared about one thing—Comigor. I wanted to burn the place down, but I couldn't do it. I was the lord, so I was responsible for the house and all the people on its lands. Nothing else seemed big enough. But then I thought of a small thing that Seri would hate.

From the kitchen I stole a bag and a flint and steel. I took the bag to the library and filled it with the lead soldiers—those beastly things that had started the bad part of my life. Then, I hauled the bag up to Seri's favorite place on the secret tower so I could burn them. Lead melts easily.

It was cold and windy on the roof. My fingers were already freezing and shaking when I untied the bag. I felt doubly stupid when I remembered that there wasn't any wood up there either. And someone was sure to notice if I started hauling wood up the stairs. But I knew how to make things hot without any wood or oil or flint. I didn't care if it was dangerous or evil, because there were people about who were a lot more evil than me. So I dumped the bag of soldiers in the firepit and thought about making the soldiers hot so Seri couldn't have them anymore. The colors started turning to black, and then the arms and legs and faces melted. Pretty soon all the bodies and horses and ships and wagons sagged together. It was a silly thing to do, but it made me feel a lot better.

One more thing I had to do before I left the castle. Mama always said that noble ladies should have flowers for every special occasion, that they loved flowers more than about anything. Lucy was finer than any noble lady I ever knew, so I slipped down into the garden and made one of the lilies bloom for her. I had already done one wicked thing that night. Another probably couldn't make me any worse. I didn't care any more.

My boots echoed through the passageways when I sneaked back into the castle. The whole place was dark and quiet like the Comigor tombs on Desfier, so that I wondered if Seri and the sorcerers had killed everyone in the place. I didn't dare look in any other room for fear someone would be lying there dead. I just hurried back to Lucy as fast as I could. I dragged her to her pallet and straightened her out so she would rest more peaceful, then I knelt down beside her, smeared some of her blood on my hand, and said, "I swear I'll remember you forever, and when I'm a man, I'll find the ones who did this to you and make them pay for it. On your blood and the honor of the House of Comigor, I swear it." Then I laid the flower on her.

"And do you know who's responsible for this reprehensible deed, Your Grace?"

I almost fell down onto Lucy I was so surprised. Captain Darzid was standing in the corner right behind me.

"What are you doing here?" I asked, trying not to sound scared.

"I've come to see your mother, but as she's indisposed, I thought to look in on you. You're not easy to find. So what's happened to this sad person?"

"This is my old nurse, Lucy. She was . . . feebleminded. I don't know why anyone would hurt her."

"Lucy?" Darzid knelt down beside me and looked at Lucy. "Your name for the nurse . . . of course. The poor woman must have been terrified to see your aunt return to this house. Probably expected this to happen every day since. Sometimes the past will not leave us alone." He acted like he wasn't even surprised.

"But Lucy never did anything to anyone."

"You know about your Aunt Seri? That she was married to a sorcerer."

I didn't look at him. "Yes. King Evard burned him. And I know that Papa killed her baby so another wicked sorcerer wouldn't live in the world."

"Yes . . . well. You know a great deal, it seems. Have you become friendly with your aunt since she's come to Comigor? Gotten to know her well?"

"No. She is wicked and condemned. She doesn't belong here. Papa wouldn't wish it. I don't speak with her."

Darzid smiled at me in that way I hated, like he was my friend and no one else was. "Of course, very wise. Well, there was a time during all of that unpleasantness about her husband, when it was necessary that your aunt be confined to the palace in Montevial. She was very well treated. Your father saw to that, for he hoped she would come to see the terrible evils she had done—allowing sorcery to exist in this world where it had no place—mortal men taking the power that belongs to the gods alone. During those months your aunt was given a serving sister to wait on her—"

"Lucy!"

"Yes. This very same woman. I saw her there several times."

"No wonder Lucy said—"

"Said? Was not the woman a mute?" The captain drew his forehead up so tight he looked like he had only one eyebrow.

"She could talk with signs and pictures. She couldn't read or write, but she could draw really fine. I could always understand her."

"I'm sure you could. And what did she tell you about your aunt?"

"She didn't want to talk about Seri, and she wouldn't leave her room any more after Seri came, so I just thought she must be afraid of her."

"Your aunt holds a great hatred for those who called her to account for her crimes, including everyone who was involved in her captivity. Ask her about me and you'll see it. I don't think she distinguishes between those like your father and me who were in authority, carrying out our responsibilities to the king and the law, and those, like Lucy here, who were caught up in the situation unwittingly."

"Lucy was the best person in the world."

"No doubt. You must watch yourself carefully when your aunt is about. In fact . . . seeing this, I'm inclined to stay with you through this night. After tomorrow she'll have no way to harm you. I've brought exciting news that will ensure your future and place you under King Evard's special protection."

"Can you take Seri away now? Can you have the king punish her for killing Lucy?"

"Unfortunately not. She's managed to cloud the eyes of the king in some way, and I don't think he'll deal with her unless we can prove her crime. He won't believe she's done murder."

"What if she had someone else do it?"

Captain Darzid raised his black eyebrows. "What do you mean?"

"I saw her with two strangers yesterday, sneaking about the garden. I wondered if they could have helped her."

"What were they like, these two?"

"One was short and wild-looking and had a strong voice. He wore a robe like a priest, only it was white. The other one was taller and younger, and—"

Darzid gripped my arm really hard, and said, "This is very important, boy. The names. Did you hear any names?"

Names. That had been very odd. Seri and the old man had called the younger man several names. "I didn't hear the old one's name. But the other one . . . They called him Dinatheel or something like that, and—"

"D'Natheil? Is that what it was?"

"Yes, but I'm not exactly sure that was his name, because they called him something else, too."

"Which was?"

"Karon."

"Karon!"

It isn't often that you can tell a grown-up something he never expected to hear, but that's what I had done with Captain Darzid. He jumped up like he had a wasp in his shirt.

"You're sure of that?"

"They called the man both names, so I didn't know which one was right. The old man said he was the one who killed Papa."

"Oh, yes. That's most certainly true, but the names . . . if true . . . Dassine, the wily bastard, kept D'Natheil hidden for so long. What could he have done?" The captain was only halfway talking to me. "What else was said? Did they know you were listening?"

"I was hiding. They said a lot of things I didn't understand."

"I've no doubt of that. The possibilities are intriguing . . . most intriguing . . . and very dangerous. Everything could be changed." He looked at me in a very different way than before. "I believe you are in grave circumstance here, Your Grace. I think perhaps we should get you away immediately."

"What about Mama and the baby?"

"D'Natheil will not care about them. It's you he'll want."

"For revenge? For Seri's revenge?"

"Yes, certainly . . . for Seri's revenge. It's very complicated. Those two are not ordinary men, even for sorcerers." He pulled me over beside him and put his arm around my shoulders. "You must come with me. I can take you somewhere where you'll be safe. Then you can tell me everything they said, and I can explain a few things to you. We wouldn't want these murderers to get away with such foul deeds as this, would we?"

I didn't like Darzid. I didn't want to be around him when he was thinking about sorcery. He knew about Seri's friends and what they were. But the night was about gone, and I had to get away. He could take me farther than I could get on my own. I would just have to leave him before he found out about me. I looked at Lucy, lying there all bloody, and decided that I would rather go with Papa's friend who carried a sword than stay with the ones who did such a thing to her.

So the two of us slipped out of the house in the quietest hour. Darzid put me behind him on his great black horse, and we rode into the clear, freezing night. It seemed like forever that we galloped, and I thought my hands would freeze from holding onto Captain Darzid's waist, but eventually I fell asleep. In my dreams a wolf howled to the full moon that shone pale and cold over the snowy hills.

CHAPTER 18

It's hard to remember much about my escape with Captain Darzid. I held on to his waist and kept drowsing off as we rode through the cold night. It didn't make sense that I could hold on for so long or that the horse could go for days without rest, but when we made camp somewhere on the far side of the Cerran Brae, several days' travel from Comigor, I couldn't remember having stopped even once.

The weather blocked the way. We came down from a pass through the mountains and were traveling north when the snow and the wind became so fierce that the horse refused to go further, even when the captain whipped him. When I buried my face in Darzid's back to keep from freezing, I could hear the curses rumbling through his bones. "Perdition to this weather and this world and all lazy, sniveling beasts."

We dismounted in a clearing, and I sat stupid and numb on a fallen tree while Darzid started a fire. "Come on," he said, kicking a log close to the fire and jerking his head toward it. "No need to freeze. The weather's a nuisance, but perhaps our pursuers will run into something like."

"Pursuers?"

"Your mother has sent out search parties, of course. Those who murdered your father and your nurse are likely among them. But we have a good day's start."

One would think that with all the sleeping I had done on horseback, I'd be wakeful once we stopped, but it wasn't so. The rocks and trees and sky all had blurry edges, and my mind seemed to slide off of anything it tried to settle on. That worried me, for it would be easy to make a slip and show Darzid that I was the very thing he was trying to protect me from. The captain gave me two blankets to wrap up in. The wind was howling, and even so near the fire, my hands and feet felt like ice.

While I wandered in and out of sleep, Captain Darzid was talking to himself. "Do they even suspect? Fate has rewarded our patience. . . . We'll need to be quick. They'll be on our heels. The test of parentage will be the key. . . . Everlasting night, to be home again, to reclaim what's mine!"

Somehow all these things got mixed up with dreams of the strange old man from Grandmama's garden and the words he'd spoken to Seri on that day. My own voice kept repeating his words over and over.

Then it was morning. The sun was blinding on the snow, the sky was bright blue, and the wind had died away. I was colder than ever, even when I drank the cup of hot wine the captain put in my hand. "Time to move on, young Lord," he said.

"Where are we going?"

"To a place of safety. I have friends—powerful friends—who have a fortress in a land far from Leire. You'll be safe there, even from such dangerous enemies as you have. There you can grow strong and plan your revenge."

"Revenge?" I still felt thickheaded and stupid.

"For your father's murder and that of your friend, the nurse. I heard you swear to avenge them. I assumed your sworn oath would be as unbreakable as your father's . . . but, of course, you are so young. Perhaps I've misjudged. . . ." He lifted my chin with his black-gloved hand and stared into my eyes. . . .

Lucy was rocking in her chair, smiling and cheerful, waiting for me. She held out her hand, but it wasn't to me. She looked curious, then scared, because the hand that held hers wouldn't let go. The person that wasn't me raised a knife, a silver knife that gleamed so bright in the lamplight that it made it hard to see anything except the crest engraved on the hilt. The knife cut into Lucy until the blood ran out all over the front of her. She tried to scream, but of course she had no voice, and she fought with the person that held the knife, but he was much too strong. She was crying and held her hand to her apron, trying to stop the bleeding. The one who wasn't me pulled her other arm away from her and cut her on that one too, and then held her in her chair until she stopped struggling. I carried her over to her bed and laid her down, but when I looked at her face again it wasn't Lucy, but Papa. He was lying on the floor of a huge chamber full of clouds and fire that was dark and cold instead of bright, and he was bleeding from a terrible wound in his belly. Before I could say anything, before I could tell him that I was sorry I was evil, his eyes got wide and scared. He shuddered and blood ran out of his mouth. Dead. On the floor beside him was a bloody sword, marked with the same crest as I'd seen on the knife that killed Lucy. The dark fire burned its way into my head, until I was full of it. . . .

"Yes!" I shouted, startling the dream away. "Yes, I want them punished. They murdered the two best people in the world, and I don't care what I have to do to make them pay for it." I was full of such hate and anger that I thought Captain Darzid would see right away how evil I was.

But he just smiled and said, "That's more like it. I'll help you grow strong enough that you can do whatever you want . . . even to men as powerful as Seri's friends. Trust me. I know you don't as yet, but I served Tomas faithfully for seventeen years, and I'll do far, far more for you."

"Help me avenge Papa and Lucy, and I'll give you whatever you want," I said.

"Exactly so," said Darzid. "Come along now. The road to our safe haven will lead us through some strange places." He pulled me up behind him on his great black horse, and we turned onto a road that was a ribbon of unmarked snow. My face felt hot, especially when I thought about Papa and Lucy, but inside all the rest of me was cold, and I didn't think I'd ever be warm again.

"What is this place?" I asked the captain when we rode across the mud fields toward the bare white walls.

"This is the destiny of those who do not know their place in the universe."

I didn't understand him. It was an awful place, a burned-out ruin of a city, every building charred and broken, bones and skulls everywhere, even hanging from posts stuck in the ground. I'd seen ruins before. Papa had taken me to Vaggiere, a day's ride east of Montevial, and to Mandebrol Castle, both destroyed by the Valloreans a long time ago. But those ruins had never made me feel sick and wretched like this one did. The bones were part of it. Anyone left alive—even if they were prisoners or wounded—would bury their dead. But then, not a blade of grass or a weed or a vine lived there, not a bit of moss, not a bird or beast or even so much as a spider or an ant creeping around. That made me think that maybe there had been no one left alive in that city.

We left our horses in front of what had once been a fine house, almost a palace. You could tell by the amount of stone fallen in on it and the broad steps that opened onto a grand commard—huge and round, paved in marble, with tall columns all around it. Lots of posts with skulls on them stood beside that house, and I tried not to look at them. The walls of the house were cracked and broken, some fallen away altogether. Charred roof timbers had crashed down into the middle of it. At least two people had died in the foyer, several more on the curved staircase that ended halfway up to the second floor.

"This was the lord of the city's house. A sad place, is it not? I need to find something here before we can be on our way." Captain Darzid's boots clattered on the stone floor as we walked in, and his voice was very loud. I wanted to tell him to be quiet. It didn't seem right to make noise in that house. But I didn't say anything, lest he think me a coward.

We stepped over fallen pillars and tramped through frozen mud and dirty snowdrifts into a large courtyard in the center of the house. Lots of trees and plants had once grown in the courtyard—all dead stumps now, of course. Several statues had toppled over. Once I stepped right into a giant stone hand. From one corner of the cloister came a trickling sound. A small fountain was still running—the statue of a little girl emptying a pitcher of water into a shallow round basin. The pinkish color of the marble made her look almost alive. A stream of clear water ran from the pitcher to the basin of the fountain, and there was not a mark or a crack or a chip on any of it. The girl had a little smile on her pink marble face, like she knew she had escaped whatever happened to the rest of the city.

"Come along," said the captain, when I stopped to look at the fountain. We climbed up steps that went nowhere, peered through doorways that had nothing on the other side of them, and pushed into dark holes under the fallen walls. "I'm looking for something like the little fountain back there, something that's not burned up or ruined, but that has writing carved on it." In and out we went until we must have covered every step of the house.

"It has to be here," said the captain, kicking aside a charred timber. "They wrote it in stone, protected it with power, so it couldn't be destroyed. Curse all Dar'Nethi bastards!"

Two days we searched that awful ruin for whatever it was Captain Darzid wanted. He said we were looking for writing that described a shortcut through the mountains to his friends' fortress. I thought that surely we could have gone the long way around by the time we would find what he was looking for. We camped in the courtyard of the great house. I slept a lot of the time and had terrible dreams. Well, I called them dreams, but they seemed real. One was about Comigor, a vision so clear that I could smell the dry grass. . . .

The tenants were tilling the fields. I could see them through the paned window on the stair landing. Nellia and James and the other servants were at their daily work. Nellia was singing. She always sang "The Warrior's Child" in her rusty old voice when she sat with her sewing. I called out to say good day, but she didn't answer, and the footman in the dining room looked right through me when I walked past him into the drawing room. Mama was there. She was very beautiful, dressed in white and wearing her favorite necklace—the one with the circles of diamonds all strung together. A harper played in the corner, and Mama was talking with her friends.

"Was there truly no trace of him ever found?" A woman in green with a crow's face leaned toward Mama's ear.

"None at all," said Mama. She dabbed at her eyes with a lace handkerchief. "The sheriff from Graysteve says that as no one has demanded ransom, we must assume he's dead. I'm going to leave this wretched place forever. My poor lamb was such an unhappy child. It's a comfort, in a way, a kindness that fate has saved him the pain of long life."

"Come, Lady Philomena, enough of sad thoughts," said a young man as he pulled her up to dance. Soon she was laughing again and drinking wine. Her diamonds sparkled in the lamplight as she danced.

"It's as well the boy is gone," said the woman in green to another woman. "He was so odd. I've heard rumors of murder and worse things . . . perversion . . . in this very house. The royal inquisitors were on their way when the boy disappeared. . . ."

Another dream came, too, and like the other, it seemed more real than any dream. I knew all the people, but they couldn't see me.

Two men—peasant men—were running through one of the rocky rifts that cut through the heath north of Comigor. One of the men carried a little girl in his arms. The other, an older man with a gray beard, was bleeding from a wound in his leg. The older man stumbled on a stone and fell. "A curse on the House of Comigor."

"Hurry, Father Castor, they're coming. We can't stop." The younger man was frightened. Choking smoke filled the air, and the young man couldn't stop coughing. The little girl whimpered, and the young man pushed her face into his shoulder. "Hush, Ceillitta."

"Go on with you," said the older man. "I'll hold them here as long as I can." He pulled himself up to lean on the steep bank, unhitching a scythe from his belt.

With a sad curse, the young man gripped the older one's shoulder, and then ran on down the gully away from the castle. He didn't get very far. Riders wearing King Evard's red-and-gold livery galloped along the edge of the rift and shouted when they caught sight of the men. Two soldiers slipped off their horses, slid down the bank, and cut off the old man's head before he could cry out. Another pair of soldiers caught the younger man and dragged the little girl away from him. The rest of the troop came up, their horses' hooves swirling up dust to mix with the smoke. They were laughing and mocking as they dismounted. Two soldiers held the young man by the hair and arms, and the others threw the little girl on the ground, pulled up her dress, and fell on her, one and then the other. The young man cursed and wept and strained to get free, while the little girl screamed, "Papa, Papa." By the time they were done with her, her scream was just a dry bubbling sound. The young man was about crazy.

"This is what happens to them as nurture sorcerers," said the captain of the soldiers. "This is the evil they bring into the world. If you had given him up, you and the child and the old man would live." Then he cut the little girl's throat.

"A curse on them all," the young man sobbed. "May they all burn."

"Oh, they will. Never fear," said the soldier. "You have the easier part." And he stabbed the young man in the belly and threw him onto the rocks.

I climbed out of the rift onto the hillside. The smoke was terrible, choking, making my eyes burn and water. When I stumbled on something softer than a rock, I didn't know what it was until I fell on top of it, and came face to face with Allard, the head groom. Only it wasn't hardly Allard anymore since his nose and ears had been cut off, and he was dead. I jumped up and ran before I could get sick, and I came to the top of a hill where I could see all around.

Comigor was burning—the roof, the stables, the barracks, the fields—for as far as I could see it was burning. People were screaming. The soldiers cut down anyone who tried to run away. A few of the castle guard were fighting to clear a way through the main gate for a carriage, but they fell one by one. When the soldiers dragged Mama and Nellia out of the carriage, others were already sticking heads on poles.

"The devil's dam—the witch! Where's fire enough for her?"

I always woke up sweating and coughing about the time Mama started to scream. I told myself that these were only dreams, not things that had really happened. But they left me feeling sick and sad, as if I'd really seen them.

By the afternoon of the second day, Captain Darzid was tearing away rubble with his bare hands. I stayed out of his way. He said we would have to leave that night if he didn't find what he was looking for. There were other ways to get where we were going, but a lot farther and more complicated.

"I'm going to get a drink from that fountain," I said. The water in Captain Darzid's flasks tasted like old boots.

"As you wish," he growled, pulling more stones away from a buried hearthstone and cursing the avalanche of rubble that followed. I left quickly, before he could tell me to help him move the piles of stone that had undone his entire day's work.

We were down to eating nothing but jack. Being so dry and salty, jack always made me thirsty, and we had used up all the wine in Darzid's pack. I hadn't told Darzid about my own supplies, because I planned to use them when I ran away from him. I had almost run away the previous night, but I hadn't seen any towns or villages close by as we traveled. Besides, I didn't relish picking my way through the ruin or the mud fields in the dark. I would have taken his horse, but the captain's horse wasn't nice at all. He was like Captain Darzid, bad-tempered underneath all his politeness.

The little stone girl was still smiling to herself in the corner of the courtyard, pouring water from her bottomless pitcher. I helped myself to some of the water and sat down on the rim of the basin, not at all interested in going back to help Darzid. The water was cool, not freezing like you might expect in the winter, and sweet, the best thing I had tasted in a long time. It seemed to clear my head a bit, too. For the first time since leaving Comigor, I had two clear thoughts together. The first thought was that this whole business of searching a ruin for the route to a friend's house made no sense at all. And the second was that those very instructions were staring me in the face from the bottom of the basin.

"Captain!" I called. "I think I've found it."

He was beside me before I could snap my fingers. "Where? Show me, boy."

"There," I said, pointing to the words carved in the bottom of the marble basin under the clear water.

Darzid looked very strange for a moment, then a smile spread slowly out from under his black beard. "Of course . . . I never thought of that. Tell me, young Lord, how do you read it? My eyesight is certainly not of the same quality as yours . . . no, not at all . . . in this dim light." He grabbed a charred stick and drew on the white paving stones everything that I read from the bottom of the pool. I didn't know the language, but the captain nodded his head as if he did.

"Now we can ride," he said. "If this storm will hold off so we can see the moon, then by morning we'll be safe in Zhev'Na."

I was happy to leave. "What was the name of that city?" I asked, as we rode toward the mountain. "Who lived there, and why were they all killed and left like that?"

"It was called Avonar," said the captain. "You'll hear that name again. It was—and is—the home of your enemies, people of no vision, people of no understanding of the dimensions and possibilities of the universe. You'll learn more of it when we're safe. For now, you've had a tiring day. Feel free to sleep as we journey."

And, of course, I did. I dreamed those terrible dreams over and over again, and when I next woke up, I was in a very different place.

CHAPTER 19

Seri

Avonar. No poet has words to describe the view from our window in the Guesthouse of the Three Harpers. The Dar'-Nethi called it the City of Light, though no such simple name could capture its glory. Stars . . . everywhere stars embedded in the night's dark canvas, so brilliant that when you closed your eyes, the image was etched upon your inner vision. Their number was so profuse that the trees of two worlds could not produce so many leaves. And they were not confined to the heavens. The pale towers of Avonar soared into the heights like long, slender hands sent to reap the sparkling harvest and shower it upon the landscape below, not only in refined and solemn white, but in palest yellows and blues.

But even such a glorious vision as the royal city could not liven my spirit. Neither could the wonder that should accompany any venture into a new world, nor the simple relief at our safe passage through the Breach. I paced the little room, waiting for Karon and news of our son.

Bareil brought food: delicately fried pastries wrapped about a savory filling and dusted with cheese, golden fruits the size of apples with pink flesh that tasted like a blending of peaches and tart cherries, and a brass pot of something fruity and pungent that he called saffria. The others unstacked the small plates and poured the hot cider into mugs of painted pottery, gathering around a low table by the fire to share the meal.

I could muster no appetite. "Why would they bring him to Avonar?" I said. "And how was Darzid able to cross the Bridge without the Heir to open the way, to guide him, protect him . . . ?"

Kellea waved her mug and amplified my questions. "And how could there be a Gate in the ruined Avonar? I thought there was only a single Gate to the Bridge in Gondai, and a single Gate in our world."

"As to the Gate," said Bareil, setting down his cup and wiping his mouth with his fingertips, "indeed only one exists in the world of Gondai with its single reflection in your world. But each Gate would have been built with multiple points of entry. Here in Gondai, all entries have been lost to the Zhid except the one in the palace in Avonar. We could not know where the entries in your world were set, of course, or how many might still exist. As for your other questions, I wish I could say. Perhaps when the Zhid followed D'Natheil to your world this past summer, the secret of the Bridge crossing was compromised. Master Dassine put extra wards at the two Gate chambers, but this entry we traveled had not been used for hundreds of years. And for the man to venture the Bridge without the Heir . . . I cannot . . ." Bareil's expression suddenly fell blank and featureless. "Well, your guesses are more likely to be correct than those of a Dulcé unbidden by his madrisson."

We filled the next two hours with trivialities. Kellea and Paulo made an inventory of our supplies, only what Bareil had carried in the small pack on his back and the rest of us had in our pockets. The Dulcé cleared away the meal, setting the remaining food aside for Karon, and then gave us a monologue on the major points of interest in the view from our window. Kellea asked about the bronze mask above the door, and Bareil told us the story of Vasrin of the Two Faces, who had existed when the universe was nothingness. But eventually these occupations flagged, and we fell into anxious silence. Heavy clouds rolled in from the mountains, obscuring the stars.

Another hour and we heard footsteps in the passage. One person. Bareil cracked open the door, peered out, and then pulled it wide open. "Holy Vasrin be praised for your safety, my lord."

Karon shook a dusting of fresh snow from his cloak, but

shook his head when Bareil moved to take the heavy garment from his shoulders. He moved directly to the fire, rubbing his hands together as he held them close to the flames. "Seems we brought an ill change in the weather." He gratefully accepted Paulo's offer of a mug of Bareil's pungent fruit cider. After a sip or two, he settled on a stool by the fire. Only then did he glance at me, his blue eyes filled with such concern and sympathy that I thought my heart must rip. He averted his gaze quickly, fixing his eyes on the fire.

"I tracked them to a house, but didn't follow them inside. Wards—protective enchantments, formidable ones—barred every door and window. It made no sense to break the wards until I knew more, lest I endanger the child unnecessarily." Leaning forward, his elbows on his knees, Karon gripped the mug until I thought the pottery would crumble. "As I happen to know that particular house quite well, I could guess where the owner was like to take guests that arrive in the middle of the night. And I know how to observe what goes on in that room without setting off any alarms. But I was too slow. By the time I realized what they were doing, the circle was drawn, the candles were lit, and the words were spoken. The space inside the circle—the portal—opened onto another place . . . and the dark-bearded man stepped into that place with the boy. Only an instant and they were gone." He flicked another glance my way before returning his gaze to the fire. "The child was asleep through everything, so he could not see what was happening and be afraid."

"My lord, did you see anything of their destination, so that we might identify it?" asked Bareil.

"Enough, I think."

"You know how to show me, so that you may command me to tell you of it?"

"Yes. Though I'm not sure we want to hear it." Karon set the mug on the table, then laid his hand on the head of the Dulcé who knelt on the floor just in front of him. *"Detan detu, Dulcé,"* he said, quietly, "tell me of this place."

For a moment Bareil wore no expression, but then his

skin lost its rich color and he closed his eyes. The rage that had been heating my veins slowed for that one moment as if everything in the world held its breath. I heard the words even before he said them. "*Detan eto, Giré D'Arnath.* Everything in my experience tells me that this place is surely Zhev'Na, the stronghold of the Lords in the heart of the Wastes."

"From what cursed house in the heart of Avonar do they send innocent children to Zhev'Na?" I had kept my seat while Karon spoke, but I could no longer hold back the storm that had been building since we crossed the Bridge. I stood in place, wrapping my arms tight about my breast, lest I fly apart in fear and fury and grief. "Darzid crossed the Bridge, a feat that I've been told is only possible with the aid of the Heir of D'Arnath. And now he's taken this child into the heart of evil. In what 'familiar house' can such events take place without fear of retribution?" Never had I felt so helpless, not even when Karon and my son had been taken from me the first time. At least then I had lived in a world I understood.

For the first time since the bandit cave, Karon spoke directly to me. "The man read secret words carved into the stone of a fountain at my family's house. We had been told the words would take us to a holy place, and we tried to use them a few times in the grotto. Without success. But we didn't know the language, and so we didn't understand about the moonlight. Now I seem to know the language. . . ." A grimace tightened his brow for a moment. "As to the crossing . . . Dulcé, can you suggest how he might be able to pass the wards on the Bridge?"

"Perhaps if you were to command me, Lord."

Karon issued his command to Bareil again. The Dulcé pondered for a few moments, and then looked up, crafting his words carefully. "Somehow the man Darzid must have known there was an entry point in the ruined city. I have no knowledge of how this could be possible. Clearly he read the inscription in stone at your family's house, just as you did. This told him of the location of the entry and how to move from the cave to the Gate. And you, my lord . . . When we joined the lady and her friends in the bandit cave, you left the Bridge passage open for our return, and thus the man was able to cross unhindered. Master Dassine knew of that risk, but discounted it, because he believed no one in your world could know of the Gates. You had no way to know. . . ."

"Demonfire!" The line of his jaw grew tighter. "And so it seems I must take the responsibility for his easy passage as well as the rest of it. To my shame and that of all Dar'-Nethi, the house where the boy was taken is the Precept House of Gondai; the chamber is the meeting place of my counselors. And so, this wickedness, too, is my responsibility, and I swear to you that I *will* repair it. But I'll not pursue my own reckoning with the Preceptors or do anything else that might jeopardize the boy's safety until he is returned unharmed. Please have my word, Lady. Whatever is in my power to do, I will do. Your nephew—"

I must have flinched just then: changed color, grimaced, closed my eyes, compressed my lips, or given some other physical sign of my impatience with lies. For he stopped abruptly and examined me, his eyes widening with newfound understanding. "Gods in the heavens, he's not your neph—"

"My lord"—Bareil shot to his feet, blocking the view between Karon and me before I could control my trembling enough to give answer—"you must command me to give you information about Zhev'Na. Not the location, of course. No one has ever found a route to Zhev'Na. Even were you to command me, I could not tell you. But I bear all of Master Dassine's knowledge of the Wastes and the evil citadel. Surely some of it will be of value."

Though his glance kept shifting to me, Karon listened to Bareil. I bit my tongue until I tasted blood. The moment of danger passed as the Dulcé drew him into several hours' questioning.

Dassine had masqueraded as a Zhid for three months, joining a Zhid war band, a feat of enchantment and courage that was unprecedented. Before he could learn the route to Zhev'Na, however, he had been discovered and taken to the fortress as a prisoner, tortured until he could not walk properly. But over the period of three terrible years, even constrained as he was with formidable enchantments, he had hoarded power enough to restore the soul of his Zhid interrogator—the most difficult of all healing enchantments. The warrior had then helped him to escape.

The Dulcé's cache of information was indeed massive: observations of Zhid behavior and training, weather and landforms, detailed descriptions of enchantments and theories on how certain ones of them were created, snatches of conversations, relative locations and sizes of Zhid encampments around the fortress. But the bits and pieces were dreadfully disorganized. We didn't know what questions to ask, and the answers Bareil provided were tangled in the old Healer's speculations on the nature of the Bridge and the Lords of Zhev'Na. Little of immediate value. Nothing of how we might broach the fortress. Nothing of what the Lords might have planned for Gerick. Nothing of how we might snatch him back.

By midnight, Karon had withdrawn from the discussion and stood gazing out of the window into the snowy night. His silence grew so lengthy that the rest of us were drawn into it like flotsam into the strong current of a river. "My lord?" said Bareil, at last. "What is it? Have you thought of something?"

Karon did not speak either to our disputes or our agreements, and most certainly not to our curiosity. His broad back was straight. Unmoving. We could not see his face. All he said was, "Impossible as it may seem, you and our friends must rest for a while."

Paulo was already asleep, and Kellea's eyes were drooping. But I could conceive of no circumstance that would let me sleep. My cheeks hot, my soul agitated, my body a series of knots like those that little girls tie in ribbon to tell their fortunes, I sat on the floor leaning against the wall, shredding the already frayed ends of my cloth belt. "I'll take the first watch," I said.

Karon left the window and crouched down in front of me, his face on a level with my own. I tried to turn away. But he gently took my head in his hands and pressed his thumbs to my pounding forehead, just between my eyes. "Sleep, my lady," he said softly. "We will need your strength. *He* will need your strength. I'll watch tonight."

As on the Bridge, his presence enfolded me. But comfort, even of so generous a giving, was not what I needed. Why couldn't he see it?

I thrust his hands aside, looked up, and saw in front of me a stranger's face. Not Karon's fine bones and slender jaw—the face I wanted and needed and yearned to see—but D'Natheil's square chin, wide-set eyes, and hard, carved cheeks. "Why should I trust *you* to watch?" I said, disappointment and grief and exhaustion bursting from me all at once. "I hold the Dar'Nethi responsible. I've found little in the people of Gondai save treachery, self-importance, and greed, all of which I can find in abundance in my own people. I've seen nothing to refute the argument that we would be better off if the Bridge had been destroyed four months ago. So while you watch, you might give serious thought as to why I shouldn't act as one of your own would do—stick a knife in you and trade your body for my son."

Bareil gasped. "My lady!"

My lips stung with the hateful words. They had come out all wrong. "I didn't mean— I'm—" I stammered, trying to think whether some apology or attempt at modification might be worse than letting the words vanish into the exhausted temper of the wretched day.

But Karon laid a finger on my lips. "You can be sure I'll give your idea my utmost consideration." He wasn't even angry.

I fell asleep before I could make an answer.

Someone laid me on the bed while I slept, for I was on the bed when I woke to see Bareil standing in a square of sunlight, looking out the window. Kellea was curled up in the room's only chair, and Paulo was rolled in a blanket on the floor. Smoothing my rumpled clothes, I crossed the room in stockinged feet, so as not to wake the sleepers, and poured myself a mug of saffria from the still-warm pot.

"He's done it," said the Dulcé quietly, his eye not leaving the view from our window. "I thought he would wait—

explore the other possibilities—talk it over with you—devise an alternate plan to allow us some recourse if Master Dassine's expectations were ill-founded . . ."

"The Prince . . . what's he done? Where is he?"

Bareil motioned to me to the window.

The morning was glorious, the pale spires of the city glowing in the dawn light. Snow lay like a white veil over the city, freshening its face for the new day. But I lost interest in the view when I saw the tall figure walking slowly across the vast commard—surely the heart of the great city. Already passersby had noticed him; several knelt and he raised them up. Others bowed or curtsied or scurried across the great square, past fountains and trees and statuary, dragging others from their houses. Karon nodded his head in return, but did not slow his progress toward the palace gates that fronted the commard and gardens. From shops and houses sleepy residents emerged wearing shifts and nightsmocks and caps. From the lanes and streets of the city trickled twos and threes, then tens and twenties, then throngs of people, in moments transforming the quiet city into a joyous mob, shouting, waving, cheering, calling out to each other and the one who moved through them, almost invisible now.

"What is it they cry?" I said, my heart as cold as first frost.

"They say, 'Our Prince has returned. Our Prince is healed. D'Arnath's Heir walks among us.' "

"They recognize him?"

"Easily. He has spoken his name to someone, and the truth of it wreathes him like the sun's aura. Everyone in Avonar will know on waking that the Heir walks among them. He tells them to be of good heart."

"I didn't think he was ready to assume this role. Has he decided to refuse Dassine's charge? Is he off seeking vengeance or royal glory?" Confused and angry, I believed what I said no more than I had meant the horrid jibe of the previous night. But when Bareil turned his distraught face to me, all other emotion was drowned in fear.

"He is *not* ready, but he has seen no choice in his course. Nor has he rejected Dassine's charge, but rather submitted to it despite his profound misgivings. He goes to the Preceptorate."

"The Preceptorate . . . He's going to murder Exeget. Is that what the old devil told him to do?"

"No, my lady. He has no means to do such a thing." The Dulcé's eyes dropped to the tangle of leather and steel in his hands—D'Natheil's sword belt, and the sword and dagger of D'Arnath. Bareil raised his eyes again, awash in grief. "Master Dassine told my lord that if the child was taken to Zhev'Na, then he must give himself to the Preceptorate for examination—and that he must go to them defenseless. When they examine him, they will probe his mind—question him without restraint. I do not know how he can possibly survive it."

By the time Karon reached the broad steps before the palace gates, six robed figures awaited him. Even at such a distance, I could pick out the giant Gar'Dena, the scarecrow-like Y'Dan, the short wizened figures of the two eldest, Ustele and Ce'Aret, all as Bareil had described them. The two other figures, less easily distinguished, would be Madyalar, "the Mother," and Exeget, traitor and murderer and abductor of children. The six bowed to their prince.

"What is it he does?"

Karon had removed his cloak, his tunic, and his shirt. Now he sat on the steps in front of the six and motioned to an onlooker, who proceeded to remove Karon's boots. When he rose again, clad only in breeches and leggings, doing something with his hands, the crowd was instantly hushed.

"He surrenders himself," said the Dulcé, laying aside the Prince's weapons. "His actions tell his people that he is their servant and that he will abide by the results of examination by their Preceptors. In essence, he states his willingness to risk everything—his freedom and his rightful inheritance—to erase all doubts as to his lineage and capacities. The silver ribbon she wraps about his wrists symbolizes his submission to their authority." His chin lifting a bit, he pointed out the window. "Note that it is to Madyalar he has surrendered, not to the head of the council—Exeget—

as would be expected. A clever move, but a terrible insult to Exeget. All will understand it, of course. Everyone in the city knows of the bitterness between them."

The six turned and walked slowly up the steps to the palace gates, which swung open before them. Karon followed, shirtless and barefoot in the cold, bright morning, and a phalanx of guards fell in behind him.

"Why?" I said. "Why would Dassine tell him to do such a thing? It doesn't make sense."

"I wish I could answer, my lady. My late master was a wise and clever man, and I knew him better than anyone living save the Prince, who cannot yet remember how they existed as one mind in the years when he had no body. Master Dassine did many things in his life that were tangled and obscure, yet—please do not think that I boast—I have always been able to unravel his plots. This one, though"—he clasped his hands tightly behind his back. "I cannot piece together any strategy requiring the Prince to present himself defenseless to those who were willing for him to die on the Bridge only a few months ago."

The crowds dispersed quickly, leaving the commard almost deserted. Kellea and Paulo had wakened and joined us at the window, and we explained what we'd seen and Bareil's misgivings.

"What are the possible outcomes of this examination?" asked Kellea.

"If he is found to be the Heir and sound of mind, then he will be able to assume his throne and do as he pleases. If it is determined that he is an impostor, he will be executed immediately. If he is found to be the true Heir, yet of unsound mind—which is what I fear—I do not know. In a thousand years such a thing has never occurred."

"I say we move ahead," said Kellea, turning her back on the window. "It sounds as if we can't count on the Prince to be of any use. If he can, then all to the good, but we can't wait to find out. We must go after the boy now—on our own, if that's the only way."

Kellea was right. The Prince—Karon—was on his own. I had to put aside fear and anger, to crush and bind the emotions that had been driving me to lash out so thoughtlessly. Our opponents were sorcerers whose powers I could not imagine. I would fight for my son, but I doubted this battle would be fought with swords and troops. "How long until the results of the Prince's examination are known?"

Bareil settled on the stool by the fire. "Days, certainly. More likely many weeks. In such a state as he is in . . ."

"Then, as Kellea says, we must prepare to do this ourselves," I said. "But I'll not risk Gerick's life by acting without thought. You've said they'll want to teach Gerick . . . train him . . . raise him in their ways . . . is that right?"

"That is the only plan that seems likely, though, of course, I cannot say—"

"That will take time. So we must take advantage of it. We have to find aid we can trust, and a plan that will work. We must learn how to live in this world: the customs, the language, the geography, whatever else Bareil can teach us of the Lords, the Zhid, and Zhev'Na. We'll need clothing that will not be remarked. If it means six weeks instead of six days until we're ready, then that's the way it must be. Proceeding rashly could cost us everything. Will you help us, Bareil?"

The Dulcé bowed to me. "It will be my pleasure to share all I can bring forth. The Prince commanded me to be of service to you during his absence."

My anger threatened to break loose again. "Do you mean he told you he was going to go through with this? Knowing the risk, you let him go without waking me?"

"He saw no alternatives and no benefit in further discussion. Though he did not understand Master Dassine's reasoning, he said he sincerely hoped it did not involve the Preceptors putting a knife in him and trading him for the boy, for such was the only rational plan he had heard." The Dulcé buried his grief in his sweet smile. "It was a jest, my lady, and he did not forbid me to tell you of it."

CHAPTER 20

Gerick

The sun on my face was bright and hot. I pushed back the blanket, only to pull it right back up again when I realized I was naked. I sat up instead. The bed was huge and high off the floor, but hard, more like a table than Mama's bed with its piles of pillows. The bedchamber was as big as Papa's room at Comigor, though this one looked even bigger because it didn't have much furnishing: a few tables, a giant hearth, some straight chairs of light-colored wood, and a few lamp-stands with copper oil lamps hung from them. Along one side of the room were the tall window openings where the sun shone in so fiercely.

I didn't remember coming here. Darzid had taken me off the horse and carried me through a doorway in a rock, but that was the last thing I knew.

Clothes that looked my size were laid out on the end of the bed. As I couldn't see any of my own things, I assumed these were meant for me. I pulled on a linen singlet and underdrawers, and then climbed out of the bed so I could look around. Some of the windows were actually doors opening onto a balcony that looked out over courtyards, lower buildings, and walls. Beyond the walls lay desert—red cliffs and dirt all the way to the horizon, smoke and dust hanging in the air. The sun that was still low on the horizon was red, too.

I had never seen true desert country. Papa had taken me to eastern Leire once to visit his favorite swordmaker. The land there was dry and flat and ugly, but Papa had said that true deserts were beautiful, with fine colors, and their own kind of odd plants and interesting animals, and mysterious water holes where everything lived together. As far as I could see, nothing grew in this place, and nothing was at all beautiful.

I turned back to the room. The bedchamber didn't have long solid walls like the rooms at Comigor. The rooms were divided by ranks of thin pillars forming arches. Metal grillwork holding candles sat in some of the arches. Strips of woven cord hung in others, moving in the hot air coming in from the balcony. Each wall had one archway that was wider than the others and didn't have anything else in it. These were the "doors," I supposed.

Beyond one of the doorway arches was a room entirely filled with clothes and boots. At Comigor I had a clothes chest where my things were folded and put away, and Mama had a huge clothes chest and a carved wardrobe taller than Papa to hang her dresses in. I had never seen so many garments at once, and they were clearly for one person, as they were all the same size. Shirts and tunics were hung up one after the other from long poles. Leggings, hose, breeches, and singlets were folded on shelves that extended higher than I could reach. Short and long cloaks hung on hooks. And rows of shoes stood under the hanging shirts—riding and walking boots of every cut and soft shoes to wear indoors. The clothes were not colored silk or ruffled, embroidered things like Mama had made for me. Most seemed to be plain, sturdy shirts and breeches and tunics like Papa wore when he went to war. On one shelf was a wooden case that held buckles and belts, and some jewelry—a man's jewelry. I didn't touch any of it.

Through another archway I found a bathing room. The floor and outer walls were covered with painted tiles of dark blue and green, and a deep pool was built right into the floor. I touched an ivory handle and steaming water gushed out of a gold pipe that was shaped like a screaming man. I'd never seen anything like it. When I pulled my hand away, the water stopped.

Other archways led to a sitting room with more tall window openings and another hearth. In front of the hearth was a table big enough to eat on and a number of straight wood chairs. Across that room, beyond another arched opening, was a wide staircase that curved downward. I thought I'd better get some clothes on before going downstairs, so I returned to the bedchamber and put on the clothes that lay on the bed: a gray linen shirt, black breeches and tunic, gray leggings and black leather boots that reached over my calves.

Laid out right next to the clothes were a sword belt and a knife sheath. They were wonderful. The knife was polished like a looking glass, and so sharp it took a sliver of wood off the edge of the table as easy as cutting a peach. The hilt was engraved with all manner of strange beasts, and fit my hand perfectly. The sword was a real rapier, every bit as fine as the knife. Even Papa would have approved the point and the finish. Best of all, the length was perfect for my height. My fencing master at Comigor, Swordmaster Fenotte, had insisted I use wooden weapons or old brittle swords that had been cut off short, so dull and nicked and blunt that you couldn't stick a hunk of bread with them. If the clothes were meant for me, then surely the weapons must be intended for me, too, or else they wouldn't be next to the clothes. Just at that moment, I heard footsteps on the tile floor behind me. I spun about, dropping the sword belt with a loud clatter.

Captain Darzid walked in through the archway that led to the sitting room and the stairs. He was followed by a man wearing almost nothing. "No, no, Your Grace," said Captain Darzid, smiling and waggling his finger at the sword belt. "The weapons are certainly yours, just as you guessed. Wear them as a young duke should. In Zhev'Na, a noble with a sworn blood debt is not treated as a child, but given his proper respect. You'll find life here very different than in a household run by women."

"Is Zhev'Na the name of this country?" I said. I didn't want to tell him that I couldn't even remember how we got here. A duke with a sworn blood oath shouldn't be stupid enough to lose track of himself the way I had.

"This land is called Ce Uroth, which in the local language means 'the Barrens.' " Darzid stepped to the windows.

"And it is indeed a barren land—stripped of softness and frivolous decoration, its power exposed for all to see. If he wants to accomplish his purposes, a soldier must be hard like this land, not decked out in a whore's finery, or wallowing in weakness or sentimentality."

He smiled then—that too-friendly smile that I didn't like. "But more such lessons later. We've had a long journey, and for the moment we are safely out of the reach of your enemies." He waved his hand in the air. "This house and everything in it are yours for as long as you stay in the fortress of Zhev'Na. It is not so large as Comigor, but finer, I think, and well suited to your situation."

"Mine . . . all of this?"

"Yes. Your hosts . . . the Lords of this place . . . had the house and clothing made ready for you when they heard you were coming. Do you approve?"

I gawked at everything all over again. "It's very fine."

The other man had knelt down beside the doorway, bowed his head, and stretched his arms out to either side. Darzid poked at the man's back with his boot as if he were something not quite nice lying in the road, but the man didn't change his position. "This slave Sefaro will be your chamberlain. He will run your household and see to all your needs. He—as all Dar'Nethi slaves—must have permission before he speaks or you must cut out his tongue. Command him as you will. Kill him if he does not please you. He is very capable, but there are many more to take his place if he does not serve."

The kneeling man didn't look at all surprised at the captain's terrible words. His skimpy gray tunic left his arms and legs and feet bare, and his hair was cut off very short. Wide metal bands were wrapped about his neck and his wrists. We didn't have slaves in Leire. Prisoners were usually killed or maimed, unless they were needed in the quarries or mines. Enemies who were not soldiers were left to work and pay taxes to our king.

As I stared at the slave and thought about what it must feel like to cut out a man's tongue, Captain Darzid went on talking. ". . . look in on you from time to time, but you'll not lack for entertainment. A swordmaster will begin your training this afternoon—and he will not be a gibbering dancing master in pantaloons like Philomena hired for you. Tomorrow you will begin lessons in hand combat and to learn to ride like a soldier instead of a child. You've never in your life ridden such horses as we have in Zhev'Na."

"But—"

"Is this not your wish? To become a strong and ruthless warrior like your father and grandfather?"

"Yes . . . yes, of course it is," I said. I was just surprised at it happening so fast. And I wasn't certain I ought to stay so close to Captain Darzid. Surely he would find out about my sorcery and arrest me. To think of burning to death made my stomach hurt.

All happened just as Darzid said. That afternoon I met Calador, my swordmaster. He was tall and thin. His arms looked like a thin layer of skin stretched over a bundle of ropes, and his eyes were strange, like the eyes in a statue where they forgot to put any pupils in them. He wore a plain gold earring in one ear. On that first day he made me run and jump, stretch, bend, and twist for hours until every muscle was sore. Never once did I get to pick up my new sword. When he said we were finished for the day, I guess he saw that I was disappointed.

"Soon enough, young Lord. We have a great deal of work to do before you take up a weapon." His voice was cold. "You have decent reflexes, but you are weak and poorly disciplined."

A whole week of sword training passed before I got to try my rapier, and then only to poke at dry leaves and shavings of wood that a slave would drop from the top of a wall. By that time I already hated Calador. He was forever taunting me and telling me how like a dainty girl I was, and how I was too stupid to know which end of the sword was sharp. When I did something wrong, he would make me squat for an hour with my hands extended in front of me, holding a brick in each one. He said he could not believe I was kin to a great swordsman and that perhaps swordsmen in my country were not of the same quality as those of Ce Uroth. All I could think of in those hours was how I had to keep getting better so I could beat Calador someday.

I rose at dawn every day, ate some fruit and cheese, and went straight to sword training for several hours. At midmorning I ate again, only a little, for after another hour of sword practice I went straight to the wrestling ground, a small courtyard of packed sand, for training in hand combat. Two hours later, after only a brief rest and a drink, I would walk out to the stables for my riding lessons. I didn't need to worry about sorcery. By sunset, I was so tired I could hardly stay awake to eat before I fell into the bed.

A big, burly slave named Xeno taught me hand combat. He was patient and coaxed me along when I was so black and blue that it hurt even to clench my fist. He said he wouldn't go easy just because I was inexperienced. But I knew he could have snapped me like a twig, and that he truly *did* hold back when things got too hard. He wore one of the iron collars, too—all the slaves had to wear them. I wanted to ask Xeno how he got to be a slave, but like all the slaves he was not allowed to speak beyond our business. All the slaves were afraid all of the time, even one so strong as Xeno.

My riding master was called Murn, and he was like Calador—not a slave. Like Calador he wore a gold earring and had eyes that prickled your skin when you looked at them. He wasn't quite so nasty as the swordmaster, but then I was a better rider than I was a swordsman. The problem with Murn was that I always came to him last in the day, and it didn't matter if I was bleeding from sword fighting or bruised from hand combat, he never changed his lesson at all. Some days I was so tired I couldn't stay on the horse when we were practicing jumps, or even control the beasts, they were so wild. It seemed like I spent half the riding time sprawled out on the ground. Murn shook his head and said that was just too bad. My technique needed to improve.

It felt good to fight and train, though. After only two weeks I had grown stronger and faster than I ever had been in my life. And no one bothered me about dressing properly or dancing lessons or being polite. This was just what I had always wanted.

Thousands of soldiers were camped around the fortress. At night you could see their fires dotted all over the plains like stars that had fallen out of the sky. In the daytime they marched and drilled and fought with each other, looking like ants there were so many. They were allowed to fight to the death in their training, which was never done in Leire. Sometimes they marched crowds of people—slaves and servants—out onto the plains and made them play the part of the enemy. They killed lots of them. On almost every day I saw bodies thrown onto piles and burned. Some days I just saw and smelled the nasty smoke that hung over the desert. You didn't have to be in Ce Uroth very long before you knew that the Lords of Zhev'Na were at war with somebody.

One day after I had lived in Zhev'Na for several weeks, my swordmaster Calador came to watch my hand-combat training. Xeno was teaching me how to disable an opponent without damaging him permanently. As our practice progressed, Calador's face turned red and angry. After a while, he called Xeno over and commanded him to kneel down. Xeno did so, which looked strange since Xeno was about twice Calador's size. "What are you are doing here, slave?"

"I'm teaching the young master hand combat as I was commanded, Swordmaster."

"You are teaching him to be killed."

"No, begging your pardon, Swordmaster. I am teaching him how to survive, how to deal with attackers that are larger or stronger or quicker, how to disarm them with guile."

"Leaving an opponent undamaged will allow the opponent an opportunity to take revenge on the young Lord. His enemies are unmatched in their wiles and cannot be dealt with in such a fashion. You are implanting weakness, setting him up to be killed."

"Swordmaster, it was never my intent to—"

"Tell me, slave, who is your master?"

Sweat dripped down Xeno's wide face. It was not from

fighting with me. "Who but the Lords of Zhev'Na, Swordmaster?"

Calador curled his lip and laid his hand on Xeno's slave collar. Xeno suddenly looked pale and sick, and began shaking like he was horribly cold or afraid. Calador stuck his face right up to Xeno's, still pressing on the collar. "I do not think you answer me, slave. Can we be a little more clear?"

"No other answer is possible, Swordmaster." Xeno was gasping and choking, his face almost purple, as if the collar were choking him.

"Tell me again, slave, and this time we shall be precise. Speak the name of your master."

Xeno straightened his back, and even though he was still shaking, sweating, and purple, his voice was loud and clear. "I call no man my master save the true Lord of Avonar, the Heir of mighty D'Arnath, the Prince D'Natheil, may he reign in peace and glory until the Wastes are restored and the Darkness is forever banished from the worlds."

Xeno did not scream until the last word was out, even though Calador opened his belly so wide that the slave had to hold in his entrails with his huge hands. Then they all spilled out, and he toppled into the dirt. Dead.

Calador put his hand on my shoulder and pulled me back a few steps. "I knew it! This stinking dog was assuredly planning to kill you."

Though it was a bit frightening to know how close I had come to death, I had a difficult time thinking of Xeno as a servant of the evil Prince. He certainly didn't look dangerous, all spread out in the pool of blood and entrails. Calador sent me in for an early supper while slaves were summoned to clean up the mess. But in truth, I couldn't eat for the rest of that day.

Harres, my new hand-combat master, was not a slave, but a warrior like Calador and Murn. He was very strict and came near twisting me in knots. One day I was slow to get up after he had pinned me to the sand for the twentieth time in an hour. My arm felt like it was half torn off. My face was scraped and raw from the hot sand. And my side had a cramp that kept me from getting a full breath, even if I could have done so in the afternoon heat.

"I said, repeat the move," screamed Harres. "You'll never get it right if you don't work at it."

"I can't," I said, barely able to get up on my hands and knees.

"Do you want me to coddle you like the slave did?"

"No, of course not." But I didn't understand why Harres couldn't go just a little slower like Xeno had. Truly I was making progress.

Harres grabbed my sore arm and yanked me to my feet. "Let me show you what your 'easy' master wanted to do to you, what your enemies want to do to you."

He marched me through the fortress, past the barracks, the servants' courtyard, and the slave pens, to a long low building made of sand blocks. If I hadn't already vomited up my breakfast that morning during sword practice, the stink in that building would have made me do so. Harres dragged me through the open doorway, past a line of empty wooden carts, each with a slave chained to the handles. The slaves were just sitting there, hot and dirty and scared-looking, waiting for something to be put in the carts. Beyond the carts were several wooden platforms and some big crates, with more slaves working busily around them. At first I thought other people were sleeping on the platforms, but when I saw one of the workers cutting the hair off of the body on the platform, I realized that the body was dead.

At another platform, a slave was tugging a boot off of another dead person. He dropped the boot in one of the crates and pulled off the next boot. He was starting to pull off the dead man's breeches, when Harres kicked him. "Here, slave," said Harres, "look here."

The slave waved his arms around his head, as if Harres was hitting him in the head. Harres had to yell at him again and kick him several more times before the man dropped to his knees and spread his arms out as slaves were supposed to do. The slave was a young man who looked very fit and strong, but one look at his face told me that only his body was fit. His mouth hung open and strings of spit dribbled onto his filthy tunic. His tongue seemed too big for his mouth and kept sliding this way and that. And his eyes . . . they were terrible. Empty in a way much worse than the warriors. And wickedly scared. He wasn't *thinking* about being scared like other slaves. He was scared as if he was going to be scared forever.

Harres yanked at the slave's short hair, slapped his cheek, and poked at his shoulder. The slave flinched and moaned, drooling and trying to shrink up into a ball. "This man was chosen to be your hand-combat trainer, young Lord. He was intelligent and obedient, his body superbly qualified as you can see. We thought him well suited to teaching—a good use of a slave. But we have discovered that this Xeno befriended him in secret, promising to help this fellow escape. When this young slave tried to report Xeno, as was proper, your kind tutor tortured him and left him like this, leaving himself in the position to be appointed your tutor instead." Harres pushed the slave with his foot until the man fell over in the sand at my feet. A big wave of stink made me step back; the slave had fouled himself. "Was this the fate Xeno had in mind for you? If you are like this, then his master, the Dar'Nethi prince, has nothing to fear from your revenge. Remember, young Lord. You can trust no one in the worlds. No one."

I shivered, even though it was blazing hot.

"Back to work now."

After a few more kicks, the slave, covered in spit and sand and filth, crawled over to the dead body and started tugging at its breeches again.

Even with the hard training and the ugly and unpleasant things, I liked living in Zhev'Na. My house was fine. I had my own things to use as I pleased and could eat only the food I wanted. The Lords and their warriors protected me from D'Natheil and the other Dar'Nethi who wished to make me like that awful drooling slave. And they treated me like a man and not a baby. I knew that the taunting was only to make me harder and better, and outside of my lessons, everyone left me alone. Best of all, I was too busy and too tired to think about sorcery.

The slave Sefaro ran my house—they called it the "Gray House." He laid out whatever clothes I needed and had my meals brought to my sitting room when I said I wanted it that way. The dining room downstairs seemed awfully big just for me. Every moment I was not training or eating, I slept. I dreamed a lot about Papa and Lucy. Xeno was in my dreams, too, holding his belly together so his entrails wouldn't leak out, along with that drooling slave that could have been me. And I kept dreaming those things about Comigor that were more real than life. Every morning when I woke up, I wanted to go right back to training. I was determined to be as good as Papa—better—because then I could kill the prince that murdered him and caused all this trouble.

Some things I missed about Comigor—though it got harder and harder to remember exactly what. Books mostly. Books were one of the few things I asked for that Sefaro could not get for me. He knelt in front of me and spread his arms wide, saying that I could kill him if I wanted, but no books could be had in Zhev'Na. I was really angry with Sefaro, because I thought it couldn't be true that there was no book in the entire fortress. I even imagined what it might feel like to stick my knife in him. But I didn't kill him. Even if he were lying about the books, it didn't seem like a bad enough thing to kill him for. Later that night, when I thought about how scared he looked when he told me, and what I had considered doing to him, I felt really strange . . . freezing cold inside. No one had ever been scared of me before. Zhev'Na was different that way. Killing was a lot more common than in Leire. I would just have to get used to it.

A few days after Xeno was executed, Darzid came to visit me. He stood at the side of the fencing yard and watched while Calador whacked me hard with his sword and then teased me while I tried to counter. Scratching or pricking me on my arms or cheeks or legs while I tried to get in a stroke was one of Calador's favorite things to do. That day he kept on longer than ever and started mocking me with his empty-eyed laugh that wasn't friendly at all. I knew Captain Darzid was watching, so I tried really hard to get in a good thrust, but Calador wouldn't stop. My arms were stinging and bleeding. Calador whisked the tip of his sword across my forehead, and more blood dribbled down my face. I was so tired I could hardly lift my rapier. Then Captain Darzid started laughing, and the horrid sun beat down, making my head pound and my bruises hurt, and before I even could think, I clenched my left fist and pictured what I wanted.

Calador's sword flew out of his hand and stuck into the stone wall. I poked the point of my rapier up to his belly. I very much wanted to push it in and make him scream instead of laugh. But Calador was not laughing anymore. Nor was the captain. All of a sudden I realized what I had done. Sorcery.

I backed away from the two of them until I was in a corner of the yard, holding my sword out in front of me and wishing it weren't shaking so badly. They would either kill me right there or call for soldiers to take me to prison. But Calador dropped to his knees in front of me and bowed his head all the way to the ground. Darzid folded his arms across his chest. Without any laughing or sniggering, he said, "Bravo, my lord. A fine move. Skillfully done. You should kill the bastard. You can, you know. Go ahead. Do it if you wish."

I just stared at the captain while blood trickled down my face and my arms, and the sun hammered on my head.

"Do you think that what you did should bother me or surprise me?"

I nodded stupidly.

The captain crouched down until his dark face and glittering eyes were close to mine. "I know what you are, Gerick. I know more about you than you know yourself. I've known about your 'talent' since the day you were born."

"You knew I was evil?"

"You are what you are."

"Why didn't you tell Papa, then? Why did you help me?"

"Tomas wouldn't have understood. He would have burned you alive, just as you suspected he would. What I've done is bring you to the one place in the universe where such things do not matter. I've brought you to a place where you belong. This is your land, Gerick. Not Leire, not Valleor, not anywhere in the Four Realms. Not anywhere green or soft or weak or common. You know what you are, and you know that this is exactly where you should be." He waved his hands at the broken red cliffs and ugly plains. Then he grinned a very wide grin. "Now teach this insolent servant a lesson, and then we will go have something to drink and a talk."

I looked carefully at Darzid, but for once he wasn't smirking or pretending. Calador was still kneeling with his forehead on the dirt. My blood boiled over like soup bubbling out of a pot. With the hilt of my sword I whacked Calador across the back of his head as hard as I could. He toppled over onto the ground.

Captain Darzid laughed and clapped me on the shoulder. "Well done. He'll think twice before touching you again."

It felt very good to teach Calador a lesson. I hated him.

We went up to my rooms, and while two slaves washed the blood and dirt off me and dressed me in clean clothes, Captain Darzid ordered Sefaro to bring food and wine. When I sat down at the table with him, he poured wine for both of us. "I've been waiting for you to demonstrate your power, Gerick. You control yourself very well."

"They don't burn sorcerers here?" I didn't want to, but I had to ask it.

Darzid laughed and gulped down a great gobletful of wine. "Not as a rule—unless they're our enemies—and in that case, any mode of death is fair. No, in Zhev'Na you are free to do as you please with your talents. In fact, there are those here who can teach you to use them to your advantage, just like your sword and your knife and your fists."

I thought about that while I ate. Darzid waited for me to speak, drinking another cup of wine. "Captain, are the Lords of Zhev'Na at war with Prince D'Natheil?"

"You have assuredly inherited your mother's renowned intelligence, young sir. Indeed, one could say that the war between the Lords of Zhev'Na and D'Natheil is a conflict beside which King Evard's adventures are no more than a chess match. This is a war for the control of two worlds. And it has been going on for a thousand years."

"When do I get to meet the Lords?"

"Quite soon, now you've shown your power and learned you are accepted here. They wanted to make sure you trusted them before revealing themselves to you. They wish to welcome you as a valuable ally."

Now he was making fun of me. I wasn't stupid. "But I'm not a valuable ally. Someday I might be so, but for now I can only do silly things, baby things. You saw my sword fighting. And I'm not eleven for weeks yet."

"The Lords are aware of all this, but, as you will discover, they deem your loyalty valuable beyond your imagining. There is power to be gained that neither Tomas nor Evard could dream of. There are battles to be fought that only you can win, and the first engagement is fast approaching. All your courage will be required, and all your intelligence and determination. I can tell you this, young Gerick. Your life will be very different from what you might have expected, but if you keep to your purposes, anything you desire—anything at all—will be yours." He tugged at my hair a little. "For now, I would advise you to continue your training. Grow strong and hard like your new home." He left without eating any supper.

No one cared if I was evil. I didn't have to be scared any more. I felt like a slave must feel if his collar is taken away. I couldn't change things and make myself good. I was what I was, no matter how much I might hate it, but there was really nobody left to care. Papa and Lucy were dead. Mama would close up Comigor, move back to Montevial, and be very happy. And I would stay in Ce Uroth, the place that looked like it was made for people like me, where no one would burn me for making the soldiers march or making a flower for Lucy. . . .

I sent Sefaro away after he put out the lamps, and then I took off my clothes and climbed into bed. I was very relieved, so it didn't make any sense at all that I would pick that night to cry.

CHAPTER 21

One morning after I'd been in Zhev'Na for many weeks, Calador received a message in the middle of my lesson. I was sparring with a slave who was considered one of the best fighters of my age. The swordmaster immediately stuck a pole between us to halt the match and kicked my opponent out of my way. I was furious. Though I had cut the boy several times, he hadn't yet touched me with his weapon. I was sure to defeat him at any moment. "I don't want to stop," I yelled.

"When you are summoned to wait upon the Lords of Zhev'Na, you do not delay," said Calador. He commanded my two slave shadows to bathe me and dress me to be presented to the Lords. A messenger would be sent when it was time.

The hot water felt good. I liked a bath really hot, and, even though I was excited to meet the Lords, I had the slaves fill the pool three times. After so many weeks, I was at last getting accustomed to being undressed around the slaves and having them wash me. I was definitely growing taller, and I wasn't so scrawny as I had been. I even had a few scars. And these slaves weren't like the servants at Comigor who talked to you, or played games if you wanted, or were interested in you as ordinary people might be. I didn't even know their names except for Sefaro. I thought perhaps they didn't have any.

I wanted to stay in the hot water for a fourth refill, but Sefaro hurried me out of the bathing pool and dressed me in a new outfit of black and silver. He strapped my weapons on and hung several silver chains about my neck. Mama would have liked to see me like that. She had always been more interested in what I was wearing than in anything I did or said. I thought it odd that Darzid had talked about her "renowned intelligence." Mama was pretty, but everyone knew she was not at all clever.

Though I was ready by midday, nothing happened for hours. I was so anxious and excited, I felt like to explode. My summons finally came at sunset, brought by someone in a long gray robe with a drooping hood that hid his face. Sefaro fastened a black cloak around my shoulders with a silver clasp in the shape of a wolf. The wolf's eye was a ruby.

Sefaro touched the back of his hand to his mouth, which was a slave's way of asking to speak. "You look quite fine, my young Lord," he said, when I nodded my permission.

I thanked him, and he bowed. Then the messenger led me away. I wanted to ask what the Lords of Zhev'Na were like. No one had told me anything about them. But it wasn't something I could ask a slave, and the messenger didn't speak as we crossed the wide courtyards that separated my house from the keep. The air was cold, something that had surprised me about night in the desert. As soon as the sun set, the wind picked up, and the heat disappeared like snow on a south slope. I was cold a lot in Zhev'Na, almost all the time except when I was out riding or running or fighting in the sun.

The keep of Zhev'Na was far larger than Comigor's, and very different. Where Comigor had thick walls and broad towers, everything at Zhev'Na seemed thin and lightweight. I wondered how the towers could stand up so tall or hold out against the wind, much less against an assault. On either side of the outer gates to the keep were the most amazing carvings of beasts and slaves and soldiers, all taller than life. I hadn't ever had a chance to look at them so close, but the messenger beckoned me to hurry, and truly, the carvings were nothing to what waited inside.

The messenger led me into a chamber that was round and huge, with great tall columns around the outside. You could have laid the tallest tower of Comigor across the floor and it wouldn't have reached the other side. The walls and columns were black. The floor was black, too, and shiny as if it were made of black glass. At first it made me feel dizzy to look in it, as if I might fall through it. And the ceiling . . . Well, I wasn't sure the room even *had* a ceiling, for above me was a moonless sky filled with stars. But I couldn't see the Great Arch or the Wolf or the Warrior or any other familiar pattern in the stars, and the air around me felt like inside, rather than outside. So I couldn't say whether there was a roof or not, even though I was sure I had seen one from outside.

Even more amazing than the room itself was what occupied it. Mostly nothing at all for a place so big. But straight across the room from the doors stood three giant statues, two of men and one of a woman, all carved of dull black stone. I thought they must be images of kings or gods, for they were seated on thrones with their hands in their laps. The smallest finger on any one of them was far bigger than me. Even seated, each was as tall as the walls of Comigor. They were the most fearful things I had ever seen.

The woman's face was old and stern, and her carved hair was drawn up in a knot on top of her head. The only color on the statue was her eyes, which were dark green like emeralds, though I had never heard that emeralds could be so large. The middle statue was of a man with a long arched nose, a wide mouth, and a forehead so broad that the rest of his face seemed small. His hair hung down to his shoulders, and his eyes were deep purple, like amethyst. The third statue was even more fearsome than the others, for it had no face at all, only blood-red rubies for eyes.

I wished that my boots didn't echo so loudly on the dark floor. This didn't look like a place where one ought to make noise. The messenger glided across the floor without making a sound.

From deep in the black floor at the very center of the room came a faint blue glow. The messenger motioned to me to stand over it. When I did so, a low hum came right through my boots and into my very bones. I didn't like it, but I stayed put. The Lords of Zhev'Na were sure to be watching me, and I didn't want them to think me a coward.

When I turned to the messenger to find out what to do

next, he had gone. I waited for a while. Nothing else happened. I decided that if the statues were the gods of the Lords, or their ancestors or heroes, then the thing to do would be to show respect, so I gave a very formal bow, like I would to the king of Leire. When I straightened up again, I almost yelled, for I could have sworn that the middle statue had moved.

The floor was still thrumming through my boots, and the pools of darkness and strange blue light kept tricking my eyes. I tried to watch without blinking, to see if the statue moved again, but I couldn't hold my eyes open long enough. When I finally had to blink, the three statues had vanished. Or, well . . . actually they were there . . . the three . . . but they were normal size, not giant. They were three people dressed in black and sitting on black stone thrones of more ordinary size.

The woman sat on the left. She looked almost exactly the same as the statue, only the knot of hair on her head was gray, and her hands and face were very pale. Over her eyes she wore a gold mask that covered half her face, each eyehole filled with an emerald.

Like his image, the man in the center had long hair, a big arched nose, and the broad forehead that made the rest of his face look small. His hair was brown, and he, too, wore a gold mask; his had amethyst eyes.

I almost didn't look at the third person, because I was afraid he would have no face, like the statue. But I swallowed and turned to the third throne. Again, I almost cried out, I was so surprised. He wore black robes like the others, and as I watched, his face shifted in the strange light. He wore a gold mask, too, with rubies where the eyes should be. Even though the mask covered the middle of his face, from his eyebrows halfway down his cheeks, I recognized him. It was Darzid.

"Welcome, Gerick. Welcome to Zhev'Na on behalf of the three of us." He smiled in his private, sneaking way. His voice sounded different—larger than a normal voice, as if he were speaking into a deep well.

"He gapes like a fish," said the woman. "Perhaps you should have warned him."

"He is only a child," said the man with the amethyst eyes. "Yet he does not flee from us in terror. I read curiosity in him more than anything. And amazement. A good start, I think."

"He is exceptional, as I've told you," said Darzid. "Blood will tell."

I didn't like them talking about me while I stood in front of them. Mama always did that.

"Gerick, Duke of Comigor, come to wait upon the Lords of Zhev'Na," I said, remembering how important visitors would greet Papa. "Is it the Lords of Zhev'Na that I address?"

The man with the amethyst eyes raised his eyebrows above his mask. "Why, yes. You must forgive us our rudeness, my lord. We are old and forget our manners. I am Parven the Warmaster. To my right sits Notole the Loremaster, and to my left . . . I believe you are acquainted with Ziddari the Exile, who has so recently returned to us after an immensely long time . . . abroad."

I bowed at each introduction, though it felt awkward to bow to Darzid who had been my father's hired lieutenant. "I wish to thank you all, my lords, for the hospitality you've shown me. I owe you a debt of honor, for I'm certain you've saved me from brutal murder. I hope to redeem my debt as soon as I'm able."

"Prettily spoken, my lord duke," said Parven. "It is our pleasure to grant you sanctuary. Consider Zhev'Na your home, and Ce Uroth as your own country. We think it is very likely that you will be able . . . "

". . . to redeem your debt of honor quite easily." Now it was Notole speaking. "We are old and selfish, and we do not step out of our way to aid young noblemen—even those so worthy as yourself—with no hope of return. Our enemies are the same as yours, and we hope to join together . . ."

". . . to make common cause against them." Darzid was speaking now. The three of them took up each other's thoughts and speech without even pausing for breath, like one person speaking out of three mouths. "You've begun your training in the skills necessary to accomplish your purposes—to fulfill the blood oath you've sworn to avenge the deaths of the man you called father and the woman you called friend. Perhaps that will be enough for you, and you will choose to return to the soft lands where your mundane king wants to burn you. But if you truly mean what you say about your life debt, then we will give you full opportunity to repay it. If you choose to make a new life here as our ally, then we will train you in other arts, and tell you truths of yourself and of the world that will change everything you know."

"It will be dangerous and exciting and difficult." Parven was speaking again. "You'll have to hear things you'll not like, and do things that are unpleasant. There will be no going back to what you've left behind. But it will be the life you deserve and your own choice. How does this strike you?"

The Lords seemed very stern, but kind, too, and respectful. My weapons felt good at my side, and I liked how strong I was becoming and how much faster I could run now. And, too, I thought of the sun-baked ugliness and the jagged red cliffs, and how the only place I felt really warm was out in that desert sun, sweating and fighting. In Leire they burned sorcerers and killed those who had anything to do with them. "I think this is the place I belong," I said. "I'd like to hear whatever you have to tell me and learn whatever you have to teach."

"Such a wise young man!" said Notole. "Let us seal our alliance, my young Lord. We are old and mistrustful and must be convinced that you take this as seriously as you seem to do. Come to me."

I climbed up the wide black step to stand in front of her. I was amazed to see that her gold mask was a part of her face, grown right into the pale, dry flesh. Each eye was a single, huge emerald. What could she see through them?

"Everything, my young Lord. Everything."

I looked away quickly. It was rude to stare, even at something so strange. Notole must be used to it, since she had guessed what I was thinking.

"We've found something that belongs to you, young duke, and have been waiting for a proper time to return it." Her hands were very dry, and the flesh hung on her long bony fingers as if it weren't connected to the bones at all. She held out a small green silk bag and dropped its contents into her hand. It was the Comigor signet ring, the one Seri had brought to me when she came to tell me lies about Papa's death. The Lords must have found it in my clothes when I first came to Zhev'Na. I had forgotten all about it.

"Thank you," I said, and reached for it.

But Notole yanked it back out of reach. "Wait one moment. As I said, we must be convinced that your heart lies here in Zhev'Na, that you will not desert us when times get hard . . . or when your pillow is wet with a child's tears."

My face got hot . . . and my blood, too. If Sefaro had seen my weakness and told the Lords of it, I would kill him. Then the Lords would know for certain that I was not a child. "I've sworn on my family's honor to avenge my father and my nurse," I said, trying to stand tall. "I consider my debt to you of equal weight. I do not swear lightly, even though I'm young." I pulled out my sword and laid it at Notole's feet. "I will serve you until you consider my life debt satisfied. Your enemies are my enemies, and I will do whatever is in my power to sustain you against them."

Notole laughed gently, her breath ruffling my hair. "We do not want your sword, young Lord. Not yet . . . though that may come when you are older. What we want is your loyalty, your allegiance . . . your soul. We want you to exchange this signet ring, a symbol of a life you have forsworn, for this"—she opened her other hand to reveal a small gold triangle, embedded with an emerald, an amethyst, and a ruby—"the token of our alliance. Else how can we trust that you will consider our common interests in preference to those about which we care nothing? A life debt cannot be half repaid or served only when there is nothing better to do."

She held out both hands then, the signet ring in one and the Lords' token in the other. "You must choose." The palms of her hands were horribly scarred, as if they'd been burned long ago.

Though none of the three moved from their thrones, I

felt as if they were all hovering about me—waiting, suspending breath until I would choose. Maybe they thought it would be difficult. But my dreams had already revealed enough of the truth. There was nothing for me at Comigor, and I wanted revenge more than anything in the world. I touched the signet ring for a moment and tried to think what to say about it. *I'm sorry, Papa. If I weren't evil, I could be like you. But I am what I am, and if those who are wicked can have any honor, mine will have to be what I make it.* And then I moved my hand to the Lords' token, picked it up, and felt such a sigh in the room that it made me think of a thunderstorm that breaks a summer's drought.

"Well chosen . . ."

" . . . we are honored . . ."

". . . our young friend and ally. Come let me show you how to wear it."

Ziddari took the jeweled token, and before I realized what he was doing, a sharp, hot pain stabbed my left ear. "There," he said, before I could protest. I touched my earlobe, and the jeweled pin was affixed firmly to it like the bolt through a gate.

Now we can teach and guide you . . .

Help make you more than you are.

My hands flew to my ears. Parven's and Notole's voices were not in my ears, but inside my head.

Any question you have, just think it or speak it, and one of us will answer. Ziddari's lips didn't move. It was amazing!

They sent me back to my house after that. Sefaro and two other slaves were waiting at the door as always. They bowed as I walked through the gate and across the courtyard. When they straightened up, Sefaro's eyes fell on the jewels in my ear. He laid his hand on the other slaves' arms and nodded toward me. Their faces grew pale and their eyes wide when they saw, and all three of them dropped to their knees. I thought that their race must be weak and cowardly to be afraid of me just because I was a friend of their Lords.

Indeed it is a truth, Gerick. Dar'Nethi are soft and corrupt—afraid of their own enchantments, their own power—

wanting every sorcerer to be as weak as they. They must be strictly controlled or they are worthless to anyone. We use them as slaves so that we can free our own kind to concentrate on battle. This was Ziddari whispering in my mind. *Try them. See how they quake when faced with strength greater than their own.*

"So they are sorcerers, too?" I said, just as if I was talking to him in person. That was a new consideration. I couldn't imagine it. I pushed Sefaro with my foot, and he fell from his kneeling position into a heap on the floor. He didn't move, just stayed there in the dirt looking up at me until I told him to get up. I would have melted with shame to look like that. "Why don't they use sorcery to free themselves? Are they too cowardly even for that?"

The collars prevent them. They are Dar'Nethi, subjects of Prince D'Natheil. They and their Prince have forbidden us to grow and use our power efficiently. We use the collars to let them know what it is like to be crippled. It's the purest torment we can offer them. And very just.

To prevent them using their sorcery did seem just. But I couldn't help but remember how it was to be afraid all the time, and so later, when Sefaro came to unstrap my weapons and take off the silver chains and the fine suit, I told him that he did me good service. He bowed a bit, but didn't ask permission to speak. I wondered if somehow he guessed that I'd thought about killing him when I was with the Lords.

When I went to sleep in my huge bed, I didn't dream at all.

My life changed on that night, more clearly even than it had when I'd first come to Zhev'Na. One of the Lords was always with me, just at the edge of my thoughts—a voice in my head that wasn't me. It seemed as natural as breathing or using the sorcery that could make toy soldiers march or flowers bloom whenever I wanted.

Sometimes the voice was very clearly one or the other of them. Notole whispered about grand things like how the universe worked and of magical power. Parven lectured me like a military tutor, teaching me attacks and defenses, and tactics and strategies that had been used in their thousand-year war. Ziddari was—well, Darzid—and he would talk about everything else, from how to treat slaves to the names of our enemies and our friends.

Sometimes I didn't hear any voice, but if I thought of a question about swordplay, Parven spoke up, or if I wondered how to use sorcery to make my bath hotter, Notole answered.

Over the next few days the Lords began to teach me about the origins of the war with Prince D'Natheil, of how everyone in their land could do sorcery, only some were better at it than others. Notole told me how D'Natheil's ancestors, most particularly the ancient Dar'Nethi king called D'Arnath, forbade those who were better at sorcery from trying new things, or from doing any magic that everyone in the land could not do just as well. It seemed like a terrible injustice, like saying that Papa could not fight with a sword, just because he was better than everyone else.

Exactly, said Notole, inside my head. *D'Arnath was afraid of losing his power to those with more talent. And still we struggle with the results of his cowardice. We fight to be allowed to use our talents as we wish. The Prince has inherited immense powers from D'Arnath, but he uses them to keep us in bondage, fearful that we will outshine his own family.*

And, of course, in all this learning that I was doing, I found out that there was more than one world. I was living in the world called Gondai, while Comigor, and all the people and places I had ever known, were in the other one—the mundane world, they called it.

That, of course, is why sorcery is such a great evil in your world, said Parven. *It doesn't belong there. D'Natheil and the followers of D'Arnath call* our *works evil, yet what could be a greater evil than introducing sorcery where it was not intended? Great injustices resulted from it; learn the history of the Leiran Rebellion and you'll understand.*

At first I was sad and a little bit scared to think I wasn't even in the same world where I had been born, but that feeling went away quickly. The Lords were teaching me so many new things, and besides, I almost couldn't remember Comigor any more, or the faces of anyone I'd known there, except the dead ones—Papa and Lucy. Those I remembered very well.

The Lords answered any kind of question except one, and that was anything about themselves. I wondered about their masks and why they wore them. I wondered why Ziddari had lived in my world for so long, and why he served as Papa's lieutenant, and why he had saved me, when he helped kill all the other evil sorcerers who lived there. When I asked those questions, I could feel the three of them with me, but no one answered. Just as well. My head was bulging with everything I was learning—and it was all so easy. I never forgot anything they taught me.

A week or so after my meeting with the Lords, Darzid came to my house. Well, of course he was Ziddari, but he looked like the ordinary Darzid again. "I have an urgent matter to discuss with you, my young Lord—one best talked about in person, I think, though you have adapted well to our new 'arrangements.' " We were standing on the wide balcony outside my apartments. Like every window and door in the Gray House, the balcony looked out over the desert. "Our first skirmish with Prince D'Natheil is about to occur, and in order for you to play your part in it, you must learn one of those bits of hard truth of which I spoke."

For just a moment, I glimpsed the light of rubies in his eyes. He was very excited, and that made me excited, too. I wanted to get on with the war, now I had committed myself to be a part of it. "Have you ever wondered how you happen to have the powers of a sorcerer?" he said.

"I thought it just happened when you were born."

"Like green eyes or large stature or red hair?"

"Something like that."

"Tell me, Gerick, how likely is it that a child has red hair and yet his mother has brown hair and his father black?"

"I don't know. Not likely, I guess."

"Then what if I were to tell you that it is far less likely

that a boy is born with the powers you have to parents who have none, than it is for a black-haired child with dark brown skin to be born to parents that are blond and fair?"

My stomach tied itself into a knot, and my skin felt cold again, though it wasn't even night. The red sun shone hot and bright on my skin. "Would it be true?"

"Yes."

"Then that would mean that Papa or Mama was a sorcerer, too—"

"You know better than that."

"—or that one of them, or both of them, were not my parents."

Darzid leaned on the balcony rail and gazed out into the desert. "Tomas was far too powerful for your mother to amuse herself with other men. And I can tell you that while Tomas had women other than Philomena on occasion, none of them were Dar'Nethi."

The knot pulled up everything so tight, I felt like there was a big hollow place in my stomach. "Then who am I?"

From the pocket of his black tunic, Darzid pulled a flat square of ivory. He put it in my hand. It had a looking glass set into it, and of course when I looked at it, my own face looked back at me. How could Papa not be my father? I could see him in my face. My chin was pointed like his. My hair was the same color, my eyes, too. And even darkened from the sun, my skin had the same red-gold cast. Nellia had said a thousand times how like Papa I was, and how no one but the children of Comigor had such coloring. . . .

The mirror clattered to the floor, and I clasped my hands behind my back as if it had burned me. I wanted to be sick.

Darzid nodded. "You've guessed it then. A hard thing to discover that what you believed all your life was false."

Seri. I was Seri's child . . . and her sorcerer husband's who had been burned alive.

"You and your cousin were born on the same day. Tomas's son was born early, weak and sickly, like all Philomena's children. There was no possibility he could survive. The serving sister who attended both mothers had overheard what was planned for the sorcerer's child and tried to switch the two of you. I caught her at it and decided that it would be amusing to see what became of you. I made sure the nurse was sent to Comigor with you and would watch out for any sign that you had inherited your father's . . . skills."

"So the baby Papa killed . . ."

". . . was his own son. He never knew it."

"Was he cursed by Seri's husband? Is that why he was born early?" Everything in the world was flipping upside down. I wouldn't have been surprised if the sun had started rising right back up from where it was setting.

"Perhaps."

I didn't know what to think. Seri. Seri was my mother. I hated her because her Prince had killed Papa, and she had brought him to kill me and Lucy. But surely that meant she didn't know the truth either. I tried to remember things about Seri, but everything was all blurry and confused. And the baby Papa killed hadn't been a sorcerer. That changed . . . something. . . . Before I could clear any of it up, Darzid tapped me hard on the cheek, calling me to pay attention.

"There's more. Worse than what you have already heard."

"I can't see how it could be worse."

"You should know your father's name, don't you think?"

"He was evil, and he's dead. I don't see why it matters except that he made me evil like him. I didn't belong there. I shouldn't have been born in that other world at all. And Papa . . . Tomas . . . was my real father."

"Don't be sentimental, Gerick. You were so afraid of Tomas that you stopped talking to him. He would have slit your throat or had you burned if he had even suspected what you are. But the identity of your father has everything to do with who you are, and what you are, and what you will be in the future, for there has come about something so unusual—even for this world that is so strange to you—that it would take days even to speculate on how it was done."

"I don't understand." My head was spinning with hot and cold and red sunlight glaring in my eyes and his words that just would not stop telling me awful things.

"It's in the names. The names will tell you. You see, Seri's husband, your father, went by the name of Karon."

"Karon? But that was the other name they called—"

"—the Prince D'Natheil. Yes, indeed. It appears that your real father is not dead at all, but has been brought back to life. He is now one and the same as our enemy."

"I don't understand how it could be possible." Two different people . . . yet the same. A dead person come to life again.

"It is indeed an immense enchantment, worked by the old man you saw talking with Seri—the last gasp of a once-talented people. We will teach you all about it and what it means for your place in the world. But for now, you must be ready to face him."

"Face him? The Prince?" I could not call him my father. I pictured the tall man who had walked with Seri in Grandmama's garden and could not imagine how the Lords thought I could fight him.

"Yes, this is the most magnificent part of the whole business. D'Natheil has made a great mistake, a mistake that could cost him his control of the universe, not to mention this perversion that he calls his life. You are the key. We didn't know your test would come so soon, but it's all to the good."

Ziddari went on to tell me of how I would be taken into the heart of our enemies' stronghold, and asked to stand in the presence of my father, the Prince, who also happened to be the man King Evard had burned to death shortly before I was born. "The two of you will be tested, to verify your relationship. The burden is on him, not on you. You have only to be present."

"Why would he admit that I'm his son if it could lose the war for him?" I was confused.

"He will have no choice. The enchantments that caused him to live past his own proper death have unsettled his mind. In a vain attempt to retain his hold on his power, he has put himself in a vulnerable position. If we play our parts well, then, before another day dawns, you will be acknowledged his successor."

"But his followers won't acknowledge me if I'm allied with his enemies." There was Darzid, thinking I was stupid again.

"Oh, they will acknowledge you. For a thousand years they've locked themselves into the stupidities of breeding and bloodlines. They'll soon discover their mistake. You are no longer the Duke of Comigor, but by sunset tomorrow you will be the Prince of Avonar, sovereign of all Dar'Nethi and Dulcé. And on the day you come of age you will be anointed the Heir of the cursed D'Arnath. D'Arnath was the only one of the Dar'Nethi who ever understood the full depth and breadth and uses of power, and in his pride and selfish stupidity, he reserved it all to himself and his Heirs. In a little more than one turning of the year, on the day you complete your twelfth year of life, all of it will be yours."

CHAPTER 22

Seri

I had assumed we would be able to approach some Dar'-Nethi, one of the Preceptors, perhaps, who might help us develop a strategy to rescue Gerick. But the Dulcé knew of no one we dared trust with the secret of Gerick's parentage, especially before the Prince was examined. And the shame-faced Dulcé confessed that, without some urgent prompting such as the threat of a compromised Heir, no Dar'Nethi would give a moment's hearing to a mundane woman who wished to go to Zhev'Na, especially in this time of tenuous peace. Even Kellea, a Dar'Nethi unknown to anyone and inexperienced in her art, would be viewed as highly suspect, perhaps even a Zhid spy. For the moment we must proceed on our own.

I believed Bareil grieved sorely for Dassine and Karon. The full weight of events seemed to descend on him the day following the Prince's departure. We had spent the morning discussing our plans to learn our way about the city. Bareil participated enthusiastically, dispensing advice, encouragement, information, and funds in the form of a cloth bag bulging with coins. But just about midday, as he was marking streets and shops on a sketch of Avonar, his voice trailed off and his hand began to tremble. He stepped away from our small table and rubbed his temple.

"What is it, Bareil? Are you all right?"

"Ah, my lady, I need— I must leave you." Indeed his olive complexion appeared sickly and washed out. He grabbed his cloak from the hook by the door, his pack, and D'Natheil's sword belt and weapons from where he had laid them carefully out of the way. "I should put these things where they'll be safe. Careless of me to keep them here. I'll be back . . . I don't know when I'll be back. Please excuse me." With no more than this, he barged through the door and hurried down the passage.

We didn't see him again until evening. He brought us a roast fowl and a thick, savory pottage of grain and vegetables, but he declined to eat with us. "I'm so sorry, my lady. I cannot remain here with you. Master Dassine's house must be set to rights in case the Prince wishes to take possession of it again . . . or give it to someone else . . . I've asked a Word Winder to reinstate the house wards." He seemed hesitant, unsure of himself as I had not seen him in our brief acquaintance. "I've arranged for you to stay here at the guesthouse as long as you wish. I would invite you to come to Master Dassine's house—Master Dassine and the Prince would be honored—but you would surely be remarked."

"Won't you be in danger? You were almost killed. . . ."

"Now that the Prince is with the Preceptors, I have little to fear. No one will bother a Dulcé without his madrisson. Nothing could be learned from such a one. Please . . . be assured I will help and advise you in these matters as I've promised."

Over the course of the next few weeks, Kellea and I worked very hard to learn the common language of Avonar. I had picked up the rudiments from the Dulcé, Baglos, on our summer adventure in the days before Karon/D'Natheil had recovered his power of speech and understanding of Leiran, and so was able to gain a reasonable understanding of the spoken language in good order. But I stumbled badly when trying to speak it myself. Kellea, on the other hand, drew on her sorcerer's power to become fluent within the first week. I was sorely jealous.

Paulo would not sit still for any teaching. He swore that his head had no more room for extra ways of saying the same thing, and spent our study hours exploring the streets and byways of Avonar.

As he had promised, Bareil came to the guesthouse every

day, but only for an hour or two at a time. His demeanor was subdued and reticent, as if he weren't sleeping well. He told Kellea how to find us clothing of colors and styles appropriate to Avonar. While only slightly different in style from ordinary skirts and tunics, bodices or breeches—the Dar'Nethi seemed to prefer loose-fitting or draped tunics and shirts rather than close-fitting—the garments were colored in vibrant, gem-like greens, reds, and blues that Leiran dyemasters had never discovered. And no Leiran or Vallorean seamstress could have imagined such materials or construction: fibers softer than silk, yet of such resilience that an Isker peasant could wear such a garment for a lifetime; stitches that were perfectly uniform and almost invisible; embroidery of such charming and complex design that the queen's whole staff of needlewomen could not produce one sample of it in a year.

But such details, marvels at any other time, were lost on us as we drove ourselves to discover some way to retrieve Gerick from the heart of the Wastes. Together we reviewed all that Bareil had told about the stronghold of the Zhid and whatever he could supply of Dar'Nethi scholarship regarding the Lords. But we were unable to discover any way to transport ourselves to Zhev'Na, much less a way to wrest a child from the Lords' clutches.

I demanded patience of myself and the others. Though my fears screamed for instant action, my brief encounter with the Zhid had taught me that I had no weapons to fight them face to face, and so far we had discovered nothing new that would give us the least chance of success. Bareil's history lessons told us that the Lords wanted Gerick to come of age in their care, so they weren't going to kill him. Kellea hinted that I was coldhearted to let my son languish in Zhev'Na, but I believed that if I were to save him, then, for the moment, I had to let him be. We would study and learn and find a way.

We heard no reliable news of the Prince. Rumors flew about Avonar that D'Natheil was dead or mad, that he was preparing for an assault on the Wastes, that he was laboring on the Bridge, or that he had gone back across the Bridge to lead the Exiles back to Avonar. Few Dar'Nethi took any of these stories seriously, Bareil told us. Most believed that the house of D'Arnath had its own ways that could not always be explained. Had not the present Heir been cloistered with Dassine for ten years, only to come forth to win a great victory and preserve the Bridge? Because of what D'Natheil had accomplished, every day brought a renewal of power that had been lost to the Dar'Nethi for centuries. The Zhid no longer attacked the walls of Avonar. Prominent citizens spoke of forming expeditions into the Wastes to rescue those Dar'Nethi still captive, but these ventures would require years of preparation. The Dar'Nethi had no more information about Zhev'Na than we did.

And so we worked and we studied and we listened, but truly made no progress at all.

On one evening more than six weeks after Karon had given himself to the Preceptorate, I was sitting before our little fire, studying a map Kellea had found in a bookshop. Though the map itself was not so old, the shopkeeper had claimed it was a rarity. Current maps delimited a vast proportion of Gondai as the unknown Wastes, showing physical features only in the narrow strip that bordered the living lands. But this map showed detailed names and locations of mountains and rivers, kingdoms, domains, and villages as they had existed before the Catastrophe.

I was alone as I pored over the inked scroll. Paulo was roaming the streets again. Bareil had taken Kellea to Dassine's house to find a book that listed ancient place names and their descriptions. From the combination of the book and the map and Dassine's tales of his captivity, we hoped to discover what place might have been transformed into the fortress of Zhev'Na. The night was quiet, and I was intent on my study, not daring to feel excited at our first possible breakthrough.

The door crashed open, filling the room with the scents of cold weather and woodsmoke. "You've got to come." Paulo was ruddy-cheeked and breathing hard. Snow dusted his brown hair and dark wool cloak. "They've got the Prince at that Precept House—Master Exeget's house. And your boy is there, too!"

I scribbled a message for Kellea and grabbed my cloak.

"I knew they'd take him there," said Paulo, frost wreathing his face as we raced through the snow-blanketed streets. "Knew it from the first. So I found the place. Been watching it every day."

We cut through a long-neglected bathhouse, our footsteps echoing on the broken paving as we circled empty pools littered with years of dead leaves and matted with snow. Moonlight poured through the fallen ceiling to reveal glimpses of richly colored mosaics peeking from behind masses of winter-dead vines. The path through the bathhouse gardens led us into a broad street of fine houses. Only a stitch in my side caused our steps to slow.

Avoiding the soft pools of lamplight that spilled from the paned windows alongside laughter, music, and the savory scents of roasting meat and baking sweets, we hurried toward a formal circle of trees at the end of the street. A high, thick wall, quite overgrown, and a severely plain iron gate with no hinges, no latches, no guards, and no obvious way to open it closed off the roadway. Through the gates and a large expanse of trees and shrubs, I glimpsed a huge house with many lighted windows on its lower floors. Signaling for quiet, Paulo led me into a narrow lane that skirted the wall.

At the back of the house, the stone wall yielded to a wooden building. The unmistakable scent of stables hung in the cold air trapped behind it. Paulo carefully removed three boards from the wall, leaving a hole just large enough for a person to crawl through. He went first, pulling the loose boards back into the hole once I had slithered into an empty stall filled with fragrant hay. Skirting the wide stableyard, we sped across a gravel lane and through a hedge, across a snow-covered lawn, and around a corner of the great house.

The addition of a massive chimney sometime after the original house was built had left a jutting corner in each side of the house. Near the bottom of the wall to the left of the chimney was a wide grate of the kind used to draw fresh air into an enclosed room. Yellow light and the sound of voices spilled out of the grate.

"However did you find this?" I whispered.

"Back when that Dulcé Baglos told us how wicked and stubborn the Prince was when he was a boy, he said how Exeget used to make the Prince spend time outside in the winter for punishment. Well, I've been throwed out in the winter a deal of times, so's I thought where would a fellow go to get warm if he was out like that? Stables, maybe, or in a corner like this where he could get a look at what was going on in the house."

We settled ourselves beside the grate and peered inside. I could easily imagine the boy D'Natheil, sent into the winter weather unclothed to crush his pride, huddling here to draw warmth from the brick chimney and watch resentfully as his warm and comfortable mentor went about his business in the Preceptors' council chamber. For that was surely the room that lay beyond the grate.

The chamber was immense, its floor well below the level of the ground on which we sat, and its ceiling out of view. Suspended from the unseen ceilings were wide lamps created, not from candles or oil lamps or torches, but from a thousand faceted globes of light hung on hoops of bronze. Tapestries woven of jewellike colors adorned the walls, hung between elegant pilasters shaped like elongated wheat sheaves. Tall bronze doors, each with a graceful tree worked in relief, faced us across the expanse. Our vantage allowed us to look down on a raised dais that stood just in front of the great hearth. On the dais stood a long table and seven elaborately carved, high-backed chairs, five of them occupied: one by a huge man wearing a wide neck-chain of gold set with rubies, another by a buxom, broad-faced woman in a robe of shifting colors, one by a skeletal, balding man, and two more by an elderly man and woman who sat in the center—the Preceptors of Gondai. Gar'-Dena, Madyalar, Y'Dan, Ustele, and Ce'Aret. A sixth man, his light, thinning hair immaculately combed, face round and boneless, looking something like a foppish clerk, must be the Preceptor Exeget. He stood just beyond the table, beside a chair that had been set to face the dais. Karon sat in the chair.

He wore a white robe, just as on the day I walked with

him in my mother's garden, but on this night his face expressed neither hope, nor joy, nor even the tired and rueful humor of that meeting. His haunted eyes were hollow, his face gaunt. His hands, resting on the wide arms of his chair, were shaking. Eyes fixed on the fire beyond the dais, he showed no signs of hearing anything that was being said. What had they done to him?

Exeget seemed to be concluding an argument. ". . . and so we have uncovered at last what the traitor Dassine has wrought: imprisoning a dead soul before it could cross the Verges, murdering our rightful Heir, and reviving him by implanting this impostor in his body, leaving us with a sovereign so crippled of mind that he could easily be molded to his master's will. Even our 'Prince' will tell you he does not belong in his office. His life should properly have ended ten years ago in the brutal fires of his adopted world. He belongs beyond the Verges."

Earth and sky, they'd told him everything!

"But no matter the method of his transformation, you cannot deny that he is the Prince as well as the Exile," said Madyalar, the woman in the color-shifting robe. "I see no difficulty here. He has answered all our questions. He possesses the Heir's power; we cannot deny him. D'Arnath's line ends with D'Natheil."

"Not so," said Exeget. "Vasrin Shaper has again shown her faithfulness, taking the matter of our dilemma and shaping a solution. The line of D'Arnath cannot end if this Prince provides us a successor."

"But D'Natheil has no children. Dassine did not let him breed," said the hard old woman, Ce'Aret.

"All true, and yet . . . If we could produce one who could pass the test of parentage alongside our crippled Prince, would you not say we had found ourselves a ready Heir?"

"Well, of course, but that's impossible," said Y'Dan, the bald man.

No. Not impossible at all.

Exeget smiled, waved his hand, and the bronze doors swung open. Darzid and Gerick entered the room and stood behind Karon, who stared at the floor, unmoving save for the unceasing tremor of his hands.

Gerick was dressed in brown breeches and a sleeveless shirt of beige silk. A gold chain hung around his neck, and a wide gold armring encircled each of his tanned, bare arms. A knife hung from his belt, the sheath strapped to his leg with a leather band. His red-brown hair was trimmed and shining, and affixed to his left ear was a gold earring, embedded with jewels. In the two months since Covenant Day he had grown a handspan, but neither that nor his deep red-gold coloring nor his exotic adornment was the most profound change.

He was no longer afraid. All the false bravado, all the sullen temper was gone; how clear it was now that they had been products of his terror. Gone also was the child who had watched with curiosity and pleasure when I made things that he could recreate for the old nurse he loved. Gerick's eyes were cold, and hatred, not love, gave life to his face.

I pressed one hand to my mouth and the other to my belly, trying to quell the dull, swelling ache just below my ribs. So profound a change in so short a time. What had I been playing at to allow this to happen? Who were these vile beings who could so easily and so determinedly corrupt a child?

"Who is this boy?" rumbled Gar'Dena. "We've been told nothing of a boy. And who are you, sir, who ventures so boldly into the Preceptors' council chamber?"

"I'm an old friend," said Darzid, "an Exile, like your Prince here."

Damnable man! What I would give for a sword to end his cursed life! Was it possible that he was Dar'Nethi?

"An Exile!" said several of the Preceptors together, wondering.

"Indeed this man is an Exile, who has by a strange accident preserved for us the hope of our royal family," said Exeget. "But here—before anything else is said—the test. The test will tell all. Once doubt is put to rest, then we can explain the happy circumstance."

Exeget stood before Gerick and laid his hands on the sides of my son's face. Gerick neither flinched nor changed expression. After a moment, Exeget took a position behind Karon's chair and laid his hands on Karon's broad shoulders. "Tell us, D'Natheil," said the Preceptor, "who is this child that stands before us? What is his lineage? Do these shoulders bear the responsibility for his life?"

Karon closed his eyes and spoke softly, no tremor in his voice. "This is my son, and with Seri, my beloved wife, I gave him life."

I pressed my forehead against the grate, gripping the iron bars. Tears welled up in my eyes, only to freeze on my cheeks in the bitter cold.

Gerick's face did not change, except perhaps to grow harder. He was not surprised by Karon's words, and he didn't like them.

Exeget stepped back. Madyalar rose from her seat and swept from the dais, the rainbow stripes on her voluminous robes teasing the eye. She took Gerick's hands in hers for a moment, examined his face carefully, and then, like a mother calming a fearful child, she stood behind Karon and wrapped her arms about his breast. "Tell us, D'Natheil, who is this child? What is his lineage? Is it this heart that beats in time with his?"

Through the aura of enchantment, Karon spoke again. "He is my son, and with Seri, my beloved wife, I cherished him from the day we first knew him."

One by one they came, laying their hands on his hands, on his loins, and on his head.

"Did your hands build a dwelling place for him along the path of life?"

"Did your loins give fire to his being?"

"Is it this mind that speaks to his mind and listens for the word *father*?"

And he answered each of them.

"With my hands did I heal and restore life where it was damaged beforetime, and so in the days of my first life, I built a house of honor for my child."

"Yes, it is my seed that called him from nothingness into the Light."

"He is my son."

"The bond of the spirit is proved," said Exeget. "And, as you see, the bond of the flesh is also true, though the flesh was not that which our Prince wears on this day. Law and custom mandate that the bonds of flesh and spirit are the true witness of lineage, and who dares gainsay what Vasrin Shaper has provided? My judgment asserts that this child is the next Heir of D'Arnath. How say you all?"

One by one, the Preceptors agreed—only Madyalar hesitating. "I believe we should wait. Let the Prince recover from his ordeals. Place him in isolation for a while. He may yet father children with this flesh—D'Natheil's flesh. Then there would be no question. Or perhaps—"

"No!" Karon roared, bursting from his seat. "Enough! You cannot make me endure this longer." Reaching across the table, he thrust his shaking hands into Madyalar's face. "There is no recovery from death. Ten breaths more and I will be unable to stop screaming. I am dead. I can do nothing for you. Care for my son. Protect him . . . please. Send for his mother to love and nurture him and teach him the savoring of life. Do not entrust Exeget with his mentoring . . . nor this Darzid who stands in the guise of an Exile, but is responsible for the extermination of a thousand Exiles."

The Preceptors recoiled in horror. The old ones gaped; Gar'Dena, Y'Dan, and Madyalar jumped from their seats, their dismay not aimed at the cursed Darzid, but at Karon, who writhed and twisted, wrestling to loose Exeget's hands that had grasped his shoulders to pull him away from the table. Then, Karon broke free and backed away from Exeget, a knife in his hand. Breathing hard, his skin gray and stretched, he held the unsteady weapon between himself and the Preceptor.

"My lord Prince, calm yourself," said Exeget. "Your mind has been savaged by Dassine's enchantments. Let us help you. I know of many things—"

"Stay away from me!" said Karon, brandishing the knife. "When I can no longer hold, you'll not want to be within striking distance of this weapon."

"Gerick . . . Your name was going to be Connor . . .

Connor Martin Gervaise." Though his gaze remained affixed to Exeget and the other Preceptors, Karon spoke to our son with an urgency, intensity, and tenderness that wrenched the heart. "I wanted to tell you about my friend Connor. I wanted to tell you so many things, but there was no time. That was the worst part of dying . . . to believe I would never see you. And now beyond all wonder, we are together, but again . . . there is no time."

Gerick spat at his feet. "Murderer! I've sworn a blood oath to destroy you for what you've done."

Karon shook his head, his lean face sculpted in pain. "So much blood on my hands—holy gods, I don't deny it—but not that of which you accuse me. If only there was time"—he staggered backward a small step—"I'm so sorry, Gerick. So sorry. Look at me . . . look deep and search for the truth." Then he closed his eyes, and with his trembling hands, my beloved plunged Exeget's knife into his own belly.

"Karon! No!" I screamed, yanking at the iron grate as if to rip it from the mortar.

The chamber erupted in frenzy as Karon slumped to his knees. The giant Gar'Dena rushed forward bellowing and gathered him in his brawny arms. His cry of grief shook the walls of the chamber. "Great Vasrin, alter this path! What have we done? The Heir of D'Arnath is dead!" Madyalar and the two old people screamed for guards and Healers, while Y'Dan slumped into his chair and laid his head on the table, weeping.

Darzid stiffened and unsheathed his sword. Grabbing the wide-eyed Gerick, he backed away from Karon and the Preceptors.

An expressionless Exeget watched the madness and did nothing.

Fate could not be so brutal, so unfair. "Why did you do it?" I sobbed, gripping the iron bars. "I could have helped you. Oh, love, why? Why didn't you wait for me?"

As if in echo of my words, there came a flutter in my head, a delicate brush of words. . . . *wait for me*. . . . Then, in a moment of grace, my mind was filled with Karon, without pain, without fear, whole, knowing everything of our life together . . . *Seri, beloved, forgive me.* . . . Then he was gone.

The guards had to peel my fingers away from the grate as I hung onto the sweet echo, straining to hear more. But strangely enough, as Paulo and I were taken inside the Preceptors' house, a different voice whispered in my head. *Do not be afraid,* it said. *Say nothing.*

I wasn't sure about that voice. Certainly it was not Karon's. I might have named it Dassine's voice, though Bareil had told me that the old sorcerer was buried in his own garden. And, too, the tenor of it was not quite the same. This sounded more as my own father might have done were he able to speak in the mind—my grim warrior father, who thought nothing of leading a thousand men to their deaths in order to slay a thousand enemies, all for the glory of his king. Once, when I was a child, my favorite pony had been crippled in a fall. After commanding a servant to slay the suffering beast, my father had taken me on his knee and awkwardly dried my tears. "The world goes on, little Seri," he said. "A soldier never dies. His blood makes the grass green for his children."

Grief threatened to unravel me, all the more devastating after the hopes of the past summer—the love and grace I had been granted after so many years of bitterness. Yet this strange and sober voice reached through the storm that racked my soul and assured me that the universe was not random, not careless or capricious. The Way was laid down, and somewhere I would find a reason for its turnings.

Perhaps it was my imagination. Perhaps I was a fool. But when Paulo and I were brought before the Dar'Nethi Preceptorate, I said nothing, and I was not afraid.

CHAPTER 23

They had taken Karon's body—no, more properly, D'Natheil's body—away by the time Paulo and I stumbled onto the fine rug laid before the council table. The patterned wool square, hastily moved, did not quite cover the fresh blood that stained the white stone floor. They had kept us waiting in a bare anteroom for several hours, able to hear only hurried footsteps and bursts of unintelligible conversation through the door. The exclamations of dismay were clear enough, though, as the word of D'Natheil's death spread.

Gerick and Darzid were no longer present—only the six Preceptors in their high-backed chairs. The one chair sitting empty at the end of the dais would have been Dassine's. I wondered, somewhat foolishly, who would be chosen to sit in the chair. Maybe no one. Maybe the Preceptorate would no longer exist now that Gerick, a ward of Zhev'Na, was to become the Heir of D'Arnath.

"Who is this woman? Where did she come from? And another boy? Is this one your own long lost son, Exeget?" said Ce'Aret.

"We should get on with our important business and interview spies later," said Ustele. "Everything is changed, now."

"Not ordinary spies," said Y'Dan, still red-eyed from his weeping, as he wiped his nose on his sleeve. "These two are not Zhid."

"Ustele is correct," said Exeget. "We have two matters of utmost urgency: how we are to announce the Heir's death to the people, and what provision we must make for the boy's care until he comes of age—approximately a year, so I understand."

Madyalar joined in. "Would that we could anoint the child right away."

"Are you planning to destroy this young Prince the same way you ruined D'Natheil, Exeget?" said Ce'Aret. "I pray this Exile Darzid is trustworthy as you assure us. The boy must not be compromised either by the Zhid or our own foolishness. We must find him a proper protector and suitable mentors."

"This Exile is eminently trustworthy," said Exeget. "And he's already taken the young Prince to a place of safekeeping. I propose we leave him there. . . ."

As the six of them wrangled, a low mutter rose from beside me. "He's not dead . . . not dead . . . not dead." Paulo was staring at the blood fading from red to brown underneath the edge of the rug. A tear trickled down his freckled face. I reached for his hand, and for once he didn't refuse it. When he looked at me, I gave him a slight shake of the head, warning him to be silent.

"Now," said Exeget. "Let us dispose of these spies, so we can get to our business. Not only are these two strangers not Zhid; they are not even Dar'Nethi."

"Not Dar'Nethi? No . . . I see not." An itchy warmth crept behind my eyes as old Ustele peered at me across the table. One might have thought I had three heads. "Mundanes."

Ce'Aret sat up straighter. "Mundane spies? Who is this woman?"

"As a spy she has severe lacks," said Exeget. He tapped the ends of his smooth, white fingers together lightly. "And one has only to look at the woman to know who she is—even if certain people are too deaf to have heard her maudlin cries."

"I'm not deaf," spat Ce'Aret. "There was a commotion."

"Yes, when D'Arnath's Heir guts himself because his head pains him, an unseemly commotion is the likely result. But come, old woman, can you not see the resemblance to our new liege? I do believe we have the honor of meeting our young Prince's mother." Exeget jumped out of his seat and stepped from the dais, coming to stand beside me. Arms folded, he inspected my garments and face, much the way he might examine a piece of furniture.

"The mother? The wife, then, of the other—the Exile that lived in D'Natheil?" said Madyalar, staring at me curiously. "Is that true?"

"The Lady Seriana Marguerite—widow of the same man for the second time," said Exeget. "A sad and most unusual case. And quite mundane. Of course, mundanes are not capable of spying as we know it. They can read nothing from our minds, nothing of the auras of life, nothing beyond the dry evidence of their eyes and ears. I cannot see how a Dar'Nethi—even an Exile—could consort with such deadness."

"Is the woman mute?" said the querulous Ustele. "Why does she stand there so stupidly?"

"What should she say?" said Madyalar. "How pleased she is to meet us who sit in judgment of her husband and her child? How delighted she is that the poor madman somehow got his hands on a knife here in the council chamber? She's committed no crime that I can see." The woman slumped in her chair, tapping her fingers rapidly on the table, her mouth drawn up in annoyance.

"Well, we can't just let the woman go free." The bald Y'Dan bit his lip and wrinkled his leathery forehead. "She might know something useful. And I don't understand—if she was the Prince's wife, why did he not acknowledge her? Why was she sneaking about here in the dirt and"—his nostrils flared—"the stables?"

"All good questions," said Madyalar. "But a more useful question might be how she can help us understand our new Heir. The boy seems so cold. What child of ten calls his father a murderer? Our examination revealed no evidence of murder in our late Prince."

"Clearly one of us must question the woman before we let her go on her way," said Exeget. "As she cannot cross the Bridge to her own world until her own son can take her, she and her young companion will need someone to take them under his wing. I consider such a matter to be my responsibility as head of the Preceptorate."

I almost broke my resolution of silence. I would not surrender myself or Paulo to Exeget.

"No, I'll take her," said Madyalar, shooting a wicked glare at Exeget. "You insisted I turn over the Prince to you for the examination, and look what's come of it. He was wreckage, already half dead before you brought him here this morning. This matter"—she waved her hand at Paulo and me—"needs a woman."

"How dare you question me? The Prince's state was Dassine's fault, not mine, and if you think I will allow the new Heir to be coddled by some maudlin female—"

"A plague on both of you"—Gar'Dena rose to his considerable height, pounding his meaty fist on the table until the floor shook with it—"and on all of us Dar'Nethi who have allowed matters to reach this pass."

Throughout the whole discussion, the huge man had sat silently in his oversized chair, his massive head resting on thick fingers ringed with emeralds and sapphires. But now his thundering rage silenced the childish bickering like an arrow in the throat. "We were saved from one disaster by our brother Dassine and this dead Exile, whom you so callously dismiss. Now we stand at the brink of another, and you quarrel about your petty prerogatives. We should humble ourselves before this woman who has suffered such loss as we cannot imagine. We have no right to question her, but should instead beg her forgiveness and implore her to enlighten us as to what might influence her son to follow the Way of the Dar'Nethi. To that end, I will take her under *my* protection, and whoever says ought against it will discuss it with my fist." A burst of white lightning spat from Gar'Dena's jeweled hand.

Leaving Exeget and Madyalar sputtering and glaring and his other fellows openmouthed, Gar'Dena lumbered down from the dais with surprising quickness, motioning Paulo and me brusquely to the door. I could no more resist his direction than a feather could withstand a hurricane. When we passed through the bronze doors, I felt slightly dizzy, and my eyes played tricks on me, for I seemed to exist in two different rooms at once.

One was plainly furnished with a thick carpet of dull blue

on the floor and padded benches of fine wood set against bare, cream-colored walls. The other room could not have been more different. A vast, opulent space, its walls were hung in red damask and gold velvet. From a ceiling painted with forest scenes and dancing maidens hung great swathes of filmy red and yellow fabric that shimmered like water, and spread on the green-tiled floor were purple patterned carpets so thick they could serve for a king's bed. Through the slowly shifting veils, I glimpsed lamps of ornately worked brass and silver standing on large tables with black marble tops and gold lions for their legs. Statuary, silver wind chimes, ornaments of glass and silver, and baskets of flowers stood or hung in every nook and niche. Two fountains bubbled in the corners where plantings of greenery, even small trees, flourished in the soft light. Exotic birds twittered from the branches, and everywhere was music: pipes and flutes and viols, softly playing every manner of melody that varied depending on where you looked.

A large hand nudged me one step further. The plain room vanished. Gar'Dena, Paulo and I had come fully into that other place. But the ebullient decoration of the vast chamber was not the whole of wonder. Gar'Dena clapped his hands three times, and three young women instantly appeared in the room with us. One was slim and short, with long, dark hair, her hand raised in mid-stroke with a silver-backed hairbrush. The second girl was blond and tall. Surprise and annoyance crossed her handsome face as she stood in the elegant room, her upraised hands and apron dusted with flour. The third and youngest, bright and fresh-faced and surely no more than twelve or thirteen, was seated on one of the swooping fabric draperies as if it were a child's swing. A book lay in her left hand, while the fingers of her right hand ran over the lines on the page. Her eyes were unfocused, aimed vaguely into the center of the room while she performed this activity, and the longer I watched, the more convinced I became that she was blind and yet was "reading" the book in some strange and marvelous way.

"Aiessa, Arielle, Aimee, we have guests," bellowed Gar'-Dena. "Look lively now. We need rooms, baths, supper."

All three girls were clad in flowing, high-waisted gowns of white, the sleeves banded in blue or rose embroidery. Their elegant simplicity presented quite a contrast with Gar'Dena himself, who was resplendent in green satin breeches and a red silk doublet in addition to his hundredweight of jewels.

"Papa, you must give us more notice," said the tall blond girl, whose flour-dusted apron was dark blue. "My bread is in mid-kneading, and there's no wine to be had in the house. You sent our dinner to Co'Meste to redeem your wager, and the guest rooms have not been swept in a moon's turning, since you frightened the sweeping girls. Not that you are unwelcome." She directed the last at me with a charming smile.

"You'll think of something, Arielle," said the big man. "You always do. Get your lazy sisters to help. I will speak to our guests for a few moments, and then they'll be ready for refreshment and beds." He bent down from his great height and planted a kiss on the blond curls of the youngest girl. "Who is kissing you, clever Aimee?"

She reached up and tweaked his outsized nose. "I'll never mistake you for anyone, Papa," she said, with a giggle far sweeter than the wind chimes tinkling in the softly moving air. "Unless perhaps a rinoceroos should come to Avonar."

"Someday when our troubles are past, I will bring you a rinoceroos, sweet Aimee. Then shall we see if you mistake him for your papa."

The impossibly strange mode of travel, the alien surroundings, the warmth and charming repartee . . . everything was at odds with the noisy rancor of the council chamber. I closed my eyes to clear the confusion, but visions of flashing knives and too much blood filled my head. My knees turned to water, and strength and surety flowed out of me in a tidal rush.

Gar'Dena's dark-haired daughter dropped her brush and grabbed my arm and my back, supporting me gently. "Would you like to sit down? Papa can be so thoughtless."

"Yes," I said. No need for foolish bravado any longer. "Yes, please."

"Papa, attention to your guests," said the girl sharply. "I'll see if I can find them something to drink, at least, so Arielle can finish her bread-baking."

Gar'Dena whirled about, his broad face everything of apology. He took my hand, wrapping my fingers about his forearm and patting them gently. "Forgive me, madam, but it always seems so interminably long between my trips home, and I miss these lovely gems of mine most fearfully. Please, let us have a seat and speak of your future plans."

He led me to one of the red draperies that swept in a long arc from the high ceiling. When I sat down, the silky stuff wrapped itself around me until I felt as cozy and comfortable as if I were nestled in a cloud. Paulo drew back when Gar'Dena pointed to a yellow drape. Instead the boy dropped to the thick carpet just beside me. Noting Paulo's sooty face and filthy clothing, I realized that I too was streaked with ashes and stable dirt. Not at all like the wife of a prince, even a dead one. *Oh, gods . . . don't think.* My chest ached.

Gar'Dena dragged a giant pillow to a spot just in front of Paulo and me and settled his bulk onto it. "Tomorrow I shall retrieve your remaining companion and bring her here. You'll be much more comfortable here than at the Guesthouse of the Three Harpers."

My face must have shown my discomfiture.

"Yes, I know of you—and of many other things that might surprise you. Ah, thank you, my loves!" On a low table of black marble that appeared just beside Gar'Dena, Aiessa, the dark-haired girl, set down a tray bearing a steaming urn made of beaten gold and encrusted with emeralds. Alongside the urn sat three gold cups and a painted, gold-rimmed plate piled high with slices of hot bread, dripping with butter. Little Aimee accompanied her sister. The girl with golden curls felt for the edge of the plate and set a crystal pot of honey beside it, at the same time knocking over the stack of cups. She giggled as she righted them again. Hardly any time had passed since the tall Arielle had left to finish her baking.

Gar'Dena was the youngest of the Preceptors, so Bareil had told us, appointed by the Prince D'Marte, D'Natheil's father, only weeks before D'Marte's death in battle. Neither the Preceptors nor other Dar'Nethi kept secret their opinions that the massive gem-worker had been appointed because of his wealth, not for his power or wisdom. Even in my exhausted confusion, I had already begun to doubt that.

I accepted a cup of hot, fragrant saffria from the urn. Aimee offered Paulo a cup and a small plate heaped with bread. The boy, slumped and listless at my feet, did not seem to notice. I nudged him. When he looked up at the rosy-cheeked Aimee, his eyes grew wide, his mouth dropped open, and his hands remained limp in his lap. I nudged him again and nodded at the plate and the cup. He shook off his paralysis and took them, but began to eat only after he had watched the giggling Dar'Nethi girl follow her older sister out of the room, passing right through a heavy brocade curtain without so much as parting it. Before Gar'Dena patted his stomach and took up the conversation again, the mountain of bread was almost gone, and Paulo's eyes were glazed with bliss.

"Now," said the sorcerer, "I know why you're here, and I stand ready to aid you in your task."

"My task?" *Careful, careful, Seri,* I told myself. *These people are master deceivers.* I had to keep my wits about me.

He leaned forward, his broad face shining with sincerity like the full moon. "Oh, madam, would that I could conjure your trust as quickly as my daughter does her baking. Our time is so short."

"Time for what?"

"To rescue your son from the clutches of the Lords. To bring him out of Zhev'Na before he is corrupted. He must not be there when he comes of age."

"How do you know he's in Zhev'Na? He was in your council chamber not an hour ago."

"He was returned there as soon as . . . the disaster occurred. They would not linger in Avonar in such uncertainty. It would risk their plan."

"You speak in riddles, sir. Do you mean to tell me that you—the Preceptors—knew my son was captive of the Zhid and you did nothing?"

"What could be done? It is not forbidden for anyone, Dar'Nethi or Dulcé or Zhid, or even one of your own kind to come before the Dar'Nethi Preceptorate and make petition, ask hearing, or bring grievance. If someone brings a boy to us, we cannot say, 'We think you come from Zhev'Na, therefore you get no hearing.' We claim that our world will be made whole again, and that all will be healed and live in peace—and when he says he brings the son of D'Arnath's Heir—we listen."

"This makes no sense."

Gar'Dena grimaced. "We could not wrest the boy from his protector while they stood supplicant in the council chamber—especially as the boy remained with the man willing. The child was not afraid and made no attempt to distance himself. It is not possible for us to trespass our laws in such a case. The Lords know our traditions and our scruples, you see, and use them very effectively against us. But we had to confirm the boy's identity. Our Prince was . . . as you saw. We must have an Heir, and even those of us who suspect the identity of the boy's protectors were powerless to change—"

"But you *knew*. Once he had passed your cursed 'test,' why didn't you take him from Darzid?" I was no longer cold, not inside, not outside. "How could you let the despicable man take him back to the Lords?"

"Because this Darzid is not a man!" The floor rumbled with the same fury that had shaken the council chamber, but his anger was not directed at me. He gripped his hands together until I thought he must crush his own fingers. "We do not know who or what he is any more than you do. We know that he has at least one ally among the Preceptors. Even if we were willing to endanger the child's life when we know so little, we dared not challenge the Lords in the very heart of Avonar. This city is our last defense. This battle must take place outside these walls. Better to appear stupid and corrupt and ineffective. Let them think they have all the time they need. And that, madam, is where you come in."

"I don't understand."

He released his hands, his shoulders sagged, and a woeful

grin worked its way through his oversized gloom. "We planned to find you. A blessing to be sure that you dropped into my not inconsiderable lap—though we were fortunate to keep you from being divided among our covetous Preceptors."

"I wouldn't have gone with Exeget. I'd kill him first."

He sighed deeply. Gar'Dena did nothing small. "Such was not an unguessable reaction, madam, though killing Exeget would not be at all simple. But since we so fortunately avoided that particular ugliness, we wish to proceed. There is a plan and help to be had if you will accept it. If you consent, we will send you to Zhev'Na to rescue your son."

Astonishment and anger would not release me as yet. "I still don't understand. If you're so worried about my son, then why, in the name of all gods, didn't you send someone to rescue him weeks ago? You don't need me."

Gar'Dena's good humor went the way of his rage, leaving only a serious intelligence that one might more properly expect from a Preceptor of Gondai. "Because we cannot send a Dar'Nethi. The rescuer must be someone from your world. You will see why as we prepare. You were the most reasonable choice and came highly recommended. Yet, we had to judge you for ourselves—to make sure that you were not overwhelmed by our world, that you were not rash or stupid and likely to make things worse instead of better. When we saw how carefully you moved, we came to believe you would do. And too, our plan was not possible before tonight. Treacherous waters must be carefully navigated. That's all I can tell you. To say more would compromise our plan."

At last I began to listen. He waited patiently as I tried to think. "Was this Dassine's design?" I said.

"Dassine knew nothing of this plan. But he would agree that we have no other possibility."

"Who are the others included in this 'we'?"

"You will not know that." A finger of anticipation tickled my spine.

"Then tell me, Master Gar'Dena—did Karon know of your plan? Was his action . . . the knife . . . what he did . . .

was that part of your plan? Did you drive him mad or did he consent to it? I need to know."

Paulo shot a glance at me, curiosity flashing across his dirty, tear-streaked face.

The big man closed the doors of his broad face and laid one ponderous fist upon his heart. "Of course the Prince's death was not part of our plan. We had hoped— But the examination was ruinous. We thought we had shown him alternatives . . . convinced him . . . Ah, Vasrin Shaper, I cannot speak of the matter. His death is a grievous blow to Gondai and our people. If we cannot retrieve his son, we are undone."

Why could I not feel Karon's loss, even after such sober speech as this? Gar'Dena's voice was near breaking. I had seen the knife and the blood and the terrible wound. I had seen Karon fall, and with the others watched life desert his pain-ravaged face. But in that precious instant we were together, he was not mad and not desperate. And if he was not mad, then I could not believe he would ever, in the farthest extremity, take his own life.

So I put him away for a while, laid aside my grief and regret and mourning. I only whispered an answer to the sweet echo that lingered in my head. *You have no need for forgiveness. I embrace your life, beloved, all that you were and all that you remain.* "Tell me your plan, Preceptor."

CHAPTER 24

Karon

The Dulcé say that life is a tapestry, the warp and weft laid down by Vasrin Shaper—the female half of the duality that is our god—and we who exist in the world are assigned our position and shading to perfect its marvelous pattern. The Valloreans say that life is a garden, each of us planted in our proper row so as to nurture or shelter those who grow beside us, or to wind ourselves about each other in mutual companionship or mutual destruction. But I think we Dar'-Nethi have it right, that life is a path laid down as you walk it and taken up behind you as quickly as you pass. That is why it does no good to look back and say "if only . . ." for where you have traveled is already unclear, and it does no good to say "tomorrow . . ." for where you are going is not yet laid down. Better to savor each moment as if it were the first or the last. Perhaps we've come to this conclusion because that is the source of our power . . . the savoring.

I had never considered myself a remarkable man, but as I sat before the Dar'Nethi Preceptorate, knowing what I did of my own life and contemplating what I was about to do, I believed I could say truly that no experience in the history of two worlds had rivaled my own. That of D'Arnath himself, perhaps—the sorcerer and king become warrior, powerful enough to build a link between worlds, reverenced so truly by his people that his successors never took his own title, but considered their highest honor to be named his Heir. But even D'Arnath had lived only one life. I had lived two, each of them twice through, once in the proper order of time as all men do and once in memory. And for ten years I had been properly dead, my orphaned soul linked to an artifact of power—a small black crystal pyramid—by the enchantments of an audacious Healer. And next . . . I could not think of next.

My trembling was quite real on that occasion, both as a result of what I had been through and in anticipation of its sequel, and when I said, "Ten breaths more and I will be unable to stop screaming," I believed that to be the literal truth.

I had known I would have to follow Dassine's instructions to give myself to the Preceptorate. All I could offer the Lady Seriana and her companions were a bit of power and a strong sword arm, and neither appeared sufficient to their needs. The problem of the child was too complex, and Dassine, the one who understood such complexities, was dead. My mentor's legacy was my life, and the only thing he had ever asked in return was my trust. I could not refuse him.

Once I had decided on my course as we sat in the Guesthouse of the Three Harpers, I considered what to tell the lady, but I couldn't think what she would want to hear from me. How stupid I was. How blind. She was so angry, and I thought it was because I couldn't be what she expected, because I kept falling off the edge of the world in front of her. And so, in the end, I said nothing but to my madrissé. I abandoned the lady, walked into the grand commard of Avonar, and told a sleepy baker's boy my name.

Dassine had not said to keep my going secret, and I hoped the crowd might provide some measure of safety. It became a much larger spectacle than I had envisioned. We Dar'Nethi are a romantic people, much given to ceremonies and rituals that draw out our emotions. Over that long night I had also decided to surrender myself to Madyalar instead of Exeget. Our meeting at Dassine's house had left me with a good impression of her.

"Come with me, my lord," said Madyalar, proceeding briskly between the columns of the portico. Her shoes clicked on the flagstones. The palace gates clanged shut behind us.

"Pause a while, good lady," said Exeget, spitting venom as he held his ground by the gates. "Despite this charming little pageant we have just witnessed, the protocols of the Preceptorate are not suspended. I, as head of the Preceptorate, will carry out the first examination of the petitioner."

"Master Exeget is correct," said Ce'Aret.

"The Prince surrendered himself to *me* and no one else," said Madyalar. "All saw it. Come, my lord." She grabbed my arm and dragged me toward a side door, tucked away under the portico beside the great entry doors.

"You overreach, Madyalar," shouted Gar'Dena. "The subject's choice has no bearing. I think that Ce'Aret, as the eldest . . ."

As Bareil had warned me, presenting myself to Madyalar instead of Exeget had caused an uproar. Each of them chimed in, wrangling over prerogatives and precedence. Meanwhile I was barefoot and shirtless, shivering, and faced with the undignified prospect of being unable to wipe my dripping nose because my hands were still bound with their confounded ribbon. And truly, there was no dispute.

"I submitted to Madyalar," I said, causing all of them to stop in mid-argument and stare at me. For me to interrupt or to speak at all was quite improper, according to Dar'-Nethi ritual. "She will determine what is best, else I will determine some other way to accomplish my purposes." I wrenched my hands free of the silver ribbon and used it to blot my nose.

All discussion was immediately ended. Being the Heir of D'Arnath had its privileges.

Madyalar was pleased, of course, and Exeget was livid, which pleased me. He bowed. "I leave you to the viper, my lord." I thought his teeth might turn to powder from his grinding them.

Madyalar led me on a long trek through the passages of the east wing, the part of the palace given over to the Preceptors who desired work space in the most secure building in the city. Her lectorium was a businesslike chamber, windowless and chilly, as were most such workrooms devoted solely to magical pursuits. Flasks and boxes of potions and powders were neatly arranged on her worktables. Small chests and painted cabinets that would hold bits of glass and metal, stones and gems were set square against the dark-colored walls. She gave me a green linen tunic and a pair of sandals to put on, as my shirt and boots had not found their way through the palace gates with us. Then she motioned me to a chair facing her across a low table.

"I'm gratified, but curious as to your course of action this morning, D'Natheil. After so long away and so soon after your mentor's death, to submit for examination seems strange. I presume you understand the depths to which you have humiliated Exeget. We all know of the unease between you, but this . . . it's most likely irreconcilable. Why me?"

"I believe you are honorable and care deeply about the future of Avonar and its people," I said. "Exeget is not and does not."

She dipped her head in acknowledgment.

"And I'm in somewhat of an awkward position."

"Go on."

"Dassine sent me to you—well not to you precisely, but to the Preceptorate."

"Dassine?" She jumped up from her chair. Her tone was sharp as a razor knife. "I understood his wounds were mortal."

"I was with him when he died."

She stepped back a bit and put her hands inside the rainbow folds of her robe. "What did he tell you?"

"Only that if certain things were to come about, I was to surrender myself to the Preceptorate for examination. No other explanation. I hoped you might understand what he meant."

She considered my words briefly. Then she sat down again. "Dassine and I were good friends, not intimate, as I'm sure you know, but allies. We had . . . business . . .

together. Perhaps if you were to tell me of these 'certain things' to which you refer . . ."

"A boy has been taken by the Zhid. Dassine said that if the child was taken to Zhev'Na, then I had to do this. The child must be rescued."

She threw back her tousled gray hair and laughed uproariously, though her laughter seemed shallow and out of proportion to her amusement. "Is that all? It sounds just like Dassine. 'I've taken the Heir and kept him hidden for ten years, letting him out only long enough to preserve the Bridge, and, oh, by the way, tell him how to rescue an unknown boy from Zhev'Na.' Tell me, my lord, what is it you want from me? Are we playing games here? I'm not a fool."

What did I want? Advice? Help? I didn't understand her laughter, but then she probably couldn't imagine the limits of my knowledge. Dassine had said I must go to the Preceptorate for examination, not for help. He had trained me well to listen to him, and he would have chosen his words carefully, knowing he had so few left. I had to believe that whatever I needed to know would be revealed by the examination—even if it was only that I was too damaged to continue.

"I wish to proceed with the examination, but I want Exeget to have no part in it."

Pleasure suffused her wide, plain face. "You realize that in the examination I will enter your mind. You'll not be able to refuse my questions or tell me anything but truth. Is that your wish?"

"Yes . . . I suppose so."

Everything happened very quickly after that. Madyalar unlocked a small mahogany cabinet sitting on her worktable and pulled out two crystal flasks. One contained a liquid of such deep red as to be almost black, and the other a substance that was clear, but thick like honey when she poured it into a silver goblet. She measured the dark liquid carefully and poured it into the same goblet, then left it for a moment while she turned down the lamps and struck a fire in a small pottery brazier that sat on the low table between us. A handful of gray powder dropped into the flames snapped and sparkled and gave off a heavy scent—agrina, an herb which enhanced one's receptivity to many enchantments. Another, subtler fragrance, almost undetectable, wafted behind the sharp, pungent odor of the agrina. Cennethar, I suspected, a powerful agent used to relax control of the muscles. From the heart of the little fire a thin trail of smoke twined its way toward me. Madyalar motioned me to move closer and breathe it in.

I almost changed my mind. Bareil had told me that Dassine trusted none of the Preceptors, yet here was I, with wounds not yet healed from earlier battles, ready to expose them to an untried physician. Leaving myself so vulnerable . . . The cennethar unnerved me. But if I were to refuse, what else would I do? Lacking any answer to that question, I released my held breath and took another, allowing Madyalar's smoke to fill my lungs.

The fumes soon had me light-headed. I was so tired . . . stupid to come after a night without sleep. I had needed quiet time to think, and so had offered to watch while my companions slept. Once I had come to my resolve, I'd wanted to get on with it—before the Lady Seriana could wake and talk me out of it or leave me a voiceless idiot once again. But here in Madyalar's dark study, watching the rising flames and breathing the choking smoke, I felt soggy and drowsy. I tried to tell Madyalar that we might better wait until I got some sleep, but I couldn't get the words out.

She stood in front of me. "Manglyth," she said, holding out the silver goblet, "the potion we use for examination."

The two liquids had not mixed. The dark one hung suspended in the clear, so that the drink looked like an egg with a dark red yolk, encased in the silver shell of the goblet. *Drink it all,* Madyalar motioned, holding the cup to my lips. The clear liquid was icy cold and sweet, coating my tongue and my throat, but the dark one boiled away the sweet coating and scalded my very bones. Panicked, I wanted to push it away, but my hands lay on the arms of the chair like tide-dropped seaweed, and the big woman relentlessly poured the rest of her potion into me. Enough of the sweet liquid remained in the cup to soothe my mouth and throat a bit, leaving them throbbing and sore, but not blistered. As for the rest of me, flesh and thought and memory were turned inside out, exposed to anyone who should desire to inspect them.

"Uncomfortable, I know"—I heaved and gasped for breath, unable to move to help myself—"but necessary. Now we begin. Your secrets . . . Dassine's secrets . . . now belong to me, as do you, in a sense. You cannot imagine. . . . And to have you present yourself to me willingly!" Madyalar sat opposite me once again, her expression that of a moneylender introduced to a wastrel baron. Not at all motherly. I began to suspect that I had made a dreadful mistake.

Quickly, brutally, Madyalar wrenched open the gates of my mind. No sound disturbed her chamber save the snapping of the flames in the brazier. Rather, her questions appeared directly inside my head. Though I could formulate my responses, she retrieved them in the same way, with no artifice of voice or limitation of words to obscure their truth. I could neither withhold an answer nor could I lie.

Came her question: *Who is the child in Zhev'Na?*

Came my answer: *He is the son of Dassine's friend, a mundane child stolen from his home five days ago.*

A mundane child! Why have the Zhid taken him?

I do not know.

And what is your interest in the child?

Dassine instructed me to find him. He said if the boy was taken to Zhev'Na before I found him, then I should surrender myself to the Preceptorate for examination.

Nothing more?

Nothing more.

And you are accustomed to taking direction from Dassine without understanding any more than this?

Yes.

Why is that?

I do not know.

She was puzzled, and I couldn't blame her, but I was unable to volunteer any information. I could only answer her questions. She rubbed her lips with an idle finger.

What have you been doing with Dassine in these past months since your return from the Bridge?

I have been regaining my memory.

Your memory . . . lost? You did not know . . . what? The deeds of a night? The happenings of a week?

I knew nothing of myself.

Nothing! Did this happen when you walked the Bridge these few months ago?

Dassine said that whatever happened at the Bridge worsened damage that was done earlier.

From the first attempt, she said. *I knew it. So Dassine the Healer was restoring your memories. Fortunately for you, he was a talented man. And so now you are restored.*

I wasn't sure whether the last was a statement or a question, but as long as there was doubt, I was compelled to answer.

No.

Madyalar's eyes widened. *Not restored . . . How much of your memory is yet missing?*

A great deal is yet missing.

She proceeded to question me about many things: about Avonar, about my family, about Dassine and the Preceptorate and the life of the Dar'Nethi. Some things I knew. More I did not. It would have been clear to anyone that I was profoundly confused and dreadfully incomplete. No one would have called me mad, but of course she hadn't gotten to the heart of the matter as yet. She was shaking her head in exasperation at my lack of information, and she blurted out her opinion with her audible voice. "You're no more than a child, scarcely past infancy. Do you even know your own name?"

She must have sensed the ambivalence her question evoked in me, for she narrowed her gray eyes and blasted her question directly into my head. *Tell me . . . what is your true name?*

I knew what I should answer, even lost in the smoky haze and the fierce compulsions of the potion she had given me. If the purpose of the examination was to legitimize my position, then only one answer would do. But under the influence of manglyth, it was not possible to speak anything but the most absolute truth. *My name is Karon, eldest son of the Baron Mandille, Lord of Avonar, and his wife Nesei, a Singer.*

She jumped up from her chair. *What are you saying? Where is D'Natheil, Heir of D'Arnath?*

And of course, I couldn't lie about that either. *I am D'Natheil, Prince of Avonar, Heir of D'Arnath.*

How is this possible? Have you put an enchantment on yourself so that you can lie?

I do not lie, and I do not know how it is possible.

Who is this Mandille? We have no barons in Avonar.

My father inherited the title of baron and the sign of the ruler from his father, Bertrand. The title Baron, Lord of Avonar, was granted by order of King Dagobert of Valleor.

These names have no meaning to me. Was D'Marte not your father? Is Mandille another name for D'Marte?

D'Marte was my father. D'Marte and Mandille were not the same man.

This is madness. How can you have two fathers?

And that, of course, brought me to the familiar ground at the edge of the precipice. *Gods save me, I do not know how it is possible.*

Are you the Heir or are you not?

I am the true Heir of D'Arnath. Hold onto that, I told myself, until the cracks in the world disappear.

On and on she went, discovering everything I knew of my two lives, of the Preceptorate, of Dassine's work, and his murder. She constantly returned to questions about conspiracies of which I knew nothing, and of what I had done to preserve the Bridge in the human world, which I could not remember, and how I'd come to believe I was two persons. Each time she pushed me to the edge, I wanted to scream at her to stop before I lost my mind.

So you truly do not know how you—this Karon of Avonar, an Exile—first met with Dassine, or when?

No.

Perhaps Dassine was able to cross the Bridge to find you.

Astonishing that you don't know. Perhaps the real D'Natheil was killed four months ago, and Dassine has mind-altered an impostor. . . . No, I would see that. Perhaps you are D'Natheil, but truly mad.

"Fires of chaos!" As her words erupted into audible speech, she kicked aside a basket of cillia branches and stood glaring down at me, the dried pods, leaves, and twigs left in an untidy heap. "Insupportable! The beast and his 'private information.' " While I sat groggy, paralyzed, and half crazed, she waved her hands and yelled at me as if I were yet a third person who understood her anger. "He thinks to squeeze me out of this matter of the boy, and every time I get the upper hand, he laughs at me. I chance to hear news of his meeting with Dassine, but arrive too late to hear anything worthwhile. And now I'm given the opportunity to become an equal partner, only to discover that my prize is a madman who believes he is two persons at once, who can tell me nothing of the boy, nothing of the one called Darzid, nothing of why the two of them were rushed to Zhev'Na. And the only way to discover the truth is to bring in the very one I detest. Damn! Damn! Damn!"

Her irritation reduced to snarls and muttering, she flopped back into her chair and picked a small blue summoning stone from a bowl of them that sat on the table. A flick of her eyes, a mumbled word, and a press of her fingers, and she dropped the thumb-sized stone into the bowl of flame, where it cracked and sizzled and disappeared. Then she threw the bowl of blue stones across the room, creating a noisy shower of broken pottery and clattering pebbles on the tile floor. The last was *not* a part of the summoning enchantment. Drumming her fingers on the table, she glared at me through the thinning smoke as if I'd made the mess. She tossed another handful of the gray powder on the flames and waved the smoke my way. "A few moments' delay," she said, sourly. "You can be sure he'll be quick."

Only slowly did the complexities of her monologue sink into my fogged mind. But sink in they did, so that by the time her smirking partner/rival walked in, I knew it would be Exeget.

Had anyone ever been such a fool? If I could have summoned enough sense to feel anything, I would have been terrified. My mind open to Exeget . . . For three brutal years of my childhood, I had resisted him, and now, in the space of an hour, I had yielded the control he had always craved.

"Difficulties, you say? A single Preceptor attempting to examine the Heir—I would expect nothing else." *Gloating* would not be an exaggerated description of his demeanor.

Madyalar was spitting like a cat, but my mysteries were evidently compelling enough for her to put up with him. "I've never known anyone capable of untruth while under the influence of manglyth, yet the answers he gives are not possible."

"What has he said that is impossible?"

"That he is two persons at once, both D'Natheil and an Exile!"

"Vasrin's hand . . ." he said, softly. Never had I known Exeget to lose control far enough to swear, even in such mild form.

And so, we went through it all again. Exeget was an immensely more perceptive and precise interrogator, and, having been my mentor, he knew how to probe deep and touch the most private self . . . but only that of D'Natheil. He didn't know Karon at all.

By the time he was done with me, I was half insensible, able to grasp only bits and pieces of their discussion. Madyalar and Exeget had made some accommodation with the Lords of Zhev'Na. The boy had somehow changed the equation. Something I'd told Exeget had made clear to him why the child was important. Madyalar was frantic to know, as was I, but I could not stay awake long enough to hear it.

For whatever reason—perhaps in exchange for knowledge of his great discovery—Madyalar released me into Exeget's custody. Muddleheaded and nauseated from manglyth, smoke, and the bile of self-recrimination, I was half carried, half dragged through passages and cold air and a portal. At last I was deposited on a pallet that was too short for me. One bleary-eyed glance told me that I lay in the same room where I'd slept for three of the most wretched years of a sorry childhood. Exeget's house—the Precept House of the Dar'Nethi. And yet, as I collapsed into complete insensibility, a soft and not unkind voice spoke in my head. *Sleep well, my lord Prince. You'll need it.*

CHAPTER 25

The bed felt like plate armor, and I was tangled in a choking knot of clothes and blankets, yet I was not at all inclined to move. If I stayed very still, then perhaps these slight pricks of wakefulness would dull into oblivion, and I could sleep the day around. Across my mind flitted the anxious notion that Dassine would soon shake my shoulder, but even after I dismissed that fantasy, the whisper of his name in my half-sleep pulled me from the domain of dreams across the border to the land of waking. Dassine was a week dead. But someone was in the room with me. I could sense his breath, his pulse, the faint warmth and disturbance in the air that told me another living person was present.

"Come, come, D'Natheil, you're too big to hide from me any more. You were never good at it."

Was my lethargy a result of his enchantments?

"More likely the residue of the cennethar. You are free to move and speak as you wish. You will excuse me if I keep a slight watch on your thoughts, however. Your first impulse has always been to violence." One might have thought he was biting down on a nettle.

I sat up. The puffy-faced man with thinning hair sat in the small, bare room's only chair. He rested his chin on one of his perfectly manicured hands and smiled, an expression as void of mirth as the room was of comfort.

"Who would have thought we'd be back here together?" he said. "Yet, you're not really the one I knew, the incorrigible little beast who spat upon the most glorious heritage in the history of all worlds. You are someone else entirely."

"That child still lives in me, and I remember everything of his time in your charge."

"How do you know that the memory Dassine returned to you is accurate? Perhaps he colored what he gave you with his view of the world and of me."

"No, Preceptor. I lived every moment of those years twice over. I knew Dassine as I'll never know any other man, and he didn't hate you half so much as I do."

"Yet hate is quite alien to your present nature. How do you reconcile it?"

Search as I would, I could find no answer to that.

"As I thought. A difficult portion Dassine has left you." He tapped his fingertips together rapidly. "Well, look at it this way: You were a child, and there were—and are—many things you don't understand. If you are to survive what is to come, you must put aside your childish view. You must accept that nothing—nothing—you believe is immutable."

"And what is to come?"

"First I'll let you eat and refresh yourself a bit"—he nodded to the boxlike table where sat a tray laden with food, drink, a pile of towels, and a green porcelain basin from which steam was rising—"and then I will restore the remainder of your lost life. Unfortunately events do not leave us the time Dassine had. We shall have to proceed a bit more brutally . . . and *not* because I will enjoy it."

"And if I refuse?"

He leaned forward, his cheeks flushed ever so slightly, his narrow eyes alight. "I saw your struggle when we pushed you to the boundaries of your knowledge. However much you despise me, I cannot believe you would refuse, even if you knew you would die in the next moment."

He was almost right. "I would do anything to retrieve what I've lost except take it from Dassine's murderer."

Exeget smiled scornfully and settled back in the hard little chair. "Have you unraveled nothing of this mystery? I'll not attempt to resolve for you the bothersome inconsistencies in your view of Dassine's death. But while I leave you to your refreshment, I want you to think about this: Dassine sent you to me. Not to Madyalar, not to any of the others. You know Dassine chose words carefully: *Give yourself to the Preceptorate for examination. Defenseless.* If your childish indignation had not been clouding your judgment, only one possible course would have presented itself—surrendering to the Head of the Preceptorate. To me."

I dismissed his jibes as quickly as he left the room. But as I took full advantage of the hot water and the mound of bread and cheese and cold meat, I could not but be drawn back to the most illogical aspect of Dassine's murder: Bareil knew nothing of the abducted child. Why would Exeget, intending to murder Dassine, have given his rival information of significance? Ever convinced of his own superiority, Exeget would not stoop to taunt a victim.

And, of course, his logic echoed my own uneasy thoughts, that I had interpreted Dassine's command according to my own desires . . . because I was afraid. . . .

Exeget returned an hour later, smirking at the broken crockery in the corner of my room. "So is it yea or nay? Remember, *your* sanity is in question, not mine."

I could not force myself to answer.

"Ahhh . . ." he growled. "When we are done, I'll put your own knife in your hand and bare my neck to you. Will that satisfy your bloodthirsty inclinations? Do we work at this or not?"

I jerked my head. He seemed to understand. "You'll need this." He tossed a white robe into my hands, his composure regained. "When you're ready, come to the lectorium. I'm sure you remember the way." Exeget, my despised enemy.

Yes, I remembered the way to the cold and barren workroom where he had tried so brutishly to shove the practices of sorcery into my nine-year-old head. Muttering oaths, I stripped, donned the soft wool robe, and padded barefoot down the stairs.

When I entered the low-ceilinged chamber, the circle of candles was already alight. The dark stone columns and walls, void of decoration, seemed to swallow the candlelight.

"How is it you know of all this?" I said, waving my

hand to encompass the luminous circle. Dassine had always claimed that his work with me was unique, unknown to any other Dar'Nethi, that I must follow his strictures if I ever wanted to be whole. Though Exeget's lectorium was cool, deep in the rock below Avonar, a drip of sweat trickled down my tailbone.

"This is not the time for questions. Take your place." He held out his hand for my robe.

Self-conscious as I had never been with Dassine, I gave it over and sat myself naked on the bare stone inside the circle. *Fool! Fool!* screamed my untrusting self.

Exeget tossed my robe onto the floor behind him with a snort, whether at my modesty or my fear, I couldn't tell. But as the light grew, insinuating itself into my head and my lungs and the pores of my flesh, he spoke softly in my mind, *Do not be afraid. I'll not allow you to drown.*

And so did I take up my life where it had been interrupted five days—or fifteen years—before, and on that very night, in the room where Exeget had so often railed at me for being soft and stupid and unworthy of my name, did I travel once again to the gracious house called Windham and meet my darling Seri in the freshness of her wide-eyed young womanhood. Her awakening intelligence soared, and she argued and laughed and studied, revealing to my Dar'-Nethi soul a universe of marvels. We walked in her cousin Martin's gardens and played chess in his drawing rooms, and when the blazing hearth of Windham faded into Exeget's circle of candlelight, I cried out, "No! Let me go back! For love of the Creator, let me go back."

"A moment. Drink this; it will sustain you." Someone poured some thick and sour liquid down my throat, and before the blaze in my eyes had dissipated enough that I could see whose hands held the cup, I was embracing the fire once again.

Every day a delight in her friendship, not daring to think of anything more. We all knew she was meant for Evard and swore that such a marriage would be like confining the lightning to a cage. Martin warned me that there could be no future for the affection and regard I tried so vigorously and so ineptly to hide, for he knew my secret and the dangers it entailed. I was a sorcerer, doomed to run, to hide, and almost certainly to burn.

How long did I journey that first time in Exeget's room? Three more times was I drawn back to the circle of fire, where I blindly gulped the murky liquid as a drowning man gulps air; three more times was I sent back again to Leire, to the happiest days I had ever known. The fifth time I came back a voice protested behind the roaring of the flames. "Enough, Master. You'll kill him."

"We'll *all* be dead or worse if we cannot finish in time. But I suppose you're right. We daren't push it farther at first. But things will get no easier as we go."

Hands, two pairs of them, drew me to my feet and wrapped my robe about me. I could not yet see for the blinding glare that filled my eyes, but as the two half walked, half carried me to my room, my senses emerged from their muffling and began to record the world around me once again. A crashing thunder growing in my ears could be traced to the tapping of a breeze-shifted branch on the window, the searing colors that soon shredded my eyes were but the muted grays of Exeget's halls, and the vicious claws that must surely be raking bloody gashes in my arms were four gentle hands as they laid me on my pallet.

"Quickly now, to sleep," said the grating voice, and the hellish cacophony of my jangled senses was deadened by the blessed touch of his hand.

In an hour, no more than two, they roused me to begin it all again.

Dassine's regimen had been nothing compared to that of Exeget. I knew no day or night, no hour or season, no word of comfort or argument, no words at all in that time. I did not eat, only drank the vile mess that kept me living and embraced the darkness when they pulled me from the circle of fire, blind and deaf and numb. I lived only as Karon, in the past, and, of course, it was not long until I understood what horror awaited me beyond my knowing.

Dead. Oh, gods, my dear friends . . . Martin, Tanager,

Julia . . . I had left them to die because I would not compromise my gift to alter the paths of fate. And my wife and son abandoned. I had abdicated my responsibilities for some Dar'Nethi ideal and left Seri to face the horror all alone. The experience of my own death, the relived torment and despair and the ten years of disembodied darkness were as nothing beside my betrayal of my friends, my wife, and my child. And Dassine had brought me back because he believed I had some holy revelation that could save the world. What kind of coward was I?

The candlelight faded; darkness and silence enshrouded me. Was the restoration of three lost souls—those three pitiable Zhid I had healed after the fight with Seri's brother at the Gate—worth everything that had happened? I could see no other return from all the pain and sorrow.

Oh, Seri, forgive me. How I understand your anger . . .

"You cannot hide forever, D'Natheil. Three days it's been since we completed our work."

The room was dark, though not as dark as my soul. He spoke softly, as if unsure of the state of my hearing. But I would not wake to Exeget. I burrowed back into emptiness.

The next time it was someone else. Hands rolled me to my back and stuffed pillows under my head. "My lord Prince, you must live. You are so much needed. Here, drink this." He pressed a cup into my shaking hands and helped me lift it to my lips. Brandy, woody and old, the smoothest I had ever tasted, yet I thought it might burn a hole through my empty stomach. I coughed and gagged and heaved, and my invisible companion helped me to sit up straight. My skin was slick with sweat.

"Holy stars!" It seemed like half a month until I caught a breath.

"It is fine, is it not? My best vintage ever."

"Bareil?"

"The same, my lord. May I make a light?"

"If it's necessary." With the glimmering candle flame came the intrusion of the world and all the burdens I had shed in my days of oblivion. "Oh, gods, Bareil . . ." I bent forward and dragged at my hair with my fingers, as if enough pain might make reality vanish again.

"I know, my lord. It is difficult. I wish it could have been slower, easier for you."

"You were there? You were the other hands?"

"Yes, my lord. Master Dassine had given Master Exeget a directive with which to summon me and command my assistance. And when I saw what he was doing with you—completing Master Dassine's work—I was happy to be of service. I hope it did not contradict your wishes."

"No." I pushed shaggy, damp hair from my brow and felt several weeks' growth of beard bristling on my chin. "Thank you."

"You must eat, even though you may not feel like it yet. I'll bring something. I've scarcely managed to get anything down you in all these weeks. And, my lord, Master Exeget is desperate to speak with you. Though he asked me to wake you, he waits just outside."

"Exeget . . ." What was I to think of him?

"It is astonishing, is it not? I was terrified when I saw you in his power. But my lord, I must tell you that never was Master Dassine so careful in his work. I have watched many of the Dar'Nethi masters work, and none other could have brought you through this as he did."

"Give me an hour."

Bareil bowed and left the room. Huddled in the corner of my pallet, I forced myself to consider the state of the world. At what I guessed to be the precise expiration of my hour, the door opened and my old enemy sat himself in the chair in the corner. He began examining his hands, turning them this way and that in the weak light, showing no sign of agitation at my delay. He would sit so all night before confessing his urgency.

"I don't know whether to thank you or not," I said, conceding the minor struggle in the hunger for understanding.

His hands came to rest in his lap, one laid calmly upon the other. "I did what was necessary. I don't expect you to thank me. Upon full consideration, you will most likely decide this is only another crime to add to my account."

"You never told me what was to come after."

"It would have made no sense at the time and may not yet. It depends on whether you were able to analyze the present situation while you lived your life again or in these past days as you lay here in your self-made tomb."

"While I journeyed, I was wholly in the past. While I lay here, I was trying to bury it all again. But in the hour just gone, I've put a few things together."

"Do you understand about the child? Who he is?"

"Yes." Seri's son. My son.

"And you see that because of your . . . unique . . . circumstances—this thing Dassine has done to you—your son is the next Heir of D'Arnath?"

"I guessed it."

Exeget's dark eyes blazed far brighter than my candle. "Do you have any concept of what it means if the Heir comes of age in the hands of the Lords?"

"The Three will control the Bridge."

"Not only the Bridge, but all the powers of D'Arnath. Only Dassine and I, of all Dar'Nethi, ever grasped their full extent. D'Arnath was able to create the Bridge because he could manipulate the forces of the Breach, forces which are the antithesis of order, the bits left over from the creation of worlds because they were defective, too odd or corrupt or broken to be included in the weaving of the universe. Before the Catastrophe, this corruption was dispersed, incohesive. But the workings of the Three, the immense increases in power they believed they created by their superior cleverness, were in fact drawing upon these broken bits and gathering them together, until, in their last disastrous working, the Breach was formed and the corruption trapped within it.

"Only D'Arnath's anointed Heir inherits his control over the Breach. One of our race at a time. The universe cannot seem to support two with such power. And so, if the Lords corrupt the Heir and control him—become one with him as they are one with each other—then, on the day he comes of age, they will be able to command the legions of chaos. None will be able to stand against them."

"The test of which you spoke with Madyalar—it is the test of parentage?"

"Yes. You are D'Natheil. Your blood and bone and spirit are indisputable witness to it. You are also the father of the child. Your wife knows it; now you know it. He is Dar'Nethi. There is no other possibility. He and this man Darzid were able to cross the Bridge. Do you understand what that requires? Yes, the way was left open, but only the boy's bloodlines—your own deeds in the mundane world bear witness to unquestionably powerful bloodlines—and whatever gifts this Darzid brings to bear could enable them to cross so easily. The man knows the boy is your son. We must assume he also knows something of what has been done to you, for he has exposed his own abilities and sympathies in order to bring the child to the Lords. Which means the Lords know the boy's heritage, as well. If you and the boy undergo the test of parentage before the Preceptorate, the boy will be proved the son of D'Arnath's Heir and must therefore be acknowledged as your successor."

I fought my way through the confusion. "Then why—if you are indeed what you wish me to believe—why, in the name of all that lives, did you return my memory? If you had left me the way I was, or driven me mad with it—not a long or difficult road as you saw—or if you had killed me, the test of parentage would fail."

His shoulders relaxed a bit, and he sighed as will a teacher who has just heard the first rudimentary evidence of progress from a recalcitrant student. "If no Heir is competent to sit for the test of his child or to name a new successor, then the Preceptorate must decide whether there is some other living descendant of D'Arnath. The only way to test a person is to send him or her onto the Bridge and see what transpires. We cannot allow what happened to you when you were twelve to happen again. We have no Dassine to make us a new and better man from a broken child. So we must keep both you and your son whole if it is possible."

How could this man be Exeget? Why had he not felt this way when I was a child?

Evidently he was still monitoring my thoughts. "I did not vote to send you onto the Bridge when you came of age. Rather, I tried my best to stop it. There was no possibility you could survive the attempt."

Nothing you believe is immutable. . . . "Perhaps if I'd received better teaching."

He waved a hand in dismissal. "I had to discover what you were. Many in Avonar said you were touched by the Lords, destined, even at nine years of age, to be their tool. If you were, I had to know. If you were not, then you would survive and be the stronger for it. My purpose was not to make you love me."

"And what was the truth?"

"I don't know. You were sent to the Bridge at twelve, and it almost destroyed you. Your soul was twisted beyond repair. My surmise is that the Lords had indeed reached you."

The room was so cold. My head throbbed, and my hands would not stop shaking. I gathered a blanket around my shoulders. "I don't know what to believe. You sent my son and his abductor to Zhev'Na. How do you know so much about all this?"

I hadn't thought Exeget could look any more disagreeable, but his smile could have wilted a dead lily. "I am the man you know. You just don't know everything. Nor did Dassine until the days before he died. Nor do those who lurk in Zhev'Na, believing I am the most faithful of servants, who has sold his soul to preserve the remnants of his power, and who so diligently carries out their plans to destroy his world and his people."

Logic and history forbade belief. "You violated the madris, commanded Baglos, your madrissé, to kill me." Seri had prevented the foolish Dulcé from poisoning me when Dassine had sent me across the Bridge to prevent its destruction, and the other preceptors tried to trade my life for the safety of Avonar.

"That was an act of desperation. I didn't trust Dassine after his sojourn in the Wastes, and I didn't know what he'd done to you. The D'Natheil I knew could never have succeeded in the task that had to be done. As long as the

Bridge exists, the world has hope. I believed you would destroy it. And so I believed you had to die. Thankfully, that was not necessary."

"And Madyalar . . ."

"Madyalar has served the Lords since before you were born. Happily for us, she is stupid and the Lords know it."

"You told her that the boy is my son."

"She would have learned it from her mentors eventually. There's no point in hiding what will be known anyway. It's how I have survived. For that same reason I sent the boy and his captor on their way and have convinced the other Preceptors that he is safely tucked away with trustworthy friends of mine. Lacking sufficient power to prevent the Lords' hold on the boy, I appear to aid them. Meanwhile, I bide my time."

"So what are we to do?" Whether or not I could accept his honesty seemed superfluous. I wasn't going to be able to help anyone. I couldn't wrestle a bird. "I'm in no condition—"

"—to fight? On the contrary, your condition is perfect. It's one reason we must move quickly. You are in shambles, yet quite competent to take part in the test of parentage. When the Preceptors examine you, they'll see the truth."

"No use putting off what will happen anyway."

"Exactly. The boy will be proved. The Lords will think they've won."

"My life will not be worth much after that."

"Also true. But we will control the situation. As you said, no use putting off what will happen anyway. I'm sorry, my Prince. . . ." And then he proceeded to tell me his plan, and how it was I would have to die.

CHAPTER 26

Gerick

"Why did he kill himself?" I asked. "If he hates us so much, why wouldn't he fight? What was wrong with him?"

Darzid paced up and down my sitting room. His eyes flashed red—true ruby red—right in the middle of the black. "He was mad. A coward who could not face his own disintegration."

I didn't see how a coward could do such a thing to himself, but perhaps if he was mad . . . "I don't understand him at all. There was something—"

There's no need for you to understand, said Parven. *This is only a momentary diversion.* The Lords were crowding each other in my head. Ziddari's anger hung inside me like a stomachache.

The fools, to allow him to have a weapon at hand! That was Notole.

"I didn't know what to do. It wasn't like I expected." I wanted them to explain things.

I knew about Avonar. It was one of the soft, beautiful places—D'Arnath's place, where his Heir guarded the Bridge he had made to corrupt the world where I was born. The man who greeted us when we stepped through the magical portal into someone's study looked soft, too, and was almost bald. Ziddari had told me that this man was a secret ally of the Lords. "A useful man, one who hates well. While you should never truly trust them, those like Exeget are worthy of an alliance, because you can always predict what they will do." Ziddari had also told me that neither Exeget nor the Lords' other allies in Avonar knew that Darzid the Exile was truly the Lord Ziddari, and that he planned to keep it that way a while longer.

The soft-looking man inspected me rudely. "Astonishing," he said, touching my ear. "He is almost not recognizable as the same child. And I see he has found favor with the Lords. Matters progress quickly."

"Gerick knows his place in the worlds and embraces it with courage and determination," said Darzid. "The Lords of Zhev'Na take his words seriously. Indeed, I would not like to stand between him and the one on whom he plans to wreak his sweet vengeance."

"His opportunity is at hand," said Exeget. "Once the boy is proved, we will hand over the Prince. He's half mad. Only the audacious fool Dassine would think of cramming the scraps of two souls into one mind. Now as to the boy . . ."

Exeget wanted to "examine" me in some way before the test of parentage, but Darzid refused. They argued about it for a long time. Parven had instructed me to be silent while in Avonar so that no Dar'Nethi could sneak into my head, so Darzid did all the talking. I trusted him to watch out for me. Our interests were the same. Our enemies were the same . . . the Prince . . . my father. The Dar'Nethi.

While Darzid and Exeget talked, I wandered around the room, looking at all the things. Shelves and long worktables held flasks and tins, packets and bundles, measuring instruments and glass lenses, small brass mechanisms of all kinds, and a hundred other interesting things.

At least a thousand books were stacked on the shelves, as well. I ran my fingers over the bindings. A few were written in Leiran. Most in the language of this world. The longer I looked at them, the more I understood. I had realized several weeks before that I no longer used the language of Leire. Even before I knew that I was living in another world, without even realizing I was doing it, I had started speaking the Dar'Nethi language. It was certainly easier to learn things here. I thought of the question about why there were no books in Zhev'Na, but neither Parven nor Notole answered me. Darzid was still arguing with Exeget.

In between two of the bookcases was a tall, narrow window with lots of small panes and an iron latch. When I first walked past the window, I could have sworn I saw a face pressed up against it—a boy's dirty face. I looked at the books for a little while, then wandered past the window again. The face was gone. It didn't seem worth mentioning.

I forgot all about the boy at the window when Exeget left the room, and Darzid called me over to the table. "Would you like to watch what goes on?" he said. "Catch a glimpse of our enemy?"

I wasn't sure I did, but didn't want to seem a coward. Darzid picked up a round, smoky glass and passed his hand over it. It was splendid! In the glass I could see Exeget crossing a room to stand before a raised platform where five other people sat. In front of the platform was a single chair with someone seated in it. The hood of his white robe was drawn down low just as I had seen him in the garden at Comigor—the Prince D'Natheil.

When he uncovered his face, his hands were shaking badly, but his face didn't look like he was afraid. Nor did he look proud or disdainful or anything like I expected. He looked more like one of the tenants of Comigor—I couldn't remember the man's name. The tenant had fallen ill, getting thinner and paler every day for half a year until he couldn't lift a scythe any longer. Papa called in a physician for fear of fever or plague, but the physician told Papa that a disease was eating away the man inside, and nothing could be done for him. The man kept on working through harvest, the other tenants carrying him to the fields so he could earn his family's winter sustenance, but every time I saw him, I wondered what part of him the disease had eaten away. The Prince looked just like that man. I believed it when the people in the room said he should be dead. The Prince looked like he believed it, too.

When the time came, Darzid motioned me through the door into the room where my father was. I tried to look like a sorcerer prince with powerful allies and a blood debt to repay. One of the Lords whispered inside my head. *Have courage, young Gerick, and do not be afraid of what transpires.* But I couldn't recognize which one of them was speaking.

Everything the Prince said . . . during the testing and then after he got the knife and threatened everyone away from him . . . it all sounded very nice. He claimed that he and Seri had cherished me, cared about me, and he said how he had been sorry he had to die before I was born. But the knife he held was the same one I'd seen in my dreams, the knife that had killed Lucy. The crest with the lions and the arch and the stars—D'Arnath's coat-of-arms—was engraved on it. The same crest I'd seen on the sword that had killed Papa.

The Lords had explained to me how the Prince had killed Papa to protect D'Arnath's evil Bridge and keep the true powers of sorcery all to himself. What kind of warrior would pretend honorable combat when he knew it wasn't possible? Papa wasn't a sorcerer. I hated D'Natheil—this man Karon—for being my father instead of Papa, and I hated him for making me evil like he was. And so I spat at him and told him how I'd sworn an oath to destroy him.

I was sure he would laugh at me then, because he was so big and powerful and I was not. Or maybe he would get angry and tell me why he wanted me dead. But instead he told me that he hadn't done what I thought, and that he was sorry. Only then, when he said he was sorry, did he first look me in the eye. Only for that one moment. Then he slit himself open right in front of me.

I guess it was Darzid who pulled me away, though the Prince was no threat any more. I stood there like a fool watching him fall to the floor and bleed everywhere, while everyone else was running around and screaming. A woman cried out the Prince's name—my father's name, Karon—and about the time Darzid dragged me through the door back into the workroom, I realized that the voice was Seri's.

"Wait!" I said. I didn't want to leave. I wanted to see Seri again, so I could decide what I thought about her. I wanted to make her tell me whether or not the Prince had known I was their son and if she had really set him to carry out her revenge. I wanted to ask her what it was the Prince had been trying to tell me in that instant before he died. No one had ever looked at me the way he did, and I didn't understand it.

Nothing that had happened in Avonar had made any sense. . . .

You did well, young Lord, said Notole. Even though she was talking to me, I could feel her trying to calm Ziddari and Parven's anger. *You left no doubt in anyone's mind that you repudiate your father and his restrictions on our freedoms. I would have encouraged you to behave just so if it had been possible to communicate with you. The Preceptors protect their chambers well. Even your jewels were closed. Our next meeting will be on ground of our choosing.*

So that was why the Lords didn't answer my questions while we were in the chamber. But then—I thought back carefully—who kept telling me to have courage and not to be afraid?

Who was what? whispered Notole.

"Nothing. It was just confusing. Everyone was shouting."

You were afraid?

"No. Not really. I didn't want to see the Prince or listen to him. But I wanted to learn about him, and why he does such terrible things."

"Well, there's no need any more. We've had a great victory this day." Darzid was leaving, beckoning my slaves to fill my bath. He didn't sound happy. "D'Natheil is dead. And it was so much easier than we could ever have guessed it would be. Only one regret. The mad Prince has robbed you of your revenge. We were going to let you kill him tonight."

From the next day my training took up again as if nothing had happened. With Parven helping me feel how to move and how to see my opponents' openings and strategies, I improved rapidly at swordplay and hand combat. Two different slave boys had to be taken away when I damaged them. I asked Calador if they were all right after, but he said it was none of my concern. When I said that perhaps he should let my partners wear leather armor like my own, now that I was getting more skilled, he said no. The Lords had commanded that my partners would wear no armor.

Parven came into my mind, then, and said that a warrior had to know that every stroke meant something. *Your hand must know the sensation of steel on flesh, and not quail from it. Your eye must see beyond blood and determination, knowing clearly which strokes will damage and which will not. These slaves could have no higher value than to aid in making their new Prince invincible. Now, continue, and do not even think of holding back, for I will know of it. The opponent you spare will be dead before another dawn.* And so I told Calador and Harres to look for more skilled opponents for me. Then I'd be less likely to injure them.

Some of my opponents were Zhid, and some were slaves. There was a third kind of servant in the fortress called Drudges. Drudges were stupid and dull and never spoke, even though they weren't forbidden it like the slaves. Drudges never fought as practice partners. They weren't allowed to touch weapons, because they didn't know what to do with them.

"They're not Dar'Nethi, thus have no true power," Ziddari told me, "so we have no need to collar them. They breed, and so make more of themselves. That can be useful. If they don't work, we kill them. They have so little intelligence that it's better for all. A mercy, in fact. They are nothing."

I'd never thought of killing people as being a mercy, but if the person was too stupid even to know what to do with a knife, it made more sense.

My training in sorcery continued, too. Notole taught me how to call my horse from anywhere within the training grounds, how to prevent my sword from getting dull, and how to make my knife cut into a rock. I asked her how I could get more power for sorcery, and if it could enable me to do bigger things. She said that someday I would be able to do anything I wanted.

CHAPTER 27

Seri

Fourteen days, Gar'Dena promised, only fourteen days of living under the very noses of the Lords of Zhev'Na. Time enough to learn where Gerick was being kept. Time enough to let the other players work their way into position. Then would come a signal I could not mistake, even though I could not be told of it in advance, and together these other players and I would snatch my son to safety. I could survive Zhev'Na for fourteen days. For my son and the future of the worlds, I could do it.

The venture would be dreadfully risky. There existed only three ways to enter Zhev'Na, Gar'Dena lectured us as we sat in his exotic sitting room on the day after the terrible events in the council chamber. The first was as a Zhid. Of course, to retain enough of one's soul to perform a selfless deed after being transformed into a Zhid was an all but impossible hope. And only the most powerful of Dar'Nethi captives were made Zhid. It was not a practical way to sneak spies into Zhev'Na.

"Unless one could counterfeit a Zhid," said Kellea, eagerly abandoning our aimless activities of the past weeks in favor of Gar'Dena's plot. "Is that possible?"

"I know of only one man who ever has managed such an impersonation," said the Preceptor. "To live as one of them, performing acts of cruelty and vileness every hour . . . how does a person with a soul reconcile it? Only a person of tremendous strength and dedication. And only one who was once a Zhid himself. No one else could know the life they lead, the words they speak, or how to work the Seeking or transform another into a Zhid."

"So, what are the other two ways?" I asked.

"The second is as a captive. Dar'Nethi of lesser power or those considered expendable are made slaves. The Zhid use weaker slaves as a source of power, leaching away the poor souls' life essence to augment their own power. They forbid the stronger slaves all use of their true talents and force them to spend their lives in unending degradation. . . ." He faltered. "You are not Dar'Nethi, and so that way is not for you."

"And the third?"

"The third possibility is yet another kind of servitude, for the Lords of Zhev'Na permit no life but servitude. Before the Catastrophe, when our worlds were closer linked, people from your lands occasionally wandered into ours. Those trapped in Ce Uroth by the Catastrophe fell under the sway of the Lords. Unlike the Zhid, who have lost the ability to reproduce, and the Dar'Nethi slaves, who are forbidden it, these unfortunates beget children. They now number in the thousands, but they have no power, nowhere else to go, and have been in the Wastes so long they know no other life. They live in desolate villages throughout the Wastes, breeding horses or food beasts for the Zhid, or they serve in the war camps or the fortress."

"And I am to be one of these?"

"We are in contact with a brave man, the one I referred to earlier, a Zhid who was restored to himself by Dassine during his imprisonment in the Wastes. This man has chosen to remain in Ce Uroth all these years, living as a Zhid in order to aid our cause as he is able. He can get you a place in the fortress of Zhev'Na itself, an ordinary duty assignment that will not be remarked. From this position you should be able to discover the whereabouts of your son, his daily routine, how he is guarded, and what possibilities exist for removing him. If we train you well before you go, and you play your part with the same courage and intelligence we've seen in you thus far, then you should be able to do what no Dar'Nethi could ever accomplish."

"This is why you needed someone from my world—a mundane," I said.

"Exactly so."

"That means I can go, too," said Paulo. He had been listening intently while munching raspberries from a silver bowl.

Gar'Dena was taken aback. "We've no plans to send anyone else. The dangers—"

"The Prince and the Lady Seri saved my life twice over. I've sworn to pay 'em back for it, and the only way I can see is to get their boy back safe. I'll go, if I have to walk all the way on my two good legs."

The giant sorcerer did not laugh as many might have done at a boy of thirteen whose ferocious loyalty was sworn with red juice smeared over his freckles. Rather he laid his wide hand on Paulo's knee and responded soberly. "The success of the plan can be our only consideration. For now, that requires the lady to go alone. But we will think on how best to use such courage as yours. As for you, young woman"—he glanced tentatively at a thunderous Kellea—"you must see that your road cannot lead to Zhev'Na. Not yet. You are Dar'Nethi, a fact that cannot be masked. Any Zhid can lay his hand on you and know what you are. But, as with this daring young man, I promise we will find ample use for your skills."

Over the next days, Gar'Dena set me to work in his kitchens, scrubbing and washing up, and to digging in his garden so as to roughen my hands. As I worked, he helped me build a new identity, to forge new habits and thoughts and patterns of speech, tempering them with constant review. I asked Gar'Dena if Bareil could perhaps be brought in to help me learn my role, but the sorcerer scoffed at that idea, saying that the Dulcé had taken no new madrisson and was therefore useless. "A Dulcé unlinked is little more than a child, you know. Young Paulo here has more knowledge at his bidding than would Bareil." I disagreed, but Gar'Dena would not budge.

Paulo grumbled that he would be happy if he was but allowed to use what knowledge he had.

"I don't know that I trust these Dar'Nethi or their schemes," I told the boy privately. "I may need you to come rescue me."

I spoke half in jest, but Paulo did not. "I'll do it," he said, quiet and fierce. "Be sure of it. I'm watching your back."

On the fourth day of my stay with Gar'Dena, Aiessa burst into our workroom with the terrible news that a Zhid raiding party had attacked three outlying settlements, killing or capturing all who lived there.

Gar'Dena practically pounced on the girl. "The names, child. What are the names of the settlements?"

"Vilkamas, Sen Ystar, and Nithe."

At the names, the sorcerer clasped his huge hands, pressed them to his brow, and closed his eyes. "Have your sisters light the war flame, my Aiessa. Remind them to take into their hearts those who have fallen and more especially those souls who find themselves this night under the yoke of the Lords. May their courage and honor light our Way." The girl nodded and hurried away, and Gar'Dena turned back to my lesson. "You must be ready to go at any moment."

We drilled for two more hours, Gar'Dena trying to trip me up with questions about the squalid work camp where Eda the sewing woman had spent her whole life, and how she had come to be in service at the fortress of Zhev'Na. ". . . And when was your mate killed?"

"The people of our work camp were honored to serve the Lords in a battle exercise a twelvemonth since. My mate did not return."

"And why were you not returned to your work camp?"

"Only I and three others survived the battle exercise. It was not in the best service of the Lords to send so few back to the work camp."

"And how did you come to Zhev'Na?"

"I've worked for these past months in the war camp of the Worships, but I was not suited to tent making. The keeper said I should perhaps be killed because I was useless, but then he heard that there was a lack of sewing women at Zhev'Na. I am greatly honored to be allowed to serve the Lords here, and I work diligently to improve myself."

"And what is your present service?"

"I sew, Your Honor, linens and tunics for the Worships, for such is simple work suited to my poor skills. I repair what needs it and change the linens in the rooms where I might be assigned. On occasion I am called on to stitch tunics for slaves, though only for the glory of the Lords of Zhev'Na would I perform any service that might benefit vermin slaves."

On and on we went, until Gar'Dena's head jerked up. A streak of blue light creased the air—a message had arrived. The Dar'Nethi would drop an enchanted stone into a flame to alert a distant correspondent that he wished to speak in the other's mind. "It is done," he said, almost reverently, after a moment's quiet as the sender communicated the message. "The first move is made. You go tonight. You may wish to sleep for a while now, my lady, as it will be many days until you can rest in safety. I will assist you to sleep if need be."

"I couldn't rest well anyway," I said. "Tonight is my husband's funeral procession. As I cannot attend"—Gar'Dena had declared it too dangerous—"I intend at least to watch what I can of it."

The people of Avonar had at last been told of the death of the Prince D'Natheil. The Preceptors' examination had revealed that his mind was too damaged by his summer's battle on the Bridge to allow him to assume his duties, so they told the shocked populace. Cast into despondence, he had taken the sorrowful step that was the final proof of his illness—taking his own life. The Preceptorate would deliberate on the succession, but, of course, nothing could be done until the Prince's son came of age.

And so in the last hours before I was to go to Zhev'Na, I stood on Gar'Dena's balcony with the Preceptor and his daughters and watched the funeral procession of the Heir of D'Arnath. Karon's funeral. As the sun slipped behind the peaks of Eidolon, the Dar'Nethi spilled out of houses and shops. Dressed in white, each carrying a glowing white sphere, they converted every lane into a river of light.

As the procession passed slowly through the grand commard, they began to sing, first the men, then the women, and then the children. They sang the story of Vasrin Creator and the dawn of life, and of Vasrin Shaper who set men and women free to walk their own paths through the world. And then they sang of D'Arnath and his Bridge and his oath to sustain it, and of the sad young Prince who had lost his father and brothers and been thrust onto the Bridge too early in the desperation of his people. They sang of the unknown Exile who had opened the Gate, and of the Prince's mysterious journey to the other world that had resulted in the renewal of life in the Vales of Eidolon.

The rite was heart-wrenching and exhilarating. Only when they carried the white-silk-draped bier past the window did I falter. But I closed my eyes and prayed that the songs of the Dar'Nethi would echo far from Avonar. "Wherever you are, my dear one, listen well," I whispered. "Let the beauty of this night give you comfort." I would not grieve. I would not.

Even after the procession wound out of sight, the singing rang through the frosty air, echoing off the mountain peaks well into the night. But time for my departure had come, and I could no longer permit my thoughts to linger on either beauty or sorrow. I donned the shapeless garb of black and brown and allowed Gar'Dena to tie a red kerchief over my eyes.

"Please forgive this," he said. "Each piece of our mosaic must remain separate lest we reveal the whole picture too soon." He led me through his warm house, scented with spices and flowers and baking bread. And then we stepped through a magical portal, so the chilly prickle of my skin told me, into an echoing room with no scent but cold stone.

"Now, my dear lady"—Gar'Dena spoke loudly into my ear, as if my blindfold might be hampering my hearing—"our honor and blessings go with you. In fourteen days you will be contacted, and shortly after, as the Way leads us, we shall be together again, rejoicing at our success, your son safely in our care. Until then . . ." He grasped my hand in his meaty one and kissed it. "Now, take three steps forward, turn immediately to your left, and then left again."

Three steps forward. A tremulous disturbance of the air. Another chilly ring surrounding me. As I turned left and then left again, a grim voice spoke in my head. *Do not be afraid. You are not alone. . . .*

One more step and the air and space around me changed dramatically. Hot. Dry. The scent of smoke and ash and seared stone. Air, stale and close. I believed I could reach out and touch walls on every side. Cool, damp hands grasped my own, and a man whispered in my ear, close enough that I could feel his warm breath. "Quickly, step forward. One moment . . ." I stood in the hot, airless darkness for a moment and felt the quivering boundary of the portal vanish. "You may remove your eye covering. You'll not see me again after this day."

I yanked off the kerchief. The tiny, windowless room was lit by one candle. My companion pressed his ear to a wooden door and then faced me. Wearing a well-tailored coat with a high collar, trimmed with a great deal of gold, and knee breeches and hose of light tan, he was almost as large a man as Gar'Dena, but a much harder man, who crowded the little room with his muscular presence. Yet, despite his robust frame, his complexion was gray and unhealthy-looking, and the hollows of his eyes were dark and sagging. My stomach tightened considerably when I saw that he wore the plain gold earring of the Zhid and that his eyes were cold and empty as only those of a Zhid can be. He bowed. "Welcome to Ce Uroth. This is quite a risk you take."

"Perhaps not so much a risk as you take, sir." To live as a Zhid, hiding one's soul . . .

"But I have a great deal for which to make amends, which you do not, and I am accustomed to my risks. Now to our business—"

From somewhere not far from this room where we spoke so politely intruded such a dreadful scream that I thought it must be an animal at the slaughter. Such a notion was banished quickly when my host bowed his head. "One thing at a time," he whispered to himself, the cast of his skin even more sickly for that moment.

Unwrapping a square of coarse brown cloth, he revealed

a thumbnail-sized slip of stamped metal. "The shipment of uncollared servants to Zhev'Na will occur at dawn. You will be added at the last moment. This is your identification tag. You know of them?"

"Yes." Gar'Dena had told me of the plain metal tag, fixed to one's left ear like the earrings of the Zhid, that carried a Drudge's name and assigned duty, and the enchantments that compelled the servant's obedience.

"To attach it will cause only brief discomfort. Your tag will carry your identification and a false enchantment—lacking any power of compulsion—but you understand that the least failure in obedience on your part will be noted and quickly remedied?"

"I understand." I said it calmly. But my fists did not unclench until the sting in my earlobe had dulled, and I had proven to myself that I could still move and think as I wished.

A loud knock on the door made my host frown. He waved me into the deepest shadows in the corner of the room. I crouched in as small a space as I could manage between two stacks of crates.

"Slavemaster Gernald?" called the intruder.

"What is it?" growled my companion, holding the candle in front of his chest and pulling the door slightly open.

"Sir, Dujene has two more collars for this lot and wants to know if you intend to set the seals. He had already sealed the first, when I told him of your desire to set more of them yourself." I could not see the speaker through the narrow opening of the door.

"Good." The man snuffed the candle and set it on a stack of crates beside the door. "Yes, I want to be there for all collarings until further notice. I've had too much work and too little pleasure lately. Nice when one can experience both together." He stepped out and closed the door behind him. The rattle and snap of a hasp left me feeling not at all secure.

For half an hour or an hour I huddled in the dark room. It seemed to be a storage room for ledgers and documents of various kinds. My anxieties were not soothed by the bone-chilling screams that occurred twice more. Shortly after the second instance, I heard voices outside my hiding place. "Is that all, Slavemaster?"

"I've no more need of you tonight. I plan to sup, to make one more attempt to find the records Gensei Seto requested, and then to retire."

"As you wish, Slavemaster."

A door closed. Shortly thereafter, my own was unlocked and opened. The Zhid shoved a small flask and a plate of meat, cheese, and bread into my hands. "I would recommend you eat this. You'll get nothing decent until your mission is complete."

"Thank you." I touched the small round loaf. It was cold and dry.

He lit the candle with a touch of his finger. "None but I have entry to this room. Nonetheless, I will lock the door until I come for you in a few hours. Do you have the scarf to cover your hair? No female servant is permitted to have uncovered hair."

I pulled the red kerchief from my pocket. "I have it."

"Don't forget it. I wish you a safe night. May our work be the redemption of the worlds." He didn't sound like a man who could have caused such screams as I had heard, but I suspected that he was. Perhaps that accounted for the diseased look of him.

The door closed behind him again, the lock snapped, and I was abandoned in the pool of candlelight. As I picked at the tasteless cheese and bread and sipped from the flask of warm ale, I imagined with a twinge of jealousy how Paulo would curl up on the hard floor and be asleep in an instant. I didn't know if I would ever be able to sleep in Zhev'Na. Of course, as is often the case when sleep seems impossible, at some point in that night, my mind let go and I drifted off. But some time later, when the key turned in the lock again, I was on my feet, wide awake, before my host reappeared in the doorway.

"Quickly. Quietly. Follow me." He led me through a large, bare room with a wide desk and a single chair, and then through a dim passageway rife with unwholesome smells. Just outside a wooden door fastened with a long bolt, he motioned me to be still. After a moment's listening, he quietly guided the bolt from its latch, cracked the door, and peered through. Beyond the door a goodly number of people were murmuring and milling about. A harsh-voiced woman shouted for attention.

The Zhid closed the door, grabbed my arm, and drew me close. He held up three fingers and pointed toward the door. I didn't get his meaning until he motioned again, counting one finger and then two. . . . When the third finger came up, he cracked the door open just wide enough to shove me through. I stood at the rear of a line of fifteen or twenty rumpled, sleepy people moving slowly forward through a cavernous room. All were dressed as I was.

Another, larger group of Drudges—perhaps fifty altogether—were being led through a wide door into another room, prodded by three Zhid with long sticks who kept yelling at them to be quiet or he'd have them eating sand for a week. Behind them a gaunt man, barefoot and wearing a short gray tunic, dragged a wheeled sledge piled high with rough mud-bricks. The wide metal collar around his neck told me he was a Dar'Nethi slave.

Near the head of the line in which I stood, three Zhid stood at a fuzzy discontinuity in the air that I now recognized as a magical portal. One of the Zhid, a woman, questioned those in line and ticked off items on a list. Another seemed to be matching the responses with the ear tag. A third Zhid laid his hand on the head of every person before they passed through the portal. Hunting Dar'Nethi, certainly.

"Name and service," snapped the woman writing the list to a hunched man in line ahead of me.

"Grigo, butcher."

"Step through."

"Name and service."

"Mag, scrub."

"Step through."

"Name and service."

"Eda, sewing."

"Step through."

And so I did and found myself at last in the heart of all my fears—Zhev'Na.

CHAPTER 28

I stepped from the portal into a barren courtyard: pounded red dirt surrounded on all sides by buildings of dark stone or red mud-brick. Gray wisps of night lingered in the dim colonnade that marked the east side of the yard, while the rising sun had already heated the broad square. Despite the heat, I crowded together with the other drab, silent bodies, all of us shapeless in our brown tunics and black skirts or baggy trousers.

The guard handed his list to a tall Zhid woman who announced herself to be Kargetha, a supervisor of uncollared servants in the fortress. Kargetha clearly did not relish being saddled with twenty dull, sleepy Drudges, and dispatched us to our duties as quickly as possible. Some were sent to the kitchens, others to the stables or the smithy, herded along by Zhid assistants.

I was the last on the list, and by that time, Kargetha had no subordinates left to show me the way, so with an ungracious poke of a sticklike finger, she pointed me toward a set of worn stone steps on the north side of the courtyard. Down the steps and to the right was a low-ceilinged, windowless room with pallets laid out on the floor—a dormitory where twenty or thirty people could sleep. The room was stifling and smelled as if it had been neither cleaned nor aired since this part of the fortress was built, long before the Catastrophe.

"This is your sleeping place. Leave your things." I dropped the small bundle that Gernald had provided me next to the grimy pallet Kargetha indicated. Then I followed her back up the steps and across the courtyard toward the long mud-brick building backed up against a high wall. She led me through one of the many open doorways into a crowded, wood-floored room. In the front of the room stood a broad table, piled high with rolls of brown and gray cloth and stacks of flat, cut pieces of the same. Two women dressed like me stood next to the table stitching the pieces into garments. At another table, three more women were hemming a huge square of raw linen. Without any introductions, I was assigned the fourth side of the square. "Do as they do."

I picked up a needle from those stuck into the wood frame of the table, threaded it with cotton from a large wooden roll, and began to fold the edge and stitch as the others were doing. Kargetha spent the rest of the morning at my shoulder, ripping out stitches that she judged too large or too uneven or too crooked. She was very particular and demonstrated her displeasure by rapping a short stick across my knuckles.

As the morning passed, the sewing room grew hot and stank with the sweat of the women. Kargetha decided she'd seen enough. "You're slow and incompetent," she said with a snort. "I don't know how you've survived this long. You'd best improve your skills or you'll be sent into the desert for hunting practice. Here"—she nudged me toward another of the women—"that's Zoe. Do as she says."

Zoe was an older woman with broken yellow teeth and mottled skin. She and the other Drudges wore the faces of brutalized women everywhere: old beyond their years, worn and battered by filth and poor food, eyes holding little intelligence and no hope. Once Kargetha had gone, the women began to talk quietly as they worked, mostly about the heat, and the dullness of the needles, and the coarseness of the thread with which they were expected to do decent work. Unlike the Dar'Nethi slaves, Drudges were permitted to speak without asking permission.

Zoe, being in charge of the group, took it on herself to question me about how I had come to be sent to Zhev'Na. She nodded sagely as I finished my story. "Aye, there's a deal of us here as have lost a mate or three in the camps." Zoe pointed her needle at a younger, slack-lipped woman.

"Dia's whole village was hit and burned for a testing. She was gone to midwife a cousin and come back to her village to find everyone dead, her mate and offspring and all. So it goes."

"How awful," I said, horrified. "Your children . . . all of them?"

The slack-mouthed girl shrugged. "Aye. There was five, six of 'em . . . I don't know. Who ever knows how many there are? I'll get more if the Worships say it."

Several of the women had similar stories. No one seemed particularly bothered, even about losing their children. My strong reaction seemed to unsettle them far more than their own horrific tales. I took the warning, and from then on did my best to keep my feelings controlled and my expression like theirs. I let them ask all the questions they wanted, which were not very many, but for the time, I asked no more of my own except about the work.

In the middle of the day a blank-faced girl carried in a tin pail and a cloth bag. Each of us took a wooden bowl from a stack of them in the corner and filled it with dark brown ale from the pail. Then we each took a piece of bread from the bag. In scarcely time enough to cram the bread down, gulp down the tepid ale, and throw the wooden bowl back on the stack, we were back at work. I thought we might stop when the light faded, but lamps were lit, and we sewed for two hours more. By the time Kargetha returned to review our day's work, my fingers were sore, my feet throbbing, and my eyes blurry. We filled our wooden bowls from a pail of thin soup. I did as the others, swabbing out my bowl with my hunk of bread, and then refilling it with ale from a second pail set by the door. While we ate and drank and stacked our bowls back in the corner, the Zhid woman inspected every piece of our work. Only after she gave her approval were we dismissed to the dormitory.

The women mostly fell on their pallets still dressed, joining others whose snoring rattled the low roof beams like a thunderstorm. There was no outer door to be locked, and in two hours of heavy-eyed observation, no guard or other watcher came to check on us.

One more venture before I slept, I thought. I wanted to get my bearings. I crept between the rows of sleeping women, through the open doorway, and up the steps to the courtyard. The night was cold, the sky hazy with smoke and dust. No stars visible. No moon. A single yellow torch burned in each corner of the yard, allowing a limited view of what lay beyond the enclosing walls.

Directly across the courtyard, to the south as I remembered from the morning light, was the plain building of two stories that held the sewing rooms and other such shops and workrooms. Behind me, above the dormitory, thin, angular towers of dark stonework rose into the night like spikes against the sky, pierced by many tall windows that shone dark blue or green. I judged this massive structure to be the fortress keep, as it extended well beyond the open colonnade that formed the eastern boundary of this courtyard—the Workers' Court, I'd heard my new home called. The L-shaped keep wrapped around the far corner to my left, forming the eastern boundary of the fortress.

The colonnade separated the workers' compound from another courtyard, formed by the keep, its eastern wing, and another towered stone building. Facing the keep across the courtyard, that building appeared somewhat less imposing than the keep, but certainly more grand than the workrooms. It also showed a few lights.

To the west—my right as I stood on the dormitory steps—were a series of low brick structures that might be guard barracks, more workshops, or perhaps dormitories for male servants. Something else lay in the dark, even farther beyond, something that smelled foul, like stables poorly maintained.

"What are you doing?"

I whirled about and faced Kargetha's empty stare. Quickly I dipped my knee and cast down my eyes. "The latrine, your Worship. No one told me where such was to be found."

"You should have taken care of that earlier. Wandering about in the dark is not permitted." She pointed to a corner of the courtyard. "You'll find what you want there. Return to your sleeping room immediately after."

I dipped my knee again and hurried to the dark corner to which she had directed me. She didn't come to check that I had obeyed her, which was a great relief. I didn't want to attract further notice. I hurried back to my pallet, pulled a thread from the hem of my skirt, and laid it carefully under the corner of my bed. One day gone.

Fourteen days. So much to learn. I couldn't ask everything at once, yet I couldn't put off my investigations until I was more settled here either.

Our dormitory was indeed part of the keep cellars. The Lords themselves lived above us, so I was told, though none of the women had ever seen them. They had heard all manner of tales about the Lords: that they were gods or giants, or creatures of spirit, rather than flesh. They all agreed that the Lords could read your soul, assuming you had one. The Zhid claimed that Drudges had no souls because we had no "true talents"—no power for sorcery. All of the women believed that it was only right that we serve such powerful masters in whatever way we were commanded. Such was clearly how the world was meant to be, and whatever else was there to do?

I asked Dia, the woman who had been a midwife, if many children lived in Zhev'Na. She looked puzzled. "No breeding is allowed in the fortress. How could there be offspring?"

"I just thought I heard a child's voice last night. That's all," I said. "When Zoe sent me to get the scraps of leather at the tanner's."

"Well, children's *voices* . . . that's different," said Dia. "I thought you meant new-birthed offspring. There's child slaves brought in from time to time, though they can't speak but when they're told. And sometimes there's young ones among the Worships"—*Worship* was the Drudge title for the Zhid—"ones they train to become Worships, too."

"I thought all the Worships were grown," I said. "Not many warriors ever came to our camp. Didn't know Worships could be young ones."

Dia glanced over her shoulder and gave a shudder. "They're not *nice* young ones."

I dropped the subject, so as not to seem too interested. But on that afternoon I made sure to stand by Zoe while we attacked the mountain of plain brown fabric that was being turned into underdrawers for the Zhid soldiers. "Dia says the Lords breed offspring. Is that true, Zoe? We never heard that in my work camp."

"Pshaw! Dia would stitch her fingers to a sheet if you didn't tell her not. The Lords are Worships, and Worships don't breed."

"But she said they made a boy that lives here like a prince, so he must be a child of the Lords."

Zoe wrinkled her pale dirty face and licked her fingers as she threaded her needle. "There is a boy what lives in the Gray House and is favored of the Lords. Gam saw him when she was called to take new towels there. She said he has the mark of the Lords on him, so she was ever so careful and respectful."

"The mark of the Lords? I don't know of that. I'm so ignorant, being new here at the fortress."

Zoe leaned close, the wrinkles around her mouth deepening into desert crags. "The jewels, you know." She laid her finger on her ear tag. "It means whatever you do or say, the Lords will know it. The boy could kill you with a look if he took a mind to. You go careful if you see the mark of the Lords, Eda."

Gar'Dena had warned me repeatedly not to reveal myself to Gerick no matter what—not until the signal came. A wise warning, it appeared.

The Gray House was the structure that faced the keep across the courtyard beyond the colonnade. On the fourth night of my stay in Zhev'Na, I decided to venture a bit farther afield and see what I could learn about it.

We had worked a bit later than usual, for Kargetha had been displeased with our day's stitching and made us rip out half of it and do it over again. By the time my companions fell snoring onto their pallets, the compound was quiet and empty. I waited perhaps an hour, then slipped through the darkness to the colonnade, crossing into the next courtyard by way of the opening closest to the corner next to the keep.

As I stood in the dark corner, shivering in the cold air, I longed for a cloak, longed to be anywhere but this awful place. The courtyard between the Gray House and the keep—the Lords' Court, the women called it—was much larger than the Workers' Court, and was paved with large squares of stone that were carved with all manner of devices and symbols. Rather than trees or plants, statues of fantastical birds and beasts were set in ordered rows across the barren enclosure. The entrance to the keep was a columned portico at least six stories in height, flanked by gigantic carvings of warriors and beasts, and lit by great bowls of flame mounted above the portico. The bowl torches were so immense and so high, no servant could possibly reach them to set them alight or refresh their fuel. I shuddered, feeling quite small and alone.

The Gray House that faced this portico across the courtyard was more modestly proportioned, but of the same severe, angular construction. No elaborate entry, but only an iron gate opened onto its interior courtyard. Despite four torches that flanked the Gray House gate, I couldn't see into the darkness beyond it. Few lights were visible in the house, but I tried to note where they were: ground level, just to the right of the gate, second level, just above the gate, and third level, to the rear.

No guards were anywhere in evidence, and I thought perhaps I'd run quickly across the courtyard and peek through the iron gate of the Gray House. Only my uncertainty as to how to proceed made me hesitate long enough to hear the quiet sneeze not twenty paces from me. Despite the chill of the night, I broke into a sweat, while attempting the difficult task of shrinking further into the shadows without moving at all.

Moments dragged past as I huddled in my dark corner, scarcely daring to breathe. At last a man stepped from the corner of the courtyard at each end of the colonnade, just as two guards emerged from the keep. The four met briefly in the middle of the courtyard. Then, while the two who had been on watch strolled back toward the keep, the other two began a circuit of the dark peripheries of the courtyard. Their path would leave them right at the posts so recently vacated. Heart pounding, I retreated into the workers' compound before they completed their rounds. I would need to go again to learn how often the guard was changed, and how long it took the two to make the circuit. Tomorrow.

Timing would be critical, yet time was very difficult to estimate in Zhev'Na. There seemed to be no clocks, no bells, no criers, no drumbeats, no time signals at all. The sewing women had no concept of time and no interest in it. What difference would it make, they responded, when I asked how they could tell how long it took them to complete a slave tunic or when it was time to eat. They started work at dawn and ended when Kargetha said they'd done enough. They ate when food was given them and slept until wakened. Yet, someone in the fortress had to know the time. The guards knew when to go on duty, and the kitchen servant arrived at what seemed to be the exact same hour every day. Someone dispatched that servant, so someone had to know. It seemed too precise to be guesswork.

Near the end of my first week, when Kargetha spent the morning teaching us to fashion a new style of legging, I finally came to understand it. Late in the morning, the Zhid woman popped up her head and said, "Blast. The last morning hour has struck, and your log brains have not even begun to comprehend what I require. One hour more, and anyone who's failed to complete one set will go hungry for the rest of the day. Your stomachs are all you care for." I watched closely, and even with no external signal, Kargetha knew exactly when an hour had passed. Her head came up. Less than a moment later, the kitchen servant arrived with our midday bread.

The signal was *inside* the Zhid somehow. We who had no "true talent" were excluded from even so basic an amenity as knowing the time of day. The realization made me inordinately angry.

So, I would have to devise my own way of timekeeping. For half a day I fumbled about, trying various schemes. None were successful until I began to count. After four long days in the sewing room, stitching had become as regular as my pulse. The interval of one stitch became one count.

Once I worked at it a while, I could approximate fifty counts quite accurately. I would begin a row of stitches, then sew without counting—not a simple matter when I was so preoccupied with it—and then count my stitches when I believed I had done fifty. I was always within one or two. It took me two hundred counts to walk to the cistern in the corner of the compound, seventy-five counts to walk from the dormitory to the sewing room. We were allowed six hundred counts to eat. I started estimating longer times, and though I was less accurate at first, by the end of two days I could estimate three thousand counts to within twenty stitches. I called three thousand counts an hour. Then, all I needed was a reference, so sunset became nineteenth hour.

At sunset on my sixth day, I began to count. I ignored the women's conversation. Our talk was so pointless, so lacking in substance, no one noticed who participated and who did not. We sewed ten thousand stitches more—three hours and a quarter, more or less.

By the time we ate our soup, and the dormitory had been quiet long enough that I felt relatively safe, it had been an hour and a half more. I hurried through the dark colonnade into the Lords' Court and took up my watch from behind a column. By my reckoning, it was first hour when the guards changed. I waited, stitching in my head until my fingers ached with the intensity of it.

Two hours until the guards changed again, and just under a quarter of an hour for them to walk the periphery of the court. Two hours later, the same. By the third guard change, the edge of the world was a deep vermilion, and I hurried back to the dormitory where the women were stirring.

All day I fought to stay awake. Zoe yelled at me several times, accusing me of slacking. My hands kept falling still, though my bleary eyes were open and my mind was counting stitches.

"I'm sorry, Zoe. Didn't sleep well. I'll try harder," I said.

"If you can't stay awake, then maybe you'd best do

something else. Her Worship Kargetha wants these leggings delivered to the guardroom at the Gray House. You'll have to do it."

My spirit quickened with excitement, but I dared not allow it to show. "I'll try not to be so slow ever again, Zoe. Don't make me."

Though one would expect that they would delight in a break of the monotony, my coworkers very much disliked being sent on errands. I didn't know whether they were afraid of doing something wrong and being punished, or if thinking had just become too difficult.

"You'll go."

"If you say so, Zoe."

"And you're to speak to the chamberlain. Some draperies have rotted from the sun and must be replaced. He'll give them to you to bring back here."

"Yes, Zoe."

I couldn't believe my good luck. Though I would do almost anything to set down my needle, I had not dared volunteer for such duty, grumbling like the others when given a mission upstairs to the threadmaker's or next door to the tannery. I had not yet come up with a scheme to get into the Gray House. Now the opportunity had fallen in my lap.

Zoe told me how to get to the servants' door at the Gray House and where to find the guardroom—just to the right of the front gate, where I had seen the lights so late. As I walked slowly through the archway to the Lords' Court with my bundle of leggings, I noted carefully the exact position of the Zhid at the corner watchpost. He looked right through me.

The Gray House was larger inside than one might expect. From the back passage where Zoe had directed me to go, I glimpsed immense, sparsely furnished rooms. All rooms in the house opened onto small courtyards by way of arched doorways, but each courtyard was as dry and barren as the rest of the Zhev'Na. A sterile house.

A dark-eyed slave girl, no more than a bony child, was carrying a basket of linens down the stairs. When I asked her which way to the lower guardroom, she cringed, shook her head, and hurried away. I came upon another slave polishing the tile floor with a rag and asked him the same. The man pointed down a side passage, then angled his hand to the left and held up two fingers. Being a slave, the man was not allowed to speak. Being a Drudge and therefore nothing, I could not give him permission, even by asking a question.

"The second turning to the left?" I asked.

He nodded wearily, then went back to his work. Dreadful scars covered his shoulders. I had never been close enough to a slave to see the collar. The strip of black metal, etched with letters and symbols in brighter metal, extended all the way from collarbone to jaw. I remembered the screams I had heard the night of my arrival, and I swallowed hard.

I delivered the leggings to the guardroom, noting that two guards were awake and two sleeping on pallets in the next room. Keeping my eyes down as I had been taught, I asked the guards where I might find the chamberlain. The Zhid directed me up the stairs.

Halfway up the tight staircase, I heard shouting and the unmistakable clash of weapons from outside, beyond a sheltered balcony that opened off the stair landing. Seeing no one to observe me, I stepped onto the balcony, staying to one side where I would be shielded from view by a column that supported the roof.

In the center of a dusty courtyard, two boys were engaged in a fierce fight, circling, weaving, swords flashing in the sunlight. One boy wore boots and padded leather armor, while the other—taller by a head—was barefoot and wearing only a slave tunic and collar. I caught my breath. The boy in leather was Gerick, his face fierce and shining with sweat as he beat off a quick blow and swiveled to attack. The speed and accuracy of his movements had no relation to the awkward ten-year-old I'd watched at Comigor.

The slave parried, and the two boys circled again. The slave was proud and unafraid, and though his left arm dangled useless and bleeding at his side, he advanced on Gerick with cool and deadly precision. What could a slave hope to accomplish by attacking the favored guest of the Lords?

I backed toward the stair ready to run for help, but a glint of sunlight on steel at the edge of the yard stopped me. A Zhid warrior stood watching from the shadowed corner. Gerick moved to attack again. The Zhid shouted something, and the slave shifted his defensive stance before Gerick struck. Earth and sky! This was practice.

Gerick missed an easy opening, and the Zhid stepped out and stopped the match, castigating Gerick thoroughly. While the warrior made Gerick repeat the required move ten times over, the slave boy walked over to a water barrel by the wall and scooped out a drink, holding his wounded arm tightly. The swordmaster completed his instruction, then stepped back and raised his hand. The boys took their positions, and when the Zhid lowered his hand, they went at it again.

As I watched them close and strike out at each other again, I decided I'd been wrong to judge this combat mere practice. In truth, it was war, both boys the casualties. When the opening came again, Gerick did not miss. His sword caught the slave youth just below the ribs, and a red stain blossomed on the youth's gray tunic. Gerick stepped back, sword raised. The slave was bent over, his sword arm clasped over his middle.

Yield, I begged silently. *Someone end this.*

The youth, not more than fifteen or sixteen, straightened, and lifted his sword. He was pale. The two engaged once more, and after only a few moments, Gerick knocked his opponent's sword away. The slave sank to his knees on the red dirt. Gerick touched the point of his sword to the boy's neck, then sheathed his weapon and turned his back. He walked over to the water barrel, scooped a dipper of water, and drank deep. The swordmaster talked to Gerick for a while, demonstrating another movement and making him practice it ten or fifteen times. Then the two of them moved off toward a shadowed doorway. The gasping slave knelt in the broiling sun, trying to keep his life from leaking away into the red dirt.

Voices from the lower level of the house set me moving again. I could think of nothing to do for the youth. Any deviation from my orders would see us both dead. Certainly my tears could do nothing for him or others like him, nor could they open Gerick's eyes to see what lessons his masters were teaching.

Quickly I slipped back onto the landing and hurried up the stairs to the second level of the Gray House. A sideways glance told me that the lights I had seen above the main gate were indeed from another guardroom. Next to it was the storage room where I was to find one Sefaro, the person who ran the household. To my astonishment, Sefaro was a slave.

"You're the chamberlain?" I asked the slight middle-aged man who appeared to be taking inventory of the pottery, linens, and myriad other items on the shelves that lined the large, windowless storage room.

The slave nodded and gestured to himself, then raised his open palms in inquiry. How were we to do our business if he could not speak?

"I am Eda, a sewing woman. Her Worship Kargetha sent me."

A smile blossomed on his face, the first I'd seen on any face in Zhev'Na. Setting down his pen and paper, he gestured me to follow. Up another winding stair and through a doorway, we came to an immense set of apartments that covered the entire third level.

The sleeping and sitting areas each opened directly onto a balcony that ran the entire length and width of the house. Filmy beige draperies, hung across the south windows of the sitting room, were showing signs of sun rot. Sefaro brought in tall stools and helped me take them down. When the load of fabric made me wobble, he gave me a hand down from my stool and bowed cheerfully at my thanks.

"I was told to find out how soon we must have them done," I said.

He considered carefully, then raised three fingers.

"Three days?"

He nodded, and opened his hands as if asking if that was reasonable.

"Three days should be fine," I said.

He smiled again so kindly that I decided to take a great

risk. In a much quieter voice than before, I said, "Are you really in charge of this house?"

He cocked his head, surprised at the question.

"I'm new here," I said. "Don't know the ways. Nobody told me that such as you . . . a slave, that is . . . could be in charge of anything."

He chuckled and waved his hand about the room, then settled it on his shoulder as if it weighed like stone. Then his fingers touched his collar, and he shook his head with a rueful smile.

"You bear the responsibilities of the house, but, being a slave, you've little power to see them done."

He agreed readily, his eyes appreciative.

I knelt and began to roll up the rotting draperies, motioning him to kneel beside me. He did so, and began to smooth the wide fabric. With my head bent over the folds, I whispered, "Do your responsibilities include checking on the fencing yard, just in case there is anything that needs to be seen to there—something left that might be damaged?"

He paused for a moment, staring at me, and then ducked his head.

"Then, I think I can finish this task alone and find my way out."

He laid a hand gently on mine, and then he bolted from the room.

At the same time that I finished rolling the fabric, voices sounded on the stair. Heart racing, I patted the red scarf to make sure it covered all my hair and bowed my head as would be expected.

"I told Calador that I wanted better partners." It was Gerick. "The younger boys don't last long enough any more."

"And what did he say to your request?" Curse the devil forevermore . . . Darzid.

"That he'd see to it."

The two walked slowly into the apartment. Weapons clanked and rattled as Gerick tossed his sword belt onto a low bench.

"I'm happy to see how you're improving. Your enemies

will not expect such prowess from one of your age. Don't concern yourself with slaves. Their lives are to serve you."

Raging inside, appalled as I considered the lasting effects of such vile mentoring on a child, I hefted the unwieldy rolls on my shoulder, dipped my knee, and moved slowly toward the stair. Neither of them gave me a second glance. I could not get back to the servants' compound fast enough. Six more hours of sewing, then to bed. Another thread in my little bundle under the pallet. Six more days, and we'd have Gerick out of this wretched place.

CHAPTER 29

As the end of my sojourn in Zhev'Na approached, I believed fortune had smiled on our venture. I had watched the Gray House through three more nights and seen no variation in the guard schedule. I had taken note of the lights on the third level—Gerick's apartments—and had seen that all of the windows were dark well before the hour I called midnight. Only one small lamp on the corner of the balcony flickered throughout the night.

I hoped to get sent back to the Gray House with the repaired draperies and even dawdled about my work so perhaps Zoe might get annoyed with me again, but Dia was sent instead. No matter how I prompted her, Dia could tell me nothing about her errand. She had seen no one, noticed nothing interesting. I considered a midnight exploration of the Gray House, but as the deadline approached, I decided not to jeopardize my good luck—not until I knew what help was available.

And so came the fourteenth day. It began at dawn just as any other day. Dia made the trip to the cistern for the pail of wash water we all had to share, and I was fortunate to be second in line, so it was still reasonably clean. I had learned to be happy to get the dirt out from under my fingernails on occasion, saving anything more for the day I would be back in my own life.

Hours passed. For once, I didn't notice my aching feet or punctured fingers. Terrified that I might miss the signal, I studied every face, jumped at every voice. Every sense remained alert, while in the back of my head I counted so as to be sure of the time. We stitched until two hours after sunset. Night . . . of course, night would be better. We retired, as usual, to the dormitory. When my eyes grew heavy in the airless heat, I decided to sit on the steps and let the cold night air keep me awake. But one of the women stirred restlessly, belching and moaning as if she were sick. I dared not move. The next thing I knew, it was dawn.

I buried my disappointment in an even higher state of alertness. We washed and shuffled across the courtyard to the sewing room, ate our morning cup of gruel after two hours of work, and the day proceeded, no different from any other day. Another night passed. Perhaps I had miscounted the days. Perhaps Gar'Dena had not meant fourteen days exactly, but only that fourteen, more or less, *should* see it done. No plan dependent on so many mysterious elements could be so precise.

On the twenty-first day, I soothed my rising panic with Gar'Dena's assurances. *They'll not forget me. If they decide the plan has failed, I'll be transferred back to the military encampment and sent back through the portal, just as Gar'-Dena said.* But my cynical self taunted me. *The Preceptors wouldn't have just sent you here to rot, would they? All these Dar'Nethi are so honorable. . . .*

I put such thoughts out of my mind. I had to trust someone.

But as more days passed, my doubts grew right alongside the calluses on my fingers. What had gone wrong? Why was there no attempt to retrieve me?

At the four-week mark, numb and terrified, I was sent to the Gray House once again, to deliver five gray tunics for the household slaves. Sefaro was in his storeroom, writing in a journal of some kind. His face brightened when he saw me.

"I've brought five tunics as ordered," I said.

He nodded and inspected them carefully, then folded them and put them on one of his shelves.

"I'm also instructed by Kargetha to ask if it is time for the new banners to be made with the young Lord's device? She has received no instructions." I gave Sefaro the wooden token from Kargetha that would permit him to answer my questions.

"We've no need for the banners at present," he said, after clearing his throat. His voice was rich and mellow. "The young Lord is no longer in residence."

The slave reached out for my arm. "Are you quite all right, Eda?"

"Yes. Yes, of course." Pressing my fingers to my lips, I fought back tears and terror until I could speak again. "I was just so surprised . . . that Kargetha didn't know. She'll want to know where he's gone. And for how long." Everything depended on Gerick being in Zhev'Na.

"Five days ago the young Lord rode off with a Zhid officer. I was not told when or if to expect him back." His gaze held mine. "Tell Kargetha that I will be here taking care of matters as I have done these past weeks: the house, the kitchen, the fencing yard . . ." He smiled and raised his eyebrows, as if asking me whether I understood. Gerick's wounded young sparring partner . . . I smiled weakly. I could not rejoice in anything.

For my first weeks in Zhev'Na, I had considered my true life as something apart and my existence as Eda the sewing Drudge only a moment's aberration. But now this soul-deadening monotony encompassed my entire existence. The sewing women had lived this way for so long that I could find no tinder in them to answer what spark remained in me. They were uninterested in ideas or stories and called my attempts at conversation odd. When I suggested that we take a few moments before sleeping to clean the dormitory, so that perhaps the mice might find it less hospitable, I got only the blank stares and shrugs that might have followed an invitation to take wing and fly across the desert.

One afternoon, after I had tried to interest the sewing women in a simple game that might enliven the hours while we stitched, Zoe mentioned to Kargetha that I was distracting the others with my foolishness. The Zhid woman touched the tag on my ear and commanded me to cease my useless conversation. I had to do so, of course, as surely as if the compulsion had actually been attached to the tag. In the days of silence that followed her command, I speculated on whether the compulsions had really been put there after all. However would I know, when I dared not disobey?

After I had gone five days without a single word, Zoe mentioned to Kargetha that perhaps her command had been too effective. She had no objection to reasonable speech in the workroom, and I had made some useful suggestions about the work in the past. Kargetha was feeling indulgent that day and reworded her command. "I release you from my bond, Eda. Perhaps you are too stupid to know what is useless and what is not. Speak as you wish, unless two of your fellows tell you to be silent."

"Thank you, your Worship," I said, dipping my knee, but I didn't resume my attempts. Two months had passed, and Gerick was gone, and I didn't have anything to say any more. The prospect of living out the rest of my days in such a fashion was abhorrent. By comparison my years of poverty in Dunfarrie seemed endlessly stimulating. They had encompassed growth and change, the acquisition of new skills, the cycle of the seasons to mark the days . . . the height of the garden . . . the flight of birds . . . such beauty and variety. That I had considered life in Dunfarrie as near death as I could imagine pointed out a singular lack of imagination on my part. But then, who could ever have imagined the life of Zhev'Na?

CHAPTER 30

Gerick

One morning, after I had been in Zhev'Na for several months, I went down to the fencing yard ready to begin the day. I had been working with a new sword, not a rapier, but an edged blade, a war sword. It was fine—a one-handed blade with a deep fuller to keep it light, a sharpened, tapered tip, and a length that was exactly right for my height. With so many new things to learn—cutting and slashing movements, different kinds of thrusting, appropriate stances, footwork, and defenses—I made sure to arrive at the fencing yard early every day and stayed at least an hour longer than usual. Though Calador never admitted it, I knew I was making good progress.

Someone new stood waiting with Calador that morning. Like Calador he was a Zhid—one of the warriors of Zhev'Na with the strange eyes. He was very tall, and his thin red hair was combed straight back from a high forehead. His whole face was long and pointed, especially his nose. If he hadn't been talking to Calador, I might have thought he had no mouth at all.

Calador bowed to me and to the tall man. "My lord Prince, may I introduce Kovrack, a gensei of the Lords' armies—our highest military rank. Gensei Kovrack has been charged with the next phase of your training, that of military command. You are to live with the gensei in the war camp of Elihad Ru, and he will teach you how to lead your soldiers. I have been honored to be your swordmaster."

"But wait . . ." I was just getting used to Calador and Harres and Murn, just beginning to improve so that maybe they would think I was worth something. I liked my house and my servants and my horses. I didn't want to change things.

It is necessary, my young Lord, said Parven, inside me. *You are to be the ruler of two worlds. You agreed to let us guide you in the accomplishment of your purposes, and we warned you that there were hard lessons to be learned. Your destiny is not to be comfortable. That will make you weak. Weakness—fear of true power—was the downfall of Avonar and the line of D'Arnath. Have we not made you more than the sniveling child you were?*

Of course, he was right. They had made me better, harder, more like what I should be. I could run for an hour across the desert and still come back and win a fight. I could pin an opponent that outweighed me by half again and break his arm to boot. It didn't make my stomach hurt any more when I cut a sparring partner's legs so they wouldn't hold him up, and I could seal the slave collar on a new captive without even hearing his screams or feeling anything but relief that there was one more of the Dar'-Nethi unable to kill kind old women. Even if Prince D'Natheil was dead, I would have my revenge on him. I had sworn my oath. "Of course, I'll do whatever is necessary."

We left the fortress immediately, without even returning to my house. All that I needed would be supplied, Kovrack told me as we rode into the desert.

Two leagues from the fortress was the heart of a Zhid encampment that stretched as far as I could see into the brown dust haze that was the horizon. I had been into the Zhid war camps only twice: once to see a new lot of horses delivered from the breeding farms, and once to watch the execution of a Zhid who had spared a captive Dar'Nethi from a punishment. The warrior's commanders had staked him out on the ground and given him only enough water to keep him alive while he baked in the days and froze in the nights. Every day they would lash him until his flesh was shredded, and the wind blew sand into the wounds until you couldn't tell he was a man. Every night they worked some sorcery that made him whole again. He was out there for days. By the time he died, he was mad.

We spent my first day in Elihad Ru touring the ranks of tents, the supply huts, and the training grounds, stopping occasionally to watch a mock battle or other exercise. At sunset, we rode to the top of a small rise where several larger tents were pitched. The gensei assigned me a tent next to his own and told me we would share a fire. A slave was kneeling in front of my tent. "The slave will keep you supplied with water, wine, and food, cook for you, and clean your clothes," Kovrack said. "You'll have no other luxuries in a war camp."

The slave looked a few years older than me. No one told me his name. Luckily he seemed to know what to do, because I didn't know what to tell him. After taking my weapons, brushing off my clothes, and putting out the light, he curled up to sleep on the sand outside the door of my tent.

On the next morning before sunrise, when the light was still dull and red, I heard Gensei Kovrack up and about. My slave was kneeling at the doorway of the tent waiting for me. I dressed quickly, had him buckle my sword belt around my waist, and stepped out of the tent. Kovrack was stretching and flexing his arm and shoulder muscles. I didn't say anything, because it looked like he was concentrating. My slave brought me a cup filled with cavet—the thick, strong tea the Zhid drank—and Kovrack flicked his fingers at his own slave as if he wanted some, too. Kovrack's slave filled a cup, but just as he offered it to his master, he stumbled over a tent stake and spilled the cavet in the sand. Scarcely interrupting his exercise, the gensei reached over to the post where his scabbard hung, drew his sword, and ran the slave through. My slave fell to his knees and pressed his head to the sand. I almost dropped my cup.

Kovrack snapped his fingers. While two slaves dragged the body away, and a third cleaned his sword, he resumed his exercise. He lunged forward in a half squat and brought his arms over his head, holding the position for longer than I could hold a breath. "You think me harsh?" he said.

I did, but would never say so. I was becoming accustomed to how things were done in Ce Uroth. I shrugged.

Again Kovrack motioned with his hand. My slave filled a cup and presented it to the gensei when he left the position and stood up again. "The first rule of command: tolerate no imperfection. Otherwise your soldiers will lose their fear of you. Slaves are not inexpensive, but they are cheaper than armies such as this." He waved his cup about us. "My soldiers know that no one of them is exempt from this same penalty. They work hard for me."

When we finished a breakfast of hot bread and soft cheese, we walked down into the camp. A troop of ten new soldiers of various ages were waiting for me. Throughout that day, Kovrack showed me how to run them and drill them, how to use my voice and my power to command them, and how to make them fear me even though I was so young and scarcely taller than their shoulders. "You are their commander and their sovereign. You hold their lives in your hand, and no one of them is worth a fistful of sand unless he obeys you without hesitation. They must be taught that you, too, will tolerate no imperfection."

The Zhid weren't like soldiers I had known in Leire. They didn't laugh or tell bawdy stories around their campfires. Though a few fierce-looking women warriors lived among the Zhid, none of the warriors seemed to have families. They talked of weapons and battles, and who they would kill if the Lords would let them. I didn't think they knew what the jewels in my ear signified.

These do not, whispered Parven as soon as I thought it. *But they're new. They'll learn.*

Gensei Kovrack supervised my training, but it was the Lord Parven who taught me the subtler things that I had to know, watching everything that went on through my eyes and my thoughts. The first weeks were anxious and difficult for I had to learn so much at once, while developing my own strength and endurance as well. Fortunately my soldiers' infractions were small, and I had no need to use any punishment beyond extra practice. I dreaded the day one of them balked at a command.

One of my men was younger than the others. His name was Lak, and he was about fifteen, only a little taller than me, dark-haired, wiry, and strong. He seemed a little brighter than the usual Zhid. Not that Zhid were stupid.

Most of them were intelligent and powerful. But if you were to think of them like metal, you'd say the Zhid were made of iron, not silver. Maybe it was because they never thought of anything but hatred, battle, and death.

That's all they need, Parven had told me. *That's how they serve you.*

By the second month of my command, we were taking long marches into the red cliffs that were the southern boundary of our encampment. We practiced disappearing into caves and niches and the long, narrow shadows, climbed impossibly steep tracks carrying heavy packs of water and food, and survived for days at a time with no sound and no movement and only the most minimal sustenance. Of course I had to do all these things with my troops, and I could not complain lest they think me weak.

Lak and I always climbed together, for we were lighter and so had an easier time scrambling over rocks and crevasses. One day we got to the top of a rocky ridge while the rest of the men were still out of sight below us. The day was murderously hot, and when I reached for my waterskin, I found it empty, a ragged rip in the side. I had not allowed a water stop for several hours. My mouth felt like iron, and my head throbbed, but I could see no remedy. I was the commander. I could show no weakness.

Lak was panting and red-faced. As he pulled out his own water skin, he glanced at mine, and his eyes grew wide. "Your water, sir."

"Unfortunate," I said, looking off in another direction—any direction but his bulging waterskin.

"But it will be hours until we reach the camp."

"It is the way it is."

"If you would honor me . . . " He pushed his waterskin into my hands, nodding his head ever so slightly down the hill. No one was in sight. It would be only moments until the others came into view, and I was already feeling desperate at the thought of the long, hot afternoon. I said nothing, but nodded in return and took a sip of the warm, stale liquid that tasted as good as anything I'd ever drunk before. I was amazed. I had never seen a Zhid share anything.

This is dangerous, whispered Parven. *You know it.*

If I don't take it, I'll risk collapsing in front of them, I thought, maintaining silence with Lak. *He'll not tell anyone.*

Lak was the only one of my men that ever smiled. He smiled on that morning when I shared his water and again a few days later when he was sparring with me and got in a decent lick that left me in the dirt on my backside.

"A commander does not spar with his troops," said Kovrack, his small mouth set hard, his empty eyes glaring at Lak as the soldier walked away.

"I choose to do so, in this case," I said. "I don't want to lose practice while I'm in the field. None of your practice slaves are the right size, and Lak needs the work, too. I can't let him be lax just because he's small."

Kovrack and Parven were both annoyed with me. But it was the most enjoyable practice I'd had since I'd come to Zhev'Na. Because Lak was a soldier, he was allowed to wear leather practice armor when we sparred, so I was unlikely to damage him severely. The work was good for both of us, and we steadily improved.

Things were going well. The move to the desert had been all to the good.

"Young Lord," called Kovrack one morning as we were doing our dawn exercises. "I clocked your men running yesterday. They were not near fast enough."

"They've been dragging all week," I said, spinning on my heel and launching my knife at a wooden post halfway down the hill. The blade dug deep, right at the mark. And I was drawing it twice as fast as I could when I first came to the desert. "I plan to run them double time this morning."

When I walked down the rise for morning inspection, I told my troop what I intended. But our morning sword practice took much longer than I had calculated, and so the sun was almost at the zenith by the time we were ready to run. "I suppose I'll have to run them this evening instead," I said to Kovrack, who had come down to watch. To run in the midday sun could be deadly.

Kovrack curled his lip the way he always did when he thought I was being weak or stupid. "Indeed you will not, my lord. You told them they would run double time this morning. You cannot back down from your word. The news of your softness would travel throughout the entire camp by nightfall."

I looked around the cluster of tents. Several of the older men were already lounging in the shade of their tents, assuming I wouldn't make them run. They were the same warriors who never seemed to draw blood when they fought each other and looked sullen when I insisted they clean and polish their weapons every night. They were on the verge of not taking me seriously. I nodded to Kovrack. I understood.

"All of you malingerers, up. Now! Run!"

I ran them two hours in the desert noonday. At the end of the first hour they were dripping and panting. When they passed by the place where I stood watching them with my hands clasped behind my back, I didn't change my expression or say anything. They ran on. A half-hour more and they were laboring. One soldier dropped to his knees, holding his belly, about two hundred paces from where I stood watching. Cramps.

I was tempted to stop the exercise, but Kovrack was beside me, glaring, just waiting for me to show how weak I was. And Lord Parven was inside, whispering. *You know what to do, young Lord. He is worthless if he cannot follow your commands. He knows it, too. A soldier has pride, or he will turn traitor when battle is hard. The warriors of Zhev'Na do not live if they do not obey.*

I drew my sword and walked across the cracked ground to where the soldier had slumped over. It was Lak. I had a full waterskin at my belt, but it might as well have been at Comigor for all the good it could do him. I touched the point of my sword to his neck. "Run," I said.

His breath came in harsh gulps, and he didn't look up.

I pressed just enough harder to break the skin. "Run," I said again. I willed him to run; every muscle in my body begged him to get up. Slowly, he pushed himself up and staggered forward through the heat shimmer.

Only nine of the soldiers returned. The oldest one collapsed and died fifty paces from the end. Lak returned with the others, falling on the ground and grabbing for his waterskin.

What should you do? asked Parven. *Has he obeyed your command completely?*

He didn't have to tell me. I already knew what I had to do, even though I hated it. "Hold, Lak," I said. "You haven't finished the course."

Lak gaped at me stupidly, holding his middle, bent double with cramps.

"You were told to run double time, but you spent a quarter of an hour on the ground until I persuaded you to continue. You'll not drink with your obedient comrades until you've done what I told you." I kicked his waterskin out of his hand. A look of such hatred blossomed on his face that I drew my sword. "Run," I said.

He stood up and stumbled away. "Neto, clock him a quarter of an hour." I turned away and watched the other men drinking and wiping their faces. It seemed like a year until the other soldier gave the call. With a loud thud Lak collapsed behind me.

Well done. Parven was still with me. *But you know you are not finished. He defied you. You had to tell him twice.*

Lak lay on his back in the dirt. One of the other soldiers was dribbling water in his mouth. He coughed it up several times until his cramps eased enough to let him hold a little of it. I stood over him and watched him heave. He was weak. I could read it in his face, and he didn't think I could. He wasn't afraid of me at all.

And he must be. He defies you with his lack of fear. What will he do when you tell him to die for you? Will you have to tell him twice?

"Bind him," I said. "Ten lashes. Five for making me say it twice, and five for thinking I wouldn't notice that he shortened the time."

Lak started to protest, but I raised my hand. "One word . . . one whimper . . . one cry, and there will be ten more . . . and ten more after that."

I laid on the first two stripes myself, as a symbol of my authority, and then gave the whip to one of the other men who could do a better job of it. When it was done, I returned to my tent and had my slave bring water to wash off the blood and flesh that had spattered on me.

The Lords were pleased: *It was necessary. . . . Not pleasant . . . Perhaps now he will live to serve you. . . . You learn the hardships of command. . . .*

I did not go out the rest of that afternoon. That way the others could clean Lak's wounds without me seeing it. It would bind them together in fear of me.

Well done . . .

For several months more I trained my nine soldiers long and hard, punishing them severely for the least imperfection. Lak and I no longer practiced together. On the day after I had him lashed, I made him get out and run with the others and do every exercise his comrades did. His hatred followed me about like the shadows of the desert afternoon.

Day after day we drilled in the broiling sun, fighting with lead-weighted cudgels to gain strength, striking at wooden posts to practice footwork and precision with swords and pikes, practicing with blindfolds to develop perception and with hobbled feet to develop balance. Finally I decided my troop was ready for testing. We brought in twenty-five practice slaves to fight us. It was a good day. Only one of my nine soldiers was wounded, while seven slaves were killed. On another day we sent fifty slaves into the cliffs. Each was given a skin of water and a supply of graybread. I allowed them a day's start and told them that they could have their freedom if they could keep it. On the next morning we started hunting, using all our skills to track them down. Some had banded together to fight or to ambush us; some had gone their own way. Within three days we had them all back, except for three who had tried to bring down an avalanche on us and were themselves crushed by it. My men had no wounds.

It was my idea to leave the slave pen unlocked on the night we put the slaves back, thinking that their short taste of freedom might induce them to run again. I was right, and my troop and I chased them all down again on the next two days. I didn't permit my men to sleep until every slave was retaken, and I had the slavekeeper lashed severely for leaving the pen unlocked. He didn't know that I had done it. He believed he deserved the beating. It made a good lesson for the men.

On the morning after we recaptured the slaves, I came out of my tent and looked down the hill to see my troop and their tents, weapons, and horses gone. "Where are they?" I demanded.

Kovrack was stretching and drinking his cavet as usual. "Reassigned. I don't know where, and you shall not."

"On whose orders?" A stupid question. I knew whose orders. *Why? We were working well. They were afraid of me. They would do anything I commanded.*

Parven answered. *You know very well why—because of who you are and what you will become. Your time in the camps is done.*

When I returned to my house in Zhev'Na, Sefaro and the other slaves were gone, replaced by new ones with no names. I was not told where they had been taken. I assumed they were dead, and if not, then my asking would make it so. A new swordmaster met me in the fencing yard, and a new teacher of hand combat, and a new riding master. All of them had strange eyes and no smiles, and they taunted and ridiculed my incomplete skills until I hated them.

I was not to be comfortable. There were hard lessons to be learned. I tried to remember what I had been before I came to Zhev'Na, but I could not, except that I had been afraid all the time. I was no longer afraid. Fear had been stripped away along with my softness and weakness until I was as hard and bare and exposed as the red cliffs of the desert. Never again would I shed a tear into a pillow. I didn't even remember how.

CHAPTER 31

V'Saro

My feet were the worst, blistered and cracked and raw. Every step was its own battle. First the stomach clenched in apprehension, and the spirit steeled itself for the violence to come. Next, the waves of blistering heat that poured off the oven of the desert sniped at the skin like the initial forays of the enemy. And last came the assault itself, as raw flesh met salt-crusted sand and wind-scoured rock, heated to broiling by the fireball of the sun.

I longed for my boots. Who would expect that a man's life could be reduced to the consideration of a single step and an unbridled lust for a ten-year-old pair of scuffed boots? They had been fine boots, coaxed into such softness and perfect shape that my foot settled into them like an egg in a nest. I had given B'Dallo's pimpled son B'Isander three fencing lessons in exchange for them. It was a fine bargain for B'Dallo, as my fee was usually higher, but good bootmakers had become rarer than good swordmasters in the last years of the war.

The last years of the war . . . We'd thought it was over when Prince D'Natheil returned to Avonar after his victory at the Exiles' Gate. Our troops—never truly an army, only sorcerers of every profession converted to soldiers—dispersed. We came out of hiding and believed we could take up where our families had left off hundreds of years ago. Fools like me said that those of us born in Sen Ystar could go back and rebuild a life in our long-abandoned village, lay down a path of beauty for our children to walk—or perhaps meet a fair Dar'Nethi woman with whom to lay down a path of beautiful children. But we learned our mistake, and so some hollow-eyed devil of a Zhid was wearing my magnificent boots, while I . . . I had to take another step.

We in Sen Ystar had heard nothing of renewed attacks by the Zhid and had gone about our business that day with hope and joy. Fen'Lyro, the miller, had called a Builder to reconstruct his wheel, and we had all been drawn to watch by the beauty of the Builder's voice. He sang the spokes and shanks into place, completing the perfection of the wheel with a burst of melody that drew sighs from several village girls who knew the Builder had no wife. Girls did not swoon over swordmasters.

My art would die away with peace. Though I rejoiced with everyone else at the happy results of Prince D'Natheil's journey, I'd not yet come to terms with that. I had thought of taking a mentor for smithing, but what I loved about swords was not the metal. I had no knack for smithing anyway. I couldn't sharpen a nail without three files, nor once done, persuade it to stay that way. It was not even the art of swordsmanship I cared for—the grace and strength so smoothly joined—but more the logical puzzle of it. Move, countermove, thrust, parry. What were the myriad possibilities, and what was the remedy for each, all perceived and analyzed in a heartbeat. No formless metal could provide the challenge that did an opponent's mind and body.

So what good had my art done me when the Seeking of the Zhid crept through the streets of Sen Ystar? The icy fingers of the Zhid took one of us and then another as we so blithely celebrated the beauty of Fen'Lyro's mill wheel. The food and wine were probably still there, abandoned on the long tables set out on the snow-dusted grass. . . .

No, best not to think of food or wine. In a single day we captives were given one fist-sized lump of bread, gray and unhealthy-looking, and two cups of water, doled out two mouthfuls at a time. And how many of those days had there been? Six . . . seven . . . eight . . .

Few villagers were left by the time we were herded through the portal into the Wastes and chained to the dolorous column of captives. It was, perhaps, not a good day to be a proficient warrior. Surely the life of the dead in L'Tiere would be better than the endless desert, and with every painful step I envied those who had found their way beyond the Verges . . . so many that I knew. One of the last to fall was B'Isander, who had learned well from my three fencing lessons so many years ago.

But no Dar'Nethi grieves for long. He takes in what is told by time and makes it part of him, and then goes on . . . another step along the Way, no matter how bitter. *Aarrgh* . . . The sand cuts like glass.

At least I had my mind still, no small matter when dealing with the Zhid. Luca the Singer, M'Aritze the Word Winder, and Bas'Tel the Smith—they were made Zhid—and they, and others who met the same fate, helped to round up the rest of us to be taken into the Wastes. No one knew for certain how the Zhid chose those who were to become like them, and those who would be only slaves. Some said it was the level of power one had attained. Perhaps that was true, for I was a slave, whereas the Builder had become Zhid and cut Fen'Lyro's throat, for whom he had spent all day singing a wheel.

"On your feet, slave," snarled a voice in my ear, and the inevitable lash followed, temporarily removing any thought of my feet. I wasn't even aware I had fallen. I managed to get up before my neck-chain played out its length, no easy matter when one's wrists are bound so tightly. I had seen two or three who had been dragged along so far by the slow-moving column that they were not recognizable as men by the time they were cut loose. I had always considered myself exceptionally strong and enduring, but after the fall I began to wonder if I, too, would be left for the vultures like so many of our number. We had started out a hundred and fifty, mostly men, a few sturdy women of middle years, but had lost at least eighteen. The women did better, a sobering thought for one who believed himself possessed of few "woman's frailties."

Another few hours and I could no longer summon a rational thought. On the horizon loomed a fortress, tall and severe and so very dark, even in the harsh desert glare.

The mere sight of it engulfed my spirit in such sorrow and desolation that I groaned aloud. I didn't notice the lash this time, for the unnamable pain inside was far, far worse.

Before too long the sun had settled onto the western horizon, and the column started to slow and the prisoners to draw close to each other to capture the heat before all of it was sucked into the frigid night. Our captors usually allowed us to do so, but not this time. "Spread out. Full speed. We're due in the pens by midnight. No rests and no slowing."

It was probably as well. I didn't know whether or not I could survive another freezing night in the open, only to face another blistering sunrise.

Two more dead men were cut from the chain before we arrived at the top of a low rise and could look down upon the army of the Lords. Those of us who remained living and able to comprehend what our eyes rested on gazed with awe upon the magnitude of our enemies, a dark mass sprawled across the desert all the way to the horizon. For twenty years I had fought upon the walls of Avonar and complained with my fellows about the endless waves of the Zhid. But never had I considered my words to be the literal truth.

We were marched straight through the crowded encampment, the mass of tents and campfires and faces forming a blurred chain of light and dark, strung together with hatred. You could feel it from every side, colder than the night wind that billowed the canvas tents and swirled ashes and sand into our burning, crusted eyes. They gathered along the track as we passed, silent except for the low hiss that we who had fought the Zhid for so long knew as the sign of their contempt.

"Don't listen. Don't let it inside you," I whispered, first to myself, and then to the youth chained beside me. Even under his sun-reddened skin he was pale, and his cracked and blistered lips quivered. It took a person years of seasoning to slough off the hiss of the Zhid. "Put one foot in front of the other."

The end of our bitter road loomed before us, a fence of

black iron rods, the upright bars spaced no more than two finger-widths apart—no, not a fence, but a cage, for the bars extended up and over the top. No doubt the crosspieces that glinted in the torchlight were the same silvery metal as our chains. Dolemar it was called, the sorcerer's binding, for it prevented any use of magical power. Some said that if a man was bound by dolemar for too long he would go mad, just from the excess of power that built up in him, impossible to spend. A Dar'Nethi could no more stop taking in the experiences of life and building his power than he could stop taking in air, so perhaps it was true. Such was our Way.

As we approached the fence, a gate swung open. Each prisoner was detached from the column, then herded into the brightly lit enclosure that was just too low to allow a tall man to stand up straight. The cage would not be pleasant in the heat of desert daylight, but I supposed that "pleasant" would have to be banished from my vocabulary, or redefined to mean such sensations as sinking onto the straw-covered ground and letting burning, grit-filled eyelids shut out the horror.

Our respite did not last long. Torchlight and voices dragged me back to the cold night from wherever a moment's dreams had taken me.

"Are they ready inside, then? We push to make the deadline, only to have them not even ready. Burns me, it does." That was one of our guards, a squat Zhid with a narrow head.

"Shut up, and get this lot sorted. We've got to get 'em collared before the slavemaster comes."

"He'll be shiv'd when he sees the poor take. Only a few likelies for the practice pens. A few for house duty. The rest'll be for the mines and the farms."

"Just get them inside and secured. Makes me twitchy just having them caged and not collared."

Using elbows and my bound hands, I forced my aching bones to sit up and lean against the bars, and immediately wished I hadn't. The bars were cold, and my back was so raw from sunburn and lashing that it felt like being speared with icicles. My expletive woke the youth who had been chained beside me for eight days and had seen fit to curl up to sleep on my legs.

"What's happening?" said the boy, who must have been somewhere near sixteen, though I was sure he'd aged a lifetime in the past days.

"No idea. They've uses for us. If we're not dead and have half a mind left, then there's hope."

The boy shivered and shook his head. I wasn't sure I believed it either.

"Wake, pigs," screamed a guard. "If you want to feed your worthless faces or wet your foul tongues, then you need to line up by the door in the far wall. One at a time."

In the early days of our march I had witnessed struggles to get free, desperate attempts to muster power enough to break the bindings, to sharpen a stick for a weapon, to lure a stone into a hand. Once, on the first night, I had believed that someone was trying to speak in my mind with images of such beauty and hope that I lay awake, awaiting the rescuers that I was sure would fall upon our captors. Two days in the desert had ended all such futile endeavors and empty visions. Then came pleas for help, for Healers, for water, and prayers begging courage and strength. Two more days had silenced us all.

As we dragged ourselves to the back wall of the cage where a steel door opened into a dark, low building, the only sounds were the clank of chains and the soft weeping of those who could not rise. We tried to help them, but at the door any who couldn't walk on their own were shoved back into the cage. My youthful comrade was among those left behind. He huddled in the corner. Shivering. Terrified.

I called back to him. "It is a wonder, is it not?" It was the tag end of an old Dar'Nethi joke. We who tried to see wonder in everything—sometimes even we were confounded by the paths of life.

Slowly a grin suffused the boy's face, banishing fear and revealing a luminous spirit. "All of it," he croaked, through his cracked and bleeding lips. "I'll see you beyond the Verges."

Several of the others left behind took up the refrain. "A

wonder . . . beyond the Verges . . ." I saw handclasps and a few kisses and even heard laughter gracing the grim night.

Ah, holy Vasrin, I thought. *From what marvelous matter have you shaped us?*

The steel door gaped in front of me, and I was pulled through in my turn. While one guard checked the bonds on my wrists and hooked a short chain to my neck ring, a second man hobbled my ankles with a length of rope. The state of my feet would have prevented me running far, but I had contemplated a few of my favorite leg-holds when I glimpsed only two guards. Too bad.

As they led me stumbling through the dark passage toward a faint yellow light and the sound of splashing water, from somewhere deep in the dark place came a cry that chilled whatever mote of resilience still lurked in my soul. What, in the name of all that lives, could cause a man to make that sound?

Turn inward for protection . . . stay deep . . . let it pass. Nauseated, horrified, I didn't even understand my own thoughts.

The passage made a sharp bend. Torches burned beyond an open doorway. As I was still squinting from the brightness, my guard led me to a wooden bench facing a bare stone wall. "Sit here and don't move."

Sitting still was not so simple a matter, as someone standing behind me took a knife to my head and began hacking off my hair in great chunks. But I did my best. When an unfriendly someone has a knife that close to eyes and ears and such appendages, it's best to behave.

"Ready for the next one!" The call came from beyond another door.

"This one's proper nasty," said the guard, dragging me off the bench by the neck-chain. My hobbled ankles almost had me on my face in the piles of hair on the floor. "Going to dance for us, Dar'Nethi?"

A retort bubbled to my lips. *No. Turn inward . . . stay deep . . . whatever you would say would only be an excuse for something you'd rather not experience. Save the wit for someone who'll appreciate it.*

The next bare room, small and square, had damp walls

and a stone floor that sloped into a drain trench. The guards hitched my hands to an iron hook above my head. Then, they ripped off what was left of my clothes and a fair portion of skin where blood had dried and stuck them to me. Though I half expected it, I could not keep silent when a pail of icy water was thrown over me from behind. "Vasrin's hand!"

"Come now, slave, you want to be nice and clean for the slavemaster, don't you?"

They used a brush or a mop or some such contrivance to swab me down, then sluiced me off with another pail of water. Naked and shivering, I almost jumped a handspan off the ground when someone began to poke and prod my back and limbs. A helpless, horrid feeling. He moved around in front of me, a short, tidy Zhid whose eyes made my skin shrivel when he looked at my face. Pulling a length of cord from several that hung from a ring on his belt, the tidy man wrapped it snugly about my neck. I jerked backward, trying to calm myself with the thought that it had been awfully stupid to go to the trouble of washing me if I were going to be throttled. Indeed he removed it right away, paying no heed to my jumpiness.

"Give this to Dujene," he said, scoring the cord with a small knife and handing it to one of my guards. "You seem to be a fine specimen."

I presumed the last was to me, but I wasn't used to making pleasant conversation with a hostile stranger who had free access to all of my vital parts.

"What is your name? And don't be stupid. We'll know if you lie."

"V'Saro of Sen Ystar."

"Age?"

"Forty-three."

"Profession?"

"Swordmaster."

"Indeed? And your true talent?"

"Minor Horsemaster. No time for anything else." Stupid to think I had to apologize for my lack of talent to a cursed Zhid.

His pale eyes and his thick hands continued to inspect

and examine me. "Too bad your true talents are insufficient to make you a warrior. Your physical construction demands it. But a practice slave will be about the best you can do. Some live quite a long time, months, on occasion. You'll have to rely on your physical prowess alone, but—"

"Dujene is ready," said one of the guards.

"Tell him this one's for the practice pens. If he's a decent fighter, he might be useful."

I was led into a dim, smoky room that greeted me with a blast of heat. My stomach knotted as they half pushed, half pulled me onto my knees on the dirt floor. The stench of fear permeated the place. That scream had originated here.

"Spread him." My hands were detached from each other and pulled forward and apart, forcing my upper body onto a slanted, and very cold, stone slab. Once my hands were fixed in place, someone removed the loose iron ring to which my neck-chain had been attached. *Good riddance,* I thought.

I couldn't lift my head far enough to see much beyond the cold granite in front of my nose. A blurry dark-clothed figure hovered about my head. I didn't like the blaze that roared behind him. Not one bit.

Someone spread a cold ointment on my neck while whispering words of enchantment. I inhaled deeply, trying to ease the dread that constricted every aching muscle. I smelled hot metal. They had talked of collars.

"This should do him," said a dry voice. "We'll see what sort of stomach such a sturdy fellow has." Hands lifted my head and slipped a strip of hot metal between me and the stone. And, of course, in the position I was, I couldn't pull back, not far enough to do any good when they wrapped it about my neck and it scalded the ointment away.

I didn't scream. It was bearable; surely it was bearable. *Go deep . . . do not feel . . . let it pass. . . .*

As the Zhid spoke enchantments that curdled my blood, the hot metal shifted and flowed and settled into position, smooth and close-fitting. Then they threw cold water over me. Sick and trembling, I thought I had come through the worst.

"Anyone important about who wants the pleasure of the seal?"

"You'll have to set them yourself. Master hasn't been seen all day, and he has no guests. I've got to get the next one ready. We've a hundred more."

"Ah, I can do them faster anyway." The guard went away, leaving only the man in black.

"Well, slave, one more thing to do. The joining. Back here . . ." He ran his finger along the narrow slot where the ends of the collar lay along my spine. "As Slavemaster Gernald would tell you if he were considerate enough to make himself available, we've discovered a substance far more effective than dolemar in controlling Dar'Nethi power. *Mordemar* it's called. Not only prevents any use of true talent, you won't be able to acquire power for it neither. No more of it. Ever again. Your collar will be with you until you die, and so you will spend the rest of your days half a man. Enjoy it."

Liquid dripped on the strip of skin exposed between the ends of the collar. Hot, though nothing compared to the searing collar itself. But as the liquid seal filled the gap, completing the ring about my neck, it gnawed its way into my being as surely as acid devours flesh. And then I screamed.

Suffocation . . . paralysis . . . blindness . . . What words can convey the loss? A soul excised, the mind uprooted and ripped apart, the world reduced to two dimensions instead of three. What would be the universe without a color like red or blue or green? What would life be if there were, all of an instant, only men, or only women, or if there were to be no children ever again?

As the seal cooled and hardened, my screams faded to weeping. I had lost the Way. I could not savor the moment because I could not see the colors of the fire, only the blaze of it. I could not see the marvelous intricacies of the granite on which my tears fell, only a cold slab. No longer could I feel the air on my bare skin and sense all the places that air had been, the faces it had touched. I could feel only the cold and the heat and the pain. Death and cruelty could no longer be fit into any larger meaning, for the ability to take them into myself and see beyond had been stripped from me. No more. Ever again. Better . . . far better if they had taken my mind, if I had been made nameless and cruel, so long as I did not understand what I had lost.

I could not have said when they removed the common shackles from my wrists, replaced them with wide, close-fitting bands of the same dark metal, and sealed them as well. When one is in uttermost despair, no pain or indignity can make it worse. After removing the hobbles, they gave me a gray tunic to cover myself, hooked a tether chain to my collar, and led me back to the slave pen. They had removed the dead and the crippled, and put down clean straw. Everyone remaining had close-cropped hair, gray tunics, and collars, and like each one of them, I huddled into myself against the bitter night.

CHAPTER 32

Morning. The sun was scarcely risen, and the pen was already stifling. Those of us in the cage could not even look at each other—not from any enchantment, but because by seeing we would acknowledge the reality of what had been done to us. It was an unspeakable violation, an unimaginable horror to be so maimed.

Step back. Observe. Learn everything there is to learn. You are not alone. . . .

Stupid. Of course I was alone. The collar separated me from all of life, from my race, from everyone I knew and everything I had ever been.

You are not alone. There are others. Watch and learn. . . . Thoughts and calculations running rampant in my head, as if I had heart or mind to care. Madness nibbling at my edges. *Listen . . . outside the cage . . . why are we left so long untended?*

"Are they to be fed then?" Someone outside the cage. "It would be a waste to have brought them this far if not. We were up half the night getting them fixed."

"I've no orders."

"Somebody's got to know."

"Bring me orders and I'll feed 'em. Not till then."

I was tempted to call after them that they shouldn't bother feeding us, but instead I leaned my head against the cage and tried to see between the bars. It was hopeless. The field of vision was so narrow. Hard-packed earth, endless movement, horses—I could smell them. Hundreds of foot soldiers marching, drilling . . .

"Have you heard about Gernald?"

"Aye. In his bath, they said."

"And he'd only been here a month."

"Looks like he ate something off."

"Someone new's been sent by. . . ."

The two passed beyond my hearing. Why did their words fill me with such despair?

More bits of meaningless conversation drifted by. Shouted orders. A great deal of activity. Sen Ystar may have been the first to feel the Zhid assault, but it would not be the last. These were not small raiding parties being prepared. *Avonar . . . oh, Avonar, be vigilant. . . .*

I must have drifted off to sleep in the heat, for when the gate to the pen opened and the guard yelled, "Up, you lazy pigs," the angle of the shadow cage had changed significantly. I considered not following, but the Zhid had shown us on the first day of captivity what disobedience would mean—the death of another captive. Quite simply, they would make you a murderer. It didn't matter that the poor soul would most likely thank me for causing his death. I couldn't do it. So I put myself in line with the rest.

Four armed guards were waiting at the gate. "This one for the mines. . . . For house slave . . . For the farms . . ." They were sorting us.

I was the first to be designated "practice slave," and was shoved back into the pen. Evidently the collars were marked with our assignment. When the next practice slave was selected, I saw the image of a sword etched into the dark metal of his collar, so I guessed mine had one also. I almost reached up to find out, but I could not make myself touch the thing.

Three of us were designated to be practice slaves. As soon as the assignments were complete and our former companions led away, we were taken inside the building again, this time to stand before a pale man with a narrow, aristocratic face. He sat behind a wide desk in a bare, windowless, stifling room, flanked by two heavily armed Zhid.

"Only three this lot?"

"Yes, Slavemaster," said the Zhid who had brought us in.

"I understand we've used up three practice slaves this week alone. We'll have to do better."

"There's another lot due tomorrow."

"Well, let's have a look at these." The Zhid officer rose from his desk and walked around us slowly, poking at each of us with the handle of a whip. He stopped in front of us. "So, my Dar'Nethi friends. You've been chosen to die in order to make your enemies invincible. The time of your death will depend on how diligent you are—and how obedient. You will be required to fight to the best of your ability, even if it means death to one of our warriors." He tapped his whip in his hand. "Because you must be able to fight effectively, we cannot bind you with the same compulsions we use on other slaves. But we do have methods to prevent your taking advantage of your freedoms. You will be penned when not in use, and— Let me show you what I mean. You"—he pointed the whip handle at me—"kneel."

I did so. Grudgingly. But I did.

"It is required that a slave spread his arms when kneeling. Ten lashes if you fail to do so again."

He stood close enough that I could smell his slightly astringent sweat. "Now, take me down." I looked up stupidly, and he spit in my face. "Are you deaf? Obey, or one of your companions will find himself without a head. Take me down."

With much misgiving, I swept my arms around to grab his knees, releasing far too much anger in the process. But I had scarcely touched him when he laid his finger on my collar. Spasms of fire rippled through my muscles, my chest, my limbs . . . everywhere. The collar constricted my throat, so I couldn't get a breath. When he took his hand away, I collapsed, gasping and shaking, huddled in a mindless knot on the floor.

The Zhid resumed his seat. "Cinnegar here is your keeper and will tell you how it is you will eat, sleep, clean yourself, and train. Speak without permission, and we will remove your tongue. You have no life that is your own, no function save what we require of you, and so it will be until you die."

For the rest of the day, Cinnegar, a short, burly Zhid with reddish hair and a nasty scar on his left cheek, put the three of us through one exercise after another. We ran, jumped, and demonstrated our skills with bows and staves, and he had us fight each other with a variety of blades and knives, and with bare hands, our only orders not to damage each other. We worked in an unshaded, walled compound, but were allowed to dip into a water barrel as often as we needed and eat graybread until we felt bloated.

One of my companions was a scrawny youth of about twenty. He was a decent fighter, precise and quick with his movements, able to present a variety of attacks and defenses, but he had no training in tactics and no endurance at all. Our second bout left him panting and lead-footed. Eight days of the desert and the horror of the collaring had done nothing for any of us, of course, and my own arms felt heavy early on. My feet were wretched. Raw and stinging, they bled as we worked.

The second man was nearer my own age, a short, blocky fellow with thick brows. He had no skills, only brute strength and such fear that it brought him near frenzy when I wrestled with him.

"Calm yourself," I growled in his ear as we rolled on the ground. "Live." I pinned him in moments. He squeezed his eyes shut, and tears rolled down his leathery cheeks. As I stood and reached out my hand to help him up, he gripped it ferociously.

By sundown we were too tired to move. Cinnegar made no comments about our efforts. He shoved us into individual cells in a stable-like block of them, giving us each a basket of graybread and a waterskin. "Bang on the bars if you need more. Someone might come or might not." He showed us how to ask permission to speak. You slapped the back of your hand against your lips, then drew it sharply away.

Even after Cinnegar left us alone, we kept silent. Though no guards were in sight, I wasn't willing to risk my tongue by saying anything.

I sank down on the straw and picked a chunk of graybread from the basket. Eating was about the last thing I wanted to do at the moment, but I forced myself. The days would get no easier, I guessed, and I wanted to live. As I leaned against the bars, staring at a second unappetizing lump, a motion from one of the other cells caught my eye. The older man had lifted his own bread to me in salute. I returned his gesture, and we matched each other bite for bite through piece after piece of the sour stuff.

With every swallow, I felt the collar. Could one ever become accustomed to such a thing? It was wide enough to prevent a complete range of motion with the head—something to be considered in combat. The Zhid warriors would know. It was as tight as it could possibly fit without choking, tight enough to keep you on the near edge of panic all the time, tight enough you could never forget it. Tentatively I reach my hand up to touch the thing. Oh, gods . . . I heaved up all the foul stuff I had eaten, and after an hour's venture into the realm of despair, I fell asleep shivering and empty. At some time in the night, though, I woke and forced myself to eat. I had to live. It was imperative that I live. I just couldn't imagine why I felt that way.

For a week the three of us trained together every day, all day, under the watchful eye of Cinnegar or one of his deputies. The work was long, hard, and viciously hot, but we managed. Each day I grew a little stronger, my principal worry being my feet. Swollen and festering, they'd become so tender that even to stand still was agony.

At the end of the week, the slavemaster came to watch our practice. "Have you decided on placement?" he asked Cinnegar.

"This one should stay here." The red-haired Zhid pointed to the older man. "He can join the battle exercise planned for next week. He is mediocre at best and is unlikely to survive more than one or two rounds. The youth has improved his stamina, but will always be unexceptional in his skills. However, he could serve us in a low-level training unit. Niemero's unit lost a slave last week, and this one can replace him. This one"—his pale eyes fell on me—"is interesting. If he were to get his feet in better condition, he could possibly begin work with the command training unit. Sword training in particular. He might do very well."

"I hear that your eye is excellent, Keeper Cinnegar. As I'm new to the post, I shall have to rely on it. All shall be done as you recommend."

Cinnegar bowed to the slavemaster, and then returned us to the pen. The youth was taken that evening. He nodded to each of us as he was tethered and led out of the pen. Not long after that, one of Cinnegar's slavehandlers came for me, linking my hands and feet and hooking a chain to the collar. The other man saluted me with his graybread one last time and sat alone in the pen as I was taken away.

The slavehandler marched me through the vast encampment to another "stable" of black bars—a long cage attached to one end of a brick building. "Here's the new one to put away," he said to a warrior who stood in an open doorway in the brick wall, drinking from a metal cup. "His first placing. Only a sevenday in."

The guard, a wide-nosed fellow with deep weather creases across his brow, poured out the remaining contents of his cup, splattering damp globs of sand on my legs. After hooking his cup to his belt, he took my tether from the slavehandler and raked an insolent gaze over me from head to sandy toes. "Big fellow." He coiled the tether chain around his hand until my face was only a handsbreadth from his own, his soulless gray eyes unblinking. His meaty finger traced a line across my shoulder. When his finger encountered my collar, I flinched. He grinned—a grotesque, unnerving expression on a damnable Zhid. But he just tapped on the metal surface without triggering the enchantment. "We'll see how long he can stay alive."

"I've got to fetch Gorag," said the handler. "Keeper says we're to see to his feet." As my escort hurried into the night, the guard released the tether to its full length and dragged me through the door.

We stood in a small open space, sheltered by the brick wall behind and to the right of us and a brick enclosure to the left. The Zhid jerked his head to two doorways on the left. "Supply room and surgeon's room. Over here"—he indicated the corner to our right where a rectangular stone sink stood half filled with nasty-looking water—"is where you will wash yourself before a match. Our commanders don't like fighting with slaves who are filthy."

Directly in front of us was a wall of the familiar narrowly spaced black bars. Taking the lantern that hung over the sink and unlocking a gate in the center of the wall, the guard led me down an aisle between the cells, some twleve of them in all. The lamp wasn't bright enough for me to see more than indistinct shapes sitting or lying on the floor in each one. No one moved as we passed.

Halfway down the aisle was an open door, leading into a cell with a thick layer of straw over the dirt floor. The guard unhooked the tether chain and shoved me inside. "Water and graybread will be brought. Down there at the far end of the stable is a pile of clean straw. You'll be permitted to change the straw once in a month, so you'll want to have a care with your habits. Remember, slaves don't speak without permission." He grinned again as he slammed the door and locked it. "I like removing tongues."

I sank onto the straw, grateful to get off my wretched feet. The cooling night breeze blew through the bars. As the guard's footsteps receded, a dreadful quiet enveloped me. Whatever scraps of resilience I had left withered in the silence.

My cell was a cube a few paces on a side. The graybread basket and the waterskin were hung on the bars beside the door and center aisle, where they could be filled from outside the cage. Nothing but the vague dark outlines of buildings was visible past the outer bars, and though the cells on either side of me were occupied, I could neither see nor hear the occupants, only feel their human presence.

An hour later, as I huddled in the corner trying to persuade myself to sleep, the stable gate opened with a clang and the lamp moved down the aisle. The guard stopped outside my cell. "Up with you."

Holding onto the bars, I dragged myself to my feet, unable even to speculate on what was coming. He led me to one of the rooms in the brick enclosure, shoved me onto a long wooden bench along one wall, and attached both my tether chain and my hands to an iron ring set into the wall above my head. Then he left me alone in the sputtering yellow light of an oil lamp.

The small room had wooden benches around every wall and more iron rings set into the walls and the floors. The room also sported a long table, a backless stool, and a small wheeled table holding a basin and pitcher. Surgeon's room, the guard had told me.

Before very long, a Zhid hurried in, carrying a large leather case. He was a small, tidy man with a short beard trimmed close around his full lips. Tossing his case on the table, he yelled at someone outside the door to bring him cavet.

He dragged the stool over beside the bench and sat down. "Let me see your feet," he said, slapping the stained wooden bench. "Here."

I propped my throbbing feet on the bench, and the Zhid took one in hand and examined it, poking here and there with his thumbs, dusting off the caked sand. His face wrinkled in disgust, he dropped my foot and retrieved his case. After fetching one of the basins and filling it with water from the pitcher, he set to work—none too gently—cutting the dead skin away, and draining and cleaning the nastiest festerings. A boy brought the surgeon a tin cup filled with steaming dark liquid that smelled strongly of anise. He gulped the drink and went back to work, mumbling about the waste of his time and talent on slaves. Several times he made odd gestures with his fingers and I felt a painful burning and stretching deep in my foot. Some devilish enchantment, I guessed, but I could not detect such things any more. I tried to concentrate on anything else, but there wasn't much to distract me.

As the surgeon covered the open wounds with ointments and bandages, and I was breathing a little easier, another slave was brought in and attached to the wall across the room. He was bleeding from a deep gash in his thigh and had a vicious swelling over one eye. I tried to engage the man's attention, but he kept his eyes averted.

"This one has to fight again tomorrow, so patch him well," said the guard. "Are you done with this lot?"

The surgeon tied off my last bandage, cut off the end

with his knife, and stood up. "Keep him idle for a day. And send the mule-brained Drudge with more cavet." As I was detached from the ring and led hobbling away, he was pulling out materials to stitch the other man's thigh. I didn't envy the poor bastard.

A Zhid Healer. The very concept made my head hurt.

The next day was long and unsettling. Left idle by the surgeon's order, I listened and learned. The other slaves were taken out one by one through the morning, assigned to high-ranking warriors who had summoned sparring partners. Evidently some of them had regular assignments, while others were moved from one Zhid to another depending on special needs and requests. One man was assigned to wrestling, one to a match with knives and axes, one to speed work with a commander who had been demoted for his lack of agility.

Over and over, I heard the rules laid down. The slave would wear only such armor and use only such weapons—real or blunted practice weapons—as the Zhid warrior specified. The slave was required to fight to the best of his abilities and to participate in such exercises and drills as the warrior or his instructor devised. The slave was not permitted to yield the match or stop the exercise. Only Zhid could call a halt.

As the slaves were taken out of the pen, led by tethers attached to their collars, none of them looked to one side or the other. Was it forbidden, or was it just too painful to see others witnessing one's degradation? Perhaps it was only fear of what was to come, for one day's watching taught me how fleeting was a career as a sparring partner for the Zhid.

A man was found dead in his cell that morning. Two more wounded men were brought back by midday, told they would be looked at when the surgeon had time. One of them was in the cell next to me, and in his shallow struggling breaths I heard an ominous gurgling. I banged on the bars of my cell. When the guard came, I slapped the back of my hand on my lips.

"Speak."

"The man next to me is dangerously wounded. I can hear it in his breathing. His chest—"

"Is that all? Call me again for such a reason, and I'll have you flogged." He spat at the dying man and walked away.

I had to do something. My hand fit between the bars, but only as far as the wrist bands. The steel loops that were used for restraints wouldn't fit through, and my neighbor lay too far away for my fingers to reach. With no talent for healing and no power for mind-speaking or anything else, words were all I could offer him. Many times in the days I'd fought on the walls of Avonar, I had heard Dar'Nethi Healers pray their invocation and found comfort in the familiar words. Perhaps they might do the same for the dying man and remind him of who he was. So I whispered the verse through the bars of the cell, hoping the guard would not pass by and hear.

"Life, hold. Stay your hand ere it lays another step along the Way. Grace your son once more with your voice that whispers in the deeps, with your spirit that sings in the wind, with the fire that blazes in your wondrous gifts of joy and sorrow. Fill his soul with light, and let the darkness make no stand in this place. *Je'den encour*, my brother. Heal swiftly."

A rasping whisper responded. "L'Tiere calls. I go freely."

"May Vasrin's light show you the Way beyond the Verges."

"I had almost forgotten. . . ."

"I, too," I said, but only to myself, for the struggling breaths had ceased with his last word. It was several hours until the guard noticed the man was dead and dragged him down the aisle. I could not see his face.

The other man survived until the surgeon came. Evidently his leg was maimed beyond easy repair. He was taken away in a cart.

The afternoon stretched long and hot and quiet. My graybread basket and waterskin were kept filled by a boy who wore no collar. I supposed he had no power that required such bondage. No way to tell. Snippets of conversation from the guards and those who passed by outside the pen drifted on the air: Someone named Gensei Senat had been posted to Zhev'Na; the previous slavemaster, who had only taken office a month before, had died suddenly; another Dar'Nethi village had been taken. The Lords were pleased with the outcome of the raid.

The Lords . . . Zhev'Na . . . No Dar'Nethi child grew up without nightmares of Zhev'Na, and yet I could not say I had ever really believed in the Lords or their fortress. I was beginning to believe.

What I did come to believe in was the Zhid surgeon. He knew his business. By the next morning, though still tender to the touch, my feet were no longer hot with festering. He dressed them again, wrapped them tightly, and cleared me to fight.

One of Cinnegar's slavehandlers came for me while the air was still cool. After reminding me of the rules, he led me through the camp to a walled yard of hard-baked dirt. In one corner was a water barrel. Piled beside it were a variety of weapons, shields, and armor. Standing in the center of the arena were a brawny Zhid warrior, clad in a hauberk and steel cap, and another slave, who was strapping steel kneecaps over the warrior's greaves. "The warrior has requested sparring with great-swords," said the handler, detaching my tether and nodding toward the pile of arms. "You will follow his instructions."

I poked through the pile and pulled out a decent sword. Strange to feel a weapon in my hand after so many days. Tempting. But the warrior's personal slave knelt beside the slavehandler. I knew the price of any misbehavior on my part.

The Zhid warrior took his stance, sword raised. "Ready," he said.

I stepped to the center of the training ground and raised the sword. Unnerving that he was armored, while I was left in my skimpy tunic and sore, bandaged feet. But the day's rest had done me good, and I liked great-swords. I had the height and weight to carry them well. Besides, I held the echo of a dying man's voice in my head, and the cursed Zhid had no imagination at all.

Five times during the morning, the warrior called a halt

to our sparring, rested, changed weapons or armor, and started again. The sixth time, he complained to the slavehandler that I'd taken a superior weapon, and that I should properly be handicapped in some way for not noting it. A hand cut off, perhaps.

The slavehandler summoned Cinnegar. The red-haired Zhid, who evidently had final say in all matters regarding the stable of practice slaves, said he would not allow me to be damaged. Being new, perhaps I'd not been rated properly. The warrior didn't like hearing that, but wasn't of high enough rank to overrule Cinnegar. I was glad for that. He sent me back to the stable.

It was made clear from the first that these matches were strictly physical combat. The Zhid did not use sorcery in their training, believing they must achieve superiority in arms as well as all other aspects of their power. Just as we Dar'Nethi hoarded our power for healing and the defense of our cities, the Zhid hoarded theirs to use in their Seeking, which stole the minds of their enemies.

No sooner had I been penned up again than I was called out for a warrior named Comus. His training ground looked exactly the same as the other, except for the dead slave sprawled on the hard ground with one arm mostly severed and his skull cloven in half. A servant shooed away an army of flies and removed his practice armor so I could put it on. Comus preferred an armored opponent. The padded leather was still warm and wet with the dead man's sweat and blood.

Comus used a great-sword, too, and was big, strong, and vicious. After slogging through a half-day with my earlier opponent, I wished this one preferred a lighter weapon, but eventually I managed to make him yield.

"This one again tomorrow when I'm fresh," Comus said to the guard, pointing his sword at me.

Without heed to heat, hunger, thirst, sore feet, or the various scratches I had collected, I collapsed on the straw and fell instantly asleep. I had survived one day.

I trained with Comus every day, sometimes with padded practice weapons, sometimes with real blades. He was good, but I was just enough better to avoid serious injury. We worked on strikes and appropriate counters, defensive strategies appropriate to certain positions, timing and balance. He began to copy a few of my moves, and it made me wonder what in perdition I was doing. It was an argument I could not resolve. To fight the cursed Zhid—what slave could ask for more than a chance to injure or kill his captors? Yet I was teaching him to kill more of my own people.

But I could not refuse to fight or to follow their rules. In my first week with Comus, I was given a clear demonstration of the consequences of disobedience. During one of our rest periods, Comus laid a wager with another Zhid that his personal slave had more impressive private parts than did his friend's slave. When Comus commanded his slave to strip to prove the bet, the kneeling man, who had not moved during the animated discussion, closed his eyes.

" . . . And arouse yourself," said Comus, sniggering. "I do not like losing."

The slave looked up at Comus in shock, then hardened his jaw and slowly shook his head.

Comus's bullish face went livid, and he belted his slave across the mouth. "I could have invoked your compulsions," he said, "but it was inconceivable that my slave would refuse a simple command." Then, without taking a breath, Comus lopped off the head, not of his own slave, but that of his friend's slave. "Now. I command you once more. Strip yourself and this dog meat, and we shall see how the cock of a live Dar'Nethi compares to that of a dead one."

The horror-stricken slave did as he was commanded, and though I averted my eyes so as not to witness his shame, I could not help but be relieved at his compliance. There was no other slave nearby. My head would have been the price of another refusal.

The days may have been filled with enough combat and sweat to block out rational thought, but the nights were long, with plenty of time for guilt and self-loathing. I did as I was told. I had to live . . . I had things to do in my life . . . vital things . . . This conviction rumbled in my belly like war drums. Was this some Zhid compulsion laid on slaves along with our collars to prevent us doing away with ourselves?

After three weeks Comus wanted to move on to some other kind of training, and I was assigned to another warrior. He was a rapier man and very quick. From the beginning, he forbade me to withhold, insisting that I fight with every skill I possessed. He certainly withheld nothing. If his accuracy had been better, I might have taken more than a few punctures and a bloody cheek while I was adjusting to the different style of fighting. I worked with him for over a month, and then I killed him.

It was a lucky thrust at the end of a long day, and I think the sun got in his eyes. He had wanted to practice a new technique with unblunted tips and had not bothered to put on his sparring vest. Caught up in the exhilaration of combat, he had expanded the practice into a full-blown duel. When I realized what I had done, I immediately looked around to see who had witnessed it. My handler had not returned. The only other person present was the officer's personal slave whose usual bleak expression brightened into a grin. He pressed a finger to his lips and motioned me away. He knew I had no binding compulsion to stay where I was.

Run . . . I had at most an hour before the handler would come. If I could get through the encampment without anyone noticing the mark of the sword on my collar, then perhaps I could make it as far as the cliffs by nightfall. Barefoot. Unarmed, for I dared not carry a weapon through the camp. One chance in a thousand I would make it to the hills. One in fifty thousand they wouldn't find me. One in a million that I could make it across the Wastes to the Vales of Eidolon. I wasn't certain even in what direction they lay. And yet, I would have tried except for the nagging conviction that I was not alone, that I had to listen and be ready. . . . Oh, gods, be ready for what?

I had lived for eight weeks, each day tallied carefully with a length of straw placed in the bottom of my bread basket. Only two men had been in the stable longer. The rest of those who had been there when I arrived were dead, and new slaves had taken their places. I could no longer imagine the taste of any food but the dry, sour graybread, nor any drink but stale, tepid water. The remembrance of savory roast chicken or frostberries soaked in wine filled me with disgust. All such physical cravings had gone dead or turned into revulsion. Food, wine, women . . . even a touch would be unbearable. The faces of my friends had faded from my memory no matter how hard I worked at reconstructing them, and I cursed bitterly when I discovered I could not bring to my mind the winding lanes of Sen Ystar. Even the memories of the beauteous Vales had blurred. So why could I not run?

I shrugged my shoulders at the eager slave and sat down in the dust by the dead warrior to wait for the slavehandler. I had to live, but I was damned if I knew why.

When a slave killed a Zhid in training, it was not taken lightly. The slavemaster came in to lead an investigation. He interrogated Cinnegar to ensure the keeper hadn't scheduled a mismatch, and the surgeon to determine the cause of death. Acquaintances of the deceased were questioned, as well as his servants and aides. The slave was placed under compulsions to discover if any person, Zhid, slave, or servant, had aided him in the match. Even when all was found to be proper, one more ritual was involved.

"Lest you forget your place," said the slavemaster, touching my collar. He sneered in disgust at my retching spasms.

And so it went on. I made it past four months and saw seventeen men—the flower of Dar'Nethi manhood—perish in that wretched stable. For every one I whispered the Healer's invocation, weeping in impotent fury at the lonely ignominy of their deaths. Only a few of them even heard the words, but I could think of nothing else to do for them. I hounded the guards and the surgeon as much as I dared, to care for their wounds more quickly, to preserve the Lords' "investment" in experienced practice partners, but soon it was rare for a guard to answer my rattling of the bars or to permit me to speak when I begged it.

I killed another warrior and paid the price again, and

then I took a wound in the shoulder that kept me out of action for a week. The surgeon said he had been given orders to make sure I was healed. "The Lords are interested in skill—even of your mundane sort."

The week of idleness was almost unbearable. The demands in my head to live and to learn became so insistent that every voice made me start. I paced my cell, unable to rest and unable to eat. I forced down the graybread and water and commanded myself to sleep, for I dared not lose my edge. Yet when I dropped off, strange dreams plagued me, of rooms and faces I didn't know, of horrors that made me wake up screaming, of words that made me weep though I couldn't capture them on waking. The surgeon examined my wound and said it was healing as expected, but I had best get some sleep or all his work would go for nothing.

I slapped the back of my hand against my mouth. "Speak," he said.

"Can you give me something to make me sleep? So I won't dream?" My own voice sounded harsh and alien to me. I had gone weeks without speech.

Gorag, the Zhid surgeon, poked around in his leather case and came up with a blue vial. "Perhaps this will help." His voice dropped to a whisper. "I shouldn't give it to you, but I have a wager with Cinnegar that you'll make it past half a year. I don't like to lose." He poured the contents down my throat and called the handler. I slept for two days straight and had no dreams at all. When he examined my shoulder and pronounced it fit, I asked permission to speak again. He shook his head. "Better not. Just stay alive two more months."

I managed it. I fought and trained like a madman, as indeed I began to believe I was. Gorag's blue vial had only suspended my strange malady temporarily. I considered asking him for more of it, but I couldn't afford to be drowsy either. The only way to sleep was to work myself to exhaustion. So even after a full day of training with a Zhid warrior, I would run in place or do some other exercise until I dropped to the straw like a dead man.

On the day I had been in the stable six months, I killed

my seventh Zhid. Nincas was a murderously cruel villain, who tortured his servants and slaves to death for the pleasure of it. I enjoyed killing him. We battled for half a day in a series of timed bouts. A bull of a man, he was not about to yield to a slave as long as there were any onlookers, and Gorag had gathered at least a hundred of them to witness the winning of his bet. I could think of nothing but death that day, and when at last I pulled my sword from his belly, I stabbed it in again and again and again, until my arms were covered in blood and I could no longer lift my weapon. I fell to my knees on the hot desert floor and began to laugh, but there was no joy in it. I could not remember joy. . . .

"V'Saro!" Hands slapped my cheeks. "V'Saro, wake up!" Straw poked at my cheek. I couldn't remember being taken to my cell. I was achy and dull and smelled like death. "Here, have a drink." My waterskin was thrust into my hands. I drained it and then promptly heaved the water up again. "Come, V'Saro. You've made me a rich man, and for that I will do you a favor. A risky matter. No one is supposed to talk to you until you've been interrogated."

Gorag. He had helped me sleep. I slapped the back of my hand to my mouth.

"Yes, yes, speak."

"Go drown yourself in your cursed water."

"You're raving. No one has ever seen such a match as you fought today. The slavemaster comes. He's heard of your feat . . . and also of how you finished it." The wiry little surgeon gestured in disgust at the dark blood that covered my arms and crusted my stiff tunic. "If you want to live, then you'd best gather your wits."

My existence had no relation to life. I could not feel life any more—thanks to the collar. But I had to keep breathing. There was purpose to my existence. I was not alone. "How much could you win if I make it a year?"

"Not enough to make me a Lord of Zhev'Na, but perhaps enough that I could get out of this blasted camp."

He stuffed a lump of graybread in my hands. "Eat, and clean yourself. They talk of sending you to Zhev'Na, where the elite of our commanders are trained. But they'll not send you if they think you're mad. They won't allow a madman to live with such strength and skill as yours. Do you understand?"

I grunted.

Gorag slipped out of the cell and locked it quietly, then scurried away in the dark. After a while, I banged on the bars, and the smirking guard came.

"Speak," he said, to my gesture. "Unless you are going to tell me about some whining slave who needs a nursemaid."

"I want to wash."

"*Do* you now?"

"I have an early match tomorrow with the protégé of Gensei Senat. I'll sleep better if I'm clean, and it will save you trouble in the morning. Perhaps you'll want to bet on my victory."

He shrugged his shoulders and let me out. Likely a small share of Gorag's winnings prompted his generosity. He sat on the half-wall and watched while I stripped and washed in the slimy sink. I rinsed the blood from my tunic, wrung it out, and hung it on the bars of my cell to dry, and then I pulled straw over me to keep out the chill.

That night I dreamed of a house in a great city, a graceful house whose owner clearly valued the refinements of art and music and literature. A silver flute lay on a music stand, awaiting its player, and books and manuscripts touching every aspect of history and nature and philosophy were poised to enlighten an intelligent eye. The library opened onto a small garden, its soft, sweet air touched with the scent of roses. I wandered through the softly lit passageways looking for someone, though I did not know who. No one was there. Only emptiness. Only sorrow.

The slavemaster woke me to the broiling stench of the slave pen and laid me under compulsions for questioning. It took him an hour to conclude that I was not mad; then he touched my collar to teach me my place and sent me to Zhev'Na.

CHAPTER 33

Seri

For unending days and weeks I ate and slept and stitched, refusing every intrusion of thought or sense until I could scarcely distinguish myself from my companions. Every so often my nagging conscience reminded me that I had purpose to my life, that people were depending on me. But impossibility and drudgery quickly stifled such uncomfortable ideas. I went for days on end without registering a single memorable word or incident or giving the least passing remembrance to my son or my friends or the perilous state of the world. My cherished hope that Karon yet existed somewhere in this world withered and died. He never would have abandoned me in this place.

The morning one of the sewing women was found dead on her pallet was the nadir. Gam had died in her sleep, and only when Kargetha asked where was our eighth did anyone think to mention it. Her body was dragged off by a slave to be stripped and burned. No sign of her remained when we returned to the dormitory that night. She had been a gregarious person as the sewing women went, and not unkind, but she was forgotten as quickly as the breakfast gruel. When I asked the others how long she had sewn in Zhev'Na, they only shrugged and went back to work.

My blood stirred. No one should finish her life in such a fashion. I had come close to it myself, in my days in Dunfarrie, when I believed I had lost everything, and habit was the only reason I could find to get up every morning. That time a mute, desperate stranger had collapsed at my feet, forcing me to re-engage with the world. Gam's desolate passing pricked me awake before I had to make that long journey all over again. If I was going to die, then it might as well be to some purpose. And so, the next time Kargetha told Zoe to send someone to the Gray House, rather than staying quiet and sullen as the others did, I spoke up.

"I think Zoe should go." The sewing women gaped at me in shock. I shifted on my feet and used my sleeve to wipe the sweat tickling my brow. "She always sends the rest of us, and never goes herself. 'Tisn't right. Dia got kicked last week, and Lun got beat bad when she dropped her basket in the Lords' house, even though she was run into by a Worship. But Zoe never gets in trouble because she never goes nowhere."

"What is your name?" asked Kargetha, staring. Incredulous.

"Eda, your Worship." I cast my eyes down.

"Ah, yes. Eda. The one who talks too much. I think perhaps you have talked too much once again. From now on you will make all deliveries from this group and fetch all the thread, leather, and cloth from the warehouses. Do you hear me?"

"But your Worship—"

"One more word and I will compel you to silence for a year." The finger pointing at my ear tag was thin and knotted like an oak twig.

I dipped my knee and covered my face with my hands, so she couldn't see my relief . . . and satisfaction.

Glowering and mumbling, I made three or four trips a day—hot, dusty journeys, carrying heavy loads, subject to the abusive whims of Zhid warriors and administrators. On the fourth day I was sent to the kitchens of the Gray House.

I dropped my scratchy load of storage bags in the wooden bin where the kitchen Drudge directed me. After rolling each bag individually and stacking them as I was told, I wandered across the hot kitchen. The Drudge woman was stirring a kettle of thin, yellowish soup that smelled of cabbage, while another woman was tossing chunks of onion into it.

I sniffed at their kettle. "Are you making this for the

young Lord?" I asked. "I never thought one so high-placed would eat the same as us."

The toothless woman stirring the pot glanced at me as if I had asked if she lived on the moon. "The young Lord gets only what is fit for Worships, not Drudge's food. And he ben't here to eat nothing."

"I heard he come back here two days ago," I said. No one was ever amazed at ignorance.

"Someone told you wrong, girl. He's gone off with the Worships long ago." The second woman blotted her oily face with her apron and began to knead a pile of sticky, gray dough.

I picked up a scrap of onion from the floor and nibbled at it. "Where do they go? When folks left my work camp, none of 'em ever came back. Nobody ever told me where folks go when they disappear."

"Are you an idiot, child? Have you not heard of the war camps in the desert? All Worships go there, and so this young Lord has done. Drudges go wherever they're sent as what our masters think best. No use to task your thick head on it."

"I am so ignorant. I never thought a Lord, one so favored and so young, would go to the desert camps. I thought that was for the *lesser* of the Worships. But I guess the young one was not so favored if he had to leave this fine house and go there. Did he do something to offend the mighty Lords?"

"Such is Lords' business, not servants. Why ever would you care?"

"I'm just new here, and . . . I shouldn't say it"—I dropped my voice low—"I am so afraid of the Lords and those who wear their mark. We heard such fearful tales in my work camp. I thought that if the young Lord who wore their jewels was not to be here ever again, then I wouldn't be so afraid to come to the Gray House when I was told."

"It's proper to be afraid of those higher," said the woman stirring the pot. "I don't know if the young Lord will come back from the camps, but he may. No one can predict the ways of the Worships."

A Zhid supervisor entered and shooed me back to the sewing rooms.

To discover a way to follow Gerick to the desert camps was a daunting prospect. I had heard mention of at least twenty different headquarters—which might be only a small part of the truth or much more than the truth—and I had no idea to which one he'd gone. The only source of information that came to mind was the slave Sefaro, the chamberlain of the Gray House.

Unfortunately, trips to the Gray House were a rarity. Most of my errands were to the guard barracks, delivering tunics and leggings and other apparel for the common Zhid warriors who lived in the fortress. Other ventures took me to the tanners and leatherworkers, to the spinners to get thread, or to the weavers for heavy rolls of cloth. On rare occasion Kargetha would send bundles of rags or gray tunics to the grim and wretched slave pens beyond the barracks and the forge. A few times I was sent into the Lords' house. No matter how bright the sun blazed, within those dark walls the light was always like the hour before dawn, when only the barest hint of color had begun to emerge from black and gray. The air felt too thick to breathe.

After weeks of frustration, I was at last sent to the Gray House with instructions to seek out Sefaro. I found him alone in his storeroom, sitting at the plain wooden table and working at his ledger. He seemed preoccupied, giving me only a cursory nod, rather than his usual smile. "Her Worship Kargetha understands there be needs in the Gray House." I gave him Kargetha's token that permitted him to speak.

Sefaro sighed and fingered the small wooden disk. "The banners. We need the banners to be made."

"The young Lord's banners?" A flush of waking life rippled across my skin.

"He returns in a sevenday, and we're to have the new banners hung for his arrival. I'll show you the device which must be placed on them." The chamberlain's hand trembled as he pulled out paper and pen and began to sketch.

"Are you not well, Sefaro?" I said, my soaring spirits restrained only by concern for the kind slave.

He shook his head and continued his drawing, gripping his pen as if it were a dagger.

I had come prepared to scatter my questions like seeds in a garden, carefully harvesting the things I needed to know. But Sefaro's disturbance hinted that this was not a day for subtleties. So, I took a step of faith. "Of all those I've observed in this place, Sefaro, you're the only one who's seemed immune to its terrors. What's changed?"

His hand slowed, and, after a moment, he looked up from his drawing. "Who are you, Eda?" His voice was very quiet. "Each time I've met you, I've wondered at it, only to call myself a fool in the next breath. What Drudge would ever think to tell me of an injured child? And now . . ."

I sat down in the wooden chair opposite him, and spoke in a whisper. "Who I am is no matter. But I know of the Way, and I grieve to see those who so embrace life held captive in this fortress of death."

His crinkled eyes grew wide. "Heaven's fire . . . what Drudge knows of the Way?"

"Just say I have more curiosity than is usual in Ce Uroth. Is there something about the young Lord's return that troubles you? Does he use you cruelly?"

"He is not cruel. At least, before this sojourn in the desert, he was not. Thoughtless, sometimes. He is very young, though he tries to be otherwise. But three of his teachers—all high-ranking Zhid—have been slain this day. And I've been told to complete my inventory and my accounts before he returns. It's unsettling. Most likely nothing." His gray complexion told his belief more truly.

"Do you think they plan to kill you, too?"

"Death has no fear for me. If you know so much of Dar'Nethi, then you know that L'Tiere holds no fear for those of us forced to live without the Way. No, it is for my people I fear. For Avonar. For the Bridge and the worlds."

"Why?"

"Because of this." He turned his sketch where I could see it. Two rampant lions supporting an arch, a device very like the shield of D'Arnath. But the arch was missing its center span, and in the gap was a four-headed beast engulfed in flame. In one clawed hand the beast held a sword, and in the other it crushed the two stars that had once been suspended over D'Arnath's Bridge.

"This is a fearsome device."

"If something isn't done, the young Lord will carry it on his shield. He wears the jewels of the Lords, and all they teach him is evil. Though I cannot fathom how it is possible, I've heard he is to be D'Arnath's Heir."

"That's true."

"Hand of Vasrin." Sefaro's shoulders slumped as if I had dropped the sky on them. "He must be turned from this path." The chamberlain glanced up abruptly. Sharply curious. "Is that why you're here, Eda? Can you turn him?"

"I don't know. If I were closer to him . . . perhaps . . ."

"I can arrange it, if you wish."

"I don't understand."

"I am to make a list of all the house slaves and Drudges that serve here, and a list of possible replacements for each one, including myself. I could put your name on the list as a kitchen servant or a scrub. We have no need for sewing women in the Gray House, but such transfers aren't out of the ordinary. I could put several of the sewing women on the list. Someone will just think it's a mistake, but it wouldn't be worth remedy. No one would believe for a moment that a Drudge would have any reason for preferring one station to another."

"If you could do such a thing, it might mean more than you know."

"I must not know anything." A sweet smile illuminated his face. "Would that I could. But I will bury this gift of your trust like a squirrel buries an acorn in autumn and take my pleasure contemplating it through whatever is to come." He gave me his sketch and the rolls of black and gray silk. "Ten of them. In the sizes I've written here. To be ready in a week."

"Be easy, Sefaro," I said. "May the Light shine on your Way."

He smiled and returned the wooden token into my hand.

A week later, when I was sent to the Gray House to deliver the banners and take up my new assignment, a different slave sat on the chamberlain's stool, and I had no token with which to allow him to speak.

CHAPTER 34

Gerick

It was sometime after my return from the desert that I first ran across the Leiran boy. I had been out riding with my new riding master, a nasty Zhid warrior named Fengara. She made Murn look as kind as the old housekeeper at Comigor. On that particular day, she had slaves set fires with some of the dry thorn bushes that passed for vegetation in Ce Uroth, and I had to make my horse carry me between them.

Zigget was the worst-tempered horse I had ever ridden, and at the first sight of the flaming barriers he went wild, rearing and kicking until I thought my arms might get pulled from their sockets before I had him through the first pair. He repaid my efforts by throwing me on the ground after every pass, snorting and threatening to trample me. Fengara was no help. She ridiculed me for my lack of riding skill and my inability to control the horse with my power. But nothing worked, no matter what I tried, words or whips or sorcery.

By sunset, Zigget was frothing and quivering and tossing his head, but I had no sympathy. I was a mass of bruises and scrapes and thought I might have torn something in my knee. No stable hands were anywhere in sight, so I wrestled Zigget into his box myself and slammed the gate. He bucked and kicked the walls until they shook.

"Bash your brains out, you stupid beast," I yelled and started out of the stable.

I didn't get ten paces from Zigget's stall when my knee buckled. I sat heavily on the straw, wishing a plague on horses and the Lords and the vile, wretched desert. When the throbbing in my knee had eased back below the point of impossibility, and I had hauled myself up to my feet, I heard a soft voice from Zigget's box. "A right mess you are. He oughtn't have done it. Serve him right if you were to bash *his* brains out. Too bad there are those that care for him, or I'd bash him myself for leaving you like this."

It was the wrong day to cross me. I hobbled back to the stall, determined to see who dared speak so of me. I would show him who could bash who. I threw open the gate of the stall, and there was Zigget, the most despicable beast in Ce Uroth, peaceably nuzzling a dirty boy who sat on an upturned barrel. The boy's head was leaning on Zigget's neck, not an arm's length from the teeth that had come near removing my fingers earlier that day.

"What are you doing with my horse, slave?" For some reason the scene infuriated me near bursting.

The boy jumped up. He was not a slave, but one of the uncollared servants, a Drudge. I sometimes forgot they could talk, they were all so stupid.

"Well?"

He shrugged his shoulders and looked vague, as if he didn't know what I was talking about. A snort and a thump from behind him distracted my attention. Zigget had kicked another hole in the wall.

I pulled out my knife. "I'll take care of you, you cursed bag of bones. You'll not live to throw me again."

"If you'd treat him right, he wouldn't go loony at the sight of you," said the boy, stepping between me and the horse.

"Get out of my way." I waved the knife at him.

"It's not his fault."

"He's wild and wicked and deserves to die." I pushed the boy aside, my knife ready to strike as soon as Zigget stopped bucking.

"I guess it's all you know how to do any more—kill what doesn't suit." The boy wasn't really talking to me, but I heard him clearly. Such anger rose up in me that before I knew it, I had him pinned to the floor, ready to put my knife in his throat instead of Zigget's. Though he was bigger than me, he was easy. He knew nothing of true hand combat.

"Go ahead, if you want," he said. "I'm nobody. That's clear enough. But you'll not master Firebreather without killing him. Then it'll be nothing but killing forever."

I held the knife over the boy for a long time, waiting for him to look scared, but he never did. My aching head was filled with darkness, and Parven stirred. *So angry you are . . . What problem is there, young Lord?*

"Nothing," I gritted my teeth and stood up, pushing the boy away with my feet. I was too tired for the Lords. They always wanted to pick everything apart—use every bruise and every breath for a lesson. I wanted no more schooling today. This was an insolent, powerless boy and a stupid horse. "There's nothing wrong. Fengara worked me hard, and I hate her, just as you wish. I'm hot and thirsty, and I have a knee the size of a melon. But since I'm not to be comfortable, it will take me a while to get back to the house, so leave me alone."

Parven chuckled in my head, and it made me angry again.

"Leave me alone!" I let darkness roll over him, until I couldn't hear him any more, and I felt like I was alone inside my head. It was oddly pleasing to know I could do such a thing.

Of course, the boy couldn't have heard Parven. He looked at me strangely and laid his hand on Zigget's neck. The demon horse nosed his hair like an old granny.

"How do you do that?" A suspicion came over me, and I laid a hand on the boy's shoulder. No, he was not Dar'Nethi.

"I call his name and tell him about grass. He likes it."

"Grass?" When I spoke, Zigget flared his nostrils. I backed away in a hurry, out of range of a flying hoof. But to my everlasting annoyance, my foot slipped, and I ended up on the floor of the stall, my knife flying somewhere out of reach, and a hay bundle toppling off a stack right onto my head. The boy turned his face away quickly and made a choking noise. His shoulders started shaking. It seemed odd that he would be afraid, after being so calm when I was about to slit his throat.

"Turn around this way," I said.

He looked over his shoulder at me and snorted, then tried to look sober. But he couldn't, and he burst out laughing. No one laughed in Zhev'Na.

"What's so damned funny?"

"Just . . . well . . . one as dignified as yourself . . . in such a wicked, magical place as this . . . coming so close to killing me not five breaths ago . . . and then getting knocked over by hay and a horse turd. It just don't seem all that fearsome."

I stared at him in disbelief. He scratched his head and squirmed and tried to stop laughing, but then he would burst out again. "I'm sorry, my lord," he said, once he was able to talk again. "I'm truly sorry you're hurt. Should I get someone to help?"

I didn't want anyone else seeing me in such a state. It was dangerous in many ways. "I don't need anyone."

"No. I can see surely not," he said.

I hauled myself up on the gate hinges, and tried to swing the gate open and get away, but the fall had made my knee worse, and I could scarcely take a step. The boy put his hand on Zigget, and said, "Stay. Settle." Then he opened the gate and disappeared into the gloomy stable, coming back with a broken wooden pole that I could use for a cane.

As soon as I was up and out of the stall, he went back to Zigget and closed the gate behind him, leaving me to hobble my way across the yard and through the fortress. I was halfway back to the Gray House before I realized that the boy and I had been speaking Leiran. It was too far to go back, and I was too tired. I wanted a river of hot water and ten hours in my bed, and I knew the Lords would be waiting to teach me more lessons. But I told myself that I would find that insolent boy again and have him explain a few things.

I couldn't do any training the next day. My knee was purple and black and had swelled up almost as large as my head. When my swordmaster came to see why I wasn't in the fencing yard, he looked at it and frowned. "You need a surgeon. You should have said something last night."

"I told Lord Parven about it," I said. I had to work hard not to yell when he touched it.

Half an hour later a bearded Zhid came into my apartments, followed by a young slave, carrying a leather case. I was sitting in a chair with my leg propped up on a footstool. The surgeon, named Mellador, commanded the slave to place a towel under my arm that rested on the chair, and then to kneel close beside my chair. The slave had the tight, edgy look to him that meant that he was acting under compulsion. It was easy to recognize.

"A nasty injury, Your Grace, but we should have no difficulty," said the surgeon, clucking and fussing over my knee. "There will be only a slight burning as I make the incision."

I couldn't imagine what he was doing when he spread a yellow ointment on my forearm, and most likely my mouth dropped open like an idiot when he pulled a knife from his case and made a neat, finger-length incision in the same spot. My arm was mostly numb, only stinging, as he'd said. I tried to pull away, but he gripped my wrist.

"Surely you've seen a healing, Your Grace. If not . . . my utmost apologies for not explaining. Your injury is too severe for ordinary means, and the Lords wish no delay in your training. We shall have it improved quite swiftly. Hold still."

Before I could come out with a single question, Mellador commanded the slave to hold out his arm. The youth obeyed, but as he did so, he looked at me with such an intense, solemn expression that I found myself shifting away from him uneasily. Mellador then cut a gash in the slave's arm just above his metal wrist band. The cut was much deeper than my own, almost to the bone, and it began bleeding profusely. The slave did not cry out, but sucked in a deep, shaking breath. The surgeon bound the slave's arm to mine with a strip of linen, then laid his hands on the slave's head. A brilliant, burning flash filled my head—incredible power, boiling red-and-black fire that coursed through my veins, so sharp and vivid that it almost lifted me off the chair.

Now to work . . . The surgeon's voice had ridden the wave of power into my mind. . . . *mmm . . . a touch here . . . and here* . . . I felt the torn pieces in my knee stretch and knit themselves together again, and what felt like chips of bone that were floating loose make their way back where they belonged. Soon, the discolor of my knee began to fade and the swelling to shrink. Instead of painful throbbing, only a pulsing warmth remained in the joint. I touched my knee with my free hand and was amazed.

I heard a gasping moan at my elbow. The slave was pale and trembling, the bones of his face outlined with pain, his eyes hot with anger. The surgeon's fingers were wrapped about his head like the legs of a huge, pale spider. Even as I watched, the slave's eyes went dead, his mouth dropped open, and spit dripped out of the side of it.

While we have a bit left, we'll take care of your other aches and pains. You have quite a healthy young body, but it appears you've taken quite a pounding this week. Mellador was still chattering inside my head, and the burning wave coursed through my veins like Papa's brandy I had stolen to taste when I was small. And as all my bruises and soreness were eased, the slave slumped heavily against my chair.

"What have you done?" I said, finding my voice far too late.

"Quite finished now. Looks like we'd have to bring in another slave if you had one more scrape."

He untied the flaccid arm from my own, and pushed the lifeless slave onto the floor, thrusting a wad of towels under him to prevent any blood from staining the tile. There was no sign of my incision, and no remnant of my injury, only a vile taste in my mouth and the boiling darkness in my blood.

"He's dead."

"Who . . . the slave? Of course. I'm glad I brought one with a considerable amount of vigor left in him, else we might not have been able to take care of all your ills."

"Get out!"

"My lord?"

"Get out!" I jumped up from the chair and backed away from the surgeon and the results of his work. "Take him with you. If I see you again, I'll kill you."

Notole spoke in my mind. *Are you not healed properly, my young Prince? Has Mellador displeased you in some way? We've not had time to discuss the process of healing.*

"I didn't know he was going to kill the slave. My knee would have gotten better on its own."

But what better use for a slave than to put his master in good health? Mellador has prescribed a day's rest, and . . .

. . . you will be able to go back to your proper business. It was Ziddari. *Why are you unsettled, young Lord? You plan to kill these Dar'Nethi pigs in war. You have killed three in your sparring already. They live only at your pleasure and that of the Lords of Zhev'Na.*

But there was a difference. Killing a soldier in battle was honorable. Killing a sparring partner—this was the first time they had told me that any of them had died—but that was almost the same. The practice slaves were trying to kill me, too. I had heard that slaves sometimes killed warriors in training, and they weren't even punished for it. But to take his life for power . . . to cure bruises and scrapes such as any boy might get . . .

It is just. Remember it, said Ziddari. *There is no difference in that slave and the rat you killed last week with your spear. Any Dar'Nethi would kill you in an instant if he was freed. We didn't expect that you would have difficulty with this.*

"I . . . I just wasn't expecting it. Of course, I understand all you say." I said what they wanted to hear, because I wanted them to leave me alone for a while. As I had the night before in the stable, I let darkness fill my head to block out their presence.

When the surgeon had gone, along with all evidence of his work, I called my slaves to run a bath. Hot, I said. Hotter than the desert. Though the midday heat hammered on the Gray House, and there was not the slightest stirring of the sultry air, I was as cold as if that red-black flood inside me had turned to black ice.

I spent two hours in the hot water, wondering what I

would do for the rest of the afternoon. I wanted to get back to my training. That was the best time of every day. Nothing to think about except what you were doing right then.

I tried to sleep, but all I could see was the slave's eyes, gray and clear. Accusing me. He had known what was going to happen—that they were going to kill him to heal me. That was what his look had meant. And then his eyes grew angry, then empty, and then they were dead.

My real father was a Dar'Nethi Healer. Was that what he did?

I threw down the sword I was polishing and pulled on my riding leathers. I didn't care what the surgeon had said.

Fengara wasn't in the stable, as she'd been told I wasn't coming. So I saddled Zigget and rode into the desert alone.

Alone? Risky you know, young Lord. Our enemies might be able to locate you outside the fortress. Ziddari.

"No one would dare attack me. I bear the mark of the Lords."

Ziddari kept picking at me, asking questions, telling me I should come back, let my knee heal. But I rode harder and faster, laying my whip into Zigget until the afternoon desert was a red blur, and soon I couldn't hear Ziddari anymore.

I didn't slow until the sun was low in the west. I had no idea how far I had ridden, but Zigget's flanks were heaving, so I headed back toward the fortress at a walk, trying to cool him down as the evening came on. But the horse took his revenge. Something scuttered out from under a rock—a kibbazi most likely, a sharp-toothed desert rat. Zigget shied and reared, just when I didn't expect it, and I found myself sprawled in the dirt.

"Curse you, devil," I said, shaking myself off and gingerly testing my knee.

Zigget looked at me with blazing hatred in his eye, and then galloped back toward Zhev'Na.

Marvelous, I thought. *A nice walk ahead.* I wasn't particularly worried. I could call on the Lords at any time, and they could have fifty warriors with me in a quarter of an hour or make a portal to take me back. But I didn't want to ask for any favors. At least I had a full waterskin at my belt. I wasn't stupid enough to go out without it, even though I was stupid enough to take Zigget on a ride alone.

I walked for a long time. Two or three times, the Lords stirred in my head, but I ignored them, shoving my anger between us like a wall. Soon I felt them withdraw, and they left me alone. It felt good to be alone in the night. Sometime around the mid-watch I heard hoofbeats and assumed that the Lords had sent someone for me. Not surprising. I knew I was a lot more valuable to them than they let on. But it wasn't the Lords. It was Zigget—and the Leiran boy.

"Thought you might be needin' a ride."

"Did the devil confess to you?"

"You might say that."

He slid off the horse and offered me the reins. Zigget's nostrils flared, and the horse shied. I kept walking.

"You should have brought another horse. This one won't carry me again."

"He's the strongest and fastest in the stable. He'd be your friend if you'd let him."

"How do you know so much about him? Is he a relative of yours?"

"He's a deal better than any kin I ever had. Do you want to know his name?" The boy was walking along beside me, leading the infernal beast.

"I believe his name is Zigget."

"Nope. Firebreather."

"And how do you know that?"

"I just know."

I stopped and glared at the idiot boy. "I'm not a fool. You're not Dar'Nethi."

"Call him Firebreather. Try it. Stand over there and call him." He dropped the reins and stepped away from the horse. I set out walking again. "Call him," the boy called after me.

"Here, Firebreather," I shouted, just to silence the Drudge. Before I had walked five paces more, the horse followed behind me, hesitant, quivering, but close enough that his muzzle hung over my shoulder. I stopped, and he stopped.

"Now tell him something nice. Tell him there's oats to be had at the stable when he gets you there." He whispered this in my ear, presumably so the horse could get the good news from me.

"Oats?"

"Tell him."

"Firebreather, there's oats. Oats in the stable if you behave yourself." I felt like an idiot.

The horse shifted his feet and blew a slightly happier note.

"Will you bite my hand off if I give you oats in it? This fool of a servant seems to think you are not a Zhid of a horse. Should I believe him?" I raised my hand slowly to pat his nose. He tossed his head. "Oats. Remember oats, Firebreather. I have the power of oats. My feet are indeed tired, thanks to you, but if you have a change of heart, perhaps I can too."

The horse bobbed his head and allowed me to touch him.

The boy took the horse's lead. "What did I say? Now he'll carry you nicely if you keep that up. Remember his name and all. He likes grass better than oats, but maybe you don't remember nothing about grass to talk to him about." He held Zigget's—Firebreather's—head while I mounted.

"What about grass?"

"How it's green and soft and grows tall to blow in the wind. How it tickles his legs when he runs and tastes so sweet, especially in the spring when there's still snow about, but there's little patches of new green peeking out of it. That's the best, but he hasn't seen it in so long."

The horse grew quieter under the boy's hand and voice.

"You'd best get up behind me," I said.

"I couldn't ride with you."

"I didn't kill you."

"True enough." He scrambled up behind me. One would think the horse had scooped him up and set him there, he did it so easily.

It was a long ride back. We took it slow, and the boy told me more about the horse and how to get him to do what I wanted.

"How do you know so much about horses?"

"Don't know. Just always had a feel for it, so my gran said."

"Your grandmother? Where is she?"

"Dead now. I don't like to talk about her."

"Why do you speak Leiran?"

"Leiran?"

"Surely you realize that the language you speak is not the language spoken here. It's not even from this world. Did you think I wouldn't notice?"

"I'm not supposed to say nothing. I'm not supposed to talk to you or even to open my mouth, because I'm too stupid to learn the proper words. Couldn't you just pretend I didn't say nothing?"

"The work camp where you were born—were there many that spoke Leiran there?"

"I don't want to get nobody in trouble."

"They won't. Not from me. I just thought it had been so long since those like you came to Ce Uroth that no one could possibly remember their old language. Do you know about the other world? Do other Drudges remember that, too?"

"I know about it. Not many others."

"That's astonishing. I've only been here a few months, and I hardly remember anything."

"There's those that wanted me to remember. Maybe no one wants you to remember nothing."

We rode in silence for a long time. When we approached the ring of campfires surrounding Zhev'Na, I told the boy to get off the horse. "You'll walk the rest of the way," I said. "And I would advise you not to expect any favors for doing me this service. If you've half a dram of intelligence, you'll spit at me whenever you see me."

"I'm always in the stable."

I rode away without saying anything more.

When I got back to the Gray House, Darzid was waiting for me. He was dressed all in black, as usual, and was sprawled out on my couch like a giant spider. I ignored him and kicked the slaves that slept on the floor of my bathing room. "Hot water," I said. "Plenty of it."

I peeled off my riding clothes and stepped into the bath. I was freezing. Darzid appeared in the doorway and dismissed the slaves. "Where have you been, young Lord?"

"Riding in the desert. You know where I was."

"We were concerned about you. The healing seemed to upset you."

"I didn't like it. You're right, of course, about it being a good use of a slave. I can see that, but I didn't like it. It left a bad taste in my mouth, and it hurt when Mellador cut me. So I decided I'd go tame that demon horse so it wouldn't happen again. I don't like being thrown about and bruised. I thought it would make me better, harder, to do something about it."

"Of course. A good thought. And did it work?"

"I think things will go much better tomorrow."

He smiled and fingered his beard. The smile did not extend to his eyes, however. If I looked close enough, would I see his gold mask and ruby eyes?

"Why did you shut us out?"

I had thought about that a good deal on the way back. "I was tired. The three of you never leave me alone. Sometimes I just can't learn any more. I think you forget I'm only ten."

"Eleven. Your birthday passed months ago."

"Oh." I had lost track. There had always been a great celebration at Comigor. Food baskets for the tenants and a round of ale for the Guard. A party with Papa and Mama's friends . . .

"And so?" said Darzid, a trace of impatience in his voice.

"It gets to where my head's about to burst with everything. Sometimes I just need to be left alone." I didn't like them knowing everything I was thinking or doing or who I was talking to.

"Don't make it too much of a habit. We are your friends and allies, and we have a great deal to teach you. Your anointing is only months away."

"And then I'll be the Heir of D'Arnath?"

"That's only part of it."

"What else, then?"

"On your twelfth birthday, the day you come of age . . .

besides taking up the sword of D'Arnath, you will take your rightful place alongside your friends and allies. No one in the universe will rival your power, for you are to become one of us—the Fourth Lord of Zhev'Na."

CHAPTER 35

My riding lessons went much better after that night. No matter how hard Fengara worked us, Firebreather and I got through it. He would carry me through roaring walls of fire and choking dust storms; he would jump over fences and burning scrub and chasms that made my stomach churn. All I had to do was call him by name and talk to him about oats and grass, and his powerful muscles and strong heart would do anything I required of him.

Whenever I went to the stable, I would see the Leiran boy, hauling carts of hay, oiling harness, or shoveling out the stalls. I took no notice of him. It was better that way.

Fengara noticed the change. "You've made a great deal of progress these past weeks, young Lord. I'd come to think you hopeless. What made the difference?"

"Practice," I said. "I just needed the practice and better teaching. You've done me good service, Fengara, and I thank you for it."

On the next day, I had a new riding master. He was a squat, vicious man of few words, quite different from the sharp-tongued Fengara.

"Where's Fengara?" I asked him.

"She was of no more use to you, my lord."

"Is she dead?"

"I could not say. Have you been riding this animal for long?"

"Perhaps six weeks."

"It seems attached to you."

"No. Fengara was getting lazy. Not challenging us enough."

That day I didn't talk to Firebreather about grass or oats,

nor did I call him anything but Zigget. I whipped him and spurred him hard. I fixed my thoughts on the horse and how vicious he was, while thinking of a question for the Lords at the same time. They didn't answer. But as soon as I let go of my concentration and thought of the question, they were with me instantly as before. I practiced all day.

By sunset Firebreather was wild-eyed and frothing at his mouth in terror.

"I want a different horse tomorrow," I said to the head groom. "This one is impossible." The new riding master nodded in approval.

That night as I left the stables, a voice called after me from the shadows by the mule shed. "Why'd you do it? Why'd you treat him like that after all he did for you these past weeks? You made him scared again."

"It would do everyone good to be scared of me. Don't forget it."

The Leiran boy watched, hard-eyed, as I crossed the stableyard.

A few weeks later, after working late with my wretched new horse and my vile riding master, I wandered down to Firebreather's box. I liked to be in the stables at night. Only a single lamp was left hanging, and only the soft noises of the horses disturbed the quiet. You could almost forget you were in Zhev'Na. I looked carefully about to make sure the Leiran boy wasn't lurking in the shadows anywhere.

"Here, Firebreather. I've got oats for you. Come here, and I'll tell you about the hills of Comigor, if I can remember. You'd like it there." I sat on the gate, fed him oats from my hand, and told him of the grassy heath where I had ridden when I was little and weak.

"I thought you'd show up here some time."

"Curse all Drudges, do you follow me?"

He was peeking down through the beams of the loft and caused a considerable avalanche of hay when he jumped down to the stable floor. I dropped off the gate and turned to leave. "I warned you," I said.

"You thought they'd kill him like they did the Zhid horsemaster, didn't you?"

"Why would I think that?" I wrenched the gate latch.

"They kill everyone who gets close to you."

I didn't want to hear it. Not out loud. "That's ridiculous. You're an ignorant Drudge. What do you know about anything?"

"I know a lot of things. I see a lot of things. Maybe I see and know more than you do."

"It's better to be ignorant."

"Maybe that's true. I wouldn't trade places with you. You're no better off than me, except maybe you get more to eat."

I pulled open the gate, but I didn't go through it. "Did they really kill Fengara?"

"She came in every morning to train horses new in from the farms. She was mean, but she could magic 'em until she had 'em doing what she wanted. That morning there was somebody watching her. She was working a big bay. Doing fine until the watcher raised up his hand. Then the horse turned on her, and she couldn't move to get out of his way. He trampled her flat. The watcher laughed when he walked away."

"What did he look like?"

"Fellow looked like a desert rat, hard and bony. Black hair cut real short, black beard, dressed fine with rubies on his belt."

Darzid. I kept one part of my mind fixed tight on the stable and the desert, so he wouldn't hear what I was thinking.

"Why do you do the things they want?"

"I have no choice. You wouldn't understand."

"I understand you quit riding Firebreather so they wouldn't kill him. And you warned me off. At first I thought you'd come to be just like them, that they'd made you evil, too, but they haven't done it yet. Not if you gave up Firebreather to save his life. You don't have to be what they want."

I hit him then, so hard it knocked him to the straw and made his mouth bleed. "You are stupid, ignorant, and insolent, and if you don't watch yourself, I'll cut out your tongue." I grabbed his filthy shirt and shook him. "You don't know anything at all. I have been evil since the day I was born. If my father had known what I was, he would have slit my throat, and if my mother had known it, she would have had me burned alive and drunk wine while they did it. I've killed people, and I've lashed them until they cried for mercy, and I've left men in the desert until they turned black and begged for water. I've had a slave killed just to heal my bruises. I am a friend of the Lords of Zhev'Na, and I'm going to become one of them, because that's what I was born to be. And nothing an ignorant servant says can make any difference at all."

I felt the Lords stirring . . . curious . . . but I kept them shut out. "Leave me alone!" I walked a long way before going back to my house.

It was many weeks until I saw the Leiran boy again—or, rather, I saw him almost every day, but in public places where I could pretend he didn't exist. I didn't want to think about him or about Firebreather. Keeping things private from the Lords wasn't easy. And mostly I wanted what the Lords taught me.

I worked harder every day at my training. I told Darzid I wanted a new master of hand combat, that I had learned all that the current one could teach me, and that only because he outweighed me by three times could he get any advantage at all. The new master taught me how to fight with knives and axes and other small weapons. I got better sparring partners and damaged several of them, so that I guessed they would die. But I learned that if they were good enough, the Zhid would send a surgeon to bandage them up. The better ones were very valuable. I would be a warrior, the best there ever was. Then we would see how the world might be ordered.

One afternoon as I walked into the stables, I saw a Zhid warrior taking a whip to one of the stable hands. "Perhaps a few lashes will improve your hearing," he was saying. "At least they might improve *my* disposition." He laid on another stroke and another. The groom was curled up in the corner of a stall with his hands over his face, but I recognized the ragged breeches and dirty bare feet. He was cut and bleeding all over.

"What's he done?"

"Young Lord!" The warrior bowed. "This insolent fool ignored my command to wipe the muck off of my boots. He acted as if he didn't understand what boots were."

"Perhaps he doesn't. He's probably never worn any, and I've noticed he's a particularly ignorant boy," I said. "Can't put two sensible words together."

"I've a mind to string him up and lay the flesh off of him to strengthen my arm. He's no good for anything else."

"I think he could serve a better purpose, more suited to his calling," I said. "That horse Zigget is a vicious beast. Look at the walls of his stall and you'll see; I'm worried he'll damage his legs kicking holes in them. Maybe he needs something softer to kick. String up this boy in Zigget's stall for a night. It will either bring some sense into his head, or remove his head where we don't have to worry about it any more."

The warrior took the Leiran boy to Firebreather's box and tied him to the wall as I watched. The Leiran boy was woozy from his beating and bleeding from the lashes. Firebreather snorted and tossed his head.

"I'll come scrape what's left off the walls in the morning, young Lord."

"Perhaps I'll come to watch. Make sure my horse doesn't have indigestion."

The warrior closed the gate behind us, and we walked away laughing.

You find an interesting way to amuse yourself, my young Lord, whispered Ziddari in my head.

"The warriors enjoy such things. I don't like it myself." I had to say that. The Lords could read me so easily that it was hard to lie to them.

Shall we amuse ourselves in other ways tonight? asked Notole, as I went to collect my horse.

"No. No lessons tonight. I'll be riding late, and then I'm going to bed. You've had all you're going to get out of me today."

As you wish. Tomorrow, then.

For two hours I practiced tight maneuvers, a tedious and boring exercise. At sunset I told the horsemaster that I was going to ride into the desert for a while to cool off. I did so, forcing myself to be patient and not return before all the grooms were asleep. He'd be all right. If he woke up, he could calm Firebreather easily. If he woke up . . .

When I got back to the stable, I heard a terrible racket from Firebreather's stall. I shoved my horse into a vacant box, grabbed the lamp from its hook, and threw open the gate. Firebreather had done a thorough job of destroying the walls of the horse box. Though his head was drooping and his eyes swollen half shut, the Leiran boy was murmuring, "Once more. Another lick, and he'll bring you oats when he comes. Oats for Firebreather. Another nice wallop. Good. It'll make you strong. Don't let him down." The hooves never touched the boy.

"Are you having fun?"

His head lifted a bit. "A barrel of it."

He drained half the contents of my waterskin. Then I untied the ropes that held him to the rear wall and helped him down to the straw, taking a quick inventory of the bloody stripes on his arms and legs. "I'm not going to clean you up. None of this looks too serious."

"Crackin' uncomfortable though." He stretched out and groaned.

"Why did you disobey a warrior? Of all the idiotic things. Would it have killed you to wipe the fellow's boots? You've done worse. You love horse muck."

He grinned, which, with his face all purple and swollen, looked pretty horrible. "Damn. Was it his boots? I couldn't figure it out. Thought he was telling me to wipe the shit off his *door*."

"You didn't know the word for boots? You mean I was right?"

"Is that a rock in your stew or what?"

I hadn't laughed in so long I'd almost forgotten how, but we both took off with that, until he rolled onto his side holding his ribs, and said, "Oh, damn, you've got to stop. Yell at me or something. This hurts too much."

"Here. I should have thought. Show me where it hurts the most."

He pointed to a tender, swollen bruise on his left side below the ribs, and I traced my finger around it to make it numb. I did the same to a couple of other places that looked particularly bad. "This won't fix them, only stop the hurting for a while."

"It's a deal better. Are you . . . are you coming to be a Healer, then?" He said it almost with reverence.

The thought nauseated me. "No. I could never do that."

"Whenever you need to go, just put me back on the wall. Firebreather will take care of me."

"Nobody's expecting me tonight. I arranged it."

"I don't want to get you in trouble."

"You won't. Do you want something to eat? I've got some things in my cloak."

"I'd eat your boots if I knew the word for it."

That set us laughing again, and it was a while until I could pull the bread and cheese from the pocket of my cloak, along with a flask of cavet that I heated up with sorcery.

After he had spent a few moments demolishing the food and drinking the cavet, he eased himself against the wall, and said, "So what do you do here besides take horse lessons from the Zhid?"

"I learn sword fighting and hand combat and sorcery."

"I know you're good at wrestling. Never thought I'd have a nub shorter'n me put me down so quick. Are you good at the other things, too?"

"I'm getting better. Swordsmanship—that's the hardest. I improved really fast when I first came here, but not so much lately. I don't think I'll ever be as good at it as I want."

"Why is it so important?"

"I've debts to pay. Debts of honor."

"Maybe I don't understand debts of honor—being who I am and all. It would be an education if you'd tell me."

It was like ripping a hole in your waterskin. No matter how small the hole, everything got out eventually. I started just to tell him about my life debt to the Lords, but ended up telling him everything while we sat in that horse box—about how my whole life had been a lie and a betrayal, that no one had been who they said they were, and how it was all the fault of one man. I dumped everything on an ignorant stable Drudge who had never owned a pair of boots.

He was quiet for a long time after I was done, then shook his head slowly. "Blazes . . . that is the damnedest story. I've got to think on it a while before I can even know what to think. Some of it's clear enough, but some . . . Why did you think this wicked prince that was really your da killed your nurse? I didn't see that."

"It was obvious. It's why Seri brought him to Comigor, to take her revenge on Lucy and Papa. And it was his knife that did it. I saw it."

"But that was in your dream you saw his knife. I've seen horses fly in dreams."

I didn't like him questioning me. "Your head's in a muddle. I don't expect you to understand. And I don't know why I babbled all of this to someone who doesn't know the word for boots."

"It's true. I don't got half your brains, and what brain I've got is full of horse muck."

"You must be about horses like I am about sword fighting. You'd like to be the best at it, wouldn't you? At training them and knowing about them. I'll bet you'd like to run a stable of the best horses there were anywhere."

He screwed his swollen face into a frown. "I never told nobody that. You didn't go picking at my head, did you?"

"No. I wouldn't do that."

"I appreciate that. Gives me the crawlies to think on it."

About that time a faint buzz in my head told me it was second watch, about two hours before dawn. "Do you want to sleep for a while? I should go soon, and once I do, it'll be harder for you."

"No need. I can sleep anywhere. It's an advantage when you're born low. Go ahead and put me back."

I tied him back up to the wall, trying to duplicate the way the warrior had fixed him. "I can't come in the morning, you know," I said.

"It's all right. It was a better night than I expected." He was asleep before I shut the gate.

It had been foolish for me to do what I'd done, but I felt a little better than I had in a while. When I went to the stable the next afternoon for my riding lesson, I wandered past Firebreather's stall. The boy wasn't there anymore. Two days passed before I saw him again, mucking out a stall, still bruised and scratched, but otherwise looking no worse for the experience. I looked right through him, and he didn't turn his head.

CHAPTER 36

Seri

Dia and I had both been summoned to service in the Gray House. We still slept in the dormitory with the sewing women, but instead of the sewing room, we reported to the Gray House scullery each morning at sunrise. A sour-faced Drudge named Gar assigned us to our duties, Dia to light the fires, prepare food for the Drudges, and deliver gray-bread to the slaves twice a day. I spent my days with a pail and rags, scrubbing floors and railings, polishing brass, scraping candle wax, and wiping layer upon layer of red dust from everything. It was a change from sewing, at least, and allowed me to see a great deal of what went on in that house. I was assigned to the lower floors, while two other Drudges cleaned in Gerick's apartments. Just as well for the present. There was always a risk he would recognize me.

I saw him for the first time on my second day in the house. My task of the morning was to scrub a tiled passage that opened onto one of the inner courtyards. The dawn provided scarcely enough light for me to see what I was doing. In the way of Drudges and slaves, I shrank back into the shadows at the ring of approaching footsteps. Gerick strode past me and into the yard.

Though his build was still slender, he had grown two hands taller and his shoulders and upper arms had filled out. A green singlet exposed his deeply tanned arms, and his brown breeches, leggings and boots were well fitted. Alone in the fencing yard, he removed his sword belt, hung it on a hook on the wall, and began to warm up. His movements were like a ritual dance, done to no music I could hear.

He was beautiful. His shining hair fell softly about his sun-bronzed face as he stretched and spun, a few thin braids dangling in front of each ear, and even as his exercise grew faster and more violent, he showed no signs of the awkwardness one might expect from a boy so young. His features were composed, peaceful, his mind seemingly focused inward . . . until a Zhid warrior appeared across the courtyard.

"What shall we work on today, young Lord?" asked the newcomer. "You fall short in so many areas, it's hard to know where to begin. Every day, it seems, our greatest challenge is to decide what you're worst at."

Gerick's only response was to halt his exercise, buckle his sword belt about his waist, and stand waiting, his face now cold and expressionless.

Throughout the morning the swordmaster continued in this manner, casting insults, taunts, and humiliation. Gerick did as he was told, repeating moves a hundred times with no complaint, no argument, and no change in his haughty demeanor.

The stone walls of the passageway became a furnace as the sun grew high. The fencing yard would be worse, as it had no scrap of shade, but the rigor of the training exercises did not diminish. At mid-morning Gerick donned his leather practice armor, and a slave was brought to spar with him. The swordmaster faulted Gerick's every move. Whenever he wished to pause the match, the Zhid would use a whip on the slave, a lithe, quick youth of eighteen or so.

After the third time the slave was left gasping in the dust by the swordmaster's lash, Gerick spoke tightly. "If you have some reason to kill this slave, then do so and bring in another."

"Shall I direct this practice like a nursery, then?" snarled the Zhid. "Childish sensibilities have no place in true warfare. Is this the weakness of your blood showing itself?"

Gerick strolled over to a barrel and drank deeply from a copper dipper. Then he returned to the sneering Zhid, who stood leaning against the wall. Almost before one could see it, Gerick had a knife pressed up against the swordmaster's ribs. "You will direct my practice the way you think best, but if you ever speak to me in that way again, I will carve out your liver and have you staked out right here until your skin cracks like an unoiled boot. I've done it before with those who crossed me. Consider it."

As quickly as he had unsheathed it, Gerick put away his knife, returned to the slave who waited in the center of the yard, and raised his sword in a ready stance. His face was expressionless again. There was no sign the incident had ever occurred.

The Zhid did not lash the slave again. When he wished the match to stop, he brought up a wooden staff between the two boys. One might think him chastened by his pupil's rage, unless you saw his smirk when Gerick's back was turned.

I had come near scrubbing grooves in the stones at the wide entry to the fencing yard. As I moved on down the passage, I could no longer see the yard, but the clash of weapons and the shouted instructions of the swordmaster continued throughout the morning. It was difficult to associate the cold-eyed youth in the fencing yard with the child I had met at Comigor. Even such a brief glimpse revealed a great deal that I didn't want to know. No need to hear the deepening timbre of his voice to know there was nothing of the child about him any longer.

Gerick trained in the fencing yard almost every morning. Even if I wasn't cleaning an area that allowed me a view, I would walk by, if only to catch a glimpse of him. I had no idea how to approach him. All midnight imaginings of revealing myself to a terrified child, grateful to be rescued from a villainous captivity, had crumbled on that first morning. And the days that followed did nothing to reverse my failing hopes.

Late one afternoon a ferocious wind storm hit the fortress, a howling, choking tempest of red sand that could flay human or beast. Gerick was in the stableyard when a horse broke from its tether, driven wild by the whirling sand. A young slave yanked Gerick aside, dragging him to the ground as the horse reared and kicked and galloped out of the yard. The slave had saved Gerick from certain injury, yet, once back on his feet, Gerick knocked the youth to the ground with the back of his hand and kicked him viciously. "Touch me again, and I'll cut off your hands," he said to the cowering youth.

On another day the entire household was called out to the Lords' Court. We gathered in awkward assembly—Drudges, slaves, Zhid—to witness the lashing of a Zhid warrior, one of the house guards whom Gerick had found asleep at his post. The Zhid was bound to an iron frame. Gerick gave the warrior two lashes, and then turned the whip over to a burly Zhid. Cold and imperious, Gerick watched as ten more lashes were administered, and the torn and bleeding warrior was dragged away.

My companions chided me for my tears. "The guard deserved his punishment," said Dia. "What if someone had come to harm the young Lord? The Worships have their duties just like us."

I didn't tell her that it was not for the Zhid I wept.

I quickly lost my fear that Gerick might recognize me. He took absolutely no notice of any servant, whether Drudge or slave. Two slaves were always within range of his call, but never did I see him acknowledge their existence by word or glance. It might have been the wind that fastened his cloak about him before he went out in the evening, or the weight of the air that deposited a cup into his hand at the end of his sword practice. Several times he came close to stepping on my hand as he walked past me, and once I rounded a corner and came near running into him. I was shaken, as his face was now almost on a level with mine, but his eyes never wavered from his destination, and he made no response to my mumbled apologies. I feared I might be too late to save him.

Then came a morning when I walked past the fencing yard, but did not see Gerick, only the swordmaster, fuming, his hands on his hips. "You, woman. Yes, you, dolt," he shouted angrily to me. "Go to the young Lord's chambers and find out why he leaves me here waiting. Be back apace or I'll have you whipped."

When I reached the top of the stair, a slave informed me that the young Lord had injured his knee and would not be attending his lessons. I reported this to the swordmaster, who summoned the surgeon. From the shadowed corners of Gerick's apartments, I watched the Zhid Healer work his vile perversion of Dar'Nethi healing. The air grew heavy and dim, laden with the foulness of that enchantment.

Gerick threw Mellador out of his rooms, forcing the surgeon to carry the dead slave himself rather than wait for others to remove him. When Gerick was alone, he began speaking—to himself, I thought. But the oppressive air made me think of the Lords' house, and the jewels in his ear gleamed bright and hot through the murk. He was speaking with the Lords.

After a moment, he gave a quick shudder, and looked around the room as if he had just returned from some other place. I didn't move, but he caught sight of me, registering no more surprise than if I'd been a convenient chair or table. "Tell my slaves they're wanted in my bathing room."

I made my genuflection, but before starting down the steps, I looked back and saw my son standing alone in the center of his fine room. He had wrapped his arms tightly about himself and was shivering violently, as if he stood in the snows of Cer Dis rather than in the heart of the blazing desert. My heart clenched fiercely. He was not yet theirs.

CHAPTER 37

V'Saro

My existence in Zhev'Na was little different from that in the desert camp. The pen itself was identical, though only five of the cells were occupied. The rules were the same. The food was the same. The stench . . . the vile washing sink . . . the storage building and surgeon's room with iron rings in its stone walls . . . the blazing furnace of the sun that sapped the body and spirit . . . the bitter nights . . . the unending fighting, blood, and death . . . the collar . . . that, too, unchanged.

The only difference was the quality and prestige of my opponents. They were the highest-ranking officers in Ce Uroth, and therefore the finest warriors, for the Zhid had no other criteria for advancement. I no longer had to run in place at the end of the day to make sure I was exhausted enough to sleep. Staying alive required everything I had.

Staying sane was something else again. Only the nagging voices in my head kept me holding on, though I tried my best to silence them. Everything seemed to be slipping away from me—my identity, my memories, my life—while my strange and terrible dreams were taking on the harder edges of reality. Who could not view such happenings as madness?

I squatted beside the stone sink, where I had just washed off the dried sweat and blood from the previous day to prepare for my morning's opponent, a seasoned warrior named Gabdil. Gabdil's slavehandler was late fetching me, so my tether chain had been fastened to a ring in the wall, and I was left shivering in the chill shadows of dawn, dully pondering how I was going to stay warmed up. I could afford no disadvantage with Gabdil.

From outside the gate came a woman's voice, asking the guards where she could find the slavekeeper. "I've a message from the chamberlain in the Gray House. A slave sparring with the young Lord has been wounded in the foot and needs to be brought back here. The house slavekeeper has no handlers to spare for the task."

I shot to my feet, my heart racing as it never did when I was fighting. It wasn't that I'd not heard a woman's voice in my time in Ce Uroth. A few female servants and slaves worked about the camps, and a surprising number of women could be found among the Zhid warriors. But this particular voice ripped through my head like a sharpened ax.

"Keeper's through the door there to the left, across from the cistern," said the guard.

I glimpsed only the back of her as she walked through the gate and into the room where the stores of graybread and tunics were kept. She wore the black skirt, brown tunic, and red kerchief of a Drudge. My cursed tether was too short, and I came near choking myself trying to get a better view. When the voice of Gabdil's aide growled outside in the courtyard, panic bade me devise some ruse to prevent me being taken until the woman reappeared. But she finished her business quickly. When she walked out of the storehouse, the full light of dawn fell through the barred gate onto her face. Only five heartbeats . . . maybe ten . . . but I knew her, and knew she had no relationship to a swordmaster from Sen Ystar . . . and neither had I.

The fantasy of V'Saro's life crumbled in that instant, but before I could even begin to sort through the rubble, the Zhid slavehandler dragged me out to the sparring ground. Gabdil, a warrior with a reach a handspan longer than my own and upper arms as thick as my thighs, had already killed a slave that week, a man who had survived three months in Zhev'Na.

Forget the woman, I told myself. *If you don't pay attention, you won't live to learn anything.*

A hundred times that day the woman's voice echoed in

my mind, and her face floated before me in the glare. Brutally I forced myself to concentrate. In our initial sparring, I took a deep cut in my arm—happily not my sword arm—and Gabdil complained that I wasn't as good as he'd been told. Fortunately, the rest of the day was restricted training, a set of patterned practice moves endlessly repeated, working on flow and control and fluid transitions between stances. There were ample opportunities to get hacked or skewered, but it was not as likely as in full combat when an instant's lapse could mean your life.

In mid-afternoon I was returned to the slave pen, trembling with fatigue, not from the work, which had been light as my days went, but from the sheer effort of concentration. The surgeon assigned to this slave pen set about stitching my arm, but I scarcely noticed, for as soon as I allowed my thoughts to wander, the world came into sharp and terrible focus, and I knew what a wicked predicament I was in. I remembered the woman's name and my own, and was already beginning to retrace the events that had placed the anointed Heir of D'Arnath so abjectly at the mercy of his enemies.

The slavemaster had died in his bath. Ludicrous. No wonder the news of it had thrown me—V'Saro—into such despair, for Gernald the Slavemaster, the Zhid whose soul Dassine had healed so long ago, had been the key to Exeget's plan. Slowly, cruelly, carefully, over the years, Gernald had worked himself into a position of power in Ce Uroth, an impregnable position, so that he could safely open a portal to Avonar itself, knowing that such a breach in the armor of the Zhid might someday make all the difference in our long war. And then, at the very culmination of his long endeavors, his heart had given out, and he had slipped under the soapy water, stranding all of us in bondage.

The plan had been ingenious, though to believe Exeget and Gar'Dena could transfer me out of the council chamber before I was dead required a great deal of trust on my part. To let me die again would be an enormous risk, and neither of them was a true Healer. But their enchantments had worked flawlessly. In four days I was completely recovered and living happily in Sen Ystar, trying to rebuild a life that had never existed. Then came the attack, and the desert, and the collar.

I was never supposed to be sealed into the collar, of course. Gernald was to be waiting for V'Saro, the swordmaster of Sen Ystar, who was to be given a seal that would leave his powers intact, and who was to have his temporary identity removed so that he would know what he was about. But the slavemaster had died in his bath, and I was left as V'Saro the slave, who had terrible dreams and believed he was going mad. And the fourteenth day had long passed.

Seri was here. Gods have mercy. I had assumed that the two who were to receive my signal and provide the information I needed to rescue my son were others like Gernald. But Seri, too, had been caught in Gernald's disaster, abandoned in this villainous place, and my son had been left to the Lords' mentoring for almost a year.

"Your scars tell me you've had much worse wounds than this, V'Saro, and much less skilled care. Why do you look like death itself tonight? Is my needle too dull?"

I just shook my head.

Exeget had found it necessary to explain fifty times over why we couldn't seize my son from the council chamber. As the man and boy had come together as suppliant to the Preceptorate, Ce'Aret and Ustele would not consider separating them, insisting that such interference would be a violation of our law. And neither Exeget nor Gar'Dena understood Darzid—who he was or what was the extent of his power. But their greatest concern lay with the jewels, the link between the boy's mind and the Lords. Take him by force in the council chamber, and the Three would destroy him, or, if they had already corrupted him sufficiently, he could possibly channel all the power of the Lords into the very heart of Avonar. Listen, watch, observe, they had told me. Anything more was too great a risk. Stealth and surprise would get him back. A quick strike into the heart of the Lords' stronghold. Stupid, how things work out.

And of course, once I remembered all these things, they did me no good at all. Neither Karon nor D'Natheil could suggest any escape from my captivity that V'Saro had not already dismissed. The terrors of my dreams were banished, but those of my days were grown far more desperate. With Gernald dead, Exeget could not get Seri and Gerick out, and the odds of my living until I could find a way to do so were depressingly slim. If I were to die, Seri would likely live out her days in this vile place, and Gerick would become the instrument the Lords had long desired. And that was only if I died undiscovered. I could well imagine the unpleasantness if my identity became known.

So I could not die, and I could not be discovered, which meant I had to keep up my deception. The difficulty was that I didn't know how long I could manage it, now I was myself again. I had no defense against Zhid compulsions. One misstep and they would have the truth out of me. And even more disturbing . . . I had to fight. I had to continue doing my best to kill whoever walked onto a training ground with me, and doubt that I would be capable of such an act consumed me.

For so many years I had believed that nothing . . . nothing . . . was worth taking a life, certainly not the preservation of my own life, and not even the preservation of the lives I cherished most. I had not yet come to terms with the dreadful consequences of my idealism, but on that night in the slave pen of Zhev'Na, I told myself that I no longer had the luxury of choice. I was fighting a war, and my son's life was bound up with the safety of two worlds. I just didn't know if that would be enough when next I faced a living man with a sword in my hand.

I could not sleep for thinking of Seri and Gerick and preparing myself for the morning. Daylight arrived far too soon. As always, I was led to the day's sparring ground by the chain hooked to my collar. Gabdil again.

"These keepers insist that you can fight, slave. I don't believe it." The big man grinned and tossed me a two-handed great-sword—my favorite weapon. "I think you are Dar'Nethi vermin who plays at swords the same way your people play at sorcery. The Lords of Zhev'Na will teach you one discipline, and I will teach you the other."

Anger stirred in my gut. No blank-eyed, unimaginative, misbegotten Zhid knew more of swordplay than the Prince of Avonar. I lifted the weapon up to the light, letting the sun glint along its shining edge, and then I pointed it at the empty eyes staring at me, as if to say "I'll put it there," and took my ready stance.

V'Saro had been but a mask, a flimsy veneer of experience and memory painted over my soul, with skills and inclinations that were very much my own. The Dar'Nethi Healer's invocation was at the core of V'Saro's being, and he risked mutilation to comfort his injured cellmates, because I was Karon, a Healer incapable of any other response to their suffering. And V'Saro knew how to wield a sword with deadly precision because I was D'Natheil, who valued nothing in life save the art of combat. It might take me a full lifetime to become accustomed to this other set of habits and instincts existing alongside my own, but when I raised my sword on the first morning of my second life in Zhev'Na, I was glad he was with me. D'Natheil did not think. He fought. And so my life continued.

"The Wargreve Damon has asked for this one?" The slavekeeper ticked off an item on his list.

The slavemaster, hands clasped behind his back, chuckled. "The wargreve asked for a challenge. Says our stock is poor these days; threatens to report unfavorably to the gensei if he doesn't break a sweat today. We'll see what he thinks of V'Saro." The slavemaster had begun visiting the stable often, especially on days I fought wager matches.

The keeper flicked a finger at a slavehandler who unlocked the cell gate and motioned me to kneel with my hands behind my back so they could shackle them together. I threw the piece of half-eaten graybread back into my basket and complied. As my wristbands were linked together and the handler's boot informed me it was time to stand, my stomach constricted in the now-familiar anxiety. Uncounted days had passed since I had learned my identity. Nothing had changed. I had to keep fighting. I had to keep winning.

"Wargreve Damon is a brilliant warrior," said the keeper.

"If he takes this one, he'll be almost as good as he thinks.

Of course, if V'Saro takes Damon, we'll have grief to pay to the gensei. But it might be worth it."

Most unsettling to hear my day's opponent was the protégé of a gensei—a general. The nearest I'd come to death in my months in the slave pens had not been from a wound of my own, but on the day I had lamed the protégé of another gensei. Only the intervention of the slavemaster on behalf of "the Lords' property" had kept me alive.

My spirits sank even lower when I was delivered to the training ground and saw Damon. He was big and young, and as I was unshackled and given a weapon and a thinly padded leather tunic, I watched him use his long-sword to hack a thickly padded practice drum into as precise, thin slices as if he were slicing butter with a dagger. This one was good.

"Is this the best you can do?" He surveyed my battered body and shabby turnout scornfully. "I said I wanted a challenge."

The handler bowed. "The slavemaster says to report any dissatisfaction."

We set right to work. Interesting. The young Zhid used incredible speed and brilliant instincts to mask abysmally poor technique. He was every bit the dangerous opponent I had judged him, but in the first hour I spotted a weakness in his defense. Stubborn and prideful, he would never evade or step away from a strike, but always chose to parry, assuming that his quickness would allow him to reset and counter. But his favorite parry was soft, his blade angled improperly, a blatant opening that would permit me to kill him easily. Yet, as I had learned before, killing the fool would be a risky proposition.

The Zhid had no children, but they were inordinately possessive of other warriors they had taken on as protégés in a murderous perversion of Dar'Nethi mentoring. To injure the wargreve would draw the angry notice of a gensei, but if I didn't exploit this weakness, Damon could very possibly wear me down enough to take me. An untenable situation.

We completed an exercise.

"Excellent, Damon," said the young man's Zhid swordmaster. "Perhaps a bit forceful, but excellent overall. Shall we try it again? Position, slave!"

The swordmaster spent most of his time praising his pupil's skills and little giving any meaningful critique. As the hours of practice passed, he showed no sign that he had noticed the glaring weakness so obvious to me.

By the time we stopped for a midday rest period, the wargreve had scarcely broken a sweat. I walked over to the water barrel, waiting until my back was turned to gulp for air and leaning casually on the wall as I drank, as if I didn't really need the support for my aching shoulders.

"Position, slave!"

I returned to the center of the courtyard. The heat beat on my head and shoulders like the hammer of Arot, the Leiran god who forged his own weapons to battle chaos. I had to act. I ducked a stroke that came near removing what hair the slavekeeper's hacking had left me and made a wide spin that brought me up next to the swordmaster, well away from my opponent. Quickly I slapped the back of my hand to my lips. The swordmaster looked puzzled—such a thing was unusual in the middle of a match—but he held up his hand to stay the wargreve's blade that hung unpleasantly close to my head.

"What is it, dog? Surely you recall that a slave cannot yield?"

"Swordmaster, there's been a dreadful mistake. You cannot mean for me to fight this youth."

"A mistake?" snarled the wargreve, not giving his instructor a chance to respond. "Our profound apologies. If you're mismatched, then you'll just die all the sooner. I'll just have to sacrifice the day's training."

"I am not the one matched above his skill. We Dar'Nethi hold our honor dear. I'm sworn to fight to the best of my ability, and that I will do, but when I've been put up against a beginner, I must issue a warning. If this fight continues, *you* will be the one to die."

The young man laughed harshly. "A beginner? I've not lost a match since I was transformed."

"I can well believe it, but I'd wager you've not fought one who was a swordmaster in his own right and sees the flaws in your training. I'll take you before your swordmaster counts a hundred."

He snarled and raised his sword. "Raise your weapon, slave. Your futile existence ends here."

The swordmaster rubbed his jaw uneasily. If harm befell the young commander, the fellow would likely not see another sunrise. "Wait, Damon. . . . Tell me, slave, what do you see?"

"A fatal flaw. If the wargreve will agree to instant immobility when I say halt, I'll show you."

The two discussed it out of my hearing. Eventually—reluctantly—the wargreve agreed. My reputation carried some weight. So we began again, and I led him through the moves that would create my opening. Praying that his curiosity would outweigh his pride and stupidity, I called, "Halt!" The edge of my sword rested on the heart vein in his neck. If he had continued his move, he would have driven it home. He looked like death—even for a Zhid.

"Though I delight in killing Zhid, I cannot fight one so overmatched," I said, speaking slowly and deliberately so he couldn't see how winded I was. I lowered my weapon.

"I'll show you who is overmatched, you insolent pig!" He came at me again. I led him again and cried, "Halt!" He dared not do otherwise. His glare might have ripped a hole in plate armor. My edge was in exactly the same spot as before. I thought it excellent that Damon was so well disciplined.

"You must show him this move, slave," said the swordmaster. "Command the slave to show you the move, Damon. Then you will be flawless."

I shook my head.

"You dare refuse me?" said Damon, with a menacing glare.

"I can show you this move, but you'll be far from flawless. You're a beginner, a brilliant one, but a beginner, nonetheless. I could move on you a hundred different ways and have the same result." A slight exaggeration, to be sure, as I could scarcely lift my arms. "Speed and instinct will never best craft. Send me back, and pick a new sparring partner of your own level."

The Zhid's glare of cold hatred shivered my gut. "For today I'll send you back . . . but only for today. I'll speak to the gensei"—he sneered and laid his hand on my collar—"but you'd best learn to control your impudent tongue. You are, and will ever be, a walking corpse. Am I right?"

Doubled over in the dirt, retching, I nodded. No chance I could forget it.

On the next day I was informed that my primary duty was now to be swordmaster to the Wargreve Damon. I would not be released from the pen and put under compulsions of obedience as might be expected, however, because I would still be assigned to fight matches as the Slavemaster of Zhev'Na would require. Evidently someone besides the surgeon Gorag had prospered on my longevity.

Though I could not see where such a change might lead, it gave me a glimmer of hope. I was required to be out of the pen for most of the day, tethered in the fortress's primary training ground, awaiting the wargreve's pleasure. Damon trained for perhaps four hours a day, sometimes mornings, sometimes afternoons or evenings, and during that time I could allow myself to think of nothing else. But in the other hours, if I didn't have an assigned match, I was able to watch the comings and goings of Drudges, slaves, and Zhid of all ranks. The training ground was surrounded on three sides by solid stone walls. The fourth side opened onto a vast stableyard. The slave pen was across the stableyard, beyond the forge and saddlery. Seri might be among the passersby sometime, but I wouldn't admit to myself how I longed to see her again. It would be better not.

Many Zhid officers shared the training ground with the Wargreve Damon. Knowing I was swordmaster to such a renowned warrior, they would ask me for pointers now and then. I made sure to ask Damon's permission before responding, but he didn't care. After a few weeks I had several pupils, although the wargreve always had priority.

On one blistering afternoon I was huddled into the tiny strip of shade within reach of my tether chain. A warrior that was not one of the regulars brought in a new slave for a practice match. I hadn't heard the new man's name as yet, but I saluted him before he went to work. The slave, a compact, sturdy man, smiled and did the same. He was good, a little better than the Zhid, but the Zhid was quite unaffected by the terrible heat, whereas the slave was soon sweating profusely. As the match went on, the Dar'Nethi's face grew pale. At every pause he would rub his eyes, and I could see his arms growing heavy and his breath beginning to labor.

When the Zhid called a pause to try a new blade, I jumped to my feet and asked for permission to speak. "May I offer a pointer or two? As you know I am swordmaster to Wargreve Damon." Volunteering for any duty was not my habit, but it might give the slave a chance to cool off.

"I take no pointers from slaves," said the Zhid with a snarl. "Damon is a fool to think a slave would teach anything worth hearing. You should all have your tongues removed."

The new slave was in the corner of the yard, fighting to keep water down, a sure sign of heat distress.

"But you lean too far forward in every stance, leaving you off-balance and slow in your counter-strikes, a vulnerability I would not expect in a warrior of your rank."

"How dare you?" The warrior was near apoplectic, knowing full well that what I said was true, and that I had revealed it to his opponent. "I'll show you my weakness. Give this insolent vermin a blade."

A stupid thing to do. I'd spent a rough morning with Damon and was scheduled for a wager match with my old friend Gabdil an hour before sunset. A small crowd of warriors and Drudges gathered to watch. Everyone was placing wagers while Damon's slavehandler detached me from the wall and gave me the weapon the warrior had discarded. My opponent heard the bettors, and his face turned purple.

The match took half an hour. The Zhid was as strong as a bull, and his technique wasn't as bad as I'd implied. Happily, he decided to yield rather than make me kill him. When I knelt and spread my arms at his command, I steeled myself for a touch of the collar, but he chose a powerful kick in the belly instead.

The forgotten slave sat in the corner to await the slavehandler, and while I worked to get air in my lungs, and my stomach returned to its proper place, he raised his open palms to me. A gracious gesture, though he was unlikely to be in the position to do anyone a service anytime soon. Most likely he could have taken care of himself—but perhaps not. He looked as sick as I felt.

The swordmaster reattached my tether, and I leaned against the stone wall, watching the crowd break up. The sun was in my eyes, so I could not make out one figure that stayed longer than the rest, standing stock still in the middle of the moving mass of people. All I could see in the glare was that it was a Drudge. No red kerchief covering the hair, so it wasn't a woman . . . wasn't Seri. Soon everyone was gone, and I drifted off to sleep.

The match with Gabdil went well. He gave me a painful slash on my back which made him feel accomplished, so that he wasn't too angry when he had to yield. The wound wasn't deep or in a place where it would cripple me, which pleased me. A number of people watched the match. Drudges, Zhid, slaves. Impossible to see through the sweat dripping in my eyes. The slavehandler bound my hands and led me back to the surgeon and my cell.

Late that night, I dreamed of snow. Seri and I had loved walking in the snow. She preferred clear winter days when the light was so brittle it would shatter on the ice-glazed gardens of Windham. I loved the quiet, blue-gray days when the drifting flakes seemed to muffle and soften the harshness of the world. In this particular dream, I stood by a frozen lake in the high mountains, while Seri strolled along on the far side of it. I was trying to pick my way across the icy boulders that crowded the shoreline to get to her, but whenever I looked up, she had moved farther away. I wanted to call out to her, but I beat my hand against my mouth and no one would tell me I could speak. At last I decided that the only way to reach her was to cross the lake, so I stepped onto the ice, trying to avoid the center where the color warned me that the glaze was thin and treacherous. But I couldn't see because it had started to snow, and the ice crystals pelted my face. . . .

I brushed my hand against my face. It wasn't snow, but straw. The cold was only the familiar dry chill of the desert night. I burrowed deeper in the straw, determined to find out if I made it across the lake, but a straw pricked my face again, and it was not the wind that whispered outside the bars of my cell. "Ssst."

I glanced around before I moved. No one stood in the aisle between the rows of cells, and the cells to either side of me were empty. With so few of us, they could keep us wide apart. So the sound was from outside the pen. Shifting sluggishly toward the outside, as anyone might while sleeping, I peered through the close-set bars . . . straight into a grimy, freckled face that split into a grin as I'd not seen in a lifetime.

"Blazes! I knew it. Holy, great damn! I knew it all along . . . it's you!"

"Paulo!" Our exclamations were muffled whispers, but no less filled with astonishment.

"I *knew* you weren't dead. We both knew it, though we didn't say it to nobody, not even to each other . . . and then today, when I saw you save that fellow's life . . . blazes!"

"You were the third. You and Seri."

"You know she's here, then?"

"I saw her. Just for a moment. Does she know—?"

"She don't know you're here—nor me. They weren't going to send me, but I made 'em do it. Were you the one supposed to give the signal then—to take us out?"

"Things didn't go quite right."

"Guessed not." He paused for a moment, a rosy flush dousing his freckles. "Except for being here like this . . . are you all right? Together in your head?"

"I remember everything."

"All of before I knew you . . . and when you showed up in Dunfarrie . . . and this time, when you fixed my legs and all?"

"Everything."

"Blazes." His gaze fell to the ground, but not before I saw innocent awe overtake him.

"I remember Sunlight, now. You told me you'd taken care of him, but I couldn't figure how you had come to have a horse of mine. You're the first one from those times—from our world—the first one I get to meet again. Extraordinary, isn't it?"

"Makes my head hurt to think on it."

"Mine, too."

We were both quiet for a moment. Life was such a wonder.

Then Paulo screwed up his face, lifted his gaze, and took up again, evidently deciding that awe of royalty or dead sorcerers come back to life was minor beside the business of the moment. "So what went wrong? How'd you get in this fix?"

"The only way I could get into Zhev'Na was as a slave. Once everyone believed I was dead, our allies put a mask on me—an enchantment that made me believe I was someone else—so I could pass the initial interrogations and be brought here. The man who was supposed to help me when I arrived—to remove the mask and leave me free—died unexpectedly. Only when I caught a glimpse of Seri a few weeks ago did I finally remember who I was and what I was supposed to be doing. But of course, penned up like this, I can't do much of anything."

His gaze roamed the row of cages. "Maybe I can steal the key and let you out."

"Don't! It's too risky—and not of any use. As long as I wear this collar, I've not a scrap of power. Even if we could get Seri and Gerick, we've no way out of Ce Uroth, because I can't take us."

"I could get something to cut off the thing, maybe."

"I wish you could. More than you'll ever know. But sorcery is the only way to take it off."

"Well, I'll think on it. We'll figure some way."

"You mustn't put yourself at risk, Paulo. I— Listen to me. To know that you're here . . . with her . . . You have to keep yourself safe. Do you understand? So there will be someone . . ."

"I understand. But nothing's going to happen to you."

"I'm not exactly in a secure profession."

A guard relieved himself just outside the cell across from me, close enough to remind me of our precarious position.

"Keep yourself safe, Paulo. It's so good to see you, to know a faithful friend is nearby, but you must stay away from me. There's nothing to be done here. Not yet."

"Well, you just watch yourself. I'm going to take care of this. You'll see."

He slipped away as quietly as he had come. I sat for a long time watching the flickering lights of the Zhid forges across the dark courtyard, pondering the wonders of a universe that would place its future so confidently in the hands of an illiterate fourteen-year-old boy. For the first time since Dassine's death, I went to sleep with a smile on my lips.

CHAPTER 38

Gerick

Something strange was happening in my house. Ever since Mellador had killed that slave to heal my knee, I had taken care of my own injuries. I could ignore scrapes, cuts, and bruises. Even gashes and sprains went away of themselves eventually. But one day a sparring partner got in a lucky slash and gave me a deep cut in the upper arm. I got back to my room before anyone noticed, and dismissed my slaves, saying I was going to practice sorcery for a while. I didn't want them telling anyone I was injured.

I wished I could use the things Notole had taught me about slowing bleeding or making wounds not hurt, but that is one of the impossible things about sorcery. You can't lay compulsions on yourself or do yourself an injury with enchantments, but that means you can't heal yourself either, even if you have the skill for it. So I ripped up a clean towel and tied it about my arm. To get the rag tight enough with only one hand and my mouth was hard. I put on a thick shirt and a dark-colored tunic that wouldn't show any blood, and hoped my arm would stop hurting and stop bleeding before I gave myself away.

When I came back from my hand combat practice after all that, I felt light-headed, sweating and cold at the same time. The pain in my arm had eased to a dull ache, but the towel and my shirt were soaked with blood. I tried again to tie up the wound, put on a different shirt and tunic, burned the bloody ones, and went to my riding lesson, but I had to cut the lesson short before I fell off the horse. I screamed at my riding master that his lessons were too hard.

I returned to the house just after sunset. All I wanted was to get to my bed, but I kept finding myself in the wrong room. When I finally came to the stairs, I made it only halfway to the first landing before I had to rest. Then I couldn't seem to get up again. I thought for a bit about calling my slaves back. Sefaro would help. But then I remembered that Sefaro was dead. Dead because of me, like all the others. I couldn't ask anybody to help me. And I had to be careful or the Lords would know everything; to keep up my barriers took concentration.

In the middle of the night I woke in my bed. Someone was doing something to my arm, and I was afraid that if I opened my eyes, I would meet the eyes of a slave being tied to it. But no rush of power burned my blood and no smirking Mellador showed up in my mind. The person cleaned the wound, put something cool on it, and tied it up tight. Whoever it was dribbled watered wine in my mouth, and I soon fell back to sleep.

The sun was already high when I woke, and my swordmaster had sent three messages asking where I was. But I told Notole that I wanted to work with her that day, that I had questions about making illusions, the most interesting sorcery I had learned so far. She agreed. When she asked why I was so sleepy and inattentive, I told her I'd been having strange dreams again—which I believed I had. But I couldn't pretend it was dreams when I touched the knotted strip of linen under my shirt. And I couldn't figure out who could have put it there.

By evening I felt sick again and came near losing my way from the Lords' house to mine. I went straight to bed without any supper. The person came again that night. The bandage was changed, and cool cloths put on my face, and I was given sweetened wine to drink several times in the night while I drifted in and out of sleep. I kept telling myself I was going to open my eyes to see who it was, but my eyes were too heavy, and I didn't really want to know. If I found out who it was, I would probably have to do something terrible to them.

Though I still felt weak, I was able to go back to training the next day, and after a few more days had passed, I convinced myself that it had all been my imagination. I must have done the things myself, but because I was feverish, it just seemed to be someone else. But then I started finding things—odd things—left here and there in my rooms.

The first was a small, egg-shaped rock sitting exactly in the center of the table in my sitting room. It was smooth and grayish blue with a clear vein through it. I couldn't imagine how it had gotten there. I tossed it into the fire-grate, but immediately picked it up again and ran my fingers over it. Just a rock. No enchantments attached. But perhaps the Lords had sent it. I threw it onto the bench where I left my grinding stones, oil, and rags for my weapons.

A few days later I found a small chunk of wood just in the same place on my eating table. The wood was dark and hard as iron, and when I looked close I could see crystals inside its seams, almost like the wood had become a stone. No one in Zhev'Na would have remarked it. I wouldn't have either, except that I hadn't put it there, and I couldn't imagine who might have done so. I put it with the rock.

And then I found a nasty-looking pit from a purplish fruit called a darupe on my bed pillows. I didn't make a connection with the other two things until I picked it up in disgust, ready to throw it into the fire, and it fell apart in my hand. It had been carefully and evenly split in two. The insides of the pit were smooth and deep brown, with dark veins like polished rosewood, and the kernel was a deep, shining red, with swirls of black in it. I tossed the thing onto the bench with the others.

Several weeks passed without anything more out of the ordinary, but then I returned from a long day's training to find a small, cracked glass dish—a piece of a broken lamp perhaps—filled with sand and sitting on the table by the stool where I always sat to take off my boots. Why would anyone collect sand in a dish? There was enough sand in Ce Uroth to fill every dish in the whole world. But as I pulled off one boot, I found myself staring at the dish. The sand in it had not been scooped up from the ground at random.

It was easy to think of the desert as an endless expanse

of red sand and rock, and to believe that any change in its appearance was caused solely by changing light, but there were actually hundreds of shades of red and brown to the land itself. Someone had collected grains of many different colors and laid them in the glass dish in layers, one and then the other, thick and thin, to make a rippling pattern. I had never seen anything like it. I turned it around to examine it from every angle. This wasn't the Lords' work.

"Well, young friend, how was your day's activity?" Darzid walked up behind me and peered over my shoulder at the sand that now lay in a heap on the tiled floor. "What's this?"

"Boots full of sand."

"I thought the horse was treating you better these days." He picked up the dish from the floor.

"Not since Fengara was replaced. I had to change to a new mount because the last one was impossible. And the new one isn't much better. I still spend more time on the ground than in the saddle." I let my anger and my bruises fill my mind, while shoving Firebreather and the Leiran boy and mysteries into its farthest corners. Ziddari was curious. I had to be careful.

"Your combat instructors report that you are progressing decently, that you work hard."

"I don't know. They don't tell me of it."

Darzid tossed the broken glass on the table, and then pulled up a few of the giant cushions that lay about the room, stretched out on them, and began combing his beard with his fingers. That always meant he was going to lecture me. "But Notole is worried about your studies of sorcery."

"Why? I've learned to do a lot of things."

"Child's magic. Illusions. Games. You are to be the most powerful sorcerer in the universe. Don't you think it's time you moved beyond calling horses and lighting candles?"

"I've done bigger things. I caused an avalanche last week. And a few days ago I melted rock into a pool so that a kibbazi fell into it and turned to stone when I let it harden again."

"Tricks. You must begin to study more serious matters."

"Notole tried to teach me how to read thoughts. I

worked at it, tried it with the guards and with slaves. But it seems like I just get started, and everything closes up where I can't see any more. I just need to practice." I threw my boots into the corner of the room and walked over to the table where a cup of steaming cavet was waiting for me. My stockinged feet left a trail of sand across the floor.

"You need power. You know that. It's not enough that you let your power grow at its own rate. You must aggressively acquire it. The time draws near. Tomas's spirit and that of your nurse cry out for vengeance. You've not forgotten?"

"Of course not."

"Then you must take the next step. Learn how to take what you need. Just as you use slaves and Zhid to improve your skills for battle, so you must use whatever is required to make yourself ready for the other battle that awaits you. The Dar'Nethi are not what they were, but strong and intricate sorcery is still to be found in Avonar. They will not lie down for you and say, 'Oh please, lord Prince, enslave us. Allow us to repay a thousand years of brutal oppression.' Tonight you will go to Notole, and she will begin teaching you about the acquisition of power. You will listen to her."

"I always listen." I hated when he talked to me as if I'd never thought of these things myself.

"Good. And you'll not refuse what she offers."

"I want to learn everything."

At least he took me at my word. I suppose he could tell I really meant it. "And so, how is your life here? Do you have everything you desire?"

"The Lords have given me everything."

"Indeed. We always keep our bargains."

After I ate and slept for an hour, Notole summoned me to a workroom deep in the Lords' palace. The chamber was dark, except for two intense green lights—her emerald eyes.

"Sit here," she said, and a path of green light showed me a backless wooden stool just beside her. "So you're ready to take the next step, young Lord?"

"I want to learn it all."

"And there is so much to learn once you have power enough. . . ." She told me all the things I would be able to do once I learned to acquire power beyond what existed in me: read thoughts and induce dreams, lay compulsions that could make a person do anything I wanted, manipulate objects without touching them, and even change the weather. "When you are sixteen or so, young Lord, you will come into your full talent. Sometimes I can see what it will be in a child your age, but you are much too dark and complex. It will be interesting to see what awaits you. But for the war to come, you will not yet be in your prime, so we must develop what skills you have. And first and foremost, you must learn about power."

All Dar'Nethi were born with the power for sorcery. It was a part of us, Notole said, just like our ability to think or to speak or to read. And just like those things, it required only a little teaching to be able to use it. But to work any significant sorcery, one needed more power than what just happened to be inside you.

The Dar'Nethi increased their power using their experiences as they went about their lives, by observing and thinking and holding on to the images and feelings. "The fairy dance," Notole called it. "They are so limited in their vision, they let the most magnificent of all gifts wither from boredom, tiptoeing through the universe like children at a glassmaker's shop afraid to touch anything. But you, my young Prince, can dismiss their foolish limitations. Look beyond yourself, and you can have all the power you wish in an instant. Here, take this stone"—she set an ordinary piece of the red desert rock in my hand—"and look on it. Consider it. Focus your inner eye on this worthless piece of nothing, and seek out its true parts in your mind, the essence that makes it a stone rather than a tree or a frog."

She guided me through the jewels in my ear, helping me to think of the stone and the gritty sand that made it . . . and before very long, I felt a small, pulsing heaviness—not in my hand—but in my mind where I held the image of the stone.

"Now take that weight . . . that morsel of life's essence that exists in this worthless stone . . . and draw it into yourself . . . into that place we have visited before where your power lies, that you can shape to your will."

I did as she said and felt much like I did after drinking cavet in the morning, a little bit stronger, a little bit more awake. And then I lifted my left hand, as she directed me, and thought about light . . . and a flame shot from the end of my fingers. It lasted only for a moment, but I had never made anything so bright. And it had never been so easy.

"There, you see, young Lord? This is only the beginning."

"More. I want to do more, Notole." The excitement of it had me ready to burst. All the things I could do . . .

She laughed. "And so we shall, but we are going to need a new stone."

I looked in my hand, and indeed the red stone had crumbled to dust. "No one will care," I said. "It was only a stone."

"Exactly so." She laughed again and gave me another stone.

Notole taught me many things in that dark room. Some were interesting and useful, and some were unpleasant, and some were vile and wicked. ". . . but necessary to know, for your enemies will stop at nothing to destroy you. You must be ready for them. Sometimes even your allies will be distasteful to you, and you must know how to control them. Your power is everything. Once you rule as you are meant to do, you can afford to pick and choose your ways of dealing with your enemies . . . and your friends."

We spent days and days working on how to build power—from rocks, from broken pots and cups and paper and yarn, from objects of all kinds. Then she brought in plants and small trees and mice and kibbazi, and I learned that the power you could take from things that lived was much stronger than what you got from rocks and pots and wood. Nothing much was left of the things when we were through with them. It was a good way to make use of things that were worthless or ugly or broken.

Sometimes I was in Notole's rooms for hours without even realizing it, for when I went back to my house, it was already night and I was ravenously hungry, or maybe the sun had come up when I thought it was only evening. Sometimes I missed my other lessons for days at a time, so that when I went back to my sword fighting, I was stiff and rusty. I was so busy with Notole and sorcery, I almost forgot about the odd things I had found.

However, on one afternoon when I came in from sword training, a smooth, flat square of wood lay in the center of my sitting room table. I sent my slaves to run a bath and set out fresh clothes for me, and while they were occupied, I picked up the thing. It was smaller than my hand, plain and somewhat crude, as if cut and shaped with a dull knife. A square of metal had been set into the back of it and polished to a high sheen, so that I could see myself in it as clearly as a looking glass. Its oddity made me remember the other things left in my rooms, and I rummaged around on the bench and found the stone and the wood and the fruit pit with the shining red kernel.

Were the Lords leaving me the things? Perhaps they were a puzzle, and when I figured out the answer to it, I would be ready for . . . something. I had no time to think about it just then, for I was going to Notole for the rest of the day, so I threw the things in a small box on the table by my bed. When I got back, I would take another look and try to decipher the riddle.

On my way to the Lords' house that afternoon, I witnessed a fight in the courtyard between two Zhid. One of the warriors watching the fight told me the two had hated each other for hundreds of years and had decided it was time for one of them to die. When I got to Notole's workroom, I asked her why the Zhid commanders didn't stop it. In Leire two soldiers were never allowed to fight each other to the death, no matter how long-standing their grievance.

"So you saw them, eh? A useless quarrel. And how useful are warriors who are so caught up in private business?" She knew what was happening—she knew everything that went on—but she didn't answer my question. "Let me show you something."

From a purple velvet bag, she pulled a dull brass ring about as big as my hand. She had me hold out my hand with my palm open. Standing the ring on its end, she blew on it and set it spinning.

"Watch the oculus closely," she said. As it spun faster, she took her hand away and it stood there on its own, beginning to shine bright gold. Faster and faster the ring spun, catching the light of the candles and her emerald eyes, creating an orb of gold and green light right in my hand. "Now probe the orb," she said. "Pull the light of it apart with your inner eye—and seek out the disharmony. There . . . you see?"

Inside the orb of light I could see the two Zhid, covered with sweat and blood and hatred, grappling in the courtyard.

So much power there, said Notole, whispering in my ear through the jewels in my earring. *Hatred is very powerful, as you know. It has made you more than you were, and can do so whenever you find it. Open your mind to it. Here, let me show you. . . .*

Through the jewels in my ear, she reached inside of me. As if she were drawing back a curtain, she pulled back a piece of my thoughts, exposing a dark, empty hole. Into the hole poured a stream of green-and gold-streaked darkness from the center of the spinning ring—pure power, an immense wave of it like nothing I'd experienced before. Fire burned in my veins, filling me, swelling my lungs and stretching my skin. My heart drummed against my chest until I felt like I was going to burst.

Notole let go of my mind and took the ring from my hand, while I gulped air. "Now, my young Prince," she said, "try it. Touch the glass there on the far shelf."

I pointed my finger at a wine goblet that glittered in the candlelight across the room, and it shattered into a million pieces at my thought. Three more beside it splintered when I looked at them. A candle flame grew to a bonfire, and then I blew a puff of air in its direction and snuffed it out again. I considered the battling warriors. I couldn't even see them, but I commanded them to be paralyzed and knew it was done because I could hear their angry and fearful thoughts. I quickly set them to breathing again, for their anger had turned into panic. They were suffocating.

I hadn't known power could be like this. Drawing a huge breath, I lifted a table with my wish and flew it about the room. A book slipped off the table, but I slowed its falling so that I could catch it before it fell to the floor. All of this as I sat on the edge of my stool. Everything that had been difficult or impossible all these months was now easy.

"Well done, my young Prince. Few in the world—perhaps no one save the three of us—can take so much into themselves so quickly. You will do well. Very well, indeed." All the Lords were with me in my mind, touching me, smiling at me, pleased with how well I had done. I was pleased, too, and could think of nothing but doing more of it.

When I left the Lords' house that night, I felt strange and excited, but I noticed that the night was exceptionally dark. Even the giant torches that burned over the entrance to the Lords' house seemed to have little effect.

A slave sat at the top of the stairs waiting for me. When he took my cloak, his eyes met mine for a moment, and I felt such a wave of terror from him that I stepped back. He averted his eyes quickly. I considered reading his thoughts, but decided I would rather take another look at the puzzle that had been set for me. Maybe I could find some enchantment that had been undetectable before. I told the slave to prepare a bath and wait for me there.

Once the slave was gone, I took the things from the wooden box and examined them again. Bits and pieces. Natural objects, except for the mirror. Not chosen idly. The sand arrangement had taken great care to make; too bad I'd had to spill it. The mirror, too, had taken time to create, yet it was not expertly made. No enchantments on any of it.

My mind flicked to the Leiran boy, but dismissed him almost as quickly. He was not one to speak in riddles, even if he could have gained access to my apartments. I turned over the mirror to look for clues, but when I saw my reflection, I couldn't think of puzzles anymore. I drew closer to the lamp and took another look. My skin crept over my bones.

My eyes weren't brown any more, but black, so dark that you couldn't see where the colored part left off and the pupil began. I threw the mirror and the other things back in the box. Cold and sick, I jumped into the hot bath and sat for an hour trying to think only about power and sorcery and what I might be able to do with them. My slaves didn't look at me. I ignored their terror and the whispering presence of the Lords who hovered in the deeps of my head telling me how well I had done at my lessons.

I didn't sleep well. When morning came, I pulled out the mirror and took another look. My eyes were brown again. I was very relieved, and decided it had just been exhaustion. Things often got confusing in Notole's rooms.

Sword training occupied the morning, but I found it difficult to concentrate on anything but sorcery. But Notole didn't call me that day, and when I spoke to her, she said she was not available for teaching.

I waited almost a week, the hunger for sorcery burning in me like a fever. At last she called, and I ran across the courtyard and down the stairs to her den, hoping she would open the purple velvet bag and pull out the brass ring. She did.

That day we let our minds travel through the Zhid encampment outside the fortress walls. A troop of warriors was being punished by their commander for lax discipline. The warriors' anger at the punishment and their desire for revenge was eating away at them as they labored in the desert, but they dared not rebel. With Notole's help and her oculus, I drank deep of their fear and hatred, and it tasted better than the first sip of water after a desert march. I was bursting with power.

We practiced control that day—holding objects, stacking them, making them move in precise patterns, and controlling the thoughts of others. The Drudges were easy; they were so dull and afraid, I could make them think anything I wanted. The Zhid were more challenging. Their minds were filled with so many things: war and strategy, fighting skills, and scheming about their fellow warriors and their superiors. I had trouble trying to intrude on their minds, but eventually one of the house guards had a fearsome nightmare in the middle of the day, thanks to me.

It was far into the night when I went back to my rooms. I worked on sharpening my sword, ate a meal, and cleaned myself up. Only then did I pull the wooden square out of the box and look into the polished bit of metal. It had happened again. This time the area of black was larger than the normal colored part of the eye. It didn't hurt. My eyes just looked strange . . . but no one but slaves or Drudges were going to see them.

My eyes were normal again the next day, and I almost brought the question about them to mind, but I decided against it. The Lords might not let me continue with Notole's lessons if it kept happening.

Another long week went by before Notole called me to her again and set the oculus spinning. On that day, we watched as the Dar'Nethi survivors of a Zhid raiding party were sealed into their slave collars. An immense surge of power filled me as I listened to their screams. I felt like a volcano, huge and rumbling and dangerous.

"This time we will travel beyond the walls of the fortress and see what we can find for entertainment," Notole said. She put out the candles, so that the only light in the room came from the emeralds in her golden mask and the green-and-gold orb of the oculus that hung over our heads. I was quivering with the power dammed up inside me. When she took my hands in her dry, withered fingers, she had to speak only one word and our minds came free of our bodies.

I could see everything, just as if I were flying. We soared through the vast temple of the Lords where the three giant statues sat under the roof of stars, and we passed through the walls of the Lords' house and looked down on the courtyards, crawling with slaves and Drudges and warriors. We sailed into the noonday and called up a whirlwind that turned the air red as it picked up sand, blasting the desert encampments and scouring the cliffs. Warriors and slaves looked like ants crawling on the desert. When I was little I had sometimes dropped grasshoppers and beetles into anthills to see what would happen; now I could do the same with people. So I picked up a few slaves in the whirlwind and deposited them behind the Zhid lines, and I sucked Zhid warriors into the wall of sand and dropped them amid the slaves. Notole laughed, but we didn't stay to watch them sort it out. Instead we soared into the vast emptiness of the Wastes. Notole showed me how to call up lightning, and for hours I practiced blasting rocks to rubble and setting thorn bushes afire.

Enough, young Lord, Notole said at last, still laughing inside my mind. *Save some adventures for another day. We've only begun.*

Still excited, I left the Lords' house and walked across the barren courtyard to my house. Lightning . . . I had called down lightning! I couldn't wait to do it again. For the moment, I was so tired . . . I rubbed my eyes and stumbled a bit. The courtyard was very dark. When I stuck out my hand to catch my balance, I realized I was about to crash into the Gray House wall instead of walking through the gate. Squinting, I felt my way along the wall to the gateway. As I went inside, I looked back over my shoulder. The torches over the Lords' gate were lit, only the fire wasn't orange and bright. The flames looked like gray veils blowing in the wind.

My skin went cold. And when I thought of some of the things I'd done that day, my stomach felt queasy. I ran into my house, stumbling up the stairs and tripping on a footstool in my room, even though the lamps were lit. I screamed at my slaves to stop staring at me and draw me a bath. When I was alone, I held the mirror in the dim circle of light cast by my largest lamp. My hand was shaking so hard, I had to lay the mirror down and bend over it.

Almost my entire eye was black. Only a narrow rim of white surrounded the deep black holes, two bottomless wells boring right down into the depths of my soul.

CHAPTER 39

On the next morning, the sun rose gray and dim. I was going to have to tell the Lords. I wasn't at all confident that eyesight would heal itself like bruises or twisted knees, and I certainly could not do any training the way I was. *Notole,* I called, *I need to tell—*

Good morning, young Lord. Before I could open my thoughts to them, Notole filled my head. *Are you tired this morning? We went farther than I had planned in these past days—you are such a delightful student—so eager—and it can be quite wearing when one is starting to develop one's talent as you are. You mustn't be concerned about it.*

"I was wondering—"

We've told your teachers that you need to rest today. Parven took up the conversation. Though his words were pleasant enough, anger rumbled in my belly as he spoke. *I will put you to sleep, my young Lord, until such time as you can take up your proper business. My foolish sister has rushed things a bit.*

They didn't let me say anything. Parven laid an enchantment on me, while the three of them talked about other exercises they planned for the next few days. As I drowsed off, it occurred to me that none of them had mentioned anything about my eyes. I had a sense that they knew what was happening, but didn't want me to know. Why else would they be in such a hurry to send me to sleep? As there were no mirrors anywhere in the Gray House, they wouldn't think I'd seen it for myself, and no servant would dare speak of it.

At least a day had passed by the time I woke again. I was famished. Once I had eaten, I steeled myself to look in the mirror. Only a trace of gray remained in the brown. I decided that as long as my eyes would turn back right, they weren't really damaged. I could still go to Notole and learn what she could teach. I needed to know about power and sorcery, so I could be strong enough to do whatever I wanted.

I worked hard at my sword training that day, enjoying moving and fighting after so many days of inactivity. Notole's lessons were tiring, but as far as I knew my body didn't move the whole time. Since I had returned from the desert and gotten so preoccupied with sorcery, my fighting skills had shown little improvement. If only I could use a little of my power . . . I tried making the air thick and heavy around my swordmaster's blade.

You will not! Parven burst into my head. *For now, true power and physical training are two separate aspects of your life, young Lord. You must be able to fight to your maximum capability with every weapon you possess.*

"All right, all right." And so I let the air go back to normal, and I slogged on, practicing one move after another. I trained with my swordmaster all day. Notole said she didn't want me that night. I wasn't surprised. The pattern said it would be six or seven days until we ventured out again. The thought of sorcery left me hollow inside, hungry, my skin buzzing like it did when you didn't get enough sleep. To call down lightning . . .

That evening after my riding lesson, I took Firebreather for a gallop to help take my mind off of my craving for sorcery. It was near midnight when we got back to the stable, though this time we made the entire journey together. When I led Firebreather into his stall, I wasn't too surprised to hear a voice from the corner. "Did he behave?"

"He expects oats."

"Thought he would. I've brought some already."

We rubbed Firebreather down and made sure he had an extra scoop of oats.

The Leiran boy kicked the straw into a pile in the corner of the stall and flopped onto it. "You've not been riding much lately."

"I've had other things to do. Have you stayed out of trouble?"

"It came out all to the good. They think I'm a half-wit. Was it you who told 'em?"

"I might have mentioned it."

"You're not the first to notice." He grinned.

I patted Firebreather's neck and gathered up my cloak and my pack to go. The Leiran boy glanced at my pack, and then looked away quickly.

"I've a packet of field rations in there," I said. "You wouldn't want it, would you?"

"If you were ever to run this place, I'd be happy to give you a word or two on improving the cooking." I tossed him the greasy bag, and he laid back on the straw, groaning in pleasure as he chewed on a leathery strip of dried meat. "Blazes! You can promise Firebreather oats, but if you want to get me anywhere, promise me jack."

"I don't have any more tonight." I rummaged through my bag and found a slightly battered darupe. "You can have this. That's all I've got."

"I'm not choosy." He dispatched the fruit in half a heartbeat and tossed the pit over the gate of the stall.

I squatted down beside the gate. "You're not good at riddles, are you?"

He blinked in surprise. "What makes you ask that?"

"Just seeing the fruit pit . . . It sounds strange, I know, but it makes me think of a riddle."

"Never thought I was good at 'em. Never had much call to. But once I helped somebody figure one out. We did pretty good."

As the stable lamp faded and sputtered, leaving us sitting in the dark, I told him about the things I'd found in my house. ". . . So what do you think? Is it the Lords' puzzle or not?"

The voice coming from across the dark stall was more serious than I expected. "I'd say somebody is trying to tell you something. Somebody that maybe can't come out and say it for fear you wouldn't allow it to be said. Not the Lords, though."

"A slave, you mean?"

"Maybe. Maybe not. Maybe it's not important the who, but only the what."

"I can't figure it out. I've tried all kinds of solutions using the names of the things, the sizes, the substances; I've tried to match their names with other words, but they don't seem to fit together at all."

"Maybe they're just to look at. No secret at all."

"That sounds like a proper half-wit."

"Bring me another bag of jack, and I'll take another guess."

"Don't count on it." I stood up, brushed the straw off my legs, and gave Firebreather another pat. "I'd best go or I'll fall asleep over my sword in the morning."

"Did you ever get a swordmaster that could teach you proper?"

"No. I've not learned anything new in a month. My swordmaster is a fine fighter, and he makes me work hard. I suppose I'm just not the best pupil."

"But you want the *best* sword fighter—one who can teach you and show you, not just make you sweat. Maybe the best one isn't one of them—the warriors."

"What do you mean?"

"I heard some of 'em talking the other day about a new slave, one that fights with the warriors, you know, to practice."

"A sparring partner? A practice slave?"

"That's it. They said he's the best they've ever seen. Stayed alive longer than any slave's ever done before. They're making him teach them what he knows and not just fight any more. Maybe he's the one you need."

"Maybe he is."

On the next day I asked my swordmaster, Drak, about the practice slave who had lasted longer than any ever had.

"I've heard of him. He's bound to the Wargreve Damon, but still does training matches with other warriors. He's not likely to last much longer, though. He fights Vruskot this afternoon, and Vruskot hasn't lost a match in two hundred years. He's had the Lords burn the words *yield* and *surrender* from his mind so he can't speak them even if he wanted to."

"I want to watch the match."

"It could be instructional. Vruskot is well known for his attacks. I'll demonstrate his basic techniques so you'll know what to look for. The match will likely be over so fast you'll miss it."

We worked until just after midday and then went down to one of the training yards just beyond the warriors' court. A good-sized crowd of warriors, Drudges, and slaves had gathered on the open side of the yard. Others were jammed around the walls. I wasn't used to crowds, and it made me uneasy, especially when they parted to let me stand at the front.

It wasn't difficult to decide which was Vruskot. I had learned early on that the Zhid didn't age. They remained the same age at which they had been transformed, and it took a considerable wound to kill one. But there was something recognizable about the oldest Zhid. They were like old trees with rough bark that you just knew had the hardest, thickest wood and had stood up through every kind of storm. Though he looked no more than thirty or forty, Vruskot was very old. He wasn't tall, but he had exceptionally long arms, knotted with muscles. His thighs were like tree trunks, and like all of the Zhid, his eyes were pale and empty.

Lots of slaves were standing along the walls, most of them personal attendants of high-ranking warriors. I couldn't pick out the one who was to fight. He must be huge and fierce to have lasted so long. And he would be controlled, not allowed to wander about. But the only slave who wasn't someone's servant was sitting by the wall with his eyes closed and his head bowed as if he were asleep or afraid. A chain ran from his collar to the iron ring embedded in the stone wall above his head.

Sure enough, when a Zhid detached the chain from his collar, he stood up immediately. He was tall, topping Vruskot by a head. His shoulders and arms were big, sun-darkened to the color of old leather and criss-crossed with scars, but he didn't look half so strong as the Zhid. Although he was lean and hard, built well for fighting, he didn't have the look of a warrior. He was just another slave, standing there barefoot and quiet as his hands were unmanacled, keeping his eyes cast down as if he were scared to look at a real fighter. They weren't going to allow him armor, so he stood barefoot on the blistering ground while Vruskot donned a thick leather cap, greaves, and a light mail shirt over his well-used gambeson. I would have bet my eyes the slave could never even scratch Vruskot.

But everything changed when they put the sword in the slave's hand. He raised his head, and you would have thought his skin had turned to steel. It wouldn't have surprised me to see a sword strike glance off his bare arms, or his eyes shoot off sparks. The small round shield they gave him seemed hardly necessary.

Vruskot didn't see it. He looked the slave up and down and curled his lip. Then he touched the tip of his sword to the slave's collar. "Through here," he said. "I'll take you right through it. You've forgotten your place, dog meat."

The slave did not even blink, which did not please Vruskot. "Position, slave!" growled the Zhid.

There was no slow beginning, no circling, feinting, or testing to ferret out weakness or crucial points of style. From the opening, they were in the full fury of battle. They used long-swords, striking so powerfully that you could feel the movement of air. Three times I had watched my father—the man I had believed to be my father, Duke Tomas, the Champion of Leire—take on the finest challengers in the Four Realms. I had thought there could be no one in the world that moved with Papa's speed and grace . . . until that day in Zhev'Na. The slave made Vruskot look like an ox.

An hour went by. The noise of the crowd—chattering, the placing of bets, gasps, and jeers—had faded into a silence broken only by the sounds of the battle. The clank and scrape of the swords, the dull thuds when sword struck shield. Harsh, gasping breaths. Vruskot's mail shirt chinked with his every move, and his boots pounded and scuffed the iron-hard dirt. The barefoot slave moved in silence.

Vruskot drew first blood, a slice to the slave's forward thigh. The Zhid pressed his advantage until the crowd had to move away from one of the walls. But he was too eager, so intent on his own next strike that he mistook the slave's acceptance of his blows for weakness. When the slave was almost to the wall, the two men close enough to smell each other's breath, the slave beat off Vruskot's next hammering strike with his thrusting shield—a move that made my own left arm hurt even to think of it—while at the exact same time whirling his own blade from high behind his head in a powerful counter. Vruskot had to step out or lose his head, giving the slave room to duck, step past, and pivot, leaving the sun in Vruskot's eyes. The Zhid wasn't slow either, despite his thick legs, and had his sword and shield up before the slave's next blow could take him. The sweat poured from the two in rivers.

Now the slave was pressing Vruskot with a flurry of cutting attacks—high and then low and then high again, moving from one to the other with fluid strength. Vruskot held his own. But then the Zhid caught the heel of his boot in a crack and went down right under the slave's upraised sword. The crowd inhaled as one. The slave waited, his sword high—aimed directly for Vruskot's neck. Vruskot just lay there breathing hard with such a murderous expression on his face that I wondered the slave could stand up before it. But the slave slapped the back of his sword hand against his mouth and pointed to the Zhid. Vruskot flared his nostrils and said nothing.

No one had told him! The slave didn't know that the warrior couldn't yield.

Instead of finishing the Zhid, the slave stepped back and allowed him to get up. What a fool! Did he think the Zhid would think kindly of him or have some code of honor that would keep him from gutting the slave if he got the chance? Vruskot's face was scarlet—with more than the heat of the battle. He attacked with a fury. They moved slowly around the yard. The slave pressured the Zhid to his knees, this time with skill instead of chance, but again he signaled that Vruskot should yield, and again stepped back when Vruskot refused.

I wouldn't have believed that either one of them could lift an arm any more, but so they did, circling and attacking as if they'd just begun. Even so, it would have to end soon. The slave's thigh wound was deep. His whole leg was covered in blood. It pained him, too, and he was favoring it. Vruskot began to concentrate on that side, getting in extra kicks and blows whenever he could. But the slave kept moving, stepping out, evading, a parry, a short thrust, a small step. And then, in a vertical cut that left the air rumbling, the slave's blade hacked right through Vruskot's sword arm, severing it just below the shoulder.

For one instant, the silence was absolute. The slave stepped back and let his sword slip to the sand. Everyone stared at Vruskot's arm lying on the red earth, its fingers still wrapped around the sword hilt. Then Vruskot bellowed in such pain and anger that the stones of the fortress rattled and the crowd shrank back from him. Dropping his shield and fumbling at his belt with his left hand, the Zhid drew his knife and swiped feebly at the slave. But the slave easily knocked his hand aside and shoved him to the ground. Vruskot screamed as his stump hit the ground and blood gushed onto the sand.

The slave, his breathing harsh and deep, threw down his shield and dropped to his knees beside Vruskot. None of the onlookers moved, even when the slave picked up Vruskot's knife. I was sure he was going to finish the Zhid, but instead he cut the warrior's shirt away, wadded up the damp linen, and pressed it against the warrior's twitching stump, holding Vruskot still with his other hand and his knees. Damn! He was trying to stop the bleeding. His chest still heaving, the slave looked around the crowd for help. For one moment . . . one glimpse . . . something seemed familiar about that face, strained and exhausted under the close-cropped hair, but before I could figure it out, the crowd erupted.

A growling warrior bashed the slave in the head with his arm, knocking him to the ground, while three others picked up the screaming Vruskot and carried him away. The slave shook his head and dragged himself up to his hands and knees, but another Zhid triggered his collar and sent him into retching spasms. Then they bound his hands, dragged him to the wall, and chained him to the iron ring. He lay there gasping and heaving in the afternoon sun, flies settling on his bloody arms and legs.

I stood staring like a fool at the deserted training ground. Vruskot's arm lay in the dirt, forgotten. The crowd had dispersed quickly. Drak, my swordmaster, shook his head and urged me to move on. "Well, an astounding match to be sure. Who could have imagined such a thing? I had no idea Vruskot had slipped so sorely in his skills."

Of course, Vruskot hadn't lost the match. The Dar'Nethi had won it. Only a blind fool would claim anything else. "Let's get away from here," I said. "I need to work."

It was Vruskot I took for a swordmaster. Zhid were not easy to kill, but the swift actions of the slave V'Saro had saved his life until a surgeon could attend to him. Of course he was bitter; a warrior without his sword arm considers himself dead no matter what. I wouldn't have been a Dar'-Nethi slave in Vruskot's service for any amount of power in the world. But he could not have failed to learn something from the slave who'd maimed him, and so perhaps he could teach me something of it, too. And, of course, Vruskot was a master swordsman in his own right—that's why the Lords kept him alive one-armed, so he could teach or command swordsmen. Once Vruskot's commanders convinced him that he had no choice, and he understood that it wasn't a humiliation to instruct the honored guest of the Lords, he got into the job with a vengeance. I had no choice but to progress.

The slave would have been a masterful teacher. But if I asked for him, I would honor him, and therefore he would die. Sooner or later it would happen. And it didn't seem at all fair to take such a man's dying out of his own hands.

The days flew by. Notole taught me to take the world's troubles for my own use. Such things existed—fear, hate, anger, pain—and I could do nothing about them, so I couldn't see anything wrong with using them to my advantage. Once I came of age and controlled my own power, then perhaps things could be different.

The Lords still said nothing about the effects of what I was doing, only that light might bother my eyes after long nights working with Notole. After each session, I would sleep for most of a day, then go back to Vruskot and training until Notole called me to her again. Just as a test, I commanded my slaves to obtain a looking glass for me. I'd been having my slaves braid my hair into many thin plaits as Isker warriors did, and I said I wanted a glass to see how it looked. They groveled and claimed there were none to be had in Zhev'Na.

But the crude gift from my unknown benefactor told me the important tale. For a while, my eyes indeed turned back to normal every time. But soon they kept a muddy gray tint. And then they stayed black, and the center of them was bottomless darkness that became a little larger each time. It got to where I couldn't go about in the noonday, but only in the morning or the late-afternoon light. I kept the draperies drawn in my apartments and moved my riding lessons to after dark.

I was afraid of what was happening, but I couldn't stop. There was still so much to learn. Notole had promised that just before my anointing she would show me yet another source of power, more rich than those I already used. It was the greatest secret of the Lords, she told me, known to no other in the universe. I had to keep going until then.

I had been so caught up in my training that I'd given little thought to the puzzle of the gifts, but late one afternoon, as I sat bored in my dim apartments, waiting for the sun to go down, I decided to look at the things again. Something new had been left in the box—a scrap of paper with hundreds of tiny holes pricked in it. I almost laughed, it was so odd. If the earlier objects had been indecipherable, then this one was totally impossible. I could see no pattern to the marks. I was on the verge of crumpling it up, when a hot blast of wind allowed a stray sunbeam to penetrate the draperies and shine through the jumble of pinholes, casting a reverse shadow on the wall, like a compact universe of stars in a tiny square shadow of a sky.

Stars! That's what it was! The paper converted the barren sunlight into stars—but not the stars of Ce Uroth that hovered behind the ever-present dust haze. There was the Watcher, the thick band of the Arch, the Bowman aiming his true arrow toward the Swan . . . the stars of northern Leire, the stars I would see from the towers of Comigor.

I hadn't thought of home in so long. I tried to remember it. Gray towers, not angular and thin like those that faced me across the courtyard, but stout and thick, stained with six hundred years of smoke and weathering . . . sturdy walls with five round towers, built to hold the garrison in safety for uncounted days from any threat that might ride across the heath. Inside the main doors were the black and white floor tiles, and the rainbow light that arched down from the tall windows of the entry tower . . . so beautiful . . .

"Maybe they're just to look at," the Leiran boy had said.

I took out the stone with the clear vein in it and held it up close to my face and my brightest lamp. The light hurt my eyes, but I needed to see these things. The vein led deep into the blue-gray stone, a secret passage allowing light to penetrate the cool darkness and reveal the secrets of the stone that would otherwise lay hidden. Deep in the heart of the stone were delicate patterns of yellow and green and blue, arranged in spirals and sunbursts and flowery splashes, a tiny garden of color.

Each of the gifts was the same in a way. The iron-like wood hid a thousand tiny perfect crystals in its pores; the ugly fruit pit masked a miniature sculpture finer than any woodworker's creation. The dish of sand had been only a piece of the ordinary desert, but presented in an unexpected way, intriguing. And the mirror . . . There my speculation came to an abrupt halt. My chest ached. Why a reflection of me?

CHAPTER 40

I had to know who it was. I had to know what someone was trying to tell me and why it hurt so much when I looked at those stupid things laid out on my table. It became a fever in me to know. I tried to read the minds of all the slaves and warriors in my house, but I didn't have power enough. I needed the kind of power I used in my sessions with Notole. For days I would jump at any word from the Lords, hoping it would be Notole's summons. At last it came. *Tonight, my Prince. A special night tonight.*

When I went to the Lords' house, I didn't usually go through the temple, that huge room with the giant statues and the roof of stars and the floor that was like black ice. Most of the time I took a side door that led more directly to Notole's workrooms or to Parven's bare stone chamber where I studied maps and strategy with him. But on this night they summoned me to a new place.

The chamber was buried in the very heart of the Lords' house, down a long tight stairway and through a winding passage that seemed to turn in upon itself. The room was so dark that it was impossible to see how large it was, or what was in it. Embedded in the floor was a glowing circle of deep blue, and suspended above it was an oculus, not the size of my hand, like the ones I'd used with Notole, but one that was taller than me. The blue light reflected off the dull brass of the ring.

"Welcome, young Lord." The Lords were there waiting for me.

". . . such a pleasure . . ."

". . . to have all of us together again. A special night

tonight." Ziddari laid his hands on my shoulders and gazed down at me. His black robes made his body fade into the darkness, so that all I could see were his ruby eyes and the gold mask that was grown into his skin. "Time has flown by us so quickly."

"You've done well," said Parven, coming up behind Ziddari, his wide, pale forehead reflecting the purple glow of his amethysts. "We had such doubts when Ziddari brought you to us. 'So young,' we said. 'So untried, and only a little more than a year's turn to prepare him.' How foolish were our doubts. You have taught us the strength of your word. You have proven . . ."

". . . that you are capable of understanding the truth of the world and leaving behind your childish past. You have seen that our interests are the same, and that rigor and discipline can build strength." Ziddari had taken up from Parven again. "As you've no doubt surmised, we've kept secrets from you. But you've not shrunk from any of our teaching, and so . . ."

". . . the time has come to reveal to you our most precious secret, and to prepare you for your initiation that comes five days hence." Notole led me to the verge of the wide blue circle scribed on the floor. The huge oculus was so close I could have reached out and touched it. "This will not be easy, as nothing in your life has been easy. You will have to give up things of value, as you have already done, but the rewards . . . they're what your blood burns for, even now."

They were right. As the ring started to spin, my heart was racing with hunger and excitement; my breath came quick and shallow; heat radiated from my face and arms. For so long only scalding water or blazing sun had made me warm, but sorcery was far better. Faster and faster the ring spun, snatching the red and green and purple light of the Lords' masks and the blue glow from the floor, weaving them into a giant ball of light. With Parven and Notole to either side of me, and Ziddari behind with his hands on my shoulders, I used my inner eye to penetrate the orb as they had taught me, and I was no longer in Ce Uroth . . .

. . . but in a land just emerging from winter, faint traces of green poking up amid the brown stubble of farmland . . . a muddy road churned up by wagon wheels and horses' hooves. Up ahead was a party of bedraggled prisoners, roped together and slogging through the mud. Mounted soldiers guarded fifty men and women, filthy and wretched and filled with . . . oh, incredible . . . such vile, unbounded hatred. The soldiers cut loose one of the prisoners, threw a rope about his neck, and dragged him through the muck. In moments, he dangled from the branch of a tree. His feet jerked. The soldiers laughed. "There's the king's justice for you. Anyone else want to complain?"

A few prisoners growled and strained at their bonds. Some wept. Some just stared at the soldiers and the dead man swinging from the tree. The soldiers lashed the prisoners, especially those who showed their anger, and soon the party was moving down the road again. . . .

Who were these people? Yet, even as my mind asked the question, I knew the answer. The prisoners cursed in the tongue of Valleor, and the soldiers wore the red dragon of Leire—King Evard's men. People of my own world! Loathing—huge and powerful and terrible—seethed in their hearts. No Zhid, no Dar'Nethi, not even the Dar'-Nethi slaves could summon half so grand a hate as these soldiers and their captives. . . .

And it is all yours, whispered Notole through the jewels in my ear. She pulled back the layers of my thoughts, exposing the gaping emptiness inside me. *Take it.*

I drank deep. Burning, cutting, drenching, drowning . . . power seeped into my pores and filled my belly and my lungs until I was breathing black fire. It ate its way into my bones. Everything I had ever experienced was made unimportant.

I could not just call down lightning, I could create it. I could make a thousand warriors turn their swords upon themselves all at once. I could blast the stones of Zhev'Na into rubble and rebuild the fortress according to my whim, a thousand times over if I chose.

"This is what your father would forbid you," said Ziddari. His voice rang clear, while visions danced in my head. "This is what D'Arnath and his Heirs have judged too dangerous for us to attempt, because they were too cowardly and too weak to control it. This is the heritage they would deny you. Yet, even this is but a small taste of what is possible. D'Arnath created his enchanted Bridge and swore his oath to bind us, to imprison our skills and our power in his own weak-willed frame. But you, our young Prince, when you come into your power, you will set us free."

Power raged within me, stretching and pulling and swelling. Nothing had ever hurt so much; nothing had ever felt so marvelous. I wanted to scream and cry out the wonder of it, but my chest was filled with fire.

Come with me, said Notole. She touched my hand, and I was released to ride the airs of Gondai beside her. I glimpsed the far boundaries of the Wastes, where the hard red plains yielded to the green softness of Dar'Nethi lands. We journeyed past the work camps and farmsteads of the Drudges, flat, endless fields of no more interest or variation than a Drudge's mind. We traveled the wild oceans, and I called up winds that flattened trees and storms that made whole islands sink beneath the waves. For hours or days we examined rocky, ice-glazed pinnacles. Then we dived into deep places where bare stones formed natural fortresses far larger than Zhev'Na, where lakes were filled with molten rock, and where grew gigantic beasts with towering fangs and razor claws, who fled in terror at my word.

Yet this is but the beginning, whispered Parven through the jewels in my ear. *Come with me. . . .*

And Parven took me into the mind of a Zhid warrior, not just to read his thoughts or mold his dreams, but to replace his identity with my own. I could feel the heat of the desert sun on my shoulders as I marched onto the training ground. I recognized the faces of my cadre and felt the brush of fear when my commander stared at me with his pale eyes and ordered me to be the first to meet the challenger who waited there. But while I knew and felt these things from the other, it was I who controlled his body and reacted in his place. My hand raised his sword, and my eyes analyzed his opponent's opening moves for any weakness. My skill directed his combat under the harsh sun, and I felt the hot surge of victory when the sword bit into the slave's flesh and struck him down. When I tired of the first man and left his body, choosing another to be my host, the first warrior fell dead. I worried that I had made a mistake. *No, no, young Lord,* whispered Parven. *Use them as you wish. Like the rocks and the rats and the dirt beneath your feet, their lives exist only to serve you.*

And now imagine, young Prince, that this *was possible in that other place—the place where you fed on passions so much more vivid than our own—the place holy D'Arnath has forbidden us to go. Imagine the variety, the endless wonders that would await us. . . .*

"Enough," said Ziddari. "Bring him back. We said we would tell him all, and so he must know what it is he chooses."

With a word and a touch, Notole brought us back across the blazing noonday desert, past the warriors' encampments, through the fortress walls and into darkness—utter, complete darkness. I thought for a moment that I'd been left alone in some other place, but I felt the Lords behind me and beside me as they had been. The orb of light had vanished along with the blue circle, yet I could still sense the spinning and feel the cool rush of air on my hot face. I turned to Notole but I couldn't see her emerald eyes, nor Parven's amethysts, nor Ziddari's blood-red rubies. I could see nothing at all.

"Do not be afraid, young Lord," said Ziddari. "It is an inevitable effect of your activities—as you have surely guessed from your previous experiences. Your desire has made you accept these limitations. The effects become somewhat more severe as you progress. But you need not worry, because we can provide a remedy."

Something was slipped over my head and fitted to my face. I saw flashes of light, which relieved me greatly. When the hands fell away, I could see again, but in a way far different than before. We stood in the throne room, the place where I had spoken to the Lords for the first time. Like the temple, it had a floor of black glass, a ceiling that was an image of the night sky, and tall columns all around.

Along one side was a curved dais and on it the human-sized thrones where the Three had sat while I pledged them fealty. Today, the columns and the thrones and everything else in the room seemed angular, as if each curve in their design had been broken into short segments that only approximated its actual shape. The brass ring appeared as a thousand-sided figure, the blue circle in the floor another.

Slowly I reached for my face, suspecting what I would find, but Notole and Ziddari grabbed my hands before I could do it. "Come with us first."

They led me through the twisting passages, and up the curved staircases into the main part of the keep. Seeing the world this way took some getting used to—everything with angled shapes, the edges gleaming with blue-white brilliance though the colors lay flat and dull. But we passed a slave, and in the moment I gazed on him with my false eyes, I knew his name was K'Savan and that he had grown up in a village called Agramante, about fifty leagues from Avonar. He was in the throes of despair. I could have named his cousins to the tenth degree and recited everything K'Savan knew about them. And I could tell that he looked on my masked face with horror and loathing; he would slay me with joy if he were not under the Lords' compulsion of obedience.

"You see," said Ziddari. "Useful, eh?"

We passed other slaves and Drudges, and nothing about them was hidden from me. When we came to a black door so massive that it would take a troop of warriors to open it, Notole nudged me forward. I swung the door open with a thought, and we walked into the temple of the Lords.

Something was changed here, too. The false sky hung above us. The black mirrored floor lay beneath our feet. The Three were there, enthroned as before, giant-sized, though lifeless this time, for the Three were also with me, shepherding me toward the far end of the row of statues. Something huge and new sat in the dark beyond Ziddari's image, covered with a purple drapery.

My heart pounded and my stomach clenched as Ziddari waved his hand and the drapery fell to the floor. It was me. In the same dull black stone as the other three. Larger than life, so that I could have climbed up and stood in my own hand. I was to be a Lord. They hadn't lied about it. And while I gazed up at the image of my face, my hand crept to the gold mask I wore and felt the diamonds that looked out from it. "And what must I give up besides my eyes?" I asked, surprised that my voice was steady.

"Very little that you've not already forsworn," said Ziddari. "Small matters of your past. Your personal quarrels might come to seem trivial beside the grandeur of possibility. These barriers of thought you have built to keep us out will crumble and fade. Your mind will not be truly separate, but one with ours, and so our joined purposes and desires may loom larger than your own. But your power will be unmatched, and everything you could ever imagine will be yours."

"I'll never use my training in battle, will I?"

"Not in your own body," said Parven. "No need to risk such a thing. We've made it so that none of the three of us may bear a weapon, and it would be the same with you. No one in any world is a danger to us save one of ourselves. And, as you have seen, we have better ways of enjoying the joys of combat. But we envision you submitting to the discipline of physical training for many years, until you have reached your full growth and have made yourself a skilled body that you are comfortable with. This is for your own safety, as well as the advantage it will give you when commanding armies or using other bodies for your pleasure. The choice is yours, of course."

"And what if I refuse your offer?"

"You will still be the Heir of D'Arnath, a friend and ally of the Lords. You may live out your limited span of years here, or make your home elsewhere if you wish. But we will expect you to aid us in our war as you have sworn upon your life and honor to do."

"But the secret of the oculus . . ."

". . . is only for the Lords of Zhev'Na and will be revealed only when you join us." Ziddari held my chin in his hand and nodded his head toward my statue. "You were born to be one of us. I believe you know this to be true."

"We are old and fixed in our ways. Your youth delights

us," said Notole, smiling and stroking my hair. "When you have lived your first thousand years, you will understand."

"It gives us great pleasure to teach you," said Parven, laying his hand on my shoulder.

"Do I have to decide now?"

"In five days, you come of age," said Notole. "At first hour of that day you will be anointed Heir of D'Arnath. If you choose to become one of us, we must prepare you in the hour between mid-watch and the anointing. You will have no second chance. This decision is for all time."

"I understand."

"For now, we will take you back to your rooms and let you sleep. When you wake, this taste of your future will be but a memory, and all will be as it was. Look well upon the face of the world and see what matches the possibilities that are open to you."

They took the mask away, and Ziddari led me back to my rooms and settled me in my chair. We ordered food. I was hungry, though indeed a lead weight sat in my stomach as I sat there blind.

"Are you wearing Darzid's face now?" I asked Ziddari as we ate.

"Yes."

"Why did you live in the other world? Why did you work for mundanes . . . a common soldier when you were a Lord of Zhev'Na?"

He laughed. "That's a long tale, and over the next hundreds of years I'll tell you the whole of it. In brief, one of us had to follow the Dar'Nethi J'Ettanne across the Bridge to protect our interests. Too late I discovered that, over a long period of time, the mundane world corrupts and confuses the memory of those born in this one. I suffered that indignity just as J'Ettanne and his Dar'Nethi did. Worse, in many ways. A wretched, despicable world is the land of your birth. As to why the task fell to me, rather than Notole or Parven . . . let's just say I lost the toss." More hatred than humor colored Ziddari's laugh.

I was sorry I had asked him any questions. I wanted him to go. I had to think—a great deal. Five days to decide whether I wanted to live forever and have all the power I could ever want, or if I wanted to live out a human life span, risking an early death like Papa who was only thirty-seven when he was struck down by the Prince D'Natheil. And what would I use to fill the emptiness inside me—the "fairy dance" of the Dar'Nethi? I didn't even know how to begin. It disgusted me to think of following the practices of the coward D'Arnath, of the murderer D'Natheil. Or would I gain power as did the Zhid—squeezing the life from rocks or rats or slaves? I could not have come all this way for that. No, there was really no choice to be made.

But if I were to leave myself behind five days from this—I wasn't stupid enough to think it was only "bits of my past" that would be lost—I didn't want to do it with unanswered questions. So I told Darzid I wasn't hungry any more, only tired.

"Then I'll leave you. Sleep well, my young Lord." He laid a hand on my head as he said it, and my limbs suddenly felt like iron weights had been attached to them. As he stood up and walked across the floor, I huddled in my chair, trying not to shiver. I was so cold . . . it must be night. I fought his sleep spell, because I knew that when I woke I wouldn't have the power to do what I wanted, only my own weak talents.

Slowly I let my mind steal through my house, and I touched a slave named Ben'Sidhe. He knew nothing of strange articles left in the young Lord's rooms. Another slave, Mar'Devi—the one who bathed me—was filled with shame, not because of the task itself, but because he felt so degraded by it. He believed he should accept his lot with better grace when so many of his brothers and sisters were bound so much more cruelly. He knew nothing of stones or wood or the stars of Leire. One after the other I probed each slave that lived in my house. None of them had taken care of my wounded arm, and none knew of the mysterious gifts left for me to find.

Drudges were so dull and stupid, I might have skipped examining them, except that I was enjoying myself; stealing thoughts was so easy now. My mind picked at one of them and then another. Astonishing that Drudges were the cousins of the people I had touched in the other world. I laid them open and found nothing—no spirit, no intelligence, no desire for anything better—until I touched the one who hovered in the shadows beyond the stair, one who stood there shocked and horrified to see me blind, left in my chair by a man she despised.

She tried to close her mind to me. Too late.

I tried to close my own mind to the Lords. Too late. I was scarcely awake, lulled into carelessness. "Seri!" I jumped to my feet.

Vainly I tried to find my way to her, crashing into the table and then the bed, trying to draw an outline of my room in my head so I wouldn't kill myself trying to get to her—to tell her I knew what she had been doing—to ask her all the questions that blossomed inside me like fireworks at a jongler fair. But even as I floundered in the dark, the Lords descended on me.

The woman! He has discovered the woman in Zhev'Na! How is . . .

. . . it possible? Inconceivable! Dangerous!

Young Lord, beware. She serves the master of deceivers. We're sending warriors to protect you.

Ziddari, get back to the boy! The tigress is ready to pounce. Such danger to our young friend . . . our plans . . .

With their shouting and jostling in my head, I hung onto the bedpost, shaking with the effort of staying awake and splitting my thoughts into those the Lords could know, and those I needed to keep private. "Seri! Run! They know you're here." I couldn't have explained why those words burst out of me. "Hurry . . . to the stables . . . hide there."

But she didn't run. I felt her arms wrap around me, and her wet cheek pressed to my face. "I would not trade this moment for a thousand years of safety." She brushed her fingers over my eyes. "Hold fast, Gerick. Look deep inside. You are strong and beautiful and good, and you know what is important. You are not what you believe. Don't let them convince you."

Boots pounded on the stair. "I'm sorry," I said. "I've got to—"

"Do whatever you have to do."

I took her arm, and as gently as I could, I twisted it behind her. Then I let a surge of anger drown everything else that was in my head. I had to protect her. And the only way to do so was to turn her over to the Lords. Any other course would have been far more dangerous for both of us.

"Young Lord!"

"I've got her. She was sneaking up on me. I was practicing reading thoughts while I went to sleep, and I found her."

"Lady Seriana," said Ziddari—Darzid, of course. I could feel it in his voice. She didn't know Darzid was one of the Three. He never came to my house as Ziddari, never let slaves or Drudges see his true form. "A pleasure, and considerable surprise, to see you again. But you have certainly come down in the world. I wouldn't think of Drudges as your sort at all. They can hardly provide the intellectual stimulation to which you have been accustomed."

She didn't say anything.

"What did you plan to do here, lady? Steal away a sleeping boy? Persuade him that you are a caring mother? Convince him to abandon his destiny? A powerful thing is vengeance, is it not, young Lord? So powerful it can make a woman destroy her child's future because he's sworn a blood oath to destroy her dead lover's kingdom. Ugly, ugly."

"Only one person in this room would I destroy, but it is not Gerick. I've seen what you're trying to do with him. . . ." I thought I had felt anger before. But my mother's fury made even the power of the Lords seem small.

Darzid didn't hear it, of course, and I began to understand why they hated her so much. They didn't understand her. "You underestimate the lad, my lady. We've done nothing but allow him to develop his true nature. He knows that and accepts it. Now, the young Lord needs to sleep. You'll have plenty of time to explain yourself . . . how you got here and who your allies are."

Sometimes the Lords really thought I was stupid. They would learn. "Remember, she's mine," I said, as I stumbled over to my bed and threw myself on it. "I've sworn an oath, and I'll not have her taken from me. Perhaps I'll have a chance for personal vengeance after all."

Darzid began to laugh. "Of course! Fortune has smiled on you once again, my Prince. You can indeed have everything you desire."

I slept for a full day. When I woke, the Lords were waiting for me . . . hovering . . . anxious. I was anxious, too, and only felt better when I saw the faint smear of gray that was the torch that burned on my balcony at night. If I worked at it hard enough, I could sense the faint outlines of doors and tables and such in the blackness.

And how are you this evening, young Lord? asked Ziddari.

"Hungry," I said.

They relaxed a bit. *Slaves can bring you what you need.* Notole was everywhere inside me and around me.

"I've already summoned them. But that won't be enough. I'm hungry for other things than food. Do I come to you again tonight?"

No, young Lord, she said, pleased. *In four days you may have all you want. Only if your craving should become unbearable would I consider taking you out again before your anointing. For now you should resume your physical training.*

"What have you done with Seri?" I tried to ask it casually.

The lady is quite safe and healthy. We've asked her some questions, but she has few answers. A traitor brought her to Zhev'Na, but he is dead now. They planned to destroy you, young Lord, to steal your future . . . your power . . . to confine you to Dar'Nethi groveling . . . to starve you . . . But their pitiful conspiracy failed long ago.

"Good."

Rest easy. Determine your future with no worries that any enemy will interfere. Do you wish to question the woman yourself? The last question was from Ziddari.

"No. I've no interest in lies. She confuses me." Yes. That was what they wanted to hear.

Then we'll leave you to your own occupations.

And so I had to figure out what I wanted. The decision had seemed easy before, and now Seri had muddled everything. My thoughts kept running in circles, and I couldn't decide what I believed, or why I had done the things I'd done, or what I was going to do about any of it.

I jumped up and fumbled about the room, gathering up Seri's "gifts." Out on the balcony, I burned the map of the Leiran stars and threw the stone and the wood and the fruit pit as far away as I could. I fingered the mirror, happy I couldn't see well enough to know how my eyes looked this time. All black, I guessed. Even reflected light made me wince. I pulled the wood away from the metal and burned it, and then I melted the metal into a lump and threw it away, too. Grabbing my cloak, I felt my way down the stairs.

There were guards everywhere in my house. I told them I was going riding in the desert and threatened to tear out their eyes if they tried to stop me or even let their thoughts dwell on what I did. After a quick stop by the kitchen, I set out for the stables. Summoning up what little power I had, I used it to help me find familiar landmarks. I put out the stable lantern, made it to Firebreather's stall without breaking my neck, and sat down to wait. Firebreather shied away from me until I'd talked to him a little. But it wasn't for the horse I'd come.

"Awful dark in here."

"Leave it that way. I'd just rather tonight."

"Whatever you say."

"I brought you some food, there in the pack by the gate. Sorry, no jack."

"I told you I'm not choosy." I heard him rummaging in the pack and then settling down in the straw. "You're in a bother," he said between bites.

"Have you started reading human thoughts as well as horses'?"

"Don't take a genius. You're sitting here in the dark. You forgot to yell at me for anything. You brought me food without me acting pitiful or nothing. You're not thinking straight."

"I needed to talk, and I get tired of talking to myself. I argue one way, and it sounds right and reasonable, and then I turn around and argue exactly the opposite, and it sounds just the same."

"I've seen it. Means you think too much."

"It's about those things I told you of. The stone and such that appeared in my house."

"Did you find another one?"

"Yes. And I found out who did it."

The silence stretched so long, I began to think he'd gone to sleep. "Blazes," he said at last. "Who was it?"

"My mother."

Another long silence, and then a totally unexpected question. "Is she all right?"

"No. Not all right at all—"

From out of the darkness a body pounced on me and pinned me to the floor, leaving me spitting straw and with both my arms twisted behind me. His elbow encircled my neck. "Damnation, you didn't kill her? If you killed her, you are dead this instant. I don't care whose friend you are, or how great a sorcerer you are, I'll break your neck. Don't think I can't do it."

He was wild and furious, and I almost believed he *could* do it. "She's not dead. Just a prisoner. How do you—? Let me up. I won't hurt you. I swear I won't. Damn, you know her! You came here with her, didn't you?" I twisted around and shoved him off me. Then I felt my way back to the wall, sat up, and brushed the straw off my face.

"I came just after. She don't know I'm here. But I've promised— Curse every bit of this place. I've promised— Oh, shit, shit, shit!" I hoped he hadn't broken his fist when he slammed it into the wall of the horse box.

"Why did you come here? Why did *she* come here? Don't lie to me."

"We came to get you. To take you back."

"To destroy me?"

"Destroy you? Why in the name of perdition would the Lady Seri want to hurt you? She grieved herself to death for you and your da for all those years, living in Dunfarrie where there was only such as me for company, and the very day she figures out who you are, you get snatched out from under her nose. She picks up and chases you through the mountains in the winter, and to a new world where she's like to get herself killed, then follows you into this cursed place, and you think she wants to hurt you?"

"She wanted vengeance on her brother. She didn't know I was her son."

"It's true she didn't at first. She didn't want to stay at Comigor, but do you know why she did? Because everyone thought you were loony. She wanted to help you because she loved her brother, but she came to love you, too. She only put all the clues together after you was gone. She about went crazy."

"That's not right. She brought Prince D'Natheil to Comigor to kill me, and Lucy, and Mama's baby . . . for her revenge."

"The Prince was getting his head put back together. He'd been half crazy for months. He didn't even remember she was his wife until that day in the council chamber. He couldn't look at her without his head trying to bust open. Don't you know anything? I know . . . knew . . . the Prince, and he never ever would kill an old lady or a child, whether it was his own or not. He never would. You don't know what all he did for me who was an ignorant nobody he'd no reason to look at, much less care for."

My head was about to twist inside out with the confusion. "He killed my father . . . Tomas . . . the man I believed to be my father."

"It was Zhid magic what killed Duke Tomas."

"How do you know? Why do you think anyone would tell you the truth?"

"Nobody told me nothing. I was there. I saw it."

This was impossible. "I don't believe you."

"Look in my head. Can't you tell what's real and what somebody planted there? What good is all this sorcery if you can't figure out when a person is telling you the truth?"

"I could tell."

"Then do it. We've got to save the Lady Seri. I owe her

and the Prince most everything, and to stop me trying to save her, you'll have to kill me first, so you'd best get on with it."

I fumbled about in the dark until I found his head, and I put my hands on the sides of it and told him to think of anything he wanted to tell me. Only that. By the time I pulled my hands away, I knew everything the Leiran boy knew from the time he first met Seri in Dunfarrie until the day my father, the Prince, had slit himself open so I couldn't be corrupted by killing him. The Leiran boy wouldn't tell me anything else—about how he got to Zhev'Na or how they planned to get me out. He wouldn't think about the Prince, except how kind he was, and how he just couldn't believe the man was really dead. But it was enough, and I could look no further anyway. Never had any injury hurt so much as the truth.

"Hey, are you all right?"

I couldn't answer him. It was not all right. It could never be all right. I was able to add so many things he couldn't know. The Lords were going to win. They had made me into what they wanted, and now I'd given them the very piece that would ensure their victory—a hold on me. They hated my mother as much as they hated the Prince. Maybe more. I almost laughed. I'd been wrong about every single thing in my whole life, blind long before my evil starting eating my eyes away. The Leiran boy had seen so clearly. He had asked how I could think the Prince had killed Lucy when I had only seen his knife in my dreams. But Darzid had twisted my dreams from the beginning.

A rustling in the straw. The Leiran boy had gone. Just as well. I would most likely betray him, too. But before I realized what was happening, a smear of light appeared in the horse box. I turned away, but not quickly enough.

"Blazing demons!" He pulled my face back around. "What did they do to you?"

I shoved him backward. "It'll go away." But it wouldn't. Not ever.

"Does it hurt?"

"No. I just can't see very well right now."

"Damn! So did you get the story out of me?"

"Yes."

"And you believe me?"

"Yes."

"Well, then, what are we going to do?"

"I'll have to get her. I think I can do it. Then I'll try to get you both out of Zhev'Na."

"And you, too."

"That won't be possible."

"She won't go without you."

"There's no other way. They'll kill her unless I do what they want. They may kill her anyway, but I'll try."

"Can you keep a secret?"

"Obviously not as well as I would like." Otherwise my mother would not be Ziddari's prisoner. *Wrong about everything. Stupid. Worthless. Wicked.*

"I mean, if I were to tell you something right now that might help . . . it wouldn't go straight to the Lords, now would it?"

"They don't know about you." At least I'd managed that much.

"What if there was someone else in Zhev'Na who could help you?"

"I don't think there's anyone who could possibly—"

"I know you don't think nobody can do anything but you, but this person . . . he'd like to help. And he's good. The best."

"We can't get Seri away from Zhev'Na unless the Lords allow it. It doesn't matter how good your friend is at anything."

"I think you should talk to him."

"Bring him here if you want."

"He can't. He's really stuck."

"This is stupid."

"You won't think so. But you got to keep it secret."

"All right."

"Do you swear?"

"Yes. I swear. Take me to him. But you'll have to lead me."

"Blazes."

CHAPTER 41

Karon

I was at wit's end. I had dabbled in madness for so long that I knew no other way to live. A day with any semblance of normality would probably have me screaming in terror. I fought and trained and stayed alive. I watched for the least opportunity, the least chink in the armor of Zhev'Na, and came up with nothing.

Paulo had been despondent after my match with Vruskot, for he'd been sure that Gerick would take me on as swordmaster. He told me of his several encounters with my son, and his belief that Gerick was desperately torn between the demands of his masters and his own nature. "He's decided to be like them, but he don't like it at all. He just don't see any other way to be."

"They want him very badly. Only the one person—the anointed Heir of D'Arnath—has power over the Breach and the Bridge and the Gates."

"But if you're still alive . . . Maybe the anointing just won't work."

"As long as I'm trapped in this collar, I'm as good as dead. And unless I'm free to use them, the Heir's powers will pass straight on to Gerick when he's anointed."

Dismal thoughts, all of this. It didn't help my morale that Paulo was almost caught on that visit. A guard chose just the wrong time to make a circuit of the slave pen with a blazing torch, and Paulo had to roll out of the light. I set up a racket on the bars, feigning a bout of madness—a perilously easy bit of playacting. On his next visit, I would command Paulo to stay away from me. A bleak prospect. His cheerful grin was the best thing in my life.

My unease was not at all soothed by what Paulo had reported of Gerick's "changes."

"They say he's come a demon, afraid of the light, and that he goes days at a time without eating or sleeping, and that he's roaming about the place inside people's heads. He told me— He told me he was going to be one of the Lords. Is that what's happening?"

Of course it was. Corruption was not enough. All the power Gerick would inherit when he came of age would be theirs, but only if there was nothing of him left that might resist them. I had long since lost count of the passing time, but weeks had gone by since I had been celebrated for living out an entire year in the slave pen. Gerick's anointing could not be far distant. The Three would be the Four. Chaos. Disaster.

The days continued.

Straw tickled my nose. Waking instantly, I rolled toward the bars.

"I've got bad news. They've got her—"

"Ah, no . . ." It was all I could do not to scream, to tear at the bars, to bang on them until a guard would come for me and I could strangle him with my bare hands. I had dared not even think of Seri lest somehow the knowledge of her presence be detected in me. It had been the only protection I could give her.

"—but I've brought someone as might be able to help."

"What possible help—?"

"V'Saro"—he was quite emphatic about the name, sharpening my attention—"this person wallowing in the muck here beside me is the new Prince of Avonar, the young Lord Gerick." He turned to the dark shape behind him. "This here is V'Saro. You saw him fight the other day. I think you ought to set him free so he can help us."

Disbelieving, I pressed close to the bars and strained to see into the darkness. The boy held his face away, but his profile was clear. It didn't seem possible. "Paulo, are you all right?" I whispered. "He hasn't—"

"He knows about Seri and says he can get her out of Zhev'Na. But he says *he* won't come. I told him that he don't have to do everything by himself, and that he has to get away from here, too. Tell him, V'Saro. Maybe he'll hear it from you."

"Seri would most certainly agree. She'd say you should be taken out first."

"She would be wrong." Gerick's voice was glacial.

"So can you do it?" Paulo whispered to Gerick.

"Do what?"

"Set V'Saro free. Undo the magic. The collar. Let him loose so he can help us get her."

"I don't know. I suppose I could get him out of the pen . . . to come and teach me. But the collar . . . I don't know. If you want your talents . . ." He didn't seem interested. But he hadn't closed the door, either. As long as he'd agree to do it, the less interested the better. I wasn't sure I was ready for him to know who I was.

"Swordplay won't win this battle," I said. "We need sorcery of a particular kind that I am able to provide. Though I've begun to think Paulo is the only true sorcerer here."

Gerick snorted at that. "He talks to horses. And gets people to say things they never meant to say."

"So can you do it?" said Paulo.

"I'll have to think about it."

"You won't be long in your thinkin'?" said Paulo.

"I can't. There's only four days. Then I won't be able to help you any more."

"All right, then." Paulo touched his hand to the bars of my cage, and the boys slipped away.

Four days . . . earth and sky . . . If Gerick could unseal the collar, and if I had not forgotten what I was about—a nagging uncertainty that haunted my nights—I could take us out of Ce Uroth. The Lords could ensure that any portal to Avonar was under their control, but I knew another way out that they could not touch. It was just that my gut heaved at the thought. . . .

The proper course would be to abandon Seri. The safety of the Bridge and two worlds was my first responsibility, and that meant that Gerick was far more important than my wife. Yet, as I lay in the straw, staring into the dark sky as it yielded to a dead gray, the more certain I became that we could not leave her behind. Some care for Seri had brought Gerick to this point. Who was to say that the act of saving her life might not be his salvation?

Late on the next afternoon I was summoned to the Gray House, trussed up like a fowl at a poulterer's shop. Gerick was in the fencing yard, sparring with a young slave under the eye of a one-armed warrior. Vasrin Shaper! It was Vruskot.

Gerick halted the match when the slavehandler dragged me hobbling through the gate. "Ah, here is the slave I ordered."

Before anyone could blink, a roaring Vruskot slammed me to the ground facedown with a bone-jarring thud, kicked me onto my back, and then fell on my belly like a collapsing tower, his knees gouging and squeezing the life out of me. As I spat out dirt and fought for breath, the sun glinted on the dagger in his hand. Twisting and wriggling, tossing my head from side to side, I tried to upend the brute before I lost an eye or worse.

"Warrior!" The world came to a stop at the command. Gerick stood calmly behind the maddened Zhid with the edge of his sword at Vruskot's neck. "If you lower that blade the width of an eyelash, your head will follow it."

Vruskot took a long time deciding. Foamy spittle dripped from his mouth, and his skin was redder than the afternoon desert.

"You *will not* damage this slave. I desire that both of you be my teachers, and if you dare trespass my instructions in this or any matter, I'll shrivel your brain and draw it out through your nose. Do you understand me?"

Astonishing. The old Zhid slammed the dagger into its sheath and climbed off me. But the stubborn devil did manage to plant a foot in my gut and trigger my collar as he stood up. While I was occupied trying not to heave up my last three days' graybread before the son I'd scarcely met,

Gerick belted the Zhid with the back of his hand. From the sound of it, a surprisingly strong hand. "Do not test me, warrior."

The slavehandler kicked me to get up. "Where shall I put the slave, young Lord? This one must be controlled and guarded at all times. You are aware that he has no compulsions of obedience? As he still fights wager matches and training bouts, the slavemaster won't allow it."

"Chain him to the wall. He can sit, but should be able to stand and demonstrate a move if I require it."

I couldn't help but wonder if Paulo had been deceived by this boy. His demeanor bore not the slightest trace of recognition or common purpose. I might have been a tree stump.

"I've informed the Wargreve Damon that you're to be mine as long as I have use for you," he said, adjusting his sword belt about his slim waist. "You will instruct me in sword work along with this warrior. You may speak at your will, until such time as I inform you otherwise or leave the training ground. Do you understand?"

I ducked my head. I never liked to push the talking.

"You will remain here day and night. I've taken a fancy to night practice, and don't wish to wait for you to be summoned."

"Is that wise, young Lord?" Vruskot's hatred eroded his discipline. "Such dogs as this should be caged."

"Do not question me, warrior." Gerick's glance could have frozen a volcano.

As the sun slid toward the horizon, Gerick resumed his practice with the sturdy young slave. Vruskot eyed me savagely as he drilled the two repeatedly on a complex move. His choice of lessons was unfortunate, for it was just the kind of unimaginative attack that had allowed me to defeat him. Only his own incredible strength and experience had made our match so long and difficult. If Gerick was play-acting then he was doing it quite believably. I had best do the same.

"Exploiting the opponent's weakness is not always the best attack, young Lord," I said. "Not unless you are also calculating his strengths that balance it. No battle is so simple that a single maxim can carry it."

Vruskot erupted, of course, but Gerick asserted his authority once again, and invited me to elaborate. For three hours we continued the lesson on attack strategies, becoming so involved that it was almost possible to forget our circumstances. He was so intelligent that he could understand my explanations as soon as I voiced them. And he could carry the implications far beyond the problem of the moment. I sensed his immense desire to be a master of the art. Swordplay was nothing I'd ever thought to teach a son of mine, but I treasured every moment of those three hours.

Vruskot seethed and blustered, but Gerick refused to dismiss him. "You are here to protect me, warrior, lest this Dar'Nethi filth make some attempt to harm me. I trust you to destroy him in such a case."

The hour grew late. When the slavehandler came to retrieve Gerick's sparring partner, Gerick told him to return later. But before too much more time had passed, the young slave began to stumble, and I suggested that Gerick would be better served to save him for the next day.

Gerick agreed and promptly ordered Vruskot to return the slave boy to the pen. "While you do that, I'll secure this slave for the night," he said.

Vruskot growled, but obeyed. As soon as he was gone, leaving only the two guards in the distant corners of the walled enclosure, Gerick knelt beside me. He linked my wrists together, shortened my ankle hobbles, and tightened the tether chains at wrist, neck, and ankle, securing me firmly to the wall. "I've found a way, but I can't do it until tomorrow night," he whispered.

"Any time is fine—" For the first time, I got a close look at his face. Spirits of night . . . He averted his face quickly, knowing that I saw. "How do they do it?" I said softly.

"That's not your business. I just need to know what you plan to do if I should set you free. I don't want you interfering with me."

"Are there plans for you to see Seri . . . the lady?"

"Yes. They expect me to kill her."

Dear gods. "Tell me when and where, and I'll be there," I said, struggling to stay rational. "Make sure Paulo is with me, too, and I'll take us all out of Zhev'Na."

"Every way out is controlled by the Lords. You've no chance whatsoever."

"I know of a way. That's why I was sent."

He squinted at me, but it was very dark, and I didn't think he could see very well. Just then, a gate squeaked and crashed shut again. When Vruskot strode from the stone arch into the yard, Gerick was leaning against the water barrel, casually taking a sip from the dipper. "I've tightened the slave's bonds, warrior, but I want you to make sure of him. Instruct the Drudges to provide his normal food and drink, and do what you can to ensure he doesn't foul the training ground."

Vruskot bowed and did an excellent job of ensuring I could not move a finger's breadth in any direction. On that long, cold night, I dreamed of my Avonar, of taking my son climbing to the snowy summit of Karylis and watching the light return to his terrible eyes.

Two Zhid stood at attention in the fencing yard throughout the next day. The Gray House was silent. No one entered the enclosure. I dozed fitfully in the wicked heat.

Sometime after nightfall, a quiet thud from the dark corner of the yard woke me with a start. One of the guards had slumped into a heap in the dirt. The second guard was in the process of toppling, even as I jerked upright.

"V'Saro"—the whispered call was from Gerick—"say something."

"Anything in particular?" I matched his quiet tone.

The boy stepped hesitantly from the darkest shadows. "Again."

"What's the matter?"

He stepped slowly across the yard, only to stumble over the chains that attached my feet to the wall. Tightly bound as I was, I couldn't catch him, but only squirm enough to cushion his fall and keep his face from hitting my knees. He ended up draped across my lap.

He wriggled backwards and got up to his knees. The Lords had been at him again. He was strung taut, quivering like a bowstring, and his eyes had terrible black centers, worse than before. His eyelids drooped heavily. I didn't believe he could see anything at all.

"Take this," he said, depositing in my hand a small, thick-walled ceramic cup—a crucible, filled with coarse gray powder. From a pocket in his tunic he pulled another crucible, slightly larger and lined with silver. "This won't be pleasant, but you must be silent."

"Tell me what they've done to you. Before you go any further. I can't let you—"

"I hear from you and the Leiran boy that the only way to save my mother's life is to set you free. I don't believe it and I don't trust you, but I've been wrong about everything in my life, so why should I expect to be right this time?" He knelt between my legs and reached around my head, fumbling at my collar, carefully avoiding the triggers that would make me convulse. "I've obtained the knowledge, the power, and the materials I need to neutralize your collar. I've very little time, but if I start right now, then perhaps I can manage it, so I would suggest you stay still." His cold fingers paused at the top of the seal. "Be ready."

"Do it," I said, feeling his enchantment taking shape, growing huge and terrible, cutting first into my flesh, and then into my mind, and then into my soul like a fiery razor.

I sank deep into myself. *Silence . . . hold . . . protect your son who has mortgaged his sight and his soul to set you free. . . .*

Slowly, relentlessly, Gerick moved his fingers down the seal, melting it away and letting the scalding, foul stuff dribble into his silver-lined vessel. My face was buried in his chest, I, who should be protecting him, comforting him, and all I could do was use his taut, slender body to muffle my sobs. No more than a quarter of an hour passed, but I became so lost in the throbbing haze of pain that I didn't even notice when he shifted position and began to unseal the bonds from my wrists.

Silence . . . hold . . . to protect him . . . It is bearable because it is necessary. It is for your wife and your son tha you never thought to see. How blessed is life . . . how glori ous the Way that can devise a path beyond al expectations . . . to come through pain and despair to finc such joy . . .

The desert breeze that chilled the rivulets of sweat cours ing down my body began to whisper of endless sand, o tiny hollows of moisture deep hidden to escape the rapa cious sun, of hardy, bony creatures that scuttered cleverly from one scrap of shade to another or burrowed deep in the cool embrace of the earth, of dry skeletal plants tha yet held a core of life. And on the very edge of the winc was the kiss of snow, blown all the way from the pinnacles of the Mountains of Light, and the faintest breath of the awakening Vales of Eidolon. "Oh, gods, young Prince . . ."

"Got to hurry." His head drooped as he carefully movec the crucible. The filled vessel radiated searing heat; the sil ver had melted away. "Can you take this? Dispose of it?" His tongue was thick with sleep.

"Lower it just a little so I can reach it." Awkwardly took the crucible and managed to empty the molten meta into the hole I had scraped out for relieving myself.

"Now I've got to replace the seal . . . so they won' notice. Give me the vessel with the powder."

"As an assistant, I have decided limitations," I said, using my feet to retrieve the cup I had dropped while he removec the seal.

Gerick held it in his hand. Heat blazed from the little vessel, and the gray powder sagged into liquid. His powe was awesome in its magnitude and villainous in its composi tion. Once I sensed it, even so faintly as in that first hou of my release, I wanted to tell him to stop, not to use such power even for good purpose. But he had already wrenchec my head forward onto his chest once more, wiped a cole ointment on the raw strip of skin between the ends of the collar, and begun to drip the hot liquid on it, guiding i with his fingers.

I dared not open my mouth lest I scream and give u away. Again I held silent, my throat constricting in pani as I felt the hardening seal. Perhaps this was his swor revenge. Perhaps he had freed me of the collar only so I would taste life for a single instant, and now he was reimposing the horror. He had sworn to destroy me, and nothing else would do it so absolutely.

Silence . . . hold . . . protect him . . .

The metal cooled on my neck. Nothing changed. The cup fell to the ground from Gerick's fingers, and he sagged heavily onto my chest.

"Gerick, what's wrong?"

He seemed to have fallen asleep. My limited range of movement made it difficult to shake him. "Wake up, lad. You've got to get away from here. Someday you'll understand what you've done tonight. There are not words enough to thank you."

He shook his head groggily.

"Do you have to return the implements somewhere?"

"No. Give them," he mumbled, holding out his hand.

"Here's one. I can't reach the other. You'll have to get it. Find my left foot—sorry, my masters don't allow me to clean it—now move right, a little more, now forward toward me."

He set the two vessels together, uncomfortably close to my foot, and blasted them into a slug of metal and stone. "I need to go."

"Can you get back to the house all right? Has someone put a sleep spell on you?"

"Always . . . after. Until I can see again. They think I don't really know what happens."

"Here, touch my hand"—and with the first glimmering of my own power, I lightened the oppression of the sleep spell—"is that better?"

He wrinkled his brow. "What you do is very different."

"Perhaps I can explain it sometime."

"I doubt there will be time. I'll be asleep all day. Then I'm to go to the Lords' temple at mid-watch. They're to bring Seri to me then. I'll see to her safety. But the Leiran boy will be here in the courtyard before I go, and you must get him away if you can."

"I'll come for you."

"You will do *nothing* unless I give you leave," he

snapped. "I can put back what I've taken away. I've freed you to take care of the Leiran boy if you can. Nothing else."

Without allowing me to say more, Gerick rose and felt his way back to his house. He looked very much alone.

I did not sleep that night, but sat and watched the turning of the cold stars behind the dust haze, felt the waning heat of the stones at my back, and observed the flickering light of the torches reflected in the chains that bound me. As the night wind told me of its travels, I embraced the long tale of death and sorrow that had accompanied my own journey. With every sensation I took a tiny step along the Way, and my power grew as the hearth's first flame is nourished by offerings of dry tinder, or as a spring is fed by raindrops until it becomes a mighty river.

CHAPTER 42

Gerick

I woke just before sunset, earlier than usual after a night of power-making with Notole. I don't know whether it was because V'Saro had weakened the sleep spell, or if I waked myself on purpose so I could watch the sun go down. Sunsets wouldn't be the same with diamond eyes.

The tight white ball of the sun grew huge and red, like a bloodleech engorged and ready to mate. The thin, dry trailers that passed for clouds in Ce Uroth reflected the swollen red light, and smeared it across the entire western horizon. By the next sunset I would be the Heir of D'Arnath and a Lord of Zhev'Na, and the world would be forever changed because of me. For better or worse would remain to be seen. I was ready, except for Seri—my mother. I had to take care of her first.

I had finally figured out what Seri had been trying to tell me with her gifts. When she held me for that one moment before they took her away, I almost believed what she whispered in my ear. But she didn't know that her mirror could show me my soul—the dark thing laid bare by my power. No beauty was hidden in me.

Odd that it was Seri's friends, the Leiran boy and the slave, who made the truth so clear. To learn what I needed to free the slave V'Saro and to gather the power to work the enchantment, I had to beg Notole to take me traveling once more. I told her I couldn't decide about my future, but that if we journeyed again, I would know. So the Three met me in the chamber of the oculus, and we observed the poorest quarters of a Kerotean city, where the air seethed with disease and starvation, and the people with bitterness and lust for vengeance. I devoured their hate, and power thundered inside of me.

Parven took me to the brink of a volcano where I could see the cracks in the earth glowing with liquid fire. And then, Notole led me into the cold, black depths of the oceans, where I touched the strange blind creatures who lived there. I transformed myself into one of those creatures, so that for an hour, all I knew was the dark and the cold and the ponderous weight of the water that was my life. "All this will be yours, young Lord."

I hated the Lords for making me leave the peaceful ocean. They laughed and promised I'd be able to travel the stars themselves once I was one of them. As we traveled, I asked a hundred questions about everything I could think of—including how the slave collars worked—and then Ziddari left me in my room, blind and spellbound. It had been all I could do to go out to the slave as I had promised. I wanted only to sleep and dream of the ocean depths, or return to the Great Oculus and travel with the Lords again.

So why had I freed V'Saro? I leaned over the balcony rail, but I couldn't see into the fencing yard where he was still bound to the wall. He was the finest swordsman I had ever seen, every bit the masterful teacher I had expected, and he seemed to be an honorable person. Kind, even. His pain and my thickheadedness had made it impossible to read his plan from his mind. But when he eased the sleep spell, I tasted his Dar'Nethi sorcery for myself. It was weak and soft and unfocused, like a candle flame instead of lightning. I didn't see how the slave could ever have power enough to stop a kibbazi in its tracks.

And so, on the evening of my last sunset, I decided I had to delay V'Saro's freedom. I had no wish to kill him or to seal him in the slave collar again, and if he could save himself and the Leiran boy, I had no objection to it. But I could not allow his grand opinion of his abilities to jeopardize my mother's life. If he failed, she would die for it, and he would, and the Leiran boy, too. I didn't want to be responsible for any of them.

As for my own future, having now experienced the reality of Dar'Nethi sorcery, I had only one choice. I could not—would not—live with such weakness, not when I had traveled on the winds of the world with the Lords of Zhev'Na. I belonged here.

"How fare you this memorable eve, young Lord?" Darzid stepped onto the balcony behind me.

"I wish it were midnight already."

"As do I," he said. *And I,* said Notole through the jewels in my ear. *I also.* Parven's voice boomed in my head like a barrel rolling down a plank.

"What do I need to do before the anointing?"

Darzid was leaning on the balcony rail. Though I wasn't looking at him, I felt him examining me—inside and out. "Nothing. All will come in due time."

"I've ordered a bath prepared," I said. "Food, too. I've had nothing since yesterday."

"The bath is fine, but no food. You must come to us fasting this night."

I didn't ask why. I probably didn't want to know. A slave came onto the balcony and knelt, spreading his arms wide. He had a linen towel over one arm. "What will happen to my slaves, my household after tonight?" I said, poking the slave with my foot and jerking my head toward the door so he would go back inside to wait for me.

"You need not concern yourself with these servants."

"I want them put to sleep. Tonight, before I go."

"For what reason?" My skin felt hot from his examination.

"I don't want them to watch me go and think about it. Perhaps, once I am a Lord, I'll decide to kill them all. Or maybe I won't." The last red crescent of the sun disappeared below the horizon.

Darzid smiled and swept his hand toward the doorway. "Your will shall be done, of course."

I hated him.

CHAPTER 43

Seri

I had never been anywhere as cold as the keep of Zhev'Na, not even the mountain passes of the Cerran Brae in the deeps of winter. The dark walls chilled my flesh and spirit until my blood seemed to slow and my thoughts close in upon themselves like a daylily deprived of the sun.

I could not read thoughts like the Dar'Nethi or live inside another's mind like the Lords, but when I embraced my son for that one brief moment, I knew I'd been right about him. In the past months I had tried to find ways to tell him he wasn't evil. Paltry things they'd been, pitiful, but all I could find or make in late nights or early mornings when the other women were asleep. I wasn't sure he had understood my message. But he had tried to save me, and he had been gentle and apologetic when my capture became inevitable. So I clung to the hope that he would yet refuse the destiny they planned for him. I doubted I'd have an opportunity to do more. I knew how many months had passed. He would turn twelve any day now.

My interrogation by the Lords was amazingly benign. An old woman had laid her dry, scarred hands on my head and taken possession of all I knew. It was over in moments. I felt as empty as if I had vomited up everything I had ever eaten, but at least I betrayed no one who could be hurt by it. Gar'Dena's care to keep the pieces of the puzzle separate had been the most successful—I suppose the only successful—part of his plan. The old woman already knew Gar'Dena was the enemy of the Lords, and she told me, somewhat wistfully, that Gernald the slavemaster had been dead for a year and could not be called to account for his part. So our failure was explained at last. The Zhid slave-master was surely the one who was to have given me the signal and taken me and Gerick out of Zhev'Na.

Once the woman was satisfied, I was left alone in a well-appointed suite of rooms. Clean clothes were laid out on the bed. The bony, dark-eyed slave girl I'd seen in the Gray House brought my meals, scurrying away in terror when I tried to speak to her. A bathing room held soap and towels, and hot water was available at a touch. It was the best I had lived in over a year. But I knew prisons, even fine ones. Though I used the bath and the clothes, and ate the food, afterward I sat and awaited the end of the world . . . or at least my small part of it.

After two days of listless idleness, I discovered paper and pens and ink in a small desk. Though I had no illusions that he would ever see it, I wrote a letter to Gerick, telling him the story of Karon and me, of Tomas and Kellea and Paulo, of D'Natheil and Dassine and all those who were a part of his life. *You have been beloved since the day we first knew you. . . .*

Late on the evening of the fourth day of my captivity, Darzid came to me. The harbinger of evil. The companion of demons. He wore his usual sleek black and sprawled languidly on a red couch, facing me across a narrow span of gray marble.

"Are you comfortable in the Lords' house, my lady?"

"As comfortable as one can be in a tomb."

"Surely you find this better than sleeping with rats and eating cold gruel. I must admire your fortitude in the face of Gar'Dena's failure at plotting."

"You may tell my son that you were kind and beneficent before your masters dispensed with me."

He burst out laughing. "It is so delightful to deal with you, Lady Seriana, and most especially to confound you. The Lords will not touch you. Your son will determine your fate entirely." He leaned across the table, his dark eyes as sharp and brilliant as obsidian. "Is he not an exceptionally fine young Lord? He is everything the Lords of Zhev'Na could have wished for: intelligent, determined, honorable, spirited—just like his mother. And he carries his father's considerable talents nobly. Unfortunate that the madman cannot see how his progeny has been nurtured to his fullest potential. Young Gerick will be the most powerful sorcerer the universe has ever produced."

"You've let him believe he is evil."

"But he is! Deliciously so. And no charming stones or mysterious star maps will change it. Did you not see his soul laid bare before you when you so foolishly revealed yourself? He feeds on the darkest passions of two worlds and begs for more. His blood is in a fever for it, and tonight you will watch as he is given a surfeit of what he craves."

"And he will do the same for his masters—give them what they crave."

"Oh, yes. On this night D'Arnath's Bridge will fall. The universe will be reborn."

"What is your part, Darzid—other than murderer, executioner, deceiver, and corrupter of children? How did you come to be the vulture that feasts on the corpses of so many noble spirits?"

"Ah, my lady, do you remember long ago when I tried to tell you of certain fantastical visions and my difficulty remembering my past?"

"Of course I remember. You—"

"I asked for your help, but you couldn't be bothered and sent me away. Now I've remembered. Come with me, and you'll see why you could never win."

He jumped to his feet and held out his arm, but I wouldn't touch him. He only laughed the more, snapped his fingers, and we were in a different place altogether.

We stood in the center of a shining black floor, a vast empty space encircled by ranks of towering pillars of black marble, each hung with a glass-paned lamp. Above us hung a star-filled night sky . . . or the seeming of it. Our footsteps caused a hollow echo as we walked toward a row of four black marble thrones that stood on a wide curved dais. Two of the chairs were occupied, one by the gray-haired woman who had questioned me, and the other by a tall man with long hair, a beaked nose, and a wide forehead. The two wore dark robes and strange masks of gold that covered the upper halves of their faces, with gems set in place of eyes. Death itself would have been a warm and cheerful contrast to their presence.

"Welcome, madam," said the tall man . . . if man he was.

"Once a man," he replied. His voice touched my mind like a clammy finger running down my spine. Depraved. Dead. "Now much more than a man. Parven is my name. To my right is my sister Notole whom you have already met. And of course you know my brother Ziddari from of old."

"Ziddari . . ." The one who stood beside me chuckled as his face dissolved. And then his own gold mask was visible, the metal not just a covering for the upper half of his face, but grown together with his flesh, its blood-red rubies flashing in the lurid lamplight.

"Old friends can still spring surprises, can they not?" Though his voice had taken on a deeper resonance, the cynical amusement was the same.

Darzid . . . Ziddari . . . the third of the Dar'Nethi who had survived the Catastrophe of their making. A Lord of Zhev'Na. Never in my remotest supposition . . . *Stupid, stupid woman.*

"How could you have guessed? You knew nothing of the Lords. And I was not exactly my usual self in all those years—a matter of being away from home in disguise for too long. Wearing a mundane face does not allow the full range of one's capabilities, and living in your world has its distinct hazards for those born to this one—else all this might have been settled long before you were born. But I think I am done with Darzid now. Your son will need him no longer. Shall you mourn your old friend?"

"I will curse your name until I am dust."

"Alas, that is very likely. Come, the boy approaches even now. Please, take your seat." He snapped his fingers again, and a plain wooden chair appeared beside me. Without willing it, I sat, while Darzid—Ziddari—took his place on the third throne.

From the depths of the polished black floor between me and the dais glowed a circle of blue light, pulsing in the same rhythm as my heartbeat. Gerick appeared exactly in the center of it, dressed in breeches and shirt and doublet of deep purple trimmed with silver, wearing his sword at his belt. He stood tall before the Lords and did not bow.

They all spoke at once, three distinct voices, yet winding sinuously together. "Welcome, young Lord," said Ziddari.

"At last," said the woman. "We have anxiously awaited you."

And Parven. "All honor to you on this night that you come into your inheritance. Have you made your choice, young Lord?"

"I have," said Gerick, in a voice cool as glass.

"And what is it to be?"

"I will be a Lord of Zhev'Na."

And so ended my hope. Perhaps I sighed or sobbed, for Gerick turned his head sharply, as if he had not seen me until then. His demeanor was neither hateful nor haughty, only solemn. But he did not speak to me and reserved his attention for the Lords.

"Yes, we have brought her here as you requested, young Lord. You can see we've taken excellent care of her. Now she is yours, to do with as you will." Ziddari's vile expectation hung over us like a cloud. "A fitting gift for your birthday."

"She is to be set free."

"What?" From all three of the Lords the word thundered, until I thought my head would burst from the sound. Though one could not read subtle expression on faces so strange, their shock and disbelief shook the floor under my feet.

Gerick's voice did not change. "I have made the choice to become one of you. But before I do so, I require safe passage for this woman. She is not important to you."

"What weakness have we uncovered?"

"Who are you to judge of her importance to us?"

"What of your oath . . ."

". . . your revenge . . ."

". . . the blood oath on the body of your nurse, your truer mother?" The twining whispers filled the vast hall like a fetid odor.

Ziddari snarled and gestured toward me. "What kind of mother is this who should never have allowed you to be conceived, knowing your only inheritance would be the stake and the fire?"

Gerick did not quail. "My oath was based on a lie. I don't know whether or not my oath of fealty to you was also based on lies. My guess is that it was. But I will live with the choices I've made, because I see no alternatives. You have fulfilled your part of the bargain, and I'll do the same. All but this one thing will proceed as you have planned."

"How did you come by these conclusions?"

"That is no concern of yours, my Lord Parven," said Gerick. "Now, time grows short. It is your turn to choose." He had them, and he knew it.

A smile crept slowly across Ziddari's bloodless lips. "Oh, brother and sister, we have done far better even than we knew. Do you not agree?" He leaped up from his chair and swept a deep bow to Gerick. "We will proceed with your preparation, my clever and immensely delightful young Prince. When the time comes for the anointing, you may release the Lady Seriana to whichever of the Preceptors you wish. They have safe passage back to Avonar after, and so will she. Is that sufficient? You have the word of the Lords of Zhev'Na, which has never been broken in a thousand years."

Gerick folded his arms across his breast, took a deep breath, and spoke softly to me, though his eyes did not meet mine. "This is the best I can do. I am what I am. It cannot be changed."

Then he turned his back on me, dropped his arms, and acknowledged the Three with a slight bow. "Let us begin."

The room grew colder, the lamplight fading until each paned globe cast only a dim circle on the black floor just underneath it. The Three seemed to grow larger as they focused their jeweled eyes on Gerick.

"You will not speak again until our work is done," said Parven. "There must be no disruption during your preparation. Do you agree?"

Gerick nodded. He showed no fear.

Notole moved to the center of the dais, carrying a crystal flask and goblet. "Have you come to us fasting?" she asked.

"He has neither eaten nor drunk in a sun's turning," said Ziddari, from behind her. "I made sure of it."

The old woman nodded and filled the goblet with a liquid so deep a red that it was almost black. "This is drink such as no mortal being may taste and remain unchanged. Drain every drop, and so from this night you will require no other sustenance save what nourishes your power." She offered the goblet, wreathed in scarlet-tinted steam, to Gerick.

"Don't drink it!" I cried. "You are not one of them!"

But Gerick either did not or would not hear me. He took the goblet, raised it to each of the Three, and put it to his lips. The first sip made him shudder, but after that he did not falter. Slowly, inexorably, he drained the glass, forcing the last drops before taking a heaving breath, clearly fighting to keep it down.

Notole took the goblet from his trembling hand. "A potent vintage, yes? You feel it in every bone, every vein, every fiber. Your body rejects it, for it is not the stuff of mortal life. But you have learned to command yourself, and so you allow it to do its work, cleansing, transforming, making your body other than it has ever been."

Notole returned to her chair, and Parven took her place at the front of the dais. "When you first came to us, young Prince, you offered us your sword. We did not take it from you then, for it was unproved, unworthy of us. But you will have no more use for such trivial implements. We now require your sworn bond that you will not raise your hand against us, your brothers and sister. Are you willing to surrender this symbol of your former life and so swear without reservation?"

Gerick unsheathed his sword, raising it high until it caught the faint lamplight, gleaming, glinting. But then he straightened his back and knelt before Parven, presenting the sword on his upturned palms.

"And you make this vow of your own will . . . freely?"

Gerick nodded.

"So be it sworn," said Parven. A beam of amethyst light

shot from his gold mask and focused on the sword. The steel blade began to glow, brighter and brighter purple, until the shape lost coherence and the metal sagged across Gerick's hands. Gerick did not flinch, but left his hands in place until the shriveled sword vanished, leaving only the stench of hot metal and scorched flesh. Then he rose to his feet, cold and solemn, his hands held stiffly open at his sides.

Ziddari stepped forward, replacing the taller Lord, and gazed down at Gerick with his ruby eyes. "You are learning the price of your power, young Lord. Not so very high. Not for this life for which you were born. You are not the sniveling child I knew in that other place. You know blood and pain as he could never know it. You know power as he could never have touched it, and the very things that made him weak now make you strong. Now it is time to bid that child farewell. Do you agree?"

Gerick closed his eyes and bowed his head, and Ziddari laid his hands on the shining red-brown hair. "And so do I remove from you the name you were given on this day twelve years past, and the shackles it lays upon your freedom. No longer will its bidding give you pause, or its invocation cause you the least concern. No longer will its bitter legacy enthrall you, but will seem as the tale of some other who is so far beneath you as to be unworthy of licking your feet. The strength and wisdom grown in you, and the passions that have shaped you are all that will remain. You are now Dieste, who is destined to be called the Destroyer, the Fourth Lord of Zhev'Na."

Ziddari raised his hands and Gerick looked up, and he was not the same as he had been. The graceful youth of his features, already roughened by sun and desert, had taken on a stony edge. No longer could I see the boy who had called for me to run away or who had been unable to look me in the eye as he apologized for losing his soul. He was no longer a boy at all.

"Now," said Notole, "receive our greatest gift to you upon this, the day of your birth, the day you take your place among the mighty of the world."

The Three gathered around Gerick. A low hum just at

the bounds of hearing set my teeth on edge. Over the glowing blue circle in the floor appeared a ring of dull brass, taller than a man. Suspended in the air, the ring began to spin, teasing at the yellow lamplight and the colored gleam of the Lords' eyes.

"You have tested the waters of darkness in these past days, but tonight you are to be immersed in them, bathed in them, cleansed of those things that will prevent the fullest expression of your power. Step into the orb, leave yourself completely open, and take your fill of what you find there. By its power and ours and your own, you will be irrevocably changed. Is that your desire?"

Gerick nodded once more.

"Then enter and claim your birthright."

Without hesitation, Gerick stepped into the very center of the orb, woven of red, green, and purple light. His vague outline was visible inside it, his arms and legs spread wide, and his face upturned as if to embrace whatever awaited him.

"My dearest son, don't do it," I cried. "Hold on to yourself. Nothing is irrevocable. You are not what they are. You were blessed and beloved from the first moment your father and I knew of your life. You were treasured by my brother who raised you as his own. And your dear Lucy, think how frightened she was by the lies the world told of those with your gifts, but how she stayed because you were so dear to her. Somehow you will know of these things again. You must not forget. . . ." And to fight off my grief and despair I repeated the long story I had written in the past days, not believing he could hear me or that it could change what was happening, but because I could not watch such evil and stay silent.

It seemed a lifetime until he emerged from the fiery orb, instantly enveloped in the smothering embrace of the Three. Notole dropped a black robe over his head, the same as the other Lords'. His hands covered his face as they led him to the fourth throne upon the dais. Ziddari and Notole stood to either side of him and gently pulled his arms outwards, uncovering his eyes. They were black pits, gaping and empty.

Parven stood behind him, and while Notole and Ziddari held his hands away, the tall Lord fitted a gold mask over the terrible hollows in my son's face. So his were to be diamonds, glittering, cold, blue-white stones that could never show fear or anger or love. I could not hear the words that Parven whispered as he ran his fingers around the edges of the mask, but as the gleaming metal molded itself to my son's brow and his cheekbones, joining itself to his flesh, I sank to my knees and wept bitter tears.

"Young Lord Dieste, we welcome you to our company," said Notole. "We are old, and you give us new life."

"You have bathed in the glories of Darkness, surrendering the flawed vision of your race in favor of the true-seeing of your brothers and sister."

"You have yielded your remaining attachments to the child you were and drunk the wine of immortality."

"We are Four, and no living hand can undo it."

CHAPTER 44

The spinning ring vanished. The Lords took turns taking Gerick's hands and kissing them, congratulating him and each other.

"Now one small matter, and then we can welcome our Dar'Nethi guests," said Ziddari. "It's not yet time for them to see you in your present aspect. You must make yourself an image of what they expect to find. If you need guidance . . ."

"I need nothing." Gerick's words were quiet and hard. To hear the familiar voice, so recently deepened with approaching manhood, coming from the face with the gold mask and diamond eyes was but another aspect of horror.

"Then we will leave you to your guests. Our allies will open a portal to bring them."

"And what of my servants? Asleep as I said?"

"They are none of your concern, young Lord. They're all dead."

"Dead? But I said—"

"You said you might want to kill them," said Ziddari. "We agreed with that. And so we have done." The three Lords vanished, leaving an echo of purest hatred and lust.

Only one black throne remained occupied. He sat still and silent, his elbows resting on the square arms of the chair, his hands knotted into fists.

What did one say to one's child who had been so grotesquely transformed? How did one counsel a youth who was on the verge of destroying what balance and hope remained in the world? Would he hear me now the others were gone? I had never thought to be allowed to speak with Gerick again, yet here was an opportunity, and I could not think how on earth to begin.

"What now?" It was all I could come up with.

His thoughts were clearly far away. "Did you say something?"

"What happens now?"

"You will be given to the Dar'Nethi as we promised. Nothing else concerns you."

How small a spark is needed to ignite a holocaust. "Do not speak to me in Darzid's words!"

The tips of his fingers tapped each other rapidly. "And whose words should I use but those of the Lords? I am one with them."

"Use your own words. They didn't take your mind from you. Think. Act. Take hold of your own life."

"You know nothing."

"Gerick, you must listen to—"

"I will *not* listen to you." He sprang from his chair and circled behind it, gripping the thick black edge of its back. His restless hands began tapping their frantic rhythm on the stone. "You are filled with incessant noise, and all I want is for you to be silent. My name is Lord Dieste, and you will show me the proper respect or I'll teach you how to do so; I'll put you back where you were found."

"And where was that? Do you even know?"

"In servitude proper to your meager abilities. You are nothing to me. Servants are nothing to me. It doesn't matter if they're all dead."

Some struggle was going on inside him. I pressed hard, hoping to find some crack, some chink in the walls the Lords had built to imprison him. "But your masters have promised to give me to the Preceptors."

"Only if I wish it. They do everything I wish."

"And what is it you wish?"

He clasped his hands together and pressed them to his chin, as if to quiet their agitation. "I don't know."

"You made them promise to save my life. Can you even remember why?"

"A stupid and childish whim. I am no longer burdened with such."

"Does it matter what I wish?"

"Not in the least."

"But if it did matter, I'd wish to stay with you. I would care for you and be your companion. You are my—"

"I have no need of companions!" He circled the throne again and sank slowly into its stony embrace, pressing his clenched hands to his forehead. "I want to be left alone. And I have no further need of servants. All my servants have been disposed of. They can no longer interfere . . . or leave their thoughts cluttering up my head . . . dead men's thoughts . . . slaves' thoughts . . ." In that instant, he might have been transformed into the same stone as his chair. Agitation stilled, cold anger muted, imperious manner quenched, his words dwindled to a whisper. "Impossible. Impossible. How could he be here?"

The diamond eyes jerked up. A searing lance pierced my forehead. "You lied! What were the two of you doing? What was he doing here?"

My mouth worked soundlessly as the pressure in my head grew . . . only to be abruptly halted when the round blue glow in the floor began to pulse rapidly. Gerick jumped up, spread his hands, and pressed his palms outward, and in a stomach-wrenching explosion of enchantment, the vast, empty darkness of the Lords' hall was transformed into a more ordinary sitting room.

Even as I blinked and gaped at soft couches, polished tables, well-stocked bookshelves, and bright lamps hung from a high, painted ceiling, the air in the center of the room shivered with the discontinuity that signified an open portal. Beyond the portal lay another room, somber gray stone, a long table and seven high-backed chairs, backing on a massive hearth. I could not fail to recognize the place—the Preceptors' council chamber, where I had last seen my husband as he plunged a knife into his belly. The Preceptors stood waiting in the center of that chamber.

First to step through the portal were Madyalar and Exeget, followed by Y'Dan and the two old ones, Ustele and Ce'Aret. Last came Gar'Dena, and only in looking at the giant sorcerer did I regain a sense of the months that had passed. His massive flesh sagged, as if he had lost a great deal of weight, and with it, the joy and genial sweetness that had illuminated his presence. His broad face was grave and creased with care.

I expected jaws to drop in horror when the Preceptors beheld the fearsome aspect of their Heir-to-be. The Preceptors were secretive, imperious, single-minded in their intents, yes. But the corruption of a few—Exeget, certainly, and perhaps some ally or two—could not blind the rest. They would never anoint an Heir so clearly the tool of the Lords. But when I turned to the one who stood beside the crackling hearthfire to greet the Dar'Nethi, my heart sank. Gerick looked entirely himself, a tall, slender youth, skin darkened by the sun, dressed elegantly in purple and silver. His eyes were the brown that matched my own. Surely it was my imagination that I saw the icy brilliance of diamonds in their depths. An image, of course . . . as Darzid's face had been . . . so the Preceptors could not see what had been done.

I jumped to my feet. "Gar'Dena, good Preceptors, don't be deceived. This is the Lords' house! They've changed my son . . . corrupted him . . ."

No one acknowledged me. All their attention was focused on Gerick. I hurried across the room, intending to grab their sleeves, to pluck their robes or hair, whatever it would take to get them to heed my warning, but my steps did not reduce the distance between us, and none of them seemed to see or hear me.

"Welcome to the house of my protectors, Preceptors," said Gerick, bowing slightly, his earlier agitation as hidden as his true face.

Exeget stepped forward and bowed deeply. "We rejoice in your ascendance to majority, Your Grace, but we cannot but wonder at its venue. Your refusal to return to Avonar even for this glorious day has given rise to great disturbance among your people. The rumors rampant in this past year are multiplied a hundredfold, and though the Gatefire yet burns white, you cannot fail to know that seven villages and innumerable households have been destroyed in the past months. The Zhid have grown bold, and your people worry about friends who do not reveal their names"—he waved his hand to encompass the room—"yet stand so high in their Prince's regard."

"My protectors have done me great service, Master. No Dulcé have been sent to poison me, as happened to Prince D'Natheil two years ago. No knife has appeared in my hand, and I suffer no madness to make me turn it upon myself as my late father did. I have lived in safety and comfort until my majority, and have put the time to good use developing my skills on many fronts. When I venture the Bridge, I will not be broken by it."

"Indeed you have grown fairly, my lord," said Madyalar, smiling. Ustele and Ce'Aret murmured their agreement.

Gerick acknowledged the compliment with a gracious nod. "Clearly I am not Zhid, and it is one hour past my coming of age. I am safe in the house of my friends, and my Preceptors are welcomed here. If the Lords wished to corrupt me, then they have made a great miscalculation, have they not?"

"Who are you?" growled Gar'Dena. "Show us your true face. Show us your friends and prove that they are the friends of Avonar."

"What greater proof of loyalty is there than saving my life?" snapped Gerick. "My protectors did so when I was an infant, condemned to death in the mundane world, and then they brought me to this haven to shield me both from execution in the mundane world and the murderous traitors in Gondai. And they saved me yet again this year when they discovered a foul plot that invaded this, my sanctuary. Some thought to prevent my taking my place as the Heir, sneaking in here disguised as servants to steal me away." His finger pointed at me.

All of the Preceptors looked startled when they saw me. But two of the astonished faces registered another emotion as well—distress, quickly suppressed. One of the two—Gar'Dena's—I expected, and the other . . . the other I most assuredly did not. I did not trust myself even to think the name, for if what I glimpsed was truth, then the implications were profound and dangerous.

"Oh, my lady—" began Gar'Dena.

"Master Gar—"

"Be silent in my presence, traitors!" spat Gerick. He whirled from me to the giant Dar'Nethi. "How dare you speak when you have so violated my trust? My first act as Heir of D'Arnath will be to remove you from this Preceptorate. I cannot trust anyone." And then he glared at me in accusation. "No one . . . no one is who they seem. Everyone lies."

Ustele, so bent and weathered that he looked like the ancient trees that clung to the windswept ridges of the Dorian Wall, glanced about the room anxiously. "Are you saying this woman has tried to harm you, Your Grace? With Gar'Dena's connivance?"

"We know nothing of this," said Ce'Aret, frowning. "We understood that your mother was caring for you all these months."

Y'Dan nodded, puzzled.

"Once we're done here today, you may take Preceptor Gar'Dena and his spy with you back to Avonar," said Gerick. "I charge you particularly, Master Exeget. Question them and dispose of them as you wish."

"But my lord, she is your mother," said Ce'Aret. "What harm—?"

"She is nothing to me! If she wanted honorable concourse, she would have presented herself to me in an honorable manner . . . told me the truth . . . "

Exeget bowed. "This is shocking news, Your Grace. Was the woman acting alone?"

Gerick turned his back to them. "Her conspirators are dead. I had them killed. All discovered. All dead."

Take me back to Avonar . . . conspirators . . . I didn't know what to say. In an instant, everything was uncertain. But my eye was on the Preceptor I had noted before. There it was again. Sorrow . . . so brief. Devastation. He had waited for over a year and had brought with him whatever glimmer of hope he and Gar'Dena had been able to maintain. But they didn't need to see the gold mask to know we had failed.

"My lord," said Madyalar, soothing. "Let us proceed with our business so we may return to Avonar and give your people the glorious news of their new hope. We have been without an Heir for too long." She urged her colleagues forward. "Come, you old fossils. The young Prince has come of age. He has been proved."

Why didn't they see? Why didn't they stop? I needed to warn them, yet something—enchantment, uncertainty, caution?—kept me silent. Something else was happening here. I watched and waited.

Exeget motioned to the others to form a half-circle, and in his pale, manicured hand he held a small round box made of gold. He removed its lid and stared at its contents. "Silestia," he said. "It grows in only one spot on the highest slopes of the Mountains of Light. The white flowers bloom only on Midsummer's Day, and it is said their fragrance fills the air for a league in any direction. From each flower we can extract only a single drop of oil. So rare and precious is it that this tiny portion I carry is the product of twelve years of gathering, since the last was used for young D'Natheil. To think—"

"We agreed we would perform no elaborate ritual," snapped Madyalar. "Since this is a private ceremony, there is no need."

Exeget looked up. "Is that your wish, my lord?"

Gerick nodded, but seemed scarcely to be paying attention. He stood staring at me, his arms wrapped tight about his stomach as if he were going to be sick.

"So be it," said Exeget. "The heart of the rite is, of course, quite brief. In the mundane world, the head of the ruler is anointed, and as the head rules the body, so does the king rule his subjects. But it is the hands of D'Arnath's Heir that are anointed, for the hands serve the body, supply its sustenance, defend it, build up the works of beauty that its soul creates. So does the Heir serve his people, sustain them, defend them, and exemplify and encourage the beauty they create. We do not know you, young Prince, yet we must entrust you with this responsibility. Some among us say we should wait and judge your worthiness, to learn of your protectors and your schooling to be sure you are the Prince we believe. But I am the head of the Preceptorate, and I say we know enough."

Exeget dipped his finger into the gold case. Madyalar, Ce'Aret, Ustele, and Y'Dan knelt before Gerick. Gar'Dena had turned his broad back, sheathed in red satin, to all of us, his shoulders quivering. I believed he was weeping. But tears would do no good. Gar'Dena should be crying out a warning. Madyalar and the others didn't understand the truth. Why was he silent?

Exeget reached for Gerick's extended hand. "Great Vasrin, Creator and Shaper of the universe, stand witness. . . ."

I couldn't believe he was going to go through with it. Exeget surely knew the identity of Gerick's "protectors," but I no longer believed he was a traitor. Exeget's face had blanched along with Gar'Dena's when he saw me revealed, and Exeget's expression had shown defeat when he heard my allies were dead. He could not allow Gerick to become the anointed Heir. Madness and frustration boiled in my heart . . . until Exeget glanced at me . . . and I knew . . . *Earth and sky!* They were going to kill him.

"Exeget, do not!" As if my own voice had burst forth in an unaccustomed timbre, a shout rang out, echoing on stone walls and dark columns and glass floor hidden behind this seeming of a room. Deep and commanding, that voice pierced my cold heart like a lance of fire. "Neither anointing him nor assassinating him accomplishes any purpose whatsoever—not while I live free."

A man appeared at one end of the room as if he had parted the plastered walls and stepped through. Tall and lean, his sun-darkened skin ridged with scars, he wore the collar, gray tunic, and cropped hair of a slave and the face of D'Natheil. One glance told me everything necessary. Recognition, completion, understanding . . . he was Karon my beloved. He was whole. I clasped his unspoken greeting as a starving child holds her bread.

Exeget lowered his hand and bowed to his prince, the corners of his mouth twitching upward in a half-smile, transforming . . . illuminating his proud face. "Never have I been so happy to see a failed pupil, my lord."

Gar'Dena whirled about with speed and agility unexpected for one of his girth. "My good lord!"

"V'Saro," whispered Gerick, staring at Karon. "They said my servants were dead. I commanded it . . . before I listened to you . . . before I knew. . . ."

The remaining Preceptors looked from Exeget to Karon to Gerick, bewildered . . . except for Madyalar who stepped protectively toward Gerick. Now I saw the puzzle solving itself.

"What treachery is this?" boomed the voice of Ziddari from every direction at once, echoing through the light and shadows, causing the floor to shudder, the homely room to seem fragile and false, and joy, relief, and hope of no more durance than dew in the desert. "How comes this slave here?"

"The anointing must proceed," said the voice of the woman, Notole. "Why do you pause in this most important duty? Continue."

"Did you not hear, mighty Lords?" said Exeget, closing the lid of the gold case with a snap. "Anointing this boy accomplishes nothing. You may bathe him in the oil of silestia, but it will gain him no power. The anointed Heir of D'Arnath yet lives in Gondai, in full possession of his power, and before you can make an Heir of your own, you must deal with him."

"D'Natheil is decaying in his grave," shouted Parven. "No impostor will delay our triumph." The air grew heavy with anger . . . with danger. . . . The lamplight dimmed.

"I would recommend that you get back through the portal, good Preceptors," said Karon, waving Y'Dan and the two old ones toward Gar'Dena and Exeget. He approached Gerick slowly, locking our son's empty face in his gaze while he called over his shoulder. "Can you hold the way long enough to get all of us out, Master Exeget?"

"You will have to hurry, my lord. A moment's earlier arrival and I would have been able to serve you better." Exeget's puffy face had crumpled into a gray ruin, as if time had leaped forward fifty years. But the Preceptor raised his clenched fists and closed his eyes. The rectangular doorway appeared in the shivering air. "Ce'Aret, Ustele, hurry," he said, gasping. "Y'Dan, Gar'Dena my brother . . ."

Gar'Dena shoved the Preceptors through the portal one by one. "My lady!" he called, gesturing for me to come. But I could not go. Not yet.

Karon gazed down at Gerick. "You must come with us."

"Why? So you can execute me?"

"To set you free. You don't belong here."

"You're wrong." And Gerick let his false image dissolve and with it the walls and the hearth and the trappings of ordinary life. He stood in the stark, black hall of the Lords, his truth revealed, his diamond eyes glittering in the darkness. "There is no going back, even if I wanted. This is exactly where I belong."

Karon did not flinch or falter. "It doesn't matter. Not even this. Nothing . . . *nothing* . . . is irrevocable. I, of all men, can bear witness to that. Come with us who care for you."

"I've freed the woman," said Gerick, folding his arms across his breast. "Take her away quickly or I'll end up killing you both." Then he turned his back on us and walked slowly toward the dais where the black thrones sat vacant.

From the opposite end of the hall where a tall, wide doorway broke the line of the colonnade, running footsteps entered the vast chamber. "My lord," cried a familiar voice, echoing in the empty vastness. "Three Zhid warriors right behind me!" A youth wearing Drudge's garb burst through the gaping door, his arms laden with belts and scabbards bristling with swords and knives. He sped across the black, mirrored floor into the light, shooting me a cheerful grin. "We've come to rescue you."

Paulo dumped his bundle of armaments on the floor beside Karon. "I come by these from the guards' stores. Thought you might have need."

Karon wrenched his gaze from Gerick's back and smiled at Paulo. "You are irreplaceable, my friend." Dragging a sword and a knife from the tangle, he took up a position between the door Paulo had just entered and the portal where Gar'Dena was disappearing into the council chamber.

"Does the young master have a sword on him—or might he want this one?" Paulo called after Karon, pulling a blade from the pile and gesturing at Gerick's back.

"I don't think he needs one. You and Seri, get through the portal. I'll wait for Gerick." His gaze embraced me, and he waved his sword toward the enchanted doorway. "Go. I'll bring him. I promise."

But before I could convince myself to leave, a nauseating wave of dark power pulsed through the vast chamber. With a thunderous boom, the portal vanished. Exeget cried out and slumped to the floor. The little gold case of silestia fell out of his hand, clattering across the dark surface. At the same time, three Zhid warriors burst from the far end of the room, swords drawn and Karon stepped forward to meet them.

While Paulo, hands on his waist, looked uncertainly from Karon to Gerick and back again, I ran to the fallen sorcerer. "Can I help you, Preceptor?" I asked, searching for some wound or hurt to ease. Sitting with his head drooped between his knees, he was bleeding from his mouth and nose, and wheezing like unoiled bellows.

"Too late." After carefully wiping his fingers on his robe, he held up his right hand. One of his fingers was black. "Unfortunate timing . . . for me, but fortunate for the Prince and the boy. At least the Lords will have nothing left of me to examine should they triumph in the end."

"You were the one who told me to be silent and not to be afraid."

Even in his mortal distress, the sorcerer managed a sly half-smile. "Dassine said you were the key to everything. May you find strength to finish it. We owe you"—he coughed and fought for breath, flailing his hand until he caught my own in an iron grip—"trust you . . . if all fails . . . you must finish . . . for the worlds . . ."

"Master, what do you want me to do?" I said. From behind me came shouts and the clash of steel.

Exeget's head dropped again as he fought for every painful breath. He looked to be beyond hearing. When his cold hand slipped from mine, a small gold canister lay in my palm, identical to the canister that had fallen out of his hand when the portal collapsed—the one that still lay beside my foot.

Exeget began choking. I slipped the gold case he'd given me into my pocket and rolled him to his side. A stream of bloody spittle dribbled from his mouth . . . his lips black . . . and his fingernails . . . the one finger wholly black . . . The silestia had been poisoned, designed to slay Gerick before he could become the Destroyer. The case on the floor was the one he had used. Therefore the case in my pocket must contain the uncontaminated oil of silestia.

A shadow fell over me, and I looked up to see Madyalar staring down at the Exeget. The Preceptor vomited up blood and lay still.

"He needs help," I said.

"I would as soon nurse a snake. The fool looks dead already. All I want from him is the silestia—" She wandered away, scuffing her foot on the floor, seeking the gold case.

"Plotting until the end," I whispered to the pale, still face. "If you can hear me, know that I understand your sacrifice. Gods have mercy . . . I will see it done." Quickly, carefully, making sure that Madyalar could not see, I switched the two, placing the case with the poisoned ointment in Exeget's pocket, and the case with the real oil on the floor as if it had rolled out of his hand. Then I backed away from him, not checking to see if he yet lived, not daring to think of what I had just done. Gerick could *not* be anointed. If we could not save him . . . if Karon died and Gerick chose to be a Lord and the anointed Heir . . .

Only moments later, Madyalar crowed in triumph as she found the two cases. The one that she found on the floor, she named as the poison that had killed Exeget and threw it, spinning and clattering, across the floor. The one that she found hidden in Exeget's pocket—the poison—she dropped into her own. I had given little consideration to gods since the day Karon burned, but on this day I needed every aid the universe could provide. *Good Vasrin, holy Annadis, mighty Jerrat, if you can hear the cries of an unbeliever, let Karon prevail. . . .*

One of the Zhid lay dead on the floor, but Karon's battle

with the other two was growing desperate. As one engaged him, the other circled and attacked from a different direction. Relentlessly. Their swords rang and blazed with sparks when they struck the floor or one of the black pillars as Karon dodged in and out of them seeking a bit of shelter. And, of course, the battle was being fought with more than swords. Karon's every stroke split the advancing darkness, every parry pushed back the night as if it was yet a third enemy that pursued him. The air was so filled with enchantments that it crackled. My hair floated outward from my head, and my skin was flushed and tingling. Then, in an explosion of green fire, Karon's blade snapped.

"We've got to help him, Paulo." I had felt him come up behind me.

"There is no help for him."

I jumped up and whirled about. Gerick, not Paulo, stood behind me, fists clenched at his side, watching the battle with his diamond eyes. Paulo had dragged another sword from the pile of weapons and was running toward Karon. "My lord!" he shouted, as Karon staggered backward, fending off two long blades with only a dagger and the broken sword hilt. "Here, my lord!"

Karon ducked, ran, and flattened his back to a pillar, dropping the broken weapon and snatching the new sword Paulo tossed him. Even from my distance I could see him bleeding . . . from his shoulder, his arms, from one leg. "Get away, boy!" he cried harshly, as another bolt of fire split the air beside him. Paulo threw himself flat to the floor, skidding twenty paces. When the two Zhid were engaged with Karon again, Paulo scrambled to his feet.

"It is Parven and Ziddari he fights," said Gerick, softly, walking slowly toward the battle, mesmerized, as if he were walking in his sleep.

I followed him. "These are just images, then? They've chosen to appear in this form?"

"No. These are real warriors, but the Lords have possessed them, using the warriors' bodies but their own skills. If these two fall, they will bring two more and fight again. Notole seeks another host even now. They won't stop. They won't die."

"You were willing to help me, to let us go free. Can you help him now?"

"Even if I chose to do so, I cannot. You heard me swear never to raise a hand against the Lords. They have called on me to fulfill my oath. I've told them that I won't fight him. But I cannot aid him either." Gerick paused and looked down at Exeget who lay in the pool of blood. He bent down and touched the Preceptor's neck for a moment, then straightened up and nudged the body with his foot. Stepping over Exeget, he moved yet closer to the battle. With silent apologies to Exeget, I stepped over the fallen Preceptor and followed Gerick.

Oppressive, soul-chilling dread filled the chamber, cold horror that rolled in like a black tide, shredding the spirit, proclaiming that all was hopeless, that the end was upon us.

There is no escape. . . .

Do you feel it, vermin prince? Make a portal to Avonar and its passage will incinerate your flesh. . . .

Prepare for your anointing, young Lord. In moments there will be no living Heir.

I believed they were right. "Gerick, he is your father. In the name of all that lives—"

Before I could finish my plea, Paulo barreled out of nowhere, grabbed my arm, and pressed a short sword into my hand. His own blade was much too long for him. "We've got to help— Blazing shit!" He stared at Gerick's face. "You damned fool! You donkey's ass! You went and did it! Jerrat's balls, I thought you had a brain in you."

"How dare you speak to me?" said Gerick, spinning to face him, stepping forward.

"How dare *I*? It's how dare *you*." Paulo waved his sword wildly at Karon's plight. "Do you see what's happening?"

"I see everything." Gerick stepped closer.

Suddenly Paulo threw the weapon to the floor, and with the flat of his hand on Gerick's chest, he shoved Gerick backward. "You're doing this, aren't you?"

"Don't touch me." Gerick did not raise his hand, but his rage swelled, fury that made the air shiver.

"This is just what you said you'd do. It's going to be killing and nothing but killing forever."

"Try me, horse boy. Do you think you could possibly take me down?"

"For the Prince, I could. For the Lady Seri, I could." With each phrase, Paulo shoved Gerick again and again, until Gerick stumbled, and Paulo threw himself on top of him. The two crashed to the floor.

"Paulo, don't!" I yelled, frantically trying to pull him away before Gerick could turn his power on him.

"Mighty Lords!" Madyalar let out a ferocious cry. "The young Prince!"

A roar like a hurricane blasted the room. A torrent of darkness swirled about us, ripping the light, dancing, screaming, tearing at clothes and hair, flaying us with its power. The air itself vented its anger; the stones about us groaned with the whirling tumult.

Kill the insolent fool, Lord Dieste! bellowed Parven, almost splitting my skull. *Blind him! Take his heart and eat it!*

Burn his skin away for daring to touch you—then taste of his pain! said Notole. *Use the power to destroy these vermin who would enslave you.*

Dread and horror gnawed at my soul, clouding my senses, threatening to tear my heart from my breast. An unseen hand slammed me backward. I could scarcely see as the two boys rolled on the floor, grunting and gasping, clawing and twisting each other in a tangle of robes and arms and legs and tunics. One and then the other was on top, Paulo pummeling away wildly, Gerick snarling and cursing, twisting Paulo's limbs until they must surely break. He's going to be dead, I thought—dear, faithful Paulo. My very soul felt bruised. The fury raged without slack . . . without end . . . slashing . . . battering . . . until Gerick staggered to his feet at last, leaving Paulo in a crumpled heap.

Silence. Utter. Complete. The tempest ceased. Thunder vanished. No clash of swords. No heaving breath. No flashes of lurid light from under the colonnade.

Madyalar screeched and chortled, extending her finger toward the still forms sprawled on the shining floor. "Four lie dead! The mad Prince has fallen!"

Gerick's turned his head this way and that, his diamond

eyes glittering in the uncertain light, as Madyalar knelt before him, dipping her finger in the gold case she had taken from Exeget's robes. "My Prince, give me your hands. Let me anoint them with the true oil of silestia."

But, of course, it was not the true oil. . . .

I could not allow it. Not even here at the end of everything. He was my son. "No!" I cried. "Gerick, don't let her touch you!"

The very same moment another voice cried out. "Wait!" Karon stepped from behind a pillar just behind us, his sword shining a brilliant green. "Still no good, Madyalar. You've miscounted—forgetting your own colleague. Exeget has won the last round between you."

The woman gaped.

"Now, quickly!" Karon threw down his sword, closed his eyes, and held out his hands, and with his deep and shaking breath, his whispered word, and a grinding rumble as if the earth had split open, a portal gaped before us. This shimmering doorway did not open into some gracious lamplit room, nor even into a cold stone council chamber, but into a pit of absolute blackness from which came sounds so fearful as to make the strongest heart blanch. This is why they had risked sending Karon to Zhev'Na. With all portals to Avonar shut down, only the Heir of D'Arnath could open another way. This way. Through the Breach itself.

Karon touched my hand. "We need to go *now*. Gerick, you must come with us. I'll carry Paulo."

My son's arms were wrapped about his middle. His terrible eyes pierced the gloom. So fragile in his darkness. So young.

The Lords' wrath spun and surged around us. Footsteps rang on the stone beyond the great doors. They were coming.

"Ah, holy gods . . ." Karon's voice broke. "We will not leave you here. If you stay . . . I will fight them until the last day of the world to set you free. I swear it."

"And I with him," I said, shaping the story yet again in my mind and heart, willing him to hear me. *You have been blessed and beloved from the day we first knew you. . . .*

"Take care of Paulo, Seri. Get him out of the way." As

Karon retrieved his sword, I stepped to the battered boy on the floor.

"Wait!" Gerick held out one hand in warning. The world paused in its turning . . . and then, with his other hand, he reached out to Paulo.

Paulo's eyes blinked open. He grabbed Gerick's hand, staggered to his feet, and leaned on my son's shoulder, grinning through his swollen eyes and bloodied lips. "We'd best go then. Lead on, my lord. We'll be right behind."

The creases of worry and grief graven on Karon's blood-streaked face softened. For one moment he took my hand, his own wide hand near crushing my fingers. "As you say. Stay close, all of you."

And as the raging fury of the Lords erupted behind us, and Madyalar crumpled to the floor, howling as Exeget's poison ate its way into her body, Karon led the three of us into the Breach between the worlds.

CHAPTER 45

We could not travel D'Arnath's Bridge through the Breach, for no Gate or entry point existed in Zhev'Na. We had to traverse chaos itself. Karon led the way through the directionless tumult, his bare, blood-streaked arms stretched out in front of him, palms outward. No solid path lay beneath our feet. Although his power enfolded us, creating a small island of stability that allowed us to move forward, he could not shelter us completely from the grotesque visions, the unending wails of souls lost in madness, the unnamed terrors that bit at our heels and nibbled at our minds until we dared not let ourselves blink lest they fall upon us.

Yet hope beyond belief bolstered my resolution, and Paulo's grin shone like a lighthouse lantern in the gloom. Though hot rain lashed our skin, and the screaming and wailing tore at our souls, we flailed and yelled with joyous ferocity at the monstrous birds that flew screeching at our eyes, pressing on behind Karon as if nothing could harm us.

Gerick's terrible eyes glittered in the fantastical light and his black robes billowed in the howling gales, until he looked like another of the grotesque creatures that pursued us through that horror. But his steps dragged, so I offered Paulo my shoulder to lean on instead of his. Left alone, Gerick huddled into himself, hunching his shoulders, bowing his head, each step a visible struggle. Soon he had slowed almost to stopping, as if the tether binding him to Zhev'Na had stretched as far as it could. A towering tidal wave of mud was bearing down on him from one side.

"Karon!" I screamed over the tumult.

Karon, the wind whipping his bloody tunic about him,

turned and saw what was happening. He closed his eyes and swept his arms around and upward, a surge of power holding back the deluge long enough for Gerick to catch up with us. As we moved forward again, Karon kept Gerick at his side, using his own body to shield Gerick from the horrors that escaped his enchantments.

The struggle was more than physical. Hour after hour, I heard Karon talking, encouraging, battling. "Hold, my son. No, this is not your place. . . . I'll not leave you. Don't listen. Surely the enchantments of this place fear you because someday you will have power over them. They smell it in you and wish to make you afraid. . . ."

Soon every step required a monstrous effort. We trudged through a hideous stew of stinking mud and pale, solid objects that looked like parts of bodies or beasts. We were shivering and nauseated, battered and bleeding, our cocoon becoming very thin.

"The Lords hound you so sorely because they know they have failed," Karon gasped, as he helped Gerick across a roaring river of black water. "You held back a part of yourself, and they didn't think you could. You are stronger—much stronger—than they believed. . . . Take whatever you need of me. They cannot follow us here. They cannot touch you here. Endure and you will be free. I swear it upon my life. You *will* be free of them. . . ."

As the hours passed, my arms grew too heavy to lift, and so my only defense against a hail of burning rocks was to turn and let them hit my back. Paulo's grin had long faded, and even Karon's voice fell silent as bitter rain lashed our raw skin.

Gerick stumbled. Half bent forward, holding his head, he gave an agonized cry and crumpled into the morass.

"Keep moving," said Karon in a hoarse whisper, as he gathered Gerick into his arms and staggered onward. "She's out there. But if I stop . . . can't find her . . . can't hear . . ."

I didn't understand him. A shivering Paulo and I clung to each other, supported, dragged, and prodded each other to take each step. We dared not lose sight of Karon through the murk.

My thoughts slipped into villainous dreaming: of the sewing women, of the slave pen, of Ziddari's blood-red eyes watching my husband burn. The vicious screams of the crowd, the stench as the flames consumed his mutilated body . . . all seemed as real as the day I lived them. Then Gerick was burning in the marketplace. . . . *No, no,* I cried, *you have been beloved from the day we knew you.* . . . And the executioner's fire became the flames of the Gate-fire where Giano the Zhid had dragged me into madness to force the Prince of Avonar to destroy the Bridge.

On that terrible, glorious day, Karon had called me back to him, over and over again. *Seri, love . . . stay close . . . come back.* . . . On this day, I heard him again, so clearly above the tumult. The voice from the vision of my past. Frayed. Worried. At the limit of his endurance. *Almost there . . . soon, love . . . hold on.* . . .

All of them lost . . .Tears flowed and merged with the hot rivers of blood and fire, and I was alone again . . . dead again . . . empty again. . . .

Another voice. *Follow my thread, my lord. Can you feel it? Hold on, I'll guide you in* . . . "Seri, follow my voice. . . . Is it really you?"

". . . Oh, my lord Prince . . . *Ce'na davonet, Giré D'Arnath* . . . and the most excellent boy . . . and my dear lady . . . Vasrin Creator be praised for his glories . . . Vasrin Shaper be thanked for her mercies. . . ."

"Paulo, child, how I've missed you . . . and Seri . . . oh, goddess mother, Seri, what's happened to him?"

Kind voices, gentle hands . . . blankets . . . cool, sweet water . . . brandy that scalded my throat and seared my stomach . . . I could hear and feel them, but I could not see and could not answer for the fire and desolation in my eyes. Then the horrific visions were brushed away, as if with some sweet magic, and I slept without dreams, except for one of strong arms that held me close as if they would never let me go. When I woke on a crisp green morning alone in my blanket, I wept, for I thought those strong arms had been only a dream.

CHAPTER 46

Paulo

I never heard of nobody from Dunfarrie ever having an adventure. Old Jacopo, the Lady Seri's friend and mine, who was killed by the Zhid—he'd been a sailor, and that was something that was talked about for a long time. But he told me about sailoring, and it didn't sound no different from working in a stable or on a farm. Work all day and half the night, bad food and never enough, folks yelling at you to do this or do that. But I guess Jacopo loved sailoring the way some folks love farming, or the way I take to horse-keeping, and that made the difference. As for adventure, though, my travels with the Prince and the Lady Seri beat all he could tell, but I'd had just about all a person could take of it.

Thanks to the Prince, we'd come back safe to the green world all together again. I recognized the place where we came out of the doorway in the rock, even though it was daytime and spring instead of night and winter like it was when we'd gone through it before. We weren't two leagues from Avonar—the dead one—and the cave in the rock was the one where we'd followed the Prince through the Gate-fire into the magic city. Kellea had guided us to the portal with her finding magic, and she and the Dulcé Bareil were waiting for us. I wanted to kiss every blade of grass, wallow in the streams, and eat Bareil's cooking until my belly popped from it.

Saving the Prince had been a near thing. I just barely heard the Prince's call in my head when I was combing Firebreather on that night, wondering if the young master was going to come for me or not. The Prince was half asleep—half dead actually—because the Lords had put a spell on everyone in the Gray House, sending them to sleep so they would never wake up. The Prince had figured it out almost too late. He'd managed to get loose of his chains with his new-grown magic, but I'd found him trying to drag himself out of the fencing yard and not making a good job of it at all. I had to get him away from the house and help him stay awake until the spell wore off. That's why we were late and the young master ended up in such a wicked way. But between us all, we'd gotten loose of the Lords and through the Breach, and I'd never been so thankful for anything in my life.

I think I slept for a whole day straight through after Kellea dragged us through the Gate and the cave. I might have done longer—I'm good at sleeping—but the Prince woke me up. "Paulo, how are you this morning?" He was crouched down by me, whispering. He looked wicked tired. The Lady Seri was rolled in a blanket, sleeping close by the fire.

"I got no complaints. Except—"

"You're hungry, right?"

I never knew somebody could smile with his whole self like the Prince, even when he was worn flat and worried.

"Are you looking in my head?"

"No need. Friends know these things about each other. Bareil has hot porridge over there, but once you've eaten, I need your help." Never thought I'd hear a prince say that to me. Made me being hungry not near so important. "I need you to stay with Gerick a while."

"How is he? Have you . . . ?"

He shook his head. "I've not been able to help him yet. I've looked at him a bit and tried a few things, but I'll need everything I can muster to attempt it. So, I've got to sleep for a while. But I don't want him left alone. Seri isn't going to wake for hours yet, and he doesn't know Kellea or Bareil."

"Sure, I'll come. Is he awake then?"

"I don't know. I'm not sure he *can* sleep any more. He's not eaten or drunk or anything since we've come here. And he's spoken not a word. Hardly moved." The Prince rubbed his head. "Get yourself something to eat, then come to us."

They had pitched a tent under the trees to shelter the young master. Bareil said they were keeping it dark inside as he seemed a little easier in the dark. All I could see at first were two white lights. Then, as I got used to the dark, I saw him sitting up in the corner, huddled up to his knees, his hands clenched into tight fists. The white lights were the jewels they had given him for eyes.

The Prince sat beside him, watching, talking to him quiet-like. I didn't know whether to say anything or not, but the Prince looked up and smiled. "Come in, Paulo. I've told Gerick that you're going to be with him for a while. Bareil will wake me at sunset. Call me instantly if you need anything." He laid his hand on the young master's head. "We'll take care of you," he said, and then he left us alone.

I wasn't sure whether I ought to talk or not. My usual is not to say anything unless I have to. More troubles can happen to you from talking too much than from not. But the young master and I had done some talking in Zhev'Na, and even though he was thinking he was going to be a Lord and had to make himself hard and alone so as not to hurt anybody by it, we had a time or two. If we'd both been born low, or both high, then one might say we'd come to be friends.

There at the last, when I thought he'd for sure turned himself evil and was killing the Prince with his magic, I went crazy and jumped him, expecting he would blast me to the ceiling—and half hoping he would. But he talked in my head, the way the sorcerers do, and told me to keep hitting him hard. He said that if the Lords were to get distracted then maybe the Prince would have a chance to stay alive. He kept telling me he was sorry, so sorry, that he hadn't understood that V'Saro was the Prince until too late, and that he'd never meant for the Lords to kill V'Saro or me. He said he couldn't hardly feel anything any more, except that he couldn't let us die—the Prince and the lady . . . and me. While we wrestled there on that glass floor, I talked back to him the way Kellea had taught me. I said that none of us would leave him in that wicked place.

And I told him that if he could keep that one bit of feeling he had left, then maybe he could find all his other feelings again. I was as surprised as the Prince and the lady when he pulled me up off the floor and came with us. But now it looked like he was in a worse fix than he was before.

"I'm sorry about all this," I said, squatting down beside him in the tent. "I thought you'd be all right if we got you out. Shows you what an ignorant horse-keeper knows."

It was just odd talking to him when you could see only part of his real face, the rest of it that mask. He couldn't blink or show that he heard you at all. But I went on babbling about horses and such stuff, thinking it might be as well if he had something to think on that wasn't fearful. He was terrible afraid. So bad it was killing him. The Prince didn't have to tell me that. The tent was busting with his fear.

When the Prince came back at sunset, he carried a handful of linen and a small leather case. I was eating some jack Bareil had brought me, and I offered to share it. The Prince shook his head. "I can't yet. It's that stuff they fed us—the graybread. It's fixed it where anything else makes me sick. I'll have to find something later."

He set down the linen and his case. "Right now we have to take care of Gerick. Light the lamp, if you would."

I did it.

"This won't be easy, Paulo," he said. "You'll have to hold him still. I'm going to try to get the mask off, and I won't be able to do it one-handed. Are you willing?"

"He saved my life back there. More than once."

"Mine, too."

He settled himself next to the young master and opened the leather case. I knew what was in it. It was his tools that he used when he healed my busted leg and put right the other one so that I hardly limped at all any more. I hoped he could do the same for his boy as he had for me.

"Remember, unless I tell you it's all right, you mustn't touch me at any time once we're bound and I've said the invocation. If you need help, call Bareil. He'll be waiting just outside."

"You can trust me."

He grabbed a handful of my hair and waggled my head with it, smiling. "I do. It's why you're here." Then he got on his knees and spread his arms and said his prayer that always started his healing magic. "Life, hold. Stay your hand . . ."

Neither of us was expecting what happened when he cut the young master's arm. I'd not heard such a terrible cry since the night I was sent to Zhev'Na and heard the Zhid putting the collars on the Dar'Nethi slaves. The Prince looked like someone had stuck a knife in his gut. But while I tied their arms together, he held his boy tight to keep him from hurting himself from his thrashing about. As soon as the knot was made and the words were said, the young master quieted.

I remembered how it had been when I was hurting so wicked and the Prince did this to me. White fire had blazed inside me, making me warm and easy, and the Prince talked to me every moment inside my head about how things were with me, so that I wasn't afraid. I hoped the young master could feel it that way, too, but I knew the things wrong with him were a lot worse than a busted leg or two. I didn't see how we were going to get that mask off. It was a part of his face, growed together with it. Made me sick to see it.

It took an awful long time. The Prince had closed his eyes so you might think he was asleep, except that he had the same fierce look as was on his face when he was sword fighting. The young master began to shake and moan, and the Prince spoke to me. "Hold him, Paulo. Just don't touch me."

And so I did. When the young master quieted a bit, the Prince had me take the jeweled pin out of his ear. It was burning hot when I took it off.

Sometime much later the Prince took his right hand and started to run it real slow around the edges of the gold mask. Over and over it he went, and after a time you could see the metal begin to separate from the young master's face. Finally the Prince said, so soft that you almost couldn't hear him, "Cut the binding."

And when I'd done that, he said, "Dim the light and have one of the towels ready."

I did that, too.

"Now hold his arms while I remove the mask. Carefully. Please, carefully."

I've never seen such a fearful sight. There was nothing there in the young master's eyeholes. When I'd seen his changes before, his eyes had turned dark in their color, but now he didn't have eyes at all, nor anything else there that I could see—just dark holes. The Prince covered him up real quick, as soon as he had the mask off.

"Take the other towels and cut them into strips." He almost couldn't talk.

I did as he told me, and we wrapped the strips of linen around and around the young master's eyes. Then the Prince eased himself into the corner of the tent, shut his eyes, and held his boy close in his arms. I poked my head out of the tent and asked Bareil if he would bring the Prince something to drink. I knew he had to be thirsty after all that, but I didn't dare go myself without the Prince's leave.

It was the Lady Seri that brought a cup of wine and a water flask. She knelt down beside the Prince and asked if he could drink. His eyes came open, and it was a fine thing to watch when he saw it was her. He took a sip of the water, then his eyes closed and he went to sleep, and the Lady Seri sat with them through the night. I stayed just by the door.

It was a week before we knew anything. Three more times the Prince worked his healing on the young master. "I can't tell you if I've done enough," he said to us after the last one. "I think the Lords' hold on him was released when we took off the mask and the jewels in his ear, but he doesn't speak . . . doesn't answer my questions or respond in any way when I'm with him. He has some places walled off so tightly that I can't touch them. I don't know if he has set the barriers himself, or if it's some part of what the Lords have done to him. All I can do is try to banish those things that don't belong, heal the places where it looks like he's been damaged. As for his eyes . . . Something exists there now. Whether he will allow them to see, I don't know."

The young master was never left alone. Though he just sat there not saying anything or even moving, either the Prince or the lady was always there talking to him or holding him, even if it was just touching his hand. Sometimes I would sit with whichever one was watching. One night the Lady Seri was coming into the tent, and she told the Prince how it was a fine night with a full moon such as they'd not seen in more than a year, as you could never see the moon in Zhev'Na. I said why didn't they go see it together, as I could stay with the young master for a while and call them if there was any change. I knew the Prince and the Lady hadn't taken any time alone together to speak of. They were shy of each other, more like two who were courting than ones who knew each other so well as they did.

They took my offer, and so I was left with the young master alone. I started talking to him as I had before—about Dunfarrie and how the folks what had called me donkey would be fair surprised when they saw me walking straight, if his lordship would ever get himself together so I could go home, that is.

"And what would you do if you got there? The village horses will have forgotten you after all this time." It was so quiet I almost missed it.

"Oh, they'll rem— Blazes! Is that you talking to me or is it my own self?"

"We don't sound all that much alike most times."

"Blazes! Damn! I got . . . I got to tell them . . . the lady and the Prince."

"Don't leave." He reached out and grabbed my arm. "Please . . . "

"No. Not a bit of it. I'll just stay right here. I might just holler out then, if that's all right."

"No . . . I mean . . . if you'd just wait a little."

He was scared. Not in the way he'd been scared of the terrible things in his head. Not cowardly scared. He told me how strange it was that he knew me better than he knew his parents, and how the Prince had been inside his head, but such wasn't like really meeting him in his own body or anything.

I agreed it was strange. My parents had been dead or

run off since I was a nub. I couldn't imagine having them walk in on me, knowing more about me than I did about them, and having all sorts of blood oaths and killing between us. "All I know is that you don't have to be afraid of them," I said to him. "They care about you more than anything."

We talked about other things for a bit, about horses and sword fighting, and about how I had worked in the stable at Comigor and he never even knew it, and how he had seen me outside the window in the council chamber in Avonar, while I'd been watching him inside. And while we talked, the tent flap opened, and the lady and the Prince came in. The young master turned his head that way even though his eyes were still bandaged up. Then he took a deep breath and said, "I think I'm all right."

CHAPTER 47

Karon

He wasn't all right, of course. It would be a long time until we knew what the result of Gerick's ordeal would be. We weren't even sure he was mortal, for he had neither eaten nor drunk anything for nine days. But we took the bandages off that same night, and he did indeed have eyes again, beautiful brown eyes just like his mother's. To our joy and relief, he could see with them, too.

Soon he was able to eat as well, not having to resort to the herbs and potions Kellea gave me to help keep things down until the last remnants of the slave food were out of my blood. On the afternoon after he first spoke, ten days after we had left Zhev'Na behind us, Gerick stepped out of the tent and went walking in the sunlight with Paulo.

He wouldn't talk about what the Lords had done to him or how much of their poisonous enchantments remained, and from the first he alternated between periods of quiet patience and intense irritability. What was most unsettling was how his eyes would take on a dark gray cast when he was angry. I saw no evidence that he possessed exceptional power anymore, only the intrinsic talents of any Dar'Nethi youth who had not yet come into his primary talent.

I believed his dark moods reflected the intensity of his craving for the power he had lost. The glimpses of his experiences I had come across while working at his healing were extraordinary, uses of sorcery alien to anything I knew of, but his determined reserve precluded any deeper questioning about them. And he made it clear from the beginning that he didn't wish for me to tell him anything of how

I or any other Dar'Nethi acquired power to support our various talents. Seri and I were uneasy at his erratic temper, but we agreed it was only to be expected. We would just have to take things slowly. We grieved sorely for his childhood, stolen away in the deserts of Zhev'Na.

"We have to talk about it, you know." I held the tangled willow branches aside so Seri could get down to the stream bank where the smooth, flat rocks were being baked by the afternoon sun.

She refused my offered hand, as if accepting my help somehow signaled agreement with my opinions. Stepping from one rock to another, she made her way across the stream, seating herself on a boulder in the very middle of the rippling water. "Not yet. We need a few more days."

"The answer will be the same, Seri. I can't stay. He can't go. We have to decide where to take him."

I had to return to Avonar. I was its ruler, and my people didn't know if I was living or dead. The Preceptorate was in shambles, the war was not ended, and my responsibilities to Gerick and Seri could not overshadow the others I had inherited with the body I had been given. But I dared not take Gerick back across the Breach, not even using the Bridge. The Lords had ripped him apart as we fled Zhev'Na, leaving him exposed and vulnerable while immersed in chaos. I had no idea what lasting effects such contact with the Breach might cause. And I wanted him as far away from Zhev'Na and the Zhid and our war as we could keep him. He needed time and distance to heal his wounds before we could risk the Bridge passage again.

"He needs you, Karon. I've no power to heal him. He hurts so badly. . . . I see it when he sleeps."

I stepped across to her rock and pulled her up into my arms. She was shaking. "*Talyasse* . . . *talyasse* . . . softly, love." I stroked her hair, trying to soothe her. "*You* are his healing, as you have always been mine. He listens to you, walks with you, allows you to care for him . . . and care about him. You've brought him so far out of the darkness; you will take him the rest of the way."

Seri was our strength. Our hope. Ever since I had known

her . . . through our darkest days . . . in my mindless confusion . . . she had been the beacon whose clear, unwavering light set our course straight. Everyone saw it but her.

Despite everything I tried, Gerick remained painfully reserved around me, scarcely speaking in my presence. Was it fear, resentment, hatred? I had too little experience of children to know—and what experience could have prepared me to understand what my son had just endured? Gerick had to stay, so Seri had to stay, and I had to go. "I'll come as often as I can."

She buried her face in my neck. "It's not fair."

"But we both know it's right. So now again to the question . . . where can the two of you be safe?"

The last thing in the world I wished was to leave Seri again. We had lost so many years, and while I believed myself to be the Karon she knew—as long as I didn't look at my reflection—it was clear we could not take up again as if nothing had happened. We, too, needed time and peace. But neither time nor peace was available, and if Seri and Gerick were not to return to Avonar with me, we had to find them a safe haven until we could be together. Not Comigor. Gerick wasn't ready to take up his old life, either, and we didn't know whether he ever would be. Not Dunfarrie. I refused to abandon Seri and Gerick to the hardships of that life, where Seri had scraped out an existence for ten years, and Dassine had sent me to find her again. To recover from their ordeals would be trial enough. More importantly, Darzid . . . the Lord Ziddari . . . knew of Comigor and Dunfarrie.

Seri pulled away and stooped to fill the water flasks she carried at her waist. "I don't know. I don't think I'll feel safe anywhere away from you."

Later that evening as we sat around the fire, Seri explained our problem to Gerick and the others. As with so many things, Gerick agreed passively to do whatever we believed best.

Kellea was the one who spoke up. "So does your friend, the scholar, still live outside of Yurevan? Seems a house like his, private, comfortable, out in the countryside, might be just the place. I'd be willing to stay for a while, keep watch as far as I'm able. . . ."

Seri and I looked at each other. It was a perfect solution. Our good friend Tennice would welcome Gerick and Seri to the country home he had inherited from my old professor Ferrante, and the private location of the house would enable me to come and go freely without raising dangerous questions.

Later, when I asked Paulo privately if he would consider staying with Gerick, he refused to dignify my question with anything but a disbelieving glare. It was all I could do to keep from laughing. If anything gave me hope for Gerick, it was his friendship with Paulo. Paulo's goodness of heart and abiding honesty had touched a place in our son that neither Seri nor I was yet privileged to visit, and we rejoiced in it.

But of course, the rightness of Kellea's suggestion meant we had no more excuse to delay. Avonar's need was urgent. We could put our separation off no longer.

Paulo had rounded up the horses we'd left in the valley over a year before, and on a clean-washed spring morning three weeks after our escape from Zhev'Na, Bareil and I watched the four of them ride off southward. I had intended to accompany them along the way, but, in one of the rare times he initiated any conversation, Gerick had reassured me. "They don't know where I am," he said, fingering the reins so he wouldn't have to look at me. "It won't occur to them that I'm not . . . what I was . . . any longer. If I stay hidden, we should be safe enough."

I had to take him at his word. For him to speak of the Lords at all was clearly difficult. And so, I had thanked him for his confidence and let them go. The jeweled earring and the gold mask with the diamonds lay at the bottom of my pack. I debated whether to destroy the vile things, but the part of me that bore responsibility for the war against the Lords surmised that such artifacts of power might have some use. Gerick had never asked what had become of them.

* * *

And so they were gone, and the Dulcé and I were left in the lovely, but so very empty, glade. "We'd best be off," I said. Up the hill, into the cave, through the Gate, and across the Bridge to this other life that awaited me. I hated the thought of it.

My madrissé smiled sadly and placed a small, wrapped bundle in my hand. "Not quite yet, my lord. You are between times. Before you take up this life, you must be sure of your path."

"What do you—? Ah." From the cloth wrapping, I pulled the plain circle of dull wood set with the black crystal pyramid embedded in an iron ring, the object I'd taken from Dassine's study so long ago. Now I knew what it was—the artifact to which my soul had been bound for the ten years I had existed without a body, ten years of darkness and pain, ten years of intricate enchantments and voracious learning, infused with the boundless energy and devotion of my Healer and jailer, Dassine. Touching the crystal would release me from this body's bondage and allow me to cross the Verges if I chose to do so. My death, so long delayed, awaited me in its enchantments.

I stared at the thing and was overwhelmed by longing, a desperate ache in the depths of my being that was far colder and far more powerful than my yearning for Seri or my worries about Gerick. "Ah, Bareil, how can I risk using it now? So many are depending—"

"He said when you were whole again, and the boy was safe. He robbed you of your choice when you died, and again when he deceived you about D'Natheil's death. And he swore by all he valued to return the choice to you. It was Master Dassine's belief that if you did not choose this new life freely, then doubts would grow and, eventually, consume you. You would never be able to enter into your life fully, and if you could not do so, then you would fail in all you would attempt. You must be one place or the other—live or die—by your own choice."

"A patronizing pronouncement from the old devil . . ." And not at all fair to give me such a choice when Seri and Gerick were out of reach. What if I could not resist the call of the Verges? I was supposed to be dead.

"I'll watch over you, my lord, and do whatever is needed . . . after." Bareil smiled, but tears welled up in his almond-shaped eyes. He didn't expect me to return.

So it was with trepidation that I stroked the smooth face of the dark crystal and left D'Natheil's body that had become my own. For a moment I saw that body lying on the green velvet hillside with the kindly Dulcé standing guard, the snowy peak of mighty Karylis looming over his shoulder. Far down the track that led to my ruined home and southward toward Yurevan, I saw the ones I loved most in the world riding into the dew-kissed peace of the morning. And then was I plunged into darkness, the ethereal pulse of the Verges beckoning me to the place of my belonging.

The long echo of my agony in the fire began to reverberate in my mind once more, but because I expected it this time, I could push it aside and concentrate on the distant light that called me into peace. I was very tired.

Where did I belong? I had lived my allotted span of years, and the Way had led me to the fire. I had accepted my fate as I had been taught—as I believed was necessary. But in doing so, I had abandoned Seri and my son and my friends to despair and death. To drown in such guilt would be easy. To run from it was tempting; beyond the Verges, perhaps, I could forget. But if I had followed any other course, made other choices, been someone other than myself, the Gate-fire might never have burned white, and the boy D'Natheil might not have been sent onto the Bridge and been destroyed by it.

I knew D'Natheil now, not everything, but enough, and D'Natheil could never have defeated the Lords of Zhev'Na. I had met the Lords in physical combat, in the slave pens of Zhev'Na, and in the battleground of my son's mind, and Dassine had been right. Exeget had been right. The Lords were the enemies of all life, a darkness more profound than the emptiness between worlds or the universe before its creation. They were a disease that gnawed on the healthy body of humankind, and what was needed to eradicate them was a Healer. Somewhere in me was the way to defeat them.

An aurora of blue and rose and violet burst into a shimmering fountain that rained fragments of light upon me like rose petals showered on a bridegroom. Such glory . . . such music from beyond the range of my vision as the luminous fragments floated through my transparent self. I reached for one of them and heard faint, echoing laughter, and the whole mass of them embraced me in a whirling nebula of joy that would transport me beyond the Verges to where unknown wonders lay waiting. My soul was filled with their beauty and with such overarching desire that I cried out. But with a soft breath I blew on them, and they drifted away regretfully like dry snowflakes, leaving me in the cold and the darkness. "Not yet," I said, and I turned my back on the Verges and set my feet upon the path that awaited me.

My eyes opened to the green and silent world. "Come, Bareil," I said. "Let's go home."

Seri

I stand upon the graceful balcony of Verdillon watching Gerick and Paulo wrestling on the grassy lawn. They've been going at it for an hour. As they separate and sprawl on the green, panting and sweating and laughing, I smile and finger the rose-colored stone that hangs about my neck, wishing, as always, that it could send my thoughts to Avonar.

"Would that you could see these moments, my love," I would say. "They are rare, but so precious, and they give me such hope. The black moods plague him as much as ever, and nights are still the worst. His cries are terrible when he dreams. One of us is always close by to comfort him, though he'll not allow it once he's awake again. But he's begun to study history with Tennice and show interest in Kellea's herb lore, and he appreciates that neither one coddles him. With Paulo he jests and teases and allows himself to be a boy again.

"Yesterday he asked me about this house, and why your name appears in the old journal that lies open in Ferrante's study. I told him, then, about his father who was a student here, and how he immersed himself in beauty, art, and history long before he became a warrior or a prince. Perhaps it will encourage him to be less shy of you.

"Peace has settled into all of us for the moment. Sometimes, though, when I hear news of the human war that rages in Iskeran, or I think of the horrors you face beyond the walls of Avonar, or I see a trace of darkness in Gerick's eyes, I believe we are like the Guardians of Comigor—you,

Kellea, Paulo, and I—standing at the four corners of the keep and waiting for the enemy to ride over the horizon. We three will stay awake, my love. No harm will come to him while we watch. Keep yourself safe, and come to us soon."

Turn the page
for an exciting preview of

THE SOUL WEAVER

Book Three of
The Bridge of D'Arnath

BY
CAROL BERG

Available February 2005
from Roc Books

Karon

My senses were deafened by Jayereth's pain. Desperately I fought to maintain my control, to prevent her agony from confusing my purpose. We were bound by an enchantment of Healing, our mingled blood linking our minds in the realm of flesh and spirit. If I shut out the experience of her senses, then I was powerless to heal her, but if I could not quiet her enough to see what I was doing, she was lost just as surely. Dark waves already lapped on the shores of her life.

Jayereth, hear me. . . . Hold fast . . . for your daughter, newly born to grace your house . . . for T'Vero who cherishes you . . . for your Prince who is in such need of your service . . . With everything I knew of Jayereth I commanded her to hold quiet—just for the moment it would take me to see what I needed to see.

She understood me, I think, for there came the briefest ebb in the death tide, an instant's clearing in the red mist of her pain and madness that let me perceive a host of things too terrible to know: ribs smashed, lungs torn, blood . . . everywhere hot, pooling blood and fragments of bone, her belly in shreds . . . Earth and sky, how had they done this? It was as if they knew every possible remedy a Healer could provide and had arranged it so I could do nothing but make things worse.

Another instant and I was awash once more in Jayereth's torment, feeling her struggle to breathe with a chest on fire and a mind blasted with fear. I could not give her strength or endurance, only my healing skill and few pitiful words of comfort. But even as I fought to knit together the ragged edges of her heart, her last remnants of thought and reason flicked out. Her screams sagged into a low, flat wail . . . and then silence. I had lost her.

Let her go, I told myself, *you can't help her by traveling the only road she has yet to travel. That road is not for you . . . not yet.* Forcing aside the wave of enveloping darkness, I gritted my teeth and spoke the command, "Cut it now."

My companion cut away the strip of linen that bound my forearm to Jayereth's, allowing our mingled blood to feed my sorcery. The cold touch that seared my flesh was not his knife—his hand was too experienced for that—but the sealing of a scar that would forever remind me of my failure in my young counselor's last need.

The red mist vanished with the death tide, and my bleary eyes focused on the ravaged body crumpled on the stone floor of my lectorium. The only sound in the candlelit wreckage of the chamber was my shaking breath as I knelt beside my fallen counselor and grieved for the horror she had known. *Cross swiftly, Jayereth. Do not linger in this realm out of yearning for what is lost. I'll care for T'Vero and your child. On D'Arnath's sword, I swear it.*

I envisioned Jayereth as she had been, short and plain, with brown hair, a liberal dash of freckles across her straight nose and plump cheeks, and the most brilliant young mind in Avonar tucked behind her eccentric humor. When I summoned Jayereth's young husband, T'Vero, I would try to keep this image in mind and not the gruesome reality.

"Was there nothing to be done, my lord?"

Two small, strong hands gripped my right arm and helped me to my feet. Bareil always knew my needs. Unable to speak as yet, I shook my head and leaned on the Dulcé's sturdy shoulder as he led me to a wooden stool he'd set upright. Padding softly through the wreckage, he summoned those who huddled beyond the door.

One by one the four remaining Preceptors of Gondai crept into the chamber, gaping at the devastation. The oak-paneled walls were charred, the worktables in splinters, the shredded books in jumbled heaps. No vessel remained unshattered, no liquid unspilled; every surface was etched by lightnings more violent than any storm of nature's making. The acrid smoke of smoldering herbs mingled with blue and green vapors from pooled liquids to sting noses and eyes. Most fearful, of course, was the corpse sprawled in the midst of the destruction—Jayereth and the rictus of horror that had been her glowing face.

"How was it possible, my lord prince?" one whispered.

"Who could have done this?"

"In the very heart of the palace . . ."

". . . treason . . ."

The word was inevitable, though I didn't want to hear it.

". . . and her work, of course . . ."

"All lost," I said. I had known it in the instant I'd heard the thunderous noise.

Jayereth's discovery should have been secured the previous night. I was her Prince. It had been my responsibility. But my own selfish desires had lured me into a night's adventure, and so I had put off duty until this morning. Too late. Before I could protect Jayereth or her work, our enemies had ripped her apart and left no place for me to heal.

With a furious sweep of my hand, I cleared the tottering worktable of chips of plaster and broken glass, then kicked the splintered leg and let the slate top crash to the floor. Only when the dust had settled again had I control enough to address my waiting Preceptors. "Search every corner of the palace, every house, ruin, and hovel in the city. No one is to leave Avonar. Ustele, you will watch for any portal opening. We will discover who dares murder in my house."

Useless orders. Useless anger. No common conspirator had wrought such destruction fifty paces from my bedchamber. The protections on the palace of the Prince of Avonar were the most powerful that could be devised. For a thousand years no enemy had breached these rose-colored walls, and no Dar'Nethi thought-reading was required to understand what every one of the wide-eyed Preceptors saw. No soulless Zhid had slain Jayereth—no lurking stranger. The murderer was one of us.

Bareil went to summon Jayereth's husband. The Preceptor Gar'Dena, a giant of a man resplendent in green silk and a ruby-studded belt, brusquely dispatched the other Preceptors to the duties I had detailed. When Gar'Dena and I were left alone, he looked down at Jayereth. "Has there been any disruption in the Circle? Any sign from Marcus or the others? This event leaves me wary of all our enterprises."

I shook my head. "No ill word from the Circle." As far as we knew the Lords had not yet noticed our most powerful sorcerers taking up positions on the boundaries of the Vales, ready to form an expanding ring of impenetrable enchantment around the healthy lands of my adopted world. "As of yesterday, Ce'Aret had almost two hundred in place. And we've had no news of our agents in Zhev'Na, but, of course, we've no way to know if they've been taken. Maybe that's what this is—the notice of their failure."

We both knew it wasn't so. The elimination of Jayereth and her work was no blind strike of retaliation, but clearly aimed. Someone knew what she had discovered and knew that she'd not yet passed on all of her knowledge. Only six people in the universe knew the secret—and to every one of them I would entrust my life.

ABOUT THE AUTHOR

Though **Carol Berg** calls Colorado her home, her roots are in Texas in a family of teachers, musicians, and railroad men. She has a degree in mathematics from Rice University and one in computer science from the University of Colorado, but managed to squeeze in minors in English and art history along the way. She has combined a career as a software engineer with her writing, while also raising three sons. She lives with her husband at the foot of the Colorado mountains.